Volume I

2nd Edition

Walter Vale

Vytameta

ISBN: 0692854053
ISBN-13: 978-0692854051

CONTENTS

Preface

It all started with a simple request from a friend of mine, struggling with the same problem I was going through about five years ago. We both wanted to write a story about the worlds and characters swimming in our heads, but we didn't have the right motivation nor the goal to reach to get us there.

That was when she mentioned to me a challenge she wanted to try: *National Novel Writing Month,* or *NaNoWriMo,* was an internet-based organization made for aspiring authors like the young adults we were. The challenge their website issued was simple: Create a 50,000 word story in one month.

It was my original intention to create a one-off background story about how a belhuayn teenager, named Kasra, became the hero of her planet. It was supposed to be short, fast, funny, and full of action. The only problem was, I couldn't create a whole world and a whole race of people in just 50,000 words. I was told by the people I asked to read the finished manuscript that it deserved much more time, and that it could develop into something bigger than what I was allowing it to become.

Most of my audience came from the college I had been attending at the time. Often, during the lull of downtime between my courses, I would tell my fellow classmates of the story I was creating. However, very few of them had the time to read the whole thing, so the feedback I received amounted to words of encouragement, like "yeah, go for it!"

Call me pretentious, but that kind of lukewarm support wasn't quite enough to convince me that I was spending my free time in the most promising and productive way possible.

One day, as I was leaving the school, I happened by someone who I mistook to be a member of the faculty. She told me she worked at the Writing Center on campus, and immediately a light switch flicked on in my head. I thought, *if anyone is going to give me useful feedback and criticism of my work, she'd be the one to do it!*

So, chancing a laugh of rejection, I asked if she'd be willing to give my work of non-academia a look over. Inwardly flinching as I braced for a verbal backhand, I was quite elated to receive a 'sure' of confirmation. Every wednesday, for the next two years, she would read over each chapter of my manuscript and help me edit it as we went. And as she became more involved with the story and got an 'insider's perspective' on the grander plot, she was able to give me useful pointers and suggestions for where to take things next.

One suggestion I took to heart was this: "the more eyes you have on your work, the better." And just like my friend from the Writing Center, I had no anticipation of where my next muse would come from next.

I met her two years ago before I heard from her again, to learn of all the changes in her life and of them, that she was writing a book of her own. And like me and my NaNoWriMo friend, it was a project that had been in the works for a while. I was pretty close to completing my manuscript by then -- about "two weeks away" as I had a habit of telling anyone who asked.

The problem she had run into was very similar to the one I started with: a strong idea of what she wanted her story to be, but had a lot of scenes jumbled about and floating around in her mind that she lacked the motivation to put on paper. That's when she turned me on to the idea of collaborating with her; giving her a fun way to hash out some of the ideas we both had, in a way that at the same time allowed us to critique each other's work.

Just like my Writing Center friend and I had made it a tradition of ours to work on my book on wednesdays, this new novelist friend of mine had made it a tradition for us to co-write on tuesdays. Were it not for her patience and acceptance with the ideas I wished to use in the entertaining and engaging settings we practiced with, I can definitely say some characters who appear in this book would not have had their debut, nor the amount of polishing they had received before they were introduced!

It was due to this same friend's helpful criticism that I was not only able to see the faults within my own writing, but that I was able to plan ahead for future volumes of this series, and leave this one off on a cliffhanger that I was comfortable with.

If there's one thing I hope this book does, is that it inspires people at the age I was at the time I first dreamt its concept to create a world of their own. But that does not mean this book should only be read by young people; it can be valued as a retrospective for the older generation as well.

This story is more than just a battle between good and evil as it was meant to be in the beginning; it's about a coming of age, and self-identification. It represents the kind of struggles that young people, the protagonist's age, deal with. It represents the mindset one develops coming out of high school, when the possibilities of one's own potential are as endless as their imaginations. It is meant to capture the gravity of making a powerful decision that can only come through critical thinking, and after weighing the pros and cons of both sides.

If you have read through this preface, I hope you will see those elements come through in this story telling. And now, I introduce to you possibly the longest Prologue you will see in any book you've ever read...

Prologue

An interstellar jaunt spanning 6,000 light years to the Perseus Arm of the Milky Way would bring star-faring adventurers to the Qualarian System, home to six intelligent worlds embosomed by a great blue star. They were called Xall, Saja, Aedaria, Vitiosa, Marden, and Inmaris. Planet Xall was heralded for having the most impressive civilization, the highest-valued currency, and largest industry in their stellar community. The robotic, Xallian people saw it as their responsibility to 'upgrade' the other worlds to fit their higher standards by impressing upon them their culture and technology. They were a trustworthy, yet intolerant empire that sought to ally themselves with other inhabitable planets outside the Qualarian System.

Despite their efforts to maintain a peaceful facade for their interplanetary neighborhood, the strengthening of their militaristic power had long been a secret priority for the Xalls. In the year 2004 of the galactic calendar, Inmaris and Marden formed an alliance to attack Xall and their allies, Aedaria and Saja, to dispute Vitiosa's neutral lands. Xall used its ultimate weapon, before then unknown to anyone in the Qualarian System, called the 'Harbinger of Dominion' -- a vital turning point in the Vitiosa Dissention. The conflict was resolved when Pulsar, the Prince of Inmaris, was captured by Arkra, the current Overlord of Xall, after threatening to use The Harbinger of Dominion to exterminate the populace of his home world. The Inmarisian government was reluctant to announce their surrender.

Inmaris was on thin ice with the Xallian Alliance ever since, but was trading with Marden in secret to bolster their military power for another attack on Xall, one day. Meanwhile, Xall investigated its neighbor, Aedaria, for its involvement in the Inmarisian slave trade, in which the people of Vitiosa were shanghaied and sold into militaries or workforces. Though their world was thereafter "forbidden" to interplanetary excursions, daredevil adventurers were known to trespass Vitiosa's dangerous lands to bring back its exotic treasures.

Vitiosa's gravity and atmospheric density not only made it difficult for an astronaut's expeditions, but it endowed its natives with tougher bodies than any other race in the Qualarian System. Belhuayns had to be tough to survive the rigors of their homeworld. Endowed with infamously sensitive ears and a fantastic sense of smell, belhuayns were also armed with serpentine tails that enhanced their strength and mobility beyond comparison to any other race in the Qualarian System.

Women were called veltas and men were called scelans. Either gender of the belhuayn race were hardy, protean lifeforms capable of surviving and adapting to any environment, but their technology only varied from swords and shields to black powder cannon in some regions. What most of them lacked in inventive intelligence they compensated with sheer, physical power and heightened senses that made them inherently effective hunters and truly terrifying adversaries. It was this brute power and adaptability that also made them particularly appealing prospects for soldiers and serfdom; it was the idea of turning their people into a slave crop that begat the war between Inmaris and Xall.

Xall believed, from their observations of belhuayn commoners, that they could be either altruistic or violent; curious of visitors, or distrusting of what they couldn't understand. One half of the population valued war and power above all things. Alliances were only made as a means to an end, and someone's word could be kept only as far as its keeper could be thrown. The other half of the population was exactly the opposite: they valued peaceful assimilation; they would help each other build homes and whole cities -- some of which were the grandest in all the world.

The elders would educate the young ones, and discouraged violence against one another. It was this minority of belhuayns that seemed to have been conveniently left out of observations made by advocates of slavery, who saw belhuayns as nothing more than what they could be made into. Those who were war-like were sold as mercenaries; those who were peaceful were sold for manual labor -- or anything else their buyer wanted from them.

Peace-loving belhuayns honored hard work and were very quick learners. It was due to their patience that the world of Vitiosa knew sophisticated tools and developed any technology at all. Their progress was only kept back by those who wished to have their 'scourge of weakness' purged from their 'perfect race.' It was this attitude of evil that predominated so much of their kind that had made the peaceful belhuayns the minority that they were. The only knowledge they took from those they killed were the weapons they could use to do it better.

"Such savage hearts!" cried an elder as he watched his village burn. "I shed no tears when the dark clouds come to take their kind away."

He and the scarce survivors behind him could see the victorious brigands fleeing with their loot, riding their graceful, black steeds away from the valley. They left nothing but the fires they set on the thatch roofs of residences built decades ago by the people they had laid waste to. From the confusion of the short skirmish, it was a miracle that anyone was able to run with their lives, much less the village elder, whose best sprint barely amounted to a cane-assisted hobble.

"Are you alright, Fyraxus?" asked a small boy, no older than 10. His purple hair was shaggy and unkempt, possibly having been undone all the more so by his haste to escape the burning village. The ragged rags he wore were barely held together by cross-stitches up the front and along the sides.

The gray-haired scelan tested his balance on his sore ankle, shifting his weight off his walking stick. "Aye, lad, I merely done turned me heel on a stone. I would've fared worse, had yer papa not hoisted me up this hill." Turning to the kindly smiling man of dark hair and purple eyes, Fyraxus finally gave his proper condolences. "I do thank ye, Undatio, but me spirit would've rested well even if ye had let me die and fought them off, instead."

The strong, darkly-tanned father in question comfortingly put a hand on Fyraxus' shoulder. His arms and chest bore the old scars of battle, and now were adorned with a few new markings, adding to the testaments of his trouble. "No one's belongings are worth their lives. It was more important that you, the keeper of knowledge, be safe; for as long as we know how to rebuild, we always can rebound from a disaster like this. The day we forget how to fend for ourselves will be the day we all perish to barbarians like them."

Fyraxus looked taken aback to hear this statement coming from the young parent standing by his side. "Ye ken more than I've forgotten!" his bushy eyebrows raised under his wrinkled brow. "A boy like yer son needs that kind of wisdom, lest he be turned like *them* at his coming of age."

"You needn't fear such a fate becoming of Kersaatz," Undatio patted his son's head, tussling his violet hair. "Not as long as his mother and I are with him. He has a sibling coming along, one day; he needs to be there to look after his new brother or sister, as well."

Kersaatz trotted along to check on his mother, who presently sat on a small plateau to rest from the flight from their village. "Mother, are you well?"

The velta of reddish blonde hair nodded, holding the slight bulge of her stomach. "Yes, Kersaatz, I am now." She looked up when Undatio came over to help her stand. "How many of us are there left?"

"Fewer than twenty," Undatio replied, with a quick glance to their remaining neighbors further down the path. "We'll have to stay with them if we want to rebuild. The elder believes he knows of another location where we can have a fresh start -- near a river, with fertile soil for grain and crops."

"But without steeds," Fyraxus interjected, "the journey could take several days. We'll need tae gather provisions as we move if we want tae arrive as soon as possible. If the Goddess smiles on us, we will make it without difficulties."

By the end of the week, the village's survivors had found the new lands on which they would reconstruct their homes. Some of them saw it as a blessing in disguise, for their territory was much larger and further open than the one they left behind. The glistening stream which wound through the verdant acreage added a beautiful landmark that the hunters could feel relieved to come back to after their expeditions into the wilderness. Within a matter of months, at the turning of the seasons, the farmers began to gather their freshly-grown fruits from the seeds they planted earlier that year.

Undatio and his family participated in the fields, taking and baling the stalks of wheat-like plants and carrying them with wheelbarrows to the windmills. They worked until the sun's rays barely peeked above the horizon. With night falling, the tired families enjoyed watching the changing colors of the twilight sky together. They stayed out and drank from the river as the first stars appeared in the blackening sky, until the whole, dark hemisphere above them was alight with white dust and grains of distant galaxies. The glow of Safiro's moon shed its ominous, blue light upon the landscape.

Just as they were speculating what the priests might say of Safiro's forbidding influence at the time of harvest, their innocently simple fears would never have begun to rationalize the curse that not even the God of Death could have wrought upon them. Their curious eyes narrowed as one of the belhuayn gatherers pointed at a strange, space of darkness moving across the sky -- like a flying creature, only faster and larger than any they had seen before. It made no sound as it made its approach, and was soon joined by more, until a whole flock of shadows were upon them. From these flying shadows emerged a horde of black beings with wings like locusts and four, glowing eyes. They swarmed to the buildings across the river, and were chased by the men of the village.

Fezerva watched her husband join their pursuit, and immediately feared for him and the safety of their child at home. Before she or the few left in her company could make a run for it to join them, one of the flying shadows shone a light upon her so bright, that she thought a cosmic being had held a magnifying glass before the sun. Her body became numb and was paralyzed; not by fright, but against her will.

She watched her limp form be raised up out of the water, as if by the hand of an invisible giant, and carried above the forest and into the sky. She was barely able to turn her head to see the great cloud of darkness looming over her, eclipsed by the bright beam hoisting her toward it. She squinted shut and averted her eyes as she was taken inside the black cloud; the humming sound it emitted grew louder and increased with intensity until suddenly, there was quiet.

From within her eyelids, she could see the presence of darkness. By the weight on her knees, she could feel a metal floor beneath her. She hazarded her sanity a glimpse of her new surroundings; a dolefully dim room made of dirty steel. There she sat, in the center of it all, on a white plinth inside of a cage. She looked up and saw what appeared to be a mirror near at the corner of the room, showing the estranged velta sitting in her small prison.

"Who are you?" came a belhuayn voice from the darkness.

As Fezerva's eyes adjusted, she could finally see the walls of the room, and saw cages like hers stacked to the ceiling, full of prisoners -- some male, some female, but all were adults about her age. Some of them did not look like any she had seen, where she grew up. She assumed they must have been from different parts of the world.

"Fezerva Jantica," the blonde finally replied, in a whispered tone.

"Where are you from?" was the same voice's next question.

Fezerva was able to identify her new acquaintance as a dark-haired velta with tangled tresses and orange eyes, staring down at her from one cage below the roof. She looked as scared as any of the others were; no doubt desiring some sort of connection to make herself feel at ease. Fezerva earnestly desired the same.

She timidly jumped when an unseen door behind her opened with a hiss. Through it came a being whose insectoid body was dressed in a black, padded armor -- the likes of which she had never seen before. His legs were long and bent, like that of a grasshopper. His head was shaped like the blade of a trowel and featured two pairs of bulging yellow eyes -- one smaller than the other. Above his brow was a sweeping pair of antennae. His upper arms were thin and frail when compared to the thickness of their fores, which were endowed with a spiky carapace.

He carried in his large, three-fingered hands what appeared to be a sort of oddly-shaped mace made of black metal; the larger, blunter end was held closer to his shoulder, while its thinner end was pointed to the ground.

The look he gave Fezerva was akin to one would accord to flotsam in the water, before turning back whence he came with a shout to someone in another room. Whatever he said sounded terse and succinct, as if confirming some suspicion that someone had about the contents of the storage room he entered. "Yep, full of belhuayns," was what Fezerva surmised he probably said.

The faulty lights flickered at about the same time Fezerva began to hear that humming noise from before outside the walls. It was faint at first, but became louder, like wheels turning faster and faster as they built up speed. Suddenly, she felt herself getting pushed into the floor, as if from the takeoff of a strider-drawn carriage.

Though there were no windows from which she could see the outside world, she knew they were moving. And though there were no sounds of crunching wheels against a dirt road, she knew they had to have been moving fast. Their travel was as calm as the wind, and like the wind, there was no telling where they were headed.

"Will they pick up more?" asked one of the prisoners.

"There are no empty cages left," another observed.

"Where will they take us, now?"

"To wherever they're from, perhaps?"

"What will happen, then?"

"We will know for ourselves, soon enough," Fezerva's questioner replied. "I've heard that relatives of friends have disappeared in a similar manner, before. They never came back."

Fezerva could tell by the shakiness of their voices that they were afraid of abandoning their homes, and that they had a commitment to the lives they were forced to leave behind. The young mother, too, was concerned for the whereabouts of her child, and dreaded to think that he may not have evacuated before he was captured, or worse.

Undatio did what he could to save them both. Remembering his sacrifice, she somberly wept. Henceforth she remained silent throughout the ride until they had arrived at their destination.

Her first warning came from the sound of the metallic door sliding open to their holding chamber, and the unintelligible clicking sounds that the dark man spoke with his segmented mouth. Against her will, Fezerva was extricated from the black cloud the same way she was put into it: by a bright, numbing light that obscured her vision.

When it cleared, she found herself in a different place -- one much livelier and full of alien chatter. She stared agape at her new surroundings: a room so vast, it had no comparison to anything she had seen on Vitiosa.

She could see stars floating over a boundless horizon outside the long, rectangular windows in the distance, as if the building they were inside were built in the middle of the sky. She watched the sun pass on by the viewing screen, as if a whole day had come and gone in a matter of minutes. She felt nauseas with consternation and bewilderment; of all the people she saw walking around, talking it up and milling about, none of them in any way bore semblance to her own kind.

Some were coated with feathers of white, black, or gray. Some were coated with rock hard scales and had raptor-like claws in lieu of hands and feet. Some had faces like creatures of the sea and slithered on the ground with tentacles instead of legs.

Then there were the beings like the man she saw before, who seemed to be watching the others with critical, untrusting stares. The multitude of aliens were brought inside the gathering hall by crafts that moved like the black cloud.

Like sailing ships, their transportation vessels were of all shapes and sizes. They could traverse both sky and land like a boat at sea. It was amazing to watch them fly and roost, and drop off their passengers.

Fezerva's starstruck viewing of this heavenly place was abruptly ended when one of the guards from the black cloud came to push her cage toward where all the alien beings were headed. Through a grand opening at the end of the gathering hall, Fezerva and her company of imprisoned belhuayns were carted onto a stage at the back of another, comparably vast room decorated with banners and furnished with tables, whereat the odd guests sat to view the prisoners. Before them stood a well-dressed man being, like those she saw before, behind a podium from where he gave a speech with a loud voice like thunder. His audience vociferated their excitement at the end of his short presentation, at which point Fezerva and her company were pushed closer to the edge of the stage for better viewing.

Then more dark men came to place a stiff piece of paper with a single glyph written on it atop their cages. The loud presenter then pointed at one of the glyphs and raised his voice once again to the audience, some of whom responded by holding what appeared to be a fan emblazoned with a similar glyph.

Fezerva thought this might've been some sort of game for the participants to recognize an alien alphabet, but wasn't too sure how exactly this needed to involve live prisoners. The loud presenter then started rattling off so quickly that it was hard to believe anyone who could understand what language he was speaking could have known what he was saying. Fewer members of the crowd than before raised their fans in response to this odd babbling, perhaps signaling for him to stop when they had enough of listening to him.

Maybe the presenter was hard of hearing, because whenever a fan was raised to cut him off, he'd go right back to talking again with the same kind of emphatic gusto as before. As he continued, fewer and fewer alien beings had the bravery or the patience left to raise their fans, until one of the seafood creatures decided he'd had enough and stood with a final wave of his glyph.

This was answered by the most raucous interjection yet by the presenter, who seemed nonetheless excited to have been told he was annoying, and then pointed to the glyph on the cage that the sea creature recognized. The sign was then taken off the cage and the cage was opened for the belhuayn inside to be ushered out with prods of encouragement from the odd, bludgeoning devices the dark men carried.

The man with the head of a mollusk then went from his table to see the much confused scelan he had won the privilege of meeting from this spectacular shouting match. The scelan was not allowed to give the creature a proper greeting, as its hands were restrained by metallic devices behind its back. Judging by the apprehension on the scelan's face, he was unlikely to touch the sea creature, even if he was allowed to.

After the scelan had walked away with the creature he met, another few rounds of this game continued, with each belhuayn being taken off somewhere by an alien being every time it finished, until only Fezerva herself was left. At this point in the game, it seemed that all the remaining participants had grown tired and simply hadn't the energy to spare to give their fans a wave at all.

It was hard to tell if the glances they gave Fezerva were out of pity or out of boredom, for having to sit through this whole process multiple times. Fezerva began to wonder what odd manner of being she'd have to meet by the time it was over. After a few minutes, the presenter, himself, who was normally so full of energy, had a difficult time keeping his audience's interest and even he was beginning to give it up.

He looked to Fezerva with an annoyed grimace before pointing at one of the dark men standing beside her and uttering a short command to him. Fezerva's cage was then pulled away from the stage as the presenter gave some finishing thoughts to his audience, who were by then packing up and leaving.

Fezerva, meanwhile, was taken on board a smaller black cloud than the one she had rode to the sky port, earlier. When she was brought inside by the beam of light, she found herself sitting in a bay behind the seat where the driver sat. This economy-sized craft was like a steel carriage that lacked a strider to pull it along, yet it had a device attached to invisible reigns that allowed the vehicle to turn and move.

Fezerva watched where the driver was going out of the single window over his shoulder. Their striderless carriage flew from the sky port and into the heavens, where much more stars could be seen than the ones she saw before. Once they had moved some distance away from the sky port, the driver secured his invisible reigns and grabbed his mace-like weapon from the wall beside him as he stood from his seat and turned to where Fezerva was sitting.

The dark man held the blunt, broader edge of his weapon under his arm, while the narrower end was pointed directly at Fezerva. She thought it was strange how he was looking at her with that weapon held so peculiarly, but her brow lowered with suspicion when she figured he knew exactly what he was doing.

All of a sudden, her current vision was overtaken by an almost dreamlike scene: a flash, then a slow fall from the striderless carriage out into the depths of the night sky. Blinking back to reality, she questioned if what she had just seen was a hint of what was going to become of her. She only had a moment to spare, but not an inch to move to change her fate. There was nothing she could have done; she saw a red glow at the end of the thin, cylindrical protrusion in the dark man's weapon. For that instant, time seemed to stop.

Fezerva looked on with a bewildered stare at the dark man's face; he did not blink. There was not even enough motion to suggest he was even breathing. Fezerva stepped forward and gripped the bars of her cage to get a closer look at the frozen driver, but her hands slipped right through, as if the steel all around her were merely a figment of her imagination. Still, the dark man did not move. She reached down to touch the weapon in his arms, and it felt hot where it was glowing, as if it were a candle.

She heard herself exhale in the pure quiet of the room. When she blinked, she heard a loud snapping noise, like the crack of a whip, only much louder. The look she gave the dark man was every bit as stunned as the one he gave her. Upon seeing that frightened look in his eyes, she pulled the weapon out of his hands and turned it on him, causing him to panic.

The dark man had no reason to suspect she'd know how to use his firearm, but having suddenly witnessed this unassuming velta vanish and reappear like a ghost beside him didn't leave him with much time to doubt her abilities. He backed off under gun point into a chamber that was barely large enough for him to stand inside of it.

Once he was inside, a rotating door closed around him. Before Fezerva could make a move toward him, the chamber then fell through the floor of the striderless carriage with a rush of wind. Fezerva felt the air being taken from her lungs; being suddenly and nearly suffocated left the velta coughing and gasping. She dropped the weapon she held and stumbled back, hitting her head on the ceiling of a chamber identical to the one she saw the dark man flee into. As soon as she was inside, the door closed, and she could breathe, but not easily. A red light above her flashed with urgency.

Glyphs similar to the ones she saw on the cages before also appeared on other mirror-like screens to get her attention, but she couldn't understand what they were trying to tell her. "Something bad," was all Fezerva could glean from the situation.

She saw no way to escape her confinement, but even if she tried the same thing that got her out of the cage, she wouldn't want to go back out there. She looked all around the console in front of her to see if there was anything she could use to drop the room she was standing in like she saw the dark man do.

All she saw was what looked like a grid drawn on a yellow tablet full of symbols. She touched one of them out of curiosity, but nothing happened. She pressed a few more, and suddenly a translucent screen appeared above the tablet. It looked like it was made of light, and seemed to have writing on it, like a floating parchment. When Fezerva touched the screen, it swirled around her fingers like water, but it didn't feel like anything. She pressed another few glyphs on the pad before her to see if another screen would appear, or if the present one would go away. Neither happened; instead, the diaphanous material remained where it was, but something else caught her attention. A blinking light brought her eyes to focus on a red button beneath the console. Not left with many other choices for things to try, she touched the beckoning button and suddenly felt her stomach leap into her throat as the chamber in which she stood had slipped through the floor.

She watched through the window of her floating cell the striderless carriage fading away into the distance as she continued to descend. She looked down and realized that there was no ground beneath her; just more darkness and more stars. In every direction she looked, it was exactly the same. It was as if she had become trapped in the night sky.

She began to think that, maybe she was too high up to see the ground -- that perhaps if she just kept falling, she'd eventually see Vitiosa come up to greet her. She imagined that she'd be the luckiest velta in the world, to have not only seen the place that so many of her kind had been taken by these mysterious dark men, but lived to tell the tale.

The fantasy she fabricated was jostled from her mind when the capsule she was trapped inside began to turn and move all on its own, like a metal barrel being carried down a river. Fezerva thought that the capsule was being pulled by a creature stuck in the sky like she was. She looked all around outside her viewing screen, but could see nothing carrying her along. Perhaps, like the reins the dark man used to drive the vehicle she departed, it, too, was invisible?

Maybe all beings in the sky cannot be seen, and that's what causes all the motion of the stars and celestial objects in the night? Maybe even the gods were carried by these transparent beasts of burden?

Inexplicably, she began to feel very tired, despite this exciting turn of events. Truthfully, she shouldn't have been so surprised; she could not remember a time she was relaxed enough to sleep through a whole night.

But certainly being caught out here in such a compromising situation was not the time to be dozing off! She wondered if it's because she was so close to the night sky that she was beginning to feel as tired as she was?

Certainly, if the night was the cause of feeling sleepy, she would be powerless to resist its effects if she was immersed in it. She let her eyes close, trusting that the creature that was pulling her along would eventually bring her back home by the time she awakened.

An unintelligible amount of time later, her eyes were attacked by the light emitted by the morning sun. She awoke to find herself still inside her metal barrel, but in an entirely different place than the one she was in when she fell asleep. The skies were of a darker shade of blue than the one she was used to seeing; she didn't feel like she had to squint as hard to look at the rising sun. The trees of the forest around her were much taller than any she had seen, before, but the plants were still green.

She could hear chirping sounds outside from animals she'd never heard of. She rested her hands on the console to peer outside the window, but found herself tumbling out of her capsule when its door swung open. The first thing she felt, besides the familiar stinging of grass against bare skin, was how oddly light she felt in this new environment.

Even the air felt thinner; she felt like she had to draw lighter breaths. She could hear things much easier than she could before; when she got up to her feet, she could hear the grass blades rising back up from being compressed under her body. Even though she could see further than she ever could before, she was unable to see any sign of civilization in the distance, in any direction she looked.

She turned around and saw that the flying bed she had been riding in had grown stubby legs to stand up from the ground. She began to worry if it had brought her to the wrong place.

Chapter 1: One or the Other

Through much of their early history, Vitiosa's lands were plagued with tumult. Belhuayns were split by a religious dichotomy that determined whether they gained strength and dominance through solidarity, or by winnowing the weak from their population. Their husband and wife deities, Safiro and Sanguina, were represented by their blue and red moons -- only one of which watched their lands at a time every lunar cycle.

The holy city of Tresantia, for four hundred years, was separated by these religious factions: one for Sanguina, the Goddess of Life, and one for Safiro, the God of Death. The Travestas Cathedral was home to a treacherous brotherhood of Safiric monks who regularly performed rituals behind closed doors, said to bring morbid misfortune upon the residents of Tresantia.

Residing within the Sachelvae Basilica, on the opposite side of town, were a cloistered sisterhood of Sanguinic priestesses, who would counter these evil rituals with their sacraments to protect those unwilling to give their lives to the God of Death. Tresantia itself was built concentric to these diametric faiths; the residences winding between these two points were built like a symbol of infinity.

The enormous energies these clashing powers created over the centuries resonated throughout the Mystic Plane, wrenching both deities from their dreaming states, resulting in a synodic event that had never occurred before or since. The moons of Safiro and Sanguina were at full attention in the night sky, like heterochromatic eyes, staring upon the landscape. The sleepless couple sought for a way to end the conflict, telepathically communicating across their heavenly fanes.

Safiro stood atop a pyramid of midnight blue, overlooking the dark, cavernous wastes filled with the hollow-eyed souls of belhuayns ancient and new. Between two torches, his throne of bone sat behind him as he stared into the sullen skies. The eaves of his pyramid were decorated with golden insignia on the mosaic floor, these symbols represented in three dimensions by the two torches on either side of the square-shaped platform.

The spirits to which his cloaked servants tended had forever assumed the appearance of the person they were, the way they looked, the moment of their death. The sounds of whipping on bare flesh begot cries of pain; dolorous groans of agony yet acquiescing to the punishment they endured. A blue luminescence was all that could be seen at first, until clarity allowed them to espy the horrific surroundings only the blind could adore.

Shoulder-to-shoulder in pits six feet deep were all the most unfortunate of belhuayn souls who died dishonorable deaths. In chains they were bound to one another and to the unforgiving ground, their strength and will sapped of them by whips of cloaked tormentors lining the holes in which they were stationed. It was a deplorable place, spoken of in legend for eons, but the campfire tales through which they were passed could not have captured the unspeakable horror of this infernal realm. One of these screaming souls somehow escaped its confines and floated over head the God of Death.

His powerful voice, like a death knell, re-inspired fear into the shackled spirit, causing it to freeze and quiver in mid flight. He grabbed it by the neck and with another, guttural shout, he imperiously swept his hand to command two shrouded bedevilers to stand on either side of him, both wielding broad-bladed axes seven feet high.

The terrified soul risked its sanity a glimpse at the faces of Safiro's servants, whom underneath their white and blue garbs were armored with silver plate. Their helms were made in the likeness of a glowering, horned skull with red fires for eyes. They lifted their mighty twibills over their shoulders, invoking the escapee to cower in fear, before it heard a loud clash of metal. Its chains broken, Safiro then cast the spirit into the starlit sky with a single thrust of his arm.

Leaning back in his chair, the God of Death dismissed his devils back to their stations. He then continued his conversation with Sanguina, sending his gravelly voice to her realm. "These people cause... too much noise. They have broken the second seal with their mystic resonance. Soon, the last seal shall be broken. We are the only gods of the Qualarian System who have not turned aberrant; we are the only ones who can save our people."

Sanguina austerely petted the chin of an unborn, belhuayn spirit at the shore of a scarlet lake, before rising from her knees to receive Safiro's message. She looked to the hemisphere above, filled with winged spirits swimming about in anticipation for their time to be conceived into the Physical World. At that moment, what appeared to be a white comet broke through the clear sky and splashed into the stagnant waters, frightening the infant spirits until they realized the 'comet' was the ghost sent from Safiro's realm. When its head broke from the rippling surface and breached through the bubbles, its eyes turned round with youth and wonderment, possessing hardly a memory of the sordid soul it used to be.

Satisfied with the transformation, albeit displeased with her husband's roughness, Sanguina sighed, frowning back at the face of his moon above her. "We must save as many as we can and find a way to bring our children together; migrate them to one location and prepare them for mass exodus. They can restart a new life on another world to escape the devastation."

Safiro was not content with her reasoning. He was infamously stubborn when it came to the salvation of his creations. "I will not retreat. I have spent too long strengthening my children for them to forsake my powers and run like cowards. They will stand and fight; they will be the only race to survive the Qualarian apocalypse. They will inherit the barren worlds left to die by the aberrant gods who turned a blind eye to their creations."

"It won't do any good," Sanguina argued. "When the judgment comes, Qualaria herself will die, too. Then everyone in her care will perish along with her. It is better for us to leave now while we still can."

"Are you suggesting that my children *surrender?*" Safiro growled.

"They are *both* our children," Sanguina's voice calmly raised. "Not all who honor peace are weak, like not all who honor war are strong. Our children have been used by the Qualarian System's empires for all this time because they are seen as primitive and lowly. If they were not so concerned with fighting each other as they were helping one another, they could build their technology and civilization to a state where they could be respected by the other kingdoms."

Safiro was not content with his wife's ideals -- he never was. He had heard it all before and it annoyed him all the same. "I will not allow the growth of my perfect race to be stunted! My children will not get the justice they deserve! They must reach their full potential to *defeat* this apocalypse! Qualaria will not die if our race can defeat its aggressors --"

Sanguina impatiently interrupted, "There is no chance they could become that strong, even if we *ourselves* turned aberrant!" She paused to await the return of a calm composure before lifting a hand in gesture towards the planet below.

"...Especially not in the amount of time we have. If we are to keep our status in the realms, we must follow the rules of Eternity." A clever smile curled Sanguina's lips, "Might I make a suggestion?" she barely waited for Safiro to respond before continuing. "We create a hero -- a Champion who can use either of our powers if she so chooses, but without either of our influences. We will observe this Champion, left to her own devices; we will be within our rights as deities to do this without facing judgement or aberrancy."

Such an idea was not exactly unheard of; during his monthly jaunts to the mortal world, Safiro heard rumors of such a person existing among his children. For a thousand years, he'd heard prophecies of a *Vytameta* -- someone who could use the ideals of Safiro and Sanguina at will. Someone who would be bound to neither faith, instead choosing a path for all belhuayns to follow.

"Yes, our children have seen this coming for a long time," a cold wind left Safiro's lungs as his fingers clenched against the armrests of his throne. "But you are as aware of the dilemma we face, when conceiving this new being into the world. The leaders of Our Faiths have begun to interrupt the cycles they were meant to upkeep, by perverting Our Will to serve themselves. The spirits I am meant to collect," he swept a hand across the canyons and pits beneath his pyramid, "are growing fewer. The population will dwindle, with the way my children currently worship…"

Her husband's admittance to wrongdoing earned a quirk of the lips from Sanguina, who was pleased to know that he was finally coming around to cooperating with her. "Then you see that something must be changed to avert the breaking of the final seal. A reversion to the Old Faith is necessary for this recourse to be made."

Though Sanguina couldn't see him do so, Safiro nodded with affirmation -- albeit half-heartedly, as if it were more out of defeat than agreement. "But this recourse cannot be made unless the Vytameta has the power to change the world. She must see the world the way we see it: For what it is. She must understand the dangers her race faces. She must be raised in the same conditions that my children suffer on the outer worlds... Then we will see if she prefers my vengeance or your forgiveness."

After some time for consideration, his wife assented to his terms. "Though I have reservations against using my children as playthings," she said, "I believe Tresantia would be the perfect place to conduct such an experiment." Ending her conversation with her husband, the Goddess of Life returned her attention to the unborn spirit floating by the pool's edge, in preparation to accept the responsibility issued by her mother.

"In your previous life, you were the founder of my promised land. Now it is time for you to be a hero again. You will not be my child, thus you will have no protection from Safiro's evil, but you can do no wrong in my eyes." She stroked the spirit with a loving hand, watching it spiral jovially at her touch.

"Neither of us can tell you what to do unless you seek our guidance. You are free to make any choices you wish, and your decisions may ultimately change the world." With a flick of her finger, Sanguina removed the golden birth ring from the spirit's neck. "But... I cannot trust that Safiro's plan will lead to the absolution We believe Our race deserves. I apologize for what I must do to ensure that our memorandums will be followed."

She placed a hand upon the spirit's crown and coated it with a pink radiance. While sheathed in this mystic light, a copy of the spirit began to emerge from the original. When Sanguina's hand had been taken back, the lights dissipated and now there were two identical spirits sitting beside each other.

"One of you will have a perfect life, filled with the kind of happiness I want for my children. That is how you will come to know me, and work to unify Our twisted faiths instead of destroy them." With an upward gesture, she commanded the twins to flap their fins and fly above the cochineal lakes, soaring upward to breach the boundary of the ethereal plane. Once airborne, the spirits twisted around each other before splitting off in separate directions to enter the mortal world.

* * *

Sixteen years later, the glow of Safiro's moon could barely be seen as a blue stain in the sour clouds over the town of Fort Pericula. The skies began to shed their first tears of rain on the straw roofs of its residences. A light breeze swirled the smoke flowing from their chimneys. The pattering raindrops drowned out the stealthy footsteps of a teenage vixy in a black cloak, creeping along the walls of a house like a shadow.

She squeezed the edge of her blade underneath the crack in a window so her limber form could slip inside like a cold wind. She let the warmth of the unknown room seep into her skin before raising her head above the countertops to find herself in a kitchen. Bowls of fruit perhaps a few days old, yet ripe for her consumption, were on an island in the center of the dark chamber.

She hadn't eaten anything in so long, and knew she'd need the energy to last another night. She made a snack for herself out of several grape-like fruits covered by hard, brown husks -- but she could have eaten the delicacies, shell and all, if she did not fear they'd get caught in her throat. Her starvation had given her a bad enough gag reflex, but pilfering food was not her main objective. She wandered the moonlit corridors, looking for any valuable possessions she could take to finally live comfortably for a while. She arrived at a bedroom where the home's owner was soundly sleeping. The middle-aged scelan barely stirred when her foot touched a creaky floorboard inside the doorway.

She approached a wooden stool serving as a nightstand by his bedside, where her eye caught the faint glimmer of gold coins illuminated by a lantern's flickering flame. She swallowed nervously, knowing it would be risky to snatch the money so close to the sleeping scelan, but she did not have the patience to wait for another chance. Just as she was slowly scraping up the coins, the wind changed direction to knock loose timber against the bedroom window. The scelan awoke with a start to see the darkly-dressed brigand in the process of taking his belongings. She froze when their eyes met; for a second, both she and her victim were paralyzed with mutual fear. "You... stupid **bitch**...!" he angrily spat, raising himself up. *"I'll kill you, thief!"*

As he reached for a wooden pole arm leaning against the headboard of his mattress, the vixy gasped and bolted for any exit she could find. She stumbled over chairs and jumped over the kitchen table on her way through the dining room, nearly bouncing off a wall as she felt her way inside the small living room.

She knocked over some knick-knacks and broke a glass cabinet with her tail swinging to-and-fro. At full-tilt, she smashed through the locked door and tumbled down the wooden stairs outside onto the cobblestone streets. As she struggled to pick herself up off her scraped elbows and knees, fighting through the pain of her bruised shoulder, she saw the scelan still ruthlessly gaining on her.

"Guards!!" he cried to the town watch. "She took my money!"

The panicked vixy's vision closed off her peripherals as she made a mad dash away from the streetlights so she could not be seen by the soldiers stationed on the battlements. Arrows zipped over her head before she melted into the backstreet shade. She wound her way around the various buildings of shops and residences until she found herself staring up the city's 12-foot barricade.

She checked with a cursory and far-too-hurried glance to really notice anything she could use to scale the heights of what was quickly spelling out a deathtrap for the desperate criminal. She could barely hear it over the sound of her heart pounding in her ears, but the sound of running footfalls aggressively beating the pavement alerted her to turn around in just enough time to avoid the point of a spear about to be driven into her back.

"HRRAAGGHH!!" the older scelan loosed a primordial battle cry as the fang on the end of his primitive weapon broke into the stone floor. Turning his forward momentum against his enemy, the thief swept her tail at the scelan's ankles, causing him to keep going and flail into the daunting barrier ahead. Just as he was picking himself up, using the sheer surface to regain his balance and return to his feet, the cloaked vixy drew a long dagger from within her robe and plunged it through his spine.

The scelan's agonized screams resounded throughout the neighborhood as she twisted the blade for good measure. His fingers curled into the wall as he collapsed below a trail of his own blood. His murderer stared with wide eyes at the prostrate body at her feet; her hands shook as she drew slow, exasperated breaths. She had no time to reflect and contemplate the act she had just committed out of blind desperation. She heard the guards' steel boots clashing against the stone roads like an avalanche of pots and pans, steadily approaching her position.

Without a moment to spare, she fled for the alleys whence she came and found a route for her escape. Her eyes darted as she made frantic motions, trying to avoid dead ends as she frenetically located the city gates. Finding that her pathway was clear, she dashed outside and continued downhill toward the outer lying woods. She looked over her shoulder and saw the torchlights of her pursuers in the distance.

Continuing beyond the fringe of the trees until the lights were no longer visible, her adrenaline rush depleted and left her exhaustedly falling into a puddle of mud. The hyperventilating vixy hadn't the energy to even crawl to the taller grasses by the edge of the mire. She felt faint, cold, and ill -- the rain poured harder as if to drown her. At that moment, such a thought was nearly appealing to her. She hadn't the resolve to go on, nor even the bravery to behold her scrapes and wounds stinging in the dirty water.

After lying there for several minutes, struggling just to breathe, she began crying; soft gasps and whimpers growing into miserable sobs that demanded imminent death as she was reminded of what a terrible life led up to the very moment she found herself in. An awful life with no qualities at all to justify her continued survival in a world that seemed to have forsaken her from the moment she was born.

Her suicidal apathy quashed her fear; she invited death with cacophonous caterwauls, but her disconsolate depression convinced her that no matter how hard she cried, her voice would never be heard and she would never gain salvation.

The sobbing vixy's eyes turned wide when she heard the sudden crunch of leaves underfoot. She rose to her hands and knees to see a lantern's light glowing in the darkness between the branches of the thicket, belonging to a hooded figure wearing blue robes and a white pallium adorned with insignia depicting a black moon. He carried a tall, curved staff, tapping against the rocks with every step he took. He stopped when he caught sight of the vixy with aubergine hair slowly rising from the mire.

"Stay the hell away from me!" she wheezed, unable to maintain a threatening posture. "I'll gut you if... *hhff*, if you take a-another step!" The violette's voice cracked before her speech disintegrated into an asthmatic coughing fit. Short of breath, she dropped to a knee and could barely hold the blade in her hand as she weakly braced herself with the other.

"Do not be frightened," he invitingly showed her an open hand. "Come out into the light."

She gave him a nearly bewildered stare, having rarely encountered a stranger so willing to offer her assistance with such a genuine tone. Though far from naíve, even at her age, the violette couldn't help trusting him. Obeying the gentle beckoning of his soft voice, she came into the open where she could see his attractive yet lifeless face.

His head tipped up with an intrigued hum, as if able to see something extramundane in her appearance. "You are no ordinary young velta, are you?... What is your name?"

"Kasra... Jantica," she breathed, staring into small pupils of his white, vade-like eyes. She hesitantly accepted his hand, ice cold to the touch, to be brought back to her feet. "Who are you?"

The monk superciliously replied with a sidelong smirk. "They call me Deniechus, the Handsome. I am a servant of Safiro -- the High Priest of Travestas."

"Travestas?" Kasra curiously repeated. "What is that?"

"You do not know?" Deniechus incredulously looked down at her. "It is the greatest Safiric temple in all the land, and it is located in the legendary Tresantia: the most sacred city in all the world, " the priest proudly smiled. "That is where I've made my home. There is no better place to be."

Deniechus brought Kasra from the swampy creek up to the dirt path where his steed awaited: a slender, four-legged creature with a coat of sublime, black hair. It had long legs, a long neck, and horns like a gazelle, but a stockier body that could support the weight of a single rider. Its flat, almost triangular head was protected by a bony shield used for fending off adversaries and competing with rivals. Its white, feather-like tail was used for attracting mates and showing dominance in a herd.

"This is Chantice, my black strider," Deniechus introduced the creature, currently grazing by the side of the road. "She was the one who alerted me to your distress as we were riding through the woods."

As Kasra was helped to climb up on the strider's back behind Deniechus, she asked, "Why did you come for me?"

"You'd expect a stranger to hear another's cries and leave them for dead?" the Priest answered with a question of his own. "Is that what you call compassion?"

"Maybe I've just never seen it for myself," Kasra quietly looked away.

"You've been in the dark too long," Deniechus remarked, kicking a heel into the side of his steed to get it moving. "But there was a time I was like you: alone and scared. I craved answers and a sense of belonging. That is how I found the temple; that is how my life changed. By following Safiro, everything became clear to me: why we are here, and what role we all play. We all serve a purpose, some of us greater than others... Don't you want to know what your purpose is?"

Despite all the wonderment he hoped his sermon would instill upon the plebeian's mind, she responded with an ignorant refute. "What does any of that matter?"

"You are selfish and green," the High Priest chuckled. "But I know my Master could make you into more than what you are, now."

"I don't care what your 'Master' wants with me," the defiant violette retorted. "I am far more concerned with relieving my pain and hunger than I am with impressing some deity who does not care if I live or die."

"You need elucidation much more than you realize," Deniechus assured her. "Once you have followed Safiro's path as long as I have, you will forget the concerns of starvation and agony. Power is the only thing that matters in this world. It is why the strong prey on the weak. If you do not strive for something, you will be some*one's* victim."

Through the other side of the forest, the city lights of Tresantia could be seen in the distance. It was home to one of the largest populations in Onteval, yet, unlike many Ontevallian cities, it was bereft of military walls to protect its people. Even without such bastions of safety, every historical siege against the town had failed. The city's lacking defenses was a testament to the lasting faith of its people.

A faith like this was a concept that Kasra was completely unfamiliar with. She had never seen a miracle like this from either god working in her favor, nor anyone else's. She saw life's events with a cynical objectivity as only someone who had always been relegated to the outside could perceive them.

She had never seen a place of worship, nor had she ever been curious to know what they were like. She figured they were full of misguided fogies who had the time on their hands to interpret a metaphysical meaning for every happenstance. Kasra only wished she could know such leisure, but considered it a fantasy, and like all fantasies, it was not meant to be dwelled upon.

It was not the first time Deniechus had detected such proud ignorance, but never before was he more inspired to make a neophyte out of this estranged individual. He rode his steed before the entrance to a cathedral made of gray stone, adorned with blue, horn-like spires atop the many angles of its roof. As Kasra gazed with wonderment at the building's enormous heights, Deniechus stepped off his strider and offered a hand to help her down. Kasra shivered under her cloak at the black, iron doors before Deniechus began to push one of them open. When she heard the hinges creak, she slowly followed him inside.

Travestas' interior was even colder than it was outside; Kasra could see the air leaving her lungs into the whispering wind with every exhalation. Though the building's single room was unoccupied aside from Deniechus standing behind her, she felt as if she was being watched from every corner.

The cathedral's source of illumination was provided by large bowls containing bonfires of blue flame, arranged in rows on either side of an aisle which led to an altar bathed in a beam of Safiro's cerulean light. More of the sapphire moon's twinkling radiance filtered in through the stained glass windows adorning the high walls, each one featuring presumably historic figures, dressed similarly to Deniechus himself.

Striking his staff loudly into the floor, Deniechus called out to an invisible audience, "Come! Let us make our guest feel welcomed!

The heavy doors slammed shut when the ambient winds grew suddenly louder. The room temperature dropped immensely, until Kasra could not tell if she were being frozen by fear or by the bitter cold. Blue, wraith-like figures appeared from the shadowed walls and dove at her from above like a rush of air on either side, grasping her with claws of steel from their wide sleeves.

The teenage vixy was surrounded and restrained from all directions. She was too languid to defend herself. It was too cold to breathe. She fell unconscious into one of their arms. The seven servants then stood abreast with a silent command from Deniechus. The High Priest then raised Kasra's head with a hand under her chin, and forced her blue eyes open to see their round pupils narrow into slits.

"You are no ordinary Pure," he snarled with intrigue. "But I think I know *exactly* what you really are..." To his servants, he commanded, "Lay her upon the altar. Let The Father determine... her potential."

The monks began softly chanting as they moved Kasra to restrain her to the sacrificial block, each one holding a separate limb to keep the vixy under Safiro's lunar radiance. A pair of tall torches in front of the altar's plinth turned alight of their own accord, filling the end of the chamber with a cerulean glow. Deniechus stood behind the altar, raising his hands toward the open window to offer Kasra's spirit to the God of Death.

"I present this vassal to your almighty holiness, to be filled with your power!"

Kasra closed her eyes and turned her head away from the blue beacon emanating down from Safiro's moon. The chants of the monks around her grew louder until they were suddenly silenced by a clacking noise. The monks turned to see what appeared to be a black rock the size of a fist bouncing on the stone floor, as if having been dropped from the blue. Before any of them could move or make a sound, the rock detonated with a blinding flash and a deafening snap. All of the Safiric servants fell to their knees in the waist-deep smoke, cawing raucously and holding their ringing ears.

Dropping in from the oculus like a black blur was a darkly-dressed figure wearing a long mantle over a leather jumpsuit. Red eyes and a red ponytail were all that could be seen outside of her mask, which hung below her chin like a veil. She pushed through the cringing monks to hoist the limp Kasra onto her shoulders and darted for the closed doors. But she was stopped when Deniechus suddenly appeared in front of her, like a wall rising from the shadows, and thrust a steel palm into her abdomen.

"Where are you going?..." he angrily rasped. A bright, blue glow began protruding from the end of his staff when he struck it into the ground, until it formed a sickle-like blade. He swung the edge of his scythe at the mysterious woman, forcing her to duck underneath. The redheaded velta performed a backward somersault; she carefully dropped the half-awake Kasra and returned to her feet in the same motion, before drawing a short sword from the scabbard on her back.

"She belongs with me!" She clashed her gladius against the side of the staff Deniechus held over his head, issuing a bright spark that jolted the straight-edged steel from the mysterious velta's hands. Undeterred by her sudden disarming, she threw a kick that Deniechus also parried, before he countered with, "I know who you are, Red Dancer!"

To Kasra, as well, the redhead also looked oddly familiar. Once she had the time to collect her bearings, she crawled away from the fray and got a better glimpse of her savior. She saw a red gem dangling from a necklace she wore, seeming to emit its a strange glow. It looked oddly familiar to a ruby pendant that Kasra's was given at a very young age by her long-lost sister. It too, emitted the same glow through her cowl. The teenage vixy's concealment could not hide her identity from her sibling. "Rozha!!"

The Red Dancer was distracted by Kasra's shout, taking her mind off her opponent for just the moment he needed to knock her down with a sweep of his scythe at her ankles. He raised his weapon for a finishing blow just as Rozha reached for her sword, grasping its hilt in just enough time to interlock their blades. Electricity flew off Deniechus' scythe and surged into Rozha's body, agonizingly tensing her every muscle.

Even if this redheaded fighter was not her sister, Kasra could not sit there and watch her die. But the violette could not summon the strength to attack their foe, even with his flank so readily exposed. She felt utterly helpless; all she could do was scream *"STOP!"*

Ironically, the very 'compassion' Deniechus claimed she did not have would serve to be his unmaking. As if forced to obey the word Kasra vociferated, his whole body froze in place. Not even his eyes could move; all he could see were star-like sparkles glistening off his arms, wrists, and the fingers that grasped the weapon he held against his adversary. Even the power he sent to surge through her veins was stopped completely.

Rozha slowly recovered, clutching her chest with disbelief at what she saw: her opponent hung above her as if suspended in time. But it was only he who was halted; everything else around her still moved, including the monks at the altar. The Red Dancer saw Kasra leaning up against the side of a pew, looking every bit as thunderstruck as she was. Blindly accepting what had happened as a blessing for as long as it might last, Rozha rolled back to her feet and carried the frightened Kasra out the doors with her.

"Where are you taking me?!" the violette exhaustedly protested, bouncing in Rozha's arms.

"To the other side of town," her sister panted. "They can't harm you there."

Puddles splashed up from the brick roads as Rozha made her mad dash from the dark cathedral. The cold downpour and the weight in her arms only made her have to push that much harder, but she only let herself rest when the face of Travestas could no longer be seen over her shoulder. She stopped underneath a stone building's wide roof to escape the rain, setting Kasra down with her back to its wall. She kept her hands on her knees, waiting for her racing heart to be quelled, as she listened for any signs of their pursuers. She stilled her breath to find the sounds of their stealthy footfalls, but it did not seem that they were being followed.

Rozha pulled down her mask and loosed a long sigh of relief, blowing a puff of warm air into the cold breeze as she slid down to a crouching position beside her younger sibling. "We've escaped, but we're still not safe," she whispered. The redhead then looked to Kasra with a hint of worry wrinkling her complexion. "Are you alright?"

"Rozha...!" the violette's eyes glistened. "It really *is* you!" she added with a smile. An overjoyed Kasra tossed her arms around her sister, who turned somewhat anemically rigid at first before relaxing herself into the velta's embrace. "I never thought I'd see you again!"

Rozha lovingly nuzzled Kasra's neck as the violette buried her face into her shoulder and broke down into a sobbing catharsis. "I've been looking all over for you ever since I left my blade dancer clan," she somberly explained. "I feared you might have been killed, but I couldn't have been happier to know you were alive on your own. I'm sorry I couldn't have been there for you, all these years."

Kasra shook her head, her fingers curling into Rozha's backside as she was overcome with emotion. "I've waited so long... I didn't know how much time I'd have left. I'm so glad you've come for me at last!"

Rozha stiffened from a sudden, strong chill crawling up her spine. "Kasra," she gently pulled away from her, "wear this, and don't move." The former blade dancer cast her mant over Kasra and swiftly moved out of the alleyway to confront a Safiric monk rising from a black pool of shadow in the street.

"Where is she?" he hissed, his voice like a sharp knife. "You are hiding her from us."

The redhead's eyes narrowed as she reached for the hilt of her blade. "Her whereabouts are no concern of yours!" With a leap into the air, she used a curved blade on her forearm to slash at the scelan, but in the fashion of a ghost, his body assumed a gaseous state to avoid her strike. Returning to his solid form a few paces away, the Safiric monk extended his palm and slammed it beneath Rozha's sternum with a flying charge, knocking the Red Dancer into the grasp of another priest having just appeared behind her.

Her first attacker then gesticulated his hands together, charging blue static between the tips of his claws, as if conjuring a spell to release her spirit. Rozha ducked away to free her arms of her captor's restraint, somersaulting beneath the oncoming blast of electric energy which was now targeted to send the monk's ally reeling. She capitalized on her foe's folly by plunging the full length of her sword through her enemy's chest, and just as she drew it back out of his screeching cadaver, jabbed the spike on her elbow into the monk's abdomen who was once again attempting to grab her. She then tripped him up with a lash of her tail against his legs, his body crashing into the wet road before she turned to thrust the point of her blade into his neck.

Rozha let the rain wash the blood off her steel as she returned to Kasra's hiding spot to see that she had thankfully been left unharmed. Kasra poked her head outside the mantle's coif when she heard Rozha's footsteps approaching, and stood up to join her. "Why couldn't they see me?" she asked, handing her extra cloak back to her sister.

"This is a *mantamina*," the redhead replied, wrapping it back around herself. "It is blessed with Sanguinic energy so that those with Safiric eyes will be unable to see its wearer's soul."

"How were you able to acquire such a thing?" Kasra asked, examining the robe with disbelief.

"From the temple on the other side of town," Rozha looked to its silhouette in the distance. "Sachelvae. They say the whole city of Tresantia was built around it because it granted Pures protection from Safiric evils."

Kasra had never heard of Sachelvae, but even from where they stood, on the other end of town, she could see the blackened edifice prominently raised over all the other structures before it. She and Rozha traveled through the midnight darkness betwixt the Tresantian alleyways until they had arrived at the grand portal to Sachelvae.

Within its spandrel were colonnettes between which were jamb figurines depicting priestesses bowed in prayer. A short flight of stairs brought them to the large, reinforced wooden doors that looked like they should have belonged to a castle. Above the doors was a tympanum, decorated with an oddly familiar visage. The velta it depicted had her face staring northward, seemingly with suspicion, to the Safiric side of Tresantia. Around her head were the engravings of belhuayn spirits. Her welcoming visage inexplicably filled Kasra with a sensation of warmth.

Sachelvae's doors opened into a vacant hall of pink marble floors and

31

tiled walls, reaching up to a convex ceiling decorated with murals and paintings of unborn spirits playing in Sanguina's realm. The huge room was almost entirely lit by the multiple oculi spanning its roof; the chandeliers hanging by the walls provided a soft, rosy radiance with their crystal lights. In the middle of this vast chamber was its most striking feature: a long reflecting pool of shiny water. On either side of this public bath were red cushions made for its guests to kneel upon. At the far end of the pool were a pair of steps leading up to a raised plinth, on top of which was a podium endowed with a red, crystal ball.

Safiro's moonlight leaking through the round windows above made blue the reflecting pool in the center, which was speckled with flower petals. It was a clean and beautiful place, perfectly befitting of the goddess in whose image it was built. Kasra could hear her every footstep on the marble floors of the quiet atrium; only the small waterfall rushing into the end of the reflecting pool accompanied her thoughts. "Are we not trespassing?"

"All the priestesses are asleep, right now," Rozha's voice echoed within the empty, hallowed halls. "But the doors through which we came will only open to those who have Sanguina's blessing."

"You seem to know this place very well," Kasra observed.

"I live here," Rozha replied. She motioned for Kasra to follow her down the end of the hall. "You must be starving," she said. "I could feel every bone in your body when I was carrying you, earlier."

"I haven't eaten a square meal in years," Kasra held her stomach, aching from the thought of food. She followed Rozha into a pantry and took a seat on a barrel by a table in the center of the room, while her sister prepared a small dinner for her consisting of a loaf of bread and a bowl of soup.

"I'm not a terrific chef," Rozha admitted, "but it's the least I can do for you."

Kasra smiled. "I can't thank you enough," she delightedly purred, feeling satiated off just the soup's rich scent. "This is the most I've had to eat in a long time." She only just then minded her soaking clothes when she was warmed by the first spoonful of broth to touch her lips.

"I might have a snack, too," the redhead collected a small meal for herself, "after all that running around I did for you."

Kasra waited for her sister to sit down across from her before asking, "Who were those people you rescued me from? What did they want with me?"

"I honestly wish I knew," Rozha wistfully sighed. "Safiro's servants are taught to kill anyone who is not of their kind. They'd have no reason to perform one of their rituals on a Pure. What you went through sounds like something the High Priestess might know about. You should meet her. I have a feeling she'd like to see you."

Kasra swallowed nervously. "I don't know about that... Would she even believe it?"

"She will," Rozha confidently answered. "I took a vow to never lie."

The violette raised an eyebrow and inquisitively cocked her head. "You're a priestess of this temple?"

"That's right," her sister leaned back and crossed her arms. "Every Sister has to swear an oath to Sanguina to be ordained. As long as you remain true to your vows throughout your life, your spirit will remain clean on the day you die. At least, that's what I gathered from Mother Diava's explanation of it."

"She's the High Priestess?" Kasra guessed.

"Mmhm," Rozha affirmed. "It'd do you good to meet her, trust me. You can spend the night in my quarters and I'll introduce you in the morning. What do you say?"

Kasra pondered her options for a good, long time, knowing Rozha to be right, but just not thinking herself worthy. "What have I done to deserve Sanguina's grace? Why would the goddess care about saving me?"

"There are some things in life you don't have to earn or 'deserve.'" Rozha solemnly raised her finger and recited the common slogan, "Mother always forgives -- that's what they all say around here, and they're words to live by. When you're not sure about something, you ask Her for guidance." Instead of giving Kasra any more time to mull it over, Rozha stood up and ushered her along. "C'mon, you can finish your soup in my room. There's plenty more to eat around here; we won't let you starve."

"Thank you," came another, unusual display of emotion from the ex-rogue.

Her sister smiled at her from over her shoulder as she led her back to the lodging hall. "I'm happy to help." She brought Kasra to the last door on their left, and opened it for her to go inside. "This is my room, here. It's a quaint little space only meant for a single occupant, but I'll spare a blanket for you so sleeping on the floor will be slightly more tolerable."

The room of wooden walls and floors was probably no more than twelve feet wide and ten feet high, and was dimly lit by an oil lamp low on its wick. The lamp was placed on top of a nightstand where it could easily be reached from the bed near the center of the room. A sliding door granted access to a walk-in closet that Rozha looked inside for some extra bedding. She laid some blankets down for her and tossed a pillow at the base of the pile. "You can hang your wet clothes out the window, there, so they'll dry overnight."

Kasra waited for Rozha to turn around before she embarrassedly took off her rain-washed robe, and knee-high boots, leaving her with only a black bandeau and a matching thong for underwear. Rozha, meanwhile, changed out of her one-piece into her much more stylish, lace undergarments, before sitting on her bed's firm mattress. She frowned of pity when she saw how Kasra looked even worse for wear than she imagined, scars stretching across her back as if lashed by whips, her hands calloused as if having bore many blisters in years past.

While Kasra made herself comfortable on the sleeping area Rozha had provided, she took off the utility belt wrapped around her waist and set it down beside her. Hearing the scabbard it carried loudly clatter against the floorboards had the Red Dancer openly wondering, "What's that sword you got there?"

Kasra looked at it with a shrug. "I don't know what it's called."

"Looks like a gladius, to me," Rozha said. "How long have you had it?"

"Since my fourteenth birthday," she answered, hugging her shins. "I turned sixteen, last winter."

"It really *has* been a while," her sister ran a hand through her hair. "I came to this temple in the summer of last year. Much of Tresantia's population is comprised of migrants from other regions. It has a certain... vibe to it."

Kasra stayed silent for a while, resting her chin upon her knees and wrapping her tail around her ankles, staring not into the floor, but into space. Rozha frowned with concern at her sister's pensive expression. "You're still thinking about Travestas, aren't you?"

The violette nodded. "How long will I have to hide from them? What will they do if they know I'm here?"

"They won't get you," the Red Dancer assured her. "Not unless you want them to. No one can hurt you so long as you stay here. And that's exactly what I'm going to get worked out with the High Priestess, tomorrow. Now get some sleep -- you look like you've been run ragged for days."

Rozha turned down the oil lamp's flame and the room went dark. The bedroom's tranquility was unlike anything to which Kasra was accustomed; a far cry from dozing off in the middle of town, or in a stranger's home. After drinking down the tepid broth she had brought with her, Kasra finally laid her head on the pillow she was provided. Despite her anxiety, her eyes began to close as the sleepless nights behind her seemed to catch up all at once.

Chapter 2: Tempting Fate

That night, Kasra found herself lying on a raft, being tossed around in a storm at sea. Looking around in an utter daze as the heavy rain pelted her face and soaked her clothes, she tried to collect her bearings but could see no semblance of a shoreline anywhere on the horizon. There was no telling how far she had been left adrift, nor from what direction she came. The single sail of her flat, loosely-constructed vessel was buffeted every which way by the cold, howling wind. She couldn't see apart from the waves crashing against her, and couldn't hear apart from the choppy surf and the roaring gale. She thought at any moment, the mast would break away from the tiny boat and she would be left in the middle of nowhere, with no way of reaching land. There were no paddles, no food -- no provisions of any kind. But the most frightening thing was that she had no memory of how she got there. She had never seen the coast in her life. She knew she grew up nowhere near a beach.

The more she thought about how confusing the situation was, the more she subconsciously drifted away. The winds grew quieter; the waves grew calmer. She felt herself lifting, as if being taken away. She turned and saw the sun peeking through the clouds; she squinted her eyes and when she blinked, she had returned to the bedroom she shared with her sister at Sachelvae. She was lying in the blanket that had been given to her the night before, now wrapped around her body like a cocoon on the floor. As she wrestled with the woolen bedsheet, trying to pull her arms free, she heard the sound of Rozha's footsteps and rustling of clothes. She rose up to peer over the bed beside her and saw her sister donning a sacerdotal gown of red and black drapes adorned with moon-shaped sigils.

Rozha gave her sister a smile when she turned to see her. "Good morning! I thought I'd let you rest for a bit while I prepared for the day's ablutions. You could probably use a bath, too, huh?"

"Yes, I suppose..." the violette self-consciously ran a hand through her tangled tresses. "Do I really look so bad?"

"Well, not terrible, anyway," her sister lightly chuckled. "I'm sure you'll feel better once you've had a chance to clean up. But that can wait 'til after you've seen the High Priestess." Moving to open the door, she added, "C'mon, she's already out there waiting for us."

Kasra was the first to step out into the sunlit passage, which now was now filled with the resonation of the priestesses murmuring further away in the gathering hall. Rozha came to join them last to ensure Kasra was seen with her, as if she didn't already feel enough out of place when she saw the forty other veltas all wearing the same gowns. They were kneeling upon square-shaped cushions on either side of the reflecting pool, facing the end of the building where a short staircase led up to a white altar adorned with scarlet curtains.

Before the altar suddenly appeared a white vortex of slowly swirling, cloud-like energy. This growing portal produced a low hum that echoed throughout the passages of the cathedral. In its center, once the gateway had reached full size, a glowing ball of white light began to emerge. The luminescent sphere filled out to the arms of the spiral, at which point the humming intensified. Then, with a whip-like crack and a shower of sparks, the portal and the lights disappeared to unveil a beautiful velta in its place. The fair-skinned abbess wore a large alb of flowing, silver drapes. Wrapped around her billowing clothes were golden bands and ribbons, each decorated with ancient writing in the belhuayn tongue.

Her white hair reached her shoulders in length, seeming to fade when compared to the fairness of her complexion; her bright blue eyes almost appearing gray. Her bediamonded tiara twinkled from the light pouring in through the ceiling with every turn of her head as she counted the priestesses sitting before her -- and noticed one was missing.

"Where is Sister Rozha?" she called.

"Forgive me, your holiness!" came the tardy dancer's voice from the back of the room.

Everyone turned and saw the teenage girl shuffling by her side, shyly bowing her head under the hood of her dirty cloak to escape their judgmental glares.

"Who is this gracious child you have brought?" the High Priestess asked.

"This is my sister, Kasra," Rozha couldn't have been happier to introduce her relative. "I rescued her last night from Travestas. I had a… strange feeling she'd be near," she added, clutching the ruby pendant she wore.

The abbess directed her gaze to Kasra, her features softening with a scant admiration for her, but it was hard to tell why. Kasra herself did not feel in the least admirable in her condition; it was flattering that anyone, especially someone so highly esteemed, held her in such regard. "I could not be more elated for you that you found this place," she folded her hands together. "But I must know: for what reason you were in Travestas before Sister Rozha brought you here?"

Before she could answer, everyone's attention diverted to a loud banging on the basilica's heavy doors. The High Priestess glanced between Kasra and the entrance before signaling for her servants to pull the doors open. Two veltas stood at either iron slab, taking hold of their metal handles and slowly walked them inward. The rest stood and gathered behind the High Priestess, who was the first to greet the ghastly monks of the Safiric Brotherhood. Deniechus stood in the company of three floating wraiths clothed in blue, tattered garbs. The hood of Deniechus' robe was down to show his face of gray skin and a deep cerulean rosage. The bangs of his wavy, black hair fell just over his pinpoint pupils staring unsettlingly into the Purity of the abbess' soul.

"We know she is here," he cryptically sibilated. "You cannot hide her from us."

"Are you inquiring about young Kasra?" Diava asked.

"We've come to take her back," he reached out a hand, as if awaiting an offering. "She belongs with us."

"Not in the least," the High Priestess narrowed her eyes to a steely gaze. "My Sister alleges she sought this place as refuge."

Deniechus pointed over her shoulder, as if looking right through her. "Bring her to us."

"I'm right here," Kasra boldly stepped through the crowd of priestesses with Rozha by her side.

"And she's not going anywhere," Rozha blocked Kasra with an outstretched arm.

The High Priest impatiently hissed, "You *dare* to oppose *the Master's* will?"

"Tell your 'Master' that if he wants Kasra, he can come get her, himself," she bravely looked down her nose at Deniechus and his lot. "And if he sends any more of his *bitches* over here, they can answer to me."

Her threats only elicited a scornful guffaw from the leader of Travestas. "Very well, 'Sister'. I will relay your message... and ensure you receive *exactly* what you asked for." He didn't take his eyes off her as he slowly turned oblique, stepping back into his awaiting company. While the rest of his followers were content with turning their hooded backs to the priestesses all huddled behind Sachelvae's doorway, Deniechus made sure to give them a troubling, parting glance over his shoulder before going on their way to return whence they came.

Rozha poised her hands to her hips, watching them reluctantly retreat, then stiffened from the unexpected embrace Kasra gave her, wrapping her arms around her guardian's shoulders. "Oh, Rozha, you're so brave! I have nothing to fear when you're by my side."

The blade dancer grinned and petted her sister between the ears. "I wanna give you a better life. I told you as long as you stayed here, you'll have nothing to worry about." Turning to the High Priestess, Rozha added, "So how about it, Mother Diava? What do you think about having Kasra becoming our newest novitiate?"

Diava tried her utmost to regain her formal rigidity, masking the fear she had of what had just transpired. "If Kasra wishes for Sanguina's favor, it is ultimately up for her to decide." "Kasra," she addressed her directly, "are you prepared to join the Sanguinic Order?"

Looking for Rozha's encouraging grin, and taking a moment to glimpse upon the faces of the priestesses around her, she turned her attention to Diava with a final, confident nod. "If that means I will no longer have to be alone and scared, then yes, I am ready."

"Sister Rozha is right," the High Priestess allowed herself a somewhat soulless smile. "None of Safiro's children can harm you within Sachelvae; a promise that Saint Sevasmia made to her disciples and has kept for four hundred years. She led them all to a promised land where they would be free to live how they pleased -- a Pure Paradise. By Her command, a sacred temple to Sanguina was built by her followers, its walls imbued with a charm that Her Righteousness was given by Sanguina Herself.

"Though many Safiric armies came to test the temple's meddle, every attack they waged failed before they even reached the doors. Hearing of the temple's legend, Pures came from far and wide to Sachelvae for its protection, and started a settlement that became known as Tresantia. You will have Sanguina's blessing now and forevermore when you begin your journey with Her. But you must first complete your rites of passage in order to be accepted as a Tresantian priestess."

"Tell me what I must do," Kasra courageously lifted her head.

"You must learn all you can about Sanguina's ways," Diava explained, "and use this knowledge to protect The Turned who have been led astray, so that they can begin to follow the path She has made."

"How will I know which path *I'm* supposed to follow?" the neophyte asked.

"Sanguina has designed one for each of us, long prior to our conception in this world." Diava answered. "It is up to us to rediscover what our purpose is, and fulfill it so that our spirits may be reborn to carry out a new path in another life. We often dream of our past lives, and from these dreams, know our purpose in this life."

Kasra's eyes blankly softened. What Diava mentioned about dreams of another life was an experience of which she had been curiously bereft, until last night. Perhaps she could impute her many restless nights to her lack of dreams before then, but she could say for certain she never had them. She began to wonder whose life she was dreaming of, and who would have been dreaming of her life, if she had died in the swamp outside Pericula. "What happens if you are led too far astray, and are never brought back?"

"Your spirit is then befouled and falls into Safiro's hands the day you die," Diava scowled at the mere mention of it. "When you are reborn from his realm, you will seek to destroy anything with fullness of spirit. Any one of Sanguina's children can turn to darkness, but any one of Safiro's children can be brought to light; that is why we are the minority, and will be slowly pushed into extinction if we do not turn more to our side."

"So when you mentioned The Turned," Kasra began, "you meant those who worship Safiro?"

"That is correct, my dear," Diava affirmed. "Shortly before Sevasmia's demise and induction into sainthood, a brotherhood of Safiric monks led by a man known as Zercius made their own church, Travestas, on the other side of town, which attracted a new population of Safiric worshipers to offset the

Pure settlers. It was their mission to overtake Tresantia through ideals rather than by force, thus dichotomizing the city's religion."

"Then, why not start with converting them?" she pointed through the open doors, in the direction of Travestas.

"If it were so simple, it would have been done centuries ago." With a wave of her hand, the High Priestess gestured her Sisters to push the doors closed, again. As they were being shut, Diava began walking with Kasra back to her place before the altar, while the other priestesses resumed their sitting positions.

"Alas, those strongly connected to Safiro's delusions cannot be swayed by methods that do not appeal to their bloodlust. As servants of Sanguina, we do not stoop to such levels of persuasion. Even the smallest willingness to inflict harm upon someone taints the soul. We can see this taint in ourself in each other by looking into our eyes," she pointed a V-shaped pair of fingers under her brow.

"Roundness indicates fullness of Purity. However, malice reduces their width. You turn more Wild with each sin and transgression, until the Brotherhood could call you one of their own..." She visibly shuddered at the very sound of such an awful fate. Collecting herself with a straightening of her dress, she added, "And no one, not even the most pious, are immune to temptation. That is why we begin every day with a ritual bath to cleanse our bodies and souls."

Kasra cast a critical gaze at the virgin priestesses genuflecting to Diava's beck and call, trying to imagine what in the world they could have done to earn the goddess' ire as much as she had.

"Sister Rozha," the High Priestess called out, "Can I entrust you to prepare Kasra for the daily ablutions?"

The blade dancer stood and took a respectful bow, "Yes, your holiness," and made her way up Diava's plinth to Kasra's side.

Diava, herself, leisurely walked down the stairs to the front of the natatorium and declared to her followers, "You may now enter the pool." The High Priestess was the first to shed her modest gown to show the one-piece swimsuit-like covering she wore underneath. The figure it concealed would not provoke an aversion of the eyes; her body was far from what would have been expected of a woman her age and could have easily belonged to someone decades younger.

As Diava's followers joined her, sitting side by side at the edges of the bath, Kasra was overcome with self-consciousness. She didn't feel anywhere near as spiritually pure or as beautiful as the women who began to fill the pool, rinsing their luxurious locks and rubbing soap along their sculpted forms. Kasra couldn't take her eyes off them. They looked like they were frolicking, without even trying to draw attention to themselves.

"I'll never fit in with them," she heaved a saudade sigh.

"This ain't about 'fitting in' or being better than someone else," Rozha corrected her. "Changing your life isn't a competition. As long as you're happy, what does it matter what anyone else thinks? No one is going to cast aspersions on you for not being perfect." Kasra didn't respond, but Rozha made sure to get her attention. "You said you were willing to do whatever it took to turn yourself around, right?" she waited for Kasra's nod. "Consider this as your first step."

She extended a hand to take Kasra's cloak as the violette bashfully unclasped the button holding her cowl around her shoulders. After Rozha placed the raggedy cope on the altar, the blade dancer then led her sister to the last, vacant spot in the pool and sat in the crystalline waters.

"It's so refreshing, isn't it?" a relaxed Rozha closed her eyes and reclined against the poolside. "I feel as light as a feather. This holy reservoir blackens not from the dirt of your body, but from the impurities of your soul."

Indeed, as the violette washed her swarthy skin clear of mud, and freed her frail hair of tangles, she was lifted by an unburdening sensation. She was so accustomed to filth and enervation; she had completely forgotten what it was like to be revivified. She had forsaken the finer things in life so much that she earnestly believed they were undeserved. She believed grace would come with a caveat; not be freely delivered to such bedraggled specimens like herself.

"I can feel it, too," Kasra beheld her newly shriven form. "I feel so warm..."

Rozha returned her companion's grin with a smile of her own. "I'll never take for granted what it does for me. I always take some time to enjoy it. Sanguina's moonlight refreshes the pool every evening, so that by morning, our tradition may continue."

As Kasra continued to bathe, cool air sent chills through her damp skin and caused her knees to quiver together. She braced her thin arms around her chest before shivering out a dainty sneeze. *"Kt-Chiew--!"*

"Salvii!" Rozha exclaimed, handing a towel to the sniffling violette. "You must have quite a guilty conscience."

"Hm?" Kasra confusedly rubbed the tingles from her nose. "What'cha mean?"

The blade dancer gave her a look that made it seem like her sister had been living under a rock. "You've never heard that a sneeze is Sanguina's way of taking sin from your body?" Kasra again, was ignorant to this apparently general knowledge. It did all the more to remind Rozha what a lacking quality of life the girl had without her. "That's why we wish for Sanguina's blessing, to celebrate the release of malice."

While the violette was washing her hair, her brow wrinkled from a mild irritation before she doubled over with a second, harder sternutation. *"Hah-KTTSCH!"*

"But if it persists," Rozha giggled, poking her sister's nose, "it means Safiro is testing you. We overcome his blight when we accept assistance from others. That's how Sanguina keeps us together." The redhead sympathetically brushed away the violette's messy bangs to feel her forehead. "I'll make sure you never feel crummy again. I promise!"

Kasra's beaming admiration for Rozha's altruism was interrupted by Diava announcing to her followers, "You may now exit the Purifier and proceed to the dining hall."

Everyone left the murky waters to begin drying off with white towels before returning to their red robes. After Rozha helped put Kasra's back on, the violette was summoned by the High Priestess, who had reclaimed her position before the altar. "Come, Kasra. I have a gift for you."

The tyro gave Rozha a parting glance as she respectfully sauntered up to the High Priestess' plinth. "What is it?" Her question lacked the clergy's traditional politeness.

"This," Diava handed Kasra a golden circlet with five crenulations, like rounded teeth, pointing down on a square of folded, scarlet cloth. "Your novitiate mantle. It is to be worn at all times, in and out of Sachelvae. The tiara is meant to show your status as a proselyte to Sevasmia's Sisterhood. One notch will be removed as you demonstrate your commitment to your goals. Once all notches are taken away, you will be inducted into the clergy."

"I will do as you ask," Kasra respectfully bowed. "What am I to do with my old clothes?" she asked, pointing where Rozha had left them.

"They will be burnt as part of your transformation to leaving your past behind," Diava pointed to the altar. "This shall symbolize your rejuvenation as Sanguina's child."

"Thank you," the violette's gratitude showed more naturally.

"When you are ready, come with us to the dining area," the High Priestess began. "We will have a meal prepared for you."

While she was on her way out, Kasra regrouped with a fully-dressed Rozha by the poolside. "Can you help me into my new clothes?" she embarrassedly bit her lip. "I don't wanna keep everyone waiting on me."

"No problem!" Rozha took the stole from Kasra's hands and began wrapping it around her narrow shoulders. "It isn't very complicated -- see, it works just like that." Rozha walk back around to face her sister and coyly tweaked her ear. "You look great."

A flattered Kasra eyed up at Rozha with a delicate smile. Her robe looked slightly different from her sister's, featuring a black crescent moon emblazoned on the chest, rather than a full black moon like the one Rozha had. Now that Diava had mentioned it, she did notice more the silver, V-shaped tiara her sister was wearing, to show her status as a full priestess. At a loss for words, she left a short pause in their conversation before Rozha patted her arm for her to follow her lead. "Let's get something to eat," she said. "You're probably still starving from last night!"

"I can't wait to see what they've got for us," the violette trotted in step with her.

At the end of the long corridor was a pair of Moroccan-style doors left open to the dining hall. The grand table was large enough to seat all forty of Sachelvae's residents. The seating arrangement for the priestesses at the table was very rank conscious; all novitiates sat at the end of the table opposite of the High Priestess, who was accompanied by two members of the faculty. The two veltas who sat on either side of her wore a robe featuring a full moon cradled by wedge-shaped extensions protruding from the black collar. Their tiaras looked similar to those of full priestesses, but were bejeweled with a red diamond in the center.

Four veltas wearing pink and black garbs came from the pantry to walk carts of food around the table, setting plates down for each priestess before reclaiming their empty chairs. They were the basilica's chefs, who each had taken a vow to volunteer their services to the impoverished. Their donations did not skimp on quality; everyone was given a plate of cut fruits along with a roll of bread.

"Kasra and Rozha," Diava addressed the two latecomers. "How good of you to join us. You may take your empty seats among your familiars."

A bit confused from what she meant by that at first, Kasra then noticed the obvious spot left open for her at the novitiate end of the table. Rozha patted her back and said, "Looks like this is where we part company, for now," leaving Kasra to shyly sit between two veltas who were probably both near her own age. Though she was nervous to have made their unspoken acquaintance, she was nonetheless relieved to see she wasn't the youngest person at the temple.

The full-figured velta of light brown hair and amber eyes gave Kasra a friendly smile as she made her approach, while the girl of dark green hair and eyes of lime sitting on the other side of her chair retained an austere frown. "Hi!" the brunette jovially greeted her new peer. Her friend less enthusiastically added, "So you're the new girl in town, huh?"

"Y-Yeah, that's me," Kasra stuttered through her failing self-esteem. She had a hard time looking up at them from the table, where her stare seemed to naturally fall.

"It's good to meet you!" the brunette chirped. "My name is Raia Bryotte. I've been a novitiate at the temple for one year."

"And I'm Layna Sladervorn," her friend introduced herself next. "I've been here for two."

Interestingly, Kasra noted that Layna's tiara had not lost a single crenulation, while Raia's had lost all but one. "Um, m-my name's Kasra," she offered them both a quick glance and an uneasy smile.

"It's okay to ease up," Layna judgingly smirked.

"We're not trying to put you on the spot," Raia encouraged her.

"I'm sorry," the violette defaulted to apology. She felt awkward being so quiet when they were just trying to engage her in conversation, but something about being in such a large place with so many people around her created a sensation of pressure, as if she were being crushed by the weight of everyone watching her.

Layna waited a minute or two before asking her first question. "So where are you from?"

The violette had a hard time finding the words to say. "Um, I... didn't have much of a home before coming here."

"You were a drifter?" Raia guessed.

"S-Something like that, I suppose," a soft spoken Kasra replied. Was it just her imagination that made her feel like she was the center of attention? What was so special about another newbie like her? Was Sachelvae having a shortage of newcomers?

"I'm from Ignalia, myself," Layna said. "It's an island about five days south of here."

"I've lived in Tresantia all my life," Raia added with a whimsical expression. "The city has grown even bigger since my earliest memories. Everyone wants to move here. I feel blessed to have been born in the most beautiful place in the world!"

Layna callously feigned gagging. "Bleh, gimme a break. I don't know why so many people would choose to live in an ugly valley like this, way out in the untamed boonies."

"I beg your pardon!" an offended Raia gasped. "Tresantia hasn't lasted 400 years because it is 'ugly.' It's the most sacred place in all of Onteval, if not the whole world! It has attracted 150,000 people from every other kingdom because it has something that no city does: a church for Safiro *and* Sanguina, providing safe havens for both worshipers to come and mingle with each other as they please. I'd say it's the most beautiful thing that's happened to the world since the Great Civilization~"

Raia's use of that unknown term had Kasra curiously tipping an ear. The novitiate's sing-song tone made it sound like this Great Civilization was supposed to be a good thing, but it was the first time Kasra had ever heard of something like it.

Raia continued, "Everyone's free to run their businesses and do whatever they want here, without fear of exclusion or exile." Turning her attention to Kasra, the brunette finished her righteous rambling. "Certainly *you* can agree that there's more to Tresantia than what Layna sees in it. I'm sure you've seen all kinds of places during your travels!"

"...I guess so." Though the brunette was certainly expecting a more riveting response, Kasra couldn't give her one with any honesty. The whole world, from the narrow perspective she had observed it, seemed like one big mire after another. There was nothing neither lovely nor sacred to her, unlike someone with Raia's rose-tinted lenses.

"How long were you on your own before you found Tresantia?" came Raia's next question, unfazed by the stranger of few words.

Kasra would have tried for a greater elaboration than "I can't really say for sure," but her memory was curtailed by a certain nasal niggling that had followed her from the Purifier. The corner of her lip irritably raised as her eyelids fluttered; her head raised back and snapped forward with a sudden sneeze onto the back of her wrist.

"Salvii!" Raia and Layna said in unison, one more repulsed than the other.

"You feelin' okay?" Raia worriedly asked.

"Could you not do that while I'm eating?" Layna impertinently huffed.

"I'm sorry," Kasra tried to sniffle away the congestion lacing her tone, but it couldn't be helped. "I'm always coming down with something."

"Well, gosh, I'm not surprised!" Raia sympathetically clicked her tongue, leaning forward to get a better look at the violette's face. "You haven't been taking care of yourself at all before you came here!"

"Spread the love with all of us, why don't you," a brazen Layna coldly rolled her eyes.

"Oh, stop it, Layna!" Raia snapped. "Can't you see she's suffering?"

Having this girl, who was barely more than a stranger to her, coming to her defense caused a warm smile to extend across Kasra's face. "I'm okay," she calmly assured her friend. "I'll get better if I just wait it out, like I always have."

Raia's lip worriedly quivered, her eyes glistening as she raised her fists to her chest. "What an awful thing to say..." her voice raised to a motherly pitch. "W-Well, at least accept this from me," she handed Kasra a handkerchief doily from the collar of her gown, "so I'll know you're not feeling too miserable."

"Great, an old snot rag," Layna snorted, "I'm sure she feels better, already."

"It isn't *used!"* Raia turned on her, resisting the blush now staining her cheeks.

Despite Layna's criticism, Kasra graciously accepted Raia's thoughtful gift. "Thank you. I appreciate your kindness very much."

A soft squeak escaped her helper's smiling lips, her facial flush now beyond her control. "You're welcome! I'm glad to help."

The congestion Kasra was being plagued with denied her the full enjoyment of the taste of her food. While it was good for the rawness of her throat, she was sometimes interrupted by short coughing fits. As much as she hoped mealtime would keep everyone's attention off her, Kasra's vexating condition attracted the disturbed grimaces of her tablemates.

Diava promised the girls that they would get their dessert after they performed their daily chores around town. Kasra, meanwhile, was given special attention by Diava as Sachelvae's most recent neophyte.

"Since you have not yet been recognized as a member of the clergy," Diava explained, "you cannot be involved with the official duties of the other priestesses. Your initiation will be complete once enough time has passed and you are deemed ready to accept your responsibilities as one of Sanguina's servants."

"Until then," she continued, "you will learn what your responsibilities are by your teachers Xanne," she gestured to the raven-haired lady to her left, "and Wanystha," she gestured to the curly-haired blonde on her right. "Xanne will teach you the laws and traditions of Sevasmia's order. Wanystha will teach you the history of Sachelvae and its significance to the Sanguinic faith."

Wanystha benevolently grinned at Kasra's nervous ambivalence. "Don't let Mother Diava scare you like that," she consoled her. "I'm the fun one to be around!"

Kasra chuckled as she watched Xanne's spiritless response to Wanystha's barb.

"You'll be joining your fellow classmates," Diava referred to Raia and Layna, "while the rest of the order completes their assignments for the day."

"As you wish, Mother Diava," Kasra bowed to her, while Raia and Layna stood to do the same.

"C'mon, Kasra," Raia lent her a hand. "It'll be fun!"

Chapter 3: The Powers Inside

The three girls followed behind their fellow classmates as they made their way down a long, torch-lit corridor with floors of ornamental tile. Picture frames on the walls contained portraits depicting Sachelvae's alumni, from graduating classes as far back as 300 years.

"I'm sorry about Mother Diava's sternness," Raia apologized, once they were out of earshot of the dining hall. "She doesn't always talk so gravely. She didn't mean to scare you, but she did want you to know what you're getting yourself into."

"This isn't just a place to freeload and worship," Layna said. "They expect you to do some work around here, and it isn't all gardening and door-greeting. We have things to do to keep our minds sharp and skills strong so that when we *do* get into a situation, we're able to deal with it."

"Oh please, Layna," Raia sighed. "You haven't even gotten yourself into a real fight. The one time you 'lost your tiara' so you could blend in with the other priestesses called to action didn't even get you to the cave's entrance."

"Hmph," Layna crossed her arms, grimacing from the memory. "I don't get why they're so stringent about their rules. Us students have nothing to do with our time. This whole discipline becomes so boring and tiresome that it's a wonder *more* people haven't followed my example."

"They *have*," Raia corrected her, "you're just lucky enough to have not been caught when you could have faced worse than a suspension. And you wonder why you're still behind some of the newer novitiates to receiving your tail band."

"I should have had my induction *months* ago!" Layna protested, the topic apparently still a very sensitive one for her. "Doesn't everything you just said prove that I've already got Sanguina's favor? I don't need these people to tell me I'm a priestess -- I already have the powers of one!"

Raia laughed, "You can't even extend your shield to cover your back, much less hand it off to someone else!"

Finally, Kasra found a place to interject in their quarreling. "Shield? What do you mean by that?"

"Teacher Xanne calls it something fancier," Layna answered with a testy twitch of her tail.

"I think the 'fancy' word you're looking for is *Masalida*," Raia condescendingly put a hand on her hip.

"Whatever," Layna dismissed her criticism. "It's not important to know the name, so long as you know how to use it."

Xanne's voice behind the small group of veltas had them all jumping to attention. "And it's for this lacking dedication that you're still behind," she said, making her way ahead of them. "Please make sure you come to class on time," she gave a friendly warning, reminding them how far the rest of the group had gotten ahead of them.

Kasra, Layna, and Raia hurried their walking pace so they could enter the classroom behind Xanne, and find their vacant desks near the back of the room. The classroom was modestly-sized and dimly lit by candles mounted on the walls. A small lamp on Xanne's desk provided soft illumination for her end of the square-shaped chamber. The Teacher stood before a chalkboard with the name of today's lesson already written on it: Conjuration Review.

Teacher Xanne tapped a quarterstaff on her desk to quell the students' chatter. Once she had their attention, she started, "You already know from the past week how to project a sphere of protection over yourself and someone else. But I must remind you to exercise caution when using this power, for it takes much energy to maintain and if it fails, you take the feedback of the attack that caused it to shatter. It is only meant to be used in a pinch and not as a main line of defense. It is much better to stop an attack before one can start: a power that freezes the opponent in place until its energy wears away. We call it *Astapsyxi.*"

Reminded of the short scuffle she had with Deniechus, Kasra interrupted, "I called it 'Stop' the first time I used it."

Her comment, though not intended to be funny, elicited the chuckles of her fellow classmates. Xanne, however, was not amused. "Are you a comedian, Kasra?"

Not sure why she was asking, the violette started, "No, I--" but was immediately interrupted by her offended Teacher. "Then I suggest you keep your jokes to yourself."

"I wasn't joking," an angered Kasra tersely snapped. "I've used this power before."

Interested, yet slightly disbelieving, Xanne said, "Would you care to give us a demonstration?" The Teacher then threw her quarterstaff with a spiral toward the ceiling, which was suddenly stopped when Kasra reached her hand, as if to grab it from a distance. Star-like sparkles, like the ones that had stopped Deniechus in his tracks, suspended the flying staff in midair.

Now Xanne was truly impressed. "Where did you learn Astapsyxi?" she asked. With a wave of her hand toward her floating weapon, she whisked away Kasra's freezing spell and let the staff fall back into her hold.

"I didn't learn it from anyone," Kasra replied. "I just knew I had to use it when my sister was in danger."

Even more intrigued, Xanne inquisitively tilted her head. "Rozha was attacked? When did this occur?"

"Last night, when I first came to Tresantia," the violette explained. "I was brought here by someone of the Safiric Brotherhood. He said I'd be safe in Travestas, but he lured me into a trap. Rozha came to save me, and they got into a fight. She was on the losing end... I was weak, but I had to do something. Somehow, by just wishing for Rozha not to be harmed, her attacker froze. I didn't know how it happened, but we used it to retreat."

"What an amazing story," Xanne tried to hide the admiration from her tone. "This might make you eligible for my advanced placement studies."

A beaming Raia turned to Kasra and happily jostled the other velta's shoulder. "Wow, that's incredible! Very few novitiates qualify for such an honor!"

Layna only gave the violette an envious stink eye. "Yeah, congratulations..." *'Who is this person, anyway? She just comes in here and she's already got everyone tripping over themselves to be her adorateur.'*

"Th-Thank you, Teacher Xanne!" Kasra stuttered, unsure of how even to handle such praise. "More than anything, I've wanted to know how better to defend myself. I'm tired of being weak... I'm tired of being the one people have to save. I want to do for others what Rozha did for me."

"That you shall and more," Xanne promised her. "If I may continue with my lesson?..." she trailed off, waiting for an embarrassed Kasra's assenting nod. "Astapsyxi works on a similar principle to Masalida, in that it breaks if overwhelmed. The only difference being that the power it failed to stop will not deliver its feedback. An attack that overwhelms Astapsyxi will be slowed and can be avoided with fast reflexes." "So, Kasra," she continued, "if you ever again find yourself in a situation like the one you described, you will know that for next time." "But do not let my warnings scare you," she addressed the rest of the students. "With practice, a power can be strengthened. The more you use these powers, the more durable they become. Once I show you how to use Astapsyxi, I want you to train both it and Masalida for next week's review. I want to make sure that sufficient improvement has been made."

Stepping around to the front of her desk, she qued her students to stand and do the same. "As with all of Sanguina's blessings," Xanne began, "Astapsyxi requires a wish, a gesticulation, and a spoken word. But with practice, this power can be used at will without preparation."

Teacher Xanne trained her students in a similar way she inspired Kasra to demonstrate her power, by throwing mock attacks their way to encourage the use of their Astapsyxi on the oncoming projectiles. Most of the students only required a second or third try to protect their fellow classmate before they got it down pat, but every time it was Layna's turn, she always failed.

"Everyone seems to have gotten the hang of it, except for you," Xanne told her. "Kasra, would you care to tutor Layna for a bit?"

"Sure," Kasra nonchalantly shrugged, much to Layna's outward disgust. "Raia? Throw that ball my way."

Raia did as she was instructed, casting the yellow, rubber missile at Kasra so she could block it with her starry telekinesis. "You have to be quick about it," the violette said. "You can't hesitate. Now you try." Kasra threw the ball back at Raia, which had its unimpeded flight strike her directly in the forehead.

"Ouch!" the brunette cried. "Layna, why didn't you stop it?"

Layna shrugged, "Teacher Xanne said the power wouldn't work unless I had a wish to stop someone from being harmed."

"See, that's your problem," Raia argued, "you're selfish! You don't care if anyone gets hurt."

"No, that's not it," Layna waggled a finger. "I just can't take this seriously, is all. I know I can make these powers work; I just see a better way to practice than playing with toys like this."

"Oh, so you're too good for our training, is that what you're trying to say?" Raia defensively rebutted.

Layna crossed her arms. "Like I said, I've got a better method."

"And what is that 'method' exactly?" Raia poised akimbo.

"I'll show you once class is over," Layna said.

"It better not involve any illegal activity..." a hushed brunette glanced at Teacher Xanne, who was busy helping a couple other students.

Layna followed Raia's eyes. "If you rat me out, you're not coming with."

"Well, I'm not going to let you throw yourself into some dangerous situation because you're pissed off and want to show off!" Raia tapped her foot.

"Hah, I knew you were too goody-goody to say no!" Layna jeered.

Even though this argument was clearly just between the two of them, Kasra felt too guilty to let them potentially run off and not be there to look after them should they wind up disappearing. The three vixies waited for Xanne to dismiss the students after everyone had performed a few more rounds of practice.

"You have two hours before Wanystha's class starts," Xanne reminded them. "I expect you to be continuing your practice around the temple grounds in that time."

"Yes, Teacher," everyone simultaneously said their goodbyes.

Since all their fellow classmates were required to be outside at the time, it gave Layna the perfect cover she needed to sneak away with her friends. "I'll take you guys to the Safiric side of town and show you how these powers are *meant* to be used!"

"Layna!" Raia worriedly hissed. "You know that Diava forbids all priestesses to cross Mediona!"

"We're not priestesses, yet," Layna pointed to her novitiate tiara.

"That makes no difference!" Raia flapped her arms. "If any of the faculty knew we went to the forbidden half of Tresantia, we'd be kicked out, immediately!"

"You may need that place, but I don't," Layna huffed. "I don't need Sachelvae to protect me from evil. I'm more than good enough at doing that, myself."

Kasra only laughed at how much the naive girl was talking. "You have no idea how good you have it. You are way too concerned with making a statement. I think you should listen to Raia and stop before you do something stupid."

Layna shot a glare over her shoulder at her fellow novitiate. "I don't know who you think you are, but I'm not afraid of you. I'm not afraid of *anything*, and I'm going to show you why."

Her courage built by jealousy and fueled by rage, Layna ignored the protests of her friends encouraging her to turn back as she dragged them along, away from the prying eyes of any nearby priestesses. The three travel mates barely avoided being seen by the veterans of the clergy walking around the fulvous streets of Mediona's bazaar. They kept their pace quick but natural as to not attract any attention to themselves as they used the colorful merchant tents as cover.

On the other side of Mediona, they could see the Safiric side of town. Everything about it looked sinister and dark; bleak buildings rising to the skyline like dilapidated towers, fashioned in the likenesses of crumbling spires, like no mind was paid to the safety of the structure's occupants. The people themselves were a diametric shift to the people who roamed the streets of the Sanguinic side of Tresantia. Diava would have called them 'Wilds.' They walked with a despondent sway, their hands sometimes concealed in pockets, their eyes never leaving the road they traveled unless to glare at someone they couldn't recognize. Not a word was spoken among them -- a far cry from the ambient chatter that filled Mediona's avenues.

Raia had never felt such a heavy sense of unwelcome emanating from the strangers and passersby. "A-Alright, Layna, you win... I don't feel safe here... we should really turn back, now."

"What're you worried about, teacher's pet?" the dark-haired velta scoffed. "I thought you were *so* well-practiced with your powers. You should be able to defend yourself if anyone picks a fight with you. That's exactly the reason I'm here. They don't like priestesses. The second they see your mantamina, they'll try to start something with you."

The sickly Kasra was feeling short of breath from the long walk through the city, and had a hard time keeping herself from coughing as they continued through Tresantia's dark depths. They followed the sound of a twice ringing church bell, from Travestas in the distance. Kasra shivered at the sight of the cathedral's eaves, watching the bell of dark silver swaying in its highest tower. Even though Raia had never seen the foreboding edifice before, she could feel its atmosphere of evil.

They stopped in the shadow of one of the black buildings near the end of town to watch a small congregation of Safiric monks forming a single file line to walk inside Travestas' open doors. They each carried what looked like silver chains in both hands, tied to orb-shaped aspersoriums issuing green smoke from a split between their hemispheres.

"They carry their *dilitrivanii* to ensure no life ever grows in the paths they walk," came Raia's whispered exposition.

It was at that moment Kasra realized she had not seen a single plant nor insect of any kind on the Safiric half of Tresantia either time she had been there. Just thinking of the poison gas being spread throughout the unhallowed earth at her feet made her asthma that much worse.

"What's wrong with you?" Layna whispered at the coughing velta under breath. "Could you keep it down?"

"Stop being so rude!" Raia came to Kasra's defense, soothingly rubbing her back. "You know she's in bad health. You hadn't stopped once to let us rest since we came here."

"Now's not the time for it," Layna said, watching the Safiric congregation slowly disappear inside the cathedral. "If she couldn't make it this far, she shouldn't have come along."

"I'm fine," Kasra growled. "Thank you, Raia," she more nicely said to her helpful friend. "It doesn't bother me."

Raia's eyes shimmered for the violette, knowing she was just pushing herself to be brave for them. She knew it was her fault that Kasra felt compelled to get herself involved in this mess. She wouldn't forgive herself if Kasra got hurt because of Layna's prideful impudence.

"They're all gone?" a disappointed Layna exclaimed. "But I've always seen someone standing outside at the end of the procession..."

Kasra and Raia also poked their heads around the corner, and sure enough, the doors to Travestas were closed and nobody could be seen near them. Just when they thought the coast was clear, a gravelly voice from behind them caught them by surprise.

"What are *you* doing here?..."

The first things the three young novitiates saw were piercing red eyes glowering from the darkness of a hooded figure. Before they could react, his fanged maw opened to give a shrieked incantation. The stones of the streets beneath them animated like vines to ensnare Raia and Layna, who lacked Kasra's quick reflexes to dive out of the way. The violette rolled underneath the floating Safiric monk, her body hitting the bricks with less grace than she would have liked, momentarily knocking the wind out of her. She coughed, wobbling as she tried to regain her footing, but the Safiric priest capitalized on her weakness.

He turned, uttering another incantation similar to the ones Xanne taught as he reached out a hand. From his fingers emitted a blue beam of light that paralyzed Kasra in place. She couldn't move a muscle despite her efforts to escape. She was pulled in against her will by the mystic force as the Safiric priest drew a short blade from his sleeve. Just as he was reeling his arm back for the killing blow, a terrified Raia closed her eyes and turned away.

"Astapsyxi!"

The evil oblate confusedly groaned when he could suddenly no longer move, and found himself locked in place by the priestesses he'd trapped. His concentration faltering, he no longer was able to keep his telekinetic hold on his adversary. When control returned to Kasra's body, she used what little flexibility her robe lent her to turn and crash her tail into the side of the priest's head, knocking him to the ground with enough force to break the magic entanglement Raia had made.

"He's down," Kasra exclaimed, rushing to her friends' aid. "We have to get out of here!"

Raia didn't look like she had an answer, and left it up to Layna to shout, *"Koptigma!"* causing the stone arms which had bound them to shatter.

"Hey, I'm impressed!" Raia said. "You remembered Xanne's barrier breaker! I suppose you're learning from those classes after all."

"You don't know the *half* of what I can do!" Layna confidently blustered. "I'm *full* of surprises!"

"You're full of *something*," a scoffing Raia narrowed her eyes.

"We've got to hurry," Kasra pulled her bickering friends along. "If we stick around, they'll keep coming for us."

Without argument this time, Layna and Raia hastily followed her along, but she was in no condition to be running anywhere. They hadn't retraced their steps halfway before Kasra was crumbling into a coughing fit.

"Kasra~!" Raia worriedly cried, going back to help her stand.

"Oh, come on!" an impatient Layna yelled. "We don't have time for this!" *"Fygidia!"* Her Sanguinic invocation caused both Raia and Kasra to suddenly appear at her side so she could help carry the weak violette. "Can you keep up, now?"

"Layna..." a star-struck Raia cooed, welling up with emotion to see Layna's sympathy.

"Don't you start that crap with me, you blubbering ditz," Layna defensively berated her. "I'm only doing this because I know if Kasra dies, I'll never hear the end of it from you."

Despite her warning, Raia just had to burst, "Oh, Layna, you really *do* have a heart!"

"I told you to shut up!" the dark-haired vixy embarrassedly shouted her down.

"How did you do that?" a bewildered Kasra started running alongside them.

"Fygidia is a transportation spell," Raia quickly explained. She was having a hard time talking between her panting breaths as she and her friends booked it in the direction of Mediona. "It can immediately take one priestess to another, either in visible range, or with a psychic connection -- via communication ring."

"A *what* ring?" Kasra was obviously overwhelmed by this dump of jargon.

"Oh *please*," an impatient Layna groaned. "You'll learn all that crap, eventually. All you need to know right now is that I just saved your ass."

Luckily, their mischief near Travestas didn't cost them another confrontation with the Safiric Brotherhood, but their luck ran out when they returned to Mediona. Exhausted and gasping for air, they rested under one of the tents and fought over who'd have the first drink of water from an abandoned flask they found nearby. Just when they thought they were in the clear and had gotten away with their mischief, they were approached by one of the priestesses finishing her chores around the bazaar. She did not wear the usual red gown; instead, she was wearing one of pink decorated with black moon insignia. By the tiara she wore, Layna and Raia could tell she was one of the faculty.

Raia was able to recognize her right away. "That's the Arch Healer!" It was hard to tell if her gasp was from fright or admiration.

"What're you novitiates loitering here for?" the aforementioned Healer started in a motherly tone. "Where have you been?" She got a closer look. "You look dirty and smell of saffron..."

"We've just been hanging around here," Layna lied. "We got bored of being cooped up in the temple; we wanted to have some fun."

"You know you're not supposed to be here," the pink priestess said, looking to make sure Diava was not nearby. "But because I was in your situation once before, I will let you get away with this. It wasn't my vow not to keep a secret."

"Thanks, nurse lady!" a relieved Layna sighed along with her friends. "We owe you one!"

"Layna," the Arch Healer quirked a brow, "you should know by now that my name is Kyrana." She frowned at Raia and Kasra, huddled around the resident hoodlum. "I would appreciate it even more if you did not make such an effort to get a new student hurt on her first day in the temple." With a proper address to the violette, Kyrana continued, "Your name is Kasra, if I recall?"

"Yes, ma'am," Kasra respectfully replied, earning the return of the Healer's kind visage.

"Well met," Kyrana bowed her head. "I hope I won't have to meet you kids again, under worse circumstances." She gave them a somewhat playful smile. "You stay safe, now."

Raia jovially waved her off. "See you later, Sister Kyrana!" As she watched the Healer take her leave, she noticed her tail had formed a ring on the inside of her gown to keep its flaps held in a perfect bell shape as she walked. Looking back to her friends, Raia said, "Wasn't she great?"

"Yeah," Layna agreed, "It's good that not everyone at Sachelvae is a stuck-up fogy."

"She's certainly different," Kasra added. She crossed her arms and smirked at her recalcitrant companion. "Well, Layna, was that enough excitement for one day?"

"Hmph..." the restive thrill-seeker irritably turned away and tapped her tail. *'What's her deal? She comes in and thinks all of a sudden that she's the one in charge?'* But the angry vixy didn't have the energy to argue. "I suppose. You really showed you know your stuff, but that doesn't mean I have to like you, now."

"Alright," Kasra chuckled, "You can continue being that way if it makes you feel better about yourself."

"If you're rested enough, Kasra," Raia got her attention, "We should head back to Sachelvae, or we'll miss the lunchtime meal."

"I can't believe I forgot all about that," Layna kicked herself, standing back up. "You two are going to have to get back by yourselves, this time. I've had enough of helping you out."

"Yeah, sure," Raia rolled her eyes, helping Kasra back to her feet.

The three of them returned to Sachelvae to find that many of their classmates had already come back inside, apparently having gotten tired of practicing the powers they learned from Teacher Xanne earlier in the day.

"I don't blame them for taking a break," Layna stretched her aching back. "I'm quite tired, myself."

"I'm going to take a bath and get something to eat," Raia said. "I'm famished from all the running around we did today! What about you, Kasra?"

Kasra thoughtfully hummed. Those ideas her friends were giving her sounded pretty appealing, but she was more curious about Wanystha, when she observed, in the distance, the teacher standing on a hill with a canvas on an easel. "Is that one of the Teachers? What's she doing there?"

"Oh, that?" Layna looked over Kasra's shoulder. "She always dinks around up there, while everyone else is doing their chores around town."

"She works on a new masterpiece every month," a starry-eyed Raia explained. "She says it helps her artistic inspiration to be synchronized with the cycles of Sanguina's moon~"

"...Whatever all that piffle means," was Layna's succinct critique.

Raia placed a hand on her hip and wagged an accusing finger at her friend. "Only because you're not an artist!"

"So what if I'm not into all that sedentary stuff?" Layna objected. "I have a heart for adventure. I don't envy people's creative talents."

"Well, *there's* a first..." Raia quietly sputtered, earning a ludic shove from her friend. She turned to a chuckling Kasra, no doubt entertained by their antics. "I know you could appreciate the fine arts a lot more than Layna can," the brunette told her. "I'm sure Wanystha would like having someone to talk to about her works. She made all the portraits in Sachelvae, but nobody seems to be that interested in her art. She looks lonely up there, all by herself."

On her way back inside the temple, Layna said, "We'll see you in a few, Kasra. Coming, Raia?"

"On my way~!" Raia followed after. "See you, Kasra!"

Finally, the violette was left in peace. She took a moment to gather herself before she made her way up the hill to see Wanystha and her current work in progress. "Good afternoon, Teacher Wanystha!"

Her greeting was met by the older velta's welcoming smile. "Hey there, Sister Kasra! What're you doing all by yourself?"

"I had the same question for you, actually," the violette returned.

"Oh, really?" a pleasantly surprised Wanystha purred. "I'm flattered! I'm just working on my newest painting."

What Kasra saw before her looked, from her untrained perspective, like nothing more than hues of orange and purple swirling together in a blue gradient taking up one half of the canvas. "It's quite pretty..." she trailed off, still trying to figure out what it was.

"Have you never seen a sunset?" Wanystha remarked. "It was here I stood, when I saw this very scene: the clouds lined up just so toward the horizon, as if following the sun behind the hills, where fulminated a fantastic conflagration of color..." she paused to sigh in longing admiration, as if her painting barely did her memory any justice. "It was a truly beautiful sight! I've always tried to capture my memories in my works, so that I can immortalize those scenes for all time and share them with the rest of the world."

"That's really something!" an inspired Kasra exclaimed. "I've never thought to do that, before. I guess I never tried to."

"I'll bet you have some very fascinating memories," Wanystha encouraged her. "I'd like to see some of them. Why don't you try showing me at class?"

"A-Alright," Kasra nervously blinked, unused to being so quickly put on the spot. "I can give it a try for you."

"That's the spirit!" Wanystha clapped. "Xanne told me that you pulled quite a move at her class, today. I'm wondering if you can impress me in the same way."

The violette awkwardly smiled. "I'm not in this to make it a popularity contest..."

"Relax!" Wanystha laughed. "I didn't ask you to compare yourself to anyone else. That's not what's important about Sachelvae. It's my responsibility to make sure you're prepared for your duties as a priestess of Tresantia. No one's got it easy, here."

What she said reminded Kasra of where Rozha must be right now. She held a fist to her lips as she looked in the direction of Mediona, as if hoping to see Rozha from so far away. Her eyes returned to Wanystha when the teacher grabbed up her easel. "Are you feeling alright, Kasra?"

Holding the back of her hand to her hot, beating forehead, the violette closed her eyes and waited to no longer feel like she was spinning. "Yeah, just give me a second."

"I'll say you need more than that," the curly-haired velta kindly riposted. Seeing the pallor of Kasra's sweating face had her frowning with concern. "Here, you need to get out of the sun," Wanystha said, taking Kasra's hand. She gently steadied the girl against her shoulder as she slowly walked her into Sachelvae's open doors. As soon as Kasra was in the shade, her legs buckled from under her and almost brought Wanystha with her onto the cool, marble floor.

"Stay with me, darling," Wanystha set down her easel and joined Kasra on her knees. She didn't want to look scared for her, but the sickly, half-conscious glaze on the violette's eyes made it difficult for Wanystha to not panic. "I know you feel tired, but you can't fall asleep," she gently admonished her. Raising a ruby ring under her chin, Wanystha spoke, "I need you to come here. One of the students has been stricken with a curse."

Suddenly, a priestess wearing a pink dress, akin to Kyrana's, appeared behind Wanystha. "Thank you, Teacher," the younger lady said. "I'll take it from here." Unlike Kyrana, this healer's hair was colored dark blue and was not cut in the traditional priestess fashion; its natural waviness was instead unkempt and left at chin-length. Her fuchsia-colored eyes had a certain peacefulness to them, albeit her cyan-colored face lacked any emotion to show it.

"Is it a disease, Platina?" Wanystha asked the novice nurse, as the azurette sat down with Kasra.

"No," Platina responded, brushing a hand over Kasra's face. "She is reacting to excess internal temperature. She is suffering from heat exposure."

"I can't see," the wide awake violette trembled. "What's going on?"

Grasping her patient's arms, Platina softly intoned, "I need you to relax." The stiff Kasra wasn't quite assenting to being eased on her back; Platina gently reclined the blinded novitiate before stabilizing her body inside of a numbing, blue fringe of light. She was held by these comforting waves as if carried by a stretcher; her body rigidly levitated above Platina's open hands. Addressing Wanystha, Platina said, "I'll keep her in the Quarantine Bay until she recovers."

Chapter 4: Trials of a True Priestess

While Kasra and the other novitiates were getting a lesson from Teacher Xanne, Rozha and the rest of the priestesses had left the Dining Hall to gather around the Purifier. They sat on their knees atop crimson cushions, all watching Diava intently. The High Priestess this time stood behind a podium, on top of which was a red, jewel-like dome. Rays of light emanated from the rubescent hemisphere between Diava's fingers stretching around it. Her eyes were closed and her head was bowed, as if deeply focusing. Her meditation ceased when the rays of light faded, like clouds passing before the sun.

Her eyes opened and her head lifted to see her audience. "All rise," she softly declared. The priestesses did as they were told, in unison assuming a standing position, not uttering a word among them. "Sanguina has given me a vision," her uplifting voice echoed melodically through the hallowed halls. "She has detected... a Safiric presence in Fort Pericula. Our suspicions from earlier in the week have been confirmed: they are attracted to the sacred Thunderstone. They have wanted to use it for something, and have just now found their means by which to do it."

But before anyone could speculate the reasons behind this unfolding plot, their attention was diverted to the sound of the heavy doors at the other end of the basilica creaking open. The sunlight pouring in eclipsed the figure standing between the tall slabs of iron, until she moved into the mild shadows to show her face. The velta appeared to be in her mid-twenties, sporting long, black and green hair styled with a priestess' straight cut. She lacked the normal red and black robes standard for her fellow members of the clergy; she instead was dressed in a blade dancer's body-fitting leather suit, outfitted with pads on her knees, elbows and shoulders. On the right side of her belt was a scabbard for a short sword; on the left was a ring holding a handful of wheel-shaped knives. Though dressed for war, she came in peace; she stopped at the position before the pool where Diava could clearly see her and took a respectful bow as she wore a cocky smirk.

"I have returned," the Messenger's apricot-colored eyes twinkled up at the High Priestess.

"Welcome back, Viasarria," the hall's high ceiling carried Diava's exclamation. "Were there any complications?"

Raking her fingers through her long hair with an arrogant flip, the ex-blade dancer replied, "Have I ever disappointed you, Mother?"

The High Priestess figured that Viassarria had praised herself enough and answered with a question of her own. "What news do you have from Pericula?"

"On the day I entered, there were only two Priests standing by the Thunderstone, in the town square," the spy explained. "The locals couldn't take their eyes off them. I asked around and they informed me that the night before, soldiers standing watch on the battlements had seen a Dark Cloud settling in the Black Swamp outside town. They feared it was the beginning of an invasion from the Dark Men, so the guards sent out a search party. They never returned."

Nodding with acknowledgment of what she had heard so far, Diava asked, "What did you see when you left?"

"When I departed at sunrise," Viasarria replied, "there were more Priests waiting around the Thunderstone than there were before. It appeared they were carrying crates, or caskets with them. The townsfolk were more perturbed by the goings-on, but the guards either didn't know what was happening or simply didn't care."

Her face darkening, Mother Diava placed her hands back on her podium's Sighted Sphere. "The town watch must have called upon the Brotherhood to assuage their fears of an impending invasion. I anticipate a great congregation will be there. If they use this plan to turn Pericula into a Safiric stronghold, all the Pures who live there will be wiped out."

Although the graveness of the urgent situation was meant to be taken seriously, Viasarria could not have waited longer to volunteer herself for what was shaping up to be a dangerous quest. "Sounds like an appointment for an ass kicking, to me!"

Diava's expression was awash with the need to be snarky, but the modest lady didn't have it in her to make a rejoinder. "Viasarria, surely after such a long journey you would wish to rest? Or at least have the decency to let your steed recuperate?"

"Jariten can handle it," Viasarria p'shawed the High Priestess' admonition. "He's an old boy, but he and I undertook jaunts like this on a regular basis, when I was still in my clan."

Realizing she wasn't going anywhere with trying to convince the messenger to stay out of the conflict, Diava settled for a huff and turned her attention to the rest of her audience. "A response is necessary, but we cannot risk meeting them with sufficient numbers; the more of us there are, the easier it will be for them to detect our Purity. For this clandestine assignment, we should limit ourselves to bringing a team of three to interrupt their sacraments. Who among you wishes to join Viasarria on what shall be known as the Pericula Initiative?"

Rozha was the first of the priestesses standing around the Purifier to accept Diava's challenge. She stepped forward to be seen clearly, ahead of the line of her companions and said, "I will join her, Mother Diava."

"Ooh, the Red Dancer, herself!" Viasarria cooed in a way that was meant to sound dryly flattered, but was clearly meant facetiously. "I look forward to working with you."

While no one else seemed to notice the subtle barb, Rozha was more than aware of the other dancer's attempt at calling her out. "It sounds more like you're looking for a competition."

"We both served Iminsun's corps," Viasarria needlessly reminded her. "The dancers in my clan all competed with each other to see who was the best. After training camp, I was awarded a medal for top trainee of my class."

"Good for you," Rozha scornfully snorted. "Who trained you?"

"My *tomina's* name was Nilsein," the raven-haired velta said, with an 'if-you-must-know' attitude.

At that, the redhead's expression soured considerably. "Who did you say it was?..." she trailed off coldly.

Viasarria raised an eyebrow, wondering what she had said that could have struck the redhead's nerve. "Nilsein Jantica," she repeated for her. "Why? Does that name mean something to you?"

Rozha wasn't going to let some jerk know what about that name offended her. She wasn't about to give Viasarria a reason to be even more inflamed about their rivalry than she already was. But just the very fact that Nilsein was her trainer irked the Red Dancer even more. The more she looked at Viasarria, the more she reminded her of her mother. "No," her tone was laced with the gravel of building anger.

Just knowing that Rozha had something to hide that put her on the verge of losing her cool elicited an even bigger grin to overtake Viasarria's smug little face. The way she wagged her tail and stood with her hands on her hips made Rozha want to knock her head off. Viasarria could sense her ire and relished every bit of it.

Diava, too, was privy to the mounting aggression between them. She was tempted to have them both stay out of the conflict so they couldn't cause problems for each other, but knew she couldn't watch over them all day. She worried what kind of dangers they could get into if they tackled the assignment with heads full of steam.

"Is there anyone else who wants to join Rozha and Viasarria?" Diava interjected her audience's collective silence.

"Mother Diava, if I may," Kyrana started, with a bowing of her head, "I would like to accompany them. Those who fight with reckless abandon need a healer by their side."

The High Priestess could not be more relieved to see her favorite member of the clergy taking it upon herself to be the mediator of these two powder kegs. "You are always qualified for an undertaking such as this," Diava smiled. "You could not be more essential to any mission, dear Kyrana."

"Thank you, your holiness," the pink-clad priestess dipped a knee and raised the hems of her dress.

Viasarria gave the middle-aged velta a gaze that questioned what place she'd have in a battlefield, but decided not to speak her mind, this time. The only thing she could think of was how she was going to sharpen her sword on the bones of the Brotherhood.

At last, someone else was given a chance to speak and get a word in edgewise. "What do you require of the rest of us?" one of the crowd piped up.

"You shall resume your chores, as per normal," Diava stated. She motioned for a pair of veltas at the back of the gathering to open the basilica's doors, for their group to leave in procession out into the temple grounds.

While everyone walked by her, Viasarria clapped her hands once to command the attention of her troops and called them to sally forth. "Alright! It's time to use our powers for the purpose they were intended!"

Diava couldn't have been more ashamed of her clerical paladin. "It was not Mother's Will for us to fight one another," she uneasily raised an eyebrow.

"We can't always rely on the enemy to kill *themselves*!" a combative Viasarria held out her open hands. "Someone's gotta take the initiative, or they'll never go away."

Her patience clearly being tested, Diava's teeth were close to gritting. "It is more important that the enemy be converted, not *neutralized...*"

"But there are some who refuse to convert!" Rozha argued.

"The High Priests are so far gone by Safiro's evil," Kyrana started, "They would be destroyed by any attempts of Purification."

"It's not possible to win them all if we do *nothing* --" Viasarria added, before being interrupted by Mother Diava's startling command, "Enough!"

All in attendance jumped and froze stiff while they watched Diava's comportment return to its normal placidity. "It is our righteous duty to defend what we have and do what we must to convert those who do wrong in the eyes of Sanguina. It is Safiro who wishes for bloodshed. If what we do pleases the God of Death, are we not the same as his kind? By destroying them, we weaken ourselves to be condemned by them. They then use our dead spirits to strengthen themselves. The more of us who are turned to them, the less children of Sanguina there will be born. We are already on the losing side. We cannot afford to lose any more ground than we have. They use their powers to instill fear in us; when we doubt our powers out of fear, we lose our strength to resist them. Resorting to murder is giving in. They have no power over us when we have Sanguina's protection. They cannot defeat what they cannot kill, for the death of their enemies is their only objective."

Everyone stayed quiet and heaved a sigh, looking at each other or at the reflecting pool, but all three of them had a hard time meeting Diava's eyes after she ended her tirade.

A submissive and soft-spoken Kyrana was the first to break the ice. "I will not doubt your wisdom, Mother Diava."

Diava waited to have the other two resound the nurse's sentiments, but Viasarria was still not convinced that her tactics should change, and she let everyone know that by staying quiet. Rozha was the only one who confessed, even though she didn't believe she was in the wrong, either. "We will do no more than what you asked of us," the redhead replied.

Satisfied enough with Rozha's half-willing assent, the High Priestess briskly walked down the stairs from her elevated stage. The long, billowing drapes of her silken dress flowed like a cloud behind her; her movement, howbeit ill-tempered, was still majestic in its form as the statuesque lady brushed by them like a coastal wind. The entire time, though her head stayed fixed in the direction she was headed, her bright gray eyes were transfixed on the unyieldingly smug look on Viasarria's face.

Viasarria and the rest of her company turned to watch, with differing expressions, Mother Diava storming out the open doors. The three of them were the last to exit Sachelvae, and stood in a triangle formation outside as they devised a plan for their route and preparations for their venture.

"I will go to Mediona to gather the necessary provisions," Kyrana said. "Pericula is a two hour journey from here, so I will collect ample rations to last the to and from trip."

"Meanwhile," Viasarria added, moving toward the stables on the temple's eastern wall, "Rozha and I can saddle our steeds and get them ready for the outing."

"Won't we have to muck their stalls, first?" Rozha asked, not even wanting to remind herself of the chore.

"Nah," Viasarria waved a hand, "I got one of the novitiates to do that for me, after I left, yesterday."

"I'm sure they were thrilled," came the redhead's sarcastic riposte.

"Oh yeah, Jariten loved it when we came back," Viasarria laughed, rolling her eyes.

"Only a member of the faculty can tell a student what to do," Kyrana stiffly cut in.

"The novitiate didn't know that," the Messenger grinned, wiggling her hips.

"I'll remember you said that when I tell Mother Diava, later," the cool-headed Kyrana turned, about to go on her way.

Shouting over at her as she continued walking, Viasarria threw in her parting shot, "Why don't you write a *note* about it, so you won't forget, you little *nark*?" She judgingly shook her head while Kyrana nonchalantly ignored her. "I can't stand sycophants like her," Viasarria self-righteously sputtered, watching the nurse shrink in the distance. "It's pathetic that some people pride themselves in making other people look bad."

'I don't think she needs any help making ***you*** *look bad,'* Rozha kept her contumely to herself. She was trying to keep from seething about how Viasarria acted up minutes ago, but the boisterous blade dancer was not making it easy to forget how much she disliked her. Instead, she settled for the less aggressive answer. "She is a member of the faculty; it's her job to abide the rules and make sure others do the same."

Viasarria looked over her shoulder after she threw a saddle on Jariten's back. "I can see they already brainwashed you," she huffed. "You've got a stick up your ass just as far as the rest of them."

If Rozha had a stick anywhere on her person, she would have been using it to beat the other velta senseless by now. "You are clearly what is wrong with the younger generation, these days."

"Speak for yourself, *kid!*" Viasarria spat. "I'm 25 and you're what, like, 19? Don't act like you know better than me!"

Giving her the most 'oh really' tilt of her head she could muster, Rozha shot back, "I'm *24*, jerkass. But it doesn't matter what your age is, if you don't *act* it."

Turning around with a start, Viasarria grasped the handle of her sword and challengingly stepped forward. "I'd love to read the rings of your bones just to see how old you *really* are!"

Rozha sneered and wrinkled her nose one last time, as she eyed up at her foe with a sly, sideways leer. In one motion -- in a single moment -- she turned her body to slap the tip of her tail under Viasarria's chin. The other blade dancer's head snapped back as the surprised fighter was sent reeling, exposing her midsection for Rozha to come back around and extend her leg for a lung-deflating kick to the diaphragm. As Viasarria fell on her back into the stable's filthy straw, the bound Jariten bucked at Rozha from his stall. The black strider's big, finger-like forelegs slammed Rozha's side and sent her clear into the opposite, empty booth. Both blade dancers shakily returned to their feet from the tremendous blows they had received. With an impressive leap, Viasarria jumped atop the wall separating her from Rozha, her feet perched on the mere inches of wooden surface as her head was ducked uncomfortably close to the angled ceiling. Dust flew from the jostled wall when Viasarria jumped, sword outstretched, down toward her ground bound foe.

Her blade bounced off the straw-laden dirt when Rozha took a step to the side to quickly evade. The other dancer countered by throwing her shin into Viasarria's neck, but the raven-haired velta kept the hit from connecting by interposing an open palm. Viasarria then ducked away from Rozha's forearm blade swinging for her head, now coshing off her padded shoulder as the unperturbed dancer came in low for a hooked arm into Rozha's thorax. The redhead's body buckled around the intense hit, for Viasarria to stand upright and send down both fists on her opponent's back. Rozha fell face-first into the odoriferous earth -- her prone body a prime target to be stomped and kicked repeatedly by an unrelenting Viasarria. The raging blade dancer used the support beam as leverage to make every contact the sole of her boot made against Rozha count.

Rozha could feel every bruise through her suit; she reached into her utility belt in-between flinches of pain to pull out her equalizer. Before Viasarria even knew what Rozha had up her sleeve, she was blinded and deafened by an awful explosion. Rozha had thrown a belhauyn flashbang beneath her foe's feet, giving her the time to roll away from Viasarria's fury. Her adrenaline and anger numbing her pain, light glinted off the redhead's bared fangs; she drew her sword and uttered a primal cry as she dove into her cringing adversary. Viasarria's arms tucked against her stinging ears left her wide open to be struck mercilessly in the forehead by the pommel of Rozha's firebrand. Any senses that were coming back to her by then were knocked clear out of her when the raven-haired blade dancer took the concussion-inducing strike between her eyes. The back of her head hit the wall behind them; the full weight of Rozha's body sitting on her waist kept her pinned down. She was only able to keep her face from turning to bloody mush by crossing her forearms to block the hammering hilt of Rozha's sword.

Rozha's tail intertwined with Viasarria's to ensure no interruptions could be made to her violent counter-offensive. The deathly desire she had in her fiery eyes showed no signs of stopping. She only let up her continuous attack when her arm felt tired from wielding her wobbly sword, not meant to be used in such a manner, and turned it upside down to bring down the pointed end like a guillotine. But the extended space between blows gave Viasarria the time she needed to stop Rozha's finisher with a sharp jab of her steel knuckles into the redhead's stomach. The grip she had on Viasarria's tail weakened, allowing the dark-haired dancer to slip her slender limb free and wrap it around Rozha's neck. With her new leverage, Viasarria pulled Rozha down and reversed positions. She used one of her sore arms to pin down the Red Dancer's sword-bearing hand, and used the other to cross over Rozha's constrained neck. Rozha could see, from the bottoms of her eyes, as her head was pushed further back into the dirt, the blood from Viasarria's forehead trickling onto her gritted teeth.

The confident agitator bent down close enough to touch noses as she huffed and puffed against Rozha's face. "What'cha think, now, hotshot? Not lookin' so tough anymore, are ya?" Waiting for a few seconds to listen to Rozha choke under the pressure of her arm, Viasarria added, "What's wrong? Haven't anything left to say…?"

Before the rival blade dancer could finish her sentence, Rozha took advantage of the close space between them to throw a punch into Viasarria's temple. Her opponent forced to back off her, Rozha was finally able to take a breath and headbutt the cut on Viasarria's crown. The black-haired dancer staggered back to her feet as she covered her wound, leaving herself open to a vengeful roundhouse kick that sent her crashing through the stable's wall. The old, wooden planks split around Viasarria's body as she fell right through them and rolled onto the clean grass outside. She was just able to use her backward momentum to return to a standing position as Rozha gave chase. Their swords both clashed as the Red Dancer performed a trademark twirl. A fast-paced exchange of parries from their blades, wielded in their hands, forearms, and tails ensued as both combatants used every practical inch of their bodies as a weapon.

This exhibition of true, traditional blade dancer skill began drawing quite a crowd when several minutes had passed. The song of steel captivated the curiosity of passersby making their rounds about the temple. Rozha and Viasarria weren't even aware of the spectacle they were creating until both ceased all motion to take a mutually-earned breather. Both drenched with sweat and covered in dirt, needles of straw poking out of their disheveled hair, the blade dancers exhaustedly slumped and eyed the small audience of thirty raving fans. They hadn't the energy to continue, nor explain themselves when, from out of the crowd, Kyrana came pushing through the excited mob.

"Who in Sanguina's holy fane dares desecrate this sacred ground with such filth?!"

Seeing as how the angrily scowling priestess was looking directly at them when she said it, Rozha and Viasarria didn't think she needed an answer to her question. The flaring emotions of the two blade dancers was doused like water splashing upon a fire when they caught sight of Kyrana's righteous outrage. The crowd of bystanders was quick to turn away, as well, certainly detecting a strong sense of unwelcome emanating from the priestess. Kyrana dropped the belongings she had gathered from Mediona behind her as she trudged toward Rozha and Viasarria, who watched her like kids caught red-handed by their parents.

They were honestly surprised she didn't slap them both across the face, but she could see they had beaten each other up enough already. "If Mother Diava saw you causing such a *detestable* scene," Kyrana spat, "she would have you both excommunicated for *life* from the temple, if not *exiled* from Tresantia!" Breathing heavily, like she had not raised her voice in years, the nurse eyed with disdain the swords in the blade dancers' hands. "Drop those ugly weapons of Safiric *devilry* when I'm speaking to you!" Immediately, Rozha and Viasarria did as they were told, casting aside their respective blades, their eyes of abject fear not leaving Kyrana's face for a second. "If either of you *heathens* convert to the Safiric Brotherhood, I will Purify you both, *myself!*"

Both blade dancers shuddered at Kyrana's every enunciated word, and wriggled and shrieked with pain when she took them by the ears and dragged them back through Sachelvae's open doors. She brought them all the way to the Purifier and pushed both of them in, not even giving them the time to change out of their suits. They fell side by side into the waters with a splash, the pristine pool then darkening considerably from all the hatred flowing from their spirits. It was the first time Rozha's eyes met Viasarria's equally frightened gaze, neither knowing what the other was thinking the whole time this situation was unfolding.

"You will stay here until you learn how to behave like proper priestesses," Kyrana started, "and more importantly, proper *adults*." With that poignant statement, the infuriated priestess finally took her leave to recollect the rations she had left behind.

Rozha and Viasarria waited for the reverberations of Kyrana's footsteps on the marble tile to dissipate before any words were shared among them. Motormouth that she was, Viasarria naturally was the first to say, "Well, looks like you're right, Rozha; it really *doesn't* matter what your age is, so long as you act it."

The Red Dancer petulantly flicked the water from her fingertips into Viasarria's eyes, causing the other velta to cringe and squeal out the door, "Kyrana! She splashed at me!"

Chapter 5: Convulsion Fugue

Kasra had slipped into unconsciousness sometime after Platina had telekinetically lifted her away from the Purifier Hall. She awoke what felt like seconds later, facing the ceiling from a white bed. On her forehead was placed a small, folded terry cloth. Its damp warmth had siphoned the heat from her shocked body, along with the zephyrs flowing from the open, stained glass windows behind her. The room of sterile brick and marble floors featured plenty of counter space along the walls, bristling with chemical equipment with alimbics, mortars and pestles, and other such instruments of alchemy -- none of which Kasra could recognize.

Beds elevated on cross-shaped legs were spaced every three or four feet apart and were separated by pink, diaphanous drapes. Each bed had its own stained glass window that a patient could look out of whilst resting on its firm mattress. All the windows depicted images of nurses and Arch Healers from Sachelvae's history. The middle row of the floor, between the beds on either wall, was occupied by small potted gardens enclosed by sleeping statues of unborn spirits. The whole chamber was endowed with a tranquil appeal and was filled with a faint yet pleasing aroma.

Kasra's bed was rather firm and creaked when she moved, the sounds eliciting the attention of Platina, whose ear turned in the direction of Kasra's activity. The light of the sun's rays from the open window reflected off the nurse's glasses when she turned away from the counter she was standing near. Behind her was a sink that she was using to wash her hands. She dried them on a towel hanging on a cabinet doorknob, all the while gazing at Kasra with the same kind of accord a scientist would give a test tube. "Please remain in rested position," she instructed her patient, "and do not move until I have checked the progress of your recovery."

A bit frightened by the unfeeling monotone of the healer's voice, Kasra did as she was told to the best of her ability -- she found it a bit difficult to relax with that belhuayn statue of a woman peering at her. Instead of the polite 'yes ma'am' that most practitioners would have expected of their clients, Kasra responded with a sideways glare as she clutched her blanket closer to her shoulders. "Who are you...?"

"My name is Platina Veremore," the nurse replied, as if reading off a serial number. "I am one of the in-training nurses of this temple."

Kasra couldn't help but notice how straight and proper the woman stood, her hands perfectly kept by her sides. It was impossible to tell if she was even breathing under that loose-fitting gown she wore. Not even her tail moved behind her. Her mouth only moved because it let her speak.

"A nurse?" Kasra repeated. "You mean like Kyrana?"

"That is correct," Platina said. "Kyrana taught me my practice as a healer, when Xanne discovered my clinical potential."

"She can do that?" a dumbfounded Kasra asked -- not that it was hard to feel particularly dumb when speaking to someone who talked like a textbook.

"It is Xanne's authority as faculty to teach all neophytes the use of their Sanguinic powers," Platina's voice nearly assumed a lilt.

"Oh," Kasra purred, having reached a eureka moment. "That's why she was so intrigued when I told her I already knew how to do asphyxiation, or whatever she called it."

At that, the nurse's expression was threatened to change from a mild twitch of her eyebrows. For about the length of a flash of lightning, Kasra saw a wrinkle form and disappear on Platina's brow. "You must have meant to say '*astapsyxi*,'" she precisely pronounced the word, with no enunciation whatsoever. "Yes, having a grasp on something few neophytes can even learn would impress Teacher Xanne."

She said that as if Kasra had asked for the results of some kind of simulation or experiment. Why did all of her answers lack any sort of tone? Why did she never smile? Was Kasra boring her that much with all her simple questions? Taking advantage of the bemused violette's silence, Platina said, "You seem to be recovering well. But may I finish my diagnosis, now?"

At this rate, Kasra wasn't even sure if she should be telling the nurse how she was feeling, or if Platina should be doing that for her. The only reason Kasra had at this point to believe Platina was a breathing belhuayn, and not a statue, is because she wore glasses -- nobody would put glasses on a statue. "Sure," Kasra nodded, laying her head back on her pillow.

Almost miraculously, the statue girl walked forward. Kasra wondered why she was surprised to not see some sort of foundation being torn from underneath her feet. "So, you're not made of stone, after all," the violette joked, just to see if Platina's face would change.

It didn't. Instead, her lifeless frown retained its 'shut up' stare, making Kasra feel all the more uncomfortable to have Platina looming right over her. The azurette removed the rolled-up towel from Kasra's forehead and brushed the backs of her fingers beneath the girl's bangs to check her temperature. "You have returned to nominal status," she concluded, turning for the sink.

After a short pause to collect her thoughts, only to realize they weren't enough, Kasra said, "What?"

In layman's terms, Platina repeated, "Your condition has stabilized. You are no longer under the duress of hyperthermia."

The third time was the charm for the violette, when most of the words matched up with Kasra's limited lexicon. "That sounds good," she replied, reaching a leg out to stand up. She hoped she could sneak away while Platina was still preoccupied with rinsing out the towelette, but no such luck.

Somehow alerted to the pindrop sound Kasra's foot made upon contacting the smooth floor, Platina said, "You have not been permitted to leave."

"You said I could, when you were finished looking at me," Kasra impatiently argued.

"I said you could not move until after my diagnosis," Platina corrected her. "You still require hydration. You must not risk physical exertion until then." The deadpan doctor then handed Kasra a short glass of water. The violette shuddered slightly when Platina held the cup out in front of her, half expecting the nurse to dump the cold liquid on her head like a potted plant.

Perhaps it was just her imagination playing tricks on her fears, but she would have sworn she just heard a loud splash of water from outside the quarantine. Apparently it wasn't just her; the statue girl heard it, too. Platina was looking in the same direction Kasra was. The azurette glimpsed down at the red glow peering through the white collar of her dress, then vanished instantly. Kasra was caught by surprise when she looked over to see the normally motionless nurse was suddenly no longer there. "Did she just *fygidia* out of here?" the neophyte got up to follow after. Then she noticed the cup of water still in her hand, and gulped it down quickly, lest she kill herself by taking another step -- or whatever it was Platina thought would happen to her.

It wasn't long into her mad jog out of the sick bay did Kasra remember she had no idea how she got there. She figured the straight hallway out the door would lead right back to the Purifier Hall, but when she rounded the first dog-legged corridor, she discovered there was more than one path to take, and more than one closed door to go through. It wasn't until her belhuayn ears identified some vaguely familiar voices echoing in the distance that she knew where to go.

She pushed through a pair of Moroccan-style doors just as her audio trail had been silenced. She saw her sister, Rozha, accompanied by a dark-haired stranger sitting at the far corner of the Purifier, nearest to the temple's grand entrance. She caught the glint of puddles scattered about the reflective floor, as if they had both jumped in, but were now oddly peaceful. They just sat there, soaking in their clothes, not saying a word to each other.

Before stepping out to greet them, Kasra looked over her shoulder to see if Platina was standing behind her. The nurse was not in the Purifier Hall, as she had expected her to be. Where did she go, if she was not there? Sighing of relief that she seemed to have escaped Sachelvae's strangest resident, Kasra emerged into the empty Hall with a shout to let the Purifier's lonely occupants know she was there.

"Hey, Rozha!"

Both the redhead and her new companion turned their heads and leaned around each other to see Kasra trotting toward them. "Where did you come from, Kasra?" Rozha asked. "Why aren't you with the other students?"

"Wanystha brought me inside after I came back from Mediona," Kasra idly rocked back and forth on her heels.

"What were you doing in Mediona?" Rozha's interrogation continued.

"Layna and Raia brought me there," Kasra replied.

"What were you doing with Layna?" Viasarria accusingly added.

"She took Raia and I to the Safiric side of Tresantia," Kasra immediately averred. "She got us into a fight with one of the Priests of Travestas, and we had to run away. I was exhausted, and I fainted when I got back to Sachelvae."

"Yeah, a long day of getting yourself in trouble would do that to anyone," Viasarria snidely chuckled.

"Shut up!" Rozha snapped at her, thrusting a finger into the other velta's cheek. "You know just as well as I do that Layna was the one who pressured her into that mess."

Slapping Rozha's hand away from her face, Viasarria scoffed, "Layna can't help that she has the magnetic ambition to lead and the charisma to get others to follow her. It runs in the family."

"Charisma?" Rozha cynically raised an eyebrow. "Is that what you call her ability to guilt others with her reckless self-endangerment into making sure she doesn't get herself killed? You're right, you two have *a lot* in common."

Viasarria arrogantly shook her head and laughed off the Red Dancer's opprobrium. "It's only mischief if you get caught. Layna's got the mind of a *true* blade dancer. I was teaching it to her since she was a toddler."

Rozha's eyes flashed as she bared her fangs and slapped a chokehold around Viasarria's throat to wipe the grin off her face. "I will curse these waters with your pickled corpse if you ever tarnish Kasra's life to defend your *idiot* sister's delinquency!"

Her hostile threat was answered with a body-quivering jab to her midsection, forcing her to relinquish her vicious grip. Viasarria stood with a start and threw a sharp punch across Rozha's jaw that sent the redhead collapsing into the pool. Kasra gasped with a hand over her mouth when she saw Rozha get knocked down, for that moment rendered defenseless. Her eyes blanked out as her vision of the current world around her was lapsed by visions of a similar past. The aggressive stance Viasarria held, the style of her wardrobe and the color of her hair, reminded the traumatized girl of a life she wished she had left behind. Seeing her hero fall before her, in an attempt to protect her, only served to be a painful reminder of the haunting childhood she could not abandon.

"Astapsyxi!"

Kasra was pulled back to reality by the shout of Kyrana re-entering the temple, followed by the diametrically casual walking pace of Platina. Kyrana had cast a Sanguinic freezing spell on Viasarria to lock the velta in place. The blade dancer shook inside of the sparkling, paralytic vice as Rozha was allowed a chance to stand back up to her hands and knees. She slowly crawled toward Kasra, trying to muddle through the neural fog caused by Viasarria's direct hit.

Kyrana glanced between Viasarria and Rozha as she kept a hand focused on the blade dancer she had ensnared, ensuring that she remained in her telekinetic hold. "I've never had a harder time trusting anyone in my life," the arch-healer grumbled. "I don't know what this animosity between you is all about, but I do not care. Such antipathy is not circumspect for a priestess of Sanguina. Your words and weapons are meant to be saved for your enemies, not to be turned against each other."

Viasarria staggered away from the pool when she was suddenly released from Kyrana's astapsyxi. The Messenger of Sachelvae had reached her boiling point and could not be forced to simmer down so easily. "Did Diava appoint you as our babysitter?" she disrespectfully retorted. "What clout do you have to give us commands?"

"Because I am a member of the faculty, Viasarria," Kyrana returned her fellow Sister's condescending language. She raised her head to let the sunlight glint off the jewel in her silver tiara, representing her higher rank in the clergy. "I appointed *myself* as your supervisor and healer. The Safiric Brotherhood relishes the opportunity to use people like you against each other." Glancing between Rozha and Viasarria, she continued, "Any one of them could see that our sacred duty isn't as important to you as settling whatever petty grudge you two have between each other. If that is truly the case, then I will take the one among you who I feel is most competent for the task."

Viasarria watched the nurse walk over to Rozha and help her on her feet so she could examine her for wounds. Seeing the tightness of her broken mandible, Kyrana placed a hand under the blade dancer's chin, filling it with a strangely soothing pulse that caused her jaw to painlessly pop back into place. "When Mother Diava finishes her errands," Kyrana began, "I will make sure that you and Viasarria both get the judgment you deserve for your actions." "Platina," she added, addressing her assistant, "Take Viasarria to the Quarantine Bay and seal it with a *masalida* so she cannot leave."

With her usual lack of intonation, Platina replied, "As you wish, Kyrana." Even Viasarria had to be taken aback by the statue girl's eyes so unsettlingly resting upon her. As if under a trance, or perhaps out of fear, Viasarria followed Platina as the nurse sauntered off like a ghost back to the Quarantine Bay.

Now that it was all over, Kasra still had no idea what she had just walked in on. Her first day at Sachelvae had already become the strangest experience she'd ever had. She started to imagine how people who live in the temple so long became like Platina -- numbing themselves to everything happening around them to avoid being driven insane by this place. Rozha still had yet to tell her what in the world brought *her* there. After seeing how everyone was pulled into doing one thing or another without significant purpose made her wonder if her sister was a resident or a prisoner of Sachelvae. The redhead herself seemed to know exactly what was going on, however, standing there beside Kasra as if unfazed by all the dramatic happenstance. There was apparently a history between her and Viasarria that Kasra was not aware of.

"Now that Viasarria will not be joining us," Kyrana said, "It seems I have extra supplies on hand for our venture."

Looking between the two adults in the room, Kasra felt even more like a nosy kid when she asked, "What's going on, Rozha? Where are you two going?"

Instead of letting Kasra's sister answer the question directed at her, Kyrana replied for her. "You shouldn't concern yourself with that," her words sounded more like a command than a suggestion. "You and your fellow students will come to know your duties, soon enough, if you are diligent with your studies."

Much to Kasra's shock, even dismay, Rozha offered no argument to the contrary. She instead joined Kyrana in staring Kasra down, until the out-of-place violette had to take a step back. From this experience, she was beginning to get the idea why Layna had the attitude she did about the priestesshood. Having just walked in on this whole event made Kasra feel like a member of the crowd peering behind the curtain of a stage. She was getting an insider's glimpse on information that none of her fellow students knew -- or were even supposed to know. Having a forbidden look at the inner workings of the temple would have eaten at anyone to discover what was being hidden from them.

"You should return to your quarters and wait for the next activity," Kyrana told the young Kasra. "You will be notified by the crystal lamp in your room. When it turns alight, you will know Mother Diava has returned. At that time, you will come back here and you will be joined by your fellow Sisters."

Once again lacking the proper courtesy, Kasra replied with a curt yet understanding, "Alright," before turning to head on her way out.

"And Kasra," Kyrana called out, stopping the girl in her tracks. "When you are given an order, your response should address the issuer of your command with a 'yes.' If you are being ordered by Mother Diava, your response will be 'yes, your holiness,' followed by a bow…" The healer demonstrated by dipping her head forward and slightly bending her knees, whilst raising the hems of her dress by pinching midway down its split drapes with her finger and thumb.

Kasra practiced immediately thereafter with an awkward stiffness, her eyes never leaving Kyrana to watch from her expression if she was doing it right. "Yes, your holiness Kyrana."

Raising a finger to correct her student, the arch-nurse fought back a little grin. "Just 'Kyrana' will be sufficient."

Smiling back at her, Kasra sweetly added, "Yes, Kyrana," before finally continuing her exit.

After the violette had rounded the corner, headed for the convent's sleeping quarters, Kyrana returned her attention to Rozha. "We've had a busy morning," she said, with some relief. "We'll be lucky if we get to Fort Pericula before lunch time."

"Shall we get going, then?" Rozha suggested.

"I will retrieve Vanix from the stable, and we'll be on our way out," Kyrana replied. "Did you have time to prepare Heschel for the long haul?"

"Not before Viasarria got under my skin," Rozha huffed, rolling her eyes.

"I can't imagine anything taking less time than that," Kyrana amiably barbed for some much-needed levity.

"I know," Rozha praisingly patted the nurse's back.

As she and Rozha started for the doors to the outside, Kyrana quietly muttered, "Mother Diava was right to not give Viasarria a communication ring. She knew she would abuse its convenience to act without her consent. Now I know why she wished for Viasarria to stay behind. She still has a lot more work to do before she becomes one of the clergy."

Raising the ruby ring on her finger up to whispering distance, Kyrana sent a message through the glittering gem, "I apologize for interrupting your obligations, but I need to inform you that Viasarria will not be joining our quest. I feel you probably had expected as much. I handled the situation promptly and in a manner you would have desired. If you wish to speak to Xanne later, I will make arrangements for the meeting when I return."

Chapter 6: History Lesson

Though the warm sunlight coming through the narrow windows added an inviting atmosphere, the room Kasra shared with Rozha was uncomfortably quiet when she entered it by herself. The floorboards creaked under her feet as she walked toward Rozha's bed to sit on its firm mattress. Her thoughts were focused on why she was currently the only resident of the temple to not be doing anything, while everyone else was either attending classes or tackling secret missions. She figured it had something to do with those 'rites of passage' Diava mentioned that one must go through to become a priestess. Kasra honestly didn't care much about becoming a priestess, but she would be fooling herself to think that she was getting along just fine by herself before she was brought to Sachelvae.

Diava's words echoed in her mind. *"We were all created with a purpose. It is up to us to rediscover what our purpose is, and fulfill it so that our spirits may be reborn to carry out a new path in another life."*

Kasra didn't see how waiting around was going to get her any closer to that end goal. She knew that she should rest, especially after what had happened earlier that day. But she also knew that her sister was going on a secret and potentially dangerous adventure without her.

"Kyrana already caught me breaking the rules once," the violette reasoned with herself. "I doubt she'll forgive me so easily for a second offense."

She didn't have any time for additional contemplations before her attention was diverted to the sound of someone's feet shuffling down the hall. Her ears perked up and her eyes lifted from the rug on the floor, to the open doorway where she saw the shadow of one of her fellow novitiates being cast outside.

"Kasra, are you here?" Raia's voice meekly called to her.

The shy brunette's submissively sweet tone made Kasra ease up and smile. "I'm here, Raia. Come in!"

Upon stepping around the corner, Raia ducked her head and nervously shifted back on her heels, almost dropping the bed tray she was carrying. Her big, bright brown eyes were stuck focusing on the suddenly fascinating 'get well' meal that she had prepared for her new friend. "I uh, I got worried when I didn't see you at the Dining Hall," she stuttered. "I knew Layna had been pushing you really hard, and you hadn't been feeling well, so I asked Wanystha what happened and she said you had collapsed after she brought you in, and you were taken to the Quarantine Bay by Platina, so I left early and... um, I made you a little something."

Raia ended her nebbish, run-on sentence and finally came forward to hand off the bed tray to her charge. The meal she had prepared consisted of a bowl of soup, and a glass of lukewarm, lime-green juice. "I hope you like it," she added, mustering the bravery to merely glimpse at the violette before her eyes went straight back down again.

Kasra's heart swelled when she beheld the girl's kind offering. Her tail slowly wagged of its own accord, curling from side to side behind her. "Thank you, Raia," she softly exclaimed, not even sure how to properly react to such generosity.

"You're welcome," Raia finally returned the violette's stare, albeit with some awkwardness.

The longer they stared at each other, the more redness Kasra could see conflagrating across Raia's face. "Are you alright?"

"I'm sorry," Raia shamefully shook her head. "I'm just not myself when Layna's not around."

"Why is that?" Kasra raised an eyebrow.

"I'm no good in social situations," Raia self-consciously averred. "When I first came to Sachelvae, everyone else was so much older than me; it was intimidating to meet them all. Layna could see that I was scared. She gave me the confidence I needed to talk to the other priestesses. She's the only person in the temple I've truly felt comfortable around. She's the only one here who understands me."

Kasra thoughtfully smiled as what Raia was saying reminded her exactly the way she felt about her sister. "Everyone needs a guardian like that, if they wanna make it anywhere," the violette said. "You can't expect to do everything on your own. Rozha taught me that, ages ago."

"Rozha always seemed really wise," Raia nodded. "I was floored when she said you were her sister! I was surprised she wouldn't have mentioned you, or introduced you sooner."

'She never mentioned me?' Kasra's feelings were hurt at the thought. 'Did she think I died? Was she trying to forget about me?'

Perhaps she thought a little too loudly, for Raia was able to catch a hint from her facial expressions that, "Something happened between the two of you?"

"Sort of," the soft-spoken Kasra reverted to her cryptic responses. "Rozha and I had been... separated for a very long time. It wasn't because of some argument we had or anything like that."

Even though Kasra was obviously trying to keep herself from saying too much, what she did say confirmed the suspicions Raia had about Rozha. *'There was always something off about her,'* she mentally noted. *'It's like there was always something at the back of her mind. Now I know what she had been thinking about all that time.'* She knew she had to be overstepping her boundaries, what with how short her charge had been to her since they met, but Raia had to know, "Then what was it?"

The morose, uninviting look on Kasra's complexion lifted to a more pitiful, almost pleading stare -- as if she had been waiting forever for someone to ask her that very thing. That peacefulness she could detect through the windows of Raia's soul let Kasra know, beyond any doubt, that this girl who was little more than a stranger to her had a heart of altruistic gold. "My parents abandoned us," she whispered, short of breath and on the verge of crying. "I don't know why they didn't like us. They were always trying to beat us into something we didn't want to be," Kasra's words quickened and raised. "Rozha was my only refuge from all the pain, but they didn't like it when she got in the way. She'd try to protect me, and they'd…" The violette dipped her head to hide the tears spilling down her face as she bitterly sobbed into her bowl.

When Raia saw her friend breaking down in front of her, she immediately sat beside her and threw an embrace around her sides. She could feel how awfully thin Kasra was when she held her so close; she dreaded to think of what she had to have suffered for so long to become the way she was. At the same time she had so much pity on Kasra, she counted her own blessings to have lived the pampered life she had, by comparison. "You're alright," Raia calmingly hushed the violette, rubbing small circles on her back. She could tell there was more to Kasra's past than what the violette could avow, but it was evident that she hadn't yet the strength to say it.

"I'm so sorry," Kasra's voice barely manifested as a squeak.

Raia reached for a doily to dab away the rivulets from the violette's cheeks. "Why are you apologizing?" she cooed.

Kasra lifted her head to face the doorway ahead. "I'm tired of crying," she sighed, trying to get herself together. "Every night it's the same thing. I'm so sick of feeling sorry for myself."

"If you're looking to leave all that behind," Raia offered an encouraging smile, "you came to the right place." Waiting for Kasra's reddened eyes to look back at her, the soft-hearted brunette continued, "You're much stronger than you think you are. Sachelvae was made for brave souls like you. It took twenty to bless these hallowed halls," she gestured an arm outward. "The worst mistake your parents ever made was letting you go. But you don't need them to be somebody here. Sanguina knows who Her children are; She will protect you the moment you come through those doors. None of us will let you down, either. We'll always make sure you have everything you need."

Raia dipped the spoon in Kasra's soup bowl to let her charge have a taste of her homemade broth. Kasra wrapped her lips around the wooden implement and felt the rich, creamy liquid soothe her throat the instant it slipped past her tongue. She took a breath of relief when her congested airways opened to the heat radiating through her body. "This is really good stuff," she commented, immediately taking another sip to increase the effects of the last.

"Thanks," Raia twirled a curly lock around her finger. "It's my own recipe of Pahoki. It's meant to be a remedy for small illnesses. My dad taught me how to grow all the ingredients on his farm."

"You grew up on a farm?" Kasra asked.

Catching the violette's subtleties, Raia looked down and smirked. "I know in my gown I may not look the type, but before coming to Sachelvae, I spent most of my years helping my dad build his fortune."

Kasra tipped an ear with intrigue. "What did you do together?"

"I wasn't able to help him with much until I was older," Raia admitted. "I started with planting whole fields of crops for him. It took almost a month to get it done, even with the help he hired before growing season. When I was about ten or so, my older brother, Malkinos, started helping dad with all the hard work, like building fences and stables. Malkinos is two years older than me -- I'm fourteen, right now."

Kasra wistfully smiled as Raia talked so cheerfully about her family. She pushed down the want to mention her own with a drink of her wriggle-inducing, citrus-flavored juice. Instead, Kasra encouraged her friend to continue carrying on. "Do you still see them, now that you live here?"

"Once per year," Raia replied with a dreamy grin, "Sachelvae holds a special ceremony called Sevasmus, which celebrates the founding of the Sanguinic Sisterhood and remembers the sacrifice of Saint Sevasmia. For that holy time, all of the Pures in Tresantia are invited to participate in a grand festival. Last year, I and the other novitiates were put in charge of decorating the temple grounds. The priestesses set up tables outside for the guests, as well as stages for the plays. We all wore costumes and performed a musical to reenact the history of our faith. The faculty was in charge of planning all the events, as well as keeping watch to make sure no one from the Brotherhood came to ruin our fun."

The glitzy holiday celebration sounded quite fascinating, like one big party for the whole town to enjoy. Kasra had to know, "Why would the Safiric Brotherhood want to do that? Don't they have holidays of their own?"

"This is true," Raia started. "The Brotherhood celebrates the death of Sevasmia for a very different reason. The only reason they'd want to interrupt our holiday is because they don't like that we celebrate ours at all."

"That's awfully selfish," Kasra frowned. "I wouldn't have expected any less of them, honestly."

"A lot of what they do is very selfish," Raia concurred. "It's their whole belief system that teaches them to be that way. They think history started with them, and that we're here to undo everything they seek to accomplish. We believe just the opposite."

Kasra's countenance hardened. After a moment's deliberation, she said with an almost graveness to her tone, "Why? Why does one religion seek to unmake the other?"

Raia found a new lock of hair to twirl around her finger, as her widened eyes trailed across the floor. She blew a long puff of air under the duress of Kasra's overwhelmingly simple question. "That all depends on who you ask," was the answer she settled for. "You'll get one side of the story at Sachelvae, and you'll get another at Travestas. This city has only been around for four hundred years, but it's a product of what happened one thousand years ago."

"A thousand?" Kasra incredulously repeated. The violette gave Raia a look like she couldn't *count* to one thousand, much less understand, "How could someone remember *anything* that happened that long ago?"

Raia laughed, "*Now* you're getting it. But a little misunderstanding of historical facts wouldn't last one thousand years. It's more complicated than that." The brunette took a deep breath, as if preparing for meditation, trying to collect all her thoughts. "The only way I can explain it is the way Teacher Wanystha taught it to us, at the beginning of the semester." Polishing her fingernails on her dress, Raia proudly endorsed herself with, "Being at the top of my history class, I can tell you the story better than anyone."

She moved on with a dramatized clearing of her throat, "It's said that Safiro and Sanguina took up residence on their moons before there was life on Vitiosa. They were told by the Sun Goddess, Qualaria, that this world was made to be special, and that they would have to work together to create a wonderful people in their image. While they thought about what they wanted their race to be like, they crafted all the world's lands to look the way they do, now. They made everything, from the sky to the oceans, the way they are now. All the plants and creatures of the land and sea were made in preparation for their children, the First Scelan and the First Velta, to nourish themselves and colonize their world. Safiro created the First Scelan to look like him: tall and strong, with narrow pupils in his eyes. Sanguina created the First Velta to look like Her: beautiful and dainty, with round pupils in her eyes."

Raia took a break during her sermon to sip Kasra's juice, which the violette had left untouched since her first trying of it. It was apparently an acquired taste that Raia had long grown accustomed to. "Safiro and Sanguina populated every corner of the world with belhuayns of every kind we know today. They made us so that we could live anywhere we wanted to -- no matter how hot, nor cold, nor dry, nor wet, nor bright, nor dark. They used Sanguina's wit to devise civilization, and they used Safiro's might to build it. Their children were half Wild, and half Pure. And unlike the people of today, they got along well with each other. They made the golden years of our race. Together, they built the Great Civilization, which was ruled by Safiro and Sanguina themselves in mortal form."

At this point, Kasra was having a hard time believing the story. She disengaged Raia's speech with another of her simple questions. "If we were all behaving so nicely and built all these great cities together, what happened to all that? Why aren't we doing that anymore?"

"Since you so *kindly* interrupted to bring it up," Raia facetiously chirped, "After eons of prospering under this perfect balance, a great meteor came crashing down that lit the whole world on fire. Legend has it that its impact was what separated the continents from each other and gave them their size and shape. Everyone who wasn't immediately wiped out fled to subterranean havens where they could survive. Safiro and Sanguina both banded together to stop the global blaze. Much of the belhuayn race was wiped out from this catastrophe. All the cities they built were lost. Almost all the knowledge they had of the world they once lived in was gone. Sanguina knew the rest of the survivors would suffer long and painful deaths out in the burnt wasteland unless She did something to spur the growth of the plants and animals they needed to live. But Safiro believed that the strongest belhuayns would find a way to survive in this different world, and would become stronger as a result."

"So Safiro did nothing while his children died?" Kasra guessed. "Why would anyone want to worship a god like that?"

"Safiro actually *did* do something," Raia corrected her. "He went against Sanguina's will to create something he called 'the Annihlus' -- an artifact that would allow whoever wielded it to have Safiro's power. He placed it atop a Great Spire, like the beacon for a lighthouse, to exert its tremendous force upon the land and everyone who came near it. The Annihlus attracted all who sought its blessing of strength. Many terrible battles were fought among Safiro's children around the Spire; so many died contesting the ownership of the Annihlus, that a round wall of stairs was built out of their bodies, so that someone could simply walk to the top."

This morbid part of Raia's tale reminded Kasra of something she once heard her father say: "Success is paved over the failures of others."

"Exactly!" an impressed Raia shot a finger into the air. "Everyone knows *something* from the Creation Story, whether they've heard of it or not."

Kasra nodded. "If someone could just traipse on up the stairs that someone else built to the top of the Spire, what was stopping them from doing it?"

"Only everyone else who had the same idea," Raia matter-of-factly replied. "Since the Spire was so tall, the staircase had to be huge to reach the Annihlus. Anyone who saw someone else climbing the stairs would have attacked them in a mad dash for the finish. But it only took the fastest and the strongest among *them* to reach the Annihlus and harness all its power."

"Who did?" Kasra's question came with a bit more excitement, as she was finally getting involved with the story.

Raia smiled that her storytelling was leaving her listener on the edge of her seat. "No one knows his name, but it's said that the power of the Annihlus was too great for him to handle. He grew as tall as the Spire itself to contain all its energies. But a mortal has no comprehension of a deity's might; he was driven insane and became a destructive force of nature. The Raging Chaos God left nothing but ruins in his wake as he uncontrollably unleashed his elemental storms wherever he went."

A fascinated Kasra shook her head in disbelief. "Someone had to have stopped him if we didn't all go extinct, right?"

"Sanguina was watching this with much the same concern you had," Raia said. "She knew this was going to be the death of Her race, and Safiro was doing nothing about it. Our Goddess created Her first Sanguinic Shield and imparted it to one of her favored children. He would be the beacon, much like the Annihlus was, for thousands of others to join him in slaying the Raging Chaos God."

"Who was the person Sanguina gave her Shield to?" Kasra interrupted the story once more.

"Like the Chaos God," Raia replied, "No one knew their names. They were only called Sanguina's Trusted. With the Shield of Sanguina protecting them, they could not be affected by the Raging Chaos God's powers -- even as great as they were. However, even with as many as they had on their side, they could not overcome the Chaos God's might. They were at a stalemate, and the Shield's power was beginning to fail. The Chaos God was able to take all of his enemies down except for the last four: Sanguina's Trusted, and his three strongest allies. By then, he had grown weak from using so much of his energy; he couldn't defend himself. Sanguina's Trusted took this moment as their opportunity to strike. They plunged their weapons into the heart of the Annihlus, embedded in the Chaos God's body, thus destroying it and the Chaos God himself."

This time Raia paused on purpose, encouraging Kasra's interjection, which the violette met with gusto. "Then good times were had by all?"

"For a while," Raia laughed. "Sanguina's Trusted were only able to breathe a sigh of relief for the moment that the Raging Chaos God was defeated. But that soon turned to fear when they saw the fragments of the Annihlus raining down everywhere. The largest four fragments were collected by Sanguina's Trusted, who vowed to hide them away in the farthest corners of the world, so that no one could recombine them and use the Annihlus' power again. But upon separating themselves and the Annihlus from each other, they were tempted by the fragments' power. Even a small piece of the Annihlus could still grant someone enough power to dominate the masses, and that's exactly what they did to become the first Emperors of Vitiosa."

"Wait," Kasra stopped Raia with a raise of her hand, "you mean to tell me that the Emperors -- the ones who exist now -- are in possession of these pieces of the Annihlus? And *that's* why they rule over us?"

"That's *exactly* what I'm saying," Raia confirmed, with a somber sound.

Kasra started rubbing her head when she felt a tension headache rising, unrelated to her fever. "Okay, so, how does the Safiric Brotherhood and the Sanguinic Sisterhood come into all this?"

Seeing that her audience was growing restless and in pain, Raia compassionately smiled and wrapped an arm around the violette's side. "All that for another time," she gave her friend a little squeeze. "I'm glad you liked my meal," she added, noticing that her soup bowl was empty. "Are you feeling any better?"

Truthfully, Kasra wasn't much better off than she was before. At least, "No worse than I usually am," she chuckled for some levity, but forcing the bit of laughter made her short of breath and break out into a dry coughing fit. She didn't even realize she had done it, much less how awful it sounded before she caught Raia's unblinking gaze of consternation.

"You poor thing!" the heartbroken brunette cried. How she sat there, holding an elbow with one hand and covering her open mouth with the other, elicited such an endeared coo to escape Kasra's lips. She laughed, "I'm not dying," albeit the way she said it came off sounding more comforting than condescending.

"Are you sure?..." Raia squeaked, her wilted ears quivering. "I should let you rest. You've had enough excitement for one day." Taking her bed tray from Kasra's lap, she stood up and offered like a worried parent, "Is there anything else I can get for you?"

Kasra kindly shook her head, and laid down on her side. "Nah, I'll be okay. Thank you for everything, Raia."

Having gained some confidence and comfortability in the presence of her new friend after having this long discussion with her, Raia's attitude was no longer impeded by her once shy lilt of uncertainty. She performed the proper priestess curtsy as she took her leave. "As you wish, Sister Kasra." Right before she turned for the doorway, she noticed, in the corner of the room, the Mission Lamp was flashing. "Mother Diava has returned," Raia provided a quick exposition.

"Should I go with?" Kasra asked, fixing to sit back up.

"No no, stay and rest yourself," Raia hustled over to ease her charge back down. "I don't want you to get all worked up again!"

Kasra chuckled, for a moment thinking it silly how officious the other girl was being with her. But then, taking some time for honest stock, she realized how no one but Rozha ever treated her this way. Raia was the first person she met in her life, besides her sister, who genuinely cared about her well-being. Kasra didn't even realize how long they had been staring at each other until Raia mentioned it.

"What'cha lookin' at me like that, for?" the brunette giggled, fixing Kasra's bangs.

"Nothing," Kasra sniffled, trying to keep her eyes from welling up with tears.

"Alright, I'll leave you to it, then," Raia stuck her tongue out at her friend. She then knelt to tenderly peck her nose against Kasra's cheek, earning a pleasantly surprised purr from the other girl.

"What was that?" Kasra asked, her tail wagging slightly as she touched the spot Raia had kissed her.

"It's just a..." Raia blushed from having to explain it. In an attempt to quickly change the subject, she waved her hands and shook her head, reminded that she had another place to be. "I should get going to the Purifier Hall. I wouldn't want them to be kept waiting on me."

"Hey Raia?" Kasra stopped the brunette when she was nearing the door. "I think I'll be good to join you."

Raia looked over her shoulder at the determined violette with the most motherly of little frowns. "Are you sure?" she asked, moving back over to Kasra's side.

The violette nodded as her friend slowly helped her stand. "I had plenty of rest; I'd feel lazy if I slept anymore." Meeting Raia's doubtful gaze, Kasra smiled and reassured her, "I can handle it. I don't want to be anyone's charity case."

Raia's heart welled up with admiration and concern for the estranged vixy. She couldn't keep herself from shaking her head as she was brought close to tears, once again trying to imagine what this poor person went through to give her the attitude she had. She was truly the product of something amazing and awful. She could probably teach everyone at Sachelvae a thing or two about the most crestfallen corners of the world.

Chapter 7: Repercussions

As Kasra and Raia hurriedly shuffled their way down the narrow passage outside Rozha's room, the violette requested, "Remind me what this activity is that we're expected to be doing?"

"Every two hours, we return to the Purifier Hall to receive our next assignment for the day," Raia explained. "The windows on the roof of the Purifier Hall were made to measure the passage of the sun across the sky; the window from which it can be seen from that room indicates the exact hour of the day it is. For us novitiates, activities are split into our classes; Xanne for the morning, and Wanystha for the afternoon."

"What about the rest of the day?" Kasra asked.

"After we've been served our dinner time meals," Raia said, "the rest of the evening is meant to be reserved for studies." With a bit of a chuckle, she added for clarification, "and the reason I say 'meant to be' is because some of us, mainly Layna, never chooses to use 'study time' for its intended purpose. For her, it's time to conduct mischief outside temple grounds, because it's when Mother Diava and the faculty have checked out for the night."

Kasra found it hard to believe that the temple's security was so lax, especially at a time that practically begged for troublemakers like Layna to get into something they weren't supposed to at that hour. "How can the faculty expect the students -- or anyone else for that matter -- to stay out of trouble?"

"Mother Diava casts a protection spell around all of Sachelvae before she goes to bed," Raia replied, gesturing out to the walls. "Nothing can open the doors once she's locked them with that magic; only a priestess of her power could undo it."

Naturally, this begged Kasra's next question, "So how does Layna manage to do anything when no one's looking?"

She honestly wasn't expecting her curiosity to have elicited a response as jarring as what Raia did next, but it forced the brunette to suddenly stop in her tracks. Kasra watched her pause for thought, as if caught in a quandary. "I... don't really know how to explain it," she started. "It doesn't work when anyone else tries it."

"What do you mean 'it doesn't work'?" Kasra prodded.

Raia shook her head, still trying to find the words to help them both comprehend what she was about to say. "She can just *push* open the doors, as if Mother Diava had never locked them. She doesn't even break the spell they're under; the doors are still 'locked' by Diava's magic, but she can open them anyway…" She confusedly shrugged, even now trying to understand the meaning of it. "If they were to ever be opened while under that spell, then all of the faculty would be alerted to an intruder's presence. But no alarm goes off or anything."

'Layna wasn't kidding when she said she knew how to use some significant powers,' Kasra contemplated. *'But it doesn't explain how she's able to use them, in a way no one else is able to.'*

"Layna would hate me if she knew I ever told you about this," Raia worriedly said, "so this has to be our secret, okay?"

As tempting as it was for Kasra to eventually take this information to one of the faculty, she had an inkling they wouldn't believe it, coming from some nobody like her. Even if they would, it wasn't worth that much to her to potentially ruin Layna's life and make Raia dislike her in the process. "I'm new here," Kasra laughed with a shrug. "Who would I tell?"

Receiving the violette's assurance made Raia smile, even if she knew the other girl were just being coy with her. Kasra had too much peace in her eyes to be distrusted. "We should get a move on," Raia nodded in the direction of the doorway further down, to their immediate left. "They're probably wondering where we are, by now."

With Kasra in tow, Raia finally rounded the corridor from the sleeping quarters and called out to her expected audience, "Please forgive my lateness, Mother Diava!" But to her mild surprise, who she saw standing behind Diava's podium wasn't the High Priestess, but Teachers Xanne and Wanystha.

"We were starting to worry about you," Wanystha gave the student a friendly grin. "You're usually nothing less than punctual when it comes to following schedule." Raia happily let out a sigh of relief, bending slightly to give her higher-ups a respectful bow. Wanystha continued, "I see Kasra is feeling much better! It's good of her to join us, as well."

"She was recovering well, when I checked on her," Raia replied. Knowing it would make her Teacher proud, she couldn't wait to add, "She was feeling well enough to let me give her a history lesson in your honor!"

"Oh really?" a successfully pleased Wanystha purred. "I can always rely on you to do a good job."

Somewhere among the priestesses sitting around the Purifier, Raia caught the face of Layna shooting her a mocking tongue. Silently replying to her friend's unspoken barb with an acknowledging squint, she returned her more well-mannered attention to the Teachers standing at the other end of the Purifier. "Thank you, Teacher Wanystha." Going against her better judgment to question the faculty, Raia had to ask, "Where is Mother Diava?"

Apparently, no one currently in attendance had yet been enlightened of this curiosity, either, for everyone's heads turned to face the two Teachers standing side-by-side on the High Priestess' plinth. This time, Xanne took her turn to speak. "She has not yet returned from Mediona. Last we heard, she was approached by a member of the Safiric Brotherhood."

"Ooh," came the collective, intrigued cooes from the Novitiates' corner.

When the rest of the clergy started theorizing amongst themselves the circumstances for Diava's disappearance, Xanne quelled the buzz by finishing her explanation. "We were given the prerogative to organize the day's events until Mother Diava comes back." Wanystha then provided her directive to the convent. "Now that we've finished our lunchtime meals, it's time for the priestesses to continue their assignments for the day. Meanwhile, the novitiates will be coming with me; it's time for my class to begin!"

Following their instructor's orders with restrained gusto, the priestesses rose and readied themselves in a single-file line to leave Sachelvae's atrium. While the line was forming, Raia made her way to the back, where she knew Layna would be waiting on her.

"See, I knew Kasra wouldn't be dying," the dark-haired velta sneered at her, over her shoulder. "If she still had the fortitude to survive one of your little lectures, she must be a lot tougher than *either* of us thought."

Raia playfully batted Layna's ear, earning herself a laugh and a shove from the other girl's tail. "This of course is coming from Layna 'back-of-the-class' Sladervorn."

Layna began her response with a 'whatever' style shaking of her head. "Say what you will about my in-class participation," which Raia quickly interrupted with, "or lack thereof," to her friend's short chagrin, before she finished, "but when it comes to taking the exams, *no one* can cram like *I* can."

"A learned trait, for sure," Raia muttered. "No one can make *tripping* look more graceful than you can, either."

"I call it a quiet protest against the impractical length of these stupid dresses," Layna huffed, minding her red gown.

"Nothing was quiet about when you hit the floor of the Purifier Hall," Raia giggled, her mockery causing rosiness to appear on Layna's cheeks.

"Hey, I was late that day and in a hurry!" the embarrassed novitiate defensively complained. The laughter of her fellow priestesses still fresh in her mind caused her to cringe.

"I'd never seen Mother Diava crack a smile like that, before," the grinning Raia continued prodding. "Everyone's reactions to what happened was even funnier than the act, itself!"

"You're all a bunch of jerks, you know that?" Layna's comment only made Raia work that much harder to contain her guffaw. "I could have hurt myself for all you knew!"

"Aww, it's okay, Layna," Raia patted her friend's shoulder, reverting at least for that moment to her compassionate nature. "I would have taken care of you!"

"Oh yeah, because that would have been *really* swell," the embittered novitiate derisively rolled her eyes. "Having you there to rub salt in the wounds would've been *just* what I needed."

"I didn't know you prefered salt," Raia prepared her hidden rejoinder. "I would have used citrus juice, first."

Layna finally started laughing and sarcastically shot back, "You are the *worst!*"

The two silly stragglers were the last to join their company of novitiates in the circle of chairs of Wanystha's classroom -- which resembled somewhat of an artist's garret. Its walls were full of lively color splashes, with an informal appeal that seemed nearly diametric to the rest of Sachelvae's sacred interior. Most of the space on the walls were taken up by picture frames, some empty and some occupied by completed works featuring landscapes of areas around the temple. Kasra almost mistook one of them for a window looking out to the setting sun. Unlike the formal seating arrangement of Xanne's classroom, the students sat in a circle concentric to a raised plinth on one side of the room, while the other fourth of the floor was open for Wanystha to stand, oddly bereft of a desk of her own.

The Teacher folded her hands together as her eyes scanned her silent students awaiting her instructions. "The end of the day is a time for reflection," the Teacher began. "You no doubt have had some interesting experiences within the past few hours! For today's class session, I would like to see each of you create, from your own point of view, a collage of today's most memorable events."

Kasra exchanged worried looks with Raia and Layna, while the rest of the students seemed confidently happy with the opportunity to have some fun with their assignment.

"If Wanystha has a reason to question anything you've drawn," Raia whispered, "she'll report it to Diava in the morning. She does these classes to hold us all accountable. She's looking for a pattern in what we all present to her. If something's out of place, she'll know we were getting into mischief."

"She looks cheery and unobservant," Layna added, "but that's only her front to hide how mistrusting she is."

Kasra wondered if that's why Wanystha was so interested in what memories she would depict in her artwork. She and the rest of the students were handed parchment sheets and ink-steeped quills with which to sketch their works. She had never practiced her penmanship in all the years of her young life, much less had a desire to draw anything. Indeed, her lineart was slowly calculated as she tried to find the shape of the image she wanted to create. She didn't try to recite the image from any of her real memories, but lacked the imagination to fabricate one. She looked for inspiration from the other students with quick glimpses at their works, but most of their drawings were too amateurishly done to really gather what exactly the illustration was supposed to depict. She could detect from her peripheral vision that Layna and Raia were occasionally watching her, too, but her progress on whatever it was she was making was decidedly minimal.

Layna's work was rather slow at best, as well, as her thoughts were on something else entirely. She restlessly shook her leg under the table, until the vibrations of her oscillating knee were getting on Raia's nerves.

"Would you *please* quit doing that?" the normally submissive brunette finally spoke up.

"Doing what?" the oblivious Layna immediately stopped her aggravating motion. Once she was pulled out of her anxious pondering, Raia kept staring at her, as if Layna were supposed to have known the answer to her question. But the confused velta was not playing coy this time. "I was just thinking about Mother Diava," Layna whispered, her eyes shifting between Raia and the Teacher at the opposite side of the room.

Although the room's size was large enough to where they would have needed to shout to be heard by someone on the other side, neither novitiate felt confident enough to take chances with their secret conversation. Raia knew where Layna was going when she brought up her sudden concerns of the High Priestess, and started shaking her head. "Oh no, you're not getting me involved in whatever it is *you're* planning!"

"Doesn't it make you curious at all?" Layna asked. "She's never went missing like this, before. Something must be going down, and I wanna see what it is."

"Is one adventure per day not enough for you, Layna?" Raia chided her friend. "I'm sure whatever it is, Mother Diava has got it under control. You know she keeps in constant contact with the faculty; if she were in serious trouble, everyone in the temple would be called to action."

"Except for us *newbies*," Layna reminded her.

"Have you ever stopped to consider it might be for the *best* that we're left out of dangerous situations like that?" Raia injected some common sense. "If we could all use our powers and Sanguinic blessings like those of the priestesses and the faculty, we wouldn't need classes to teach us those things. We're kept out of peril until we're ready for it."

Layna scoffed, "So what, you get into one little fight with a priest and you suddenly have a new lease on life?"

Glancing once again to the Teacher's side of the room, just to make sure she didn't somehow overhear Layna's louder-than-whispered exclamation, Raia hissed, "I didn't want to get involved with that mess, anyway! You dragged Kasra and I into it, and it took everything we had to escape with our lives. Just think what would have happened if anyone other than Kyrana saw us hanging around Mediona!" She paused for a moment, and when she realized Layna wasn't going to respond, she continued, "Your mom can't always bail you out of trouble, you know."

Layna shot darts into Raia's eyes when she was given that last push. "Stop acting like you've got a perfect record! I'm not the only one here who has a cushion from facing expulsion."

Smirking a bit, Raia said, "If you're referring to my grades and attendance that convince people to absolve me from blame, then yes, I *do* have a perfect record."

"Hmph," a jealous Layna turned her head away from her. "The only reason you even follow me around is so that you can feel better about yourself when you watch me screw up. You're really a cold-hearted bitch, you know that?"

"Speak for yourself!" Raia laughed. "The only reason you *let* me come with you on those excursions is because you need *me* to come up with believable lies."

Squinting her eyes and raising a brow, Layna leaned in closer to her. "What'cha trying to say?"

Unperturbed by the other girl's pseudo-threatening posture, Raia answered her glare with a playful poke to the tip of her nose. "Exactly what I said. For someone who's so wily, you're not very good at deceiving others."

"Nah," Layna shook her head. "What you're *trying* to say is that you've had more *reasons* to lie than I have!" Raia was shocked that her friend would accuse her of such a thing, but like a prosecutor in a courtroom, Layna continued denouncing her. "I knew that your angel act was nothing more than a front for your *real* desires. You follow me because you want to be more like me."

'A delusional failure?' Raia tried not to let her full disbelief escape her thoughts, but couldn't keep it from showing too much on her face. But Layna seemed to be convinced that she had her motivations pegged, and knowing how headstrong she was, she wasn't going to let up until Raia confessed to it. "Well, yeah," the brunette's voice quivered, trying to think up one of those 'believable lies' she mentioned. "I get bored with the way things are, sometimes. I crave a little action to break the monotony of daily events."

Seeing Layna's grin made Raia wonder if she went too far with validating the troublemaker's analysis. "You really *do* know all the right things to say," the dark-haired velta chuckled. "I was testing you because I know you can't help it but to be on everyone's side. That's why you have no enemies here. They all love you because they know they can always rely on you to be a shoulder to cry on. You're tired of people treating you like nothing more than a blanket -- you're tired of them using you to comfort themselves. *That's* why you join me. I'm the only one here who doesn't use you like everyone else does." Wrapping an arm around Raia's shoulders, she asked, "Have I ever come crying to you for anything?"

Thinking back for a moment, this time with all the honesty she could muster, Raia said, "No, you haven't."

"Have I ever vented to you?" Layna continued.

"Only when the faculty caught you doing stuff," Raia uneasily smiled.

"Okay, bad example," the young criminal laughed. "But you know what I'm saying. You're a pathological liar; you're used to saying you care when you really don't. You even like coming up with falsehoods when the truth doesn't sound interesting enough!"

Although Layna was more proud of Raia's sins than she was arraigning them, these assertions did more to hurt Raia's feelings than instill her with self-gratification. She sighed and softly spoke, "I guess you're right, but --"

"Hah, that's all I needed to hear," Layna waved a hand at her. "The only time I've ever seen you be yourself is when you're with me. It's a little ironic that you'd only be mean and critical to the people you actually like!"

'No, I'm mean to you because you deserve it,' Raia inwardly countered.

Layna oddly paused, as if to hear something closely, then gave Raia a calculating, if not knowing, sideways leer. "You're only quiet when you don't want to say what you're thinking." Waiting for Raia's inquisitive, if not somewhat fearful stare, Layna added, "But you're an open book to me."

Raia watched as Layna propped her elbow on the table so that she could comfortably recline her chin against her hand. "What do you mean?" the brunette asked her.

"Exactly what I said," Layna wagged a finger, turning the conversation full circle. "I've known you for a while, Raia; I'd like to think that, in that time, I've come to know a lot about you."

"No," Raia argued, "knowing someone well does not give one insight into what their exact thoughts are…" she trailed off, hardly wanting to believe what she was about to say next. "Can you read minds?" Layna smirked as her friend was finally catching on to her secrets, but chose not to say anything to avow this fact.

Wanystha, though she tried to look busy in the background, couldn't help noticing that Kasra and her group of friends were the only ones looking amongst themselves the whole time they were working. The other students were typically untalkative, but Kasra's group was oddly conversational.

*'Mother Diava has the **sight**,'* Wanystha thought to herself. *'She probably already knows.'* After waiting another half an hour, seeing that most of the students seemed to be finished with their pieces, she clapped her hands once to get everyone's attention. "Alright, let's see what you've made! I'll start on the left and go clockwise so everyone has a turn to explain their artwork."

The youngest of the novitiates typically focused on either Diava or a favorite dish they had from the dining hall. Some of the older girls featured their chores in their drawings. But everyone's collages had some take on Xanne's visage when she saw Kasra perform her power trick in the classroom. After about the third mention, the bashful violette was trying to hide her face behind her paper.

"Sounds like you put on quite a show!" Wanystha chuckled at her. "Xanne told me about that, herself. Would you mind explaining what that was all about?"

"Um, yeah..." Kasra nervously swallowed. She shrank in her chair under the weight of everyone's stares. "She was talking about that astapsyxi thing, and when she described it, I said I've already done it once."

Wanystha nodded, holding a hand on her hip. "She was quite chuffed, I'll have to say! Nobody expects a novitiate of Sanguina's order to already be versed with one of the Goddess' gifts. These special powers are only reserved for those who have earned favor in her eyes. Very few Pures can summon them at will -- much less without knowing what they are."

Kasra tilted her head with her typical ignorance. "What does all that mean?"

Wanystha smirked. "I'd like to know that myself!" "So," she raised her voice, suddenly back on task, "let's see what you've got for us, Kasra."

What Kasra had created, after all the time she was given, ultimately resembled a road curving over a colorless hill to a vacant horizon. "It's just this," the violette held up her simple masterpiece. "A road... to nowhere."

"Hm..." Wanystha frowned. She stepped closer, as if to analyze something deeper in the rather plain and empty drawing. "It's not... quite what I expected. But... it lends itself to some interpretation." She traced her fingertip along the contours of the pen marks in the vellum. "The thickness of the lines bleeding through the paper show a certain... indecisive thoughtfulness. As if nothing was for certain, but everything was deliberate." Taking a step back, she held a hand to her chin as a calculating smile crept back on her face. "With some training in the right direction, that kind of effort can do wonderful things."

Layna's eyes enviously narrowed at the dumbstruck Kasra while Raia's eyes sparkled with admiration. All she could do was tap her foot and judgingly shake her head while Wanystha gave Kasra her generous criticism. The jealous velta then beckoned for the Teacher's attention. "What do you think of this one?" she called out, waving her picture around.

"I'll get to yours, next," Wanystha raised a finger to signal for patience. "Let me look at Raia's, first."

The brunette hopped in her seat when her name was called. "Oh! I just made a picture of --"

But before she could even complete her sentence, a priestess with long, blue hair -- almost like Platina's -- came fretfully barging in through the wooden door. "Teacher Wanystha, please forgive me, but we have an emergency!"

Briskly walking over to the distraught woman, Wanystha replied, "What is it, Cinté?"

"The priestesses who were sent to Mediona were attacked by members of the Safiric Brotherhood!" Her aghast exclamation had all the students present gasping with fear. "I was so scared, I had to get away -- I don't know how many are still there, but I had to come here to tell you!"

Wanystha remained diametrically calm as she held Cinté's shoulders so that the panicked velta could get a grip on herself. "Does the rest of the faculty know?"

The shivering Cinté swallowed timorously, "Teacher Xanne just left!"

"Then I'm going, as well," Wanystha said, an unusual look of seriousness hardening her face.

Mouthing like a fish out of water, the azurette stuttered, "Wh-What am I supposed to do?"

"Stay here and watch the kids," Wanystha ordered, then added with a whisper, "Make sure they don't leave the temple."

Wanystha brushed by the shaky Cinté on her way out the door behind her, and left the shocked priestess on her plinth with all the equally terrified students staring at her. Only Layna had an expression other than blank fright; the resident hoodlum couldn't have been wearing a more ecstatic beam.

"A-Alright, then," Cinté uneasily shifted back and forth on her heels. "So this is history class, huh?" She was answered by the quiet nods of the students around her. "That's cool," she trailed off, searching her scatterbrained mind for anything remotely relevant to say. "She's got you working with the easels this time? I liked doing these art projects when I was a novitiate. You don't know how lucky you are to have all this leisure time," she chuckled, forcing a smile that looked every bit as uncomfortable as everyone felt.

"*Man*, this **blows!**" Layna raucously interjected, stretching back in her seat.

"Layna!" Raia hissed, pulling the girl's arm back down. "What're you doing?!"

"She isn't even one of the Teachers," Layna scoffed. "She's such a candy-ass, we could do whatever we wanted with a nervous *pushover* like her."

Having gained a greater semblance of a spine, Cinté piped up, "Wanystha left me in charge, so as your superior, you have to do what I say!" She punctuated with a threatening finger wag.

Layna intimidatingly slapped her easel and shot up out of her seat. "Make me!" she truculently made her way up the raised platform.

Cinté cringed at first, but quickly regained her ground to face down the recalcitrant teenager. "Don't make me have to do this!" she held her hands out, preparing a sparkling radiance with a dance of her fingers.

"What're you gonna do with that, anyhow?" Layna smirked, holding a hand on her hip. "I'll bet you don't even know how to cast a proper *astapsyxi!*" And with that smooth utterance, Cinté squealed as she was suddenly frozen to the spot by Layna's magic bind. The dark-haired girl wasted no time running by her, going straight for the door. She only stopped to turn around and beckon her partners in crime, who were every bit as shocked as the rest of the students still sitting around them. "Would'ja get a move on, already?"

Looking once to the struggling Cinté, Kasra and Raia rose from their chairs and swiftly made their way to join their friend's escape. Raia stopped before Cinté for a moment to apologetically bow to her appointed superior, before joining up with Layna at the door. "That was a terrible thing you did back there!" she reprimanded, as all three of them were dashing full tilt down the temple's corridors.

"Is that to say you'd rather be stuck with little Miss Jitters back there?" Layna huffed and puffed along.

"Well, no, but --"

"Then I did the right thing!" the troublemaker tersely argued, while the tired Kasra lagged behind.

"I'm never going to hear the end of this one," Raia would have sighed, if she had any breath in her at all to do it.

"Not unless we become heroes," Layna optimistically stated, "which is exactly what we're going to do."

"You can't be serious!" Raia squealed. "This is just as much of a suicide mission as any other you've made."

"They're not 'suicide' when I come up with them," the other vixy corrected her. "They just *become* that way, later on."

"Oh great," Raia laughed, rolling her eyes, "so they're more like death traps, then."

"Sheesh," Layna glanced at her friend. "Maybe you *would* have been better off hanging out with Cinté -- you have a *lot* in common."

Chapter 8: Rising Stars

In the events leading up to the Sachelvian Sisterhood's order to scramble, Mother Diava had been wandering the streets of Mediona to watch over her clergy. Her psychic eye following the activities of the priestesses was distracted by what she wondered her volunteers were doing while gearing up for the Pericula Initiative. She received word from Kyrana just a few minutes ago that Viasarria wasn't going to be joining them. She could only surmise that meant the ex-blade dancer couldn't control herself and had flown off the handle again.

'Rozha can barely be trusted any more than Viasarria,' Diava mused. *'Now that her sister is living with us, there's no telling what will happen between those two.'*

"They're an interesting pair, aren't they?" came a startling response to her private thoughts. Diava merely jumped in place and immediately turned in the direction she heard the man's voice. All she could see was the contours of his face in the shadow of a nearby building, on the Safiric side of Tresantia.

"You are Deniechus," the frightened Diava surmised.

"I have something important to tell you," he replied, beckoning her with a curling of his fingers. "But it would be much easier to explain if you saw it for yourself."

The High Priestess raised her nose and steeled herself. "Under no circumstances will I ever enter your turf."

"Those rules are not followed so stringently by the youngest in your cloister," the Priest hinted. "Or did you send them, yourself?"

Diava could have groaned, had the matter not been more serious. "What have they done, now?"

The Priest tapped his walking stick on the golden cobblestones as he stepped forth into the light, his aged complexion wrinkled by a ghastly grin. "They attacked one of my monks," his voice softened as the distance between them closed. "And the one I was looking for was with them."

"Kasra?" Diava disbelievingly backed away from him.

Deniechus paused to revel in her fear, as he watched the High Priestess maintain her space. "She's been causing... trouble for us. But the Master does not wish us to punish her actions of violence. It is worth more to him if she lives. The deaths of a few monks can be overlooked, so long as they are… repaid, somehow."

Diava's eyes narrowed. "Are you saying Kasra *killed* a member of Travestas?"

"*Caused* him to be killed," Deniechus clarified. "Weakness has no place in the Safiric Brotherhood. If he could not defend himself from a few novice priestesses, he stands no chance in my temple and deserves to die, for shame shall not live in Travestas." His dark tone lifted when he added, "However, it seems that shame has made a home for itself in Sachelvae, where its priestesses are allowed to gallivant as they please and stress the fragile bonds that keep peace between Tresantia's temples."

"Are you looking for an apology by playing the victim?" Diava sternly asked. "Are you pretending that Travestas is not responsible for the disappearances of Sachelvian Sisters for centuries?"

"What you are saying then, is that these acts are *justified*?" Deniechus intriguingly raised his brow. "Such a bold statement for a lady of Sanguina! In the time that Travestas has been in my care, its record has been clean regarding the activities of its priests. We have exercised patience under the duress of numerous discriminatory acts made against us --"

"Insofar that the priests being attacked could not commit murder 'out of self-defense,'" Diava finished for him. "I make no excuses for the conduct of my novitiates, but know that their reprimand will be more severe to ensure that repeat violations are not made."

Deniechus smirked at her attempted diplomacy. "Your words mean little to us, 'your holiness.' Time and time again, promises have been made for a change in behavior, but no progress to the former has been forthcoming. It is evident that you either are incapable of disciplining your students or have had no desire to from the start. A debt is owed to us and it is time we collected it."

Diava's breath caught in her throat when she saw the blade of Deniechus' scythe emerge from the end of his walking stick. She took a step back to retreat, but she was stopped by the crossed quarterstaffs held by a pair of monks behind her. The High Priest of Travestas bound forth, as if flying across the ground, to swing the massive fang of steel through Diava's side. In a fulvous burst, a lustrous, transparent dome appeared around the High Priestess, causing Deniechus and his servants to be thrown in separate directions.

The sound of their cries and the sight of the powerful masalida's radiance had everyone in Mediona halting in their tracks and turning their heads. Those who did not flee the scene stuck around, but kept their distance, to watch the unfolding conflict.

Raising himself up from his crouched position, an enraged Deniechus commandingly shouted to his gang, *"**DESTROY HER!!**"*

Upon this monstrous vociferation, more monks and priests entered the fray from the Safiric shadows, and aggressively converged on their single foe with ghostly blasts fired from their hands. Diava's masalida was constringing under the combined power of what was becoming countless enemies all around her. She used the maximus of her spiritual energy to keep the shield holding true, but she couldn't outlast her foes forever. The ring on her right hand sparkled as she telepathically eked out a cry for help, which was answered promptly by the priestesses performing their duties around Mediona's avenues. Like the priests who had seemingly emerged from nowhere, the priestesses, too, appeared behind each of them to hold them still with their astapsyxies.

The dilitrivanni orb Deniechus wore around his neck began issuing its green smoke from the holes in its hemispheres. When he struck his scythe into the ground, a wave of pressure burst from him and rippled through his servants, causing the priestess' magic entanglements to shatter. Once freed, the priests turned on their attackers and pushed them back, causing them to scatter about Mediona.

The fight was quickly growing out of control as the Safiric Priests caused the destruction of many shops; entire carts were blasted into airborne shrapnel as their attacks were being evaded by their targets. The civilians and bystanders couldn't get out of the way fast enough as the warring clergies ran rampantly down the bustling avenue.

Diava preferred this unbridled madness to be reserved for the Safiric side of Tresantia, but she currently didn't have a choice in the matter as she was being pegged down with nowhere to go. Her shield couldn't move with her; she would need to take it down in order to move anywhere, but she couldn't take the risk until more help arrived.

She called upon her faculty, Xanne and Wanystha, to drop whatever they were doing and come to her aid posthaste. Before they could arrive, Deniechus forced Diava to drop her masalida when, with a rising gesture of his hand, he summoned a pillar of flame to shoot up from underneath her. Her holy gown was torched by the Safiric blaze; Diava shed her burning clothing before she could be caught up in it, too.

She was left with the sacerdotal bathing piece she wore underneath -- a much less restrictive attire that, despite all it covered, left virtually nothing to the imagination. Even though it was far from lewd by belhuayn standards, the High Priestess would not dare be seen outside the temple wearing it.

Now without her masalida, Diava felt all the more vulnerable to be without the dignity of her dress. But she didn't have much time to think about the embarrassment it would cause her, with Deniechus continuing to press the attack. The High Priest rushed her once more, forcing Diava to dodge by teleporting away behind him.

Apparently having anticipated this evasive maneuver, Deniechus countered by turning around and throwing his scythe like a boomerang. Its blade whirling toward her was stopped in midair by Diava's astapsyxi, before the weapon suddenly disappeared. Expecting it to have reappeared back in Deniechus' hands, Diava's eyes flicked back up to where she last saw him, but he was not there. She had no time to realize where he had gone off to before she heard Xanne shout, *"Astapsyxi!"*

Diava looked to her left to see the dark-haired velta coming toward her with a hand outstretched, facing the sky. Diava looked directly overhead to see Deniechus suspended over thirty feet in the air, frozen solid by Xanne's glistening shell of magic. "Where is Wanystha?" the High Priestess desperately importuned her.

"She should be arriving any minute, now," Xanne replied, "Unless there are more than we thought."

"We need her *here*, now," Diava demanded. "Let the priestesses sort the rest of them out."

With the sound of breaking glass, Deniechus willed himself free of Xanne's astapsyxi with enough force to make its caster shudder. Capitalizing on his foe's opening, Deniechus summoned another pillar of fire directly behind her so that when he dropped from the sky and came bounding toward her, she would back directly into the flames. But when she did avoid the strike of his scythe, she did not get burned, for she had the protection of an invisible masalida of her own.

The shield put out the flames as she stepped through them, and still had enough strength to endure another slash of Deniechus' blade as the High Priest spiraled into the air. Once he made his move, he vanished again, only to reappear moments later to fire another barrage of attacks from behind Diava. A flurry of white, cloudy Ectobolts flew from the Safiric alleys outside Mediona, and chased Diava back to the Sanguinic edge of Tresantia.

She didn't have enough energy to project a new shield; she couldn't outrun them and they couldn't be stopped with astapsyxi magic. All she could do was brace herself when they caught up with her, but when she threw an arm to cover her face and heard the white clouds make their bursting impacts, she beheld a new masalida had been made for her. Once again, her life was saved, this time when Wanystha came to her rescue.

"How're you holding up?" the Teacher informally asked the High Priestess, as she moved to stand by Diava's side.

More properly, but with her usual lack of emotion, Platina also offered her assistance. "Are you wounded, your holiness?"

Answering neither of their concerns, Diava directed their attention to the imperative situation at hand. "It's Deniechus," she pointed, gasping for air. "He's attacking Mediona. We have to help Xanne fend him off."

"Rest and get a second wind, Mother Diava," Wanystha suggested. "Platina and I will do what we can." The Teacher and the assistant nurse then took off ahead of their leader, toward Mediona, where Deniechus had begun to give Xanne chase.

The High Priest threw his boomerang scythe to cover the distance between them; the weapon's spiraling blade repeatedly hacked into Xanne's barrier like a circular saw grinding a plate of metal. Seeing that she was unable to move, he took his opportunity to advance, summoning a blazing tower to singe the priestess within her shield.

Xanne was knocked down just in time for the scythe to fly inches from her head once her masalida was broken. While Deniechus' scythe was returning to his awaiting hand, he jumped forth and slammed a fist into the cobblestone street. The power of his magic punch opened a fissure spewing blue fire toward his adversary. Xanne was taken by the flames, and while they did not physically burn her, she was accosted by the psychic sensation of her whole body being set alight.

While Deniechus' ghostly inferno kept the Teacher distracted, he prepared a finishing blow, stirring a mystic radiance between his hands. But the charging of his power was waylaid by the combined astapsyxies of Wanystha and Platina. Having been abruptly stopped in the middle of focusing his energies caused the power emanating between his hands to destructively fulminate.

With a loud bang, the double astapsyxi was broken and Deniechus was sent hurtling back into his enemies. Wanystha and Platina were both staggered by the forced cancellation of their telekinetic bonds; they nearly fell to the ground as Deniechus uncontrollably came flying toward them. But just when it looked like he was going to crash, his body turned transparent and intangible, allowing him to slip through them for just that instant.

He then sprang off the ground with the scythe in his hands and landed on his feet with impressive acrobatic finesse for someone who was wearing a full-body robe. After performing this swift maneuver, he paused and slowly turned to look over his shoulder, waiting for his opponents' next move.

"Where are the rest of you?" he sneered. "There's no point in holding back now; this place has already become a warzone."

"If we can already stop you with what we have," Xanne replied to his challenge, "then there's no reason to risk anyone else's lives with this madness."

"How noble of you to offer yourselves up as sacrifices," Deniechus chortled, throwing his scythe down between them.

The two priestesses stepped aside to get away as the blade bit into the ground, but they couldn't move far enough to escape the electric aura it emanated. Wanystha and Platina were stuck in a paralytic vice of blue sparks, unable to escape the Ectobolt volley they were attacked with next.

Xanne used a "Fygidia" spell to call her friends to her side so they could escape the electric entanglement and avoid being constantly barraged by Deniechus' power blasts. They were already wounded by the draining bursts of mist; they could barely stand beside her -- until all three were inexplicably shielded in a dome of light.

"I feel warm," Platina gazed skyward, looking for the agent of this saving grace.

"Mother Diava has returned!" Wanystha pointed to where the High Priestess had emerged.

A fully recovered Diava now stood between her faculty and Deniechus as the High Priest faced her down. "You're foolish," he shouted, "leaving yourself open to save their pathetic lives."

The leader of Travestas, with hands outstretched, began slowly rising into the air by a tremendous gale underneath of him. Diava had to steady herself against the vacuum-like force of the wind against her back, threatening to push her into the street. "You children of Sanguina," he continued through gritted teeth, as a white glow was cast over his eyes. "When confronted, all you can do is run." Before him now materialized his scythe; its fringe of blue light started to resemble smoke drifting from a flame. "But in the end, you'll still *die!"*

Six pillars of blue fire exploded from the ground and encircled his foes all huddled inside. The towers grew larger, their heat more intense, as they began converging on Diava and her allies. She had nowhere to go; they couldn't escape. She could only use her masalida to save herself or them.

But Diava refused that to be immolated by Safiric fire was the price she had to pay for being a feckless leader.

Like Deniechus, she had a great power of her own waiting in the eaves. While the tremendous heat was intent on cooking her alive, Diava stilled her mind with a meditation so focused, that nothing could be seen, nor could be heard, nor could be felt. She was sheathed in a white glow that immunized her to all pain and sequestered herself from all distractions. The winds stilled and the fires too ceased their movement. For a moment, all was calm; even Deniechus was frozen with confusion and fear.

"Spexuaross!"

Then the winds reappeared, only to shift in the opposite direction. The anti-cyclonic forces slammed Deniechus into the ground with an awful thud that separated him from his scythe. The reversing winds even caused the pillars of flame to disperse and dissipate. The dazed Deniechus arose to a crouching position, and called back his scythe to his hand to weakly brace himself, as he disbelievingly beheld his greatest power be nullified right before his eyes.

"Mother Diava!" Xanne admiringly exclaimed, albeit just as shocked as everyone else. "I've never seen a power like that before!"

"It's made to invert the effects of Safiric energy," Diava heavily breathed. "It works so long as the caster's power is equal to her adversary."

"Th-That cannot be!" Deniechus stammered, quaking back to his feet. "I did not live four hundred years to be outmatched by an unpracticed priestess, so weak in her own faith!"

"Speak for yourself, Deniechus!" Diava spat back. "You children of Safiro may have the privilege to enjoy a long life by imbibing the souls of others, but we children of Sanguina need not be on this world a thousand years to have a lived a thousand lifetimes. I am an old soul -- one of the direct descendants of Saint Sevasmia's disciples. I have lived a very long time through many different bodies, and have carried many different names. I was called by the Goddess of Life Herself to guide the people of Sachelvae. In all my previous lives I was sworn to protect my fellow Pures from the evils of the Safiric Brotherhood. None of you could kill me then, and you won't now."

Deniechus' scowl turned to a truculent grin, as if accepting the challenge of the High Priestess' haughty vows. He turned his scythe as if ready to strike, but before he could commence the attack, he and his opponents turned when they heard Layna shout, "Let's finish him!"

The young velta emerged from behind the wall of a tanning shop near the Sanguinic entrance to Mediona, armed with a throwing knife in hand. *"Koptigma!"* She used her barrier-breaking cry to throw the sharp projectile with a telekinetically-aided push from the palm of her hand. The knife's blade went flying straight like a bullet into Deniechus' chest.

"Layna!" Diava was just as shocked as the High Priest, himself.

"What're you doing, you foolish child?!" Xanne added for her.

"What does it look like?" Layna turned on them. "I'm ending what he started!"

Their short-lived argument was answered by Deniechus' chuckling. The High Priest laughed off his pain as he slowly straightened from his agonized coil, clutching the knife's handle stuck through his robes. He shot a glare into Layna's eyes, for that instant holding her still with a jarring fear, before taking the blade from his sternum and throwing it right back at her.

Layna cowered as her attack was reciprocated with the same force it had been instigated. When she opened her eyes and saw that she was still alive, she found herself standing behind a transparent lens of air. The knife's blade had been caught inside this swirling field of curious energy, which distorted her perception of everything behind it.

Raia once criticized Layna's shield for being unable to cover her back; indeed, it wasn't like any masalida she was taught to cast by Xanne's classes.

The telling expression the High Priest wore indicated that even Deniechus recognized it as something entirely different. In a calculating manner, he watched Layna's shield begin to fade until the knife embedded in its center dropped to the ground.

"Your confidence is strong," he finally said, "but you can do even more than you realize." He then looked to the building that Layna had been hiding behind and squinted his eyes, as if trying to see through it. "Where are the others?" he asked. "I can see one of them. I know she is here with you."

Layna turned toward her friends, Raia and Kasra, who had been both huddled at the corner of the wall since their fearless leader brought them there. Deniechus' scythe reverted to its walking stick form as he held out his hand and calmly said, "Tell them to show themselves. I mean them no harm." Considering his current surroundings, he added, "We have caused enough devastation today."

The novitiate did as she was told, and waved for Kasra and Raia to stand beside her. Hesitantly as they should have been, Kasra was the first to emerge and face her enemy, then was joined by Raia seconds later.

Deniechus' head imperiously upturned to stare Kasra down when he saw the violette's familiar face. "There you are," he whispered under his breath. He then cast a somewhat judgmental glance at Diava and the faculty standing behind her, who were without words of their own to say. "You are wasting your time with them," he addressed the clergy, as if they weren't standing right there. "They don't know how to handle someone like you. They want to keep you from becoming what you are." Turning back to Layna, he added, "I knew you'd come when you sensed they were in danger. You are here because you crave it. You are here because you *yearn* to be different."

Smirking, he said with attention to Kasra, "You are here because your heart is poisoned with guilt. You couldn't live with yourself if she was killed. You don't want to watch *anyone* die." Deniechus shook his head. "Such irony. The Father must be disappointed."

The High Priest then turned his back on the speechless novitiates as he headed in the direction of the Safiric side of Tresantia. Before he left, he gave a final consideration to Diava and her ilk. "You have so much power, yet… so little control." Though the High Priest could have just disappeared into nothingness, he settled for sauntering away.

Once they could finally drop their guard, Diava turned off her masalida and with the Teachers in tow, approached the novitiates who Deniechus had blamed for causing all this trouble. Layna stood rigid, her eyes squinting up at the High Priestess' darkened visage as she prepared herself for what she expected to be a tremendous haranguing. Raia almost wanted to hide behind Layna for cover, as if waiting for Mother Diava to explode. Kasra didn't think she'd fare much better than her cohorts, but was as surprised as any of them when the exhausted Diava didn't have a whole lot to say.

"I tried to keep you out of this," she started. "All I've done is protect you. But now I see my efforts aren't enough. Even if you must suffer your sister's fate, it must be done."

Glancing back and forth between Diava and Xanne, Layna asked, "What's she talking about?"

Xanne deferred to Diava's explanation. "Like Viasarria, you will be incarcerated to the Quarantine Bay and be supervised for all activities outside of there. I can no longer trust you to keep anything to yourself nor to stay out of danger."

"What?!" Layna squeaked. She clung pleadingly to Xanne's dress and desperately begged her, "You can't let her do this to me!"

Xanne swallowed nervously under the pressure of the girl's teary-eyed stare, but once again looked to the High Priestess for support. "I gave Mother Diava my permission to do what was right for you."

Layna pulled herself away from the Teacher with a self-righteous huff and a clenching of her fists. "This *isn't* right, this is *torture!*"

"You have made enough appeals," Xanne chided her, brushing a hand against the young velta's ear. "I didn't bring you here to exercise special privileges over your fellow novitiates. Viasarria set a bad example for you and that is why she is following the same correctional actions you are."

Before Layna could make her enraged rebuttal, her attention was diverted to Xanne's distracted gawk, staring over her head at one of the priestesses rushing down to see them. "There you are!" Cinté cried. "I caught you!"

"Cinté?" Wanystha finally spoke up. "What's going on? How did these three students get loose? I thought I told you to look after them."

"I did my best, Teacher Wanystha," the azurette apologetically bowed. "But *this* one, here," she accusingly pointed at Layna, "*zapped* me with an astapsyxi so the other two could escape with her!"

Suddenly, Kasra and Raia started looking particularly sheepish under the glares of the faculty. Meanwhile, Layna was trying to hold back a laugh from Cinté's retelling of her precious memories. Xanne looked like she was ready to slap her forehead. Platina's countenance had remained untested throughout the conversation, but that came as a surprise to no one. Everyone was more shocked that Diava didn't have something inflammatory to say about the matter, but she simply didn't have it in her after the battle at Mediona.

Cinté crossed her arms and gave the group of kids a disdainful scowl while she awaited Diava to smite them with her righteous fury. But the victimized priestess practically deflated when she heard her great leader say, "I must repose, but I will seek Sanguina's council on the matter." The frustrated Diava then began massaging her temples. "For now, the best I can do is control what I can. Sister Cinté, you will be rooming with Layna. I want you to keep watch over her at *all* times outside the Quarantine Bay. She is not to leave the temple grounds under any circumstance."

A bit overwhelmed by the new responsibility her mistress had just heaped upon her, Cinté shakily affirmed Diava's request. "Yes, your holiness…"

"Furthermore," the High Priestess turned to Platina, "you will be staying with Viasarria at all times, inside the Quarantine Bay and out. You will be rooming with her from now on, until her behavior shows signs of improvement."

With the proper rigidity expected of the statue girl, Platina also gave Diava the respectful priestess curtsy. "Yes, your holiness."

Chapter 9: Laeyudi Town

Rozha and Kyrana had traveled west of Tresantia through the soft earth of the marshes for about an hour before their steeds set foot into Virluti Forest. The limp branches of the weeping trees around them barely touched the ground with their tasseled leaves and hanging moss. The shore of the forest was the first spot of dry land either Vanix or Heschel had seen since leaving Tresantia.

The black striders had the slender legs and thin frame for walking smoothly through Onteval's swampy terrain; their species was accustomed to grazing on the mosses and grasses floating in the shallow waters they passed on through. But such rations weren't enough for the constant movement they endured; both steeds were eager to stop on the solid ground and sift through the dead leaves for the precious greenery at their feet.

Their riders also took this opportunity to have a snack of their own -- a more proper meal than the bite-sized portions they had been using thus far. Kyrana made sure to pick up a carry-on lunch while she was gathering supplies at Mediona, earlier, for she and Rozha to share midway to Fort Pericula.

"We've still got a way to go," Kyrana ruefully admitted, peering at the sun through the trees. "I would normally not take this path to Pericula, but under the circumstances, we don't have the time to take our usual detour."

"Why not go through here to start with," Rozha openly wondered, "if this path is shorter, anyhow?"

With some hesitation, the Arch Healer said, "There have been… odd sightings through Virluti Forest, in the past. Some say the Safiric Brotherhood have an outpost there, but it isn't known for sure. For as long as I've been serving at the temple, we've been told by Mother Diava to take a longer route through the thinner forest further north. Where there is light, there are less places for the Brotherhood to hide."

Rozha squinted her eyes over Heschel's head, as if expecting to see the aforementioned danger so far away. "It gets pretty dark in there, I take it?"

"The foliage gets thicker and the space of the canopy gets smaller," Kyrana pointed upward. "It is like the Black Swamp, northwest of Tresantia. We know the Safiric Brotherhood has established a stronghold there, within the heart of the Black Swamp's darkness. The territory is so large and dangerous, Mother Diava has forbidden us from ever entering it."

Rozha nodded for a moment to take all this information in. "But it's worth risking our lives this one time to go through the Black Swamp's little brother, just to put a stop to whatever's going on in Fort Pericula?"

With some semblance of a chuckle at her partner's cynicism, Kyrana said, "Yes, that is *exactly* what it means."

Once the traveling duo had ample time to rest, they continued their adventure into the the wooded vale. The shade of Virluti Forest was a welcoming contrast to being out in the hot, humid air of a Tresantian summer day. The invisible choir of insects was nearly loud enough to mute the footsteps of the black striders crunching through the leaves.

Rozha gazed up at the heights of the treetops to see a family of four-legged creatures crawling across the vines overhead, strung between the branches like ropes and bridges. Much of Virluti's wildlife took up residence either in the water, or in the trees. They utilized their darkly-colored bodies and plant-like appearance to hide in plain sight.

Vanix stopped and turned his head with every out-of-place sound these swamp creatures made, but Rozha's steed was trained to not be spooked by sudden rustles or splashes. Heschel quickly became the leader of the pair, his movement undaunted by these benign distractions. His confident pace was only slowed when the Virluti's darkness began closing in a half hour later.

The dry land was getting smaller and the trees were getting closer. The spots of light amid the shade started to disappear; the bright, noon sun was being eclipsed by the overcast sky. Onteval was known for its rainy season; the last storm passed through just the night before. Now another shower was beginning to fall.

The forest canopy was as good as a tattered umbrella against the cold rain; it could barely impede the flow of droplets from falling on the travelers, below. Though always expecting such inclement weather, Rozha's and Kyrana's only means of defense was to pull up the hoods of their garments to protect their heads from getting soaked.

"Mother preserve us," Kyrana sighed. "This is the last thing we needed, to make our mission more difficult."

Rozha could only hope that the gray clouds weren't planning on doing anything worse than unleash the soft shower they had already issued. "This would be the worst place to be during a windstorm," she woefully commented. She imagined being crushed by a falling tree, or knocked off her steed by branches whipping across her face.

"Your masalida can protect you," Kyrana said. "If you do not use it at full power, you can carry it with you."

"Really?" an intrigued Rozha tilted her head. "I never knew that. I would not have considered trying it, before. Since when did you ever need to know such a trick?"

The nurse chuckled at the blade dancer's hidden barb. "Us healers have to be quick to recover priestesses fallen in combat. That means we have to be able to defend them and move at the same time. Desperation often calls for innovation."

Rozha only wished she knew that when Viasarria was attacking her, earlier. Her military training kicked in so instinctually when Viasarria drew her sword, she completely forgot about her Sanguinic powers. The use of them didn't come as naturally as it did to someone like Kyrana.

"You've only been a practicer of the faith for a year now," Kyrana continued. "You can't expect to know everything, yet."

Indeed, Rozha felt almost stiff when she was using her special powers. She'd much rather go in for a close-combat attack than wait for her enemy to strike her, first. But if she could somehow combine the two disciplines, and make her Sanguinic powers come just as naturally as her fighting skill, she could be a much more formidable foe.

Kyrana went on to say, "But that takes continued training, and *that* requires applying yourself into situations like this."

"So being a priestess is a lot like being in the military," Rozha finally replied. "It's all about your experience in a combat situation."

"We do not prefer likening it to those terms," Kyrana nodded a disclaimer. "We'd rather it be called 'prevention--'"

"I know, I know," Rozha rolled her eyes, "because you're *so* sensitive to fighting words, I get it. Well, I still stand by what I said to Mother Diava before we set off on this little quest. I don't believe the Safiric Brotherhood is going to be stopped if all we do is push them out of their territories. They're just going to hide somewhere else and grow in power like a wound left to fester, so they can come destroy our strongholds later."

Kyrana truthfully had no argument to make against Rozha's points, but she was more concerned with upkeeping Mother Diava's credibility. She knew that a revolution would be impossible unless they had a means of defeating their adversaries beyond a point of banishing them from their sacred havens. Throughout history, temples had fallen on both sides. It was a constant back-and-forth that had been maintained since the beginnings of the two faiths.

"Sachelvae has been around for four hundred years," Kyrana defaulted to the simple facts. "If they haven't destroyed it by now, they never will."

Rozha almost wanted to laugh at the nurse's delusional confidence. "Maybe like Pericula, they're only waiting for the right opportunity to present itself."

Kyrana wasn't about to doubt those odds, either. She stayed quiet for the rest of their trek into the depths of the Virlutian wilderness. Darkness was closing in faster now; in a short amount of time, it was difficult to tell what hour of day it was.

The sun was nowhere to be seen; the broad leaves of the forest canopy had blotted out all sources of light. The noises of creatures calling to one another became louder and more commonplace, inspiring stillness in Kyrana's steed as he would stop to listen for approaching predators. The waters through which they walked muffled all sounds of distant footsteps; it wasn't until Heschel stopped, too, that the travelers realized they were not alone.

Rozha held up an arm to signal for Kyrana to halt when Heschel perked up in the direction of something they couldn't see. Black striders' eyes were made for seeing perfectly at night; the darkness of Virluti wouldn't have been a deterrent for beasts like them. They could also hear much farther than the average belhuayn; Rozha relied on her steed's senses as an extension of her own. "We're being followed," the blade dancer whispered to her partner.

"Where are they?" Kyrana looked all around, but could see nothing through the falling curtains of moisture. Vanix also seemed to have been confused. Her strider had been glancing every which way since they entered the forest, but no direction he chose to look would have been the wrong one to see where their pursuers were coming from.

Peering out from the shadows between the twisted trunks of the sleeping trees, were the ghastly globes of white eyes belonging to unseen monsters. Their feet silently splashed through the black water as they came hobbling forth. As they closed in, their horrible faces could be seen -- six small eyes clumped together on a small head armed with claw-like mandibles dripping with raindrops.

Kyrana cried the name of a spell, *"Fashaina!"* that cast a dome of light around her and Rozha like a stroke of lightning. The nearing creatures shrieked through their gnarled teeth as they reared up on the last four of their six, spindly legs and stamped into the murk. Vanix, too, rose up on his hind legs and forced an unsuspecting Kyrana to tumble off his back.

The frightened, giant insects beat their massive wings like a cicada's cacophony, and each took their segmented bodies into the air like a swarm of wasps. They turned their thoraxes to face the two veltas huddled underneath Kyrana's light, taking aim with their dagger-like stingers. Rozha drew her sword to block the first wave of attacks as the flying bugs took a dive at her.

A fearless Heschel even joined in with kicks and upward thrusts of his plated horns. Rozha dismounted her fighting steed so he could be freed from the weight of his rider to better defend himself, at the same time allowing her more freedom to dodge the oncoming assault.

Kyrana was weighed down by her drenched gown as she pulled herself up from the knee-deep, stagnant water. She did what she could to prevent the monsters' flurry of attacks and held them still with astapsyxi spells, for Rozha to deliver her swift and skillful condemnation.

With the help of Kyrana's well-timed reactions and Sanguinic magic, Rozha slashed off the barb of one of the monsters about to strike her from behind. Once the wailing creature had been so painfully disarmed, it broke through Kyrana's holding spell and came back for a second dive to pin Rozha down. The Red Dancer disappeared into the shallow waters; only her blade could be seen as it came up to sever the front leg of her large adversary.

The monster staggered and reared back up for the moment Rozha needed to plunge her blade through the heart of her enemy. The screaming insect's innards bubbled out of its exoskeleton like a green foam, crawling down Rozha's sword, as she mercilessly drove her smooth steel deeper inside its flailing cadaver. The bug's head shook with fury as it gnashed its huge jaws; its legs kicked and wrapped around the blade dancer with the last of its waning strength. When monster was forced onto its back, Rozha delivered her killing blow.

The scared Vanix, while not quite the experienced battle beast as his partner, Heschel, had a few shining moments of his own when he scored a lucky shot, goring his horns into one of the narrow marauders' bodies. With his superior strength, he rose up on two legs and threw the stuck monster to the muck. The black strider then repeatedly stomped the giant bug into submission with a ferocity that would have made Heschel proud. Heschel, meanwhile, had already downed two of the bugs and was currently engaging another, with the scars striping his body to prove it.

By then, Kyrana had helped Rozha decapitate another one of the flying monsters and slice a third in twain. The last insect of the swarm at least had sense enough to know it wouldn't last much longer than its fallen allies and retreated for the trees whence it came.

Their adrenaline petering out shortly after the unexpected ordeal had been resolved, Kyrana slumped against her shaken steed for a much-needed rest. "I don't know how much more of that I could have handled," she gasped, her heart slowing just enough to hear the pattering rain.

"You think *you're* exhausted?!" an exasperated Rozha sheathed her bloody blade. "I was the one killing them all!"

Minding the severed bodies littering the waters around them, Kyrana looked as if she were on the verge of fainting. "A priestess like me is not meant for battles like these," the nurse lamented.

"What it sounds like you're trying to say," Rozha smirked, "is that you're getting too old for it."

Immediately perking back up, Kyrana defensively raised her nose to the air and straightened out her dress. "A priestess' age is inconsequential to her stamina. We only get stronger as we get older."

"Sure," Rozha rolled her eyes, meanwhile hardly breaking a sweat. "I had my doubts about you, but I think we made an effective team. Even Vanix showed he had a heart for battle."

Turning to her steed, Kyrana saw the telltale discoloration on his horns from the insects' guts. "Did you, now?" she rewardingly stroked his neck.

"If this is the worst Virluti's got for us," Rozha continued, "I'm pretty sure we'll make it out of here just fine."

No sooner did she make that remark than they found themselves surrounded once again. "You no move!" cried a belhuayn's broken vernacular. A shocked Rozha and Kyrana then beheld an advancing party of spear-toting men wearing leather strips of clothing and camouflage body paint. Their long, messy hair was done up in different styles, usually tied around the bones of fish or lizards. The only one speaking demandingly pointed the edge of his spear at Kyrana. "Where you from?"

The nurse rose her hands and backed away. "I am a priestess of Tresantia."

Rozha scoffed at her from over her shoulder, "Like *they* know what that is!" before she was subsequently flanked by two other tribesmen. She grabbed the hilt of her weapon and threatened to draw should they come any closer.

"You kill all Dovistra," the self-appointed leader of the tribe minded the insectoid corpses. "You come in peace, we no do harm."

Although it must've been hard for them to believe they had no ill intent, what with the bodies of the creatures lying in their midst, Kyrana did her best to assure the gang, "We mean no malice to this place. We were passing through," she gestured in the general direction they were headed.

After looking thither to see nothing of note, the leader then returned an untrusting stare to the nurse. "You say you priestess?"

"I am," Kyrana affirmed. "I'm the Arch Healer of Sachelvae."

"If you healer," the leader said, "you must help Laeyudi elder."

"What ails him?" the nurse asked.

"He sick. No cure. Is dying."

Kyrana nodded; those three short phrases sounded urgent enough. "Take me to him and I'll see what I can do."

Easing up from his battle stance, the Laeyudi tribe leader then pointed at Rozha. "She healer?"

"Fighter," Kyrana clarified. "She's my friend. She won't hurt you, either."

The leader frowned and crossed his arms as he thought it over with a growling hum. "She can come, but no see elder. Only you. You no leave unless you make better."

"I will do what I can," the nurse vowed again. She mounted her steed and waited for Rozha to do the same.

Rozha would have much sooner thrown hands with the primitives than agreed to assist them with their pointless troubles. Whatever ills betided them they probably deserved for being out in such a wretched place like this. *'We did them a favor by killing those disgusting things. Now they have the unmitigated gall to take us prisoner?'*

Ushered along by her two pushy escorts, a reluctant Rozha climbed atop Heschel's back and rode away to follow the Laeyudi through their detour. Interestingly, their tribe wasn't far from the path they had been taking, which could have explained why they encountered the two veltas on foot -- and how they were able to sneak up on them without even their striders noticing.

The Laeyudi's village was built on piers suspended above the watery terrain; all buildings were raised on wooden struts alongside rickety walkways teeming with moss. It appeared that the Laeyudi village was constructed by borrowing from the native land, intertwining it with their civilization: The stairways and bridges were woven with the giant trees, larger than they did anywhere else in the forest.

The roofs of their hut-like houses were insulated with branches and leaves. The village heights extended far beyond the ground; its twisting ramps and stairs rose almost as high as some of the biggest trees, themselves.

'As detached from modernity as these people are,' came Rozha's inward monologue, *'their ingenuity is impressive -- I'll give them that.'*

What didn't impress the blade dancer was the workmanship with which these structures were built. She didn't expect that she could bring Heschel up the boardwalks, but she couldn't much traverse them, either, with any glint of safety.

The first flight of stairs seemed sturdy enough when she took her first step, but after so casually planting a foot up on the pier, she almost thought she was going to fall through. Now she knew why the men ahead of her took their time and walked in single file line. As leisurely as Kyrana's pace was, Rozha wasn't left wondering why the nurse didn't seem to be having any trouble. The sure-footed blade dancer had to harken back to her training days just to be able to move around on these crumbling highways.

Now that she was allowed to have a closer look of the buildings on either side of her, as she passed on through, she noticed below the corners of each roof was hung a paper lantern. Above the leather skin doorways, she noticed a similar, square-shaped lantern decorated with a kind of honeycomb design. They emitted an odd, but not quite foul odor that Rozha could vaguely recognize. *'That's what they use to deter predators from their homes. Burning ikaq wax emits fumes that certain creatures don't like.'*

Just when she was about to give the Laeyudi some credit for their unseen intellect, what she saw next once again took them back down another opinionated peg. Rozha was reluctantly relegated to standing outside in the rain, while Kyrana was brought by her escort to a large house of rectangular shape and high, angled roofs.

When the tribespeople opened the leather 'door' for the nurse to go inside, Kyrana was treated to the view of white mildew forming a crust on the walls within the building's humid interior. She could even smell it when she stepped on the wet, paper mats inside. If she didn't think it would look rude to her hosts, she would have raised a kerchief to keep from breathing it in.

As soon as she saw the town elder, lying shivering with a fever in a cot that served as his bed, she wasn't terribly surprised to see him in that awful condition. His skin had developed an awful rash, from his face to his toes. Some poor woman, probably his sister or wife, was dabbing a cold sponge across his brow. Kyrana couldn't keep herself from grimacing when she noticed the bucket she was using had the same water in it that was outside.

The balding, white-haired woman shot up on her bent knees when she saw Kyrana emerge through the door. She gaped with missing teeth and backed into the wall until she saw the two huntsmen with her. Assured by their somehow calming presence that Kyrana was no enemy of theirs, the nurse braced her stomach to kneel in close to the blind, old man lying before her.

"I mean you no harm," Kyrana reassured her, with a peaceful raising of her hand. "I am here to cure this man."

The nurse looked to the ceiling -- though any direction would have sufficed -- to give Sanguina a silent prayer before closing her eyes for some meditation. She raised the splayed fingers of her ring-bearing hands above the midsection of her quivering patient. Her hands were tightly hugged by a building sensation of pressure, like reaching into the depths of a pool. Her fingers were then sheathed by a pink radiance, as this pressure grew beyond the confines of her touch to the elder's body.

She heard him release his breath with a surprisedly relieved tone. Kyrana's audience leaned over her shoulders to get a closer look at her patient, to see his pale eyes beginning to close of their own accord. He seemed peaceful. His body no longer shivering, his limbs stiffened. His pain was entirely abolished. Now the glow of Kyrana's hands issued droplets of light to come slowly falling into and throughout the elder's numbed form. As the particles danced throughout his system, from the crown of his head to the tips of his toes, the rash of his skin began to disappear. Underneath the burning redness, his olive complexion was revealed.

Everyone in attendance gaped with astonishment to behold the priestess' magic. When Kyrana was finished, she opened her eyes and arose from her crouched position. She then whisked her healing spell away with an outward wave of her hands. She waited, and the elder came to shortly thereafter. His eyelids raised to reveal a new, vivid color of green his irises did not have before. He raised from his lying position and the first thing the grinning elder did was hold Kyrana's hands with the most heartfelt, unspoken gratitude the practitioner had ever seen. He bowed his head multiple times to her, saying repeatedly a word or phrase in a language she didn't quite understand, before jumping out of his bed and embracing the female assistant at his side.

The elder looked like he could have done a dance if he was so inclined; he moved like he hadn't felt such vigor in decades. He shuffled a quick lap around the room and stopped before Kyrana, once again unable to keep his hands to himself when he placed one on her shoulder. "You are... priestess, yes?" he tried his best to find the correct words.

"I am," the healer affirmed. "My name is Kyrana Rejinam, of Temple Sachelvae."

"Ah, Sal-vee-chay," the old man verbally butchered the holy place's pronunciation. "You come from Tresantia. I know that place." He then invited her to sit down with him on the floor.

As much as the nurse hardly wanted to stay in the squalid shack another minute, much less acquaint any part of her body with its interior, she couldn't say no to the old man whose life she had just saved. She settled for sitting on her knees; she could at least wash her clothing if any residue happened to brush off on it.

"You cure me," the cross-legged elder started. "I dying from disease, but you save me. Tell me how I no will catch again."

"Well," Kyrana minded the moldy walls, knowing where she might start. "There are some medicines you can take that will strengthen your resilience to illness." While she'd be surprised if any word at all that she said didn't go straight over the old scelan's head, she went on to say, "However, I do not have the herbs to show you how to make them. One day I will procure these for you and let you see them for yourself --" Kyrana inwardly added, *'Assuming he doesn't catch something else by then.'*

"I most grateful," the elder grinned. "I in debt to you. I want you have something -- I give you anything you want in village."

As generous as the offer sounded, Kyrana knew it would be better for her health if she politely declined. "I cannot tarry here long," she said. "My friend and I were undertaking a dangerous mission through your lands."

"Ah," the old man gravely frowned. "Virluti bad place, but," he smiled with a proud wag of his finger, "Laeyudi know the night. We know... *badder* things appear when dusk."

"*What* appears?" Kyrana naturally asked.

Looking over her head to the hunters standing behind her, as if they knew what he was about to say, the elder then replied, "Mire Fiend. She wait at night, and then," with a quick, snatching motion of his hand, "eat anyone come through."

Kyrana raised an intrigued eyebrow and gave the elder a sideways glare. "Where does this Mire Fiend live?"

Holding his knees, the old man bent in closer as if to share a secret. "Mordax Swamp." He then pointed toward the wall, in the general direction of the place he mentioned. "It out there, to west of village. Sun no rise there." With a jocular grin and a cackle just hoarse enough to be ominous, he said, "Maybe she eat it, too."

Kyrana's lip curled with a tinge of disgust as she raised her head for a kind of half nod. He seemed to be the type to tell stories; she wasn't sure just how much of what this man said could be taken literally. But after what they had just encountered before entering town, in broad daylight, no less, she wouldn't be surprised if something as awful as the rumored Mire Fiend actually did exist.

Regaining his serious composure, the elder leaned in again to share another bit of pseudo-secret information. "You no see her coming. She taste you before you know she there. Mordax is belly of Mire Fiend."

Frighteningly enough, this fabled territory just happened to be in the direction that Rozha and Kyrana were headed before they were picked up by the Laeyudi. "Is there any going around it?"

"Only in morning," the elder shook his head. "At night, certain death." His expression then lifted as he began excitedly wagging a finger toward the ceiling. "You stay here and leave in day, when safe to go."

Kyrana couldn't keep the grimace off her face this time. "A servant of Sanguina has no fear," the self-conscious priestess turned her look of discomfort into an uneasy smile. "If it is Mother's Will, today I shall not perish."

His countenance awash with admiration, the elder almost pleadingly asked, "You slay beast for us?"

"That is not my prerogative," Kyrana admitted. "I will leave that to my fighter friend."

Though he still had yet to meet Rozha, who had been waiting outside all this time, the elder seemed convinced enough to believe in their abilities. "You very brave. Most courage in all village."

"You flatter me, old scelan," the nurse modestly bowed her head.

"Ghanius," the man finally introduced himself.

Standing back up, Kyrana said, "Maybe we will meet again, Ghanius."

"You need something for quest," the elder stood up with her, "to resist evil lair." Ghanius shuffled to the corner of his bedchamber, where, beside a tall chest of drawers, a group of small barrels was kept. He searched the contents of these make-shift junk containers, reaching in elbow-deep to finally extract a small, corked vial of green liquid, hanging from a string. "This shield body from poison," he indicatively rubbed his belly. "You drink when see mist. Then mist no harm you."

After Kyrana was handed this special potion, the priestess asked, "What's this 'mist' I'm supposed to be wary of?"

"It burns skin," Ghanius gestured up and down his wrinkled arms. "Inside and out. You no survive long if no drink potion. It made from plants near Mordax." Returning to his cache of odds and ends, the elder grabbed a larger, glass bottle from a different barrel. It was filled with an orangish-yellow gel; air bubbles as if locked in time were frozen inside the viscous substance. "This protect from Mordax water. You no touch if you no wear it."

Very curious about this unknown ointment, Kyrana asked as she examined it in her hands, "What is this, Ghanius?"

Pausing with a melodramatic frown, the elder said, "It come from Mire Fiend. It found near Mordax. It only thing left of soldiers who no come back." Kyrana's eyes widened with a more fearful stare at the grisly ooze. Seeing her repulsion written on her face, Ghanius gravely warned, "It will be insult if you not use it. No let brave soldiers die in vain."

Kyrana's skin crawled at the thought of slathering this disturbing substance on her body. If her life depended on it, however… "I will make sure this will be the last time this liniment must be used," the priestess promised.

"You come back?" his question was spoken more like a request. "You tell of adventure?"

Allowing herself the first, little smile to grace her face since their conversation had begun, Kyrana promised, "I shall," then went through the door to be on her way. The priestess was greeted by the much more pleasant scent of the post-rain air, and the impatient Rozha who had sought shelter underneath a leaky roof from the chilly showers.

Upon grouping up with Rozha, the blade dancer asked, "So did our sick buddy make it?"

"He contracted an illness that Sachelvae has not seen for a hundred years," Kyrana explained, "no doubt a result of his substandard living conditions. I don't know how all the rest of them haven't caught similar diseases; it must've been his age that made him susceptible." The priestess sighed and went on to say, "Nevertheless, I was able to cure him. He gave me some useful information of what lies ahead." With a bit of trepidation, she added, "He calls it the Mire Fiend, of Mordax Swamp."

"Mordax?" Rozha repeated. "What did he tell you about it?"

"All Ghanius said was that it was really dangerous there," Kyrana replied. "The Mire Fiend is a creature that has apparently claimed the lives of many Laeyudi hunters."

Casting a critical gaze at the spear-toting men wandering about the narrow, bridge-like streets, Rozha huffed, "Like *that's* saying much. Whatever they're so worried about can't be that tough."

Kyrana smirked. "Still coming off your battle high, I see? I'd say you're developing a bit of overconfidence from our recent troubles."

"I feel more like I'm developing a rash," the aggravated blade dancer hissed, incessantly itching at her feet through her boots. "Are we ready to get the hell outta here?"

"Ghanius said we could have anything we wanted from the village," a ludic Kyrana held up her hasty friend. "Are you sure you would not like to take him up on his offer to get dried off, first?"

"Using whatever rotten materials they have around *here*?" came Rozha's expectedly curt response, earning a chuckle from the priestess.

"No, I suppose not," Kyrana sardonically sighed, as if needing time to think about it. "Shall we be on our way then?"

Briskly ambling out of earshot of their company, an increasingly irritated Rozha growled, "You couldn't have asked that fast enough."

Chapter 10: Mordax Swamp

Regathering their steeds where they left them, Rozha and Kyrana hurriedly set back off to continue their way from Laeyudi Town to the fabled and feared territory of Mordax. "We have wasted enough time as it is," Rozha huffed, "We can't afford to take any more long routes. This is the way it'll have to be."

'Easy for her to say,' Kyrana thought. *'She likes doing all the fighting. A hard-headed blade dancer like her isn't afraid of anything.'*

The whole time they had been plodding westward, Kyrana kept trying to imagine what the Mire Fiend could have been. *'They referred to it as if it were female; how would they know that unless it wasn't some creature?'* She knew that Safiric terrors grew in all shapes and sizes; she never claimed to have seen them all, but, *'I've never heard of anything that fits that description.'*

The open waters of Virluti Forest began shrinking the further the travelers went, the more rife it became with vegetation. Far beyond the regular moss and lichen-coated rocks, grew new, hateful plants, each which Rozha was able to call by name. "Toxic lilies, needle ferns, and marsh thistles, just to name a few." The trees themselves were decorated with the swirls of vines, from which grew carnivorous plants like amber curls. They lured insects to be eaten by its sticky 'nectar,' and blood roses, which dripped an aromatic liquid that was intensely poisonous. Rozha recognized them almost immediately for being useful for assassinations. "They can be mixed with drinks or even delivered along a string; one drop in the mouth will kill the average scelan in minutes."

Kyrana grimaced and Vanix also shrunk away when the squeamish priestess found the half-eaten corpses of rodent-like creatures caught in various stages of digestion by the nearby gallow flowers. The beautiful and equally dangerous plants were so named for the way they hung from high branches. "The false 'stamen' serves as the plant's tongue," Rozha explained. "When a small enough creature pokes its head into the flower to approach the stamen, the flower encloses the creature's head, which the tongue then begins to devour."

"They don't come in any larger sizes, do they?" Kyrana fearfully asked.

"The more they eat, the bigger they get," Rozha said, pointing at one in particular that was big enough to swallow a belhuayn skull. "This one's been busy! We were told when we found ones like this," the blade dancer drew her sword, "that we should err on the side of caution." With that, she sliced the gallow flower's head off its curled stem and watched the man-eating plant fall into the water.

Kyrana's expression contorted as her stomach turned. She gazed up into the gallow flowers above her and made sure to sit low on Vanix's back as they made their way under the shallow field.

"While you've got your head down," Rozha said, "make sure you're looking for trip roots and water spikes, so your steed doesn't walk into them."

The more hostile this environment became, the more Kyrana felt sorry that she had dragged Vanix into this whole mess. Her black strider may have been born for traipsing through such dangerous wilderness, but he admittedly had been pampered by the priestess in the long time he had lived in her stable. But Vanix wasn't quite the mama's boy that he had been before this mission started; having Heschel to impress motivated him to stay strong in a place he where he normally would have retreated. When he saw himself falling behind his leader, he would gallop to catch up with him.

"You better be careful with letting him do that from now on," Rozha warned, upon the last time Vanix hurried to Heschel's side. "The water is getting deeper in certain areas." Indeed, most of their travel thus far had been ankle deep for a strider; now the waterline was creeping up on their knees. "We might have to divert course to find dry land, or we'll have a good chance of falling in up to our necks."

Thinking it might've been a good idea to find some of this fabled, dry earth now, Rozha stopped for a minute to take a look around. "Moreover," she continued, "Some really nasty things live in the deeper waters." Before she could get into what exactly these dangers were and really spoil Kyrana's appetite, Rozha pointed to her immediate right, "I found a shoreline over there! If we're careful, we might be able to get there without running into anything."

Heschel picked up his pace slightly as he made his way in the direction of Rozha's grassy peninsula, but Kyrana had Vanix keep moving slow. When Rozha and Heschel had made it to their spot of terrafirma, Vanix started to panic when he felt something slithering around his legs. He kicked nervously at the invisible predator and picked up speed, despite Kyrana's efforts to calm him down. Heschel pulled at Rozha's reigns when he detected Vanix's distress, but Rozha halted him from running anywhere. "What's going on, over there?" Rozha shouted to her companion.

"I don't know," Kyrana quickly replied, "I think he's found something --" but before she could finish, Vanix's lower half suddenly disappeared into the water with a big splash. Kyrana was up to her shins in the churning surf as Vanix fearfully bleated.

"Fygidia!" Rozha cried, teleporting Kyrana to her side. The shocked priestess' legs collapsed from her quivering knees; she turned around once she hit the ground and gasped to behold her beloved steed being viciously thrashed about by an unseen monster.

"Astapsyxi!" Kyrana commanded her Sanguinic magic to hold still whatever was attacking Vanix, but she didn't have a clear line of sight to her target. "I can't stop it!" the nurse held a hand to her mouth.

"Fathvit," Rozha uttered a belhuayn execration not related to any spell. "It's a damned zhyraboid." The blade dancer stood up on Heschel's back to grab the nearest branch overhead. After briefly testing its strength, she hoisted herself up to wrap her ankles around it. She crawled across the tree's thin limb, which began sagging under her weight the more she moved closer to its tip. She continued climbing until she was suspended right over where Vanix was struggling, before she plucked a belhuayn flashbang from her belt and tossed it between Vanix's legs.

The bright blast broke Kyrana's spell, but shocked the creature holding the strider into releasing the frightened beast from its jaws. An equally surprised Vanix threw himself up onto his hind legs and turned away before falling back into the water. His injured front limbs couldn't keep his head above water; he had to flail to keep himself from being submerged.

Once Vanix was away and in the process of retreating to Kyrana, Rozha drew her sword and dropped into the water. The depth of the swamp's murk was well over her head when she went splashing in. The blinded blade dancer could hear the muffled sounds of Vanix kicking beneath the surf.

She could barely open her eyes wide enough to see a pair of glowing eyes on either side of a creature's jaws peering through the floating silt. Its head was protruding from the bottom of a sinkhole, wavering as if stunned by the concussive force of Rozha's grenade. Its mouth was open just wide enough to invite the blade dancer's sword down its throat.

The angered creature gargled on Rozha's steel as its teeth clamped down to take her with it into the silt. Rozha gouged one of its eyes out with the spike on her heel to force the burrowing monster to relinquish its hold on her weapon. She popped back to the surface to retrieve a breath of air, but just when her head breached the water, she was pulled back down by the zhyraboid grabbing her feet.

Choking underwater, she desperately kicked it again with her free leg until it let her go, but not without it dragging its teeth down the length of her calf. She had to cough out the water she swallowed, but that was all the time she had before the zhyraboid was biting at her tail. She reeled in the heavy beast with her strong tail and blindly slashed its neck with the curved saber on her forearm.

She could see a cloud of blood underneath the water's foliage when the monster let her go, only to come back in again to clamp its teeth into her sides. Rozha loosed an agonized cry as she was punctured by its powerful mandibles. She raised her sword with both hands and thrust the tip of its blade as hard as she could straight through the zhyraboid's neck.

The enraged blade dancer then turned her sword and pulled it inward to widen the wound until its head split in two. She kicked what was left of its carcass like refuse to the bottom of the swamp as she came trudging toward Kyrana.

"Get me outta here!" Rozha impatiently demanded.

Kyrana quickly teleported her friend before her with a 'fygidia,' at which point the exhausted Rozha crumbled to her knees, buckling from the pain of the wounds she suffered. The arch healer wasted no time with mending her serious lesions. She closed her hands and uttered a short prayer to Sanguina, until a pink light surrounded her fingers. Like she had done with the Laeyudi's elder, by covering the zhyraboid's bite marks on Rozha's sides, she was able to close them and nullify her pain.

"He tore me up pretty bad," the relieved blade dancer beheld her shredded clothing. "I'm actually surprised I didn't fare worse, but that was about the worst I've ever had."

"You are lucky, Sister Rozha," Kyrana calmly smiled. "Those wounds were close to some vital organs. Anyone else in your situation would not have survived, if they did not have a healer's touch."

"Yes, I know too well how lucky I am to have you," Rozha laughed, eyeing up her companion. "I saved your life and you saved mine since we began this little excursion. Shall we call us even, then?"

Kyrana smirked and shook her head. "This isn't about keeping some unwritten score. A child of Sanguina does not give help to someone merely because it is owed to them. Have you fallen asleep in your faith, dear Rozha?"

The blade dancer looked puzzled. "What do you mean?"

As Kyrana went to heal Rozha's wounded leg, she answered, "I seem to recall that you were much more practiced as a novitiate. You weren't like many that I've seen who resent being the oldest students in a class. You were patient and diligent. And it was due to these traits that you made your way up the ranks so quickly. The faculty and I were always impressed with the rate of your advancement. We knew you'd make something wonderful of yourself as a priestess."

Just when Rozha was starting to feel flattered by all these kind compliments, Kyrana added with a bit of a scowl, "You're not going to tell me that your good behavior was only to last insofar that it could be used to your benefit."

Rozha was silenced by the weight of the disappointed look Kyrana was bearing down on her. Eventually, she mustered the courage to say what she believed, and met the nurse's eyes with determination. "I do what I must to get by. It's what I've done all my life."

She trailed off as her expression softened. "At least, that's the way it was before I came to Sachelvae. When I thought I lost Kasra, I resented all notion of faith. I knew my parents worshiped Safiro, but I didn't care about the excuses they used to treat Kasra and I the way they did. They told us to hate what we were. They said Pures were 'the rot of the world,' and that they must be eliminated from it."

Checking her armor's weapons for any damage they may have sustained, she continued, "My mother wanted me to be like her -- a blade dancer. My father pushed me the hardest because I was his first born. He punished me if I broke because he wanted me to be an example for my sister. I learned not to fight back, but when I saw him attack Kasra, I'd lose it."

Wincing and gritting her teeth at some of the memories of the fights she had with her parents, Rozha trailed off, "The only thing he didn't do was kill us..." She idly traced a finger across the contours of her forearm saber. "If I had the chance, I wouldn't be so merciful."

The more Kyrana learned about Rozha's past, the less she could fathom how the Red Dancer and her sister turned out as well as they did. Their worst qualities were not as bad as they could have been -- Viasarria's family was proof of that. As much as Kyrana wanted to use this golden opportunity to get to know Rozha better, they were still in the middle of very dangerous territory, and the day wasn't getting any younger. Once they had some extra time to rest and snack on some of their rations, Kyrana got back on her steed and decided it was time to press on.

The twilight sun nearing the horizon peeked its orange rays between the branches of the trees, giving Virluti Forest its first spots of light since they had reached its darkest depths. The long shadows the trees cast on the swamp's waters and muddy earth began to fade into the night-time darkness. A cold chill crept up the spines of the Pures plodding through the swamps; though they could not see Safiro's moon hanging above the forest canopy, they could feel its presence and evil.

Virluti became uncomfortably loud with the chaotic sounds of its nocturnal wildlife. Visibility by the darkness was cut very short. Kyrana cast a golden bubble of light around her and Rozha to extend their range of sight and ward off any Safiric creatures. Just when things were seeming for a while peaceful enough for the two travelers to let down their guard, their striders began slowing of their own accord.

"They can sense something isn't right," Rozha explained with a whisper. She scanned her immediate surroundings, looking to all the plants and the thin trunks of the tall trees barely touched by Kyrana's illumination. But she saw nothing nearby that was out of the ordinary. "They'll know it's there before we do."

Rozha halted Heschel and raised her hand for Kyrana to do the same. "Do you smell that?" Suddenly, both she and Kyrana were on full alert again. While the arch nurse was going through mental flashcards of the names of all the spells she knew, Kyrana curiously raised her raised her nose to the air and took a deep breath to imbibe the odd odor swirling through the still, cold atmosphere. "I don't know what that is," she started. "Is it made by an animal?"

Rozha doubtfully shook her head. "It's too weak yet to tell for sure. But it was getting stronger the more we moved forward."

"Should we keep going and risk finding out what it is?" Kyrana asked.

"Have we any other choice?" Rozha turned to her.

Kyrana felt Vanix lazily swaying beneath her, as his head started to droop. "It might be best if we turn back and find a safe place to set up camp. We can continue by daybreak."

"We can't afford to do that," Rozha argued. "We don't have that much farther to go until we reach Fort Pericula. The Safiric Brotherhood waits for nights like this to perform their rituals. If we sleep through whatever ceremony they had planned, all this time we spent going there would have been pointless."

"You're right," Kyrana heaved a reluctant sigh, seeing nothing but a much longer evening ahead of her. This had already been the longest 'two hour' trip she could remember. "We lost a lot of time with the Laeyudi tribe and the fights we had along the way." As much as she didn't want to admit it, she was fresh out of ideas for coordinating a better route than the one they had. "What do you suggest we do, Sister Rozha?"

The blade dancer could tell Kyrana was scared, and as much as she didn't want to test the nurse's nerve, she knew there wasn't a more efficient option for plotting their course. "We keep going the way we have been," she shrugged, much to the healer's dismay. Trying to inspire a chuckle out of the anxious woman, Rozha added, "We can't let some bad perfume scare us off! Not after what *we've* been through!"

Her tactic to inject jollity seemed to work for the moment; a smirk tugged at Kyrana's lips as she bowed her head, as if to hide it from her brave friend. "Let's do it. This is the final stretch, after all!"

With a new liveliness to their step and some courage regained, the two priestesses continued their mission. As they moved closer and closer still to the source of the strengthening smell, they could see strange bands of green fog swimming through the trees, up ahead. By now, that curious odor had become like the pervasive stench of death -- bad enough to have Rozha using her veil as a respirator. Even when she could no longer smell it, she could still taste it in her mouth. "What *is* this awful place?" she cursed under her breath.

"It must be Mordax Swamp," Kyrana suddenly remembered its name. She raised her sleeve to cover her face, but it didn't help much to keep her from choking on the burning fumes.

"That's where you told me the Laeyudi's 'Mire Fiend' supposedly lived," the blade dancer skeptically started. "You sure he wasn't telling you ghost stories to keep you away from there?"

Kyrana couldn't deny the possibility that only something terrible could make a home out of a territory like that. "I don't think he needed to come up with a lie to advise people to keep their distance. I'd think most people would do that instinctively."

Apparently, she hadn't known Rozha long enough to realize that the hardened blade dancer lacked such emotions to distract her from danger. The redhead couldn't have given Kyrana a more dismissive look when she voiced her concerns. "I don't care about all that. I've got ways to protect myself from almost anything, and you have your Sanguinic magic to keep you safe from whatever may be lurking in there. I'm not going to be scared off by some rumors spread by a bunch of primitives -- just because they can't handle what's in there, doesn't mean we can't either."

Kyrana made sure to roll her eyes only after Rozha had taken point. The nurse almost laughed at the thought of what kind of trouble they'd be getting into if Viasarria had come along for the ride -- not that their situations hadn't been bad enough -- indeed they were only about to get worse. Kyrana took this moment to drink the small potion that Ghanius had given her. *'If anything Ghanius said about these medicines were true,'* Kyrana thought, *'If this works the way he explained, this will prove it.'* She wasn't the kind of person to just drink any odd thing that someone offered her. For all she knew, it could kill her immediately.

But seeing as how the very atmosphere of Mordax could have resulted in a quick demise, she didn't have much a choice in the matter. The tonic that was meant to protect her insides from being corroded by the air filled her parched throat with a very cold, howbeit relieving sensation. Almost the instant it entered her body, she no longer was choking on the toxic air.

Rozha looked over her shoulder when she heard Kyrana uncorking her vial and watched her drink the blue liquid inside. "What was that potion you just used?" she asked.

"Ghanius said it was meant to resist Mordax's noxious air," Kyrana explained. "He didn't give it a name."

"It's probably some kind of tinvaath," Rozha said, tugging at her veil. "During my training, we were told to use that tincture on our masks to prevent from breathing in any poisons." Thinking for a moment, she then held out her hand for Kyrana to share the vial with her. "If it can be used to grant immunity to these fumes," she started, "it could probably have an effect on the Mire Fiend, itself."

"I'm willing to give it a try, if you think it'll help," Kyrana agreed to share her potion.

Rozha then unsheathed her sword so she could pour a few drops of the tincture on its blade. Using a polishing cloth to spread the liquid throughout the length of steel, she then used what was left of the small bottle to steep her throwing knives. "If this thing really is so dangerous," she said, "I'll want to keep as much space between us as possible."

When Rozha's steed breached the boundary of the green stripes of fog, it suddenly stopped in its tracks and stomped its front legs. "What's wrong, Heschel?" Rozha peered around her black strider's antlers to see the land rejoined the swamp's water, which had turned a sickly, yellow green color.

The steaming pond before them was unsurprisingly devoid of any plant life; not even the typical mosses could be found floating on its surface. The sounds of the forest were nonexistent here. Everything living was very much behind them. *'This is a deathtrap if I've ever seen one,'* Rozha thought, grabbing a shoot from a nearby branch. She tossed the unsuspecting sprig into the water and watched it dissolve like a lump of sugar before her eyes.

"Unbelievable!" Kyrana's aghast whisper echoed the sentiments of Rozha's expression.

"This is no work of nature," Rozha added. She followed the shimmering reflection of Safiro's moon to the foreboding fane itself, seen clearly hovering over the acidic pond. "I don't know how I'm supposed to get around this," she scanned her surroundings. Most of the area around the water was blocked by trees; it wouldn't be easy for Heschel to walk through them.

"You may lack faith in the Laeyudi's shrewdness," Kyrana said, "But Ghanius gave me a couple of things to defend us from what lies in Mordax," she pulled off her pack to search it for the special items she mentioned. Kyrana handed the grim bottle of Laeyudi remains to Rozha, first, so she could examine its contents.

"What is all this?" Rozha squinted her eyes, concentrating on the gelatinous fluid as she held its container from all angles.

Sparing her friend the grotesque origins of this special ointment, Kyrana skipped to her sales pitch. "Ghanius said it was supposed to protect you from the water, here. If you rub it on your skin, you won't be harmed."

Rozha raised an eyebrow at her friend, having never heard of a substance that could protect her from acids. She uncorked the bottle and proceeded to pour its contents, slowly oozing in her palm. Kyrana grimaced as she watched Rozha rub the greasy lotion on her gloves, face, and any other armored place she expected to come in contact with the water of the evil swamp.

Deciding to test the effectiveness of this ointment, Rozha climbed down from her steed to touch the corrosive pond. She felt nothing when her hand sank into the bright, opaque liquid. When she drew it back out, her glove was unscathed; the water slipped off the slick film she had applied to herself. "I'm impressed," a satisfied Rozha returned to her feet.

Meanwhile, although Kyrana was glad that the lotion worked -- especially for the high price paid to make it -- she was more so relieved that she was not the one wearing it. "See if you can use it on Heschel and Vanix; they will need it as much as you will." While Rozha was heeding the priestess' advice, Kyrana kept a lookout for anything strange stirring in the vicinity.

At the east of the acid pond's edge, Kyrana heard what sounded like the snapping of a twig. She and Vanix both turned their heads attentively in the direction it came from, as if expecting to see something come wandering out of the thicket.

When she narrowed her eyes to focus on what looked like a shadow or a silhouette peering from the shrubs and tall grasses betwixt the bald trunks of spindly trees, she saw what could've been mistaken as a creature about the size of a person in crouching position. But it wasn't moving. Maybe it was staying still because it knew it had been spotted?

Her curiosity besting her judgment, the priestess dismounted Vanix to have a better look. When Rozha heard Kyrana's feet squishing into the wet earth, the blade dancer asked, "Where are you going?"

"I have to see something. I don't think we're alone here." The priestess then carefully jaunted around the pond as the foliage forced her ever closer to the water's edge. No matter how close she got to the object of interest, whatever the 'creature' was didn't move. Not even when she crept into the dry, yet prickly blades of the grassy weeds.

It was then that she realized it wasn't a creature at all that she had been stalking; it was the open husk of a headless victim. She almost wanted to gasp when she saw its unusual features; its torso, with a bit thinner of a waist than regular belhuayns, had been torn asunder. All of its insides had been removed. Its skin was like a bug's exoskeleton; dry and free of decomposition.

The only parts of the dead being's body that had been withering away were its arms, bent up as if fending off an attacker that had pinned it down. One of its hands had broken off; probably the source of the noise that had brought Kyrana to see its corpse. She examined its body further to see the hand it had left had three, long fingers, shaped almost like a scissor. Its legs had an extra bend at the knee and sported spiky protrusions at the calves. Its feet were split into two, large toes, with a talon-like claw on the heel.

"What do you see over there?" Rozha called over, after watching the dumbstruck Kyrana just staring down at the odd specimen she found.

"I have no idea…" the mesmerized nurse shook her head. Her gaze was then distracted to another shadow she caught out of the corner of her eye. She looked to her immediate right to see, deeper into the forest, were more cadavers of this alien being littered amongst the weeds. It looked like the aftermath of a battlefield. It was hard to tell how long they had all been there, but Kyrana surmised it was some time fairly recent -- assuming that these creatures rotted like regular belhuayns.

Both her and Rozha's attention were thereafter transfixed with a start when they heard a distant splash, as if it had come from another pond beyond the trees. The jarring noise had both Rozha and Kyrana holding their breath as their minds and hearts began racing. Vanix took a step back -- Heschel, too, even turned and prepared to run. Knowing her strider was ready to bolt for the woods, Rozha carefully clambered off her steed and grabbed the hilt of her sword.

A gentle yet chilling breeze, like the final breath of a dying victim, stole the air the priestesses had caught in their lungs. Their crawling skin broke out in shivers; their steeds stepped closer to the refuge of the trees, all while intently eyeing the lifeless water. At the spot of Safiro's reflection, a white foam of bubbles rising to the surface began to form. Rozha's fingers tightened their grip on her sword's handle, albeit losing the nerve to pull it from the scabbard.

Another, ominous wind rushed through like a vicious roar, rustling the creaky branches of the dead trees around them. Emerging from the rippling water were a pair of eyes -- green, glowing orbs like moonlight shining behind an overcast sky. The rest of its body was obscured in shadow as it slowly rose from the acid pond. Its arms were bent upward at its sides, like a marionette hanging by its strings.

As the belhuayn silhouette crept toward its frightful visitors, a slimy film secreted from its pale, turquoise skin. The Mire Fiend's fish-like tail swayed behind her with each step she took. Her breath came in prolonged rolls of gargled air, as if pushing through thick fluid bubbling from her throat. Nearing her prey, the Mire Fiend flashed her fangs; strings of gunge extended between her parting lips as her jaw widened to let her long tongue hang to her chin.

Upon seeing this creature's ugly visage, Rozha quashed her fear with a spring tide of aggression and drew her sword. Just as she was reeling back to slash it through her disgusting adversary, the Mire Fiend lashed a whip of slime onto its blade and wrenched it from the Red Dancer's hand. A shocked Rozha's knees bent and stiffened when she saw her weapon irretrievably plunge into the water. When she heard a splash and saw the Mire Fiend lunge forth, she guarded herself with her forearm blade.

The Mire Fiend latched her corrosive grip onto Rozha's wrists, and fastened her tail around the blade dancer's ankle to throw her victim to the ground. Rozha's arms were pinned above her head and the Mire Fiend's knee was in her stomach. She was overpowered by the creature's strength and couldn't shake free from her sticky hold. She could do nothing but grit her teeth and vainly struggle as the Mire Fiend's salivating grin grew nearer.

"Astapsyxi!" Kyrana shouted, stopping the evil belhuayn when her teeth were just inches from the Red Dancer's neck.

Rozha used the opening she was given to kick the frozen Mire Fiend off her, before the creature's acid slime could melt through her wrists. Kyrana's spell broke as the bestial velta crashed down on her side between them. Rozha rolled to a crouching position just in time for the inflamed Mire Fiend to retaliate with surprising force and quickness, delivering a slash across the blade dancer's face with her needle-like fingernails.

Rozha could feel every point of contact the Mire Fiend made with her burning on her skin, as if by an invisible fire. With anger, she ignored the infernal slime burning through her glove when she blocked the Mire Fiend's second strike. Rozha twisted the Mire Fiend's elbow and slashed her curved saber across the demoness' face with enough force to split a skull in twain.

But it merely left a scar from the Mire Fiend's chin to her forehead -- it hardly made the demoness cringe. She punished her enemy's efforts by spitting a gout of acid into the blade dancer's unprotected eyes.

Rozha immediately staggered back and covered her face, praying that she hadn't been blinded. She defensively lashed her tail out in front of her when she expected the evil creature's lunge, but the Mire Fiend was stopped by a flash of light when she collided with Kyrana's masalida. The priestess' golden shield let Rozha recover her strength and mend her wounds, as well as repel her adversary's attacks.

But Kyrana couldn't use two shields at once. The slimy belhuayn hunched over and slowly turned her head to face her open target. Kyrana stepped back from the Mire Fiend's intimidating glare, but before she could utter an "astapsyxi," she was pulled into the demoness's arms, catching her with a sticky web of gunk.

The Mire Fiend sunk her claws into Kyrana's back and tore into the front of her dress, burning holes into both sides of her body. The Mire Fiend was about to tear out a chunk of Kyrana's flesh with her teeth before the priestess loosed a "koptigma" burst, knocking herself down while sending the demoness flying back into the trees.

She stuck her feet to the tall trunks with unexpected grace, and like a spider, swiftly crawled up into the obscurity of their branches. Kyrana nervously watched for the Mire Fiend to reappear, and tried as hard as she could to listen for its movement in the foliage. After a few seconds of finding no sign of the creature, the priestess approached her resting ally. "Are you alright, Rozha?"

Before she could receive an answer, Kyrana felt a warm breath ripple through her hair. She turned around and saw the Mire Fiend's face suspended upside-down just inches away from her. Kyrana wasn't given time to scream before her throat was being crushed and burned; she couldn't cry an invocation to stop her attacker, and soon found herself pinned on the ground beneath her. The helplessly writhing priestess prepared to be disemboweled by the Mire Fiend's teeth, but was more shocked when the darkness and weight of the demoness' body was suddenly lifted off her.

She gasped for air and rolled onto her knees to see Rozha crossing an arm around the Mire Fiend's throat from behind, while a knee was stabbed firmly into the demoness' lower back. The thrashing creature wrapped her tail around Rozha's waist while her hands reached for the blade dancer's chin.

The Mire Fiend sank its claws into Rozha's cheeks once they found their grip, but even still, her opponent was unrelenting. Rozha only tightened her grip and turned her arm to contort the demoness' neck. The desperate Mire Fiend began oozing a thicker, stickier, more pungent slime as she struggled about until she could slip from Rozha's deathly embrace.

The blade dancer then found herself coated with the slimy velta's caustic mucus, while the creature scurried into the safety of her pond.

Rozha weakly staggered to her feet and stepped away from the shoreline, waiting for the Mire Fiend's reappearance. The blade dancer reached for a small knife dangling from a ring attached to her belt. Kyrana slowly stood and followed suit; both veltas watching for signs of life from the acidic pool. The tension stifled all other sounds beside their hearts pounding in their ears. The weight of the suspense kept their legs bent at the ready.

The waves began to fade from the water's surface -- no bubbles nor stirring could be seen to indicate motion inside the shallow pool. Just when they thought they could breathe a sigh of relief, thinking that perhaps the Mire Fiend had retreated, they saw air frothing up at the middle of the pond. The Mire Fiend re-emerged to lash out a whip of slime at Rozha's ankle. Like a lasso, she pulled the blade dancer's legs out from under her and dragged her toward the pond's edge.

Rozha used the spiked heel on her free foot to anchor herself, but even the added leverage of her forearm blade gave her hardly any advantage to resist the Mire Fiend's superior strength. The demoness continued to pull and crouch lower into the water, until Rozha's legs had been taken into the deathly pond.

Kyrana used an "astapsyxi" to stop the Mire Fiend from going any farther, so that Rozha could cut herself loose from the creature's slimy rope. She saw the demoness shivering inside her paralytic vice; the sparkling barrier holding her still was about to give. Using what little time she had, Rozha sprang to her feet and threw her one of the small knives she had washed with Kyrana's tinvaath across the pond. Unlike her sharper, larger forearm blade, the short, potion-steeped steel buried itself into the Mire Fiend's chest.

Kyrana's entanglement spell shattered as the creature clutched the dagger and loosed a horrid shriek that echoed for miles in the quiet forest. Another great wind swept through the valley and rattled all the dead trees in the clearing. With her dying breaths, the Mire Fiend spat her vile sludge at her enemies -- neither attempt making its mark as it staggered back to the edge of the pond.

The monster's oozing hands wrapped tightly around the handle of Rozha's weapon embedded in her sternum. Rivulets of blue-colored blood continued to pour down her abdomen until the Mire Fiend finally collapsed against the shore of her acid bath. Green wisps of steam rose from her skin as the slimy film began to evaporate. Even in death, her eyes did not lose their piercing glare. It was as if she still sought to wreak damnation upon her adversaries, even though she no longer was alive to do it.

After watching the Mire Fiend's body slowly slip into the waters that now marked her grave, the two priestesses waited several minutes in that one spot to assure themselves that the monster was truly slain. It wasn't until then that Rozha was the first to let herself fall to the ground, her surge of adrenaline and excitement giving way under her wounds.

She gave Kyrana an exhausted gawk as the healer tended to her friend -- neither one able to believe what they had just seen. Now that their most harrowing encounter had been resolved, there was still the issue with finding their steeds and replacing Rozha's lost weapon. "I'll have to make do without it," the blade dancer regretfully accepted her fate.

Thankfully, Heschel and Vanix hadn't scattered too far away; the two striders happened to stick together when they wisely fled the conflict, and were found just a minute or two outside Mordax Swamp.

The whole party was terribly tired from all they had been through, today, but they still couldn't give themselves a moment's peace. The edge of the forest was just barely in sight. Through the small and dangerous domain of the Mire Fiend, they saw the space between the limp trees growing larger.

Unless their eyes were deceiving them, they could see the glow of city lights ahead.

When they picked up their pace to leave Virluti and all its horrors behind, they couldn't have been more awash with solace when they saw a beautiful dome of radiance over Pericula's wooden walls.

Chapter 11: The Pericula Initiative

Rozha soaked in the sights of the fort atop the hill while her strider grazed and Kyrana muttered a solemn prayer to Sanguina, requesting a blessing for their survival. The torchlights of Pericula's battlements cast an orange glow at every corner of the walls, built from tree trunks sharpened like spears. Rozha could tell they hadn't been spotted yet; she could vaguely see the silhouettes of guards in the nearest towers looking in another direction. Had they emerged standing at the front doors, the town watch would've been no doubt suspicious of what a pair of priestesses could have wanted at this hour.

"We must leave our steeds behind," Kyrana suggested, proceeding to dismount Vanix. "Even with the protection of our mantaminas, they'd only make us an easier target to spot."

Agreeing by following suit, Rozha joined her ally at ground level. "Just to be sure, we should split up, as well; these cloaks don't cover our Purity, entirely -- especially from the eyes of Elites." Her warm breath swirling in the air, Rozha calculatingly added, "They'd have the gates closed for sure if the Safiric Brotherhood really were trying to do something in there. I'll have to find an alternate way for us to get inside."

"It won't do us much good, if you're the only one who makes it in," Kyrana replied. She reached into the collar her gown to retrieve a locket she wore around her neck. She opened the clam-like box and held it out for the girls to see its contents: a golden ring with a red signet of a crescent moon. "This is a communication ring," the nurse answered Rozha's clueless stare. "If you wear it, you will be able to speak with me, no matter where you are."

Kyrana pulled back her sleeve to reveal she was wearing one such ring of her own. "These rings only work with another that was made at the same time. All of Sachelvae's faculty wears one, even Mother Diava." She slipped the new ring on Rozha's outstretched finger, causing her own ring's jewel to turn alight. "Now that our rings have a bond, any time you want to speak with me, just call my name into that sanrisma," she tapped a fingernail on the crescent, red gemstone. "Once you're inside the fort," she then gestured to the torch-laden walls, "just say 'fygidia,' and I'll appear right beside you."

Rozha nodded with acknowledgment, impressed by her teammate's sound plans. "You certainly are quite experienced with these kinds of operations. You're pretty clever!" She poised her fists to her hips and straightened with pride. "Now, I know you won't like the sound of this," came Rozha's disclaimer, as the blade dancer looked to the nearest tower, "but I need you to help me neutralize our first target."

Having just asked for Sanguina's assistance and for her forgiveness, Kyrana's stomach sank at the thought of becoming an accomplice for another cardinal sin. "So long as Mother understands this as being part of our mission, I am sure the right penance will suffice for my actions."

"All I need you to do is hold him still," Rozha assured her. "Just light him up for me, and I can be rid of him before anyone notices."

One 'astapsyxi' later, the guard was held by the tell-tale sparkle of Kyrana's Sanguinic entanglement. Using the bright fringe around the silhouette's form, Rozha was able to more accurately target a lethal shot when she threw a knife straight for his throat. Without a sound, the guard collapsed behind the tower's window. Having heard no whistles being blown, nor any other indications that they had been spotted, Rozha relievedly turned to a very much distraught Kyrana, who had refused to watch what was going on since she trapped the guard.

"Thanks, arch healer," Rozha placed a hand on the nurse's shoulder, causing the uptight velta to jump slightly. "I can handle it from here." With that, the veteran blade dancer quickly and quietly advanced up the hill to the walls. Using the saber on her forearm, Rozha slowly carved a notch just wide enough for her fingers to slip inside so that she could begin rising herself up the stone wall. She steadied herself with the spiked heels of her boots; every step she took made it look like she was scaling an invisible ladder.

A couple minutes later, with a dexterous whip of her tail, she grabbed the ledge of the tower's window and hoisted herself inside the battlement. She crouched low to keep her head from being seen, at the same time checking on the mess she had made of the nameless guard on the floor. His face was stricken with fearful confusion; her dagger's blade was steeped with his blood seeping into the slats of the floorboards beneath him. Rozha gripped the window's edge and peered into Pericula's interior to see who was lurking inside.

The blade dancer's eyes widened when she saw the number of monks and priests congregating around the carved boulder, serving as Pericula's centerpiece. They had lit eight torches alight with blue fire in a circle around the Thunderstone. Their unholy flames casted an eerie glow on the four coffins standing upright against the rock's white surface. The men in indigo robes stood in a similar pattern, one ring encircling another around the sacred menhir.

Raising the ring on her fist to speak within whispering distance, Rozha sent a telepathic message to Kyrana. "You won't believe what I'm seeing up here."

"Don't make me guess," came the nurse's reply. "Send me up there with you."

Casting a glance back to the dead man lying behind her, Rozha decided to spare Kyrana with a suggestion of her own. "I'll have you join me once I'm on the ground. We'll have a better idea of what to do by then."

After a short, perhaps resentful pause, Kyrana said, "Alright, but don't keep me waiting."

"Believe me, you'll wish I had," Rozha grimaced at the thought of confronting the massive congregation. She knew it'd be suicide to charge into them, now, when they were all standing idly by for whatever it was they were waiting for. It was at this point she was wondering what risk it would've caused for Diava to have allowed the entire Sachelvian Sisterhood to deal with this situation. *'There's no way all these guys are from the same temple,'* Rozha thought. *'Pericula's church is too small for this many people to be cloistered inside there.'*

As she was imagining what evil plot this small invasion force had up their enormous, collective sleeve, the congregation moved to open a space between their standing positions. Rozha watched as a new, curious figure began sauntering toward them, emerging from behind the shadows of a small building by the cobblestone road. Unlike his cohorts, this man didn't have his hands tucked inside his sleeves; he seemed to lack their sophistication and organization.

His robes appeared tattered as they flowed behind him with every step he took. As he came closer to the light, Rozha could see the finer details of his garments, which, despite the damage they took, were far more elaborate than any of his fellow priests'. Instead of moving through the opening they provided for him, he stood outside their huddle and raised his arms, his hands facing the Thunderstone.

Even though she would lose her vantage point when she left the tower, Rozha knew this was her opportunity to advance. From this position, she was able to survey the lands below her. There was no way to cause a soft enough landing to where she wouldn't be heard if she dropped off the wall. But she wasn't about to waste more time digging a ladder for herself down the other side.

She espied the slight angle of an A-framed roof about a short jump away from where she was standing. With a bending of her knees and an outstretching of her arms, she leapt through the window to the building she spotted, sticking the landing like a lizard to a leaf. She let her body slip down to the gutters of the roof, feeling with her tail how much further she had to go until she was touching the ground. With a scuffing of stone that only her feet could hear, she was back to solid earth.

"Prepare yourself, Kyrana," she warned her partner, "I'm bringing you in." Upon intoning the sacred word, "Fygidia," Kyrana appeared beside her.

Before any words could be exchanged between them, both their gazes were averted to the great ring of light blasting like a shockwave overhead with a thunderous boom. The terrific sound rattled the walls of all the residences and even shook the ground.

This tremendous display was then followed by a massive spire of light shooting into the sky. Unable to stand still any longer, both Kyrana and Rozha rounded the alleys until they caught a glimpse of the Thunderstone congregation, and saw that this narrow ray was emanating from the top of the Thunderstone itself.

All of the priests in attendance had misty, blue auras surrounding them. Their leader was wrapped in the largest glow, drifting off his body like a hazy inferno. His cohorts began performing a frenetic wave of bows, falling to their knees with their hands on the floor, before rising back up again -- all while chanting some short, mystic phrase. The priests on the outer circle were shaking some sort of crystal, rattling instruments that altogether produced a sound like wind howling through an icy cave.

The Thunderstone itself began to radiate in seven colors, the length of its aura gradually increasing over time as the priests' spiritual energies were filling the boulder to its capacity. When this threshold had been reached, the beam of light dissipated with a flash of sparks. Suddenly, the chanting and the music stopped. All movement halted dead in its tracks as the priests continued gazing skyward.

For the first time since this chaotic exhibition started, Rozha could hear herself breathe. Soon after, their eyes were treated to the sight of a rather large shooting star in the center of the night sky. This was later joined by a shower of many, smaller streaks -- the scale of which neither Rozha nor Kyrana had seen in their lifetimes. And unlike any time in their lives, the very sight of it filled them with immeasurable dread.

Their sensation of doom was met with another horrific sound, like the crack of a god's bullwhip, as a black rift was torn in the sky itself. This opening, like a split in smooth steel, widened as if clawed through by the other side, into a circular doorway of darkness. This black hole was filled with aubergine swirls, like the reflection of stars stirring inside a maelstrom.

The Safiric priests slowly approached the Thunderstone, now pulsating with its radiance, to place their hands upon its surface. One by one, in waves they were taken into the portal it created, their bodies zipping upward like the shooting stars they summoned.

"What kind of devilry--?!" Kyrana finally shouted in a hushed tone.

"Now's our chance," Rozha interjected, with an encouraging slap to the nurse's arm. Without telling her what she was going to do this time, the brave blade dancer sallied forth into the fray, getting the jump on the doubtlessly surprised members of the remaining congregation.

She made her presence known with a belhuayn flash bang aimed for the space between the gathered priests and their leader. As soon as they were all disabled by her hostile greeting, Rozha laid into her nearest, nameless targets. She dismembered every limb she struck with a single slash of her forearm blade, taking down three monks in the time it took for the ones who recovered first to surround her.

The mad assassin danced around their entanglement spells as stones and roots reached from under her feet to bind her. She dexterously deflected ghastly globes and parried swipes of swords, before countering with kicks and bone-crushing blows. Kyrana assisted from a distance by stopping would-be lethal strikes from Rozha's adversaries, at the same time leaving them open for the blade dancer's killing attacks.

Even the priestess who feared death was immersed into the excitement of watching her bloodthirsty rogue slice their evil enemies into ribbons. Seeing Rozha make short work of them, now slathered head to toe in their gore, Kyrana now understood the origin of her nickname: The Red.

The crazed blade dancer looked like a tornado of knives when in motion. When she stopped amid the broken bodies of her decimated victims, she faced down their leader, who had been silently watching the carnage unfold with ever waxing interest. And how the blade dancer's eyes widened when she saw, hovering over the Elite's hand, was a great ball of white energy -- collected from all the souls of the priests she had so proudly slain. The vacuum this ghostly orb manifested toward itself pulled away the Elite's hood so that his grinning face could be seen: manic eyes of gold over his yellow, belhuayn rosage.

Fun time was officially over when the Elite cast the ball forth with a flick of his wrist. As large as the projectile was, like a cannonball, it crashed into Rozha with a force every bit as astonishing as its speed. The overconfident and reckless blade dancer was humbled with unconsciousness after she was taken by the spiritual grenade's mighty burst.

Night turned to day when the ball exploded with a blinding flash. Kyrana had to cover her eyes and turn away, but hardly fast enough to prevent being dazzled by its destructive fulmination. She could hardly imagine that Rozha would've been in one piece after being directly struck by such an awful attack.

But she had no time to consider her fears before something even worse was staring her right in the face. When her sight had returned, the first thing she saw was the Elite himself, standing directly in front of her.

"Is there anything *else* you'd like to contribute to our sacrament?" he said with a measured, albeit sarcastic tone. As soon as he saw her mouth begin to move, he thrust a knee into her stomach and pushed her up against the wall with his tail. "Such a pretty face," a purr rumbled in his throat, as his arm crossed over hers. "You wouldn't wish to die and let all that go to waste, would you?" He loosed a decidedly creepy chuckle, puffing softly against her cheek as she desperately craned her head away from his face.

She couldn't intone any spells to break herself free, but she still had one tactic Xanne didn't teach in her self-defense classes. She knew her ankle had hit its mark when one well-placed kick later, the Elite's countenance contorted with pain. With an uncomfortable gasp of air, his grip softened and his knees buckled, giving Kyrana the opportunity she needed to slip herself free of his grasp.

The Elite's eyes flashed, his recovery coming much too fast for the priestess' liking, as he angrily threw a punch right for the pretty face he complimented just seconds before. Had Kyrana not ducked out of the way, she dreaded what would have become of her skull when she saw the priest's fist smash through the wall behind her. Her quick reflexes saved her again when she stepped out of the way of a clawed swipe aimed to tear open her torso.

With a well-timed "Koptigma," the enraged Elite was sent flying into Pericula's barricade, allowing Kyrana some time to start running for the center of town. She'd have to bring Rozha back to fighting fit if she wanted a chance of leaving this place alive. But that evil bastard wasn't going to make it easy on her; as soon as she rounded the corner of the building she had been hiding behind, the Elite came diving out of one of its walls like a ghost.

Kyrana deflected his tackle with a barrier, sending him back into the building whence he came. She ran just a bit further down the alley before she was tripped by roots coming out to grab her feet. She turned her ankles on her way down, but had no time to resist the pain. Kyrana had to project another shield to reflect the Elite's Safiric blasts as she koptigma'd her way out of his trap. She kept looking over her shoulder to see if the Elite was going to come diving at her from the smoke cloud his attacks had made when they hit him.

After no sign of him, she started the struggle to pick herself up off the ground and begin her mad, crawling dash for safety, but barely made two steps forward before she was stopped by the Elite now blocking her path. He sent a brain-jarring uppercut into her jaw that had the priestess leaving the ground for what felt like two seconds before she was laid out in a daze. She wasn't sure if the stars she saw crossing through the sky were from the meteor shower or from her malfunctioning eyes when she came to. She felt like her extremities were a mile away from her head, and all she could do was wonder where she was.

Although her thoughts were fuzzied by the intense, cranial blow, the priestess still had enough of a mind about her for her Sanguinic intuition to warn her of impending danger. At first she couldn't tell if the tingling in her spine was from a concussion, or from the admonition she had received to look up and see what was coming.

She heard the Elite's seemingly distant voice muttering an ancient incantation, and lifted her dizzy head in time to see a ball of hot energy growing between his hands swirling apart from each other. Acting fast, Kyrana used a fygidia spell to instantly rise to a crouching position, so she could then swiftly prepare a masalida to protect her from what was coming next.

"For 'tigyamah!" the priest cried with a forward thrust of his arms. The grand spell he had been charging was unleashed as a fantastic cloud of blue fire, like the eruption of a volcano. The head of the explosion resembled the face of an angry lion, and crashed into Kyrana's shield with such force as to push the priestess across the ground on her knees.

She could feel its immense heat slowly leaking through her shield as it was beginning to give under the attack's duress. She could hear her masalida cracking like glass with every second that the screaming wave of flame continued to pass by her. She could see the visages of tormented spirits distorting in the rushing blaze.

Kyrana's clothes began to burn moments before her shield finally shattered, and let the priest's power overcome her. She knew she had been rendered unconscious before she even collapsed to the ground, but did not know for how long until she was pulled from her dreaming state by the Elite's voice.

"I have no time for you!" the priest boomed, disgusted that his power failed to destroy her. "The portal to my new world won't last long."

"New world?..." Kyrana repeated, stirring weakly. Smoke drifted off her scorched dress like a snuffed candle.

"My own world to conquer," the Safiric priest clarified, looking back to the portal above them. "For the glory of Safiro, I will cleanse what lies beyond that gateway to lay waste to all the vermin who have victimized our species."

"Vermin?" Kyrana rose from her crouching position. "What are you talking about?"

"The Dark Men," the Elite said. "They are the ones whose form resembles the insects who prey on our fields. They come like a pall from the stars at night to seize our kind and take them away, into the skies. Whole villages have disappeared before sunrise, without a trace that anyone lived there the day before. Only The Father knows what woes betide our people when they vanish and are never seen from again."

"So you feel it is your righteous duty to mete out justice?" Kyrana insightfully assumed. "And you created that magic door with your evil sacraments to accomplish this unholy crusade of yours?"

The Safiric priest scoffed at his enemy's vindictive, demonizing language. "It is amusing how the defeated become so defensive," he pretentiously started. "I've waited two hundred years, since founding this town, to wash the Thunderstone with the blood of the Dark Men. On the last night I could see Safiro's face in the night, I saw a Black Cloud descending toward Fort Pericula. I gathered my Brothers from this temple to engage our unwelcome visitors and headed them off at Virluti Forest, in the east. The Dark Men had some impressive weapons and even more impressive nerve for such small and fragile beings... I relished stomping their cadavers underfoot as I destroyed them with Safiro's blessing. We massacred a multitude of the vile creatures before the rest had sense enough to abandon their heist of our people. I even took a few of their bodies as a gift for the demoness of Mordax. I thought perhaps the flesh of the Outsiders would appease her from feasting on us, for a while."

Though Kyrana was impressed by the mention of the Mire Fiend -- that someone else had indeed heard of her, before -- the arch healer was more curious about a more pertinent issue. "What happened to the others you had killed?"

"I used them as reagents for the ritual," the Elite explained with a chillingly nonchalant tone. "After I had exsanguinated their green innards on the Thunderstone, I placed their empty corpses into coffins and ordered my Brothers to wait until the next time Safiro's face could be seen in full. I wanted The Father to watch what we had done in His name, and to give us His guidance as we undertook this sacred honor, to quench his anger on the souls of the Outsiders."

His expression souring, he turned around to accusingly point down at his vanquished foe. "And you... You were sent here to stop us. You daughters of Sanguina are so selfish to *prevent* this justice from being exacted! Have you no empathy for the rest of your own kind -- who have been so tragically and barbarically stripped of their lives and dignity to be *harvested* by the Black Clouds?!"

He aggressively postured with an outward sweep of his arm, "All you do is stifle growth with your ignorance! All you can hope to achieve is to bring us back to the dark ages we left by the *graces* of Lord Zercius! The Safiric Brotherhood was made to give teeth and *strength* to those unable to fight back against the oppressive forces who, for all millennia, have *beleaguered* our brethren!"

As the Elite dramatically turned to depart from his soapbox, Kyrana halted him with a shout, "What can you gain by destroying others?! How many will have to die until your victory is secured? Is there an end to the madness? Or is it your plan to be the only ones left?"

At that, the priest offered an indicative smirk. "The throes of the Father's enemies shall continue... until *everyone* obeys. So try and stop us all you want. I don't *care* if I have to kill you. The world will be much better off *without* your deleterious ideals!"

"Then why bother letting me live?!" Kyrana spat, returning to her feet with a spring tide of energy and courage.

Unperturbed by her aggression, the Elite replied with a surprising lack of fury. "Because, like you, I believe there is a second chance for everyone to see the light. I have faith that even someone like you will join us one day, once you see the Father's might. I want to let you live to see that day, for someone with a spirit as strong as yours could easily become a High Priestess of our clergy."

Kyrana's brow defensively lowered. "You know as well as I do that I will do no such thing for you."

"Of course you won't," the priest knowingly smiled. "But in time, you will."

As much as she was taught to despise the Safiric Brotherhood and everything its worshipers stood for, Kyrana had never come across someone like him, who could make sense of everything she was told to ignore. With much less hostility than her words had before, Kyrana genuinely asked him in a conversational tone, "Who are you?"

"My name is Atherator," the Elite finally introduced himself. "My Brothers call me 'the Future-Seeing.' I'm always looking ahead to broader horizons, for both the Brotherhood and for Vitiosa itself. I see nothing for the way it is now, but for the way it *can* be -- its potential. Some have said I'm *too* optimistic…" he trailed off as he looked in the direction of the portal looming above the Thunderstone. "I have enjoyed talking with you, fair priestess, but I must be on my way. May you fare well, so that one day, we can meet again."

Kyrana had to blink when he turned away, just to ensure her eyes were not still deceiving her. She caressed the back of her head, thinking that perhaps she had a contusion from when she fell. She refused to believe that what she heard came out of the same person who just minutes before was threatening to kill her, if not worse.

Mother Diava had warned her to always stay away from members of the Safiric Brotherhood, and had even said of the beautiful lies they could tell. She had never heard what one might've sounded like until now, but she knew for certain that a lie was all it was.

Even now that she had rationalized this to herself, Kyrana had no gumption to call out Atherator's hypocrisy; she didn't want to give him any reason to finish her off. She was spellbound as she watched him so confidently and deliberately rise into the invisible vortex created by the portal. He faced into the doorway with the kind of smile one would have if they were on their way to visit an exciting, faraway land. Kyrana couldn't imagine what this place he was expecting to go would be like -- the realm of the Dark Men.

"Rozha, can you hear me?" Kyrana called into her communication ring, but she received no response. Picking herself back up, the priestess wobbled her way to Pericula's streets, to find them filling with wandering people, all wondering what happened while they were hiding from the terrifying goings-on. Upon seeing the priestess walking toward the Thunderstone, the strangers approached her, demanding to know the meaning of all this. Most of them feared the portal hanging over it, and wanted her to tell them how she could close it. She only wished she could tell them; she had a hard time believing it, herself. The only thing she could say was that she was there to stop it, but had not succeeded.

"I am looking for my partner," she shooed them away, "so if you would excuse me…"

"Kyrana?" Rozha's voice weakly called out, as if from the bottom of a grave.

The nurse looked all around to see if she had been standing behind the crowd, but caught no sight of her. As she pushed away from all the people either following her around or otherwise milling about, watching the waning meteor shower, Kyrana heard Rozha calling for her again. This time, she was able to catch it clearly enough to know it was coming from behind the Thunderstone. She rounded the pillar of rock to find her friend in the middle of a large, shallow ditch, excavated by the explosion of Atherator's attack. Rozha barely managed a smile when she saw Kyrana, looking in much better condition than the blade dancer, herself.

"I can't move a muscle," Rozha gasped. "I feared he might've got you, too."

"I was surprised he didn't," Kyrana relievedly chuckled, kneeling by the blade dancer's side. "Even though it is a night of Safiro," the priestess dolefully minded the moon, "I will do my best to heal you."

While the nurse went about her work, the Red Dancer said, "You won't believe what I saw, when I thought I was going to die."

"I told you already that I don't like guessing," Kyrana playfully chided her.

"I saw my soul, hanging above me," Rozha replied. "Her eyes were plenum of pity. Her hand reached for me, as if pleading me to hang on. For a ghost freed from her body, as beautiful as she looked, she was not at peace. She seemed worried, as if under pressure to get something done. I feel like she knows this is her one chance to do it."

The way Rozha referred to her spirit in the third person made Kyrana more curious to know what symbolism her Sister saw in this near-death experience. "What do you believe this means? What do you think she desires of you?"

The blade dancer shook her head, when she felt enough feeling in her neck to do so. "I don't know. But what I do know is that I've seen her in my dreams before. I've seen her in other places, too, but none so clearly as I did, tonight. I feel like I should know who she is, but I can't remember her name." *'I don't want to believe it is her.'*

145

As if reciting Atherator's words, Kyrana replied, "You will, in time, dear Rozha. For now, I believe it is best for us both to rest and reflect on what we have learned today." Having finished her healing process, the arch nurse offered a hand to Rozha, which at that point she was able to accept and return to her feet as if unscathed.

"I agree, Kyrana," Rozha happily sighed, as if unburdened. "I believe these fine people here," she motioned toward the wandering strangers, "will gladly provide us with a place to stay this evening."

While Rozha proceeded to ask around and use her priesthood to buy them a free room at the local inn, Kyrana joined the wanderers in staring at the open rift. *'Atherator,'* she mused. *'Is there a chance he's still alive, wherever he is, now?'*

Chapter 12: A Two-Way Door

Rozha and Kyrana entered the only inn Pericula had to offer, and were greeted by its warmly-lit interior endowed with a wonderfully homely atmosphere. The atrium was unremarkably vacant for this time of night, and was heated by its fireplace located at the furthest, right-hand corner of the room. The rectangular space was furnished with tables on top of straw mats to protect the wooden floor. The ceiling was supported by rafters, between which were support beams, each holding two torches about eight feet from the floor.

The inn's owner made himself known almost the moment they stepped onto the doormat. "Hullo, there!" the stout scelan with a bushy mustache waved them over. His thick accent was not native to these parts of Onteval, but his jolly smile couldn't have made the two, exhausted travelers feel more welcome. His skin was colored a dark bronze, and the spiky ring of hair atop his balding head was colored a light yellow, as if it might've been a shade of orange in his younger years.

When Rozha and Kyrana approached the counter to their immediate left, and faced him eye-to-eye, they saw that he stood probably no taller than the Arch Nurse -- Rozha was not used to seeing men shorter than herself. Even as languid as she felt, Kyrana could still manage to keep her formal grace and politeness. "Good evening, sir," she dipped her head and held her dress.

"I'm quite surprised to see you come in," the innkeeper admiringly said, "What with all the commotion y'caused out there, I'd have thought ye'd all left b'now."

Rozha raised an eyebrow and cocked her hip to the side. "What reason would we have for retreating?"

The old scelan chuckled, "Nobody just scraps with th' Brotherhood and gets away with it, y'know." Upon closer inspection of his squinted eyes, Rozha could see the man was of Wild blood, himself. "I'd never seen a thing like it, but I watched it all from out m'windah! What was that all aboot, anyway?"

"We have known for some time that this was about to happen," Rozha began to explain. "We were called to task to prevent this situation from occurring." Never one to like admitting defeat, the blade dancer sneered, "but we came too late."

"Too late?" the innkeeper inquired. "Fer what, eh?"

"Our mission details are confidential to the Sachelvian authority," Kyrana answered for her frustrated friend. Upon seeing the old scelan's reaction to what she said, she realized she probably sounded a bit stern. "It's not because I don't trust you enough to tell you what I am here for, but it's because I haven't been given permission by the High Priestess to discuss our purpose nor findings with anyone but her."

The innkeeper gave her a sideways glare, as if calling to question her trustworthiness for challenging his own. But, who was he to turn away good business? "Would you be lookin' fer a room to stay the night, then?"

"We'd be most appreciative of that, sir," Kyrana more submissively replied, in the hopes that his attitude would return to be more favorable.

As much as it brought the smile back to his face, it was hard to not be shocked by the next thing he said. "It'll cost ya fifteen silver divitias."

"*Fifteen?!*" an appalled Rozha exclaimed.

"What's the problem, Miss Priestess?" the innkeeper sardonically twirled his mustache.

"Oh, I was not aware of all the *rich folk* you had in this *bustling metropolis* of yours!" Rozha continued ranting. "That price could buy *three* meals in Tresantia! Ain't no way I'm gonna pay that much money for *one* room!"

"Bein' a priestess won't get ya nuttin' free, here," the innkeeper laughed. "Especially not if yer dressed in all black and brandishin' bloody knives on ye."

Slamming her hands aggressively down on the counter between them, Rozha shouted, "You want your blood added to them, old man?!"

"Rozha, stop!" Kyrana finally added her commanding voice as the one of reason. "Mother can only forgive so much of her children. Against my better judgment, I already let you get away with several acts not circumspect for a member of our clergy. Need I remind you again the memorandums you follow as a Sister of Sachelvae?"

Much to the cowering innkeeper's relief, but to Rozha's added disgust, the blade dancer reluctantly eased up and let Kyrana talk some sense into her. "No," she heaved a heavy sigh. "You know what's right." Shooting a deathly stink eye at the scelan she so utterly wished to put down, Rozha stepped away from the counter, eyeing Kyrana before she said, "Even still, I refuse to pay such an outlandish amount of coin for such a simple service."

Almost argumentatively, the innkeeper pulled himself away from the wall and declared, "My rooms are th' finest in all o' town."

"That's not saying much," Rozha crossed her arms with a huff. "They're the *only* ones here."

"Exactly right, lass," the old scelan grinned. "Either stay 'ere, or rough it ootside."

Defaulting back to her blade dancer charm, Rozha threateningly riposted, "Not if you value your head --" her steely-eyed glare and vindictively shaking fist were interrupted by Kyrana's growl, "Rozha..." thus thwarting the stingy redhead's second attempt at the innkeeper's life. Rozha muttered some unspeakable words under her breath as she took the coin pouch from her pack and sifted through its contents for the amount her greedy host required.

After carefully counting to make sure that every divitia he wanted was in his possession, the innkeeper approvingly nodded and waved off his clients on their way upstairs. "See ya in the mornin'!" came his rehearsed, jovial goodbye.

The short flight of stairs led to a narrow corridor, on which either side were a hall of doors. The sounds of muffled chatter could be heard coming from some of the distant dorms, no doubt discussing the recent event that swept the town. But most of the small chambers were quiet; Kyrana wondered how anyone could have slept through such a calamity. Upon settling into their room for the night, Rozha leaned her back against the door after closing it behind her.

She was still very much in a huff about the egregious charge she had to pay; her arms were crossed and her eyes were giving the floorboards a deathly stare. "I'm already starting to regret not sneaking back out of here," the tip of her tail tapped the floor. "I feel bad about leaving Heschel to fend for himself. I'd rather sleep outside with my steed than overpay for any service offered by some Wild curmudgeon."

Sitting on the side of their shared bed, Kyrana tried to ease the mind of her angered ally. But even she was having a hard time keeping a smile on her face. "I understand the source of your trouble, but it would do neither of us any good to make things harder on ourselves than they've already been. After all we've done today, isn't fifteen divitias a small price to pay for ending it all with a warm bed to sleep in?"

Rozha once again held her fury. "It's not the cost that bothers me, it's the principle of the thing. The sheer *arrogance* of that man--!"

Kyrana raised a hand to once again silence her friend, when she saw the redhead's teeth clenching. "Us priestesses aren't treated with reverence wherever we roam," she reminded her. "Some see our dress as a mark of evil. Mother Diava has often said that the people of Tresantia are the most exceptional in the world for their equal treatment of both faiths. I daresay she might be right."

"Kyrana?" asked a tired groan from within Kyrana's own mind. At first she thought by uttering her name away from her presence, she had summoned Mother Diava's voice. But after a moment to recollect herself, she realized it was a result of wearing her communication ring. "Yes, Mother Diava?" the Arch Healer responded.

Rozha confusedly perked up to hear Kyrana utter that phrase, and looked around as if expecting to see the High Priestess somewhere nearby. She wasn't used to using communication rings, since she was never allowed to have one.

"I must speak with you and Rozha," the High Priestess said. "I will use my clairvoyant visage to see you both." Upon her mistress' request, Kyrana held out her ring-bearing hand at chest-level. The large, rectangular ruby the silver band held cast forth a cone of light, like rays from a projector. At the end of this short beam of radiance, a translucent bust of Mother Diava began to form, floating at the abbess' height in the middle of the room.

"Forgive my disturbance at such an hour," Diava's avatar forced back a yawn, "but have you any news from Pericula?"

"I am sorry, as well, for having not remained in more constant contact with you," Kyrana returned her matron's apology. "We arrived at the Fort a long time behind schedule."

Though the High Priestess was anxious to know what had happened to her imperative mission, she had to ask first, "What were the causes of these delays?"

"We were waylaid as we trekked through Virluti Forest," Rozha explained.

"We were beseeched by the Laeyudi tribe to save their village elder," Kyrana added. "Ghanius was his name."

"Lae-yu'di?" Diava uncomfortably sounded out the syllables. "I've never heard of such a place. Did they give you trouble?"

"Well, besides wasting our time," Rozha tersely admitted, before she could be interrupted by her more couth acquaintance. "I couldn't turn them down in good conscience," Kyrana started, "even with what we had at stake. I had a feeling if we refused, they wouldn't take no as an answer."

"You were blackmailed, then?" Diava surmised.

"They trusted us," Kyrana answered. "I could sense grave desperation when I spoke to them. I don't think they would have done us any harm; they were just looking for anyone who could keep Ghanius alive."

"What was so important about him?" her mistress asked with a rather indifferent tone.

"He warned Rozha and I about an impending danger," Kyrana said. "He gave us some reagents and medicines we could use to combat her and resist her effects."

"*Her* effects?" the High Priestess indirectly demanded elaboration.

"The Mire Fiend is what they insisted on calling it," Rozha said.

"It was a demoness unlike anything I've read about before," Kyrana added. "Its whole territory was tainted with a kind of Safiric evil that only the worst of worshipers could instill upon the land."

Diava nearly shivered from having to imagine the existence of such a creature. "And you dealt with it?"

"It took Rozha and I both to handle it," Kyrana replied.

The arch nurse could hear Mother Diava's disapproving hum at the mention of Rozha's name. "Was it able to be Purified...?" she asked, with an equivocal hopefulness.

Kyrana knew the High Priestess wasn't going to like the truth, but the nurse maintained her honesty. "Its body fell into the waters whence it came. We couldn't retrieve it from there."

"I see," Diava heaved a sigh of acceptance. "And what about Pericula? Have you any... *good* news at all, to report?"

The nurse swallowed when she heard the disdain in Mother Diava's voice. She suddenly had a hard time relaying this information to her, face-to-face. Rozha decided to save her friend from the High Priestess' denigration. "We got here just in time to witness what the Safiric *Brotherhood* had planned. They were using the Thunderstone to open a gateway --"

"-- to another world, as I understand it," Kyrana jumped in to return her friend the favor of sparing Diava's criticism, before Rozha could get into the dirty details of dispatching the Brotherhood's subordinates, as the blade dancer was wont to do. "We thought they'd use the portal for demonic means, but it seems their leader, Atherator, had more ambitious plans. Atherator believed that he was charged by Safiro to conquer a new land in the name of the God of Death. He had gathered together the bodies of Outsiders -- Dark Men -- to use as a sacrifice."

Diava's austere frown turned a bit further down, gaining a hint of seriousness. "Has this gateway closed?"

"Not to my knowledge," Kyrana replied. "It was still open, last I saw it."

"This bodes ill tidings to our lands," the High Priestess warned. "If that doorway lets things from our world into another place, what is keeping the evil Dark Men from using that gateway to come here, as well?" Obviously, Kyrana and Rozha didn't have an answer for that one. "The portal must be sealed."

"How?" came Rozha's necessary inquiry.

"You must destroy the Thunderstone," Diava commanded. "It is what holds the portal in place."

A defeated Kyrana shook her head. "How could we do that?"

"That thing is huge --" Rozha added, "it must weigh several tons. We'd have no hope of toppling it by ourselves."

"Remember that a priestess relies on strength in numbers," Diava said. "It is the Safiric Brotherhood that relies on strength alone. I only sent you two on this Pericula Initiative because I could not risk having too many of our Sisterhood being detected and ruining any chance we'd have of ending their ritual. Now that it's no longer an issue, we can unfetter what we have at our disposal."

While Diava was convinced this course of action was the right thing to do, Kyrana couldn't help feeling like it was beginning to sound like a trap. "I do not mean to interfere, your holiness, but I believe that having so many of our numbers here in one place would only serve the Dark Mens' purpose."

"What do you mean?" Diava and Rozha both faced their ally.

"Atherator told me that the Dark Men come to capture our kind, and take them away to their world," Kyrana explained. "If there will be so many of us out there to respond to this threat when they come, would they not try to kidnap us all?" Truthfully, Kyrana wasn't as concerned with being killed by the Dark Men as much as she was worried about what they did to the belhuayn prisoners they captured. "If they take us from this world," the arch healer continued, "will Sanguina be able to save us? Indeed, is Atherator not a fool for wanting to leave Vitiosa to battle the Dark Men on their own ground?"

"You say that as if you *expect* to be taken," a determined Diava scowled. "So long as we remain here, we have Sanguina's protection. It is our enemies who shall be without whatever foul gods they worship."

Just then, a flash of light came through the window to their room, followed by a thunderous rumbling. At first, the party of priestesses naturally assumed that it may have been a lightning strike, but there was no indication of any storms before then. Kyrana and Rozha rushed forth and opened the glass pane to peer out into the town square. There they saw, standing atop the Thunderstone, was a truly foreign man clad in all black armor. Above his red, insectoid eyes were long antenna, like eyebrows. It was joined by two more Dark Men, standing at the base of the Thunderstone.

They looked like a much more alive version of what Kyrana had seen in Mordax Swamp -- the beings Atherator had claimed to dispose of there. The priestess gasped when she saw it move. "It's the Dark Men!"

The Dark Men's cicada-like wings fluttered intermittently as they idly clicked their fingers and scanned their surroundings. Their leader left its tall perch to float to the ground, and examined the coffins leaning against the Thunderstone. With a strong sweeping motion of its arm, it tore open the locked door and beheld the carcass of its fellow Dark Man inside. As if piecing together the puzzle, it then looked up to the portal through which it came, before drawing a weapon resembling a crossbow from its backside.

"Kyrana," Diava's disembodied voice called her from behind, "what's going on?"

The shocked priestess didn't have time to give the abbess an answer before one of the Dark Men's weapons was trained on her. Almost instinctively, the arch nurse ducked behind the window, narrowly avoiding a streak of red light from disintegrating her where she stood. The laser blast zipped by like the crack of a whip -- the hole it left in the ceiling looked as if it was made by a giant's fist. The smoldering debris fizzled out Diava's holographic image. Kyrana and Rozha looked up to see the embers above slowly working their way into a blaze. While the arch nurse went running for the door to escape, Rozha leapt out the open window and gracefully tumbled into the street.

The three Dark Men faced down their adversary as they and Rozha, for that while, were frozen with mutual fear. The insectoid beings were much more imposing up close -- their leader stood at least seven feet tall on its slender, jagged legs. It began slowly lowering to an aggressive, crouch-like stance, during which it moved its ant-like mandibles in such a way they clicked and grumbled. It emitted a noise that could have been mistaken for speech, but what language it was, Rozha could not tell. The word it spoke had an intrigued tone; if Rozha tried sounding it out with her own tongue, it would have sounded like *"Ikaxit."*

This foreboding word led up to the Dark Men's next move, which was to shake their wings with such speed that they loudly rattled together. The deafening, shrill pitch of the awful noise had Rozha covering her ears and crumbling to her knees. She couldn't even hear her own shrieks of pain over the horrendous, piercing sound.

She was completely defenseless to stop the Dark Men's leader from aiming its next laser blast right for her head. With a destructive burst, all sounds ceased -- Rozha's screams and the Dark Men's fluttering wings. But through the clearing smoke, the Dark Men were surprised to see a pink shield standing before their enemy. Behind the unconscious blade dancer stood Kyrana, holding her nearly-broken barrier with a telekinetic hand.

"Koptigma!" With a thrust of her arm, Kyrana commanded the spent shield to sally forth, and crash into the Dark Men's leader like an angered bull. The moment the insect in the middle was incapacitated, its two friends retaliated. They drew their guns and were about to open fire on her, before they were distracted by arrows being shot at them from the guard towers.

One of the arrows struck into the ankle of one of the Dark Men, earning its undivided attention. The town guard's efforts was joined by several belhuayns leaving their houses to see the cause of the raucous disturbance. The sleepless scelans were mostly middle-aged and armed with knives and other simple weapons, but they didn't stand a chance. The Dark Men's laser guns, just between the two of them, were able to cause the kind of devastation that only the cannon of an Emperor's army could to a fort under siege.

The rapid blasts of this destructive power came like a band of gods beating on their drums. While one of them targeted the residences of the innocent, the other aimed to destroy the battlements. Whole houses were torn apart and immediately thereafter consumed in a raging inferno. Roofs were set ablaze in instants -- even if the Dark Men could be stopped, there wouldn't be much left of Pericula to defend after they were gone.

In the middle of the Dark Men's rampage, a group of voices all cried in unison, *"Masalida!"* A great, dome-shaped shield suddenly appeared to encompass all of the town within its walls, and caused every laser blast the Dark Men fired to chaotically ricochet in all directions. The frightening fireworks this caused had the alien marauders ducking for cover as their last bullets exploded all around them like an air raid.

Kyrana could barely see her saviors through the clouds of dust and dirt, but she knew it was her fellow priestesses of Sachelvae. How her heart swelled when she saw all forty of them standing by Pericula's perimeter, led by Mother Diava and the faculty. As soon as the Dark Men rose to their feet, they realized they were outnumbered. They threw down their guns, but not as a gesture of surrender.

They instead unsheathed what looked like claws of flame from their scissor-like hands, and took off with breakneck speed in separate directions to engage their adversaries. While its two compatriots hacked through the giant barrier to get to the priestesses standing safely on the other side, the Dark Men's leader swiftly attacked the unprotected Kyrana. But what he seemed to have forgotten was that he'd have to get through Rozha, first, to do it.

The blade dancer ceased feigning death and arose to give her attacker a vicious surprise. With a single uppercut, her forearm blade sliced in half the Dark Man's breastplate and left a nasty scar across his chest. The insectoid screeched and staggered back as green blood sprayed from its large wound. Rozha followed up with a haymaker aimed for the Dark Man's jaw; the mandible she struck hung from his face if by a loose hinge after the leader finished recoiling. He raised an arm to block Rozha's next attack, and kicked her down with one of his powerful legs.

Instead of capitalizing on his prone foe, the Dark Man swiped his glowing red claws for Kyrana, who stopped him in mid-swing with an "Astapsyxi." Rozha rolled to her feet and used the opening Kyrana provided her to sweep her tail at the Dark Man's ankles, causing Kyrana's holding spell to break as well as knock her tall adversary on his back. She was fast to pin him down and deliver the coup de gras, severing the Dark Man's head in a burst of green gore.

Rozha and Kyrana then fearfully beheld the spirit-crushing sight of several more Dark Men flying into the fray, emerging from the portal still looming above the burning town. Like the ones before, they came dressed for battle -- armed and armored with the standard fare of their brethren. When they saw two of their kind fecklessly hacking against the shield the priestesses were hiding behind, they trained their guns on the barrier, unknowing what ills would betide them next.

Knowing better, Kyrana protected herself and her companion with a small masalida of her own, which was just barely able to weather the hail of laser fire raining like brimstone all around them. The Sachelvian Sisterhood's combined power was just barely able to contain the violent volley, this time; it began flickering as the energy of its casters was giving out.

"Had the weight of Safiro's stare not been tainting the air," Diava said to her despondent Teachers, "our masalida would have held true!" With that, their powerful shield was forced to fade, and thus released the snow globe of dirt it had contained within. While the fog of war dispersed, and the debris finished falling, the remaining Dark Men rose from their cover upon the cratered land to see nothing but ruination in their wake. Pericula had been transformed into a war-torn wasteland. Even the Thunderstone had taken severe damage; the pockmarked meteor looked as if it could barely remain standing. Everyone in attendance turned to the portal to watch it begin to shrink.

When the confused and disoriented Dark Men realized their time to return home was closing fast, they turned into a raving panic. Seeing that their enemies were currently unprotected, they grabbed the weapons they dropped and fired upon the priestesses as they hastily took off for the skies.

The members of the clergy dropped back to evade the mortar-like blasts exploding at their feet while the Dark Men covered their escape. In the midst of their frenzied fluttering about, some of the invaders bumped against the Thunderstone, providing the last push it needed to topple over. The damaged meteorite crashed into the earth and fractured into a hundred pieces as soon as the last Dark Men had left; thereupon the shrinking portal it held blinked from existence.

The new atmosphere of silent desolation seemed almost eerie by comparison to the horrendous cacophony of war that it replaced. All the priestesses wanted to collapse with relief and exhaustion after what they had just experienced -- especially Rozha and Kyrana -- but their work was still not done.

"Help! Is anyone there?" came the weak cries of the few survivors, from beneath the smog-laden wreckage.

The forty priestesses sifted through the ruins of Pericula to find the sources of the various voices beckoning for their assistance. While Kyrana joined the rest of the Sisterhood to heal and save the injured and the dying, Rozha dug through what was left of the crumbled inn for something else she hoped had survived the terrible calamity.

"There's a chance it's still here," the determined blade dancer thought, as she clawed her way through splintered beams and pushed aside broken walls.

Sometime later into her search, she uncovered the body of the innkeeper, who was lying face down in a space that used to be the counter behind which he once stood. Rozha brushed away the shards of glass on his back and didn't even bother checking for a pulse before she pickpocketed his apron. She couldn't have had a bigger grin on her face when she retrieved a fistful of divitias -- even more than the amount she had given him for her room. Holding true to her blade dancer training, Rozha glanced over her shoulder to make sure the clergy were keeping themselves busy before she began looting the inn for everything it was worth.

Meanwhile, the survivors of the Periculan catastrophe were gathered at the ruins of the town square, which was the only spot of clear ground left amid the wreckage of buildings. The disheveled and now homeless masses were crowded among the priestesses, who awaited Diava's instruction on what next to do with them. While the High Priestess watched her younger servants walking around, she wore an expression that showed a certain anxiousness leaking through her calm and regal exterior.

"There are fifty three in all," Xanne relayed the head count to her mistress. "We won't have space in the temple for everyone."

"This is to be expected," Diava's eyes remained facing forward, her words not matching her troubled thoughts. "Even without proper shelter, they will still be safe within Tresantia's walls. We can at least spare them what we have to supply them with warmth and food to last the night. We'll work on providing them with residences in the morning." Checking the time by the position of Safiro's moon, Diava said, "It's far too late to concern ourselves with anything else until then."

The High Priestess was then approached by Kyrana, who genuflected with the priestess curtsy. "My fellow healers and I have restored everyone we could find to nominal health, your holiness. Is there anything else you require of me?"

Diava smiled at the arch healer. "No, Sister Kyrana, you have done most splendidly. I wish to congratulate both yours and Sister Rozha's efforts..." she trailed off a bit awkwardly as she looked over the nurse's head to search for the blade dancer in question. "Where is she, by the way?"

"Rozha?" Kyrana's question became more of a hopeful calling out, as she turned around to realize that the Red Dancer was nowhere in sight.

"Do you need something, your holiness?" Rozha's voice suddenly came from behind the priestesses walking about. The blade dancer came sidling up to Mother Diava on her steed, with an unusually cheery gait.

"Nothing more than the wish to congratulate you for your exemplary services," the High Priestess bowed her head. "You and Kyrana will be rewarded for your efforts."

Rozha had a hard time imagining what Diava had in mind to give her as recompense for nearly losing her life twice on this journey, but what she had taken from the innkeeper already made it all worth it. "Oh really?" the blade dancer asked, as if not in the least expecting to be disappointed.

"I always had the belief you'd make something special of yourself, from the moment you entered Sachelvae," Mother Diava explained. "A Sister of your skills and with your level of dependability is a uniquity that should never be overlooked. I nearly feared you would be like Viasarria, considering your similar backgrounds, but I am glad to see I was wrong."

The blade dancer's eyes narrowed as she suspiciously cocked her head, but tried not to let the contradiction she noticed take away the gift she was about to receive. Thankfully, if Mother Diava noticed this expression of concern, she didn't have the intuition to pay it any heed. "I once thought if Viasarria never showed any signs of improvement, I'd never allow another blade dancer to ever set foot in Sachelvae."

The High Priestess chuckled at the rash sound of her own words, and went on to say, "But thanks to you, dear Rozha, I have seen the light. I have seen the potential for greatness I did not know was there before. It is because of this that I have chosen to create a new classroom for Sachelvae, and I want you to be its Teacher."

Kyrana's eyes couldn't have been wider when she heard what Mother Diava had to say. Xanne did better at hiding her surprise, but the announcement their leader had made had both she and Wanystha turning their heads. Rozha couldn't believe it, either. She reflexively opened her mouth when she was expected to say something, but she had no idea which words to say first. "Th-Thank… I mean… why?"

Diava beamed at the blade dancer's flattering surprise. "I had been thinking about what you said for a long time after we had that argument in the Purifier Hall. I considered that perhaps there should come a time when it is acceptable, even in Sanguina's eyes, to fight fire with fire. I consorted with The Mother Herself on this matter; I invoked Her divine providence throughout the day to receive an awakening."

Closing her eyes to concentrate and sharpen her memories, Diava continued, "What I saw in this awakening was a world that was set ablaze so that it could restart anew. Just like in the Creation Story, something had to end before what we have now could begin."

Rozha remembered the Creation Story from one of her first history sermons she had at Wanystha's classes. She thought it rather grim that the world in which they now lived had supposedly come after a great civilization had ended. It seemed this 'resurrection by fire' only resulted in something worse than what came before. Why would that trend be something to look forward to, in this case? Should they not try to hold on harder to what they already have, instead of searching for another revolution to ruin it even more? Rozha wasn't sure if she liked this new twist that Diava was trying to put on their faith -- and worse yet, what she thought the blade dancer could do to bring this change about.

"What class is this that you want *me* to teach?"

"One that I have perhaps been ignoring far too long," Diava started. "Self-defense training; a course that goes beyond the simple practices of Sanguinic magic, and enforces realistic uses of it in combat."

With a stern frown, she added, "I think it's time to stop hiding from the novitiates what they already know. If they are one day to become priestesses of our clergy, then it's only fair that we should tell them the truth of what will be expected of them." Even though she had seemed confident with the decision she made, the High Priestess paused to raise the edge of her hand to her forehead for meditation. *'I am sorry, Mother, if my gambit shall be a failure.'*

Detecting her obvious distress, Rozha placed a hand on the High Priestess' side and offered the abbess a smile when she opened her eyes with a start. "I will gladly accept this responsibility. It'll be an honor for me to be inducted into the faculty."

The rest of the Teachers were aghast with swelling envy. Even Kyrana, the youngest of the faculty, served as a priestess and then a nurse for ten years before she became the Arch Healer of Sachelvae. Xanne and Wanystha entered the priesthood at the top of their classes, then served five years just to be voted in to replace the previous Teachers. Now Rozha came along and in merely two years after her graduation ceremony was already the newest member of the faculty? Teacher Xanne managed to encapsulate all these concerns in two, simple words: "I'm impressed."

Diava could tell, by the lack of elation or any feeling at all to Xanne's statement, that the Teacher was none-too-pleased by her decision. "I am full aware of the personal tribulations it takes to enter the faculty and rise through the ranks of the clergy. After all, it's only been twenty years since I became the High Priestess of Sachelvae. I am not granting Sister Rozha this privilege to undo the reputation of the temple. I believe we have been in need of this awakening for some time. Indeed, Sister Rozha's induction to the faculty should not be measured by the amount of time she has spent in the temple, but by the amount of time the temple has needed her."

While Rozha wondered how nice it would sound when everyone would start referring to her as "Teacher," Kyrana began to wonder what *her* reward would be for this supreme act of valor that Diava was so enthralled with.

Perhaps the abbess had truly gone mad and would abdicate her status as High Priestess to her?

Deciding not to press her luck, the Arch Healer instead retreated to her usual politeness and deferred to Diava's wisdom. "I eagerly await Rozha's ceremony," Kyrana said, trying to make her smile not look so strained. "It has been a long time since I have bore witness to the festivities that come with having a new Teacher. I'm sure all the novitiates will be excited, especially dear Kasra."

"Yes," Diava nodded, "it will be a special day for all of us, and for the history of Sachelvae." The High Priestess' eyes glistened as she imagined what the textbooks of the future would say about the good she had done for increasing the temple's institutions.

"But that for another time," she pulled herself from her fantasies. "We have more immediate issues to attend. Getting us all back to Tresantia will be as simple as a 'Fygidia' spell." Raising her communication ring to speaking distance, Diava asked, "Are you ready, Sister Platina?"

"Yes, your holiness," the nurse's almost bored voice telepathically muttered. "I am standing outside the temple doors."

"Everyone join hands, or you will be left behind," Diava instructed her priestesses and refugees. "We are about to leave." Once everyone was prepared, the High Priestess commanded, "Alright, Sister Platina, say the word."

One unheard 'Fygidia' later, and by their next blink, Diava and everyone she was with at Pericula were teleported back to the front yard of Sachelvae. Platina found herself in the middle of this massive group of people, who had literally appeared from nowhere, yet the indifferent look on her face showed no hint of surprise whatsoever.

"Thank you, Sister Platina," Diava told the sleepy nurse. "You may return to your quarters, now, and continue watching Viasarria."

"As you wish, your holiness," the azurette hid a yawn behind her sleeve as she bowed, then sauntered back inside the temple. Even as proper as she was, she could barely keep herself from slouching and barely noticed her tail dragging on the ground.

While the rest of the clergy were tasked with making arrangements to shelter the Periculan refugees for the night, Diava let her exhausted heroes off the hook. "You, as well, may retire to your quarters. You both have well-earned it, at the very least."

Truthfully, Rozha would have begged for it if it wasn't going to be offered to her. After all, the newest member of Sachelvae's faculty had a lot to think about. Feeling like a real winner, with the grin to show it, Rozha patted Kyrana's shoulder as she proudly strode on by her. "We really accomplished quite a feat, huh?"

"Indeed..." the nurse's half-hearted response was distracted by her thoughts. Kyrana was starting to feel a bit ignored by the High Priestess, who had yet to mention what her reward was going to be for putting herself through the Pericula Initiative. But such thoughts were beginning to make her feel a bit petulant; she found solace in the resignation that she would know, in time. Managing a smile to the abbess, the Arch Healer parted ways with a customary bow. "I will see you in the morning, your holiness."

Rozha returned to her room and had almost completely forgotten Kasra was staying with her. Her mind was so transfixed with collapsing on her bed and sleeping in as long as possible, that she was quite surprised to see her younger sister currently curled up on her mattress. The violette was wearing some very comfortable pajamas that Raia had probably donated to her, since they looked a little small on her. Kasra awoke with a gasp when she heard the door open. Rozha laughed at the vacant, frightened look on her sister's face. Apparently she was confused after having been jarred from a sound sleep. "It's just me," the redhead sweetly chirped to calm her sister's nerves.

"Oh, thank goodness!" Kasra relaxed, her voice having a slight buss of congestion. She grabbed a nearby handkerchief and held it to her nose, which appeared to have been tended to frequently. This, of course, prompted Rozha's next question: "Are you feeling okay?"

Kasra paused to think about it for a moment, then slowly shook her head. "I've been feeling ill all day. Raia has been taking care of me, though. I was a lot worse off before she started helping," the sick vixy coughed and sniffled. "She taught me how not to spread germs by covering coughs into this hanky she gave me."

"She sounds like quite the sweetheart," Rozha smiled, placing a hand on her hip. "I guess it'd be rude for me to ask to have my bed back?"

"I'm sorry," Kasra sheepishly clutched her covers in an attempt to look more pitiful. "I know you've been out all day." Unable to hide an excited grin, the violette almost bounced in place when she said, "Tell me about it! Where did you go? What did you see?"

Rozha let out a laugh as if it pained her to do so, then took a step forward and tousled Kasra's hair. "Can we save all that for tomorrow, please? I'd rather not spend any more time awake than I need to."

The tired blade dancer sat down on the corner of her bed to take off her armor. She started with her boots and was surprised to not have any blisters beginning to form when she removed her stockings, although she had been very good about drying out her boots from time to time as she and Kyrana moved about the swamp.

Kasra, too, was rather surprised to see that, of all the dried blood on Rozha's gear, none of it belonged to her sister. She hadn't a mark on her underneath her form-fitting pads. It made the violette admire her all the more, to think that Rozha had braved such a terrible excursion and suffered no injuries -- at least, none that hadn't already been healed.

As much as Kasra liked to think her sister was invincible, she was far from indefatigable. The next thing Rozha did was lie across her bed, stretching from corner to corner in what was perhaps the least comfortable position possible.

Even still, she could feel herself drifting off to sleep. She'd take her chances catching whatever her sibling had if it might exclude her from another dangerous activity, for a while. It was on nights like these that she would have hooked up with some lucky scelan and run up a tab on a heroic amount of drinks to wash the day away. She'd be in a much better mood for telling stories, then -- to the best of her ability.

As tempting as the idea sounded, she knew she nor Heschel were in any condition for any more traveling tonight. She planned to save all that for her sick day -- whether she was actually sick or not. The concerns she had for tomorrow seemed to fade away as her dreaming state took over.

Chapter 13: Sparking Interest

In the depths of her sleep, Kasra laid eyes on a beautiful couple of smiling faces: a husband and wife, embracing each other around their sides. The man, maybe just six inches taller than the woman, had short, dark green hair and long bangs swept to one side to cover his left brow. He wore a brown bowler hat in addition to the nicest suit Kasra had seen in person. His face was colored purple, his eyes were a dark shade of brown.

The woman had long black hair that boasted a lustrous shine. Her facial color was a verdant green, and her eyes the same. She had dark skin whereas his was lighter. She too was dressed nicely, in an expensive-looking white garb, featuring puffy shoulders and an old-fashioned collar of frills. She had no shortage of jewelry, either.

It was a fuzzy image, like a portrait through a haze, or a clouded window in the middle of winter. Only it wasn't cold. There was no feeling at all, except for an inexplicable hatred. *'Why am I feeling this way? I've never seen these people before.'*

She didn't know whose parents they were, but they looked a lot nicer than hers. Just as she was thinking this, red droplets began to fall on their image, like a pen dripping with ink of blood. A burning hole was torn through the portrait, as if a candle had been lit underneath of it. Her vision was clouded by smoke so thick and plentiful it was invading all her senses. She could smell it, taste it, and feel it crawling across her skin. She could feel its wispy fingers climbing through her hair. It stung her eyes and filled her throat. She couldn't breathe.

Rozha was awoken to the rather unpleasant melody of Kasra's hacking coughs. She slowly stirred and languidly picked herself up on her achy joints to see the violette standing in the corner of the room with a kerchief clasped to her face. The creaking bed had Kasra's ear twitching to turn around and offer her sister an apologetic grimace. "I'm sorry for disturbing you," she hoarsely rasped, rubbing one of the dark circles under her eyes.

"How long have you been awake?" Rozha's ears tiredly drooped.

"For a bit," Kasra cleared her throat. "I could hardly sleep. I kept waking up and had the hardest time getting comfortable."

"I think Diava will understand if you decide not to show up to the Purifier Hall today," Rozha nodded. "I'll tell her you're still feeling yucky when I go out to see her."

"Thanks," Kasra daintily smiled with a rising of her shoulders. "With any luck, I'll at least be feeling good enough today to partake in the after-class activities."

"You're really enjoying them, huh?" Rozha returned her sister's delighted expression.

"Oh yeah," the violette proudly smirked. "Teacher Xanne looked so surprised that I had such a handle on her magic stuff. She even had me tutor Layna a little bit because she was lagging behind."

Imagining what Viasarria would have had to say about that earned a chuckle out of Rozha. "I'm sorry I had to miss that." With a bit of an inquisitive wink, she added, "Might that have anything to do with what you, Raia, and Layna got yourselves into that day?"

Looking down somewhat bashfully at her foot as she idly brushed her toes against the wooden floor, Kasra began with an elongated, "Yeaahh… she got really jealous and wanted to prove that she could do magic stuff too. So she took us over to Travestas to pick a fight with the Safiric Brotherhood."

Rozha raised an eyebrow and stiffened her neck, as if wanting to reprimand her, but knowing it was too late to start yelling at her for what she had done. "You know they're hunting for you, right? Why would you agree to follow her over there?"

"She wouldn't take no for an answer!" Kasra defensively complained. "And if I didn't go with her, then she would have just dragged Raia down there. If I wasn't there to bail them out, they would have gotten themselves killed!"

Seeing the strong convictions in her sister's words and body language made Rozha smile. "You felt you had to do something, as the voice of reason?"

"Something like that, I guess," Kasra vacantly blinked, having not expected Rozha to agree with her.

"There's nothing wrong with wanting to play hero," the blade dancer said. "Someone's gotta stand up when no one else will. The fact that Layna needs to throw herself into a situation to show how 'great' she is, proves that she's got no game. The most talented fighters never make challenges. They are the ones who beat up the idiots who do."

Kasra's bright-eyed stare and impressionable grin soaked up her sister's words and took them all to heart. "I'll bet you could have finished off Deniechus, had you been there when we were."

At that remark, Rozha curiously tilted her head and curled her tail. "What're you talking about?" Suddenly she began to wonder just how much had happened while she and Kyrana were away.

"When I was taking Wanystha's class," the violette recalled, "a priestess named Cinte came to tell us that Diava was being attacked by the Safiric Brotherhood. Wanystha had to leave, but put Cinte in charge of the classroom so none of the students would go anywhere. Layna didn't want to stay put, so she froze Cinte so Raia and I could run off with her." At this point in the story, Rozha was already rolling her eyes.

"We got there just in time to see Diava do this amazing magic trick that used Deniechus' own powers against him. When he got knocked down, Layna stepped out of the hiding place she had brought us to and threw a dagger right into Deniechus' chest!" The raising of Rozha's brow and the lowering of her chin said it all for her. "...But, he threw it back," Kasra went on. "Layna caught it in a shield I've never seen her use before. Deniechus was pretty impressed by it, too. He told her a few things I didn't really understand and then made fun of Diava a bit before gathering up his cronies and walking off."

With an analytical nod, Rozha's eyes trailed across the room as she thought about what Kasra said. "What were some of the 'few things' that he said?" she eventually asked.

Rubbing her temples to clear the fog of her fever, Kasra recollected, "He said that she was 'wasting her time with them,' and something about how 'they can't understand' her.'"

'There's something strange about that,' Rozha thought. *'The Safiric Brotherhood never shows mercy to Pures. They wouldn't just leave them alone if they thought they could kill them, instead.'*

Her concerns must've been written in her face, because Kasra could read that Rozha was thinking about something. "What's wrong?"

"This whole Thunderstone business must've brought them all outta the woodwork, yesterday," Rozha shrugged. "I've never seen them out in force like they have been. They aren't usually so... around, and busy."

Now it was Kasra's turn to look curious. "Thunderstone? What's that?"

What 'was' that, might be the more proper tense, now. "It was a point of interest in Fort Pericula. Kyrana and I were charged by Mother Diava to investigate some activity relating to the Safiric Brotherhood."

"Pericula?" Kasra couldn't help interrupting, as the name sounded familiar to her. "Is that place pretty close to here?"

"It's *supposed* to be," Rozha laughed, remembering the so-called 'two hour' estimate. She then went on to explain her encounter with the Laeyudi people and her battle with the fearsome Mire Fiend at Mordax Swamp. After her telling of the story, Kasra was stunned. Certainly if Rozha had so much respect for this adversary, it must've been one of the most wicked and vile creatures to have ever lived. "But you're alive now to tell the tale," the violette casually observed. "Did you have to run away?"

Rozha could see her sister was on the edge of her seat, worried for her, but she wasn't quite a good enough storyteller to capitalize on her suspense. "Psh, *hell* no," she dismissively waved a hand with a haughty chuckle. "When it tried to pull me into its bath water, I threw a knife into its ugly face and killed it right there."

Kasra had a hard time getting herself immersed into Rozha's sudden change of mood. She was more distracted by trying to picture in her mind the visage of this miserable demon. "What did it look like?"

Rozha bit her lip and eyed the ceiling as she tried to the best of her ability to remember. She honestly didn't want to see the monster any clearer than she was allowed to during their confrontation. It'd probably be better if she forgot about its face entirely, but that look the Mire Fiend gave her as it laid dying was the most poignant thing she saw the whole night. "It was the most belhuayn creature I've ever seen," Rozha started. "It even looked female enough to where the Laeyudi called it a demoness, but it was hard to believe..." the blade dancer trailed off. "I don't know what has to happen to someone to become something that grotesque. Everything about it and its dwelling was made to kill anything that came in contact with it."

Kasra's newly-awakened artistic spirit was so fascinated by Rozha's monster that she wanted to draw something that matched its description in her next history class. "I'll bet Teacher Wanystha would be really impressed if I could capture its image onto paper."

"Oh, I'm sure she would!" Rozha laughed, knowing Wanystha would throw a fit if Kasra tried to draw *anything* Safiric in nature. "If she lets you keep it, I'd like to see it, myself." Out of the corner of her eye, Rozha saw the ruby lantern turning alight in the opposite corner of the room. "I'm afraid the rest of my story will have to wait til later. My presence is needed at the Purifier Hall." Standing up from the bed, Rozha grabbed her priestess robes from her wardrobe. Holding them in her arms, she went to the doorway before she turned and performed a sort of jocular, half-curtsy for her sister. "But I shall return."

Rozha changed into her priestess garb as she made her way down the corridor to the Purifier Hall. As it had seemed to have started becoming habit for the Red Dancer, she was the one of the last priestesses to arrive. But this time, the cushion that was normally reserved for her was taken by a different priestess. Instead, there was an open space for her at the faculty's end of the sacred bath, between a smiling Wanystha and a diametrically uncaring Xanne.

"Over here, Teacher Rozha!" Wanystha waved the Dancer down.

And already it had begun. Rozha couldn't help smirking upon hearing her new title as she accepted her fellow faculty's invitation. While she made her way over, Viasarria, who sat by a closely-watching Platina, filled the whole chamber with an appalled yawp. *"Teacher?! Since when?!"*

"Since last night," came the unseen Mother Diava's voice from behind the raised altar. The High Priestess then made herself visible to her followers by approaching her special Seer's Podium. "Rozha's commendable acts of valor from her undertaking of the Pericula Initiative earned her this honor -- this new position that I felt Sachelvae had needed for a long time."

Viasarria knew her next reaction wouldn't be acceptable as a member of the clergy, but she was far too offended by the recent events to care. "You've gotta be *kidding* me!" the enraged rival blade dancer started. "I could've done what Rozha did and *then* some, and everybody here *knows* it! I'm a much better warrior than her -- *I* should be the one getting this praise, not *her!*"

While everyone in attendance was running something through their minds at that very moment to put the envious ex-priestess in her place, they all deferred to Diava's wisdom to give Viasarria her official what-for.

"Your lack of discipline is what holds you back," a stern Diava argued. "Your abilities in combat are inconsequential when it comes to your knowledge of how and *when* to use them. Because you are far too apt to disobey direct orders and act of your own volition, you have been thusly demoted from your priestess status until you can regain the same level of trustworthiness that you had before. The role you played in Pericula, before the Initiative, was merely for reconnaissance -- and even *then*, I was taking a gamble with you. But I had faith you would not fail me. And for taking this crucial step by staying within your boundaries, for once, I have begun to reconsider your demotion. So long as you continue to prove yourself, I may one day return your silver crown. Until then, I expect you to show the same dedication expected of any novitiate here. Perhaps you can learn something from Teacher Rozha's example."

As if it weren't enough to be humiliated in front of all the clergy by the High Priestess herself, she had to invoke the name of her rival on top of that. Viasarria cast the most disdainful scowl she could muster at her enemy from across the Purifier. So much hatred flashed in her eyes, the sacred waters began to darken by just being near her. Even the usually indifferent Platina could sense that Viasarria had reached her low boiling point.

"Please try to repress your emotions," the statue girl suggested, as if speaking to a machine. "Such troublesome feelings will only cloud your judgment. Strength comes from willingness to reason; stupidity comes from a propensity to lose one's temper. Mother teaches us to reconcile because the destruction of our problems does not eliminate their cause. Our greatest problems come from within. We can only be destroyed when our enemies can exploit our weaknesses."

"Sister Platina is right," Diava confirmed. "Even the Purifier can only undo the sins you are willing to forgive. It cannot fix their roots, as well; that comes from personal introspection. You can only become a priestess when you accept this accountability -- when you are willing to admit your wrongdoings. Rozha has renounced her past, but you have not. And so long as you retain that prideful immaturity, I cannot call you a true child of Sanguina."

Though Viasarria had managed to control her outward enmity, the still, cold emptiness in her eyes were an obvious enough indication of her apathy for everything Diava was telling her. She could think of nothing more than how she had been wronged and ignored by the High Priestess, and how her fall from grace was now placed on a pillory for all her former colleagues to see.

Diava only pretended that she didn't take heed of Viasarria's quiet warnings as she directed the daily ablutions. But she knew there was nothing better she could do with her recalcitrant blade dancer other than forcing her to remain in the Quarantine Bay, under Platina's supervision. And it was back to the Quarantine she returned after mealtime had ended.

"It's not fair what they're doing to her," Layna complained, as she and Raia were on their way to Xanne's classroom.

"You heard what Mother Diava said," Raia replied. "Viasarria has been violating the rules of conduct for a priestess of our clergy. Her correctional imprisonment is justified if the faculty believes she cannot be trusted."

"You're far too adamant when it comes to obeying these stingy rules," Layna was quick to criticize. "Viasarria and I were born into this whole life. We've known it almost as long as Mother Diava has. She just doesn't like that Viasarria is always one step ahead of her judgment -- she'd never abdicate her status as High Priestess so long as she lived."

Raia had to bite back a laugh. "What you're saying then, is that Mother Diava is *not* suspicious, but rather *jealous* of Viasarria?"

Layna squinted her eyes, as if studying her friend's expression. "Yes, that's exactly what I'm saying. Think about it: she just awarded the Red Dancer for doing something that not only could Viasarria have done, but *has* done multiple times."

"Do you not see what the difference is between her and Rozha, though?" Raia raised her finger to make a point. "Viasarria killed members of the Safiric Brotherhood and has disrupted their rituals in the past, yes. But every instance this was done, was acted either on her own or even against Mother Diava's will."

Layna shrugged, "So what you're saying then is that the High Priestess favors sycophants." She disgustedly scowled, placing her hands on her hips and tapping her foot. "So long as they do what she says, she likes them just fine. But when someone does something she didn't ask them to, even something she'd approve of, they're treated like her worst enemies."

"That's the way *any* system has to work," Raia argued some common sense into her. "You can't just act like you know everything when you first come into a place, and expect people to treat you like some savior. That just makes you sound irrational and impatient. Nobody respects people who are rude and constantly challenging authority so they can claim it for themselves. Nobody wants to serve someone so *selfish*, either."

Instead of being terribly miffed by Raia's harsh words, as the young novitiate was starting to think Layna might be once her rant had ended, the dark-haired vixy was surprisingly understanding about the whole matter. "Huh, so this is what you're *really* like, when you finally speak your mind," she calculatingly examined her. "It's refreshing to see you come out of your kiss-ass closet and stick up for yourself, for a change. However," Layna's comportment hardened, "what you said changes nothing about how I feel. If authority is never challenged, a revolution will not come. And that's what this world has needed for a long time."

"A revolution?" a perplexed Raia gasped. "What're you talking about?"

"Something both sides -- both faiths have sought, but has constantly eluded them for all time," Layna continued. "It is because they would rather retain the status quo than seek change. They have sealed their fate to perpetuate an endless cycle of war and death. They are thus divided and wish the world to remain broken. What they need -- the worshipers of Safiro and Sanguina -- is something to make them whole again."

This first insight into Layna's deeper thoughts left Raia bewildered. It was growing increasingly apparent to the novitiate that her friend had much bigger ideas than the brash remarks she could loose at the drop of a hat. "Why are you telling me all of this in such confidence?" Raia quietly asked, having now stopped outside the door to Xanne's classroom.

"You're the only one who could make use of it," Layna replied. "Everyone else here is too stupid to understand what I have to say. Their typical response to such a lamentation is simply, 'oh, you're so smart,' or some other useless crap. I don't have time for people like that. If they ever approach me, I just tell them off because they're just distractions."

"If you're so smart," an unimpressed Raia challengingly smirked, "How come I'm getting better grades than you are?"

"Pff, *again* with that shit?" Layna rolled her eyes. "I already told you that the only reason people do well here is because they suck up to the faculty. I don't like kissing rings and licking boots, so I don't move up the ranks like everybody else."

"Then why are you wasting your time here?" came Raia's second remark. "If you're already so far ahead of everyone else, why not just graduate yourself? You don't seem to need us for anything."

"If I thought I was ready for that, I would have done so by now," Layna riposted. "I never said I knew everything. But when I do, then I'll move on."

Raia wasn't sure if she could believe that. Something about Layna's body language was unusually insincere. Of all the words one could use to describe Layna behind her back, 'honesty' was her only virtue. "That's not the whole truth," if it was even part of it at all. "There's something you want, that you know is here, don't you?"

Once again, Layna gave Raia that odd smile she would wear when she was catching on to one of her schemes. But the troublemaker wasn't about to let her know what she was thinking this time, and didn't have the time to, even if she felt like it. Both of the vixies' attention was diverted to the sound of the red, wooden door opening behind them. On the other side, Xanne poked her head out around the corner. "What are you two whispering about, out here? We've been waiting for you to come in so class can start."

"I'm sorry, Teacher Xanne," came Raia's angel-faced apology, as she ashamedly held her dress. "I was just talking with Layna about Kasra," she lied. "She hasn't been feeling well, and I haven't seen her leave her quarters all day. Layna didn't seem to think that it was any big deal, but I'd like to check on Kasra, if I may?"

Xanne would usually have smiled at Raia's excuses, but she could tell there was something amiss, this time, about their palavering. "You two have been acting strangely ever since Kasra moved in," the Teacher observed. "As commendable as it is for a novitiate to care for her fellow student, it is not necessary to keep poking around in someone's business at all times. There are some things Kasra can do for herself."

Realizing that sounded a bit cold, Xanne added, "But I know Kasra's health has never been in the best of sorts. She might need all the help she can get to fully recover. Mother only knows what she has been through to get herself where she is…" She looked over Raia's head as she gazed wistfully down the way, in the direction of the student bedchambers. "If you can get her to come to class," Xanne said to Raia, "please do, but do not take long with it. I do not want you to miss out on our newest lesson."

"Yes, Teacher Xanne," Raia performed the proper bow, "I will return shortly."

As she turned on her way back down where she came, Raia caught a pair of familiar figures out of the corner of her eye -- one dressed in white, and the other in red. She was a bit taken aback to see Mother Diava with Rozha just to her immediate left, further down the hall. They both were standing before a great rectangle drawn in red paint on the marble wall, between Xanne's and Wanystha's classrooms. Diava was holding onto a beautiful, ivory staff that looked like a long tree branch, decorated with several antler-like limbs at the top, resembling a crown.

"This will be where your new room is constructed," Diava's voice faintly echoed. "Tomorrow, I will have a crew of builders come and tear a new doorway inside this rectangle marker," the High Priestess traced said imaginary doorway, with the point of her finger. "Until then, you can draw up plans for what you would like to be in your new space. The room will be sized 30 feet long by 20 feet wide. You can make a list of materials for any furnishings you may need, and I will have a team of priestesses go to Mediona to procure them for you."

"That is most generous of you," Rozha graciously dipped her head. After opening her eyes upon finishing her curtsy, she saw Raia standing at the corner. Diava followed Rozha's distracted gaze and turned in the direction of the eavesdropping novitiate. "Sister Raia," the High Priestess called to her, "why are you not in Xanne's room?"

"Forgive me, your holiness," Raia submissively clasped her hands by her waist. "I was on my way to see Kasra. Teacher Xanne requested me to retrieve her."

"That's good of you," Diava praised her favorite novitiate. "You may hurry along now, dear Sister."

"Yes, Mother Diava," Raia started on her way off, but paused in mid-step to say one more thing. "Congratulations, Red Dancer, for joining the faculty! I can't wait to be a part of your first class."

Even Rozha found herself enthralled by the vixy's charm; her cheery attitude and bright smile were virtually contagious. "Please, call me Rozha! I'm looking forward to seeing how well you and Layna do here." She gave the brunette the kind of smirk that indicated she might have known about Raia's and Layna's 'hands-on experience' in dealing with the Brotherhood. Raia said nothing, but laughed off her nervousness, as to not give herself away in front of Mother Diava. "You be on your way, then," Rozha shooed her off, which Raia did not hesitate in doing, this time.

After the vixy had disappeared around the corner and her footsteps could no longer be heard on the tiled floor, Rozha turned to the oddly unsmiling Diava. "She's real endearing, isn't she?"

"What she's doing mixed up with someone like Layna has me worried," Diava disapprovingly shook her head. "She's protecting Layna, but I don't know why."

This curiosity also had Rozha wondering why Kasra had taken a liking to them. Kasra had already told her one story of what they did together when they first met. *'They're so close-knit and trusting of each other,'* Rozha mentally noted. *'It's like they're forming a gang, and Layna is the one leading it. What does she need Kasra and Raia for?'*

Her mulling the situation over was truncated by Kyrana calling to her and Diava from the opposite corner of the U-shaped corridor. "You wished to see me, your holiness?" the Arch Healer came briskly walking over.

"Yes, Sister Kyrana," Diava replied, "it is about your reward for taking on the Pericula Initiative."

Kyrana blinked as her neck stiffened. Truthfully, she had been wondering if the High Priestess had perhaps forgotten since she had taken so long to even mention it. But on the outside, she gratefully said, "I would be most happy to accept anything you would like to give me."

"Then I am all the more confident that this will suffice to satisfy you," Diava smiled, holding out her tree-like staff to her. "This is a Branch of Life. It is said that the very first Branch was given to Saint Sevasmia by the Mother Herself -- built from the Life Giver."

"That is the sacred tree of ten thousand limbs," Kyrana recalled.

"You know your history well," Diava affirmed. "The Life Giver resides on the northernmost edge of Sanguina's Moon. It bears the fruit known as Vikanti, which feeds all the unborn spirits of the ethereal realm."

"But not all Branches of Life are made from the Life Giver, itself?" Rozha guessed.

"Correct, but the tradition of fashioning them from sanctified trees continues to this day," Diava explained. "Only a High Priestess has the privilege of crafting these holy artifacts. They are created as part of Purifier Beacons for Sanguinic Crusades." Pointing to the crown-like top of the staff, she noted, "The leader of onesuch Crusade would place a gem, known as a Sanrisma, inside this staff, thus completing it. The Purifier Beacon works to magnify the powers of any priestess who wields it. Once established to consecrate an area from Safiric evil, it cannot be removed."

"I have never heard of a Sanrisma before," Kyrana commented. "Where do they come from?"

"They are precious stones found very deep underground," Diava said. "Sanrisma are considered holy artifacts of Sanguina because they are the only things found in nature that repel Safiric poison. It's said that sanrismae are fragments of Sanguina's moon, and that is why they shed light like Her holy fane. Their fragments are used like candles in funeral ceremonies to commemorate the deaths of high priestesses. Sanrismae are more often carved into guidance charms and communication rings."

"If they are such an important part to completing a Purifier Beacon," Kyrana asked, "Why does my scepter lack one?"

"Because sanrismae are so rare, and only one that is found whole can be used to complete a Purifier Beacon." Diava explained. "They are typically only used when a Crusade is issued. Since sanrismae have many other uses, at least one is reserved in a temple for this very purpose. It is very dangerous to wield a completed Purifier Beacon because they who are not repelled by its light will seek to destroy whomever carries it. But even without a sanrisma attached to it, a Branch of Life still extends the Sanguinic energies of its user."

At last accepting her award, Kyrana could feel the Branch's power flowing into her. "It will be my honor to serve in this new cause, when it arises."

"I was given a Branch of Life, myself, a short time before I was inducted as High Priestess," Diava stated. "Since I have served, I have only had to use one in a Crusade. We can only hope that this trend of peace will continue..." she trailed off with a knowing frown, "but I fear it will not. I have received auguries during times of meditation and have seen black clouds forming over the outer lying swamps. I have seen Tresantia being overcome by the wilderness and consumed with darkness... but I do not know what these visions mean."

Watching Mother Diava silently staring off into space, Kyrana insightfully surmised, "You believe that we may know what these dangers are, soon enough?"

The High Priestess somberly nodded. "We cannot be ill-equipped for what lies ahead. The Brotherhood is on the move and arming up like I've never seen before. Whatever opportunity they have found, they have seized upon. It will be all we can do to fight and banish them from reaching their goal. That is why I have taken the steps I have to prepare us, by appointing you, Sister Rozha, and you, Sister Kyrana, to your higher positions. If it is Sanguina's Will, we will know Her mercy. And still I have fear...."

"In the interest of preparation," an inspired Kyrana began, "I have a special run I'd like to make to Mediona. I want to gather a few medicines to give to the Laeyudi tribe. I promised their elder, Ghanius, that I would bring him something he could use to ensure his health does not falter again."

"This is very commendable of you, Sister," Diava curiously tilted her head. "You are not planning on making that delivery *today*, are you?"

"Perhaps not," Kyrana had to think about it for a moment. "I would like to give Vanix a reasonable amount of rest before taking him on such a dangerous jaunt, again. Especially if we run into the same kind of dangers we encountered before. But..." eyeing the Branch of Life in her hand, "I feel we will be better prepared, this time around."

"Fair enough," Diava understandingly nodded. "You are not required for any particular activities today, so you are free to do as you please, Arch Healer. However, I'm sure Sister Platina would appreciate your guidance in dealing with Viasarria. I feel guilty about putting the stresses on her of watching such a loose cannon all day."

"I will do what I can to make my errands quick," Kyrana bowed.

Rozha then asked, "Is there anything you require of me, your holiness?"

"You have earned your sabbath, Teacher," Diava smiled. "I will grant you this day, as I have Kyrana, to do as you please."

"That is most kind of you!" Rozha relievedly exclaimed. "Because I have something I'd like to do at Mediona, as well. I lost an important weapon that I wish to replace. So I will go to see Reaventyr the blacksmith and ask what he can do for me."

As much as the thought of using murderous weapons sickened Diava, the High Priestess was well aware of what kind of times they were in. She knew this was no longer the time to condemn the use of killing tools by members of her clergy. "As you wish, dear Rozha," she gave her permission with an obvious reluctance. "Just remain cautious; our recent confrontation with the Brotherhood in Mediona has left people there nervous and wary of the conflagration of more conflict between our faiths."

Her eyes softened, her expression more troubled than it was before. "Even earlier today, I detected the presence of murders on the Safiric side of town. Whether they were sacrifices to Travestas or defectors from the Brotherhood, I cannot say for certain." The High Priestess made sure that no novitiates were around to hear what she had to say next. "Rumors are beginning to spread that the Brotherhood may be establishing battlements on their side of Mediona to secure themselves from our side. If Deniechus is trying to turn the populace against the Sisterhood, then our efforts should be to undo whatever rumors he is spreading."

"I'll keep a lookout," Rozha tried to assuage Diava's fears. "I will take no actions to further jeopardize the Sisterhood's reputation."

Diava relieved Rozha from her attention and let her newest Teacher be on her way. After Kyrana courtly bowed to her and left the High Priestess in peace, she thought to herself, *'It isn't so much I fear what Rozha will do, but what the Safiric Brotherhood will frame her for.'*

Chapter 14: Preparing for the Future

While Rozha, Kyrana, and Diava parted ways, Raia had entered Kasra's room and found the violette restlessly lying on her bed, staring at the ceiling. When she heard the door's hinges squeaking, she eagerly sat up, expecting to see her sister, but was nonetheless pleased to see her good friend peeking around the doorway. "Oh, hey, Raia!" Kasra greeted her. "What brings you here?"

"I apologize for barging in!" Raia held her chest, stepping the rest of the way inside. "I was expecting you to be asleep. I know you're still not feeling the best."

"Don't worry about me," the sickly violette shook her head. "I'll bounce back from this soon enough."

"As long as you don't need me for anything," the brunette continued, "Teacher Xanne's giving her lecture -- she said it'll be about a new power we haven't used before. Do you think you can join us?"

"Of course!" an excited Kasra rose from her bed. "I hate sitting around -- I don't want poor health to keep me from doing what I want."

Her headstrong comment elicited a matronly furrow of Raia's brow. "Alright, but don't overdo it," the vixy turned to lead her friend outside, "I'll try to keep Layna from getting you into any more trouble, if she gets any ideas."

Even though she felt like hurrying to keep herself from missing anything, Raia kept her pace normal for Kasra to keep up. By the time they had reached Xanne's classroom, they could overhear her saying from the other side of the door, "...Now we will begin the practice session." Whatever was about to begin was put on standby when Raia came into the room. Xanne and all her students were standing from their desks, in preparation to try her newest, magical ability.

"How good of you to join us, Kasra," Xanne said. "Thank you, Raia, for convincing her to attend."

"I didn't have to persuade her," Raia admitted. "Your lessons are always the most exciting part of my day." She could see Layna giving her a silent jeer from the opposite corner of the room, behind all the other novitiates standing between them.

"Your seats are open at the back," Xanne pointed forward, and waited for her stragglers to stand at the empty desks to Layna's side. "Are we all ready now?" she scanned over the heads of her class. Now that Raia and

Kasra were in a location where they could see the chalkboard, they saw that "Masalida II" was written in large, bold letters behind their Teacher. Oddly, and somewhat disconcertingly, they found a scowling Cinte standing in the corner of the room by the door. Her arms were crossed and her eyes were fixed on Layna.

"Now that you have been given a week to train yourselves on the use of your masalida," Xanne started, "I believe you are now ready to begin learning how to strengthen it. Better than merely defending yourself from an attack you cannot dodge, nor prevent with an astapsyxi, you can use your masalida to reflect a Safiric power back at its user. I know by now you have mastered the technique of englobing yourself and others with your shield, but because you will just be starting out," came the Teacher's caveat, "I suggest you use just half of your masalida to start with. This will reinforce your reflexes to deflect an attack aimed directly at you. Once you have had some practice, you will be able to use your full shield to deflect attacks aimed at you, or anyone else. Just remember that the masalida can only reflect an attack the moment before it makes contact -- it is a dangerous tactic that should not be used by a priestess acting on their own."

Raising her hand for permission, Raia asked, "Can the masalida only reflect an attack from a distance?"

Xanne somewhat reluctantly admitted, "The masalida can bounce back someone who attempts a physical strike as well, ...but I must warn you against this, because the consequences of failure could be much more dire. The use of your masalida in such a way is simply foolish; if you can see your opponent advancing and have enough time to prepare your shield, you could also have used an astapsyxi to stop him."

For some reason, Raia had an inkling that Layna would want to give this example of 'foolish use' a try, anyway. She was always more than willing to take a huge risk, especially to receive a big reward.

Because of the noise made by the stonemasons breaking down the wall between the pre-existing rooms, Teacher Xanne moved her class outside. Her students enjoyed the weather while they continued practicing their Sanguinic spells. "So when we go outside," Teacher Xanne continued, "don't let me see you using anything but our rubber projectiles to practice with." She gave a forewarning glance to Layna, who suddenly tried to hide her indicative grin. "If you have any questions, you can ask them, then. For now, I wish for you to partner up with someone to practice with." Then addressing the violette, she continued, "Kasra, since we have an odd number of students here, would you mind having Layna and Raia as study partners, again?"

Something about how she asked that had Kasra wondering why Xanne was giving her a choice. It was as if the Teacher was hoping she wouldn't say yes. Kasra glimpsed at the other eyes all staring at her around the room, before Xanne added, "You can join up with any other pair you like. I assumed you'd choose Layna and Raia since you three seem to have taken a shine to each other."

Kasra quietly looked between Xanne, and Raia's almost pleading stare, a few times until she finally made up her mind. "I think I'll be good with these two," she motioned toward her friends.

Xanne nodded and heaved an awkward sigh, "Alright then," before turning for the door. "Line up and follow me then."

While they waited for the students ahead of them to make their way behind Teacher Xanne, Kasra whispered to Raia, "I don't even know how to do this masalida thing -- how am I supposed to do this exercise?"

Of course, Layna couldn't help overhearing and making her own remark first. "How can you not know how to use a basic shield, but you can somehow use an astapsyxi? Are you just *trying* to draw special attention to yourself?"

"Shut up, Layna!" Raia came to Kasra's defense. "Unlike *you*, she never claimed to be ahead of everybody else. Teacher Xanne said that some Pures can use their powers without even knowing what they are, during situations of extreme distress. It's Sanguina's way of protecting Her children and making sure they come to Her faith. As you can see, it worked in Kasra's case," she smiled at her friend.

A disgusted Layna derisively dismissed Raia's saccharine words, but this time, didn't feel like speaking her mind. She could almost feel Cinte's goofy, forewarning glare looming behind her. She'd gotten in trouble with the faculty enough, this week; she didn't want to continue pushing their buttons by continuing to make a scene.

Xanne, for one, was pleased to not hear any whispering from the back of the line as she made her way through Sachelvae's halls. She knew whenever Layna and Raia were having a secret conversation, she could expect them to 'disappear' outside when she wasn't looking. Now that she had Cinte to watch over them, the Teacher felt like she could relax a little bit. It was almost a second job to make sure Layna and Raia didn't get themselves into any mischief.

It was the first time Kasra had ever seen the temple's backyard. Sachelvae's courtyard was fenced off from the outside world by a short, brick wall barely six feet tall and hedged with flowering bushes. It contained a tranquil orchard of frupom trees, which were still in their smaller stages of youth, but had enough space between them and the building to allow them growth to their full size.

The frupoms themselves had trunks no wider than a belhuayn standing beside them, and had leafy branches from which dangled their eponymous fruit. A frupom's natural produce was colored blue when ripe, and at full maturity was about the size of two fists put together. When the tree was full grown, its fruit grew a hard husk of spines that was difficult to remove, but the fleshy bulb within was considered an Ontevallian delicacy.

Sachelvae's beautiful garden was where the students of the clergy would practice their Sanguinic magic and would do their daily chores. Of these, their chores included picking frupoms and managing the flower gardens by the walls, as well as trimming the hedges. Raia was quick to point out Layna's known dislike for such menial tasks, which spurred her adventurous spirit to skip out on them.

Every time she looked at the temptatious, short barrier, she was reminded of the first time Layna ever asked Raia to help hoist her up and over the wall. There was just enough cover given by the trees that a Teacher distracted by a distressed student wouldn't notice someone trying to make a break for it. But the introduction of the hedges was made to prevent any more breakouts of this sort.

"Come to think of it," Raia said in the middle of her exposition, "lots of the new defenses Sachelvae has added have been directly related to Layna's mischief."

"It's not like I'm the only kid to ever wanna *leave* this place," the troublemaker argued.

"No, but you are the only kid who's ever left and came back," Raia returned, "*numerous* times."

Kasra chuckled at the dark-haired vixy, "You really are spoiled, you know that?" earning herself a death glare from her rival. "If I hated it some place, I would have left *long* before I could have built up the kind of reputation you have here."

"Oh yeah?" a testy Layna invaded the violette's personal space. "And what brings *you* here, anyway? You weren't good enough to make it out on *your* own, either."

Unlike so many of her fellow novitiates that she had challenged before, the ex-rogue didn't give Layna an inch. She called her bluff with a much more threatening stare, as only eyes that knew murder could have. "I lasted a *hell* of a lot longer than you could've, little vixy."

Seeing that Layna was nearly standing on the stalwart Kasra's toes, Raia interposed herself in their developing conflict. "Would you two *stop?!*" she pushed them apart, and prayed that she would be left with her arms intact. She hated watching people fight, but knew it was a lot easier to end one before it began. "Seriously, what kind of idiots would start something like this in front of the faculty? Are you *trying* to get yourselves kicked out of here? Because it isn't hard to leave if you don't want to stay. They don't *force* you to stay if you don't like it here."

Kasra crossed her arms and gave Layna an oblique squint of her eyes from over Raia's shoulder. "No," she frowned, "I don't want to ruin the one chance I have to live in peace with my sister. Perhaps family doesn't mean that much to some, who are so *ungrateful* with what they have that they believe the world *itself* owes them something more."

Instead of responding in her usual way, Layna's aptitude for a barb seemed to have been quieted by a certain thoughtfulness. The way she looked at Kasra showed that she was finally beginning to study the other vixy for more than what was on the outside. She had been so distracted by how much she disliked her outward appearance and attitude that she had forgotten to assess her spirit. It made her all the more curious to know where Kasra came from, and who Rozha was. Perhaps the reason she hated Kasra so much is because she resented her for having lived through the experiences she wanted to have?

"Maybe that's it," Layna said, just loud enough to be heard. "Maybe we have *too much* in common."

Kasra raised a brow as if to say "I beg your pardon?" and probably would have, had it not been for a yellow, rubber ball bouncing off the side of her head.

"Please forgive us!" shouted a blonde vixy of long hair and shoulder-length braids. She was standing under one of the nearby frupom trees with another novitiate, whose shorter, bob-cut hair was of a chartreuse color. "We were just practicing our deflection technique and weren't watching for anyone who might've been too close."

"I forgive you," a smiling Layna spoke on Kasra's behalf. "You want your ball back, then?"

"If you wouldn't mind," the blonde came a little closer for Kasra to toss the practice projectile back into her hands. "My name's Lavelle, by the way..." trailing off when she finally caught heed of who she was speaking to, she suddenly realized, "Hey, aren't you that new girl? Kasra, right?" The violette nodded. "What're you doing with *Layna?*"

"Listen jerk," Layna threw a finger at her, "what's it to *you* who she hangs out with?"

Raia had to do a double take when she thought she heard her friend coming to Kasra's defense. Lavelle, however, didn't see Layna's outburst in the least charming. "I'm *sorry* if I offended you by the way I said your name with such an *inflection*," she stuck out her tongue and raised her hand in a funny gesture -- a belhuayn 'loser salute.'

Turning her attention to her original audience, she said, "If you want to have one notch on your tiara in one year rather than *wait* a year to have one notch removed, I suggest you play with a nicer crowd." Gesturing to her friend, she added, "Tassie and I wouldn't mind if you wanted to be a third in our team. We'll even help get you caught up on the lessons you missed when you weren't here."

Truthfully, the proposition sounded like a rather attractive one to Kasra. She had only met Raia and Layna because she was seated between them at the dining hall. She potentially could have been in anyone's group, and known anybody in Sachelvae on her first day. Some may have called it fate that she was paired up with the biggest troublemaker and the best student in the convent, but Kasra wasn't of that mind. She had no reason to believe in preponderance of any sort.

At least, that's the way things seemed before she met Deniechus. Ever since Rozha brought her to Sachelvae, the whole 'Safiro' and 'Sanguina' thing started to make sense -- how good and bad things seemed to happen, depending on which deity was smiling upon her that day. Even Rozha believed in fate, or at least that Sanguina was guiding her in some way. But Kasra could tell her sister wasn't quite as staunch a believer as a Diava or a Kyrana.

Perhaps she had been thinking to herself too long and let time slip her by, for the answer she could have used was stolen from her by motormouth Layna, once again. "Bah, you two would get whipped by the first Brotherhood spook to cross paths with you! I've only been held back because I seek a *real* source of experience, to apply these powers in the way they were *meant* to be used. You guys are good at walking a line and obeying the rules, but when it comes to actually doing your duties in the *real* world, what good are you?"

"Oh dear, here we go again," Lavelle rolled her eyes. This time, the usually taciturn Tassie got to make her case. "Of course we wouldn't be any good against a priest, if we were to go picking a fight with one. Even the faculty and Mother Diava, herself, were once novitiates like us." Turning to her friend, Tassie cooed, "imagine that, a *young* Diava!" eliciting the aggravating giggles of both. "So what's it going to be, Kasra?" Lavelle finally turned the conversation full circle. "Layna or us?"

She might as well have just said 'the evil you know or the evil you don't.' After speaking to the gossipy Tassie and Lavelle, Kasra knew she had a much better chance of hating herself less for staying with Layna and Raia. At least they were *outspoken* about who and what they didn't like. "No, I'd rather just stay where I'm at," was the most polite way Kasra could manage her thoughts. "I don't want to make a habit of being pulled around all over the place. It would distract me from trying to learn new things."

"Have it your way, then," Lavelle shrugged, both she and Tassie on their way to leave. "I'd think there'd be no greater obstacle to intelligent pursuits than 'Teacher's Pet' Sladervorn, over there."

"Teacher's pet?" Kasra repeated, giving Layna a funny look. "Why'd they call you that?"

"I don't know," the dark-haired vixy defensively rebutted. "They must think Raia's last name is Sladervorn. She's the only 'teacher's pet' I know."

Kasra then turned to Raia, who had been oddly excluded from the conversation, as if she wasn't even there. The brunette had a sour look on her face, as if in pain and on the verge of crying. "What's wrong, Raia? Are you feeling okay?"

She hadn't even paid Kasra any mind until she started talking to her. The obviously troubled vixy had been looking in another direction the whole time. "Uh, yeah," she lied. "My stomach hurts a little. I'm just stressed -- I'll sit down for a bit." She then turned to depart, heading in the direction of the main building.

"Hey," Layna shouted at her accomplices, "are we gonna do this practice thing or what?"

"Um," Kasra glanced between Layna and Raia, watching the brunette slowly retreat. She wanted to follow Raia to comfort her, but she knew Layna wasn't the most sympathetic of friends, and thought it would be better to divert her from Raia's problems. "Sure. Raia said she wasn't feeling well, so I guess it'll be just you and me."

"Oh please," Layna shook her head, "that drama queen's probably just suffering indigestion. She'll get over it. We don't need her for our training session, anyhow." Energetically juggling the ball in her hand, the young rebel said, "I'll be the pitcher, and you can be the blocker." Stepping back for some distance between them, Layna then threw her small missile right at an unaware Kasra's chest.

"Hey!" the stunned violette coughed, "you didn't ask if I was ready or anything!"

"Sorry!" the snickering Layna couldn't have meant it less. "I forgot you didn't know how to use your shield."

Kasra picked up the rubber ball with every intention of returning the cheap shot, but glancing out of the corner of her eye, she saw Xanne walking through the garden. The Teacher was keeping tabs on her students, making sure they had perfected their lesson. She had just given pointers to Lavelle and Tassie, probably warning them not to get so 'advanced' with their trick shots when she saw them lose their rubber ball in a tree -- probably from intentionally bouncing it off the top of their shield. A couple of other students had gotten particularly creative with their masalida technique, and were currently engaging in a game of 'touchless catch,' involving deflecting the ball back and forth between their shields.

Xanne couldn't help but notice that Kasra and Layna were the only two students in the whole courtyard who hadn't even practiced their deflection trick once. But she pretended not to notice. "Have you two already got this down pat?" She acted amused. "Where is Raia?"

"She took one hard to the stomach," Layna casually fibbed. "I guess she wasn't ready for my fast throw."

"Oh dear," Xanne groaned, at least willing to believe that scenario. "I told you that this is a *practice* session, not a combat simulation. You can save all that unnecessary aggression for Rozha's first class." Layna sneered at Kasra when she heard her sister's name, just to see if the violette would have a smug look on her face. Of course she did, and so obliviously, too -- only making the envious vixy that much more irritated.

"If you feel that you have done all you can," Xanne continued, "then you'll be ready for the game I have planned." She suspiciously added, "*after* I review Kasra's progress. It is important that our newest student have the basics reinforced before we move on." Taking the rubber ball from Kasra's hand, the Teacher then moved to Layna's position and asked, "Are you ready?"

Having no time to really consider her options for being forthright or honest with her Teacher, Kasra could only nervously nod and hope for the best. When Xanne threw the ball at her, a lot more delicately than Layna, Kasra flinched and held out her hand, as if to catch it with her eyes averted. Without even realizing it at first, she felt a release of energy from her body accompanied by an odd, airy whirring sound -- the likes of which had no comparison in nature.

She, Xanne, and Layna were equally surprised to see that not only was the ball blocked, but it was even perfectly reflected by Kasra's barrier. The Teacher was so silently awestruck that she forgot to catch the ball before it dropped at her feet. *'How did she do that?'* was all she could think. *'I watched her the whole time -- she never did it once. No one even told her how to.'* Returning to her usual austerity, Xanne finally said, "I am impressed. You have done well."

"Thank you, Teacher Xanne," Kasra bowed, with some awkward hesitation.

"This concludes today's exercises," the Teacher replied, looking to Layna. "No doubt she learned so quickly from your expertise."

"Oh, yeah, of course," a taken aback Layna timidly nodded, not in the least bit ashamed to take credit for something she didn't do. "You really owe me one, Kasra!"

"Huh, sure," the violette huffed and raised an eyebrow at her. Teacher Xanne was tempted to do the same, but crossed her arms instead. "There is no reason to make deals with your fellow novitiates," she warned. "Your intentions as a priestess are to remain altruistic, even when called upon by others."

"I know that!" Layna groaned and rolled her eyes. "Nobody can understand my sense of humor!" She playfully shoved Kasra's shoulder. "You know I was just kidding."

As much as Kasra wanted to push Layna back and say "no, I didn't," she retained her air of quiet dignity and played the role of the stronger person in Xanne's presence. Thankfully, the Teacher came to Kasra's defense by saying exactly what was on the vixy's mind. "I don't believe she's known you well enough by now for you to be joking with her in that manner."

"Whatever," the teen tossed her head with a shrug. "Can I start my chores now?"

"Yes, I suppose," Xanne muttered, sharing the novitiate's impatience. "You can weed the gardens. Any refuse plants you collect will be burned later. Kasra, you can collect any ripe frupoms you find from the orchard. Those will be shared at mealtime at dinner hour."

"Yes, Teacher Xanne," Kasra bowed, then shot a look at Layna, as if daring her to mock her politeness. While the vixy certainly seemed tempted, she refrained from her petulant behavior to go about her duties. Once Xanne had left the immediate vicinity, Kasra decided to check on Raia on her way to collect her basket. She found Raia near the courtyard's entrance, sitting on one of the benches outside in the shade. The look on her face was not of pain, as she expected it might've been, rather it showed a certain pensive guilt.

"Everything alright?" Kasra asked, sidling up to her friend.

Raia's demeanor seemed to turn a little more cheerful when she saw Kasra approach and sit down beside her. "I didn't mean to leave you out there, by yourselves. I just didn't want to be a part of the conversation anymore."

"I don't think they said anything about you," Kasra then immediately second guessed herself, as she tried to think back to something Raia could've been offended by.

"That's the problem," Raia replied, "they like to pretend I'm not here. Not just Lavelle and Tassie, but almost all the novitiates around here. I'm not very popular, as you can tell; they all avoid me like they do Layna, but I never did anything to them."

Kasra smiled. "You know why that is, don't you?" Raia quizzically glanced at her, but wasn't in the mood to guess. The violette continued, "They're intimidated by what you've accomplished. You're just two notches away from being a priestess, and you're younger than a lot of the other novitiates. They don't want to admit you're better than them, so they don't want to ask you for help."

"I feel bad for them, if that is the case," Raia sighed, staring at her knees. "They should be putting that kind of attitude aside if they want to be in the clergy, some day."

"I'm sure you've noticed it isn't as important to some as it is to others," Kasra winked, knowing exactly who both of them were thinking of when she said that. "You can tell the ones who were told to come here, apart from the ones who came of their own free will. The students who like this place will do well here. The ones who don't will eventually drop out."

Returning to her original point, Kasra added, "There's no reason to beat yourself up because you can't be everyone's friend. What use do you have for apathetic fools like them, anyway? The only thing they're good for is slowing others down and convincing winners to quit. People who are serious about making something of themselves will come to you like a light in the darkness."

Raia laughed. Not because she had never been given a pep-talk before, but because the way Kasra said it made sense to her. "You know, Layna told me something like that when we first met. I only listened because she was the only one who wanted to talk to me. But as I've gotten to know her, all those things she said I've come to realize was just her cajoling me to be her friend. I can't take any of it seriously anymore. But you're different; I know your heart is in another place than hers. The background she wants everyone to think she has -- you actually lived it. While Layna is trying to turn me into her worshiper, I can actually admire you, Kasra."

"Awh, gee," a clearly flattered Kasra batted her eyes and sheepishly turned. "You're way too nice to me, Raia," she curled her tail around her legs.

"You say it like it's a bad thing," the brunette poked her friend's puckered cheek. "I just treat people in a way that would make my father proud." Upon that remark, Kasra's once bright smile turned to a puzzled frown, as she started imagining what kind of home life Raia had -- that she was missing out on. Kasra didn't even want to think about what she'd have to do to that would be worthy of her parents' praise.

Xanne then broke the collective silence by uttering an announcement to her class that their break time was over. She asked that they all gather in the vacant meridian separating one half of the orchard from the other. She organized the students in two equal teams for what she called a 'fygidia relay race.' "You can only progress toward the designated finish line by teleporting to the person ahead of you," the Teacher explained. "It is a great test of your quickness with the intonation and your focus under pressure. The finish line is the temple wall, over there," she pointed to the other side of the orchard. "You must touch it with your hand, then teleport back to your last teammate to complete the full lap."

Just to avoid any potential tricks, Kasra was placed in the team opposite of Raia and Layna. But Layna only saw it as an opportunity to outdo her classmate. They just so happened to be at the end of their respective lines; they shot each other challenging glares as they awaited the game to begin. Raia was the first of Layna's line, and she gave her team a great headstart with her nearly perfect reflexes when Xanne signaled for the race to start.

She tagged Lavelle, who then teleported to tag Tassie ahead of her, then six students later, Layna felt a tap on her shoulder from the student preceding her. She shot a quick glimpse at Kasra, who had been tagged a mere half second after her, and watched with shock as the violette beat her to the wall of the temple. She tagged the wall of Sachelvae with a slap while Layna gave it a kick from about two paces back, giving her just the extra step ahead she needed to tag the last student in line simultaneously with Kasra.

Layna and Kasra watched with bated breath their teammates teleport down their lines until Lavelle's hand touched Raia's back. It was truly too close to tell who came in first place, but Layna immediately assumed herself the victor. "I win!" She ebulliently jumped, shamelessly taking all the credit for herself.

"You mean 'we,' Layna," came the derisive retort of one of her classmates.

"How do you even know Raia was tagged first?!" Kasra squeaked.

Before an argument could break out, Xanne interposed herself between the squabbling students and reminded them, "There are no prizes for this competition; there is no need to fight over who won and who lost. I'd say both teams performed very well; the balance of speed between them was virtually even."

"Laaame!" Layna cried out. "What was the point of teaming us against each other if there was no reason for winning or losing?"

"It is easier to see who is faltering in their exercises when I can observe the performances of smaller groups, as opposed to a single large one," Xanne explained. "These prize-giving competitions you're referencing are creations of the Safiric Brotherhood. It is Safiro's will to pit belhuayns against each other. Sanguina wishes for solidarity; indeed, we are much stronger when we act as one rather than when we are divided."

"Oh come *on*," Layna once again voiced her displeasure. "Is *that* the moral of this activity?"

"Yes," Xanne tersely responded. "As a priestess, you will not always be working with those of your convent; at the time of a Crusade, you might group with members of other temples across the land. You can't succeed in working toward a common goal if you are more concerned with working against your peers. The Safiric Brotherhood knows when a Sister is weak in her faith and she will be the first they prey on."

This time Layna had no further remarks to make; Xanne took this as a good sign and encouraged, "Let's continue with today's games. Now that we've had a fast-paced fygidia race, I want us to have a similar exercise using our masalidas."

Inspired by the game she had seen Lavelle and Tassie playing yesterday, she said, "I want you to line up the way you were before, only this time in a zigzag orientation. I will toss this rubber ball, and you will have to deflect it to the person behind you, until it has reached the back of the line. If I see a group drop the ball midway through, they will have to start over until they get it right."

Scanning the uncertain expressions of her students, Xanne asked, "Is everything making sense so far?"

"Of course, Teacher Xanne," Raia bowed, just to earn the jealous glares of everyone around her.

"I am not surprised you would make ease of my instructions," Xanne smiled at her top student. "Perhaps if anyone in your group falters, you will be able to correct them for me?" With that, Teacher Xanne commenced her game of touchless hot potato and saw that during the process, only two students in either group dropped any of the projectiles as they were being passed down the jagged lines. Understandably, these mistakes were made toward the beginning of the game and were corrected after a couple tries.

To mix things up and add some difficulty to the training session, Xanne increased her pace with tossing the rubber missiles at her students; there would be two passing through the lines at once, or one even thrown into the middle just to try and ruin their rhythm. She never ran out of these projectiles because she was always able to teleport the ones she had thrown back into her hand. Once their practice had been perfected to the point that, no matter how she tried to shake things up, neither team dropped a ball, Xanne was satisfied.

"I'm very impressed with you all!" The Teacher proudly stated, as her students tiredly panted and puffed air through their dresses. Even Xanne, herself, was breaking a bit of a sweat. "You may rest yourselves in the shade of the orchard, and you may each have a drink from the well," she motioned thither, as she went to the stone structure. She cranked the lever for the giant rope pulley to bring a full bucket of water from the bottom of the reservoir to the surface. Inside was a ladle, and around the well was a table built like a semicircle, full of wooden drinking cups.

She used the ladle to pour an equal amount of water for all her students to drink, allowing them to take a break in the shade. Many were happy to just sit down in for a moment, but some had gotten the keen idea to use light koptigma blasts to free frupoms from the tops of the trees and have themselves a snack, too.

Meanwhile, Rozha and Kyrana had just arrived in Mediona on missions of their own. Rozha proudly sauntered her way down the golden avenue, passing by tents and tables on either side of her, whilst listening to the funny music of the lone street performer who had been frequenting Mediona so long, he was pretty much a part of the scenery anymore. She never asked for the scelan's name, but she knew every time he was near.

He wore colorful clothes like those of a court jester and was commonly seen with an odd instrument that looked like a cross between a harp and a guitar. The melodies he played were always fun and inspired people to donate some coin as they infectiously danced on by. Even Rozha found herself in a good enough mood to drop some divitias into his bowl. *'Why not? I've got the money to blow, now.'* She still wanted to make sure that she had enough to pay for her replacement weapon, and there would be no skimping on quality with this one.

She heard of Mediona's famous blacksmith, Reaventyr, who had been running his shop for at least 20 years. She never had much of a reason to head in his direction, which happened to be on the southernmost edge of town. From this end of Mediona, travellers could leave Tresantia and head toward the outer-lying farmland. Even from where she was, she could see the verdant, colorful hills of patchwork fields rolling toward the horizon.

The farmers would typically use this entrance when bringing in their wagons full of goods to sell during harvest season. It wasn't quite the time for harvest yet, but there were still some perennial goods, such as meat cuts, that would inevitably find their way to Mediona at about this hour. Lunch time was nigh, so that meant plenty of hungry, working customers coming to look for something to eat before they went about their business.

Rozha walked by plenty of them as she pursued the sounds of a hammer banging on steel. In the distance, she could see a stout, gray-skinned scelan slouched over an anvil, repeatedly striking an unfinished slab of metal. Each strike of his sledge slowly shaped the hot alloy to his will. When the metal lump began to turn a darker shade of red, he lifted it with a pair of tongs and placed it back into a white-hot furnace belching with fire. Standing behind him, like the mouth of a cave, was the doorway to his workshop -- a rectangular, stone building full of tools and probably a shelf of finished items.

The scelan of a long, scraggly beard hadn't even noticed Rozha until he turned away from his forge. The aged man swiped a hairy arm across his sweat-soaked brow and managed a grin that looked more like a pained grimace to greet her approach. "G'mornin' t'ya!" he beckoned her over.

"How can I be of service t'ya, lass?" The way he talked made it sound like he had coughed on his fair share of black smoke.

Rozha couldn't keep herself from smiling back at him. Even though he was of Safiric blood, she could detect a peacefulness in his eyes, unlike the innkeeper she met the night before. "Well, if you happen to be Reaventyr, I might have a job for you to do."

"That I be," the gruffly-voiced scelan nodded, brushing a hand across his balding head. "Bladesmithin' be my trade, but I've got a staff workin' in the back who're experienced goldsmiths, gem cutters, and even trap-tinkerers if that strikes yer fancy."

"Bladesmithing, you say?" an intrigued Rozha rocked on her heels, as if she hadn't heard the rest of what the man said. "What can you make for about, hmm…" the blade dancer raised a bag full of coin, as if trying to guess the amount inside, "Five hundred gold divitias?"

"Five *hundred?*" Reaventyr's squinted eyes widened. He began chuckling as if he didn't believe her, at first, then turned around to pull his hot metal from out of the forge. "Fer that, fair lass, I'd get ya a sword fer an *Emperor.*"

"Sold!" Rozha threw the bag of money his way. With reflexes unlike anything he had in his youth, Reaventyr snatched the bag from the air while at the same time nearly dropping the hot metal on his feet. Had it not been for his quick, untried juggling technique, the old scelan might've finally felt what it was like for his grandfather to have lost his middle toe. Reaventyr cast her a glare that was on the verge of shouting at her, but he couldn't be mad if the payment she mentioned was actually inside the brown sack of cloth.

He laid down his tongs as he glanced between her and the bag of coins, so that he could untie the string keeping it closed and peer inside. He was met with the most sunlit gold he'd ever seen in one place -- many embossed portraits of Emperor Iminsun imperiously stared back at him.

"I'll be honest with ya," the nearly breathless blacksmith said, "I've been doin' this twenty five years and I've *never* had someone pay me so much for one thing. What I said I won't rescind; I will make ye the very best sword I've ever made. I'll even put this one," he minded the hot steel on his anvil, "on hold til I've finished yers." His eyes then regained their squint, if not with a bit of suspicion, as he thoughtfully scratched his beard. "Now, I'd never normally be questionin' a customer, 'specially not one payin' so nicely… but I'd ask what a priestess would want with a weapon like this."

Rozha looked down at herself, as if only then remembering that she was wearing her sacerdotal gown. "What, you think I *stole* this money?!" came her Freudian slip. Judging by Reaventyr's slight recoil and the raising of his brow, she realized she must've sounded a bit defensive with her remark. She toned herself down when she added, "If you must know, I was sent on a mission to have a masterly-crafted sword be made that was fit for blessing."

"Ahh," Reaventyr nodded, her persuasive lie having earned his belief. "You goin' on some kinda crusade, priestess?"

"I cannot give too many details," Rozha replied, her demeanor undaunted by her practiced falsehoods. "I can only tell you what I have said, up to now."

"I've served Sachelvae since b'fore Diava was a Mother," Reaventyr proudly replied. "It'll be me honor to make a masterpiece of m'trade fer them."

"You knew Mother Diava *that* long ago?" Rozha asked. "You hardly look a day over 50!"

Reaventyr chuckled, slightly flattered by the blade dancer's accidental compliment. "We Lasuisians don't age like other belhuayns. I've done my *trade* over 50 years." The blacksmith's smile then turned more inquisitive, as if he had seen Rozha somewhere before. "While I haven't *personally* crafted all the tail rings fer holy vows, I do remember many that've commissioned my shop over the years. Yer Rozha, aren't ye?" He smirked, "Yes, it was hard for me to recognize ye at first, but I couldn't forget those devious eyes o' yers."

"Devious?" Rozha frowned. "What do you mean?"

Reaventyr laughed again, "Well if mem'ry serves, yer vow had somethin' to do with tellin' the truth. Mother Diava seemed t'think ye were quite the rabblerouser."

The blade dancer smirked and looked at her feet, ashamed of the memories that brought her such scorn. "That was almost two years ago, now. I've changed a lot since then."

Perhaps it was due to the age difference, but the way Reaventyr heard it, it sounded like Rozha was trying to convince herself more than she was trying to convince him. He could see hardly more than a young kid standing in front of him -- whether she had that battle-hardened stare or not. He simply acknowledged her statement, then decided it was time to go about his work. "Well, priestess, I wish my best o'luck to ye, and yer secret mission. Come back at about this time one week from now, and I might have somethin' special to show ye."

"Ah, you test my patience, good sir," Rozha jokingly replied, with a respectful bow. "I can hardly wait to see what you will do. Thank you for your business!" No sooner did the blade dancer turn on her heels than did she see Kyrana's unmistakable figure standing across the way. The Arch Healer seemed to be speaking with a nice-looking and quite fashionable middle-aged scelan, alongside a kid who appeared to be his teenage son. The two were running a kiosk, selling some produce they had brought from their farm.

Judging by the looks of the boy's father, he must've been the farm's owner. Rozha could tell the rancher wasn't comfortable in those dapper clothes he was wearing; it was like he was trying too hard to look professional and stately.

Even though Rozha couldn't hear what they were saying from the distance at which she stood from them, the way they carried on with Kyrana was as if they had met, before. Feeling that it wouldn't be too terribly intrusive to introduce herself, Rozha sidled up to the Arch Healer and made her presence known with a pat on her back. "Hey there, Kyrana! Fancy crossing paths with you, here!"

"We walked to Mediona *together*, remember?" Kyrana embarrassedly hissed, staring down her acquaintance.

Pretending that she didn't hear her, Rozha motioned toward the nurse's friends, "Who're these fine gentlemen you're speaking with?"

Believing it proper to introduce themselves, the rancher started first, "My name is Drathnifere, and this is my son, Malkinos. I am the owner of Bryotte Farm, down the nine mile road outside town," he casually pointed in that general direction. "My hired help and I toiled for months to bring before you this season's harvest: fresh qinchao herbs and hakota seeds. Both can be used for special teas and various recipes, making them very valuable to many buyers."

"I was very interested in the qinchao, myself," Kyrana stated, "for the very reason he mentioned. At Sachelvae's pantry, I have access to many other ingredients and reagents that I can use to complete medicines to share with the Laeyudi people."

"And flaunting the old priestess charm to get a discount I see?" Rozha indicatively winked, earning the most offended look she had seen from the Arch Healer yet.

"I beg your pardon?!..." Kyrana had to keep herself from causing a scene in front of Drathnifere and Malkinos, who were clearly entertained by the blade dancer's barbs.

"Well, I do have to say," Drathnifere began, "her charm comes quite naturally."

The nurse paused for thought when she saw the rancher beaming so kindly at her. *'Perhaps he was just being nice?'* Certainly he had to be married to have children. No Pure would have started a family without The Mother's blessing. She didn't need to concern herself with such things, anyway; a servant of Sanguina needn't such diversions in her life. Even still, she was tempted to check his hands for any rings -- which she could've done if they weren't currently hidden in the pockets of his jacket.

"I'd give her what she wanted for free," the glittery-eyed Malkinos added, then caught his father's disapproving glare out of the corner of his eye. "Who are we to profit off of the Sister's holy mission?"

Seeing that the boy acted like he had a crush on her, too, put the nurse's mind at ease. *'Maybe casual flirtation just ran in the family?'* "If I wanted to be a better sweet-talker, I'd take some lessons from you two, first," the successfully beguiled Kyrana smiled. With attention to Drathnifere's son, she remarked, "You could make a girlfriend jealous with such blandishments."

Malkinos shyly chuckled, "Maybe one day."

"I am surprised a boy your age wouldn't be looking more often," Kyrana verbally prodded, "especially when you live so close to Sachelvae. There are plenty of girls living in the temple."

"I know," Malkinos nodded, "my sister is one of them."

"Is she?" Kyrana asked. "What's her name? I probably know who she is."

When Malkinos gave the answer, the nurse wondered why she didn't see the resemblance sooner. "Her name is Raia. She's been a novitiate for about a year, now."

"How interesting!" Kyrana cooed. "She never told me she was raised on Bryotte Farm. She probably just didn't want to draw attention to herself... How long has it been since you've last seen her?"

"Oh gosh," Malkinos thought back, "it's been since the last Sevasmus, I think."

"That was several months ago, now," the nurse feigned a gasp. "Certainly she'd like to see you again! This is about the time she and the other novitiates would be doing their chores in the courtyard. We never normally let guests into the temple when Mother Diava is not there, but I would gladly be your escort if you'd wish to visit Raia."

Malkinos couldn't tell which mental image brought more heat to his face: the chance at getting to enjoy a long walk with Kyrana, or getting to see a bevy of beauties playing around outside, afterward. Obviously, this called for some careful deliberation. He could just feel his father smiling at him from behind, but he didn't want to make it conspicuous that he was going to enjoy it so much. "Umm... Okay!" his tail nervously coiled around his ankles.

"Don't be gone too long," Drathnifere reminded his son, waving him off as Malkinos began walking away. "You'll have to be back in time for us to return home."

With her eyebrow raised and her arms calculatingly crossed, Rozha stood there like she was still analyzing what she had just witnessed. She honestly couldn't wait to see where Kyrana's game of match-maker was going to lead. But she couldn't simply depart without properly addressing her new acquaintance. "It was good to meet you, Mr. Drathnifere," Rozha gave him one of her unrefined bows. "But my business in Mediona has come to a close. I am needed back at Sachelvae."

"Well met, indeed, Sister," Drathnifere replied. "I would be remissed if I did not know your name, however."

"It's Rozha," the blade dancer smiled. "I'm soon to be Sachelvae's newest Teacher."

"Is that so?" the impressed rancher poised akimbo. "Well I'll be praying for your continued success, then."

"Thanks!" Rozha chirped. She looked in the direction of Sachelvae, and suddenly remembered she hadn't stopped for any lunch yet, since she arrived in Mediona. "Maybe I can have something for the road?" she asked, pointing at Drathnifere's kiosk.

"Sure," the rancher chuckled. "Take some hakota seeds; they make excellent trail rations."

"Sounds good!" Rozha gathered up a small sack full of the aforementioned victuals. "I'll have to stop by again, if I see you around."

"It'll take me another couple of weeks to sell everything I've stored up, this season," Drathnifere said, "but what I'm really waiting for is lakusha season to roll around -- that's when I make my big profit to hold me over through the winter."

"I see," Rozha nodded. "Must be how you made your fortune, huh?"

"Lakusha plants were native to the more temperate regions of Onteval, west of the central swamps," Drathnifere explained. "They only grew in soil that was neither too arid nor too moist; the consistency had to be just right.

Tresantia is special in the sense that its soil is unlike the rest of central Onteval; the wetlands out here aren't fit for lakushas, but something about this one spot of land is different."

He frowned as he paused for thought. "It really is a strange thing; there's no reason for this one valley to be so different from the rest of the climate, here. If anything, its elevation would suggest an even wetter ground than the area around it. Instead, these fields are famous for producing crops of all kinds. *Anyone* could make a fortune out here, if they knew the right stuff to import."

Ever since she moved into Sachelvae, Rozha had heard from not only Mother Diava, but everyone else who lived there how wonderful the city was. After spending so long traversing the slums of most any small town she came across, none of which were as prosperous as this metropolis, she had to agree -- there really was something exceptional about it. The Sachelvians would have her believe that it was all due to Saint Sevasmia that Tresantia turned out the way it did, but Rozha couldn't help but think that wasn't the whole reason. She looked over yonder, to the Safiric side of town, to see the tall angles of Travestas' roof poking out over the twisted towers. "It takes a little bit of both to make things work," she thought out loud.

"Both?" Drathnifere curiously tilted his ear. "Of what?"

"Fertile lands and the knowledge of what to grow in them," Rozha replied. "Things don't prosper in a place they're not meant to grow. Indeed, what good is a fertile land if it has nothing to provide?"

The rancher may not have been the most insightful scelan, but even he could tell that there was something deeper than crops and soil on the blade dancer's mind. He chose not to pry, however; he didn't know her long enough to be asking such personal matters. Besides, he hadn't much time to wonder what she was thinking about, before his next batch of customers showed up. By the time he greeted the newcomers and watched them examine his wares, Rozha had departed.

'She isn't like most of the bright-eyed priestesses at the temple,' Drathnifere thought. *'What's she doing in Sachelvae?'*

Chapter 15: Matchmaker

With a purse-like bag full of fresh produce acquired from Drathnifere's store, Kyrana left Mediona with Malkinos, listening to the boy palavering about his life on his father's farm. He seemed to be proud of himself, especially in how strong he had gotten from his years of fieldwork. Building fences and stables for the animals, as well as tossing around bales of feed for the livestock was not a small person's work, after all. He knew quite a bit about taking care of brown striders, Onteval's larger beasts of burden, as well as making sure the more prim black striders looked their best. "Mine even won a contest for 'Best in Show,' last year," he said.

Indeed, he went on to describe the yearly Harvest Festival that was famous around Mediona. It all started about a century ago on the ranches outside town, with arguments between farmers about who had the more prosperous fields or who had the strongest beasts. "Some say it was old Olkarn's grandfather who started the very first Harvest Festival," Malkinos explained. "He gloated to his neighbors that he had the biggest brown strider of them all -- it was over *twenty* feet tall! Or so the legend goes..."

Before Drathnifere settled there, it was said the last owner of his acreage once grew the tallest frupom tree in all the land. He was also told that if he found its stump, where the tree was eventually cut down, he could dig nearby and find all the wealth of its former resident. It didn't take long for Drathnifere and his family to realize this was a tall tale told by some of the farmers who didn't take kindly to 'newcomers.' "We've been here almost 17 years now, and Olkarn still asks us if we ever 'found that treasure,' yet."

"Ah, I see," Kyrana nodded, "a bit of a troublemaker, is he?"

"He doesn't trust people who haven't lived here as long as he has," Malkinos said. "His family's roots have been in Tresantia almost 200 years; we're all 'newcomers' to him."

'200 years, hm?' Kyrana thought. *'He might be a useful source of information if his family's had a history in this region that far back.'* "Well, it's too bad he isn't more friendly," she stated out loud. "Is he the one with the long, white beard and the straw hat I see about twice a year?"

Malkinos chuckled at her succinct, yet wholly accurate description. "Yep, that's him. He owns the biggest farm of anyone outside Tresantia. I think he said it was over 400 acres."

"Really?" an impressed Kyrana raised a brow. "An elderly gentleman like him must have a lot of help to tend to all that land."

"Of course, he isn't going about his business by himself," Malkinos replied. "But he tries to keep running the whole thing in the family. He's got an extensive range of relatives whom each have built houses to occupy their own swatch of his land. My father plans to expand his property in a similar fashion, when Raia or I get married and have families of our own."

Kyrana smiled. "You've still got a long way to go yet before you have to start worrying about that!" Then, realizing she'd never asked for his age, she indirectly did so by guessing, "You look barely sixteen, to me."

Malkinos dipped his head to hide his bashful blush and rubbed the back of his neck. "What gave it away?"

"The innocence in your eyes," the nurse shrugged. "That glint of youth can shine through even the hardest of hearts. I've seen many different kids from many different backgrounds in my time at Sachelvae; I've come to recognize a fair amount of unique personalities among them. Even when they become accepted into the clergy, I can still tell they haven't totally left who they were as novitiates behind."

Gazing up at the impressive edifice of Sachelvae looming before them, its entrance just a few more steps away, Malkinos sighed, "It's too bad they don't let boys into the Sisterhood. I'd like to learn the kind of stuff that Raia does."

"It isn't entirely true that the Sanguinic Sisterhood omits members of the opposite gender," Kyrana explained. "Sachelvae is a boarding school that has it firmly written in its tenets that females have an inherent closeness to our Goddess, because She made us veltas and vixies in Her image. This isn't to say that males are incapable of empathizing with Mother, but they do so at a much slower rate, and maturity has a lot to do with it. There are other boarding schools for the Sisterhood that are male-only, but I am not familiar with any particular ones."

"How come they can't co-mingle?" Malkinos asked, with all the naivete in the world.

Kyrana chuckled and put it lightly, "The clergy believes that this 'mingling' would cause unnecessary distractions for our students, studying their duties. Indeed, this lack of mixture creates a more focused atmosphere. Members of the Sisterhood can still talk to boys, of course, so long as it remains outside temple grounds." Walking her guest inside Sachelvae's open doors, the Arch Nurse added, "but for this one meeting, I will make an exception."

Malkinos was taken aback, his eyes full of wonderment as they gazed upon the historic architecture of Sachelvae's interior. He had the same kind of reaction one would have of coming to a famous place they had only seen in books, and told of in tales. He was fascinated by the sheer size of the Purifier Hall, and in awe of the crystalline waters, themselves. He could see the marble tile shimmer beneath the reflective, almost glassy surface. He admired the tapestries hanging on the walls, as he walked betwixt the columns, depicting Saint Sevasmia and the Goddess Sanguina.

Kyrana smiled at her whimsical guest and waited for him to rejoin her at the next corridor. "Try not to tarry too long, now," her voice echoed across the way. "There are some areas of the temple that are off limits to visitors. If Mother Diava has any reason to suspect I might've let you see them, I'd be in big trouble."

"Sorry, Sister," Malkinos called back, walking to her side. "Raia's told me so much about this place; I just lost myself when I got to see it all for the first time."

"I understand," Kyrana graciously replied. "But this won't be your only time to enjoy Sachelvae's sights; you and your father both will be invited to come to Raia's induction to the priestesshood."

Malkinos' eyebrows raised as he fought his weakening jaw to turn agape. "Are you saying that Raia is going to be a priestess, soon?!"

"I have full confidence that she will not be a novitiate forever," Kyrana amended with a laugh. "I cannot make promises as to when Mother Diava will feel that your sister has done all she can as a student. But when that decision arises and the faculty are called to a vote, Raia will certainly have mine. She has all the graces of someone who has the Goddess' favor. It wouldn't even surprise me if she became a healer, one day."

"No way..." Malkinos' eyes turned alight, almost unable to imagine Raia looking as stately as Kyrana. Suddenly feeling unimpressive by comparison, he added, "Y'know, my dad says I'll be the owner of his ranch when he's no longer able to run it."

"Seems that you both have some very bright futures ahead of you," Kyrana nodded. "I always look forward to see what someone will make of themselves when they come through those doors for the first time. I know it's not nice to make predictions of where a novitiate will end up, but the longer I've been here, the more accurate my secret assertions have been." She sighed, "sometimes I don't like being right."

Malkinos could tell that she was thinking of someone in particular when she said that. He even had a feeling he knew who it might've been, but chose not to delve any further into the matter. He was having fun with

Kyrana's company and didn't want to ruin it by bringing up something depressing like that.

He wouldn't know what to say to cheer her up, anyway; she didn't look like she'd have Raia's sense of humor. He was admittedly intimidated by her gentleness; she had that presence about her that made him feel like he had to act like more than what he was to be worth her time. But she spoke to him not with an imperious tone, but in a much more inviting manner that simply had him feeling conflicted -- as if he *should* be able to approach her, but was too unsure of himself.

He found himself silenced by his inability to level with her, and was so for long enough during their walk around Sachelvae's halls that Kyrana began to notice it as well. "You're being rather quiet, all of a sudden," she said.

"I, um, I was just looking at the paintings," he stammered out a likely excuse, albeit in truth, he had barely noticed the framed pictures on the walls. "They're all beautiful," he added a cursory observation, before he tried to make a more judgmental one. "Some of them look older than others."

"Some of these paintings go back to the founding of Sachelvae," Kyrana explained. "Some of them depict the lands as they were before Tresantia was built around the temple. We keep them as a visual record of the temple's history. Teacher Wanystha was appointed by Mother Diava a few years ago to continue this tradition. It was she who made all the portraits of the current faculty, and is now in the process of creating a collage -- one landscape for each season of this year. Once her time capsule is completed, in another decade, we might have another artist to do her work all over again."

"Every ten years, you have a new faculty?" Malkinos asked. "What about the High Priestess?"

"The High Priestess serves until her passing," Kyrana replied, "but yes, almost every decade, some students become priestesses and some priestesses become Teachers. Most members of the current faculty got their start as an assistant to their predecessors. I was the assistant of then-Arch Healer Diava before she was appointed as our High Priestess."

"Do all Arch Healers become High Priestesses?" came Malkinos' next question.

"I certainly hope that is the case!" Kyrana chuckled. "A High Priestess must have special credentials in order to be appointed. She must have a mastery of all Sanguinic magic and an exceptional understanding of her own providence, but doesn't necessarily need to possess a healer's touch."

Tempted to roll her eyes, she added, "We can't *all* be Saint Sevasmia in the flesh."

"Is that what a High Priestess is meant to be?" Malkinos was even more impressed by these heightened standards.

'That's what Mother Diava thinks she is,' Kyrana thought to herself, then uncomfortably frowned; if Mother Diava really was listening in on her, she could expect to hear from the High Priestess, later. "Perhaps she didn't want people's perception of Saint Sevasmia to change," she settled for a kinder explanation. "After all, the tenets of the Sanguinic Sisterhood were based upon Saint Sevasmia's practices."

Even though this metaphysical macrocosm was well beyond the farm boy's head, Malkinos vacantly nodded, as if understanding the situation to some degree. Now it was she who remained taciturn, as the weight of her guilt slowed her footsteps. But she had what little grace was owed to her left, to finally arrive at the last corridor of Sachelvae. The hallway ahead of them featured a rounded roof and an arch-like door, framed by flowered vines to indicate the entrance to the courtyard.

The door was open and the twilight sun pouring in made the rest of the chambers behind them seem dreary by comparison. Malkinos smiled, his tail wagging behind him as he watched the quiet winds rustle the trees outside. As he caught glimpses of the young novitiates walking about the orchard, he was nearly overcome with the excitement to go running out there with them. The only thing that kept him from giving in to his natural temptation was Kyrana standing beside him -- and the curious baskets of fruit lining the walls.

"What're all those sitting there, for?" Malkinos pointed at the freshly-harvested frupoms.

"Teacher Xanne must have decided for them to pick from the trees after class," Kyrana surmised. "Novitiates are always given chores to do around the temple while the priestesses go on their missions."

As Malkinos and Kyrana were just about to step into the doorway, they narrowly avoided a collision with Kasra, whose figure was silhouetted by the light behind her. "I'm sorry--!" her apologetic squeak was truncated when she laid eyes on the curious sceli that Kyrana was standing with. Her heart jumped slightly when she saw his comely face, and had a hard time breaking the silence between them when it made her think all the more about the condition she was in. Wringing her hands around her basket's handle, Kasra breathed a quiet "Hi," like she had never seen a teenage sceli before.

"Hi," Malkinos blinked back at her, his mind immediately drawing a blank for anything flattering to say to her. "You're, um… you're not Raia." Right after that awkward stutter, the sceli felt his stomach sink. *'Good going,'* he beat himself up. *'If she wasn't taken by **that** response, what else would have worked?'*

"Nope," the violette shook her head, too dumbstruck to notice the boy's mistake. "My name's Kasra. Are you Raia's brother?"

"Yes, that's me," he smiled, "Malkinos. Nice to meet you."

"Likewise," Kasra nervously shifted on her heels. Setting her basket aside, she pointed a thumb over her shoulder and said, "We're all working out there, right now. I can take you to Raia if you wanna see her."

"Sure," Malkinos followed her outside. As soon as he stepped through the doorway, he was stopped by Teacher Xanne. "Um, *excuse* me," the velta confronted her intruder. "Who *are* you?" Malkinos' heart leapt into his throat as he turned, beckoning for Kyrana to save him.

"I'm sorry I didn't inform you of this, earlier," the Arch Healer emerged, rubbing the communication ring between her fingers. "I met Raia's brother at Mediona when I was running errands, earlier. He said he'd like to visit his sister, so I didn't see any harm in letting him in the courtyard for just the afternoon."

Teacher Xanne sighed with a disapproving frown. "You know what Mother Diava would say if she were here," she crossed her arms, her politeness tested by a brow-furrowing irritation.

"I know," Kyrana nodded. "But I only did this because I knew you wouldn't make a big deal of it. Besides, Malkinos is a fellow Pure; he won't get into any mischief."

Glancing between her and Malkinos' blameless if not sheepish grin, Xanne replied, "Alright, but you might want to explain this to Sister Cinte. She's here as well, keeping an eye on Layna."

"I'll stick with him, don't worry," the nurse said. Turning to Malkinos, she added, "Shall we continue our visit?" Without any further objections, Kyrana followed him as Kasra led them to see Raia, at the tree that they had left off. Of course, having Malkinos around was attracting the attention of all the novitiates passing by, but seeing him being escorted by Kyrana had them keeping their distance.

Kasra's destination was somewhere near the back of the grove; her company began to see the wall behind the trees when they could all hear Layna's voice cursing Kasra's name. "What, did she get *lost* over there?! It doesn't take *that* long to put a basket away!"

This aggravated hissing was followed by a sigh from Raia, who rolled her eyes at just the moment Kasra was coming around the corner. "Malkinos!" The young brunette threw her arms around her big brother the minute she saw him. "What're you doing here?"

"Kyrana let me come see you," Malkinos tousled Raia's hair. "I wasn't gonna say no, even if it might get me kicked out!"

"Aww~" Raia stood on her toes to teasingly nuzzle his cheek. "Are you starting to miss me?..."

"Yeah," Malkinos smirked. "Ever since you left, dad's been pushing me a lot harder on the farm!"

"Oh, *that's* all it is?" the brunette cordially laughed, pushing him away from her. "You're such a wimp, needing a little vixy like *me* to lighten your load!"

"*Little* nothing!" he stared down his smaller sister. "You're practically half a man, yourself!"

"What's *that* supposed to mean?!" Raia shot back, whipping him in the side with her tail.

Reminded of the way she and her sibling would bicker, Kasra was too busy stifling her laughter to have a comment in either one's defense. It wasn't until an agitated Layna started shouting from the top of the tree did their playful squabbling cease. "Who are you *arguing* with down there?! Is that slacker back yet?" With a pitifully girlish shriek, the dark-haired vixy fell bottom-first onto the frupom tree's lowest branch, with a loud clash of rustling leaves. Malkinos was as surprised to see her popping in from out of nowhere as Layna was to see him standing there. "Uh, hey," the teenager's confidence began faltering.

"You were *saying?*..." Kasra tapped her foot with a testy smirk.

Picking a twig out of her hair and brushing a leaf from her bangs, Layna continued, "Yeah: what was *taking* you so long? You're not gonna tell me you stepped out just long enough to make a boyfriend."

Taking any excuse to get one up on Layna, Kasra glanced at Malkinos, who was offering nothing to the contrary, before saying, "Sure, if that's what it looks like to you."

"Puh," Layna sputtered out a chortle. "He can't be all that if he got into *you* so fast."

"Well, he's better than what *you've* got right now," Kasra fired another shot at her.

"Oh please," Layna dismissively laughed her off again. "I'm not gonna take the first hinterland tumbleweed chaser who throws himself at me --

sorry, Raia," she half-heartedly addressed her friend, who was not in the least bit willing to exempt her from offense. "I'm reserving myself for better stock."

"Let me know how that works out," Kasra snickered, feeling great to give the ill-tempered vixy a taste of her own medicine. She even held a rather uncomfortable Malkinos' hand and bumped her side against his arm to see Layna's expression change. The whole time, the poor sceli was wondering what he had gotten himself into. Kyrana, too, couldn't believe what she was seeing. Her innocent effort at trying to get Malkinos to meet a nice girl was falling apart like she never imagined it would. *'Why do they always go for the damaged ones?'* she inwardly sighed.

Shifting his eyes from place to place, unable to affix his gaze on Kasra or any particular person, Malkinos turned to the violette and said, "I didn't agree to be in a relationship with anyone! What's going on, here?"

Kasra was at a loss for words when she met his pleading stare -- anything she could have said was then interrupted by Layna's heckling. "Oh, this just gets better! Well, I see my work here is done; now he thinks you're a psycho! Serves you right!"

The angered violette jumped at Layna's legs dangling above her, threatening to pull her out of the tree and silence her guffaws. "Why don't you say that to my *face*, you coward?!" Layna nearly inadvertently obliged; she braced herself with her tail so she wouldn't go falling to the ground as she held her sides. "Yeah, that's right, come get me!"

"We don't need any of that," Kyrana chided. The nurse caught Kasra in an astapsyxi and teleported her back to her side. Turning to her guest, who had been thinking about backing out or even running away at that point, Kyrana said, "I'm sorry for getting you mixed up in all this, Malkinos. A nice boy like you deserves better."

"It's okay," he gave an uneasy grin midway toward a grimace, his tail curling around his ankle. "I think I'm ready to leave. I wouldn't want to overstay my welcome, here. Dad's been waiting for me to get back to him, anyhow."

Patting Malkinos' back, Raia apologized for her friends, as well. "I'm sorry about what happened -- I swear not everyone here is like them."

"I'll take that one as a compliment!" Layna interjected from afar.

"That's enough out of you," Kyrana reprimanded her. "You just get back to your work and mind your *own* business for a change."

"Fine. I would have been able to get a lot more done if Kasra were any quicker with getting that basket back over here," the dark-haired vixy complained. "So how about it?" she motioned toward her less-than-willing partner.

"Yeah, whatever," Kasra huffed, handing the basket up to her. *'I'm sure she's **so** proud of herself, right now,'* she derisively clicked her tongue, watching Malkinos and Raia walk away from her. *'The way she made a fool of me like that... That little brat knows she can only get away with her crap in here, where she's protected by everybody. I'd like to see her try me **outside** Sachelvae. I'll teach her to mess with me.'*

Albeit knowing that Kasra was brooding over what had just transpired, Kyrana had to leave her behind so that she could take Malkinos back through Sachelvae. She had to make sure he didn't lose himself in the halls anywhere; he needed to be gone before Mother Diava returned. While she went away to escort him back to Drathnifere, Raia regrouped with Kasra and Layna to play mediator, even though she was a bit frustrated with the both of them for scaring off Malkinos like that. *'Of all the people in the world who could have ruined such a sweet thing for me,'* she inwardly trailed off, trying not to let it bother her too much.

She did her utmost to concentrate on her chores until they were finished nearly an hour later. All the novitiates could have monitored the time by their empty stomachs; at just the time when everyone was starting to think about food -- some had already snacked on some frupoms -- Teacher Xanne called out to her students that dinner had been served. On their way to the dining hall and for all the time during their meal, nary a word was spoken among the usually chatter-filled trio. Raia, Kasra, and Layna still walked in line and sat by each other at the table, but there was an obvious tension between them that silenced the silly banter they were infamous for.

It wasn't until everyone was on their way to Wanystha's classroom did Raia pull Kasra aside to have a private word with her. "I need to talk to you," she finally broke the ice, "because it's all I've been thinking about since we came inside..." She took a breath to still her nerves, and began a hissed tirade with a shortly whispered prayer, "Mother forgive me, but, what the *hell* was that all about? I'd expect that kind of behavior from Layna, but I thought I could trust you. Why did you do that?"

The bottled anger Kasra could see behind Raia's eyes had her powerlessly mouthing the words she wished she could say. That stern look Raia gave her, and the hushed albeit forceful tone she used made her feel like no excuse would've been good enough. But like the fool she knew she'd been, she had to say something. "I'm sorry, Raia," she submissively slumped against the wall, trying to make herself look smaller to the shorter vixy. "Layna just... got under my skin. After how her sister hurt Rozha, I wanted to get back at her somehow."

"What do you mean?" Raia tipped her ear. "What did you see Viasarria do?"

"She and Rozha got into a fight yesterday," Kasra explained. "I didn't see the whole thing, but I saw the aftermath of it. They were about to start another brawl in the Purifier before Kyrana came and stopped them. It sickened me so much..."

The violette turned her head away and squinted shut her eyes, as if willing herself to forget what she had seen. "Layna reminds me too much of the kind of person Viasarria is. Viasarria wants her to hate me the same way she does Rozha. I saw the way she goaded my sister into fighting with her... it reminded me of the way my mother would insult us. She'd keep pushing us just so she could beat us down..."

The tensile strength of Raia's heart strings were brought to their limits by Kasra's story, but it wasn't enough to smooth over the raw edge of her pain. "I had no idea you've been through so much," she sniffled, trying to keep a tear from trickling down her cheek. "But you still hurt my feelings when you used Malkinos like that. I accept your apology... but it'd mean more if you explained the same to my brother, as well. He'll be staying in Mediona with my father for the rest of the week. While it is forbidden for novitiates to enter Mediona, they can do so if they are accompanied by a member of the clergy."

"Fair enough," Kasra shrugged. "I'll ask Rozha to take me down there tomorrow."

For the first time since their conversation began, Raia allowed herself to smile. "Thank you, Kasra," she sighed with a measured tone of relief.

Standing back upright, allowing herself to breathe, an equally elated Kasra replied, "I'm sorry, again, for offending you. I will set things right with Malkinos -- I didn't mean to hurt him. But I think it'll do me some good, too, if I avoided Layna for a while."

"Maybe," Raia laughed. "I think that's exactly what everyone else around here believes, too. I can't say I blame them; she does have an uncanny knack for getting on one's nerves... But I don't think she means to, half the time. I think she's bitter because she wasn't accepted right away, so she seeks to hurt everyone else's feelings before they can hurt her..." *'At least, that would have been fine if that was really the case,'* Raia confidentially added.

"There's no harm in wanting to be someone's ray of sunshine," Kasra said, "Just don't delude yourself into thinking you're the only one who can help them."

Raia had to pause for thought at that one. What she said virtually summed up how she considered her friendship with Layna. She was almost tempted to ask why Kasra saw that 'delusion' as so reprehensible, before the violette began walking to Wanystha's classroom. "We really should get going," the violette beckoned her to come with. "I don't know how many more times they're going to excuse us for being late."

Although they hadn't been holding up the works for very long, the impatient Layna was starting to notice a trend in their absences and she was growing weary of it. All this did was give her ample time to sulk up some nasty ideas in her mind. *'So she wants to start something with me, huh? She doesn't give me any credit at all. Alright, I'll show her why she should revere me.'*

Chapter 16: Making Amends and Making Enemies

Kasra refused to speak at all to Layna during Wanystha's history lecture, much less acknowledge her existence, even though she was only in the second seat over from Raia. There was still that lingering, cold tension between them from before. The rest of the students were doubtlessly happy that they didn't have to hear Layna's whispered snickers underneath Wanystha's preachings, but the Teacher was the only one in the classroom who was concerned about their lack of dialogue. She could tell by the way they avoided looking at each other that there was something going on, but she didn't know what. It wasn't enough to cause her complete suspicion, yet, but after having been told by Cinté what happened last evening, she couldn't let her guard down.

"You know well by now that the Safiric half of Tresantia was made to be a perversion of our own," Wanystha's teachings continued. "It was built this way as a mockery of the sacred city Sevasmia founded. Everything we do here, the Safiric Brotherhood orders be done in reverse on their own side, in their own image. They do this to copy our prosperity while refusing to be a part of it. This is why we must *stay together*," she emphasized her words, casting a critical gaze at Kasra and her troubled friends.

"Solidarity is imperative to all Pures if we wish to survive in a world that is hostile to our well-being. We have separated much since the fall of the Great Civilization; as we have found, and continue to find, more and smaller differences among us that further keep us apart, we may never be whole again. But it is important that we breach divides with our faith and unite others with our beliefs. No matter how 'different' we are from each other, spiritually we are all children of Sanguina -- we all seek the same thing."

Her ad-libbed statement succeeded in resonating more strongly with the portion of the audience she indirectly targeted. Feeling a tinge of guilt seeping in from the Teacher's poignantly chosen words, Raia was the first to glance between Kasra and Layna, subsequently drawing their eyes toward her and begrudgingly at each other. Both Kasra and Raia could tell, by the unwavering frown on Layna's face, that she still had no compunction to change her attitude. She felt like she had done nothing wrong and wasn't going to apologize.

To that day, Raia had never heard Layna utter the word "sorry" for anything, unless it was said in a blatantly sarcastic tone. There were times she thought reproach was beyond the troublemaker; she'd never once been seen asking for Sanguina's blessings nor forgiveness. But every time they sat in the Purifier, no darkness ever came off her. Even Diava was not free of sin; why was Layna somehow exempt? Had Sanguina *Herself* given up on her?

That look Layna gave Kasra when Raia drew their eyes to meet, for that split second, was not of a kind Raia had seen tainting her countenance before. Layna's regular, smug cheerfulness was replaced by a stone-hard contemn. Her odd quietness was all the more foreboding; Layna was rarely at a loss for words. Raia feared what she might do in a situation where deriding someone was no longer working in her favor. She knew this ire was directed at Kasra, but couldn't determine wherefore. Layna had been seemingly very successful in making Kasra regret she ever met her, while also making her time at Sachelvae as unpleasant as possible. *'What else did she want to get out of the poor thing?'*

If Layna could truly hear Raia's thoughts, she wasn't keen on answering any of her friend's curious contemplations. She might not have even been listening -- she definitely was not paying attention to what Wanystha was saying anymore, but that wasn't really anything new. Instead, she retained that frigid demeanor of hers, like a captain watching the advances of an enemy army.

Kasra meanwhile seemed oblivious to this possible plotting, and Raia wanted to make sure that she informed her friend about it when Wanystha's class was over. While all the students were making their way to their sleeping quarters, Raia once again stopped Kasra when she caught her away from prying eyes and out of earshot of anyone else. "I have a bad feeling about Layna," she started. "I don't know what she's thinking, but I know it's nothing good. I don't want you to get hurt, Kasra, that's why I'm warning you."

"You think she wants to pick a fight, huh?" Kasra poised akimbo, channeling her inner Rozha. "I'm not afraid of some spoiled little vixy like her. She's just like every other bully who's all talk and no game. I'll bet she's never been punched in her life -- I can't wait to show her what it's like."

Raia, however, could not share her friend's excitement. She looked every bit as concerned as Kasra would've expected a girly-girl like her to be.

"Look, I don't want *you* doing anything stupid, *either*! I wasn't telling you this so that you'd want to fight her; I was hoping you'd try to *avoid* conflict!"

"Some people don't learn until someone else *teaches* them," Kasra subconsciously clenched a fist at her side. "Layna's problem is everyone's been too soft with her -- she's never been challenged. I think that will change once she's got an ass-kicking."

"Mother preserve us," Raia raised the side of her hand to her forehead, "you're just as bad as *she* is! It doesn't matter who wins; when the healers see you all beat up, they'll know exactly what happened, and they'll tell Mother Diava about it. Layna thinks she's got everyone on her side, so she doesn't care if she gets caught. She just wants them to kick *you* out."

"Has this worked, before?" Kasra asked.

"Honestly…" Raia trailed off to think about it, "I've never seen her try anything like this with anyone else. She's never wanted to scare anyone off this badly."

"Ah, so I'm a special case, then?" Kasra raised a brow, not in the least taking this threat seriously. "I don't know what it is she hates so much about me, but I don't care. I've seen what she can do, and she doesn't scare me. If she wants to tear me open to see what I'm made of, it won't be before I'll see what *she's* made of, first."

Unlike when Layna made those kinds of haughty promises, which made Raia want to see some kind of validation, she knew Kasra's background well enough to believe she could back up what she was saying. Truthfully, she wasn't so much worried for Kasra getting hurt as she was Layna, but she was much more concerned with never seeing Kasra again. "Can you just promise me you won't let her goad you into doing anything stupid?"

The violette stoically paused as if taking a moment for deliberation, blinked, and simply replied, "I'll think about it."

Raia rolled her eyes and threw up her hands. "You're totally hopeless! Fine. Have it your way. I'll just stay up all night worrying myself sick about you two," she began walking away.

"Good night, Raia," Kasra complacently shouted to her down the hall. She then shrugged, as if wondering what got into her friend, before turning to enter her own room. It was just then she realized she hadn't seen Rozha since she woke up that morning. Right before they parted ways, she said "I'll see you later," like it was such a transient thing. Kasra was almost beginning to feel comfortable with the long stretches of time had without her sister; whole days of being apart felt like mere seconds in comparison to the years she thought Rozha was dead. *'She must be busy,'* Kasra wistfully comforted herself. *'She's never lacked an excuse for not being there.'*

Sometime while waiting for her sister to come back, Kasra fell asleep on her bed. She hadn't been sleeping but for an hour or so until she was stirred back awake by the sound of the door opening. She couldn't recognize the silhouette at first when she opened her eyes; the odd way she was standing in a bit of a slouched posture wasn't like anyone she knew. "Rozha?" Kasra confusedly uttered. "What happened to you?"

She didn't look wounded, but walked forward with a clumsy stagger and a gormless smile. "Hey, babe," Rozha weakly chortled. Her tail even wagged with an awkward sway, as if unable to tell in which direction it wanted to swing. "Sorry for waking you up, I was trying to be quiet..." She stumbled forth and collapsed chest-first against the foot of the bed, then muffled her uncontrollable laughter into the mattress.

Kasra raised her eyebrow, as if unsure of what to make of all this. Even though Rozha looked like she was having a good time, the violette's spine tingled with nervousness just watching her barely able to walk. "A-Are you... drunk?"

"No," Rozha immediately denied the obvious truth, but her lack of inhibitions couldn't keep the smirk off her face. "I was just out havin' a few drinks at the Safiric side of town. I needed somethin' to keep me sane after what I went through, yes'rday!"

Her fear for her sister's safety couldn't have been greater when she was immediately reminded of what Wanystha had taught her, earlier in the day. "You were over *there*, wearing your robes?!" The violette gasped. "You could've been killed!"

"Psh, naw..." Rozha carefully climbed up on the bed beside her. "I've went in there a couple of times before. They think it's cool to serve drinks to a priestess like me. They treat me like one of them because I'm a 'bad girl' -- oooh~" she derisively crooned with a waving hand gesture. She laid her head on the pillow as if ready to zonk out right then and there. After she was finished cackling, she looked up to see Kasra was still worriedly frowning at her, too uncomfortable about the whole situation to speak her opinion on the matter. "Stop looking at me like that," Rozha lazily shoved her. "Y'know, your problem is you don't know how to live. Y'never loosened up since we left mom and dad -- you need a release, or you'll always be a tightwad."

"Alright," Kasra agreed, only because she knew it was the only answer Rozha would settle for. She still didn't like how Rozha looked. It frightened her to think what could've happened to her while she was out at the tavern.

'I'll bet this isn't the first time she's done this,' Kasra thought. *'At least she still had enough of her wits about her to make it back to Sachelvae in one piece.'*

She didn't notice it before, but now that she had a chance to look at her face more closely, Kasra saw a slight redness on Rozha's forehead as a result of her inebriation. She curiously brushed the back of her hand under her sister's bangs and definitely detected an abnormal temperature. "Are you gonna be okay?"

"Hm?..." the sleepy Rozha fought her eyes to stay open. "I'll worry about that when I'm sober. Right now, I could use a snuggle buddy," she patted the mattress for her sister to lie down.

Albeit with some hesitation, Kasra did as she requested, but made sure she was facing away from the alcohol in her breath. What with how the situation had unfolded, she wasn't going to be getting much sleep that night. Even when she was in the process of dozing off, she'd be interrupted by Rozha's jerking around or adjusting her position. There was even one instance in which Kasra awoke to find her sister's long ears covering her face.

By the time she was pushed onto the floor by Rozha's tail, Kasra finally decided the bed was not large enough for the both of them, and settled for sleeping in her spare blanket. It wasn't any more comfortable, but at least she could make it through the rest of the night. She woke up to the morning sun peeking through their open window with aches and pains from lying on the floorboards, but that wasn't anything new. Her stretches and groans as she sat up were echoed by dolorous moans of Rozha's own.

"How're you feeling?" Kasra asked with a yawn.

"Is it my stomach that's hurting, or yours?..." an addled Rozha tied her arms around her belly, and her tail around her waist.

'What?' was all the bemused violette could think of to respond. She didn't sound drunk anymore -- at least, not as much as she was before.

"Is the lamp blinking?" Rozha asked, not really in the mood to look for herself.

Kasra had to stand up over the bed to check for her. "No, it's still a little early," she replied.

"Good," Rozha moaned. "I think I'll have to wait a bit until I'm ready to go out there. I really did it to myself, this time."

"Why'd you do it?" the naive Kasra openly wondered.

"Why else?" the blade dancer weakly snickered. "It numbs the mind of all worries. It lets me be clear and carefree for a while -- unconcerned about the responsibilities of being a Teacher and all that. Once I'm inducted into that life, I won't have the opportunity to do anything like this, anymore."

"So you really meant what you said last night," Kasra's ears despondently wilted.

"I guess?" Rozha honestly couldn't remember much of anything she and Kasra discussed. "What did I say?"

"You told me I needed to 'loosen up,'" Kasra paraphrased.

"Oh, that," the redhead laughed. "Well, it couldn't hurt," she more politely doubled down. "You don't wanna become like everyone else who lives here, or Sachelvae will be all you know. Of course, nobody who loves this place would tell you that's a bad thing. They all take their dedication to Sanguina as seriously as they do breathing."

Something about the blitheness of Rozha's statement made it seem rather uncaring for someone who had just been recently appointed to Sachelvae's faculty. "You mean you *don't* take it seriously?"

"I never wanted it to be my life," Rozha admitted. "Even though they put this silver tiara on my head, I don't think they really accepted me into the clergy. They just saw me as a useful asset -- a weapon for their own means. The Brotherhood started calling me 'The Red Dancer' after I went out on my first mission as a priestess, and the name stuck. Now it's being used as a pejorative term among my peers, who do not approve of murder as a means of self-defense. It wasn't until just recently that Mother Diava finally saw it my way, which is why she made me a Teacher. So even now I'm not 'one of the girls,' -- I'm still just their tool. They only like people who are rougher around the edges, insofar that we can be used to their benefit. Once we've served our purpose, they'll think of a reason to get rid of us. Nobody but a bunch of virgin priestesses will ever fit in here."

"But Sachelvae's been around for so long," Kasra argued. "You can't mean to say that in all this time, they've never changed their ways."

"Religion is hugely based in tradition," Rozha explained. "It's all they teach here. You can become very powerful in the faith, so long as you do what they tell you to. But you'll give up a very large half of a life you could've had. It's true that Pures are not born like those of Wild blood; we're inherently different in what appeals to us and what doesn't. But this isn't to say that neither of us are immune to the temptation of dabbling into one another's side. You can see it happening all the time in Tresantia; Wild and Pure belhuayns mingle in Mediona, but you'll rarely see one from the other side crossing into ours. Sometimes choice is all it takes for someone to reach enlightenment, but so few people believe they have it. In the end, we're born to serve one deity or the other: Safiro or Sanguina. We can't have both."

Something about how Rozha described how the faiths worked was much easier for Kasra to grasp than if Wanystha or Xanne had done it. "Even if it isn't what you desire, I believe that you'd make a fine Teacher, Rozha," Kasra smiled.

Before Rozha could roll her eyes at her sister's kindness, she glimpsed the slowly flashing light of the red lamp in the corner of the room. "Diava's ready for us," she said. "Time to get out to the Purifier."

After they had joined their friends to participate in the daily prayers and ritual ablutions, Rozha was called up to Mother Diava's platform while everyone else was heading off to have breakfast. "You wish to speak with me, your holiness?"

"I wished to inform you that I have reviewed the plans you made, and that construction for your classroom will begin today," the abbess replied. "I also have a special gift for you," she added, turning to the altar behind her. Rozha saw, over Diava's shoulder, a neatly-folded, red and black dress sitting on the clean, white surface, on top of which was placed a bediamonded tiara. "This is your new faculty attire."

Minding Rozha's current half-nakedness, the blade dancer sporting only her bathing suit, Diava added, "You may change into it before you enter the Dining Hall. A new seat will be opened for you between Teacher Xanne and Sister Kyrana." With a smile so gentle yet so amazingly heartfelt, the High Priestess declared, "It does me great pleasure to officially induct you into Sachelvae's faculty, Teacher Rozha."

"Thank you, your holiness!" The blade dancer respectfully performed her expected curtsy. Despite what she had said about not feeling accepted into the clergy, she never felt a greater sense of pride than when she took her new spot among the Teachers near Diava's end of the table. She was greeted by the congratulations of Wanystha and Kyrana as she sat down with them, and the seemingly forced smile of Xanne, but she was never much of one to show emotion.

She could certainly say that the biggest thing she appreciated about being a member of the faculty so far was the upgrade in quality and portions for her meals; it was like the chefs actually cared enough to give her more than the usual frupom juice and egg salad. Seeing as how the chefs were also a part of the assistant nursing staff -- Platina among them -- and had their own seats opposite the priestesses at the table, Rozha couldn't complain aloud about anything she didn't like.

Her seat was closer to Diava than it ever had been, but that also meant that it was even further away from Kasra. At least, at this distance and angle, she could peer far enough around the heads of everyone else to see her sister at the farthest end. She was sitting right in the middle of Raia and Layna -- a seat much feared by all the newest novitiates that ever entered Sachelvae. She could remember many more times she had seen that chair vacant than occupied.

It impressed Rozha all the more that Kasra not only stuck around longer than most would have, but she had even made friends with them. But something didn't seem right when she looked upon them, now. There seemed to be some issue between them that wasn't there, before. Kasra didn't mention anything about any problems she was having, but Rozha didn't necessarily ask her, either.

'She must think I'm so selfish,' Rozha worriedly thought. *'Every time we have a chance to catch up at the end of the day, we only talk about what I've been doing. No wonder she doesn't even think to tell me about anything she's been up to; she probably doesn't think I'd care.'*

She'd have plenty of time to think about how she was going to make it up to Kasra once she had begun her chores around Mediona. Since she didn't have a classroom yet, she wasn't considered a true Teacher, therefore still had to act as a priestess until it was completed. "It's a lot easier being one of us than you'd think," Wanystha said, whilst working on her latest painting. "It's nothing like being a priestess at all, but you do need to have a lesson planned out every day. Xanne sometimes keeps me awake at night, because she'll be up til the wee hours with her lamp on, preparing a syllabus for the morning."

"You room with Teacher Xanne?" Rozha probably shouldn't have been so surprised. But she kind of expected that faculty would at least get to have their own rooms. "If my seating arrangement at meal time is different, will I keep my room with Kasra?"

"If you wish, I suppose that can be arranged," Wanystha replied. "Sister Kyrana is currently without an occupant in her quarters. If you move out of your current room, that would be the only other one you could take. I would suggest it, honestly," the Teacher continued. "Faculty quarters are much more spacious than those of students and priestesses, and each come with their own desks and paper. You would find those very useful for lesson plans."

"Maybe," Rozha considered it. "Given what I'm teaching, I don't know how much talking is going to be involved. But I suppose it'd help to write *some* stuff down. I'll think about it." She honestly was more concerned with leaving Kasra by herself, alienating her further than Rozha already thought she was. *'She'd think I was trying to completely avoid her if I did that. She only started living here because I am. If I'm away from her all the time, she might think that impetus to stay no longer exists.'*

Truthfully, it wasn't weighing as heavily on Kasra's mind as Rozha feared. The violette very much had her own problems to worry about, what with Layna potentially scheming against her and all that. She knew Raia and Layna roomed together on the other wing of the building; they probably talked about private matters such as these sometimes. But the way Raia's body language was speaking to her, she could tell that the situation hadn't been resolved.

Indeed, the brunette looked very tired on the way to Xanne's class and lagged behind a little bit. *'Poor thing really **was** up all night,'* Kasra thought. She wondered how she was going to make it through the physicality of Xanne's next lesson, which by the blackboard's rubric was covering an advanced technique for their astapsyxi spell.

"You learned yesterday a new trick for your masalida," the Teacher said, "and I was very impressed by some of your skills," she nodded in Kasra's direction. "Now you will learn deeper control of your astapsyxi. Before, you were told that astapsyxi can be used to stop an opponent's whole body and even a weapon in its tracks. But this powerful spell can be minimized to target single limbs, leaving the rest of your attacker vulnerable, but still active. Like the masalida's deflection technique, this is very risky but also very rewarding in the right circumstances. For instance, you would be able to trip an attacker in mid lunge by aiming your astapsyxi at his feet."

"I'd advise you to exercise caution with this technique during practice, however, as careless use on your fellow students could cause them serious injury…" she trailed off with a forewarning tone, her eyes narrowing at Layna. "We do have nurses standing by for this practice session, but they can only cure so much." "Since this requires substantial space to perform," and more importantly, a more vacant space to watch over, "this session will be done on the front of Sachelvae's estate."

Cinté still shadowed Layna as all the students were lining up to head outside, but this didn't perturb the troublemaker from carrying out her plan of attack. She had no reason to fear her babysitter before and she wasn't going to start now. Kasra could feel Layna's eyes drilling through the back of her head. She knew she meant her nothing but harm, and was going to stay on her guard the whole time they were outside. *'She'd be a fool to try anything,'* the violette's self-assurance did nothing to calm her nerves. *'With everyone watching us out there, she'd be stopped before she could even start something with me.'*

Instead of attempting any measure of foul play, Layna seemed to regard this fact much more than Kasra assumed she would. While Raia assumed the role of Kasra's sparring partner for this practice session, Layna resigned herself to watching them from a distance. She seemed to lack the drive she normally had to cause mischief to others; when another pair of students asked if she'd like to join their group to practice with them, instead of taking it as an opportunity to cause one of them harm, she played along just fine -- albeit with cold indifference.

This change in behavior was nearly fooling Cinté and Xanne into thinking that Layna was finally coming around for the better. She had a kind of autonomous, monotonous attitude of going through the motions which started to bore the other students, who'd rather her be mean to them than continue this new, creepy strangeness she was exhibiting. *'Nothing else matters until I get what I want,'* she coldly gazed over her shoulder at Kasra.

Meanwhile, Kasra and Raia continued their friendly practice session by stopping the swings of their tails with their selective astapsyxi spells. They laughed amongst themselves as they had some fun with it by temporarily freezing each other in the middle of dance poses, generally having a good time until class was finally over.

For a while, Kasra was so busy enjoying Raia's company that she had forgotten Layna was even there. The way they played off each other and even seemed to empathically share a similar sense of silly, harmless humor made Raia feel to Kasra like a member of her family. When Teacher Xanne called everyone inside, and the two vixies had to stop their games, they only then realized how uncomfortably hot it was for such exertion.

"I'm almost sweating through my clothes," Raia repeatedly puffed the collar of her gown.

"Same here," a panting Kasra concurred. "You think they'll let us take a quick dip in the Purifier?"

"I don't see why not," the brunette shrugged. "I've seen some other people do it after coming back inside from their chores or whatever. I'm sure Mother Diava would commend any excuse to cleanse one's spirit."

After they had gone back inside and had found the Purifier Hall, Kasra began disrobing to her bathing suit, "Once I get myself freshened up, I'll see if Rozha can take me to Mediona so I can visit with your brother. It's almost lunch time now, isn't it?"

Looking up at the clock-like windows in the temple's ceiling, Raia checked which of the twelve oculi the sun was peering through. "Yep," she confirmed, "so she and the rest of the clergy should be coming back, anytime now."

Something about her activity being unmonitored by the High Priestess made it feel taboo when Kasra's toes touched the Purifier's water. "Are you sure it's okay to do this without permission?"

"Of course!" Raia confidently laughed, bravely sitting herself into the novitiate's end of the pool. "The worst anyone will think is that we were thrown in here as a punishment for something."

"Judging by our current record," Kasra followed suit, "that might just be exactly what they'd think." Looking around for a particular someone she was suddenly reminded of, she added, "Speaking of, where'd Layna run off to? I haven't seen her since she ditched us during practice."

"I hate to say this," Raia whispered, leaning close, "but I kinda like it better this way. I wasn't exactly missing her, you know?"

Kasra's back turned rigid with surprise as she fought back the urge to chortle at her friend's honest brashness. She'd never heard the sweet brunette ever say something so callous -- it was almost unbecoming of her. Still, she had a hard time disagreeing with her. "I know what you mean," the violette nodded. "There's a... word for people like her that I don't like using."

"Tankta?" a smirking Raia guessed, earning another naughty grin from her friend.

"You're gonna blacken this whole pool with your spite if you keep using remarks like that!" Kasra playfully tweaked the vixy's ear.

"Hey, that's what it's here for, right?" Raia mischievously stuck out her tongue, then calmly reverted to her more bashful demeanor. "I'm sorry if this seems so unlike me. I've never had an opportunity to just... vent what I feel to anyone. Layna's all I've had to talk to since I came to Sachelvae. Everyone else uses me as a source to unleash their emotional burdens, and I can't shoulder it all anymore. I know Sister Kyrana thinks that patience and understanding are the calling cards of nascent healers, but I don't think I could make a living doing what I've always done for free."

Even though Kasra was bereft of sound advice for Raia to take to heart, she was happy just to think that Raia had come to like her enough to continue opening up to her. She felt, maybe one day, she would do the same for her when the time was right. After a long pause in their conversation, Kasra's attention was brought to the droning chatter and footsteps she heard approaching the basilica's doors.

She and Raia stood up from the pool in time to see the first wave of priestesses re-entering the Purifier Hall from their outdoors activities. Apparently, they had much the same idea that the two novitiates had, because as they amiably talked amongst themselves, they prepared to cool off in the pool as well. And rightfully so; it was a hotter day than it had been in a while. Central Onteval was known for its cloudy, foggy days and for its cold, rainy season. When the sun was allowed to shine upon the wetlands, it did so with intense heat and humidity -- the likes of which would leave any priestess gasping through her heavy gown.

Amid the wandering clergy who had not yet entered the bath, Kasra could spot her sister, who looked a little more comfortable than her comrades. She looked a lot more impressive, too, in her new Teacher garb. "I almost mistook you for Kyrana when I first saw you!" Kasra laughed, approaching a preening Rozha.

"Well thanks," the redhead untied her curly ponytail. "I'll assume you meant that as a compliment and not barbing my age."

"Not at all!" a smiling Kasra shook her head. "I think it's a nice look for you."

"What's got you suddenly in such a cheery mood?" Rozha playfully poked her sister's dimpled cheek.

"I just had a good time today, that's all," Kasra swiveled her hips as she hid her hands behind her back. "I was wondering if, after lunch, you wouldn't mind taking me to Mediona with you."

"I'll see if I can get it worked out with Mother Diava," Rozha inquisitively tilted her head. "I don't want to strain my reputation with her, right after becoming a new Teacher and all. What do you want to do in Mediona?"

"I want to talk to Raia's brother," Kasra casually replied, earning a little sideways smirk from her sibling.

"Ohh, this is about a boy, is it?~" she teasingly pinched her embarrassed sister's shoulder. "You mean Malkinos? I met him and his dad, yesterday. Seemed like a nice kid."

"Layna got me in a bit of trouble with him," Kasra sighed. "I promised Raia I'd set things right between us."

"Well, I'm sure Mother Diava will understand the situation," Rozha was about to saunter off, before Kasra desperately grabbed her by the arm.

"Wait, you can't tell her about it," the violette implored her.

"Why not?..." Rozha suspiciously closed an eye.

"She's not supposed to know that Malkinos visited the courtyard," Kasra said. "Raia told me it's against the rules to let boys come here."

"Oh great," the redhead slumped her shoulders and heaved a long sigh toward the ceiling. "What have you gotten me into, now?... Alright," she straightened herself out, "I'll do this little favor for you, only because I think you two would make a cute couple."

"Rozha~!" Kasra squeaked with a petulant pout. "Thanks," she endearingly batted her eyes.

"But if you do anything stupid to get yourself in trouble," Rozha waved a finger at her sibling, "you're on your own -- I'm not bailing you out if you get caught around here, together."

"I--I hardly know him yet!" the pigeon-toed violette defensively raised her shoulders and clenched her fists.

"With a boy of *his* stock?..." Rozha sardonically whistled, "it won't take long for you to get better acquainted."

By now, Kasra wanted to fall through the floor. She just knew Raia had to have been standing behind her, listening to the whole conversation. She didn't even want to turn around to make sure; she felt like a fool enough as it was. The only thing that could've made this situation worse was if Layna overheard everything, too.

"So you're going on a date in Mediona, huh?" Layna's voice suddenly spooked her from behind.

'Nope, too late,' a needle of pain shot through Kasra's temples. She contained a groan as she slowly turned around, expecting to see that annoyingly smug look staring back at her, but was rather surprised to see Layna was sporting a more genuine smile.

"I wish I could accompany you, but Viasarria is still locked up," the vixy regretfully held her hands together. "So it looks like I'll be without a responsible adult as my porter for some time. Anyway, I'd like to give you my best. See you at the Dining Hall!" And with that charismatic wave, off she went, leaving a dumbfounded Kasra and Rozha in her wake. Both were stuck processing what they had just witnessed for several seconds after Layna had disappeared into the crowd of priestesses.

'There's no way that was the same person,' Kasra's wide-eyed expression remained unblinking. *'What's going on?'*

When mealtime came, lovesick Kasra could barely touch her portions -- she was too nervous about what she was going to say to Malkinos when she saw him again. This time, she wouldn't have Raia to fall back on for support. Rozha would just make Kasra all the more awkward if she was standing there, watching the whole time.

Of course, when she approached her sister about it before it was finally time to be on their way, the redhead just needled her some more. "Awh, are you afraid I'm going to embarrass you? It's okay, I won't say anything while you're working the charm~" Rozha walked her fingers along Kasra's ears, causing the violette to shrink away from her. "But, if you want to make a *real* impression on him," she added, "you should wear some perfume and doll yourself up a little -- let him know that what he saw before isn't all there is to you."

Kasra wasn't sure if she understood her sister's advice. "Why should I do all that? Then he'll just like me when I'm making an effort, instead of for who I really am."

"With the right cosmetics," Rozha replied, "you could hide some of those scars," she began pointing out her sibling's imperfections. "Some eyeshadow wouldn't hurt, either, to draw his eyes to yours." Lifting the side-sweep of Kasra's bangs to reveal her red eye she normally kept concealed, Rozha added, "If you're going to live with that weird heterochromia thing, you might as well make it work for you."

Starting to believe her a bit more, Kasra helplessly tossed her arms, "Okay, but how am I supposed to get that stuff?"

"That's what I'm here, for," Rozha wrapped an arm around the violette's shoulders, showing her a bag of coins.

"Where'd you get all that money?!" Kasra exclaimed in a hushed tone.

"I've been saving it," the blade dancer slickly lied, ushering her outside. "And I can think of no better use for it right now than to help my little sister with her first date." Rozha then took Kasra to a few shops around the Sanguinic side of Tresantia to procure the items she needed. Their first stop was a dome-shaped cottage with red siding and a thatch roof, from which a short chimney billowed puffs of smoke.

"That's the clothier's place," Rozha said. "You don't want Malkinos to think the temple is your life. He might be intimidated to go out with a staunch little priestess."

The door of green wood was closed, prompting Rozha to peer through one of its circular windows to check if there was anyone inside. "Looks empty, to me," she curiously stated. After tugging the door open without any struggle, the blade dancer looked to Kasra and shrugged, "Door's unlocked; must be honest people who live here."

The clothing store's round interior was warmly lit by the midday sun. Its straw-insulated walls and thatch flooring seemed to glow from the sunlight pouring in from the windows. Its single, spacious room was made quaint by the large rolls of colorful fabric hung up on either wall.

Standing before the rolls of fabric were short tables with scissors made for cutting out the designs and shapes of each layer of cloth. Whatever was left after this process was sitting in a pile beneath either table. It was admittedly a messy workspace, but it seemed to work for this business' owner. Between the tables was the only clear walking area, leading directly to an open doorway and another, larger room. It was from there that Rozha could hear the whirring of a loom's wheel.

"Are you guys open?" Rozha called back to the unseen employees.

"Yes," someone shouted back at her, over the sound of the rolling loom. "I'll be with you in a moment."

Meanwhile, someone else came out to the work area to keep their guests company, for a while. It was a middle-aged, dark-haired velta who stood slightly shorter than Rozha and Kasra, wearing a puffy, long-sleeved blouse and a ruffled dress that gave her a rather pampered look. Whomever she was married to obviously knew how to spoil her -- and probably at her behest. Her long, wavy hair was styled to a prim perfection; each lock was endowed with a lustrous shine. The glistening rock on the necklace she wore was practically impossible to overlook.

"Are you priestesses of Sachelvae?" her voice was a silky smooth contralto, almost flirtatious due to the natural narrowness of her gray eyes. "Is there something I can get you girls?" By the judging look on the fancy velta's face, she could see that the two of them didn't seem the type to be ordering custom outfits.

In any other financial situation, Rozha would have known she had come to the wrong place to buy clothes. But since she was now in the money, her spending habits begged to differ. "My sister here is going on her first date, this afternoon," she gestured toward a nervous, out-of-place Kasra.

"Mmhm," the fancy velta critically nodded. "Well, we have something that might be in her size on the rack..." she motioned toward the back room.

"No no," Rozha corrected her with a wave of her hand. "I want something *custom-made*, just for her."

Again, the fancy velta didn't seem ready to believe her. "I doubt we have the ability to prepare something under such short notice. It takes our seamstress at least a week to complete her finest dresses, and that's *including* advanced priority."

Rozha addressed her subtly snarky tone by stepping closer and dropping her coin bag on the table beside her with an impressive, metallic clash. "I'll give you *three hours*," the redhead stared dead in her eyes and watched the fancy velta's austere expression slowly be overcome with a fearful reverence.

She remained where she stood, but despite her efforts to appear unperturbed, the fancy velta couldn't keep the tense squeak out of her voice. "I will try my utmost. I will explain the situation to Janelle. Follow me, please." She turned back into the room from which she came and weakly trilled, "Miss Janelle, a customer wishes to speak with you."

The loom stopped as Rozha and Kasra walked in, and saw its operator sitting there with what looked like part of a half-finished gown in her lap. The older, short-haired brunette set down her knitting tools and pulled up the round, white cap on her head to see her customers. Her light, amber eyes shifted between them before settling on the shy Kasra. "Is she the one?" she stood up and peered all around her, as if taking her measurements. "She certainly looks like she could use a boost of confidence."

"Thanks," Kasra self-effacingly croaked.

"Is there anything you can do for her?" Rozha acted like she was speaking with a doctor.

"Well, I must say, red is a fine color on her," the seamstress began, tugging on the sleeve of her priestess gown. "But what you want is something she can be comfortable in outside, I take it? It's never really warm here, even in the summer; it'll have to be something that can breathe, but not too much…" she thought aloud. "Mabella, record this vixy's measurements," she whisked away the fancy velta. "Meanwhile, I think some black would be a nice look for you," Janelle squinted at Rozha. "Yes, all that red on the gown clashes with your hair. You need something that helps those features stand out. Especially since you have such light and fair skin!"

"I-I wasn't here for myself," a flattered Rozha crossed a hand over her chest.

"My customers are never so modest!" Janelle laughed. "Here, I have something you might like." She led Rozha to the immediate left of the room, where on the wall, there were fine dresses suspended by hooks on racks running from corner to corner. "I use these pieces as examples of my works, for newcomers," she said.

"Because you are a priestess of Sachelvae, and a Teacher by the looks of it, I will give you this outfit for free." Janelle reached up high for a black dress with round shoulder pads, and white bows on the sleeves and pleated skirt. "It's made of a thin material for hotter days like this, so you'll want to wear something tight under it when the weather cools back down."

"This is really nice!" Rozha had a hard time maintaining her smooth demeanor as Janelle held the dress out in front of her. She accepted her gift with gusto, almost wanting to try it on the moment it was in her hands. "I wonder if Malkinos has an older brother I can go out with," she joked.

"It pleases me to serve the Sisterhood," Janelle proudly replied. "The first owner of this shop was my great-grandmother. She started her business by selling custom gowns to the clergy of those days. Any time they had a new Teacher, they'd come to her to make a dress in her size. In fact, at the risk of dating myself, I was the one who made the High Priestess' gown when she was inducted!"

"How about that?" an impressed Rozha chuckled. "Everyone here has a connection to the temple in some way."

"Of course!" Janelle smiled. "Sachelvae brought this whole town together. We all owe it something for being a driving force to living in Tresantia and keeping us all safe. It's the only haven of its kind for us Pures in all the world."

After she was done webbing up Kasra's body with measurement tape, Mabella gave Janelle what she had recorded on a piece of parchment. With a quick review of the numbers, the older velta nodded and hummed, "Yes, I can see this coming together quite well." Glancing back at Rozha, she asked, "And eh, Miss Teacher? What was your deadline?"

Suddenly Rozha felt a bit guilty at the way she had treated Mabella earlier, but the fancy velta certainly hadn't forgotten how harsh her attitude was. "She said she wanted it done in three hours," Mabella replied for her.

Janelle looked like she was about ready to faint, and fell back in the chair of her loom. "I-Is that so, eh?"

"She gave us this as payment," Mabella added, showing her the sack of coins Rozha had left for her.

"My gracious," Janelle checked to see if her heart had stopped beating. *'The temple's richer than I realized,'* she kept her remarks to herself. "Seeing as how this is an emergency and all," the older velta raised an eyebrow, "I can put what I've got on hold for you and do what I can to meet my deadline. If I'm unable to make it, I'll refund you the difference for what I had not completed."

"That is very kind of you," Rozha bowed her head, giving Mabella a slight glare from the corner of her eye. "I will return in three hours and see what you have got for us." With that, Rozha and Kasra set back off for Sachelvae. "Since we've got some time to wait, we'll go to the other stores around town and see what they have for you." Catching a worrisome glance from her sister quietly walking beside her, Rozha reassuringly added, "Hey, I know what I'm doing! Malkinos will be the one apologizing to *you* when he sees how you look!"

Chapter 17: Before the Grand Reveal

Their next stop was a large, purple tent decorated with golden swirling patterns. Out front, on either side of its opening, were tall torches currently unlit due to the time of day. As Rozha and Kasra approached, they could smell a rich mixture of fragrances emanating from the silken structure. Across the front of the tent, just above the opening, was a hand-painted sign that read "Perfumist" in bold lettering.

"I think we have the right place," Rozha observed, raising the tent flap for Kasra to walk inside. She ducked in after her, but neither were able to get a good look of the dark interior before they were greeted by the business' owner.

She was a middle-aged velta of long, wavy black hair streaked with purple highlights. Her mauve, Wild eyes were her most fetching feature, and were outlined with an almost scar-like tattoo, with three dots in a line across on her cheeks. She wore a wide-sleeved, transparent black dress that showed a more form-fitting garb beneath it. Both layers of clothing featured loops of bejeweled fabric hanging from their hems. Her necklaces were similarly studded with gems.

"Welcome~" this mysterious velta eccentrically raised her arms. Her green fingernails and the many rings she wore glinted from the candlelights on her decorated table. Each candle was positioned in the center of a white circle, drawn onto the dark wooden surface. Between these candles were large cards chaotically scattered about. Suddenly, Rozha wasn't so sure if she had the right place, anymore, and was even tempted to leave when she saw the velta begin to move.

"Don't tell me…" the gypsy gestured toward them, holding her forehead as if in deep concentration. "You have come to help your sister."

"Maybe," Rozha nonchalantly shrugged at the psychic.

"You play the fool," the nomad smirked, strangely wiggling her fingers, "but I know why you're here. I saw your colors before you stepped through that door."

"My colors?" The blade dancer frowned, curiously curling her tail.

"I can see the feelings of others," she cryptically responded. "I detected your compassion hours before. Your sister wants to impress someone."

"Alright, hot shot," a chary Rozha defensively poised, "what *else* do you know about me, Wild-blood?"

The psychic demurely held a sleeve before her mouth as she cackled, "I know you are troubled and in a desperate situation. You are feeling overwhelmed. You are tense -- but I wouldn't need to be a third eye to notice that."

Instead of continuing to argue with this woman who simply knew far too much than Rozha was comfortable with, the blade dancer asked, "Are you really selling perfume, or did you put that sign out there to goad me into some kind of trap?"

"My my, aren't *we* harboring a guilty conscience?" The gypsy feigned vexation. "Don't be so testy until you have seen my wares," she added, pointing to the darkness behind her. The void was inconspicuously lifted by ghostly wisps of light appearing from nowhere, revealing bookcases and shelves full of little glass bottles of various shapes and colors.. "Come, child," the psychic motioned for Kasra to follow her, as she rose from her seat. "Show old Shikaina what strikes your fancy."

None of the containers were labelled, and there were so many all around her, it was impossible to know where to begin. Kasra was too scared of the strangeness of this encounter that she was at a loss for words; she hardly wanted to be near the weird lady, much less go following her into a place that she could turn dark at any moment. The violette looked over her shoulder to see if Rozha were still there, and indeed, her sister hadn't taken her eyes off her.

"Don't mind her," the fortune-teller dismissively waved, redirecting her attention to the shelves. "What's the first one you see?"

Upon being given that directive, Kasra's eyes settled upon a tall container shaped like an upside-down 'V,' full of dark liquid that was endowed with enough of a tint to be called aubergine. It was on a shelf directly in front of her, and at just her eye level. "This one, I guess," she pointed her finger against the bottle.

"I *thought* that would be the one," Shikaina smiled, taking the container from the shelf. "But I never like choosing for my customers. Everyone likes the illusion of choice."

Kasra had to double take at that deep statement from out of nowhere, as Shikaina passed her by. The psychic returned to her table and placed the container upon its surface. As soon as Kasra returned to Rozha's side, the darkness that concealed her wares closed upon them once again. "That's one of my finest fragrances," Shikaina remarked. "Your sister has good taste -- she's not quite as modest as she looks." Before Rozha could make a riposte in Kasra's defense, the psychic held out her hand and said, "That'll be 30 divitias."

"Daylight robbery is more like it," Rozha huffed. "But you probably already knew I'd say that," she mockingly muttered, digging through her coin bag for the required change.

"You'll come back, won't you?" The chortling Shikaina waved her off.

"I don't know, *will* I?" Came another over-the-shoulder response, as the moody blade dancer sauntered off.

When they were back out in the sunlight and out of earshot, Kasra laughed, "What was wrong with *you*? I've never seen you like that!"

"I hate psychics," Rozha petulantly crossed her arms. "A blade dancer's secrets are meant to be hidden. My thoughts and feelings are nobody's business but *mine*, damn it!"

"You're acting ridiculous," Kasra rolled her eyes. "What would she care about all that, anyhow?"

Rozha gave her sister an incredulous glare, as if to scream 'duh' without saying it. "She could've been with the Safiric Brotherhood, for all you know!"

"Oh *please*, the creepy perfume lady?" Kasra doubtfully squeaked. "She was right; you really *are* paranoid! If you throw a fit like that, of *course* she's going to be suspicious."

"Whatever," the redhead changed the subject. "I can complete the rest of your makeover, myself. I've got a set of cosmetics in my room that we could use."

Upon returning to their dorm, Rozha sat Kasra down on a molded stool in front of her vanity, and began applying makeup to her sister's face with the same kind of concentration that Wanystha had with her canvas. "You gotta hold still now," Rozha circled a small brush on the apples of Kasra's cheeks. "Keep your eyes closed, but not tightly," she continued, then adding applying a red eyeshadow to complement her purple bangs. "You're starting to look like a work of art, already," Rozha remarked, letting Kasra see herself in the mirror. "Now you don't look so sick and run down!"

"I suppose," Kasra cynically frowned. "At least, I don't *look* as gross as I feel, anymore."

"That's the spirit!" Rozha patted her sister's back, accidentally causing her to cough. "Don't go anywhere yet," she pushed her shoulders back down in her seat. "I haven't done your hair."

"What's wrong with it?" Kasra impatiently huffed.

"Besides that it looks like a rodent nested in it?" Rozha rustled the disheveled, purple mop on the violette's head. "You've got the Jantica curls," the redhead flauntingly held her ponytail over her shoulder. "Your hair will make you beautiful if you know how to manage it." Within a half hour, the amateur stylist turned Kasra's unkempt tresses into proper, wavy bangs and long, flowing curls extending to her lower back.

"I think we really have something here," a pleased Rozha commented. She and her sister both took a moment to admire the work she had done, as Kasra turned her head to see her reflection from all angles. Perhaps it was just her imagination, but the way the light glowed against her cloud-like curls made it look like pink rivers were swirling through her shiny waves.

"I like it a lot," Kasra was at a loss for words. She could hardly even recognize herself. "Thank you, Rozha."

Never the best with accepting compliments, Rozha just gave her sister a little hug around the side. "Just don't ruin it, okay?"

"I'll try not to," Kasra gave Rozha a look as she stood back up.

"Well, with any luck, Janelle might've finished your outfit by now," Rozha glanced out the window to check the time. "If she's any good at keeping her word."

"We really shouldn't have rushed her," Kasra fretfully began. "What if she gives us something crummy just to teach us a lesson?"

"I don't think she will," Rozha shook her head. "She seemed genuine enough about wanting to help out. She gave me that free dress, after all."

"She was probably just doing that because she was afraid you were gonna burn her store down," Kasra pouted.

"Did I really look that tense?" The blade dancer laughed.

"Yeah…" the grimacing violette trailed off. "It was kinda scary, honestly."

"I guess I take more after our father than I thought," Rozha bit her lip with a saudade sigh. "It's strange. There's nobody I'd like to resemble less, but the longer I've been apart from them, the more I've noticed how similar we are."

"So what?" Kasra tried to cheer up her sister. "That doesn't mean we're going to turn into the kind of monsters they are."

"Maybe not, but we're not the only ones they've tried to transform," Rozha said.

Kasra tilted her ear. "What do you mean?"

"Before Viasarria and I fought, she told me the name of her trainer," the redhead dramatically paused. "It was our mother."

Kasra flashed back to the moment she saw Viasarria attack Rozha in the Purifier -- for those few seconds, her eyes glazed over in a trance. "That's who she reminded me of."

"I never knew Nilsein became a tomina," Rozha went on to say, "but it makes too much sense for the way she treated us. She raised us like a blade dancer trainer would treat her students. She must take pride in turning Pures into killing machines," she disgustedly scowled at the floor. "She didn't succeed with us, so she tried to do the same with Viasarria and it worked. That's why she hates us so much. I'll bet Nilsein told all her students about us."

Kasra's jaw nearly hit the floor. "You think she sent assassins after us?"

Rozha nodded. "If not to kill us, to return us to her. To finish what she started."

Kasra's stomach fell into a pit; her tail turned nervously around her ankles. "Do you think... she knows we are here?"

"That's what I'm most worried about," Rozha poised akimbo, taking a deep breath to calm herself. "The way Viasarria looked at me when I first came to Sachelvae was the most striking thing I remember about her. It was as if she was trying to recognize me, but didn't know where she saw me before. Mother Diava calls her 'the Messenger' of Sachelvae, because she's almost never here. But I doubt sending letters to other temples is the only thing she's been doing," Rozha looked to their open bedroom door. "I'll bet she's been keeping in contact with Nilsein, as well."

"And what better spy than a Pure," Kasra added, "who has direct access to Sachelvae. Nilsein knows she can't come in here, so she sent Viasarria to look for us. Do you think Mother Diava knows what she's up to?"

"Not if Viasarria has been good enough at hiding it," Rozha replied. "Although... if what I thought about her is correct, she must've been corresponding with Nilsein the entire time she's been here." Placing a finger to her chin, she concluded, "I'm going to go look in her room for evidence." Without a moment's hesitation, she turned on her heels to do just that and had Kasra chasing after her.

"Wait, Rozha!" The violette pleaded. "How do you know it's safe to go traipsing into her bedchamber like that?"

"Why wouldn't it be?" The Red Dancer cocked her hip. "She's cooped up in the Quarantine Bay with Platina, who I believe is her roommate now. Neither of them are going to be in there -- that means it's ripe for the picking." As if suddenly coming to an epiphany, Rozha turned back around and whispered to herself, "Just in case it's locked..." She reached under her

229

bed and fished out a small, thin, rectangular box held shut by a metal clasp. She tucked it in her sleeve before Kasra could inquire about it, then continued on her way. "Come with me," she beckoned to her sister. "I'll need you to look out for me."

"This doesn't sound good," came Kasra's pessimistic response.

Since everyone was outside, the halls of Sachelvae were empty and devoid of activity. Thankfully, the doors to the Quarantine Bay had been closed off, so they wouldn't be interrogated by Platina, if she happened to see them walking by. Rozha and Kasra had walked all the way to the other wing of Sachelvae until they finally arrived at Viasarria's dorm, which happened to be the first door after passing the Quarantine Bay. "Yep, it's locked," Rozha casually stated, after testing the doorknob. She dropped the box she had been carrying in her sleeve into her hand and opened it up to reveal a set of lock picking tools.

"I knew I had a bad feeling about this," Kasra muttered under breath.

"Put a lid on it and make sure no one's coming," Rozha carefully fidgeted with the door lock's innards. While she finagled the lock open, Kasra felt an odd breeze go through her hair. She turned to the side, as if imagining someone had just brushed by her. A fearful numbness crawled up her spine -- the same kind of fear one might have to a poltergeist's presence.

"Did you feel that wind?" Kasra whispered to her sister.

"No?" The blade dancer irritably hissed. "What're you babbling about?"

"Sorry, it must've been my imagination," Kasra anxiously held her hands.

"Stop distracting me," Rozha tersely truncated the conversation. She listened for the clicks of the lock's teeth as she moved her thin device further inside its opening. After the third click, she turned the knob a full 90 degrees.

"Ha, I think we're all done, here." Sure enough, when she pushed on the door, this time it swung open without a fight. The room that Viasarria and Platina shared looked much like the other dorms of Sachelvae: two beds and two dressers, both with their own nightstands. In these nightstands were drawers that Rozha assumed may have been hiding little secrets -- in particular, any letters for Viasarria.

Rozha's eyes lit up, her heart racing as her mind was excited back to all the memories of her blade dancer days. She was tempted to search every corner of the room for its goodies now that she had free reign of the place. But she held herself back when she knelt before one of the nightstands to check its contents. The one near the bed on her left opened to unveil a stack of papers, on top of which was a well-detailed drawing of what was unmistakably a nude scelan posing provocatively.

Rozha almost forgot to breathe as she gave the picture a puzzled look, and out of curiosity lifted it up to see more of the same risque illustrations lurking underneath. Most of the models were leanly muscled and well-endowed. *'Looks like our quiet nurse has a bit of a kinky side.'* She knew after seeing that, she'd never look at Platina the same way again. She hoped that the other nightstand, which she assumed to be Viasarria's, would turn up something a little more intriguing -- in a high-brow sort of way. Indeed, it already had when she found that it was locked shut.

'Well isn't this interesting,' she inwardly hummed. In a matter of seconds, the blade dancer was able to use her tools to trick the simpler mechanism into opening. Before her sat a messy pile of parchment curling slightly under the weight of the ink on which messages were addressed to Viasarria. *'Some of these are dated as far as two years back,'* Rozha noted. *'But none of these letters have a signature.'* She had never seen her mother's handwriting, either, so she couldn't know for sure if Nilsein was the one who wrote them. *'She doesn't even mention Kasra or I by name, but there are constant references to two 'targets'.'*

As she was reviewing the messages, she felt a puff of air on the back of her neck. She turned over her shoulder, half-expecting, if not hoping, it was Kasra standing behind her. But when she checked, no one was there. Kasra was still standing at the doorway, wringing her hands as she watched the halls. Rozha then glanced all around the room, from the ceiling to the corners of the walls, for any shadows or evidence of movement. But there was nothing at all to suggest she wasn't alone, aside from a gut feeling.

"Rozha," a nervous Kasra called to her in a hushed voice, "have you found anything, yet?"

"I'll say I have," the blade dancer stood, finally shutting the drawer and returning to Kasra, "I found orders that Viasarria was given to find us. None of them were signed by our mother, but I know far too well that she is the one behind this…" Just then realizing something again, Rozha nearly wanted to kick herself. "That's why she told me who her tomina was -- she was hoping I'd know Nilsein's name if she brought it up, so she'd know she had the right people."

"What do we do now?" Kasra timidly squeaked.

"We report this to Mother Diava," Rozha simply replied. "As long as Viasarria is in the Quarantine Bay, there's nothing she can do to us. If

Mother Diava kicks her out of Sachelvae, she'll put a seal on the doors so that Viasarria will never be able to come back in."

"We can't just *hide* from her, though!" Kasra argued. "Even if she's no longer in Sachelvae, she'll still be able to get us when we're off temple grounds."

"If she attacks us *anywhere*, we'll have the whole clergy to deal with her, then," Rozha said. "Don't worry, it'll be alright."

"What about Layna, though?" Kasra asked.

"If she can't deal with it and starts acting up, then she'll get the boot, too." Rozha comfortingly pet her sister's head. "You worry too much! I think Raia's been an influence on you."

"Speaking of," Kasra motioned in the direction of the Purifier Hall, "Should I postpone my date until after we've told Mother Diava about what we've found?"

"No," Rozha said, "You let me worry about that. You're not supposed to know about any of this stuff -- you're just a novitiate, remember? Mother Diava thinks you're doing your chores right now. If you tell her you were sneaking around with me, you and I both will be locked up like Viasarria is. Let me break the news to her. If she wants to put me away until she can prove to herself there's something to my story, that's fine. But I'm not going to ruin this date for you."

Rozha's expression softened as she stared into Kasra's eyes, seeing how damaged she was on the inside. She couldn't stand to think what her sister went through in the time they had been separated, but she was going to do everything she could to make it up to her. "You should really stop worrying so much!" The Red Dancer moved Kasra's hands back to her sides. "I don't want your hair to start turning gray after all the work I put into making it look nice!"

Kasra was inspired by how unfazed Rozha was by this whole situation. Anyone else would have been encouraging her to panic, but her sister was seemingly unperturbed by fear. Nothing, not even the threat of death, was going to stop her from living how she wanted to. Even with Rozha walking by her side, the strange presence she felt in that room made it difficult to forget her fears.

She wanted to bring it back up as they made their way to Sachelvae's atrium, but knew her sister well enough that even if she had experienced it, too, she would have dismissed it all the same. *'Rozha's right,'* Kasra steeled herself, *'I should stop doubting my confidence. I shouldn't be aloof to danger, but I shouldn't be constantly stressed about it, either.'*

Rozha could tell, by Kasra's quietness, that she was thinking about something but chose not to ask what it was about. It wasn't until they had went back outside that Kasra was able to put her thoughts into actions. The refreshing sunlight of the open world reminded the violette of what she had to live for. When they went back to Janelle's clothing store, Mabella was the first to notice how dramatically Kasra changed. "Oh my, aren't you adorable!" She admiringly held the violette's chin. "Janelle will be most excited to complete your look. She just finished your wardrobe not too long ago."

Chapter 18: Kasra's First Date

"Kasra, my dear~" Janelle exclaimed, presenting her with a two-piece dress. "You are simply ravishing. The whole time I was working on your special outfit, I was thinking back to how I felt for my first date. It was an amazing time in my life, and I wanted to do what I could to ensure you would have a similar experience. But with the time constraints I was given," she trailed off, eliciting a funny grin from Rozha, "I was forced to split the dress in two pieces to complete it as quickly as possible."

And what she was left with was a nicely-constructed, ruffled top and a matching skirt, neither of which looked like they would cover much. "Even still, I have to say I am pleased with what I made. I was inspired to create something that would play off the energy of youth and tastefully flaunt your Mother-given assets."

Kasra bashfully brushed her toes into the floor at all the new attention she was getting, and even more so when she imagined how much of her body would be showing in that outfit. "I'm a little thin," she quietly averred. "I'm not quite that confident in myself."

"I knew this would be the case," Janelle replied, turning back around, "which is why I also prepared this for you:" she retrieved a folded set of tights and leggings. "You can wear these under your dress. They won't make you sweat in a warm day like this, and you stay covered while pleasing your boyfriend's eye."

"Well, alright," Kasra's ears fell as she blushed. "Let's do this, then."

"I have a dressing room in the back, here," Janelle pointed. "I can help you into your new dress, if you'd like?"

Rozha and Mabella waited by the loom while Kasra prepared herself for the mortification of having to disrobe in front of the older velta. Janelle led her to a sliding door with wooden slats barely wide enough to see anything through, but allowed for just enough vision to tell if the room was occupied or not. The room itself amounted to a closet space barely large enough to fit two people comfortably; Janelle had to stand on a short bench so she could see over the taller Kasra's head. On all three walls, there were tall mirrors where Kasra could see her reflection from all angles -- something she hadn't expected to add to the already embarrassing nudity she was confronted with.

She was certain that no one had ever seen her bereft of clothing and was equally confident her body was nothing special to look at. The high-strung violette wasn't sure whether or not she'd prefer Rozha to be standing in the small closet with them, as Janelle helped her out of her priestess gown. Her arms were tightly tied around her chest, her tail wrapped around her legs, as she shivered mildly without the cover of her gown.

"Are you cold?" Janelle asked her customer.

"No," Kasra honestly replied, but made no further comment.

Janelle offered a soft, compassionate smile for the shaky vixy, turning her attention to one of the mirrors to see Kasra's profile view. "I don't think there's anything wrong with how you look. I think you'll love how my new outfit looks on you."

For the first time in her life, she let someone else be the judge of her outward appearance. "Wh-What if I'm trying too hard, and none of this works?..." a trepidatious Kasra bit her lip, refusing to look in any direction but the carpet at her feet.

"I may not know this boy you're going out with," Janelle said, "but I do know that any kid his age won't be expecting a young lady like yourself to make such an effort to leave a lasting impression."

Kasra only felt like she was trying to be something she wasn't -- or even worse, *hide* something she *was* -- in an effort to impress someone who hadn't even agreed to go out with her yet. "That's not who I am," she quietly averred. "If I know it, won't he see that, too?"

"How much does this date mean to you?" Janelle asked her own question. "You act like you don't even want to go through with it. Believe me, if you don't, you'll spend a long time wishing you had."

Without any prior experiences to relate Janelle's warnings of regrets, Kasra heaved a long sigh. "Maybe…"

Even though Janelle's airy clothing was easy and comfortable to wear, 'uncomfortable' was the best word she could use to describe how she felt when the seamstress had finished putting it all on her. "Oh, darling," the older velta cooed, "it's even better than I imagined!" It was at that moment that Kasra finally mustered the courage just to look at her completed outfit in the mirror. Even inwardly, she had to admit it was a great look. It made her think of a young princess. "You really think so?" The violette chirped.

Holding her shoulders and ushering her forward, Janelle excitedly encouraged her, "Let's go see what your sister and Mabella have to think about it."

The instant the door slid back open, Kasra was greeted by the pleasantly surprised stare of her sister, standing with a slightly less impressed Mabella. "Wow," was the first thing to escape Rozha's nearly gaping mouth. "I don't know who that pretty girl is, but she doesn't look like the Kasra I used to know!"

"Thank you…" Kasra's face was weighed down by her embarrassed flush, along with her wilting ears. She couldn't believe the reaction she was already getting from just the three veltas around her. She grinned, her tail starting to sway as she imagined what Malkinos would have to say about her.

"You did wonderfully, Janelle," Rozha finally complimented the seamstress. "I'm sorry I was so rude to you guys, earlier." Turning to her sister, she said, "If Malkinos can't appreciate all the effort you put into looking this good, then he's not worth your time. If you don't knock his socks off, *I will!*"

"Don't worry, Rozha," Kasra looked up at her, smiling confidently. "I think I can handle it."

"No, you need one more thing," Rozha retrieved her sister's perfume. "You better use it after what I paid for it!"

"Okay, sheesh," the violette huffed, taking the vial. "How do you use this stuff, anyhow?"

"Like this," Rozha gave the bulb at the end of the container's hose a squeeze. A sparkling mist sprayed from the bottle's brass cap into Kasra's face -- her reaction eliciting a laugh from her prankster sibling.

"Bleh!" Kasra recoiled, batting her stinging eyes. "Wh-What did you do *that* for?!" She angrily shrieked, coughing into one hand and wiping away her tears with another.

"That's what you get for being difficult," Rozha held her hands on her hips. "Hold still before you ruin your makeup," she added, turning Kasra's head by her chin so she could dab her face with a handkerchief. "You ready now?" She poked her sister's snout, to which she responded with an indignant sniffle. Kasra couldn't have been more ready for this whole thing to be over. "C'mon, let's get moving while we still have daylight!" Rozha pulled her along, leaving a flabbergasted Janelle and Mabella in their wake.

Even in the time it took for Rozha to take Kasra to Mediona, the violette's eyes were still burning from the perfume. She tried not to let it show how much it was bothering her by the time Rozha had walked her over to Malkinos' table.

"Hey Drathnifere!" Rozha called and waved to them. When she was within normal speaking distance, she continued, "Good afternoon to you both," nodding toward Malkinos, who kept glancing between her and a shy Kasra.

"Good to see you, Rozha," Drathnifere smiled, looking up at the blade dancer's new tiara. But her simple jewelry was easily eclipsed by the beautiful, albeit clearly nervous young lady standing beside her. "What brings you here? Are you the Sister Kasra I've heard so much about?"

"Indeed she is," Rozha replied for her silent sibling. "I brought her here because there was something she wanted to say to your son." She nudged Kasra with her tail for her cue to speak, but the violette was too embarrassed to even look at Malkinos -- she had spent all this time preparing for this encounter and still had no clue what to say. Having the boy's father standing right there didn't make it any easier on her, nor did the growing tingles plaguing her sinuses. *'Damn this perfume,'* Kasra inwardly cursed.

After shuffling her feet two little steps forward, she swallowed her fear and watched her hands trying not to shake down by her waist. "Um, I-I'm sorry for the way I acted, yesterday," she stammered with a sniff, suddenly wishing she had brought tissues.

"I didn't mind," an equally dumbstruck Malkinos feasted his eyes on Kasra's new looks. "Y-You're, um… I mean, a-are you f-feeling okay?" His tail wrapped around his locked up knees.

"Huh?" A confused Kasra finally met his gaze. It took her a moment to realize what he was talking about. "Oh, I'm fine," she self-consciously blinked her slightly reddened eyes. By his unperturbed frown of concern, she could tell he didn't believe her. "W-Well, actually, I have a bit of a cold -- it's nothing serious…"

"Were you wanting some stuff for medicines?" Malkinos asked, his twitchy hands fumbling through his father's merchandise. "I've got some hakota seeds right here you can make a soup with -- I could show you how, if you wanted me to."

Kasra raised her shoulders and batted her eyes again, this time unrelated to her perfume. Before she could make a response, Drathnifere prodded his distracted son, "You're not gonna give more of my stuff away for free, are you?" To which a panicked Kasra glanced between him and Rozha, who had a fist clasped firmly over her mouth to avoid giggling at her sister's blossoming romance. "I, uh, I'm sorry!" The violette bit her lip. "I didn't bring any money…"

"I'm only messing with you," Drathnifere laughed. "Malkinos, why don't you take Kasra to the fair? It just opened up at the other end of the avenue there," he pointed in the general direction.

Malkinos followed his father's finger toward the horizon, where he saw a larger crowd of people gathered around a group of tents with colorful flags and banners in the distance. Managing a goofy smile at his crush, he asked, "You wanna go check it out, Kasra?"

"Sure!" The violette walked closely beside him, all the more eager to finally part with Rozha. The blade dancer exchanged looks with Drathnifere, who hadn't stopped smiling since the whole rendezvous had begun. "Shall we wait for them to get back?" The rancher asked.

"Nah," Rozha smirked, "I've got a more fun idea."

While her sister shadowed them amid the street-goers, Kasra pretended not to notice when her swaying tail would brush against Malkinos' behind her. "So, I know you haven't been at Sachelvae for very long," the boy tried for some small talk. "What do you think of it there?"

"It's been a fun experience," Kasra honestly replied. "There's plenty to do all day and lots to learn -- when I'm not hanging out with Layna, that is."

"You got mixed up with her, too?" Malkinos sympathetically chuckled. "Raia says she scares away all the new novitiates who come to the temple."

"Well, it hasn't worked on me, yet," Kasra proudly shrugged. "I'm not scared of her."

"You'd be the first in a while," Malkinos smiled. "She even frightens me, sometimes."

"It's probably why Raia's never had a boyfriend, the poor thing," Kasra scoffed and shook her head. "The cutest girl there in the world wouldn't have a chance if she was with a man-repellant *that* strong."

Malkinos laughed, "I'm honestly in no hurry to see Raia start dating anyone. Dad said when that happens, I'll have to vet the boy she's with to make sure he's right for her. That sounds like it'd be really difficult... I don't like most guys my age. I don't think Raia does, either."

Kasra curiously tilted an ear. "Why do you say that?"

"She's never shown any interest," Malkinos thoughtfully hummed. "I know she's only 14, though -- maybe she's still too young for that. With all the time she's spent at Sachelvae, I'm surprised she isn't feeling lonely, yet."

Kasra could understand being a late bloomer; when she was Raia's age, she had just left her parents and was living on her own. Meeting boys and settling down with someone were at the bottom of her list of concerns at that time. She didn't want to bring all that up, though, and decided to change the subject instead.

"Well, I don't know about Raia, but I like boys~" she held Malkinos' hand, smiling as he blushed at her. His mind preoccupied, he wasn't watching where he was going and bumped into something before he finally stopped. He saved himself from doubling over against the side of a wooden counter, on which a tall sign was placed that read "Cakes and Confections."

The stand was roofed in by a striped tent and was being run by an out-going scelan sporting long, light green hair, wearing a matching vest over a stained apron. "Well, how's it goin'?" He flashed them an inviting grin. Judging by his tanned skin and nasal accent, he wasn't native to Onteval. "Can I get ya kids somethin'?"

"What're you selling, here?" Malkinos peeked over the counter to see racks of hooks behind him, each one holding something sweet and sugary on it.

"Gee, lemme take a look," the sardonic chef turned to face the forest of donuts in his small kiosk. "A li'l bit of everythin', it seems! I'm sure if anythin' strikes your fancy, you'll more than likely find it heah."

"Is that so?" Malkinos chuckled, reaching for a coin pouch on his belt. "What would you like, Kasra?"

The violette stood on her toes and leaned over the counter to give everything a once-over, but truth be told, she couldn't recognize anything the chef was selling by name. She couldn't even say that she knew what any of the confections tasted like. "I'll have whatever you like, Malkinos."

"Alright then," the farm boy said, "I'll take two lignugoes," he pointed to a collection of colorful kebabs hung like torches on either side of the counter. The lignugoes featured a small mass of multicolored spun sugar at the end of an edible, striped handle. Kasra could hardly wait until after Malkinos paid the vendor to have her first bite of the stuff.

"It's sticky and melts on your tongue," she noted, "but it's really good! Thank you, Malkinos~"

"I'm glad you like it," he smiled, having a taste for himself. "What to do, next," he resumed holding her hand as they both had a look around. Upon seeing a row of targets amid a large, fenced-in field, Malkinos exclaimed, "Ohh, that looks fun!" Waiting for Kasra's agreement, the violette said, "Let's check it out."

They passed through a small crowd of strangers either standing in line or walking between the various kiosks on the sides of the street, as they made their way to a small group of people standing around a barker wearing a gold and black patchwork garb. A vaguely axe-shaped symbol was emblazoned on the hat he wore, made to look like a soldier's helmet. The scelan himself certainly looked tough enough to have been a soldier for real, but he lacked the stoic exterior and was instead much more kind-hearted. His brashness was merely a front for his audience, as he tried to goad them into the contest he had on display.

"Why don't you commoners try your hand at a *warrior's* training?" He loudly shouted to anyone who would listen. Malkinos puffed out his chest at the mere invitation to a challenge and walked up to the front of the line with Kasra, to confront the haughty scelan. "I'll bet it's not so hard!" The farm boy confidently stated, earning a single laugh from his challenger.

"So you wanna test your mettle, kid?" He arrogantly poised. "Come see if you can throw these javelins into those ringed targets, there," he motioned toward the table beside him first, then to the rather far away targets. "You gotta stand behind the line there when you do it. Still think you can handle it?"

His nerve untested by the scelan's condescending tone, Malkinos all the more confidently asserted, "I *know* I can do it."

"Then step right up and prove it," the mock soldier grinned, opening the short gate for Malkinos to enter. The farm boy looked back at his girlfriend to see her watching intently as he stepped to the table. The soldier handed him one of the black javelins sitting against the fence, which was a little bit heavier and more unwieldy than he had expected.

Even still, Malkinos' concentration was undaunted as he raised the large bolt over his shoulder and sized up the distance for the throw. With a slight running start, he threw the spear across the field and its bronze tip barely stuck into the bottom of the target across from him.

Even though it wasn't a perfect shot, for his first attempt, he was pretty pleased with himself. His small feat earned an applause from Kasra, but the soldier wasn't as impressed. "Let's see if you can do it again," he handed him another spear, convincing Malkinos to make a fool of himself.

But Malkinos wasn't about to choke for this guy's benefit. With the practice he had gained from his first throw, he was better able to gauge how much harder and higher to aim the next one. With exceptional strength that even had the soldier taken aback, Malkinos' second javelin was buried nearly halfway down its handle through the center of the same target. The barker had a look on his face that spoke all the words he couldn't say for him. "I've only ever seen a *real* soldier do that!" He finally managed. "You're somethin' else, kid! You ever thought about joining the military?"

Malkinos' toughness shrunk away as soon as he was faced with the difficult question. He bashfully brushed a hand through his hair and said, "A little bit, I guess. I'm pretty good with some weapons, but I haven't had any real practice."

"Tell you what, kid -- what's your name?" The soldier asked.

"Malkinos," the farm boy replied.

"I was never in the service, myself, but I was part of the town watch for a while," the soldier continued. "My brother actually did join Iminsun's corps -- I can tell you where he trained, if you wanna give it a shot?"

"I don't know about all that," an intimidated Malkinos blinked. "Aren't I a little young?"

"They take 'em as young as 16," the barker said. "You won't be out on the front lines, of course. You'll probably be an archer or a cannoneer until you've gained some combat experience."

"I'll give it some thought, for sure," Malkinos affirmed. "Thanks for the offer!"

Upon stepping back through the open gate, Malkinos was greeted by an elated Kasra clinging to his arm. "You were so impressive out there!" She admiringly purred. "I've never seen something like that, before."

"I can do it again, if you want?" Malkinos vacantly offered.

Kasra giggled, "As much fun as that would be, my feet are actually pretty tired from all the walking around I've done, today…"

"Shall I take us to a place we can sit down for a bit, then?" The boy led her to a picnic table across the street. He let her be seated on one side while he went to occupy the other, and reclaimed his lignugo from her to take another bite out of it. "Feeling better?" He asked.

For the first time since their date began, Malkinos found himself at a loss for words as he stared into his girlfriend's mystifying gaze. The two colors of her eyes made them that much easier to lose himself in. Perhaps it was just his imagination, or he'd been in the sun too long, but the way the full, afternoon light radiated off her shiny, purple hair made it glisten like star-like glimmers. "Your face is like the night sky," he absently commented.

Kasra wasn't sure what he meant by that, but assumed it was a compliment. Her face was consumed with a hot blush, and she tried to hide it from showing on her cheeks by covering them with her hands. The beaming Malkinos then softly intertwined his fingers with hers and pulled them away from her rosy face. He couldn't help admiring her eyes again as they so endearingly watched him back. "You're really cute," Malkinos wagged his tail. "Can I kiss you?"

Kasra felt the insides of her ears turn ablaze as she was suddenly put on the spot to answer such a simple, yet emotionally-tasking question. "Yes," she barely audibly creaked, her eyes wide and unblinking. She stayed frozen to the spot for a few moments as she watched Malkinos lean his way to the middle of the table, before forcing her knees to bend her upright. Their lips lingering mere inches apart, Kasra hesitated as if unsure of what to do from there. She had seen people kiss before, and it was never such a dramatic thing. It was usually short and casual -- sometimes even anemic.

Perhaps hers was, too, but the mere moment it lasted felt like several minutes to her. Her heart stopped the second she tasted his kiss; she held her breath until they separated. She opened her eyes to see Malkinos' staring quizzically into hers, with an almost disappointed look to them. "A-Are you alright?" He returned to his bashful stammer, upon seeing the awestruck, if not frightened expression on Kasra's face.

"I'm sorry," the violette breathlessly began, not even sure why she was apologizing. "It's just... that was my first kiss. I didn't know what to do." She only realized how stupid her excuse sounded after she said it.

"It's okay," Malkinos chuckled. "Maybe we'll get better with practice?" Just before he could lean back in, he was stopped by a poke to the tip of his nose. Malkinos blinked his eyes back open to see Kasra holding him back with the tip of her finger. "Can we save it for a second date?"

"Yes," Malkinos' ears timidly folded against his back, falling on his bottom from his quivering knees.

"How about tomorrow?" The violette asked.

"S-Sure," Malkinos' twitchy body turned itself around as he stood up from the table. "I'll see you then, Kasra~" He relished saying her name with such a romantically sing-song lilt. He couldn't stop glancing at her over his shoulder, while she just sat there watching him depart. It wasn't until he was no longer in her presence did Kasra come back to reality.

Her insides sank when she imagined all the people around them and walking by could have seen everything they had done together. At least nobody would fess up to that.

"Oh my~!" Came a sardonic whistle from an all-too-familiar voice.

Kasra's shoulders and legs fell into a slump as her head turned upward, wishing she could fall into the ground and disappear. "Oh no," she groaned. She didn't want to turn around and see the silly look on her sister's face.

"If you had a strider of your own, I don't think I'd ever see you again," Rozha obnoxiously tapped the mortified Kasra's back, as she plopped down on the bench beside her. "You two looked ready to elope, just now!"

The violette spun around to defend herself. "We just had a little date, that's all."

"*Little*, nothin'," Rozha scoffed, taking a sip of some warm tea. "That kid's totally into you."

"You think so?..." Kasra regained her girlish lilt.

"Yeah, I'm pretty sure," the redhead straightened up her sister's bangs. "I can tell you had quite a time, too."

"You watched us the *whole* time?!..." Kasra's jaw dropped.

"I was making sure you two weren't going to run off anywhere," Rozha argued. "I hardly knew this boy before he met you. I wanted to make sure he wasn't going to try and take advantage of you." This time without a condescending tone, but with motherly pride, Rozha added, "I don't think I've ever seen you smile more than you did the whole time you were with him."

"Oh gosh," the violette clutched her dress and turned her eyes to the street.

"I can't get enough of how cute you are right now," Rozha held Kasra's shoulder, causing the violette to jump slightly. "Let's get back to Sachelvae so you can be ready for Wanystha's class. She'll complain to Mother Diava if you keep being late. You don't want to end up being watched like Layna, or you'll have to say goodbye to Malkinos."

A peppy Kasra smiled, "I'll be good! I promise!"

Chapter 19: Self-Defense

On their way out of Mediona, Kasra merrily told Rozha about what happened on her date with Malkinos -- as if her sister didn't already know -- from her first-person perspective. Kasra's description of the 'odd feelings' she experienced during her kiss with Malkinos made the sexually confident Rozha uncomfortably blush. She wondered when might be a good time to explain the purpose of courtship to her sister, or if she should outright forbid it so she wouldn't have to worry about Kasra being cursed by the Jantica fertility, as well as the 'Jantica curls.'

"Those urges you feel," Rozha started, "Don't let Malkinos satisfy them. And if he pressures you after you say no, kick him between the legs."

"Wait, I don't get it," Kasra confusedly shook her head, warding her sister's hastiness with a waving of her hands. "First you dress me up like this so that he'll want me, and then you tell me to push him away when it starts working. What's the point of all that?"

"You don't just want to *give* yourself to him," Rozha waggled a finger, "nor *any* boy who suddenly strikes your interest! If they're worth keeping around, they'll devote their loyalty to you, rather than expect you to submit to their desires. Malkinos is a nice kid; if you go slow with your relationship with him, he'll kiss the ground you walk on. If you bend to his whims, he'll begin to think he can control you. He's still young; his mind hasn't been conditioned to think like most scelans, who just want everything to be their way all the time."

"I don't want to be his *mistress*," Kasra timidly replied. "I'd rather us remain the way we are now."

"That's a middle ground you'll have to find, yourself," Rozha said, "but at the rate your relationship is progressing, I'd suggest you slow it down. And if he truly respects you, he will have no problem doing that. Chastity outside of marriage is very important to the Sachelvian Sisterhood. If Mother Diava has any reason to suspect you've been getting frisky with this kid --"

"I know, I know," Kasra impatiently interrupted her, nodding with a dismissive wave. Her narrowed eyes then widened and she nearly halted in her tracks as she came to a sudden realization. "Rozha, does that mean you've never... *hooked up*, either?..."

The appalled blade dancer snickered and scoffed at the very thought of admitting such a thing. "What, do I *look* like I've never seen action?" She held a hand across her chest.

"But you said--!!" An indignant Kasra squeaked with a stamp of her foot.

"Hey, I'll bet some of those other priestesses aren't as innocent as they look, either!" Rozha defensively pointed in the direction of Sachelvae. "If *you* saw what I did in Platina's desk, you'd *know* that!"

"Platina's desk?" Kasra curiously repeated. "You mean when you were searching her room? What did you see?..." She gave her sister a funny, sideways glare.

Rozha paused for a moment, flashing back to the raunchy images she rummaged through before shaking the thoughts from her mind. "The point is that nobody's perfect. In fact, some of the priestesses at the temple were reformed troublemakers of one sort or another."

"How do they all get away with it, then, if you said Diava can sense these things?" This made Kasra wonder all the more how the High Priestess could detect when someone was being naughty.

"Who says we -- I mean *they* -- have?" Rozha rebutted. "Like I said, and as I'm sure Layna knows very well, we're all given another chance so long as we genuinely repent and show a willingness to improve." It was a statement that didn't really work so well in Layna's case, because she never repented for any of her wrongdoings. "The most sinful thing is conception outside of wedlock. That's entirely intolerable in the Sachelvian Sisterhood and is punishable by immediate expulsion. That's why the chastity rule is so strictly enforced, to ensure that doesn't happen."

"So," Kasra began her summation, "as long as they don't have a reason to suspect you've been getting frisky, what's stopping me from trying~?" She insinuatingly raised and lowered her eyebrows, earning a flick on the nose from her sister.

"If *I* have any reason to believe you're fooling around, I'll be watching you like a katsiski," Rozha suspiciously stared her down. "The reason you should be more careful is because you take more after our mother than I do. She didn't bring us two into the world because she was infertile. For a Wild velta, having more than one child is very uncommon. Pures like us are naturally fertile, and if you come from Wild parents, there's an even higher chance you'll have many offspring... *When* you find a husband," she immediately amended her statement.

The two sisters had finally left the cheery avenues of Mediona and found themselves walking down the red and brown cobblestone streets of the Sanguinic side of Tresantia. The lampposts between the cozy brick houses were providing just enough illumination in the twilight sun to show they had been lit.

By the clock of their stomachs, they knew it was close to dinner time and that they'd be expected at the Dining Hall soon. Kasra and Rozha could see the grand edifice of Sachelvae atop its lofty hill barely a quarter mile away, short walls bent outward like inviting arms to come through its open doors. But what had been a leisurely stroll back home was about to end in the most unexpected of ways.

With the whirring sound of a sharp object spinning quickly through the air, a short knife had been thrown directly in front of Rozha's feet. Both she and Kasra immediately stopped and looked around, but their attacker was nowhere in sight.

"Tell me," a familiar voice shouted to them from behind and above, "Do I know your mother?"

The traveling sisters turned around and looked up to behold the benighted image of Viasarria, holding onto the roof of a stranger's house with one hand on its chimney, and her knee on its shingles. Her other hand was gripped onto the hilt of the sword she carried on her back.

"You!" Rozha pointed at her, squinting her eyes to get a clearer look. "How'd you get out of the Quarantine Bay?!"

"Layna bailed me out after she caught you snooping through my stuff in Platina's room," Viasarria replied, grabbing another dagger from her belt.

"Layna?" Rozha repeated, exchanging looks with Kasra. "No one was in that room but us the entire time we were there!"

"Or so you thought," Viasarria snidely smirked. "Layna isn't wrong when she says she's capable of magnificent things. I don't know how she's able to defy the laws of Sanguinic magic, but I know it's why Mother Diava is keeping her there."

"If you think Layna's powers are so great," Rozha argued, "why isn't she with you, now?" This curious statement had Kasra trying to detect the same feelings she had from before when the invisible Layna was nearby.

"I had the good sense to never let her know what I was up to," Viasarria said. "Even now, she's at the temple, playing nice. All I told her was to keep an eye on you two for me when I was locked up. After she told me she caught you looking through my letters to Nilsein, she distracted Platina to get me out of the Quarantine Bay."

"So that's all Layna is to you, then?" Rozha spat. "A tool for your own ends?"

"The only reason she even disliked you is because I *told* her to," Viasarria proudly proclaimed. "She's as competitive as all the demons in Safiro's hell, and will become a wonderful killer one day." She laughed at imagining her younger sister with blood-stained hands, standing over the bodies of her first victims.

"I regret nothing for making my mission so personal. Every blade dancer trained in your mother's corps are all told what failures her children are, and how it pains her to have wasted her body on their birth. I knew nothing would please her greater than to have their ravaged corpses be brought back to her. It's the least I could do to repay her for what she has done for me."

Just before Rozha could make a rebuttal, Viasarria threw a fistful of knives at both her and Kasra, one of them making its mark through the violette's ankle. With an agonized shriek, Kasra fell into a narrow alley. While Rozha was dropping back to block, the wide sleeve of her Teacher's gown unveiled her forearm blade, off of which one of Viasarria's knives was deflected. Another stuck into her chest, but the pointed blade couldn't pass through the armor padding underneath her dress.

Viasarria gracefully leapt off the roof and vanished in mid-air. The invisible assassin only gave herself away when she tumbled on the ground, kicking up dirt and crunching stones, giving Rozha the warning she needed to block her strike with a blinding clash of steel -- her sword's edge scraping against the short saber mounted on Rozha's armor. Viasarria reappeared and disappeared in a blink of an eye upon the moment she made physical contact. After she deflected Viasarria with her parry, Rozha extended a leg through the slit in her dress, but struck only air; her unseen opponent countered with an upward lash of her tail. The curved blade attached to its green-colored tip sliced Rozha's dress in twain.

Now that her movement was no longer restrained, Rozha could make a proper comeback. Even still, she'd have to make do with one less weapon to defend herself against her rival dancer's entire arsenal. Viasarria only let up in her assault now that they were on equal footing because she could see Rozha's lacking offense, too. The fires in her eyes dared her rival to make the first move, because she knew she could counter it twofold.

"You hesitate because you know I'm the better fighter," Rozha incited her invisible adversary into acting first.

"If you're so good, prove it!" Viasarria called her bluff with a slap to her face. Rozha's heart pounded in her ears as her adrenaline rose to a fever pitch; she threw a punch directly ahead, but once again missed her transparent target. She was then frozen in mid-swing by an astapsyxi before she was kicked in the back, and fell on her face when her legs were grabbed out from underneath her by Viasarria's unseen tail. She made herself visible when she sat on Rozha's back and used her legs to restrain her opponent's arms. She secured a chokehold that put even more pressure on the Red Dancer's spine. "Do you think your mother would be proud of me?" she taunted her grimacing foe.

Kasra entered the fray with a koptigma, causing a telekinetic burst to separate Viasarria from her sister. But as soon as Viasarria was no longer touching Rozha, she turned invisible once more. Rozha got to her feet and spun around, only to be struck between her shoulder blades and have her head bounce off the iron shaft of a light post.

She could barely shake off the dazzling shove before her neck was once again at Viasarria's mercy, this time tied to the street lamp by her rival's tail. The visible Viasarria kept herself high up out of arm's reach by hanging onto the lamp upside down by her crossed legs. Once more, Kasra came to her sister's defense with a koptigma blast, sending Viasarria flying back to the street.

The unexpected separation had no effect on the blade dancer's acrobatic finesse, who used the momentum of this magic push to land on her feet with a graceful stunt. Though she had been rendered invisible again, Kasra gave her position away with her astapsyxi -- its sparkling effect tracing the outline of their opponent's body. Thinking fast with a flourishing twirl, Rozha slashed her forearm blade into to Viasarria's armored abdomen. The cut didn't make it all the way through her rival's protective padding, but the force of the blow did knock the wind out of her.

While the black-haired velta was doubling over in pain, Rozha sent her staggering with a kosh of her elbow on the back of Viasarria's unprotected head. The Red Dancer then attempted to knock her down with a straight-legged kick to her midsection, but Viasarria proved her finesse at using momentum to her advantage by rolling back to her feet after she fell on her back. She used the new space between them to throw her last knife, forcing Rozha to block and open herself to a charge attack.

This time, anticipating the aggressive maneuver, Rozha ducked down to dodge Viasarria's overhead swipe and grabbed her shins between her legs.

The grounded blade dancer turned her body to take Viasarria down with her, where her sword was rendered useless.

Viasarria dropped her blade as Rozha sat on the small of her back and pushed her rival's face into the gravel-laden street. Their tails intertwined as Rozha kept Viasarria's from reaching around her neck; the whole time, her suffocating opponent was struggling to stand on her knees. As soon as Viasarria got a knee up and was able to release the pressure Rozha was exerting on the back of her head, she was able to twist her body and reverse positions.

Small pebbles fell from the wounds of her face, almost completely reddened with blood, as the angered blade dancer pummeled Rozha into submission with repeated kicks of her spiked heels. Once her tail was freed from Rozha's grasp, Viasarria was able to break away from their deadly ground game and return to her feet. She swiped the crimson liquid dripping off her brow in just enough time to see Kasra send a blast of invisible force right into her face. The unexpected attack was like a jab to her chin; the pain-resilient blade dancer recovered a bit too fast for the surprised Kasra's liking, who now earned herself her enemy's undivided attention.

With a cartwheel to pick up her weapon and an astonishing leap, Viasarria cleared the gap across the street and nearly cut Kasra in half with a strong swipe of her sword. The violette stopped her in mid-swing with an astapsyxi, causing the raging velta to drop from the air and lose her balance when she hit the ground. Kasra followed up by taking a step back and shooting another burst of energy from between her hands, this one much more pronounced than the first. A purplish wave of light struck the sword out of Viasarria's grasp as she tried to use its edge to deflect the unknown attack.

Rozha was nearly speared by the tip of the falling blade when it stabbed into the ground nearby. The redhead relegated herself to quietly observe whilst she recovered her strength; she was every bit as interested in her sister's abilities as Viasarria was. Unperturbed by Kasra's unpracticed talents, Viasarria continued her assault, advancing with a blade dancer's spin in an attempt to catch her with the remaining two weapons in her arsenal. She moved too fast for Kasra to freeze her this time; the violette flinched behind a masalida that shattered from the first hit.

She wasn't able to project a second one fast enough, before Viasarria's tail came around to smite her with its spiked bracelet. Taking the hit to her arm caused it to go numb with pain; Kasra was certain she had broken the limb when she was knocked onto her side. Under the weight of her teeth-clenching agony, the violette could do no more than wail and squirm away from her attacker. Viasarria dropped a knee on Kasra's stomach and reeled an arm to finish her foe, before her tail was entangled by Rozha's own.

The rival blade dancer was pulled off Kasra, her head meeting Rozha's armored elbow causing her to momentarily lose consciousness the instant before she hit the ground. Viasarria saw her blood smeared on the cobblestones as she slowly raised her face from the street, before Rozha planted the heel of her boot into her neck.

"Is a miserable life like yours even worth ending?" A victorious Red Dancer threatened to end her with a coup de gras. "I should send your severed head back to Nilsein after I carve my name into your face so she'll know who your killer is."

Before this vengeance could be exacted in the manner she described, Rozha was stopped by a silent astapsyxi from out of nowhere. The weight of Rozha's foot being lifted off her neck allowed Viasarria to turn her head and see where her savior came from. But it was not who she imagined it would be. Instead, she was rather surprised and equally miffed to see a wounded Platina clutching her side as she extended an arm toward the fighting blade dancers.

The nurse appeared to have been beaten mercilessly; she was slowly healing a bleeding gash near her hip as she limped toward Rozha and Viasarria. She waited until she was within her anemic speaking distance before finally uttering a word to either of them. "You must stop," the delivery of her words were oddly unaffected by her pain -- which even this she did not show in her face.

"I should have known better than to let you live," Viasarria coughed, her fingers digging into the dirt.

Platina teleported Rozha to her side and freed her from her binding spell. "Mother Diava knows everything about you," she told the injured villain squirming to her knees. "You are hereby excommunicated from Sachelvae. Teacher Rozha, you are exempt from blame as you were acting out of self-defense." She laid her hands on the Teacher's face to begin healing her wounds, once her own were fully mended. "Viasarria," the nurse addressed the assassin, "your only prerogative is to flee as soon as possible. For your betrayal, you are now treated as an enemy of Sanguina, and the Sisterhood will see to your exile from Tresantia. A seal has been placed on the doors of the temple against you. You will never be able to enter Sachelvae again."

Kasra was amazed that Platina wasn't reading all these vows from a textbook, the way she so casually said them. The moment she thought of the statue girl's name, she earned the unsettling attention of her eyes. "Kasra," came Platina's tremble-inducing voice, "I will take you to the Quarantine Bay to heal your wounds. You will not be allowed in the Dining Hall until then."

Instead of carting her off on a paralytic stretcher as she had done once before, Platina settled for the more traditional method of hoisting Kasra's arm around her shoulders to help her stand. She let the novitiate use her to balance on one leg as she carried her back up the hill to the temple. Kasra wasn't even aware of the wound on her arm until Platina wrapped it around herself.

Rozha stayed behind and made sure Viasarria wasn't going to try anything while her sister's back was turned. She could see the ire written in her rival's bleeding face as she wobbled to her feet. Despite her unwillingness to admit defeat and her reluctance to surrender, Viasarria was smart enough to know she was in no condition to be fighting anymore. She took this opportunity to stagger for the cover of the residences around her, her mind too fuzzy to carry her legs any faster than an awkward walk.

Rozha kept her eyes on the place she saw Viasarria disappear as she backed up toward the slowly advancing Platina and Kasra, until they were finally within the safety of the temple's doors.

Chapter 20: Diava's Judgment

Once they were inside and had the iron doors pulled shut, a pair of priestesses playing gatekeeper assisted Platina in preparing a magic seal to lock the doors from Viasarria's hands. They seemed confident that this would be enough to keep the blade dancer out, but a concerned Kasra knew better. "If Layna was able to get Viasarria out of the Quarantine Bay, what's keeping her from getting her back in the temple?"

"A psychic alarm will sound when the doors are opened by anyone but Mother Diava," Platina explained, upon completing the casting of her spell. "If Layna was able to break this seal, the High Priestess would know about it and be able to stop any interlopers from getting inside."

This fact made Kasra even more curious. *'Raia told me the same thing, once before. But she said when Layna opens the doors, it was as if they weren't sealed in the first place. If Mother Diava was made aware of this every time it happened, why wouldn't she stop them from going out?'*

Just as the violette's mind was being filled with conspiracy theories, Platina gently set her down on the marble floor to tend to her lacerations. She started with laying her hands on the violette's ankle; the moment her foot was sheathed in the healer's warm radiance, the pain of her wound subsided. Feeling the weight of her company's stares on her back, Platina requested, "Teacher Rozha, you are expected at the Dining Hall. Please do not tarry."

"Yes, Nurse Platina," Rozha respectfully bowed, along with the priestesses behind her. Platina continued her work as she watched them leave the atrium. She heard one of the veltas whispering something about what kind of food they'd be having and saw Rozha shrug as she refused to comment.

"I am impressed that she was unscathed," Platina remarked, when they were finally out of sight and earshot. "Usually the target of an ambush does not fare so well. Why do you think Layna went to such lengths to free her sister? Does she realize what Viasarria was up to?"

That was the first time Kasra had ever heard Platina ask a question -- she was usually the one with all the answers. What did she need a young novitiate's input for? "I, I dunno…" the violette played dumb, to avoid possibly incriminating herself. "Maybe she was jealous of my date with Malkinos?"

Platina gave her a look like she wasn't ready to buy that excuse. Although truthfully, *any* look the nurse gave someone would seem indifferent, at best. "This is why boys are not allowed on the premises of Sachelvae," she said. "It tends to spark competition and jealousy. These emotional disputes are to be avoided because feelings are fickle things. People contrive emotions as a way to manipulate others. I look for the logic in what people say, rather than the passion with which they say it; that's the only way to winnow lies from the truth."

'She'd make a good judge,' Kasra thought cynically. *'She treats everyone's words like writing.'*

With a forward bluntness reminiscent of Layna's, Platina said, "You are… quite transparent, Kasra. Your expressions often convey the things you fear to say. But do not take my criticism as negativity; there is nothing wrong with being open and honest. Sanguina does not like secrets, for they are often used to hurt someone else. The more we know about one another, the more we can have in common."

'That's an ironic statement, coming from her,' Kasra mentally riposted.

Platina continued, "I made my sacred vow to keep my mind pure and clean at all times; all I do is focus on Mother's desires."

Now Kasra really wanted to know what Rozha found in her room. *'It must be **really** bad if she couldn't tell me.'* Then openly asked, "Does Sanguina not wish for you to find someone to love?"

"She is the Goddess of Love as well, this is true," Platina could not argue, "but love is a distraction that elicits inefficient behavior."

Having been caught off guard by Platina's point of view, Kasra asked, "What do you mean by that?"

"I am referring to what so many stricken by love call 'the chase' --" the stoic nurse explained, "the will to do anything to earn the affection from the person they desire. Their minds become so focused on winning the heart of their partner that they forget other pursuits and at worst alienate other people. I cannot put my missions nor my ambitions on standby for so long. I will lose sight of my purpose in this world."

"What do you believe your purpose is," Kasra began, "if it is not to find your soulmate and aid the procreation of our kind?"

"I am a healer," Platina plainly said. "My purpose in life to make sure other people do not lose theirs. I am one of the beams that keep the structure of the Sisterhood whole. Without healers like us, the Sanguinic Order would cease to be."

"And you feel like having something so simple as someone to love would end that for you?" Kasra insightfully, if not skeptically, asked.

For the first time since their conversation began, Platina paused for thought, as if reaching a barrier in her mental calculator. "Perhaps," she said with unusual measure, and even emotion.

"Have you never had even a crush on someone before?" Kasra dug deeper into the young woman's subconscious.

Again, Platina was forced to deliberate; her face, usually austere and stiff, softened with what appeared to be a frown and a raise of her brow. Her irises moved to the top of her eyes, having that familiar look that normal people have when the proverbial wheels are turning in their heads. "I can't say for sure if what I felt was a semblance of love or not. I have favored some people over others. But I don't think that's the same thing."

Kasra smiled. At last, she saw a crack beginning to form in the statue girl's outer shell. "Have you ever wanted to see someone more than anyone else?"

Platina nodded slowly -- what could have been mistaken as a smirk started curling a corner of her lips. "Yes. Before I came to Sachelvae, when I was a young girl like you, I met a boy who I liked very much. We'd always meet at lunchtime every day, when we'd go to the same vendor to buy food. He'd talk to me about the work he had done throughout the morning. He helped his father tend the fields. He knew so much about working with his hands and growing crops. My parents wanted me to be a mother who did housework, and be married to a man like that. They were Pure, like me, but they weren't particularly strong to the faith. They wanted me to go to Sachelvae so that I could learn how to be the most refined and sophisticated woman that a man could marry. But after I got here, my plans changed."

The nurse eased herself to a more comfortable sitting position before continuing, "When I met Teacher Xanne and learned of my potential to be a healer through her exercises, I was told to see Sister Kyrana. Kyrana was responsible for unlocking the powers of healers, of which there are said to be one in every thirty four Pures. Therefore it comes as no surprise that we would be considered such an important, and rare commodity. I was told if I wanted to be one of the Sachelvian nurses, I would have to be more dedicated to achieve this position in the clergy. They said I could almost never leave the temple, unless in dire circumstance, like to perform healings on a priestess who had fallen in combat. I had to remain ready to save someone's life and know every spell to cure every ailment. I couldn't let myself be distracted by anything. I had to choose the future my family wanted for me, or the future that Sanguina wanted for me." Taking a dramatic pause, she looked at Kasra, who wore an expression like she knew how Platina was going to end her story.

"You must be wondering if I regret it now," she asked herself the most poignant question. "I cannot say with confidence that I didn't make the right decision. I know the path I have been traveling was the one I was made to go down. I never wanted my parents' lives of humble mediocrity. But I never considered myself an adventurer, either. I wanted to be someone whose responsibilities fell in between that."

Kasra knew how Platina felt. She never dreamt of having a perfect life - - just one that worked. "I'm glad I've gotten this chance to know you better, Platina. I think what you've become is a very interesting person." The violette wasn't even sure the proper response she was supposed to have when Platina turned her head to show an undeniable grin on her face. "Thank you, Kasra. You are most kind to think of me in such high regard. Perhaps one day, I will come to know you better, as well." As if realizing she was beginning to show any unsightly emotion, she returned to her austere complexion and added, "You must forgive me for having kept you so long. I know everyone must be wondering the reason behind our hiatus."

Kasra stood up along with Platina, graciously holding the nurse's hand. "I'd be happy to talk to you again, sometime. You're not so scary after all!" Letting her go for a goodbye wave, the violette chirped, "See you!" And departed for the Dining Hall. On the way, she nearly bumped into Raia as she traversed the temple's corridors. "What're you doing, wandering around out here?" the violette's voice echoed in the narrow, torch-lit chamber.

"You were taking a while to show up," Raia half shrugged, "so Mother Diava asked me to go look for you. Is everything alright?"

"Yeah, Platina and I were just talking about love, of all things," Kasra raised an eyebrow, glancing over her shoulder.

Raia chuckled with disbelief. "What? Platina has emotions?" the brunette laughed harder. "What brought all this up?"

"Malkinos and I made amends, today," Kasra started, shyly brushing the sole of her boot on the marble floor. "And we had a little date, too…" her tail innocently wagged with a sway of her hips.

Raia's eyes glistened as she beamed with elation. "You went out with him?!" She excitedly gasped, trying to refrain from hopping in place. "I'm so happy for you! You have to tell me what you two did together!"

An embarrassed Kasra rubbed the back of her neck. "C-Can I save that for a later time? We've been holding up dinner for a while, now…"

"Alright, I get it," Raia rolled her eyes, calming herself down. She flicked her head, motioning for the two of them to get moving. "Malkinos was so lonely living out at the ranch all by himself. He's always had difficulty talking to girls, but I don't think he could have had a better girlfriend than you."

"Nahh," Kasra blushed, earning herself a little hug from Raia.

"I mean it!" The brunette squeaked, jumping up to nuzzle Kasra's cheek. "You're the best thing that's happened to him since I started living here."

"I have plans to see him again," Kasra tweaked Raia's ear, "sometime soon, I hope!"

A ticklish Raia giggled and squirmed away from her friend's grasp. She had the most submissively pleading of stares as she batted her bright eyes up at Kasra's. She even leaned back against the wall to make herself look slightly smaller. "Um, I know Rozha is faculty right now, so that means she's likely going to be leaving your room to dorm with Kyrana," came the start of her pitch. "At the risk of sounding hasty, I was wondering... since your room will have another bed in it, soon, if you wouldn't mind me moving in with you?"

Kasra's face lit up at the mere thought of it. "Of course I wouldn't mind!" She knelt to give Raia a nuzzle of her own. "You've been my best friend since I came to Sachelvae!" Which wasn't exactly a fair statement; she was the *only* friend Kasra had made. But this made no difference to Raia, who was happy to be sharing a room with someone she actually liked, for a change. The short brunette threw another hug around her friend, then playfully whispered in her ear, "You'll protect me from Layna if she gets mad that I've abandoned her, won't you?"

"No one's going to be laying a hand on either of us," Kasra said, "except the faculty if we don't show up to the Dining Hall any sooner!"

When the two novitiates finally arrived and claimed their open seats at their end of the table, Layna greeted Kasra with a stink eye. "Ooh yay, you finally made it," she derisively monotoned. "I was starting to get my hopes up that you wouldn't be here."

Kasra stayed coldly silent as she took her seat, believing her rival undeserving of a response. Layna's eyes flashed at the violette, as if begging her to respond and light her ire; it took Raia to pull her back by the ears to stop them from getting into an argument. "We don't need this, right now!" The brunette hissed, glancing fearfully at Mother Diava's end of the table. "Can you two just sit next to each other without bickering, for even a minute?"

"She wasn't here for Diava's announcement," Layna bitterly stabbed a fork into her salad. "Viasarria's been kicked out of Sachelvae, thanks to *the Red Dancer!*" She whimsically wiggled her hands.

"Thanks to *herself*," a frowning Kasra corrected her. "She was the one who attacked us, *not* the other way around."

"I don't believe that for a *second*," Layna crossed her arms. "Why would Viasarria pick on someone right after she got out of the Quarantine Bay? She only got in there in the first place because Rozha *framed* her for starting a fight!"

"That's a load of shit and you know it!" Kasra jabbed a finger at her. "Rozha didn't start anything! *You're* the one who freed her from the Quarantine Bay -- Viasarria *admitted* it!"

"What?!" A bemused Layna incredulously squeaked, her ears standing on end. "You expect me to believe all *that*?! You're *delusional!*"

After studying Layna's countenance and hearing the overly-defensive tone of her words, Kasra was reminded of Platina's teachings, to look for the logic rather than the emotion of her argument. Kasra already knew Layna was lying, but now she could see how she looked when she was trying to acquit herself. "I think you know very well how you could've gotten away with it. It's not like you haven't, before."

Minding Raia over her shoulder, who had been trying to keep herself out of the conversation as much as possible, Kasra added, "Raia told me about what you can do. The only reason they keep you here is to understand why. The only reason you *won't* leave is because you're scared."

Layna's eyes narrowed as she leaned in to test if Kasra would flinch. "I'm not afraid of *you*!"

A stalwart Kasra merely shook her head at the sassy vixy's threat. "You just use aggression to mask your insecurities. If you *really* wanted to start something to prove yourself, you wouldn't have used Viasarria to do it for you." Layna returned to sitting back in her chair with a sneer and a powerless chuff.

The troublemaker was short of a comeback this time, allowing Kasra to continue. "I've had powers like you all my life, and I don't even know what all of them are yet, but they've become clearer to me the longer I've been here. That's why you go running off, to test yourself."

Just when Kasra thought she had done something profound to open Layna's mind, the brash vixy shot back, "Stop talking like you know everything about me! You're so arrogant because you think you've been

through it all. You think you know what I'm going through. You're wrong -
- we have *nothing* in common!"

At this point, the other novitiates had noticed their erupting argument. It
was only then that Layna realized they were being scrutinized. Interestingly,
the High Priestess was having a secret conversation of her own, amongst the
Teachers at her end of the table. Suddenly, Platina rushed into the Dining
Hall and said something in her ear that caused both the High Priestess and
Layna to freeze with concern.

Suddenly, Diava stood from the table with an authoritative shout,
darkness falling over her face like a cloud before a storm. "Layna," her voice
thundered across the hall. "Come with me. Now."

The unexpected and imperious summoning of the troublemaker earned
everyone's alerted attention. Everyone but Rozha and Kasra shared a look of
shock and puzzlement; all eyes were on Layna as the dark-haired vixy
trembled out of her seat.

Of all the looks she had gotten from Diava in her time at the temple, she
could say for certain none were as disapproving nor angry as this. As she
apprehensively sauntered around the table, down the long walk of shame
toward the High Priestess, she desperately glanced to an equally worried
Teacher Xanne, as if expecting her to say something in her defense. What
with how Diava stared her down from six feet high, she was surprised she
wasn't pulled by her ear away from the Dining Hall.

Instead, the High Priestess hooked her tail around Layna's back,
ushering her along outside of the room. "No one is to leave the Dining Hall
until I return," Diava commanded her followers. Teachers Wanystha and
Xanne then stood up to follow the High Priestess and Layna. Their footfalls
faded to silence before anyone at the table risked moving a muscle.

"What's going on?" one of the novitiates whispered to Raia.

"Is she dusting off the old torture room?" a priestess of lavender hair
darkly joked.

"There's no such thing!" a green-haired velta was appalled by her
Sister's sense of humor. "Such a dungeon is merely a myth."

"Dungeon?" Rozha piped up, upon hearing the less-than-hushed
comment.

The dismissive priestess rolled her eyes, pointing at her jocular friend
across the table. "Brynita's referencing the old scare story that our former
history Teacher used to tell, to discourage bad behavior from her novitiates."

Brynita then spoke for herself, "Ex-Teacher Penitha said Sachelvae was
originally built with a great cellar, which could only be accessed if the

Purifier was drained; a secret door on the floor of the pool is said to lead to St. Sevasmia's tomb. Of course, only the High Priestess has the right to drain the Purifier."

"The Purifier's water is only renewed once per anointing of a new Mother," another priestess explained, turning everyone's heads to her. "To complete the ritual to become a High Priestess, it's said that the Mother abdicating her status must take her successor to St. Sevasmia's tomb. It is there she recites the oaths and vows of Motherhood, which only High Priestesses are allowed to know."

As enlightening as this dialogue was for Teacher Rozha, it still didn't answer her original question. "What's all this got to do with the cellar being used as a dungeon?"

"Well," Brynita proudly smirked, "as the others would have you believe is all conjecture, Teacher Penitha told my generation of novitiates that any vixy who makes repeated violations against Sanguina's Will are sent to St. Sevasmia's tomb to be forcibly re-educated until their behavior is up to Sachelvian standards."

"It's completely ridiculous," the first priestess exclaimed. "St. Sevasmia would never have allowed for such abject conduct from any of her disciples! Our temple was built to be a haven, not a prison, for our fellow children in Sanguina. Novitiates come because they want to, and stay because they like it here -- *not* because they're captured and forced to never see the outside world."

After seeing what happened to Layna, Raia wasn't entirely convinced. "Then for what reason was Layna taken off like that?"

This time, the righteous priestess could make no argument in Diava's defense, allowing Brynita to rest her case. It was at this point, during the silence in their conversation, that Teacher Wanystha returned to the Dining Hall. Her countenance lacked its usual, passive cheerfulness. Instead, her smile seemed a bit awkward -- even forced, as if trying too hard to maintain an optimistic disposition for her students. "The novitiates may excuse themselves from the Dining Hall and prepare themselves for today's lesson."

Truthfully, after what had just occurred, Kasra and Raia weren't sure if they could so easily take their minds off what was becoming of their friend. Indeed, their fellow classmates seemed equally concerned; not that any of them were going to miss Layna, but they certainly wouldn't have wished the sort of mysterious punishment that she was facing at the hands of Mother Diava. Teacher Wanystha saw it as her duty to distract the students as much as possible from worrying so much; when she was asked after Layna's well-being, she simply dodged the question by feigning ignorance.

She dared not let them know that Viasarria escaped the Quarantine Bay; she thought it was much safer to simply leave the students in the dark about Viasarria's excommunication from the temple. *'I really wish Mother Diava would have been less forceful with Layna's extrication from the Dining Hall,'* Wanystha lamented. *'It's put me in a rather difficult spot to explain it all away. The more fearful these students get, the less they'll tolerate our rules.'*

Teacher Wanystha was starting to guide her students to her classroom, and Kasra wanted to make sure she wasn't late this time. But Raia had been oddly quiet after their dinner -- even now, she was shyly lagging behind, when she was usually the one leading Kasra and Layna to these events.

When everyone else had went inside Wanystha's classroom, Kasra held the brunette back outside. "Okay, I can't stand to see you moping around like this," she placed her hands on Raia's shoulders. "What's going on with you?"

"It just makes me feel sick when I see people fighting," a pouting Raia pursed her lips. "I know it's going to sound awful, but I've never seen Layna hate someone more than you, before."

Kasra's hardened stare softened to a caring smile. "Is that what this is all about? I told you not to worry about me! I think Layna and I are going to be alright from now on."

"What?..." Raia disbelievingly gawked. "But I just heard you arguing, again!"

"For a brief moment," Kasra explained, "I saw what Layna really thinks. She's trying to prove to herself that we're not similar."

Raia laughed, "Where'd she get *that* idea from? You two are polar opposites!"

"Ideologically, yes," Kasra said, "but I've had powers like hers all my life. I don't think I've even seen what they all are, and I don't think she has, either. That's why she puts herself through those tests, to learn more about what she is. These things only became clear to me when I arrived in Sachelvae. If we truly are opposites, she needs to experience what I already have gone through, or she'll never be enlightened."

"You can't be serious," a shocked Raia exclaimed in a hushed tone. "The faculty would never let her leave Sachelvae."

"If she wants to, no one can stop her," Kasra replied, both she and Raia knowing this to be the truth.

"I don't know what I think about this," Raia uncomfortably looked away. "I never thought I'd miss Layna if she decided to leave, but I can't imagine being without her, either. I'll feel guilty if anything happens to her."

"I wouldn't blame you for getting tired of Layna," Kasra chuckled, "but I think it's time you moved on from her. It's not your responsibility to take care of everybody."

"We're nearing the end of the week," Wanystha said to her students, as Kasra and Raia took their seats. "Tomorrow, we'll be entering Sachelvae's sabbath day. I'm only making this announcement for our newest student, Kasra, who has never joined us for this occasion."

Naturally, when put on the spot, the violette quizzically glanced to Raia, demanding elaboration. "What's she mean? What's a sabbath?"

Raia proudly smiled at a chance to show her smarts, making sure her response was loud enough for the Teacher to hear. "That is a day designated by Sanguina for Her worshipers to rest. It is based on the cycle of Sanguina's moon -- once every two weeks, the Goddess enters Her resting phase; when the Goddess takes Her sabbath, so do we."

"Exactly right, Raia," Wanystha happily nodded with acknowledgement to her star student. "When Sanguina is at rest, Her moon is gone from the sky; Safiro's moon is in full bloom."

"When one moon is resting, the other moon is full," Raia clarified. "Only one deity watches us at a time."

Wanystha noted with an intrigued hum, "It was said, back in the time of the Great Civilization, the moons of Safiro and Sanguina were in perfect synch; they would enter and leave cycles at the same time. Ever since the calamity that split our faiths, the moon's phases have been altered. For thousands of years, we have observed them the way they are now. Until, just sixteen years ago..."

She trailed off as her gaze traveled across the faces of her class and settled on Kasra's, whom she just now noticed had her hair parted to show both eyes. She couldn't help tilting her head as she stared a little closer; *'That's interesting,'* she thought, examining the violette's red and blue heterochromia. Her lips parted as the temptation within her grew to ask Kasra how old she was. Most of the students in that room wouldn't have even been born before the date the Teacher described.

"What happened?" Raia got the Teacher back on track.

With a ruminative grin, Wanystha said, "I remember standing outside in the courtyard with her when it happened -- I was still just a priestess, then. We had been celebrating the day of Sevasmia's sainthood. The whole day, from the first ringing of the morning bell, Mother Diava seemed tense about something. I assumed it was just her anxiousness about the festivities; we all knew the Safiric Brotherhood waited for times when Pures congregated to attack us. Thankfully, our numbers were able to dissuade anyone interested in starting any trouble while we celebrated with the local population. We were out clear into the evening and watched the sky grow dark. Two weeks before, neither moon was present in the night. Since then, we had watched both moons moving through their phases in synchro. That night, we beheld something truly remarkable: we all were speechless as we stared at the sky. Safiro and Sanguina were staring back at us, at full attention. While everyone whispered conjecture amongst ourselves, we could see blue lights from far in the distance, coming from Travestas; the Safiric Brotherhood was also observing this occasion with much the same interest we had."

The way Wanystha said that made Raia feel like the Teacher had the idea that the Brotherhood was up to no good, as usual. "Do you think the Safiric Brotherhood has a different opinion about this event than we do?"

"It wouldn't be surprising," Wanystha half-heartedly chuckled. "Regardless of what this means to the Brotherhood, Mother Diava believes..." she fell silent again, still slightly distracted by Kasra's unveiled facial features. "That this synodic phenomenon was a gateway to a new era."

Naturally, this led to Kasra's next question: "Is this 'new era' good or bad for us?"

Wanystha had a hard time believing she was about to break this news with her young students, but she knew she had to. *'Mother Diava told me to take the gloves off. I only hope she's right about them being ready.'* Even still, she began with a kind of dramatic hesitance. "Back then, I heard Ex-Teacher Nalina ask Mother Diava in a hushed tone what caused her so much consternation. Diava hesitated and leaned in close, hoping no one would overhear when she said... the deities were preparing to pass judgement on us."

This startling revelation caused many exchanged looks and whispers among the student body. Twenty pairs of innocent eyes hardened with worry and demanded the Teacher to expound on her hypothesis. Raia was overcome with curiosity and asked the question many were thinking. "Safiro and Sanguina are angry with us?"

"I can't say for sure," a heavy-hearted Wanystha admitted. "Mother Diava thinks they have been unhappy ever since the end of the Great Civilization. Instead of trying to find a compromise and work together like

262

they once did, the gods are at odds with each other; one is seeking to undo the other."

"The gods are fighting?" Kasra confusedly remarked.

"In their own sort of way," the Teacher explained. "Safiro nor Sanguina can be 'defeated' through the kind of physical means by which we mortals are familiar; one must remove the other's influence by destroying their worshipers."

"So what you're saying is," Raia surmised, "Safiro and Sanguina want to create a single religion?"

Wanystha gravely nodded. "It would take something truly momentous -- as earth-shattering as what destroyed the Great Civilization -- to bring about such change."

Of course, the mentioning of an apocalyptic cataclysm spurred the fearful attention of all the Teacher's students. "Another meteor is going to fall?" one of the more pessimistic vixies whispered to another. "But everything is going so well!" Another commented. "It's so sudden --"

"Which side will win?" Kasra interrupted their chatter with a simple, yet insightful question.

"I wish I knew," Wanystha shrugged. "Safiro and Sanguina have set something in motion that only their believers have any control over. I think this scary time might prove to be a uniting force -- a worldwide rallying call to awaken those who were never faithful to either deity to make a choice." She paused with a somewhat indicative, yet cryptic smile at Kasra. "We need as many children of Sanguina as we can to join forces against the enemy. Mother Diava believes Tresantia will be pivotal in that role."

"What can we do about a threat so big?" Raia trembled. "Is that not a bit beyond us?"

"For now, yes," the Teacher honestly gave her disclosure. "You as students are not expected to join the front lines in this effort. But I am telling you, those of you who are so close to your graduation, what you can come to expect of your duties when you finally join the clergy. We're living in very different and decisive times. But..."

Wanystha tried to boost everyone's drained spirits with a rather forced smile, "as you can see, the sun is setting and will rise once again tomorrow. Nothing is going to stop you from existing as you are and as you have been. After all, although Sanguina will be at rest, Her magic still protects us; She does not wish for Her children to live in fear."

She realized it was probably not the best timing to unload such a heavy, dreadful warning on her students shortly before they would begin their once biweekly day of frivolity. She doubted if even she herself could enjoy her sabbath, now that she was worried about what was going through the minds of her students. She inwardly cursed Mother Diava for wanting her to create such an awkward situation. *'I know she's afraid of losing Layna, but that doesn't mean she has to take it out on everyone else.'*

Layna's lack of commentary during Wanystha's didactic sermon wasn't missed, however; lots of the students who even remembered she wasn't there were all glad she was absent. Even Raia felt at ease; she always got more out of her classes the less Layna had something to say about everything.

She could actually enjoy Kasra's company for once, instead of having to constantly defend her when Layna wanted to attack every last comment she made. She didn't feel like she had to wait for everyone else to leave ahead of them so they could engage in secret gossip at the back of the line -- instead, she was much more open about what Kasra wanted to discuss and knew nothing that Kasra had to say was going to get anyone in trouble with the faculty.

Seeing Raia so carefree didn't have the same effect on Kasra's mood, however. After trying to carry on a jovial conversation with her away from their classmates, the brunette was beginning to notice the distraction in Kasra's smile. At last, Raia grew concerned enough to inquiringly stop them from moving any further down the candle-laden corridor. "What's wrong? I know something is bothering you."

As if having waited for Raia to bring it up, Kasra replied, "Aren't you even a little curious about what Mother Diava has done with Layna?"

The brunette laughed, "Are you still thinking about Brynita's silly rumor?"

Kasra shook her head, wondering why her friend wanted to shrug off the whole incident. "Don't you think it's odd how Wanystha looked and acted the whole time afterward? Xanne didn't even come back to the Dining Hall after Diava left -- it was a weird occurrence for everyone."

This time, Raia's comportment immediately shifted to a frustrated groan. "Can I not just enjoy the one day off I've had all month without having to worry about some huge dilemma?"

"The world doesn't stop just because you want to take a break," a determined Kasra narrowed her eyes. "You have to keep moving with it, even when it's inconvenient for you. Well, I don't think having a rest is more important than what's going on behind the curtain, here."

Raia wanted to slap her forehead when she felt a growing tension between her ears. "You sound just like Layna," she muttered under breath, just loud enough that Kasra might've been able to pick out a few words. She stopped pinching her temples when she said more aloud, "Don't you think that it might be *better* that we don't know some things that are going on around here?"

"Why?" Kasra shot back. "Is that what the Teachers say? I learned a long time ago not to listen to what someone says just because they're the only one talking. Layna's right about one thing: you do well in Sachelvae when you stringently obey authority. But a place that's hiding this many secrets from the people who live here is not one that's meant to be trusted."

Raia took a long time of looking into Kasra's eyes glaring back at her before she finally let herself ease up. Her shoulders slumped and her brow furrowed, her voice returning to that childlike tone she normally had. "You really think we have to investigate this, don't you?"

Kasra smiled, trying to comfort her shaken friend. "I'm not asking you to be up all night and sacrifice your day off. It'll only take a moment to see what's going on."

"Alright," Raia tremulously sighed. "Let's go, then."

Chapter 21: Secrets of Sachelvae

Raia let Kasra lead the way back to the Purifier Hall. As they made their way down the marble passages, they started to hear something that resembled a faint hum. Following the sound to its source, its volume raised to a level high enough to where Raia or Kasra would have needed to almost shout to hear each other talking. They took a left turn away from the wide passage they had been walking down, away from Wanystha's classroom, which took them into a narrower hallway, leading them straight for the east entrance to the Purifier atrium.

The source of the sounds they had been tracking made itself apparent; Raia's eyes widened the moment she caught a glimpse of it, as they continued to make their approach. It was emanating from a translucent, red screen of watery energy. "It's huge!" She loudly remarked for Kasra to hear. "I've never seen a masalida so powerful before!"

The curious students stood almost close enough to the barrier to touch it, but neither of them dared to put a finger on it. The barely transparent wall seemed to glow slightly, as if warning against potential attacks. It was difficult to see much at all through the thick, red lens before them, but they could definitely see a small amount of the Purifier Hall through the Sanguinic door. Their visibility of the room was cut down just enough to see the pool, which was strikingly bereft of water. The empty natatorium revealed a staircase down its halfpipe-like interior, leading down to a bottom that neither vixy could see from their current position.

"They drained it!" Raia gasped. "That's the first time I've ever seen what's inside!" She wasn't sure whether she was scared or amazed by this revelation.

Kasra, however, knew exactly how she felt about it, and it only made her all the more frustrated that she couldn't explore it further. "They really don't want us to see what's down there," she growled.

"And it's for the best you don't know," came Xanne's startling voice from behind them. The dire glare she gave her students had Raia and Kasra taking a step back from her looming presence.

"Teacher Xanne? What're you doing here?"

The older velta faced her with an expression that was especially dower, even for the austere lady. "You both knew her better than anyone else. She was competing with you from the moment you two first met. I know it was not due to any pressuring on your part that she felt compelled to prove herself; she changed much since I brought her here."

"You knew Layna before she came to this temple?" Raia asked.

"She and her sister, both," Xanne replied. "I raised them, after all."

Raia and Kasra exchanged expressions of equal shock, neither having been enlightened of this fact. "You're Layna's mother?"

Xanne slightly tilted her head, as if Raia was only half right about her assertions. "I am their aunt," she clarified. "I took them in after their mother was murdered…" her expression fell further, her gaze trailing to where the wall met the floor of the narrow corridor.

"We left the coastal city of Li'Mez three years ago so that I could save them by pursuing Sanguina's Path of Truth. But they resented me for taking her away from her home city. Sometime during our travels to Tresantia, Viasarria abandoned our carriage. It wouldn't be for another year that I'd find out she went to be a blade dancer. During that year, Layna became more recalcitrant with me. She frequently complained that she missed her father and detested her mother for leaving him. She refused to be taught Sanguina's ways, because she only correlated the goddess with her mother… She did not want a second matronly figure to replace the one she lost."

The Teacher turned away from her audience to hide her misting eyes. "I wanted to believe it was all due to her youthful arrogance -- that she would one day grow out of this phase. She wanted to be with her father so badly, but I told my sister from the beginning that he was wrong for them…"

She grit her teeth and took a deep breath, trying not to show the anger she had kept long repressed. Her fingers clenched inside her sleeves, but the quivering of her voice she could not hide. "I told them he was of Safiric blood -- he would reject Sanguina's ways, even though he promised my sister he would not! He said his eyes did not dictate his faith, but he was a liar, like all of them are! He did not want a family; only the satisfaction of his… libertine avarice!"

A heart wrenched Kasra clutched an empathic hand to her chest. "Teacher Xanne…" she quietly trailed off.

"Where is he, now?" Raia openly wondered.

Xanne's head dipped down as she let out a sigh that sounded curiously like a chuckle. "…What does it matter?" was the controlled response she gave. Her composure seeming to have returned, she brought her full attention back to the novitiates standing behind her. "You should go back to your rooms, now," she gestured thither with an outward stretch of her quarterstaff.

Instead of genuflecting to her authority as the Teacher was expecting them to, Kasra recalcitrantly resisted her demands. "No," the violette steeled herself, stubbornly crossing her arms. "I want you to tell me what Mother Diava has done with Layna. Why are you imprisoning her?"

"After all I've avowed to you, I am in no mood to explain anything further." Xanne imperiously looked down her nose at the brave vixy. "What you've heard is all you need to know."

Kasra's eyes narrowed at the Teacher's attitude shift, seeing that her allegiance to Diava was stronger than it seemed. "What're you going to do to stop me?" the violette challenged her once more.

As Xanne's serious composure started to turn to a sour anger, a fearful Raia became short of breath. "K-Kasra..." the brunette weakly grabbed her friend's shoulder to jostle her attention. "I think we should go...!"

The violette flicked her eyes away from Xanne's unblinking countenance to see Raia feebly shaking on her bent legs. Kasra glimpsed back to the Teacher to see her arms reeling in preparation for an unknown spell; immediately thereafter, Raia's grip on Kasra faded. The violette heard her friend faint beside her just before the end of Xanne's quarterstaff was swung at her forehead. *"Rakshasti,"* the Teacher intoned.

Kasra flinched, expecting to be struck, but the weapon paused just inches above her crown and issued a strange pinging sound -- like a melodic vibration inside a brass cylinder. Kasra's whole body, from head to toe, was then filled with this vibration, causing her to feel very weak and languid. She felt heavy and tired, as if she had been awake for days. She stammered confusedly as she wavered in place, her bending knees bringing her closer to the floor as she tried to fight the power's effects.

After her world turned dark and her senses were suspended, Kasra awoke some time later to find herself lying in bed, staring at a ceiling that looked like it might've belonged to the room she shared with Rozha. Of course, as many bedchambers in Sachelvae were made to look identical, she couldn't get a full scope of the room she was in until she lifted her head to get her bearings. At first, it didn't seem very familiar, due to the presence of another bed being right beside the one she was in.

A dramatically reposed Raia was laid upon the mattress, with a damp terry cloth folded on her forehead. Seeing the poor, unscathed damsel looking like she had been rescued from a battlefield had Kasra cracking a smile, in spite of the stressful series of events that led up to their current situation.

This jocular emotion was dashed by the sound of footsteps on the polished stone floor outside. Kasra's muscles stiffened, preparing to jump if Xanne poked her head through the doorway. To her relief, what came through to greet her was the face of her sister. "You've awakened," Rozha paused momentarily, upon stepping in the room. Her mildly surprised frown grew to a knowing smirk as she crossed her arms and reclined against the wall. "I came and got you after Xanne told me what happened."

"I couldn't help it," a blubbering Kasra sat up, vindictively clutching her bedsheets. "How can they expect no one to wonder what's going on when someone's carted off like Layna was? Do we all just have to act like we don't know any more than what we're told?"

Rozha ducked her head to hide a quiet chuckle -- not to mock Kasra's case, but because she knew how she felt. "I know you're upset," she showed a grin, "but if you start going around, acting like everything is a big conspiracy, you're going to get in trouble. They hide things from everyone around here; it isn't because they don't think you 'deserve' to know or that they are plotting something against you. You can't be skeptical about *everything* you hear; no one you meet is going to spill their guts for you just to satisfy your curiosity."

Rozha raised a hand to prevent Kasra's predicted protest. "Look, I know things are getting weird around here, too -- my induction to the faculty is evidence enough of this. Mother Diava is trying to transform this place. Whether it's for some legacy of hers, or if it's because she's afraid of something, I couldn't tell you. But…"

She looked over her shoulder as if checking to see if anyone could have been listening in on them, before slapping the door shut with her tail. Minding the still sleeping Raia as she came in closer to Kasra's bedside, the redhead finally added, "I'd be lying if I said it had nothing to do with you. All these changes started coming about as soon as you entered these doors. She's panicking about something and isn't doing a very good job of hiding it. The faculty is responsible for keeping things under control, but Mother Diava's attitude isn't making it easy for them. She doesn't know how to handle what's going on. If you keep making her nervous by getting onto her case about what she's trying to sweep under the rug, she's going to take a radical step to make sure you don't do it anymore. That's why Layna is where she's at, right now."

Kasra felt an empty pit open in her stomach as sweat cooled her furrowed brow. "So the moral of the story is simple," she nervously concluded. "Keep your mouth shut and your head down."

"That's right," Rozha smiled at her sister's understanding. "Remain inconspicuous, and no harm will come to you. That doesn't mean don't be curious; just don't question authority. I recognized this rank and file system very well from my time in the military. Now you know how a couple of 'heathenous' blade dancers like Viasarria and I were able to make it here."

Kasra was impressed with how her sister was able to play the system to forge her way through the ranks of the temple. "I'm not the least surprised," the violette proudly swelled. "I'm happy you told me all that, Rozha; I wouldn't have believed it if anyone else told me. But..." came her dramatic hesitation. "What does this mean for me? You said that Diava is reacting to my being here."

"Like I said," the redhead averred, "I wish I knew." Upon seeing her sister's brow furrow with a hint of aggravation, Rozha added, "Don't think I've sold out my loyalty to you because I'm one of the Teachers now. I'll always be your big sister, okay?" With a purse of her lips, she offered a little smile and a teasing flick of Kasra's ear. "You can trust me to always tell you the truth!"

"Okay," Kasra chirped, her sister's playful attitude alleviating the twisting of her stomach. She knew if she didn't try to get her mind off what was going on behind the Sachelvian scenes, she'd never get any sleep that night. "What're you going to do on Sabbath Day?"

"Well," Rozha's eyes upturned as she thoughtfully poked a fingertip to her chin. "The blacksmith might have my new sword done by then. I'll have to go by his shop and see!"

"New sword?" Kasra curiously swiveled an ear. "You never told me anything about that."

"You never let me finish my story about the Pericula Initiative!" Rozha jokingly protested. But instead of actually delving into the details of her battles with the dark men, she skipped to the ending. "I got a lot of money out of that town for helping out -- more than enough to pay for a replacement for the weapon the Mire Fiend snatched from me."

"Is that how you were able to pay for all those other things for me?..." Kasra asked, her head turning suspiciously to one side.

"Hey, what're you looking at me like that for?" Rozha defensively retorted, guilt swelling inside her. "Do you think I *stole* all that cash?"

"No," Kasra raised an eyebrow. Now that Rozha seemed so shaky about it, she was actually starting to wonder if her sister was hiding something.

But the redhead wasn't going to give her enough time to draw a conclusion. "Then it doesn't matter! Point is, I need a new sword and I'm getting one tomorrow."

"If you'll be going to Mediona then," Kasra began her pitch with a smile, "would you like to be my chaperone to another date with Malkinos?"

Rozha couldn't keep out a laugh, giddy that she could facilitate her sister's budding romance. "Yes, I will most certainly do that for you. And, I'm going to do you another favor," she raised a finger as she paused for dramatic effect. "This is going to be yours and Raia's new room," she gestured to the sleeping vixy she mentioned.

Kasra's eyes sparkled, but just for a moment until she came to a rather disheartening realization. "Where will you be moving to?"

"I'll be sharing a room with Kyrana from now on," Rozha explained. "Diava said my classroom will be completed tomorrow. After Sabbath Day, I will have my official first class at Sachelvae!"

An elated Kasra nearly threw herself in her sister's arms, sharing in her excitement. "Oh Rozha, that's amazing! I just think you'll look so cool doing your new Teacher thing~"

Rozha chuckled and petted her sibling's ears as they pulled back apart. "Thanks, Kasra -- I'm really looking forward to it, myself."

"What's your lesson going to be about?" Kasra bounced in place.

The redhead showed a slight indication that she nearly gave into the temptation to spoil her sister with this hidden information. "I have a few ideas," she eventually said, "but I'll let them be a surprise for later. For now, you should be getting some sleep."

"Alriiiight..." Kasra disappointedly trailed off, watching Rozha take her leave.

"I'll see you in the morning," the Red Dancer gave her a charismatic wave, as she shut the door behind her.

The sound of the door's tooth clicking shut inside the pit of the wall had Raia finally stirring awake with a groan. Kasra's head turned to the half-awake brunette shifting to her side, trying to brush the hair away from her eyes. "You alright?"

"I couldn't be *worse*, thanks to you," a groggy Raia petulantly pouted.

"I'm sorry, Raia," Kasra bit her lip. "But we're not hurt and we're still here in the temple! That's what matters, right?"

"I told you we shouldn't have overstepped those boundaries," Raia continued protesting. "Now we'll have a Cinte of our own watching every move we make."

"That's fine, because Rozha just told me how we can get out of this," Kasra said, much to Raia's unspoken disapproval. "If we pretend we learned our lesson, they'll get off our case."

"What do you mean 'pretend?' " Raia shook her head. "We knew we weren't supposed to have come near the Purifier, in the first place."

"So?" Kasra shrugged. "They never told us to stay away."

"Sure," Raia argued, "except that Teacher Xanne overheard any intent you had of getting through her barrier."

"If *anyone* saw it, they'd want to know what was on the other side, too!" Kasra made her case.

"Not me," Raia self-righteously turned away and closed her eyes. "Everyone knows I follow the rules around here. That's why I'm one notch away from receiving my silver tiara," she pointed to the bronze circlet on her head. "If you want to be a paranoid screw-up like Layna, be my guest, but count me out. I've had enough of these silly adventures between the two of you. Nothing that you think the faculty is hiding from us could be worth losing my one and only chance of becoming a Sachelvian priestess."

Kasra thumped the bed with her tail, showing a hint of building aggravation at the brunette's selfishness. But upon having such vindictive thoughts, she took a mental step back for some introspective clarity. *'I'm the one being selfish for pulling Raia into our latest debacle. She's right; I'm no better than Layna if I act like this. I don't want to be like her and lose Raia, too.'* Having allowed herself to calm down, the violette expired an apologetic sigh. "Well, like it or not, we're roommates now; I guess the faculty thought I might be a better influence on you than Layna was."

"What?" Raia snapped back to attention. "You mean, this is going to be my room?"

"Rozha apparently was going to tell us that after we got out of Wanystha's class, but..." Kasra awkwardly tittered, "you know..."

Raia tried to keep the smile from spreading across her face, her voice regaining its girlish lilt. "I suppose I can be happy about this, so long as you promise me we won't do anything so stupid again."

After a long, solemn stare into her friend's eyes, as if considering deeply the decision she had to make, Kasra calmly stated, "I'll think about it."

Taken off guard, Raia couldn't contain her laughter. "You are the *worst*! What am I supposed to do with you?" She had the hardest time being upset around the violette; something about her presence always made her feel better. *'I don't know why I should even be trusting her like this,'* she shook her head, looking up at the ceiling. *'I guess it's because if she really was like Layna, she wouldn't have even tried at making me a promise. She doesn't lie nor manipulate like Layna does.'*

Relaxing to a more comfortable position on her bed, Kasra asked, "Are you going to be able to get any sleep?"

"This mattress is a little stiffer than the one I'm used to," Raia commented, testing the springs with kneading motions.

This would have been Layna's cue to make a weight-related remark about the full-figured vixy. Even though such a temptation never crossed

Kasra's mind, the way she said what came out of her mouth was immediately taken the wrong way. "I'm sure you'll be able to break it of its firmness, over time."

"Gee, thanks..." Raia shot a hurt, albeit slightly desensitized glare over her shoulder.

"I-I didn't mean it like that!" Kasra apologetically gulped, hastily waving her hands.

"It's okay," Raia sputtered at her friend's reaction, proceeding to peel the blankets down from her pillows. "I'm used to that kind of mean stuff, by now. Layna wouldn't have even apologized if she had said something like that."

This spoken fact didn't surprise Kasra in the least. "I'm sorry I hurt your feelings. I'd never do it on purpose! I'm so awkward with compliments that they get dizzy and stumble on the way from my head to my mouth."

Raia laughed a little more jovially, finally lying down on her side. "You act like people never say nice things about you, yet you scored a date with my brother."

"It was both our first time out," Kasra bashfully admitted. "He was the only boy my age I've ever met before who actually noticed me. Most people avoided me before I came to Sachelvae."

Raia's expression softened. Her estranged friend had come close many times to explaining her background, but she still never got a full disclosure from the violette. "Why is that?" She asked, hoping that she could eventually probe into Kasra's secrets.

It was evidently something she was still rather uncomfortable with dredging up. Her attentive stare on Raia's eyes faltered and took off to no place in particular. "You know I didn't quite grow up like everyone else," she started. "I didn't have the kind of home life you did, with a loving family and all that. I was never told anything about my relatives, nor even where or when I was born, for that matter. I just assume that I get one year older at the beginning of every year."

"That's awful!" Raia covered her mouth with a gasp.

"That's certainly the way it felt," Kasra bitterly sneered. "I thought if I got away from them, they'd forget about me. But Viasarria's attack made it clear to me that not only have I not been erased from their memory, but they want me back -- dead or alive."

Raia's expression pensively softened. At a loss for words, she rested her head against her pillow, but couldn't take her eyes off her troubled friend. *'No wonder she's so aggressive. Maybe if I'm more patient, I can help her.'*

Chapter 22: The Second Side

In Kasra's sleep, she was given visions through her dreams of the unseen events that had enraptured her curiosity, from the evening before. She could see, as if from the perspective of an invisible, intangible watcher, Mother Diava taking Layna to the Purifier Hall. She ordered Teacher Wanystha to drain the holy natatorium by manipulating the wheel on top of a spigot, which was fashioned in the likeness of an unborn belhuayn spirit. The way the spigot was designed made it look like it was flapping its fin-like wings to breach the waters, as if leaving the pool to begin its life in the physical world.

After Wanystha had turned this wheel thrice in a counterclockwise motion, a whirlpool began to form in the center of the Purifier. All of the water was swirling down into a round drain, large enough for someone to fit inside -- were it not for a metal grid covering the hole. This metal grid was outfitted with a handle. The step on which the priestesses sat for their ablutions continued as a staircase down the pool's half-pipe structure all the way to the bottom.

When the pool was dry, Mother Diava ordered Teacher Xanne to project a barrier on all access points to the Purifier Hall. The High Priestess then took a shaky Layna down into the empty Purifier, where she pulled the metal grate open to unveil its dark interior. Xanne seemed nervous as she stood guard, while Wanystha hurriedly made her way back to the Dining Hall.

Once they had begun their descent, Mother Diava issued a silent spell to cast a ball of light over her hand, so that her arm acted like a torch for her and Layna's safe passage through the wet, spiral of stone stairs leading to the secret subchamber of Sachelvae. The staircase descended what could have been sixty feet until they reached the bottom. They stood on an iron vent covering the subterranean pipes, where the water from the Purifier had spilled into. The rest of the rectangular room before them was made of mossy stone that looked like it hadn't been touched in several decades.

The ceiling was spiky with short stalactites and loops of vines growing from cracks between them. The cavernous cellar smelled of humidity and waterborne vegetation. In the middle of the room was a square-shaped indentation. Outside of that, on either of the room's far corners, was built a marble statue of Saint Sevasmia's likeness -- one with wings, and one without, both with her hands folded and head bowed in prayer. Between these large sentinels was a round, red door made to resemble Sanguina's full moon.

With a whisk of her light-bearing hand, Mother Diava mystically commanded magical torches on the walls to turn alight -- not with fire, but with a divine radiance that defied explanation. She took a starstruck Layna to the center of the room; now standing in the square indentation, the High Priestess began to assume a similar stance to Sevasmia's statuary. Seconds into her concentration, a phantom sound like the chiming of bells resounded from everywhere and nowhere at once. A sparkling mist descended from the ceiling, like snowflakes falling and melting in mid air.

Cracks of light began to shine through the square-shaped striation carved into the floor around them, getting taller and brighter until it formed a floating banner. As these effects coalesced, Layna was overcome with an odd stiffness -- as if she would be unable to move even if her frightened legs had the strength to carry her. She powerlessly watched as Mother Diava muttered a prayer to the Saint whose guidance she sought.

"Sister Sevasmia, you have given me the Sight -- in the auguries you have endowed me, I have seen the holy waters turning foul. I have seen the bones of priestesses shimmering in their depths. Oh Saint of Sanguina, I ask for your wisdom in these troubling times. I ask for you to impart me the knowledge of the Goddess' Chosen for this student's preservation. For I fear... if she drifts into the hands of madness our world will descend into darkness. It has come time for you to show her what I cannot. I bow in deference to your sacred honor, to teach her what I have failed to."

Her humble wishes were answered with a reactive shine from the statues, as if Sevasmia's avatars had suddenly grown consciousness. Orbs of light appeared before their closed eyes; red haloes materialized above their heads as a great rumbling shook the floors and loosened strains of dust from the ceiling. The vines overhead wobbled as the round door split in half -- both sides sliding back of their own accord to slowly unveil pink rays of light bursting from the seams.

Layna had to shield her eyes to avoid being blinded by its radiance, filling the once dark room. She hazarded the longevity of her vision a glimpse over her arm at what laid beyond the doors. At first, what looked like a rose-colored setting sun filling the passage dimmed to a flat, rippling spiral -- as if a rock had been thrown into a pool, and the waters themselves had been turned sideways to disobey gravity.

White sparks starting from four quadrants of this gateway spiraled into its center, like streams of sugar being blended into a rich tea. However, this portal did not emit onesuch pleasing aroma -- rather it sang a single note of a melodious hum. Its hypnotic depth pulled Layna chest first toward it, her eyes glassy as she wobbled unsteadily on her feet. An urgent touch of Diava's hand against the backs of her shoulders brought the starstruck vixy back to reality.

"This is the gateway to the Elnastha Realm," The High Priestess pointed toward the open doorway. "Within that peripheral dimension, not even your godless powers will allow you to escape. You will be able to harm nothing and no one. You will be kept there until the date our sacred Mother has divined upon me for your release. I believe Sanguina let me live in this time and place to guide the Vytameta into Her arms. Sachelvae was never meant to be your permanent home. The residents in my care have just made it a living for themselves because they enjoy the protection it provides. You deserve so much more than to be associated with such vain and hollow nobodies as the people who haunt the basilica's halls."

The banner of light around them then opened for Layna to move through it. She appeared to feel compelled to do as Diava requested, even though there was nothing to stop her from running away. She approached the portal until her figure was eclipsed by its solar glow. She stopped before it and clenched with pain, trying to resist the geas the High Priestess put on her.

She shouted back at Diava over the Elnastha Gate's ambient droning. "You can't control me," Layna grit her teeth, bracing her hands on the edges of the doorway. "My fate is not yours to decide. Your banishment can't stop me from being what I am! Once I've learned the secrets of my powers, you will be the first to feel them all!"

A tense Diava showed a color of panic as she gave the spiteful vixy a shove with her koptigma, pushing her into the Elnastha Gate. As Layna disappeared through the portal, everything was engulfed in a fulmination of whiteness.

Kasra's vision ended when she awoke with a start. She winced as her eyes were attacked by the sun's rays shining through the window of her bedroom. Her long ears lifted from her pillows when she heard Raia opening her wardrobe at the far left wall. As the violette peeled the pajamas off her sticky, sweat-laden skin, she tried to disbelieve what she dreamt was real. She held her face in the palms of her hands as she rubbed her eyes and mulled it over with a tired groan. *'It must've been my imagination being overworked,'* she convinced herself.

The almost-awake violette nearly freaked out when she suddenly realized she had slept in; with a gasp, she clumsily struggled to an upright position, rubbing the water veiling her sight. "Oh no, I'm going to be late!" she kicked herself with a slap of her hands on the mattress.

"Calm down, Kasra," a half-dressed Raia laughed over her shoulder. "Mother Diava is off today, too -- she's not expecting us to be out there."

Kasra looked to the red signal lamp in the corner of the room to see if its light was glowing, but the post stayed dull and dim. "She isn't?" Kasra relievedly squeaked, letting herself breathe. After all the trouble they had gotten into yesterday, the last thing she needed was to make it worse by not showing up on time. As she swung her legs off her bed, she couldn't help but notice, "What're you wearing, Raia?"

Indeed, the brunette hadn't donned her priestess gown, but instead was clasping the buttons of a brown, leather shirt decorated with bronze tassels at the shoulders. At its hems was the top of a knee-high skirt clad in fur of a similar color. Below that were wide-topped boots with v-shaped openings and bronze trim. "You like it?" Raia smiled, turning to the side to show off her ensemble. "I bought it for myself last year. I'm wearing it now because we're allowed to dress in casual attire today."

"It's quite pretty," Kasra commented. "It's the first time I've seen you in anything other than a red dress. I've got a special outfit of my own, actually." The violette strode across the room to her own dresser on the other side to pull out the dress Rozha bought for her. It was a bit of a challenge to put it all on, herself, however. Raia had to chuckle at Kasra's tussle with her tights, until she finally felt pity enough to go over there and help her. When it was all done, Kasra gracefully teased her hair with a flick of her fingers, pretending like she hadn't been fighting with her outfit earlier. "So what do you think?"

"Well I do have to say," an impressed Raia started, "I can see why Malkinos fell for you so fast!"

Kasra's demure facade faded the moment she was hit with her friend's flattery. "Thanks," she bashfully held her skirt, her tail swinging around her legs. "Ready to see what we can get ourselves into today?"

Raia rolled her eyes with a disconcerted groan, "I'd rather not!" Knowing that Kasra was only joking, she returned to her more cheerful demeanor before getting ready for the daily ablutions. "I'm more than ready to forget about Layna for a while and enjoy my time without her, honestly." This candid catharsis earned a quizzically shocked look from Kasra, begging elaboration. "It was during times like Sabbath Days that Layna would try especially hard to take me on one of her adventures. I can remember one in particular, very vividly, as a matter of fact, because it happened the winter before you came to Sachelvae."

According to Raia's memory, it was within the last couple of weeks of that winter season; snowfall had all but disappeared from the ground, but permafrost and blistering cold temperatures were still very much a side effect of every rising and falling of the sun. The trees of the outer lying swamps were barren, and the lakes from which they grew had been frozen over by thin sheets of ice. "Layna hated the winter because she was from the warm beaches of Onteval," Raia noted, "but she said that the night before, she had caught a glimpse of something happening far away that really caught her attention. No matter what the weather was like, she said we just *had* to go check it out."

~~

"Have you no respect for a Sabbath Day?" the appalled past Raia argued with her friend.

"What better time to conduct a search?" a determined Layna had spread out her arms. "Everyone else will be ignoring us to do their own thing. Even the Red Dancer won't be breathing down our necks."

At the time, Mother Diava had become aware of the two's 'extracurricular activities,' and assigned Rozha to intimidate them from getting into any more trouble. It was only last fall that Rozha had gained her own reputation as 'the Red Dancer' for having gone postal on members of the Safiric Brotherhood during her first mission as a priestess. With good reason, the High Priestess surmised such a fear factor would have been great enough to dissuade Layna from coming up with any more hijinks, "but of course when she saw something so attractive, nothing was going to keep her from jumping."

"What did you see, anyway?" Raia had asked, suiting up in her extra layers of clothing.

"It was right outside the bedroom window," Layna started, pointing to the panel of glass in question. "I thought it was a really bright star at first, but it kept getting bigger. It flickered between orange and blue as it grew, then when it was about the size of the space between my fingers," she pinched the air for illustration, "it streaked down for the trees and became bright enough to where I could see the shadows of the frozen swamp. It wasn't like any meteor -- it moved and changed direction like something in controlled flight."

"I dunno," a skeptical Raia crossed her arms, "sounds pretty weird to me. What were you doing up late enough to see this happen?"

"Mind your own business!" Layna retorted. "I need a witness if I find anything, or no one will believe me. You coming with or not?"

Not that Raia had had any reason to believe Layna would have taken 'no' as an answer, she reluctantly replied, "Sure. I guess I was fooling myself into thinking I could have had a break today."

"That's the spirit!" Layna mocked her friend's lack of enthusiasm with an energetic fist pump. "Now just make sure you've got yourself bundled up; that swamp's a mile or two away, so we could be out there for a while."

Raia derisively grinned like she could hardly wait. Everyone else in the temple was currently outside doing their chores -- among them caring for the sick, as illness in this season was a constant problem for the Tresantian residents, keeping both Travestas and Sachelvae busy. Rumor had it that Rozha was secretly dirtying her hands with the blood of Safiric monks who may have been trying to cull the herd of its weakness on the Safiric side of town.

Present Raia elaborated to Kasra, "We were supposed to leave them alone, but Rozha once had a falling out with the faculty when she argued that if we were to leave the Brotherhood to its own devices, they might try to bring their filth over to our side of town. No one was willing to admit it at the time, but even Mother Diava feared she may have been right. Whenever she agreed with something she didn't like, she stayed quiet -- that's how we knew she was pretending not to know what the Red Dancer was up to. So long as Rozha could keep her activities a secret and not get found out by the Brotherhood, we wouldn't have to worry about getting into fights with them, later."

Layna had believed that what she saw coming into the swamp that night was probably related to some kind of Safiric activity -- she thought that the Brotherhood knew more than they let on about what Rozha was up to. "I bet they're preparing a counter-attack with some crazy ritual," Layna said. "Imagine if we could uncover something like that and sabotage their plans! Not even that stuffy Diava could deny that we're heroes, then!"

Raia didn't feel like a hero when her teeth were chattering and her hands were scraping up and down the sleeves covering her arms from the wind's biting chill. As the traveling pair made their way up the hills from the Tresantian valley, they could see the frozen wetlands and beyond them the frosted trunks of the swamp trees. "How far do you think we'll have to go in?" the brunette worriedly adjusted her scarf.

"Probably not very," Layna had hopefully guessed. "The light I saw looked really close to the edge of the forest. I'll bet those Safiric spooks aren't too bright if they only went just past the fringe of the first trees to hide whatever spells they were casting." The more she talked about it, the more believable of a scenario it seemed; the Brotherhood would have thought that Sanguina's resting moon would provide the perfect opportunity to smite their enemies with the full power of Safiro. The closer they got to the forest's entrance, the more frightening the prospect of a secret Brotherhood gathering became.

"What if they set up guards to watch over their congregation?" Raia went down a short list of scenarios. "What if they could see us coming because of our Purity? Do you think they're already onto us?"

"Stop!" Layna suddenly grabbed Raia's shoulder, causing her to jump and shriek. "Shh!" the dark-haired vixy quieted her friend, her eyes shifting to check for a potential ambush. "They can sense fear," she whispered, staying still for just a few seconds longer. There was no noise other than the wind blowing through their ears and the sound of Raia's less than calm hyperventilation. "I think the coast is clear," Layna finally eased up, before giving her friend a slap on the arm. "Don't freak out like that again, or you'll get us killed!"

"You're gonna blame *me* for that?!" Raia had pointed at herself. "*You're* the one bringing us into this crazy mess!"

"It's only a mess if you make one of it," Layna responded with her confusing wisdom. "If you know how to handle a situation, then it won't become dangerous." Without waiting for Raia's next comment, she gestured onward with a twitch of her head.

The crunching of frozen grass bristles under their feet were soon accompanied by an enigmatic droning sound, emanating further beyond the trees ahead of them. The odd melody rose and fell, as if its source was moving to and fro at regular intervals. Upon breaching the brush of the forest, where ahead of them laid lakes of ice filled with foliage, the vixies saw what could very well have been their first contact with the unknown epicenter of Layna's discovery. The orange and blue lights she had described from last night were glowing through the trunks of the trees further ahead, and in greater view than she had seen them before. The pea-sized, star-like object she had seen then had grown into several beams of light peeking through the trees, as if coming from several origin points.

"It looks like it all belongs to a single, round beacon of some kind," Layna had observed.

Raia was dumbstruck with what she was seeing. She suddenly didn't feel so silly for letting Layna convince her to join this excursion, but she was beginning to feel a greater dread now that there was indeed something here. "I don't get the sense that this is something we're familiar with," she began somewhat cryptically, not quite understanding, herself. "It doesn't even smell like it's from around here, whatever it is."

They urgently pressed on to get a closer look. The frozen water cracked underfoot as they scampered over the ice -- Layna would have slipped on her face had she not have been able to brace herself on the nearby tree, marking the edge of the clearing up ahead. It was there, when she and Raia both stepped through, that they finally met the creation of their curiosity. It was a giant, metallic, egg-shaped structure, standing vertically on what appeared to be four thin legs. A deep striation was carved like a belt around its center, splitting the object into hemispheres.

On the bottom hemisphere, was an unmistakably door-shaped indentation, bereft of a knob or handle with which to open it. Underneath of this presumed entryway was a short flight of stairs reaching to the ground. On the upper hemisphere were circle-shaped windows, but they were too high up to see what rooms were inside. Spanning the circumference of either hemisphere were mysterious objects that glowed far brighter than any torch -- possibly on par with some Sanguinic spells Raia had seen before.

A masculine, raspy voice from behind them had brought both vixies whirling around to face their invisible stalker. "That's as far as you go." With a V-shaped burst of smoke, a young scelan dressed in dark blue robes endowed with Safiric insignia appeared a short distance before them. He pulled down his hood to unveil his face of indigo rosage and darkly-tanned skin, then swept aside his black, straightened bangs to show his sinister, red eyes. "I found this outpost, and am awaiting its occupants' return so that I may slay them for the glory of Safiro."

"Looks like we're not the only ones who got the idea to come here," Layna fearlessly stood her ground, while Raia took a step behind her. "I knew you guys would have something to do with this. Where are the rest of you, huh?"

"I made it my personal mission to come here," the teenage monk said. "No one in my clergy knows of this but I."

"Why don't you ask him for his name, Layna?" A smiling Raia playfully nudged her friend's shoulder. "You two have something in common!"

Smirking from this flattery, the Safiric servant replied, "My name is Voxus. I am one of the novitiates of Travestas," he pulled back a sleeve to show a thick, bronze bracelet constructed of segments, featuring a red, eye-shaped symbol in the center.

Exchanging looks with Layna, Raia then asked, "Travestas has a school for their own priests in training?"

"Of course," Voxus shrugged. "How else do you expect anyone learns to become crusaders for the God of Death?"

Seeing that his mind wasn't yet brainwashed by the members of his religion, Raia had believed that she could make peaceful discourse with the young scelan. When she stopped hiding behind her friend, it was Voxus who then seemed taken aback by her brave advancement. "So tell me," the brunette started, "what got you interested in joining the Safiric Brotherhood?"

"It started for me like it does for most people:" Voxus simply explained, "my birth under Safiro's moon. These eyes show the promise we were given," he pointed indicatively to his slit-shaped pupils, "that if we seek His guidance, Safiro will give us His Power to right the wrongs of this world."

Naturally, Raia had to know, "What problems do you see that need to be corrected?"

"My Teachers tell me that it all started after the fall of The Great Civilization," came a familiar phrase. "Safiro saw His children in trouble, and He wanted to give them assistance to rebuild the Civilization they had lost. He created the Annihlus: a tremendous artifact endowed with all His Power, meant to be shared among His children. But His experiment with the Annihlus ended in tragedy when Sanguina sent four of Her Trusted to destroy Safiro's artifact. She feared His Power and wished it not be used by anyone! But the Annihlus' destruction was not total; its fragments were spread throughout the world, each endowed with fractions of His Power. Every one of these shards has a pull toward one another, each desiring to be recombined. And the greatest chunks of the Annihlus were owned by none other than its destroyers: Sanguina's Trusted, who wished for them to remain fractured."

Voxus dramatically bowed his head, as if the ending of the story were a sore subject for him. Then, his eyes opened and shot back at his audience with a determined fire. "We the Brotherhood wish for the Annihlus to be *whole* again! Our religion was founded on the belief that the Great Civilization shall forever be in ruins unless Safiro's Power is in *all* of us."

Had this story been said to more pious members of the Sachelvian Sisterhood, the young monk's passion would have been countered twofold and a fight would have ensued. But the short time Layna and Raia had spent in the Sisterhood wasn't long enough to instill such a grounded stubbornness in their minds. Their allegiance to the faith was still liquid, insofar that they were willing to hear the second side to the story. While Raia had not seemed so ready to believe everything she had heard, Layna had been more willing to give the story some consideration. "So that is why the Brotherhood believes there is no room for Purity in this world?" the raven-haired vixy gathered. "Purity is the one and only problem you see that's keeping this goal of perfection from being accomplished?"

"That would all be a very nice take," Raia said, "if it were to be the whole truth. But you're missing a crucial bit: The Annihlus was, in fact, used by a single belhuayn who was unable to harness its power. It was he, the Raging Chaos God, who was defeated by Sanguina's Trusted so that the Annihlus' evil could not be abused."

Voxus laughed, as if having heard it all before. "That's impossible! The Annihlus was never designed to be used by any one person. It was meant to be a beacon of prosperity that would attract all of Safiro's children to its beckoning light and give them strength by its radiance. It's only typical that the Sanguinic Sisterhood would demonize an ancient story to fit their purposes."

Raia had quirked an eyebrow at this romantic retelling of a much darker side of the story, of which she was more familiar. "You don't think at all that men would fall to the temptation of trying to take this wellspring of power to themselves? It was for the competition for His power that the Annihlus encouraged that begot the advent of the Raging Chaos God."

"There was never any such thing!" Voxus defensively argued. "The very name of such a fictionalized character was all made to scare the non-religious into avoiding and distrusting His Power. Safiro is the God of Death, yes, but He is not evil. The Father is aware a cycle must be upkept and that only the strong survive. It does Him no pleasure to winnow the weak from a population, but it must be done for the greater good. If the Sisterhood had its way, our race would be overcome with weakness and disease until it would cease to be."

The star student's teachings had fallen on Raia's deaf ears, who had resigned herself to ignoring the rest of his confab, but Layna had been still very much interested in what he had to say. "But you know as well as I do that power alone does not complete us. It's why the Safiric Brotherhood takes the advancements that the Sisterhood creates. The problem with the world is that there's not a balance between the two…" Layna trailed off in thought.

~~

It was at this point that Raia stopped her reminiscing, leaving a fascinated Kasra in eager suspense. "And then?!..." the violette prodded. "What happened next?"

In the fashion of a proper storyteller, Raia smirked and chidingly waggled a finger. "The rest I shall save for another time! Right now," she pointed at the flashing signal lamp, "it's time to head to the Purifier and start our day."

Chapter 23: Sabbatical

"What say we get Rozha to take us to Mediona, so you can see Malkinos again?" Raia suggested, placing a hand against the violette's back as she ushered her out the door. "If we don't hurry, your sister might leave with plans of her own!"

The Purifier Hall was oddly disorganized for its morning ritual; all the priestesses were almost unrecognizable in their 'normal' clothing as they stood about the pool and talked amongst themselves in groups. Some of them were sitting in the waters just because they could -- Diava was giving no direction to any of the activities, even though she was atop her stage where she normally was every day. There was something funny about her stoic demeanor as she carried on with members of the faculty, especially when everyone else was in such jovial spirits. *'Poor old thing can't lighten up at all,'* Kasra remarked. *'Not even when she's supposed to.'*

The grand doors to the temple were wide open, and Kasra could notice that not every priestess she used to see every day was in the room. "Darn, I hope Rozha's still here," she said to Raia, standing beside her.

"Hey there, troublemakers!" came Lavelle's deceptively sweet-spoken greeting, approaching their flank. The blonde was wearing a black vest over a dark blue blouse endowed with white ruffles at the low-cut neckline, as if she was trying to look tough and cute at the same time. Her black leggings and matching, ankle-high boots didn't look like they'd offer much protection in the Tresantian wetlands. She was joined by her bespectacled friend, Tassie, who opted for a look to really bring out her inner nerd, completed by a light green dress shirt with long sleeves sprouting from its puffy, round shoulders. She was at least not trying to fool anyone with her fashion sense -- not with those dorky, yellow slippers she was wearing. *'But I'll bet she found the little bows on them irresistible,'* Kasra's eyes judgmentally flicked from Tassie's feet, back to her face.

"What do you want, *Lavelle?*" Raia forced herself to say the vixy's whole name, rather than substitute it for a word that was closer to the tip of her tongue.

Lavelle crossed a hand to her chest and exhaled an insulted huff, exchanging looks with her shorter friend. "Did you hear how she said my name?" began the start of a wonderful conversation. "Sounds like Sanguina's gift comes early for some of us, this month," she stage-whispered to Tassie, watching Raia out of the corners of her eyes, eliciting a roll of the brunette's own. "I was just going to ask what special plans you two had to get yourselves kicked out of here, now that Layna's not going to be able to help you."

"We really do apologize for the unfortunate incident that landed her in the slammer," Tassie disingenuously bowed her head. "Um, what did she do, again? I don't believe I ever heard Mother Diava say anything about it."

"At this point, does she really need an excuse?" Lavelle cocked her hip and half shrugged, with an upturning of a single hand.

"Either way, it's none of your business," Kasra crossed her arms, eyes narrowing at the both of them.

"Ooh, did you see the aggression?!" Lavelle acted scared, pointing at the violette while her friend held her hands and nodded like a lying sycophant. "There's no way you don't know about what Layna did -- it must've been *really* bad if Mother Diava put her away like that."

"Why don't you ask her, yourselves?" Kasra frustratedly shook her head, motioning toward the High Priestess' plinth.

"Training for your vow of secrecy, are you?" Lavelle gave her a fist-clenching wink. "I really do feel sorry for you, that you had to get wrapped up with her on your very first day in Sachelvae. You would've been better off with anyone other than the brain-stunting likes of miscreants like *them...*"

At this point, Raia had lost her patience and finally said what was on her mind. "Is there anything *else* you wanted to say, besides your usual *bitchy* self?"

Lavelle raised an eyebrow and flicked her tail to one side. "Wow, look at you! So brave, even without your girlfriend around! Does that mean she can put a *spine* in you, too?"

The expression on Raia's face showed the exact moment her heart stopped beating. "Shut up, jerk!" she recovered, her ears rising. "You don't even know what you're talking about!"

"Well, it's not exactly a *secret*," Lavelle leaned some weight back onto her foot. "I wonder if it's got anything to do with why Mother Diava locked her up? Maybe you'll be next?~" She mockingly wiggled spooky fingers at Raia.

Kasra sneered, giving both her and Tassie a death glare while Raia was getting so angry she was on the verge of tears. Neither could have been more thankful for Rozha's impeccable timing when she showed up behind Lavelle and Tassie. The two vixies didn't even hear the blade dancer walking up to them; her footfalls were silenced within the torrent of chatter filling the Hall.

Kasra almost didn't recognize her at first, what with how well she had blended into the crowd with her new look.

She was wearing that black, fancy dress Janelle gave her, and let her ponytail down to frame her face like a fiery mane. "Maybe you should share your ghost stories with Brynita, instead of antagonizing these two with your conspiracy theories? It's not acceptable of a servant of Sanguina to engage in such sinful behavior when our Mother's back is turned."

Lavelle only minded the new Teacher over her shoulder at first, before turning fully around. A more timid Tassie, however, was at immediate attention when she heard Rozha's voice sneaking up on them. "Yes, Teacher Rozha," the vixy of chartreuse hair replied. "But it was Lavelle who was making such crass allegations; I was merely an observer."

Tassie's leader gave her a stare that indicated she didn't appreciate her fair-weather friend betraying her so quickly. As badly as she wanted to say something in her own defense, or mock Rozha's sudden righteousness, she gave the redhead a dishonest smile and popped a quick bow with her knees. "We'll be on our way," both vixies gracefully retreated, parting ways around the taller Teacher.

"Well then," Rozha was left to properly address her sister, "you're all smiles today! I'm guessing that means you approve of your new roommate?"

"Of course," Kasra gave Raia a friendly smirk and a nudge with her shoulder. "I think this is going to work out well for us."

Rozha nodded, as if relieved. "Do you have any special plans?" she asked the two of them.

"Actually," Raia started, "we were hoping you could escort us to Mediona." Responding to the redhead's ear tilt, the brunette concluded, "Kasra wants to see Malkinos again; I'd like to visit my family, too."

"Sure, I have no problem with that," Rozha coolly shrugged. "I've got stuff to do down there, myself. I've gotta see Reaventyr about a special…" Even though she was far away enough from Diava to where she was certain the High Priestess wouldn't hear, she couldn't be too cautious. "…something I commissioned from him."

Knowing her sister's secret, and Raia knowing better than to ask, both vixies lacked further comment but unanimously were excited to be the Teacher's tag-along. The simple mission required no permission from other members of the faculty, nor even Diava's acknowledgment; Rozha was allowed to leave and bring whomever with her as she saw fit, "so long as we're back before the temple closes at sundown," the redhead reminded them.

Rozha treated them to breakfast at a local inn, which currently was having a special discount on one of their popular dishes: an Ontevallian favorite called *buuntash*. "It's a venison cake," the chef explained, "prepared fresh daily and cooked rare." A single serving was meant to be shared among four patrons. To Raia's weak stomach, the dish sounded a bit unappealing; it didn't look a whole lot better when it was brought to their table in a tin skillet, thirty minutes later. The crimson strips were stacked much like a pie, nearly three inches high and about twelve inches across.

Dark red grease, or what Raia's conscience wanted to believe was grease, pooled around the buuntash's base and dripped off each brisket when stuck by a fork. Kasra thought it at least smelled decent; it was the first bit of meaty victual she had had in a long time. But upon taking a look at the other customers sitting at their own round tables, she surmised she and her companions might've been wearing the wrong outfits for this kind of place.

Rozha almost felt like she'd need a bib to catch the yucky, oily drips before they'd stain her expensive outfit. At the risk of being rude, when she had an opportunity to have a taste of her meal, Rozha plainly remarked, "I've had stuff in the wilderness that's better than this."

"No way," Kasra argued in mid-chew. "You must've just cut a bad piece -- this stuff is great!"

Meanwhile, a sheepish Raia lightly jabbed the strip she took from the buuntash stack, as if expecting it to yowl at her. "Do you think they'll let us take home what we can't finish?" was the most polite response she could manage.

"I'm surprised you don't like it, Raia," Rozha waggled a fork at her. "I thought you'd be used to this kind of stuff if you grew up on a farm."

"My father didn't raise livestock for eating…" the brunette swallowed, her stomach sinking. "He made his fortune on lakusha plants. We kept our beasts of burden to plow the fields and to provide us transportation to the city."

Kasra suddenly wondered if she looked like a monster to her friend and refrained from going back for seconds. Rozha was unperturbed, however, taking another piece for herself. *'That's two whole divitias of food she's not eating!'* the blade dancer judgmentally noted, before saying outwardly, "I'm sorry, Raia; I didn't mean to create an uncomfortable situation for you."

"No worries," the farm vixy pushed away from the table. "I'll just have something that my dad is selling when we see him, later. He knows of the Sachelvian holidays just as well as any of us do; when he expects a high turnout of priestesses like us, he'll mark down his prices."

"In fact," Rozha concurred, "lots of people who frequent Mediona have gained awareness to the holidays of both temples. I wouldn't be surprised if there was some festival scheduled to go down there, today."

"Say...!" a bouncy Raia tapped Kasra's arm. "That's something we -- I mean, you and Malkinos could do together!"

"You better be careful if you're planning on attending a big gathering like that," Rozha warned them. "The Safiric Brotherhood is also aware of our Sabbath Days. They don't need to see you in a red dress to know you're from Sachelvae."

Once the three travelers had their fill, Rozha left a couple coins of Iminsun's riches on the table as payment and gathered up the leftovers of their buuntash. She divvied up the wrapped remnants between herself and her sister after requesting some salt with which to preserve them. "Rationing food for small meals throughout the day is never a bad thing," the survivalist said. "You pay less for new stuff when you make more use of what you already have."

When Rozha, Kasra and Raia had arrived at Mediona's golden avenue, they encountered an interesting new development: along the Safiric side of town was what appeared to be the framework for a currently unfinished wall. Gray bricks of various sizes were scattered about the uneven, knee-high barricade. The wall got taller the further to the south they looked, and was capped by a battlement just twenty feet high. "I don't like the look of that," Rozha quietly said. "Nothing good comes out of a town inside a fort."

"That is so strange," Raia scanned up and down the thin barrier. "It doesn't look deep enough to stop anything like cannon fire, and it isn't tall enough to keep out catapult boulders. Why are they sealing themselves off like that?"

"They must've started last evening and worked through the night to get this much done," Kasra observed.

'I'll bet they heard about what happened in Pericula and freaked out,' Rozha guessed. As soon as she said that, she caught a glimpse of a dodgy stranger. A scelan wearing dark robes half crouched behind a portion of the wall, ducked his head to avoid her stare and continued looking busy laying brick in the corner. "Something's definitely going on down here. They're probably taking advantage of the Sabbath Day to get away with things unseen."

"Do you think Mother Diava already knows?" Raia asked.

"Whether I think she does or not, I'll be giving her my report shortly," Rozha replied. "As of right now, I have some business to attend. I'll be off to see the blacksmith -- you two have fun now!"

"Wait, Rozha," Kasra held out a hand to stop her, "aren't you supposed to stay with us?"

"If anyone of the temple knows we've been anywhere by ourselves," Raia added, "we'll get busted for sure!"

"Don't worry," the Teacher whisked away their concerns. "I'll be keeping an eye on you and you won't even know I'm there."

Of this, Kasra was certain; remembering how her first date ended brought back a shudder of embarrassment.

Raia was excited to see Kasra on her way to her second date, and couldn't have been happier to help her get there, despite their worries from yesterday. Malkinos, too, looked just as pleasantly surprised to see her and Raia together as they approached Drathnifere's shop. Malkinos immediately stopped setting up their belongings when he saw the two vixies from the corner of his eye. "Kasra," he smiled, unable to keep his feet from idly turning on the ground. "What brings you here?"

As tempted as Raia was to deliver a snarky remark about how Malkinos hardly even noticed her, she let Kasra be the one to do the talking. "It's my Sabbath Day -- I wanted to see if you might be free to enjoy it with me. I had a great time with you a couple of days ago... Maybe we could find something else fun to do together?"

Malkinos swallowed timidly, his embarrassment building as now his whole family got to watch him make moves on his nascent girlfriend. "Sure, I'd like that a lot." He added quickly, "I had a lot of fun with you, as well."

Drathnifere smirked. "Don't be out too late, now," he warned, much like last time. "I want you back at the inn by dusk."

"Yes, father," Malkinos respectfully nodded.

"Raia," the rancher addressed his daughter, "are you here to make sure Malkinos stays in line with your friend?"

Malkinos blushed at a smiling Kasra, while Raia stuttered out an excuse. "A-Actually, I -- um, yes I was." It wasn't what she initially wanted to say, but she didn't think her dad's idea was a particularly bad one. She offered an apologetic grin to Kasra, who was no doubt a little displeased that Raia would suddenly want to moderate the progression of her date.

Drathnifere chuckled with a proud twinkle in his eye, as if admiring the young lady his daughter was becoming. "I knew I made the right decision when I let you go to Sachelvae. But I've been missing seeing you around as much as I used to. You're growing up all by yourself, without me."

"Aww, dad," Raia rushed into his arms so she wouldn't have to see him work himself up to tears. "I promise I'll come visit more often! I'm sure Mother Diava will understand if I want to use more of my free time to be with family. Once I'm a priestess, I'll be able to see you guys much more often."

Drathnifere wistfully pet his daughter's hair, his expression a mixture of happiness and acceptance, as if knowing he was doing well, but was beginning to regret the sacrifice. Raia finally looked up to meet his eyes and added, "I won't forget about you!" She couldn't help noticing the distant stare he returned to her. Fixing his vest for him, she motherly chided, "Now stop that guilt-tripping of yours before you ruin everything for Kasra and Malkinos!"

He flicked up his gaze to the young couple standing before him. "We'll be going now," Kasra offered an awkward wave and a funny smile. She and Malkinos began to turn around slowly, as if expecting to be stopped. But Drathnifere hadn't any last words for them other than, "Have fun," allowing the kids to walk hand-in-hand down the avenue.

Raia, Kasra, and Malkinos followed the colorful flag banners and jovial music to Mediona's Sabbath Festival, held at the eastern gate of Tresantia once per month for the Sachelvian residents. "Another is held at the western end for Travestas, every other month," Raia explained. "The Sabbath Festival starts when the sun rises and ends by sunset. The one for Travestas starts at sundown and ends by dawn."

"I'll bet nothing good happens at the one for Travestas," Kasra naturally supposed.

"Brynita would tell you it's a dark carnival full of drinking, carousing, and even volunteer sacrifices to insult the full moon of Sanguina," Raia said. "Truth is, none of us priestesses would be allowed outside at such an hour to see what goes on there."

Kasra had to believe, "You and Layna probably know by now, right?"

Raia gave the violette a knowing smirk and laughed, "Ohh yes, Layna wouldn't have let *that* rumor escape unnoticed! However, her adventure of the 'dark carnival' was a little bit before my time. Layna claimed that, a month before she and I met, she snuck out of the temple to see the Safiric Carnival the last time one was held. She said most of the attractions were in large tents, hiding the party-goers from the light of Sanguina's moon. But she swore she saw intoxicated stragglers stumbling about the streets and shouting execrations at the sky."

"What else was she able to see while she was there?" Malkinos asked, prompting his sister to continue her storytelling. "Layna said she was somehow able to get close enough to one of the tents to peer inside its flaps. She saw, amid a ring-shaped crowd of people, a wheel-shaped torture rack made to spin while its occupant was being flogged by two executioners."

"No way!" Kasra cried. "That's crazy!" Malkinos added.

"Shortly after witnessing that," Raia went on to say, "Layna was discovered by a Safiric Priest standing guard, and had to run away. I had a hard time believing her testimony, myself, but that's why she wanted me to come along with her on all of her other outings -- to prove to me what she saw was real."

"So have you ever seen one of these Safiric Carnivals, yourself?" Malkinos prodded.

"As brave and bone-headed as she can be," Raia replied, "Layna thought I wouldn't be able to hide as well as she did and would only slow her down if we needed to retreat."

'Probably because Layna can turn invisible and Raia can't,' Kasra inwardly scoffed. *'Still, if Layna can make herself unseen like that, how was she found out by that priest? Unless she didn't actually go, and was making the whole thing up.'*

"I'd be lying if I said I wasn't curious, though..." the brunette's ears guiltily wilted. "After all the things Layna and I have been through in the time we've spent together, I've become more willing to believe the story she told me."

'Poor thing's such a sucker for a good fable,' Kasra shook her head. *'Layna never knew what she was doing; she was just as shocked as any of us when things went awry.'* She was all the more glad that Layna wasn't there to add anything in her defense. *'We'd probably be scoping out what's going on with the whole wall situation in the Safiric side of town by now.'*

Their conversations accompanied them to a large trellis forming the entryway to the Sachelvian festival, ornately decorated with vines whose bulbous red blossoms were made to resemble Sanguina's moon. A banner stretched across the whole street of Mediona was hung between two flag poles and read "Sabbath Day" in painted, belhuayn writing. Raia was the only one of the group who could read or write, and assumed the role of tour guide for much of their perusal. Illiteracy was actually the norm among most belhuayn cities; Sanguinic schools were the only institutions that stressed reading and writing as a learned skill. "I was taught how to read within my first year at Sachelvae," Raia said. "I'm still not the best at writing, however."

Most of the attractions were set up in booths alongside the street, plenum of candy similar to the kinds Malkinos and Kasra sampled at the fair they attended for their first date. "Every time I come here, there's always some party going on," Malkinos remarked.

"In all my travels, I had never come across a place where everyone is so happy," Kasra nodded, holding her hands behind her back.

"Mediona never sleeps and it never stops finding reasons to have fun," Raia smiled. "I love the atmosphere and joyous spirits here. It's too bad that Mother Diava doesn't let us come here more often!"

It didn't take long for the three kids to find food vendors selling snacks to capitalize on the hungry lunchtime traffic of passersby. Upon acquiring some salty meat sticks for Malkinos, some veggies for Raia, and sugary goodies for Kasra, their attention was drawn to a group of colorfully-dressed youngsters wearing costumes and frolicking about in what looked to be a wooden pen. The small, short fence was merely meant as a boundary to separate their stage from their audience; the children weren't playing a game as much as they were putting on a well practiced show. Most of them were no older than ten years of age, but they each had a better attitude and discipline during their act than a few novitiates Kasra had seen during her time at the temple.

"You'd have to use a collar and a switch to get Layna to cooperate like that," Kasra ruefully remarked, eliciting a humored laugh from Raia before the brunette pointed to a familiar face.

"Hey, isn't that Teacher Wanystha?"

Indeed, the frizzy-haired azurette could be seen supervising the youngsters' show, sitting cross-legged in what almost looked like a director's chair near the back corner of the play pen. It was at this point in the children's effervescent reenactment that a blonde vixy wearing a vaguely sun-shaped, cyan headdress skipped on by and sang, "The beginning of the next day~"

Her fellow performers took their cue to scale big building blocks made to represent towers of a city. Half of the kids were dressed in red, the other half in blue, but all of them had their short tails arched to attention as they gazed around the sky.

A twelve-year-old sceli standing near the front of the pen supplied narration. "Heeding the seer's warning, some people of the Great

Civilization waited for a star to fall on their capital city. But nobody else believed them, and made fun of them for doubting the gods' will."

"Sanguina will save us," shouted a red-dressed vixy. "Sanguina rebukes all evil wishing to harm us."

"No, Safiro will!" a blue-dressed sceli shouted back at her. "Safiro destroys all evil to ensure it can harm no one."

"But no amount of arguing would save either of them, as their faiths in the gods were becoming increasingly polarized," the narrator concluded.

Suddenly, a sceli wearing a big, poofy, ball-shaped costume came swinging from the nearby scaffolds of the 'heavens.' As he rode the rope hanging from a higher platform above the stage, the yellow tassels of his costume fluttered behind him, resembling fire flickering off a meteor. His short descent ended with a ceremonious crash when he collided with the 'city,' made to represent the Great Civilization.

All the building blocks comprising the towers were toppled as their vigilant believers ducked for cover to escape the avalanche of painted wood and dyed cloth. The vixy representing Sanguina's mortal likeness nearly lost her red halo as she backed off in surprise. The sceli who was made to look like Safiro meanwhile reclined a large mallet against his shoulder and laughed boisterously.

"Now is my chance," the mock Safiro exclaimed. "It is time to do what I've always wanted: ensure that my children are the only ones left."

"No!" Sanguina cried, rushing over to shake some sense into her counterpart. "Can you not see what has happened? The first seal has been broken! If we do not come together, it will mean the end of our world!"

"I don't care about all that," Safiro blithely pushed her away, then straightened with his fists to his hips. "None of that matters so long as my children take over whatever's left!"

While the avatar for the God of Death continued his contrived chortling, a rather dejected Sanguina turned to face the audience, her hands clasped to her waist as she prepared her monologue. "Why doesn't he get it? Why won't he understand me? The stars have fallen, and the sky has been shattered. Now anyone can get in and mingle with our people. If that happens… what shall become of us, then?"

It was by then in this strangely eye-opening skit that Raia and Kasra turned to exchange looks with each other, no doubt thinking the same thing. "What kind of message is Teacher Wanystha trying to send?" the violette asked. "This wasn't in any of her lessons before."

"This play expounds upon the creation story I told you once before," Raia replied. Then with glitzy eyes, added, "Teacher Wanystha has just found a masterful way to incorporate the old story of the Four Seals into a single retelling, chronicling the beginning of our race to the prophesied end."

"Prophesied?" Kasra's ears wilted. "Since when?"

"Since all *this* took place," Raia pointed back to the stage.

As Sanguina was sharing these final thoughts, a sneaky Safiro was tiptoeing to the wreckage of the Great Civilization and planted a flag in its midst. The banner flying from its pole was emblazoned with a rough drawing of a sapphire. "My children shall gather around this beacon of prosperity and together shall forge a new civilization, made for Wilds only! Then we shall see whose way is better!"

"You fool!" an aghast Sanguina turned around to see what he had done. "That's not at all how it was meant to be done! But if a contest is what you want, I shall be the winner -- for peace and forgiveness is the only way to achieve healing and solidarity."

"Blah blah, whatever," Safiro jejunely gestured a mouth-like motion of his hand. "What's all that *forgiveness* good for against someone who has no mercy? My ideals make change while yours do nothing. Change is what this world needs, and that's what I'm gonna give it, whether you like it or not."

"Try as Safiro might to end the world," the narrator returned to say, "the Great Civilization springs anew in Tresantia! And so long as it remains, the fourth and final seal shall never break."

"The fourth?" Kasra's curiosity escaped into the open air. "If the meteor was the first, what were the other two?"

"As with most things that decide our history," Raia started, "that all depends on which side you ask. The Safiric Brotherhood would tell you that the second seal was when the dark men started coming to our world, and the third was when Tresantia was founded. The Sanguinic Sisterhood believes the second seal was when the Annihlus was broken and the third seal was when Saint Sevasmia died." She and Malkinos pensively watched Teacher Wanystha congratulate her young volunteers for a job well done, their emotions mixed from what they had just seen. While the play was constructed to have such a lighthearted tone as told by children, the impactfulness of the message was not hindered by its method of delivery.

"Either way," Kasra finally said, "the destruction of Tresantia is believed by both sides to be the fourth seal?"

Raia solemnly nodded. "Ask both worshipers of Travestas or Sachelvae, and they'll tell you that Tresantia is the keystone to the apocalypse." It was hard for Kasra to believe after what she just said, she could turn around with a smile on her face. "It's the successful intertwining of both faiths that make this city the last bastion of hope for Sanguina's Will. Saint Sevasmia died to ensure the fourth seal would never be broken. If Safiro wants this place gone, it's going to have to come from somewhere beyond His influence."

Chapter 24: Only Joking Around

As Kasra, Malkinos, and Raia continued down the street looking for more things to do, they came across a road block of people dancing to music that practically vibrated the bodies of its listeners to move with its upbeat tempo. It was being performed by a small band of young scelans, standing with their instruments upon a tall stage. Every one of them was wearing colorful clothing that was difficult to ignore. Their flamboyant outfits were made to match each other, likely crafted by a talented seamstress. But their style of clothing was certainly not of these lands; the fabric looked much too light and showy for the Ontevallian climate. Indeed, the performers themselves looked quite foreign to most Ontevallian natives; each one of them looked like they came from another part of the world.

"Ohhh, I've heard of them!!" an exhilarated Raia gasped, unable to stop herself from bouncing. "They're the Outland Four -- they travel all over the world to wow their audiences!"

Malkinos rolled his eyes while his little sister was in the process of swooning. "I don't see what's the big deal with them," he muttered. "They all look so superficial with their long hair and fancy clothes…"

"I dunno, I like them…" Kasra found herself being absorbed into Raia's dreamy state.

"You've gotta be kidding," Malkinos tipped his head back with a groan.

Upon noticing a discarded flier for the event laying in the street, Raia picked it up and clicked her tongue, "See, if Mother Diava ever let us know what was going on, I could have been here sooner!"

"They're not that good," Malkinos pretended like he hadn't been reacting to their music, earlier. He then found himself getting pulled along by Kasra, following Raia into the middle of the crowd. It was certainly an event for all ages, bringing in everyone from children to their parents, to even their grandparents, sitting on the sidelines. Everyone who wasn't swaying or skipping around were holding hands -- "It makes me sick," Malkinos' thoughts escaped his mouth as a bitter murmur, his head facing away until a doe-eyed Kasra hung onto his hands.

"You wanna dance with me?" Kasra smiled at her boyfriend.

Malkinos' lips made a fish-like motion as his heating cheeks melted away his reservations. "O-Okay," he powerlessly stammered, stiffly trying to move his legs.

The awkward farm boy didn't have much rhythm, but thankfully for him, Kasra's first time trying to wiggle didn't look a whole lot better. Raia, however, was a natural at dancing by herself or with anyone else for that matter. She looked like she was born to be on stage, whether anyone was watching her or not. It got to a point where people around her were starting to notice and stopped what they were doing as they were captivated by her moves. Even Kasra's and Malkinos' heads turned.

She was totally unaware of the style she was inventing at this spur of the moment, but it didn't escape the notice of her favorite band. At the end of their number, the attractive scelan of auburn hair and an open-vested shirt to show his sculpted physique of dark brass skin, pointed a finger into the crowd directly at Raia.

"Hey you," his distinctive voice carried as if by a horn, "come up here and join us!"

Raia froze with disbelief and trembled with excitement. She wasn't even able to move on her own until Kasra gave her some encouragement, patting her on the back and saying, "Go for it!" The brunette glanced once to her friend and again to the stage, raising her fists with all the want in the world, but a fearful tail wrapping around her legs kept her where she stood. Kasra played hero for the vixy's fantasies, nearly having to carry her past the crowd and up the stairs so she could see the band members up close.

All eyes were on her as she was ushered to the front most corner; the pressure had her breathing as if she had dashed a marathon. But when the music started again, the new piece's pace was slow and soothing, endowing Raia with waves of courage to shake off her tension and move once more. A pleasant sway and bob of the knees eventually grew into a swivel of her shoulders and a rocking of her head, until even her tail was swinging along with the rest of her body.

The crowd started clapping to the percussion beat of the band's Lasuisian drummer, who looked flattered to be part of the action. Any one of the Outland Four could have admitted that they had never encountered a small audience brimming with as much enthusiasm. Upon ending their show with their most energetic song yet, the band's leader, the one who invited Raia to come up on stage, gave the short brunette a one-armed hug and a peck on the forehead that happened so fast, she was hardly aware that it occurred.

The exhausted vixy looked like she had been touched by Sanguina Herself when she locked eyes with the Ardinsulaian. When he began so casually walking away to regroup with his band, all her mind could think of was to follow, but she forgot to remind her legs. Chest first she leaned forth until gravity had her falling on her elbows.

"Sheesh," Malkinos bit his lip with an exasperated slump, the crowd bursting out into a collectively demure giggle.

Kasra once again found herself coming to Raia's rescue, taking the brunette by the tail and slowly pulling her off the stage, back to the ground. Raia's legs still weren't with it; when her feet touched down, her full weight leaning against Kasra nearly knocked her friend over. "You alright?" the violette restrained a laugh, raising Raia back up with her hands under her arms.

"I'm so sorry!" the dizzy brunette's eyes were vacant. "I don't know what happened!"

"You're acting like you fell outta the sky," Malkinos dusted her off.

"I didn't," Raia began collecting herself. "But I think I know which one of them might've~"

"Oh please..." her brother sighed, "you don't even know his name."

Giving him a look that just screamed "oh yeah?" Raia unfolded the leaflet she was carrying in her shirt. "He's a great singer and he can play any woodwind instrument --"

"Wonderful," Malkinos cynically interrupted, "so he's good at blowing into things."

Raia glared at him, taking a deep breath and releasing it into an impatient huff. "His name is Taifonn -- he's from Ardinsulai," she pointed to the illustration of the scelan in question. "Erigath plays the pipe and tabor -- from Lasuis, Katal is the lutenist -- from Cataenas, and Runo plays the organetto, from our very own Onteval."

"I'll bet if you took any of them out to a farm, they wouldn't last a minute," Malkinos raised his head, earning a jab in the stomach from his sister.

"They don't *have* to work on farms," she hugged her leaflet and turned away. "Any velta would be lucky to be with one of them."

With a mischievous smirk, Kasra held her friend's shoulder and whispered, "Why don't you ask him out, Raia? I saw how he was looking at you."

Raia swallowed nervously, slowly eking her head to gaze upon the musicians still collecting their belongings. "Uhh..." But she was unable to make a coherent response. "I-I'm sure a Wild blood like him wouldn't have any interest in me --" She shook her head to regain her religious faculties, patting down her skirt. "I mean, he's gotta be ten years older than me, anyway. Besides, I must remain chaste for my induction into the Sisterhood."

"He totally just kissed you a minute ago," Kasra teased.

"Not where it counts," Raia blushed. "Although, if he wanted to, I wouldn't say no..."

Malkinos began to look nauseated. "If he doesn't have a girlfriend by now, it could only mean one thing."

"Shut up!" Raia defensively slapped his side. "That doesn't matter, anyway. Sanguina nor Safiro have any opinion when it comes to that."

"There's no need to be jealous of them," Kasra nudged Malkinos' arm. "It was just something for us to do. I had fun!"

Malkinos' toughness disappeared. "So, um, wanna find something else to do?"

"They really could have made a flier for a schedule of all the events," Raia muttered, trying to see over the heads of all the taller people around them.

That's when a voice belonging to a stranger said to the group, "I heareth there shalt be a fireworks display this evening." This unexpected response of such a dated tongue had the three of them turning from their huddle to see a vixy whose age was probably between theirs, with strikingly white skin that emitted a soft, moonlike glow in the twilight sun. She was clad in flowing, red drapes; her airy clothing almost seemed to float off the ground as its long, flag-like hems trailed elegantly behind her.

She moved barefoot with a soundless saunter; the golden aglets on her ankles and the bracelets on her wrists tinkled together like windchimes. When she stopped before the young trio, she made her tail a halo for her legs. She brought the slender, pink-tipped limb before her to show what could have been mistaken for a priestess' ring on it.

The bright red rosage of her cheeks puckered under her Pure, crimson eyes as she gave her new acquaintants a soft smile. Her hair, as white as her skin, flowed like a curtain to her lower back.

If it was somehow possible, Kasra was more awestruck than the rest of her friends when they saw this teenage vixy's extramundane appearance. She was certain that she had recurring dreams of this person long before she ever came to Sachelvae. Her voice, though it had been a long time since she heard it, stuck out in her mind as clear as a crystal bell. She had seen this bright and charming vixy coming to give her words of encouragement in her times of deep distress. She remembered waking healed at times she had fallen asleep broken.

Since entering Sachelvae, these dreams seemed to have ceased. Instead, she began having dreams of the kind of life she wished she could have had, with the kind of parents she was woefully without. Kasra could hear her heart pounding in her ears as her synapses were flaring from the mere sight of this almost otherworldly vixy. The question was on everyone's mind, but only Kasra had the nerve to actually speak it for her friends. "Who are you?"

"Thee asketh for my name?" the vixy started, as if it was unimportant. "I am Yalikai."

Malkinos raised an eyebrow at the lack of a royal title attached to her introduction. "Are you not a princess?"

"I doth not hail from any special land," the albino's tone was almost melodic. "I have come hither to witness the festival. What doth thee bethink of this joyous nonce?"

"I, I… uh…" Raia looked to her less educated compadres for some backup, but Kasra nor Malkinos could provide a translation for her. Even though she was not well versed in old-timey belhuayn speech, she couldn't help but think there was something rusty about the way this albino vixy was talking. It was as if she didn't quite know, or remember how to speak the language, herself.

"It's been great," the brunette allowed herself to grin. "I never imagined the Outland Four would be here~"

"Some do attempt to avoid it," Yalikai started, "but everyone returns to whither they did get their start, some day."

Perhaps ignoring the overarching symbolism in the vixy's statement, the brunette replied, "The band was organized here, in Tresantia?" This was a new piece of information to which Raia was surprisingly not privvy.

"This city is a drawing point of change and inspiration," Yalikai gestured to the rooftops on either side of them. "Uniquity is drawn to the energies its people emit." Her eyes swept back over Malkinos and Raia, but gave a lasting acknowledgement to Kasra. "Tis my first time being here," she went on to say, "but I hath heard many legends about Tresantia. I desired to see it all for myself."

Kasra found it a little strange that of all the people she saw at the festival so far, this Yalikai person was the only one who seemed to be going around by herself. She also thought it was a bit stranger that none of the passersby were acknowledging her existence -- as if nothing about this vixy's appearance was out of the ordinary. "Did you come with anyone?" the violette asked. "You must've come a long way to get here."

Yalikai's head tilted somewhat inquisitively, yet her smile remained untested, as if impressed by Kasra's insightfulness. "I doth dwell very far hence," she affirmed, "but I hath grown accustomed to such a long sojourning."

"All alone?" Raia cooed, her lips assuming that 'pity pout' she'd always do when she saw someone in need. "Well, even if you can handle yourself well enough, you can join our little group if you want. I've lived in Tresantia for as long as I can remember; if there's anything you want to see here, I can take you to it."

Yalikai purred so subtly, it was barely audible to her acquaintances. "Thou art most gracious," her elegant tail gracefully swung behind her. "I'm joyous that thee is my tour guide."

Raia smiled, "If nothing else, I can at least show you where you can get some good food around here -- I've made a second meal off the candies and snacks at the fair. You must be quite hungry, yourself!"

"Thee needn't worry thyself," Yalikai showed a hand. "I'm very interested in seeing the various attractions the festival will provide." Looking out to the stands and fences further down the road, she noticed such carnival staples as lifting competitions, fencing matches, archery contests, and dubious betting games. "It looks like a place to discover many latent talents. Case in point, thy recently-discovered knack for dance," she earned a shy look from Raia.

"You saw that, huh?" the brunette awkwardly grinned, her tail lowering to the ground.

"Have no shame of thy abilities," Yalikai said. "Our passions stem from our talents because people art born to do all sorts of things. Tis a shame that most fail to realize their potential and fall short of their dreams."

The vixy's words filled Kasra with such wonderment that her constant staring could have been mistaken for suspicion. "What do you like to do, Yalikai?"

"I love to observe others," the albino replied. "I can oft learneth just as much about a person by seeing those folk from afar as I can from meeting them directly."

Kasra looked like she was having a hard time understanding, rather believing, how a talent like that could have worked, but her boyfriend was quick to give it a test. "What can you tell about me, just by looking?" He asked, complacently raising his chin and arching his tail.

While Raia was wishing she and Malkinos weren't related, Yalikai exhibited a kind of extrinsic calm that reminded Kasra of Platina's demeanor.

But instead of showing no emotion at all, Yalikai was consistently contented. "I can bid thee hast many arts," she started, turning Malkinos' head back to her. "...which hast not yet revealed themselves to thee"

The accidental, caustic finish to her statement left Malkinos crushed. Raia couldn't help herself from laughing the instant she saw her brother's smugness disappear. Yalikai added, "Thee has't the potential to becometh a very responsible, howbeit incorrigible scelan upon thine coming of age."

The teenage sceli confusedly glanced between his girlfriend and his smarter sister standing on either side of him. "That's a good thing, right?"

"We can at each moment maketh something valorous out of our predeterminations," came another indirect answer from Yalikai. Her eyes were then brought to bear on the pensive expression Kasra was gawking at her with. "Thee hath doubt for my words?"

Kasra was taken aback by this candid scrutiny -- her friends, too, were now looking at her. "What makes you think that?"

"Thy silence vilifies thee," the albino replied. "I bid thee more loquacious around the people thee knoweth. Thine wariness of strangers due to past hurt. But having cater-cousins hast been a healing process for thee. Thee did crave it. Tis wherefore thee hath chosen those folk thou art with."

"I *chose* them?" a confused Kasra tipped an ear. "I didn't make a conscious decision to meet them; it just happened that way."

The deliberate measure with which the violette replied elicited an intrigued twitch of Yalikai's tail. "Who art thou convincing? Me or thyself?"

Kasra's brow furrowed, a hand now perching upon her hip. *'She doesn't even know my name, yet she acts like she can just peg me down within moments of meeting us. Who **is** this weird girl?'*

Her contemplations were interrupted by an attention-commanding shout coming from the stage on which the Outland Four had previously held their concert. "Hear ye!" The funny, nasally voice had everyone turning their heads. Prancing with a grin-inducing effervescence was a scelan, perhaps in his mid-twenties, sporting a green and blue court jester's attire. He wielded a harp guitar, and with every leap, gave a strum of its strings.

Upon reaching center stage, he tapped a foot and jingled his hat along to the beat of his guitar solo, for a moment becoming a one-man band. After setting down his odd instrument, the music inexplicably kept playing. He ended his dance with a dizzying spin on his curled-toed boots, and flourished with a bow facing away from his audience. "Greetings! Laritat, at your service."

While Raia's laughter joined much of the crowd, Kasra showed an impressed ambivalence to the jester's introduction. Malkinos reverted to his prior grump and crossed his arms. "Oh great, another nut heard from."

Turning around to properly face his observers, Laritat smiled and pulled a small scepter from his sleeve. "Now that those *third rate* performers have left," he scoffed over his shoulder toward the stage curtain, "I can treat you to some *real* talent!" The jester twirled his staff and tossed it high into the air, where it exploded into a colorful cloud of smoke. And from this cloud came raining down multicolored orbs, which Laritat then caught with both hands, his tail, and one foot.

The dextrous jester proceeded to juggle these eight, fist-sized balls whilst performing a balancing act. The phantom background music became faster paced and included a drum roll of increasing tempo as the speed of his juggling also intensified. Suddenly, the dramatic music ceased and all the balls were simultaneously tossed skyward. Laritat and his bewildered audience watched the projectiles continue to fly, but they didn't come back down. Instead, they burst like missiles into colorful flashes beautifully contrasted by the darkening skies; some of these nebulous explosions resembled objects like pinwheels. From these rapid fire detonations, Laritat's magic scepter fell back into its owner's hands.

His eccentric, premier exhibition earned the applause of his audience of ever increasing size. "See, us Wild boys ain't all so bad!" Laritat pointed at his Wild eyes. "Every month, I see a bunch of dour city folk with bored faces wandering about Mediona looking for something fun to do at these festivals. I came all the way from Cataenas to give you what you're all missing!" After another applause of agreement and a bow of courtesy, Laritat less-than-humbly said, "Yes, thank me, thank me~"

"I can't stand this guy," Malkinos was unsurprisingly unimpressed.

"For my next trick," Laritat started, "I'll require an assistant from the crowd." The jester deliberately ignored the few people who were excitedly beckoning for his attention as he scanned over their heads. "You there!" he pointed at Malkinos. "You'll do nicely!"

"What?" the stunned farm boy froze to the spot. "Me?" Before he could make any demands, in a blink of an eye, he found himself teleported to the stage. He was suddenly face to face with the intimidating Laritat. The jester mischievously twirled his scepter in one hand whilst bringing a thoughtful finger to his chin.

"Yes, in fact you'll do so nicely, I'm jealous of you!" Laritat then tapped Malkinos' forehead with the green pommel of his staff, causing the kid to flinch. When he opened his eyes, he looked down to realize he was wearing Laritat's clothing. Correction, he *was* Laritat! He stared at himself as if looking into a mirror -- suddenly, his former body sported a very jester-like grin and even chuckled like Laritat did.

"Yes, I can get used to this body!" 'Malkinos' wiggled a foot and shook a wrist. "I might just keep it for myself."

"Wait, that body is mine!" 'Laritat' reached for the boy, but was unable to grab him before he backed off and started running away.

"You'll have to catch me if you want it back!" 'Malkinos' taunted him, forcing 'Laritat' to chase him in circles on and off the stage. 'Laritat' followed his body snatcher under the wooden platform and back up the stairs until he was too exhausted to continue. "You know what," 'Malkinos' said, "on second thought, I like my old self better." He then swiped the scepter from 'Laritat' into his hand and tapped him on the forehead again. After another jarring flinch, Malkinos found himself back in his own body and Laritat pretending like nothing happened.

"Thanks for your help!" the jester grinned. "Here's a gift for you:" He grabbed the pommel of his scepter as Malkinos continued to hold its shaft, and pulled the gem-like end to transform it into a bouquet of red flowers. "You like?" Without giving his flustered assistant time for a response, Laritat shoved him away and waved him off. "Ta-ta for now!"

A thoroughly mortified Malkinos sauntered off the stage, weighed down by the pressure of the audience laughing at his expense. "I got these for you," the farm boy meekly said, drained of all emotion, as he handed the bouquet to his girlfriend.

"That's so nice!" a hysterical Kasra happily accepted her present.

"Indeed it is," Laritat overheard. "But you better find a vase for it soon, because it won't stay pretty for very long without water."

For the first time since they met, Yalikai's smile had been replaced by an untrusting scowl. "I heareth those flowers bloom better in darkness," she whispered to Kasra.

"We'd better go take Laritat's advice," Raia said into Kasra's other ear. "It's getting late; we'll be expected at Sachelvae, soon." Looking around, she added, "Where's your sister?"

"She said she'd be around," the violette conducted a cursory search of her own. "I'm surprised she hasn't made herself apparent, yet."

Chapter 25: Trouble Town

While her sister was out perusing the fairgrounds with her friends, Rozha was away and busy relocating the familiar plume of smoke of Reaventyr's store, emanating over the roofs of all the other awnings and tents lining the sides of Mediona's stone streets. She heard the blacksmith hard at work, hammering out his latest masterpiece for another high-paying customer, no less, in need of his expert service. He recognized Rozha's loud voice the instant she called his name from afar. "Hey, Reaventyr!"

The aged blacksmith wiped his brow with a burly arm as he set his hammer down on the anvil, next to what looked like shoes for a strider. "'Ey, ye came back! Yer quite the punctual one; finished yer sword last eve, I did!" He held up a finger signaling her to wait a moment while he ducked back into the dimly-lit shed behind him, where could be heard other metallic banging noises coming from his assistants.

Rozha came a bit closer to the forge to peer into the entrance of the blacksmith's shop. Standing just outside the space between its fiery mouth and the anvil Reaventyr left outside, she was able to see another hearth belonging to a furnace.

The light of its hot flames silhouetted the scelan standing in front of it, hunched over a lump of gold he was pouring into a blazing mold. It was hard to tell if the stout scelan's skin color was due to a trick of the eyes played by the flaming light source, or if his tan really was orange as an ember. His braided hair, long and dangerously close to the fireplace, was a coppery red. Similarly to his boss, he had a coarse and thin, neck-length beard that like the hair on his head, was also braided on the sides.

The goldsmith was of a much younger age than Reaventyr; he was probably in his mid-thirties, and about ten years into his profession, what with how skillfully and focused he handled himself. After Rozha had took this minute to study his appearance, her eyes gave a closer examination to the ring-shaped mold in which he poured his molten gold; it looked like it could have easily fit around a velta's tail.

At this point, Reaventyr had just reemerged back out into the open, narrowly avoiding hitting his head on the entrance to his shop. In his hands, he carried a very exquisitely designed scabbard, colored black with a gold pattern of swirls that resembled the back of a dragon's hide. Protruding from this finely crafted sheath was the hilt of a sword, topped with a dangling, red cloth tied almost like a ponytail to its pommel. On the edges of the hand-conforming grip were red eyes with round, Pure pupils.

With a proud beam and a twinkle in his eyes, Reaventyr held out the completed sword to Rozha and said, "Go ahead, pull it out -- tell me what ye think!"

The blade dancer couldn't have been more ready to do just that. She with gusto accepted her new weapon and with the smoothness of second nature, slipped the sword from its shell with a characteristic swoosh and ting. What she beheld, reflecting the light just above her head, was a creation unlike anything with which she was familiar. The weapon's blade was endowed with curves from hilt to tip, as if it was a tongue of frozen fire turned to polished steel. "It's beautiful…!" a gawking Rozha gasped.

"It's my favorite creation yet," Reaventyr poised with fists to his sides, puffing out his chest whilst his tail curled against his back. "It's a flamberg -- I call it *La-mor'bel*, ancient Lasuisian for 'War Cry.'"

"A sword like this could inspire many wonderful names," the mesmerized Rozha watched the magnificent metal course near-weightlessly through the air. "It feels so soft in my hand, like an extension of my mind."

"Wanna give 'er a test?" Reaventyr was almost as excited as the blade dancer to see his creation in action. He placed an old cut of wood from the cord he used to feed his fireplaces out on its end in front of her. The oaken block was surprisingly lightweight for its size from years of dry rot, but its thickness would've still been intimidating for an axe to chop.

Rozha held her hilt with both hands, taking and releasing a single, long breath. With precision and concentration bolstering her fast swing, La-mor'bel cleaved the block of wood. She hardly knew she hit the target before she saw it fall over in two pieces. Her eyes flicked back up at Reaventyr, who looked every bit as impressed as she was. It was hard to tell if it was her technique or the grade of his weapon that allowed it to perform such a feat.

"Well, I fair say I'm stunned!" The blacksmith held his broad-brimmed hat. "Where'd ye learn how to do somethin' like that, bein' cooped up in a temple?"

"I wasn't always a priestess," Rozha sheathed her sword. "And I'm not called the 'Red Dancer' for nothing, either. Sanguina is trying to guide me to Her Light, but there are elements of my past I cannot forsake..." She looked to the scabbard as she held it by her side. "I believe Sanguina took me to Sachelvae, not because I need the temple, but because the temple needs me."

She looked back out to the unfinished wall on the Safiric side of town, and was filled with a curiosity that could not be quenched by standing around. From her end of the street, she was at a high enough altitude to where she could see that the barrier was more complete at the southern side of Mediona; the barricade of dark bricks became shorter the nearer to the north they were; they had tapered off just outside Reaventyr's shop. She watched the traffic of pedestrians flowing across Mediona, waiting for a gap between them that she could slip through on her way over.

Amid the wandering people paying her no mind, passing her by like a fog of colors, she picked out a steely gaze coming from a strikingly familiar face. Tiny black pupils centered into his purely white eyes peered at her from underneath his indigo hood. She stopped and stared to get a closer look, but one blink later, he was gone. Rozha began to recall the warning she gave to her sister before they parted ways, about how the Brotherhood was braver on nights like these. She reflexively clung a hand onto the hilt of her new sword, and continued her way with increased caution. She could see, albeit faded by the atmosphere of the setting sun, the full face of Safiro's moon glowering down at her.

Her gaze returning to the place she was headed, she caught the same face she had lost a minute ago, once again, this time appearing from a different place. Almost to her flank, she had to turn around as if expecting to engage. Her adrenaline ignited; now on her toes, she stood avast, one foot behind the other. A glint of steel showed from her scabbard -- the sword so close to being drawn this time. But once again, the ghastly figure retreated from sight.

A bead of sweat cooled her temple. She swallowed, releasing her breath but could not release her tension. She was on full alert -- the people passing her by began giving her funny looks as her actions accorded undue attention to herself. Their attitudes soured all the more the closer she approached the Safiric side of town. Their eyes all showed to which God they belonged, and they all could tell by a cursory glance that the incognito priestess did not belong there.

Having passed by the shortest end of the Safiric wall, the music of Mediona had almost entirely dwindled to a hush behind her. The river of people she had crossed through were gone. There was nothing now to block her vision of the ashen towers and sullen streets of Tresantia's twisted half before her. The blackened grounds crunched underfoot; the grasses, unlike the lush greens of the Sanguinic half, had decayed to ochre bristles. She could smell the dying odor of dilitrivanni gases still lingering in the places where it had choked out lesser lifeforms. Their last breaths coagulated into a white fog rolling along the ground, getting thicker the deeper into town she looked.

'It gets worse every time I come here,' Rozha thought. *'And it's been getting a lot worse as of last week.'* Considering how tirelessly they were working toward their mysterious goal was also unsettling. Armed guards brandishing pikes and other spear-like weapons were standing and milling about behind the incomplete barricade, while the peasantry continued to work at gathering and setting the supplies. Further down, where the wall was closer to being finished, people pushed wheelbarrows full of gray bricks and dumped them off into piles. The workers on their knees would then stick these blocks, some of them ranging to a cubit in length, on the barrier while someone else trowelled on a coat of tar.

"Are you impressed by our progress, Sister?" a gravelly voice said from behind her.

A surprised Rozha spun around to see her speaker. A priest whose face was almost entirely concealed by his cowl, held over his shoulder the shaft of a weapon tied to his back. Rozha's attempts at drawing her sword were halted magically by a telekinetic vice; her bent arm was immovably restrained by what looked like a pulsating, blue amoeba.

"I am not here to fight, unless you start one with me," the priest said. He waited for Rozha's assenting quiet before whisking away his Safiric astapsyxi. "I can tell you now," he looked to her sword, "a priestess so weak in her faith would not last a minute against one as experienced as I."

"What makes you so sure?" Rozha challengingly riposted.

"I am one of the Teachers of Travestas," he outstretched his arms. "Bildarius is my name. I coach my students to infuse their weapons with Safiro's Power."

"Is that right?" an unimpressed Rozha shifted her weight back on one foot. "I happen to be a Teacher, myself, of Sachelvae. I train my students how to use any means necessary to destroy such haughty fools like you."

Bildarius mockingly laughed, "What a revolutionary waste of time. Your teachings are merely perversions of Safiro's Will. Sanguina's children have no place in combat." He showed her an enlightened grin, " Your skills would do you much better on our side. Yes, you know too well how much power matters in this world. For what other reason would you seek protection through an extension of your body rather than an extension of your spirit?"

Rozha glanced to the weapon by her side, then back at him. "Sometimes it's not enough to have just one or the other. I believe we live in a time where the ideals of Safiro and Sanguina are closer than ever to being recombined."

"Recombined?" Bildarius spat out the blasphemous word. "And to what end? The age of the Great Civilization is over. It was a time we were not meant to see again. The Father cannot be satisfied by the stagnation that the intertwining of our faiths would cause. Our people want one ideal, or the other."

"How can you live in Tresantia and earnestly believe a statement like that?" Rozha argued, gesturing to the bustling Mediona behind her. "What makes this city different than any other in the world is that both Safiro and Sanguina are said to smile upon its people."

"No," Bildarius refused, "it is their craving for revolution that both sides grow equally. As one population grows to upset the balance, so too must the other increase its advances to keep both in check."

But Rozha could not be convinced by his logic. "Is that really all you think this prosperity boils down to? A common want among one side to defeat the other? Where is this hatred -- this madness among our people that you see fueling this uprising?"

"It all started there," Bildarius pointed to the distant Sachelvae. "The creation of that landmark transformed these lands and threatened to overthrow them entirely into a world of weakness. Were it not for Travestas," he spread an arm to the diametric cathedral, "the heart of Onteval would forever have changed... and our history would forever be ruined."

"History?" Rozha repeated. "What're you talking about?"

"It was here, in these lands, that Sevasmia was sainted," Bildarius explained. "It was here that the Annihlus was destroyed. If these lands are corrupted by Sanguina's magic, the history of what happened here will be re-written by the Sisterhood; the Brotherhood's greatest stronghold will cease to be. It is for this reason that we must protect so fiercely the provenance of our faith..." he pointed to the wall, which begot their conversation, "...by preventing outside interference."

Following the direction of his finger, then looking back to him, Rozha lifted her chin and declared, "As a servant of Sanguina, whose mind is so blighted by her faith that she refutes all recourse, I draw but one conclusion from your story." She paused and began to draw her weapon. "I think you know what that would entail." Although the Red Dancer was once again left without the full arsenal of her stealth suit, she still had faith enough in the one weapon she had to fight without them.

A pulse of light flashed off Bildarius' eyes as his once ambivalent frown grew to a confident smirk. With a single hand, he pulled from the sash on his back the mighty hammer it concealed. Then, as if pushed by a gust of wind, jumped to crash its steel sledge upon Rozha's head. The blade dancer made no foolish move to block the massive weapon with her own, and took a backward somersault to evade Bildarius' tremendous impact.

With a thunderous peal and a blue flash of energy, the Safiric Elite's weapon excavated not only the ground it struck, but also a trench forming a direct path to his adversary. The unprepared Rozha was slammed by this wave of light and backed into the unfinished wall behind her. Seeing his opponent dazed encouraged Bildarius to press the attack; he advanced with a spinning motion, his feet levitating inches from the floor as he moved with astonishing speed. Rozha leapt atop the shoulder-high barrier, and with an explosion of bricks, narrowly avoided being crushed by the spiky edge of Bildarius' hammer.

Rozha was barely able to land on her feet when she fell back to the ground; the staggering blade dancer left another opening for her opponent's continued assault. The sharpened points of Bildarius' sledge came rising from a downward angle to cleave Rozha's side, if the Red Dancer hadn't rolled away. The Elite's hurried and risky attack had his momentum carrying him another few paces before he could stop; now it was Rozha's opportunity to turn the tables in their conflict.

La-mor'bel had its first taste of Wild blood when, with a dancer's twirl, she slashed her kris across Bildarius' exposed back. He cried with anguish when a crimson wound was torn across his spine through the indigo robes he wore. He turned back around to see Rozha's sword now dripping with his life force and grimaced with rage, baring his sharp, gray teeth. A cyan smoke began drifting off his weapon as his red eyes flickered with fire.

His wide sleeves pulled back to unveil brass bracers on his forearms, endowed with ancient symbols. Rozha was pushed away by a shield of wind when she attempted to advance, and paid for her mistake immediately thereafter when Bildarius threw his hammer like an arrow into her sternum. After a loud clang of steel, the Red Dancer was bashed against the wall; all the air had been taken from her lungs as she was left choking and gasping on her knees. She hadn't even realized that she had dropped her weapon in mid-flight until she rested her hazy eyes on her empty right hand clutching the black ground.

Bildarius' hammer floated on its own back to the Elite's clutches, his anger subsiding while he watched his foe struggling on her last legs. "It's a shame to kill you here, when you could have served a much greater purpose for the glory of Safiro. You could have done so much more with His Power, but you have been hopelessly blinded by the veil of Sanguina's deception. Death is the only cure for a Pure like you. You will have your restitution when your life serves to extend mine."

A sheen of energy glowed with a mystic screech around Bildarius' weapon. It was then raised above his head as he came flying forth to deliver the coup de grace on his weakened adversary.

"Masalida!"

With a bright flash and a horrible scream eclipsed by an explosion of power, Rozha lifted her head to see, beyond the shimmering lens of a half-spent masalida, her foe now laying on his side. Smoke drifted off the holes burnt in his robes as he stirred, slowly lifting himself up on his elbows. He turned a bewildered gaze to Rozha, who was none the wiser when it came to the identity of her savior. She hardly recognized the voice of she who cried the name of the Sanguinic spell floating so elegantly between them. That was, until the Arch Healer of Sachelvae suddenly appeared with a burst of sparks.

"Kyrana!" a relieved Rozha shouted. She summoned the last of her energy to shoot back up to her feet, but her body simply didn't have the strength to help her remain standing. She fell back against the wall and clutched her chest as she started coughing again.

"Rest yourself, fool," Kyrana's hardened stare softened slightly after she saw the smile on Rozha's face. Her attention was then brought to Bildarius' shaking form; the sucker-punched priest rose to a more-or-less standing position, using his hammer as a crutch.

"It would have been better for you to have stayed hidden," he admonished the Arch Healer. "Do you not see the full power of Safiro above us? You have no advantage here, priestess."

"Oh no?" Kyrana coyly tipped an ear. "Two against one is not an advantage?" With the side of her hand raised to chest level, she channeled her energies into Rozha, sheathing the blade dancer in a pink radiance that lifted the weight of her pain. When the revived Rozha picked herself back up, she saw her sword being telekinetically lifted for her by Kyrana's magic. "Take your weapon, blasphemer," the Arch Healer smirked at her friend.

With hesitance, Rozha staggered forth to do just that; now both she and Kyrana were staring down the Safiric Elite, who seemed oddly unperturbed by being cornered like this. Instead, he was rather humored. Leaving his hammer standing beside him, he outstretched both arms and proceeded to guffaw skyward. A swirling darkness appeared beneath his feet and grew outward; suddenly, Rozha and Kyrana found themselves contained within a cloud of pitch darkness.

"Destroy them."

Suddenly, the blinded Rozha and Kyrana found themselves being accosted from all directions by invisible attackers, biting into them with sharp claws raking into every inch of their bodies. Rozha couldn't fend them off; it was as if none of her foes had a physical form. She couldn't hear them coming and she could barely feel the weapons they used as they continued lacerating her.

The torrent of darkness grew colder the longer she stayed within it, until it became difficult to breathe. She could only think of how to break free, but the pain of her wounds made her too weak to run. She tried to call out for her friend, but her voice echoed as if she were in a hollow box all to herself. She fell over as she tried to flee; the second she hit what felt like the ground, she was unable to stand.

Something was keeping her pinned down. She was now weightless, but could feel herself sinking. She held her last inspiration as now her throat was being restrained. She gagged on the liquid darkness; what she heard was barely audible, but sounded like it was coming from above the surface of a deep pool. As she was losing consciousness, she thought she heard someone say *"Spexuaross!"*

Suddenly, Rozha inhaled through her decompressed windpipe. The attacks ceased. A ray of sunshine pierced the darkness, before the rest of the black cloud dispersed. Her eyes slowly adjusted to her new surroundings, which came to be nothing more than the very section of Tresantia she was in before. She looked all around, to find a badly-wounded Kyrana lying nearby.

Rozha knew she couldn't have been in much better condition, herself, but had no time to think about how much worse for wear she was. She saw, straight ahead, the familiar shapes of Diava, Wanystha, and Xanne surrounding a levitating black ball -- like a hole torn in the air, itself. Their arms were stretched forward as if keeping it back; a hexagon of pink energy was wrapped around them and a few other participants eclipsed by the darkness they were containing.

Kyrana came to in just enough time to behold what happened next. The ball of darkness began sparking, like a thundercloud, as it grew in size. It expanded like a balloon being filled with breaths of air; the dirt beneath it dispersed like the debris of a small tornado. Diava and her priestesses were unable to remain standing where they were; they were pushed back and had to retreat. The purple flashes of lightning increased with frequency -- the ball of darkness then exploded like a loud rumble of thunder, and from it came an unconscious Bildarius and a company of Safiric priests spilling out into a pile of bodies.

Diava commanded her priestesses to grab the score of Safiric acolytes with their astapsyxies and telekinetically carry them off one by one back to Sachelvae for later Purification. Rozha then saw the distant Diava turn to face her and Kyrana, and imperiously point as she gave an unheard order to her remaining helpers. Suddenly, Platina appeared by Rozha's side and knelt to mend her wounds.

"Remain still," the stoic nurse said. "The extent of your injuries are beyond my current power to fully heal. I will do what I can for you and Kyrana, then take you both to the Quarantine Bay so you can rest." Seeing the silent desperation on Rozha's face, the healer added, "Mother Diava has everything under control. The faculty will assist her in rectifying the situation. Any further assistance from you will be unnecessary."

The way she said that had Rozha thinking it wasn't coming from Platina's own mind, but was rather a message that Diava herself wanted the healer to convey. "Diava didn't like it that I jumped the gun, did she?"

Platina paused for a moment, then replied, "Mother Diava would have preferred that you stayed put after you provided your reconnaissance. An accident of this kind could have been avoided if protocol was more closely followed."

Rozha gave the nurse a funny, sideways glare. "A simple 'yes' would have sufficed." But the blade dancer should have known by now that nothing about Platina was simple besides her demeanor. She ignored the rest of what her patient had to say while she was laying her hands on Rozha's wounds to fix the ones she could. "I must conserve my energy to stabilize Kyrana," the nurse minded the Arch Healer over her shoulder. "You should be able to move on your own, but do not make any hasty actions."

Platina stood up, on her way to tend to Kyrana's injuries, but the second she turned around, she stopped as if taken by surprise. Rozha peered around the other velta and first caught sight of the hems of tattered robes swaying like tassels in the wind. This dark cloth of disrepair belonged to the High Priest of Travestas. A creepy smile adorned Deniechus' lifeless face as he stared down at Kyrana's motionless body, his large scythe firmly in hand. A green mist from the dilitrivanni orb he wore around his neck drifted toward the Arch Healer, lying at his feet.

"Do not come… another step," the High Priest warned.

A shaky Platina rose a tremulous arm to speak into her communication ring. "We have trouble."

Diava was distracted from supervising her servants, and upon seeing with whom Platina was speaking, she requested Wanystha and Xanne to keep watch while she handled the situation. Deniechus watched as the High Priestess made her way over to them, and waited for her to be within talking distance before he said anything to her. "So here we meet, once again, *Mother* Diava," he spoke her title with a sarcastic respect. "I thought we were at an agreement that no one from your temple would muddle with Travestas' affairs. For what reason have you sent your attack beasts to lay waste to my congregation and destroy our wall?"

Diava had no patience for smooth-talking with Deniechus and wasn't about to play any more of his games. "Don't pretend like you don't know what's going on, here."

"Bildarius told me why you were building that wall," Rozha stepped in to Diava's defense.

"Did he, now?" Deniechus' calm composure was unperturbed, as he looked in the direction of his fallen Teacher. "Then his vow of secrecy is allowed to die with him. I will let you Purify Bildarius in exchange for your Arch Healer's life," his tiny pupils shifted down to Kyrana's body.

"You want us to let Kyrana die?" Diava spat.

"Right now, her fragile soul is being kept in her body by my dilitrivanni," Deniechus explained. "I could take it out of her and into my hand at any time. If you do not agree to my terms, you are to release Bildarius and I will let your Healer live."

"And then what?" Diava continued her impatient interrogation.

"The wall shall continue to be built without further interruptions from your side," Deniechus replied. "If you destroy what we have done, our non-aggression pact will cease."

All eyes were on the High Priestess as she hesitantly made her deliberations, looking to the procession of priestesses carrying off Deniechus' congregation. Bildarius was the last to be gathered; as soon as she saw an astapsyxi wrapped around him, she looked to Rozha, whom she knew had been nearly killed by the Elite, then to Kyrana, whose life was hanging by a thread. Closing her eyes, Diava swallowed her reluctance and raised the communication ring under her chin. "Release him," pain shuddered her words.

Deniechus' smile brightened, his eyes widening slightly as if pleasantly surprised by Diava's acceptance. The High Priestess watched him with distrust, as if expecting him not to keep his end of the deal. Deniechus' wrinkled, spider-like fingers unclenched from his palm and enclosed one by one over his dilitrivanni. Its green smoke ceased issuing from its pores. He took a step back, and released Kyrana from his deathly hold; the Arch Healer took in a deep gasp and coughed, as if she had been suffocated.

"Hopefully you have learned something from this," Deniechus turned oblique to his audience. "I will let you Purify the priests you have already gathered; there's always more of Safiro's children who wish to satisfy their violent urges. They might actually appreciate their renewal as children of Sanguina, rather than suffer forever at the hands of our disappointed Father. How good it is…" he started with a snide smirk, "that Mother is always so willing to forgive."

Deniechus walked deeper into the Safiric side of Tresantia, but not quite out of earshot of the Sachelvian Sisterhood. He raised a communication ring of his own to relay a message to an unknown listener, "Make sure to keep them busy. The wall must be finished before the Vytameta is ours."

Chapter 26: No Way In

Raia, Malkinos, and Kasra spent their last hour together bringing Yalikai on a short tour of the Sanguinic side of Tresantia. Now that Kasra had seen a couple of the businesses in town, she had a bit of a working knowledge of the city, herself, and was able to impress Raia with her limited lore. Yalikai gave little in terms of a response to this sight-seeing; when asked for her opinion, she seemed rather lost in thought. Although she was physically there, observing the buildings and venues pointed out to her, it was as if her mind was in another place.

Their tour skirted around the grandest edifice on purpose, so that Raia could save her favorite and most obvious part of the city for last. "...And that is Sachelvae," her eyes dreamily glistened, "the most beautiful place in the world."

Yalikai stared up high at the cathedral's tall heights, beyond the decorative retaining wall capped with the squiggled statues of unborn spirits. The ancient, ornate barbican was left open, bereft of gate, so that anyone could walk through into the Sachelvian courtyard. The temple was framed with at least three acres of ground on all sides, which was used mainly for growing food and keeping livestock. The self-contained farm was typically tended to by the novitiates during their daily chores.

Layna had a notorious dislike for 'smelly behemoths' and would try to skip out of doing her chores as often as she could. She had fooled the faculty with enough repeated complaints of supposed allergies to livestock that she could be exempt from mucking stalls or feeding grain. Raia liked to joke that her city friend wouldn't know a hard day's work if it kicked her in the chest with both hooves. Kasra honestly wasn't the most appreciative of this honest farmwork, but since she had begun dating Malkinos, she liked to fantasize how he might've been impressed to see a little lady tending to the fields with the best of them.

Of course, none of the temple's yard was as impressive as the hand-crafted stonework of Sachelvae itself. The corners of the castle-esque keep's face were jointed by turrets, featuring slats for windows under their cone-shaped roofs. Beyond the crenellated walls were the tall angles of the temple's roof, their tops outfitted with flags and weathervanes blowing in the wind. Yalikai hummed as she gazed at the regal depiction of Saint Sevasmia in the round, stained glass window, above the red doors currently shut to outsiders. "Yes," she finally said, with a somewhat wistful tone. "It most certainly is the most beautiful place in the world."

Raia turned from the temple's face to gaze up at the multitude of stars spanning the belt of the Milky Way, but she couldn't ignore the bluish hue Safiro's full moon cast on the sky and everything in its sublunar radiance. She could only imagine what kind of horrid devilry the Brotherhood could be up to on a night like this. Her stomach soured all the more when she realized they hadn't regrouped with Rozha, nor had seen anyone else from the temple while they were out in Mediona. *'I hope they're alright...'*

Malkinos looked back in the direction of Mediona when he caught Kasra staring out into space, probably sharing much the same consternation Raia had about her sister. "What're you thinking about?" His sudden question startled the violette.

"I'm wondering where Rozha is," Kasra glanced up at him. "She was really concerned with the wall the Safiric Brotherhood was building. I wonder if she gave her report to Diava and just forgot to come back for us."

"She's probably just in the temple, then," Malkinos comfortingly held his girlfriend's hand. "Besides, your sister is really tough, isn't she? I'm sure she wouldn't have gotten herself into any trouble."

"I guess not..." Kasra trailed off, squeezing Malkinos' fingers.

"You know," Raia said to Yalikai, "the temple is always looking for new Pures to join its cause. Would you like to come to Sachelvae with us?"

Yalikai smiled, but had to politely reject her offer. "I'm sorry, but I cannot stay. My family will expect me home, by the end of the week."

"You were just passing through?" Raia asked. "Where does your family live?"

"I hath kin scattered about the globe," Yalikai cryptically replied.

"Even here, in Tresantia?" the brunette guessed. "How have you liked the city, now that you've had an opportunity to see it all up close?"

"Splendiferous," Yalikai's tone was filled with wonderment. "I doth feel as if I was once here."

It always made Raia swell with pride when she got to meet someone who shared her love for her favorite city. "I hope you'll come back, soon!"

"Aye, mayhap we shall meet again." Yalikai turned around, and gave a curious look to the bouquet Kasra was holding. "Yonder lady," she softly called to the violette, "T'would be my regret if we parted without hearing thy name."

Kasra snapped out of her distracting thoughts when she heard Yalikai's voice addressing her. She couldn't help thinking it was odd how she happened to know the names of her friends but didn't know hers. She faced her with a kind of half-smile. "It's Kasra Jantica," she finally introduced herself.

"Ah," Yalikai nodded, closing her eyes with a short purr, as if having heard a pleasant sound. "So it is. I won't soon forget."

"I'd wish to stay longer," Yalikai added, minding all her new friends, "but I must depart."

Raia looked like she didn't want Yalikai to leave so soon, but knew she couldn't convince her to tarry any longer. "A-Alright, is there anything I could help with? Kasra has some buuntash rations I'm sure she could share for your journey -- there's a stable just a little bit east of here where you could rent a steed…"

Yalikai raised a hand, trying to bite back a chuckle before the brunette could work herself into a tizzy. "I'll be fine, my dear. Thee art most gracious with thine concerns. I would like to give thee a token of my gratitude." Reaching up between her ears, she unraveled something on a string that she had tied into her silvery hair. She hid it under her rosy fingers and held it out for Raia, so that she could see the brunette's reaction when she unfurled her hand and revealed her gift. It was a ruby crystal cut into a teardrop shape, attached to a thin pendant.

"Yalikai…!" Raia covered her mouth with a gasp. "This is a sanrisma!"

The albino affirmed, "Wear this, and no harm cometh to those you care about. Thee will always be able to help thine friends, even when thee art far apart."

"Oh gosh," the brunette blubbered, shaking her head, "I can't take this from you -- these are so valuable and so rare, only a High Priestess…"

Yalikai hushed her by clasping her gift into Raia's hand. "Tis worth more with you than anyone else."

Raia's breath caught in her throat, her legs so taught they almost quivered. "Thank you," she squeaked with a wilt of her ears.

"I hath not a bounty of recollections of times in which I hath met a heart like the one thy keeps," Yalikai admirably said. "Thee art in the right place at the right time. Many wait their whole lives to be where thou art now."

A flattered Raia blushed, looking away as she rubbed the back of her neck. "You wouldn't say that if you knew the kinds of things I've done up til now…"

Yalikai shook her head. "What thou art is a testament to what thee hath accomplished. Thou art an amalgamation of trials, both bad and good. Upon which hour thy feeleth lost, tis time to reflect on what thee hath learned."

After a short pause, the albino added, "As a priestess thee should know, that once thee hath begun Sanguina's Path, thou canst not be led astray."

After a moment to think about Yalikai's wisdom, Raia smiled and nodded, as if having come to a soothing epiphany. "Yes, I understand."

With a final, addressing glance to Malkinos and Kasra, who had stayed equally quiet for these enlightening revelations, Yalikai took her leave. "Twas a wonderful meeting between us this evening. I feeleth I hath learned enough to make you my friends. I bid thee all good tidings, till we meet again." After giving them a priestess-esque curtsy, the albicant vixy sauntered down the path whence they came. Kasra and her friends watched her depart until she descended a flight of stairs and was out of sight.

"She was really something else, wasn't she?" the violette reminisced.

"She never did say where she was from," Raia curiously purred.

"Nor where she was going," Malkinos finished for them.

"Speaking of," the brunette turned to her brother, "aren't you expected back at the room dad rented at the inn?"

"Yeah, I guess..." the taller farm boy brushed his foot on the cobblestones. Then with a little smile at Kasra, he said, "It was great seeing you again~"

"You, too," the violette rocked on her heels, her tail bashfully wagging.

"Dad and I will be leaving town for a while, come daybreak," Malkinos sighed. "We won't be back until our lakushas are in season."

"Well, then I suppose you'd like something to remember me by, huh?" Kasra winked. She stepped forward and stood on her toes to give her boyfriend a little kiss, lacking any shyness while Raia cooed behind them.

An embarrassed Malkinos blinked at Kasra after their lips popped apart. He tried not to look at his little sister, whom he knew had to be impishly grinning at him. "Do you think you'll be able to visit on your next Sabbath Day?"

"Ooh, *there's* an idea~!" Raia tapped Kasra's shoulder. "I'd love to take you to Bryotte Farms! It's so pretty -- you'd like it there. I'd get to show you all the places Malkinos and I liked to go when we were growing up there."

"Oh please," Malkinos rolled his eyes, with a little smirk. "What do you mean 'growing up?' You're *still* just a kid!" He poked his sister's nose.

"I am *not*," Raia defiantly sniffled, crossing her arms with a twitch of her tail. "Mother Diava and Teacher Wanystha have called me 'young velta' many times."

"Terms of endearment," Malkinos not-so-quietly muttered to Kasra's ear.

"You're worse than Lavelle!" Raia squeaked, whacking her chuckling brother in the side with her tail. "Hurry up and go see dad before you make me hate you more."

"Okay…" Malkinos sighed, then leaned in to give his sister a hug. "Goodnight, Raia."

"See ya next Sabbath, Malkinos," the brunette held his hands and let their tails slip apart before he started walking away.

"We should get back inside," Kasra pointed to Sachelvae's entrance. But by the time Kasra and Raia got to the temple's grand, iron doors, they refused to budge. "Oh no," the brunette groaned. "We're too late! Mother Diava has already locked us out!"

Even though she was sure the doors would be just as shut if she tried them, Kasra instinctively gave the handle rings a vain couple of tugs, herself. "Alright, then we'll have to find an alternate way in."

Raia, admittedly, wouldn't know any other ways to access the temple. "The only other door I can think of is the one that leads to the orchard, but I'm sure she would have sealed that one off, too."

Picking up a rock alongside the trail, Kasra threw her fist-sized projectile at the nearest, stained glass window. Raia's heart jumped when she saw the stone fly twenty feet, only to unceremoniously bounce off the painted window. Although they were still stuck outside, she heaved a sigh of relief, but not before reprimanding Kasra's efforts. "I can only imagine what Mother Diava would have said if she saw us break in like that…" She shook her head and clutched a hand to her chest as her mind raced with visages of disdain, surrounding her upon getting inside the temple.

"Well now I know why the Safiric Brotherhood had such a hard time getting in," Kasra said. "Everything this building is made of is completely invulnerable." Noticing a keyword in her phrasing, she remembered, "Those windows in the Purifier Hall -- one of them right above the Purifier is just large enough that I might be able to squeeze through…"

It sounded like a good idea, except, "I'm sure the Safiric Brotherhood would have tried that, too, by now," Raia doubtfully hummed.

"If they had a reason to think it was even there," Kasra rebutted. "You can only see the oculus from the inside. They probably wouldn't bother trying to break a hole in the roof if they couldn't get in any other way."

"I dunno about this…" Raia trailed off, once again, as she gazed up at the frightening heights of the temple's roof. "The angles are so steep, I don't think you could hold on, even if you *could* get up there."

No sooner did she say that than did Kasra want to give it a shot. "This isn't my first time breaking into some place," she confidently averred, handing Raia her bouquet. Armed with nothing aside from her bare hands and boots, Kasra grasped a few uneven bricks and began scaling Sachelvae's vertical heights towards the temple's turrets. Her progress was slow and calculated, like a mountain climber finding footholds in a rocky surface. But without even needing to carve a slot to sink her fingers into, the agile vixy was able to use her tail as a counterbalance to make her way up to the hundred-foot-high eaves.

"Once I find a safe place," the dangling Kasra shouted down to her friend, "I'll teleport you up here!"

"No no, that's okay!" Raia timidly laughed. "I'll just wait until you're inside before you fygidia me anywhere!"

While she took a moment to rest, Kasra held onto the edge of a turret's overhanging roof, which at its tip was over eleven feet tall. Her feet were reclined against the nearest merlon, which was closer to about four feet in height. Her body rested a bit diagonally between these two points; her tail was once again used as a counterbalance to keep the steady winds from pushing her off. She could hear the nearby flags flapping just twenty feet overhead. From the top of the turret, a regular priestess starting from within the temple could access the battlement she fought so hard to illegally reach.

While it was the first time Kasra had been at these heights, she was told by Layna and Raia once before that it was a part of a novitiate's chores, once per month, to clean the moss and lichen growing from the shingles. From where she was sitting, she could see the roof was constructed into a kind of funnel shape, leading forty feet down to the timekeeping oculi she mentioned to Raia before her ascent, spanning over the Purifier Hall.

The rest of the roof beyond the funnel resembled a mountain range of peaks; it made her think of a giant, sea monster's maw opening up from the ocean's depths to swallow its victim whole. It wouldn't have been difficult for a hapless novitiate to fall off the catwalk leading from the battlements and slip into the deep bowl. *'So that's why I saw the rain flowing into the pool when I first came inside,'* Kasra remembered. *'The roof wasn't designed to keep water out, but rather drain it in.'* She could only imagine how much more difficult it would have been to climb up there had it been raining, in addition to it being dark outside.

Feeling like she'd had enough rest, and had avoided looking down at the dizzying drop below long enough, she finally stepped onto the battlement proper and from the catwalk continued her way into the funnel. Transitioning from a cautiously crouched position, she rested her side against the top of the bowl-shaped slope, which didn't offer her much in the way of anything to hold onto. Rather, like the mouth of the creature she imagined, its smooth shingles acted like much more of a slide.

Her descent toward the oculus started slow, but gradually picked up speed every ten feet, until she covered the distance rather expeditiously for her liking. The violette shrieked with fear as she tried to scramble away from the approaching oculus, which had become a lot larger up close. It was big enough for her whole body to slip through. Just as her legs were entering the hole, she extended her arms for something to hold onto. When she felt herself at the mercy of gravity, she flinched; somehow, in the blink of an eye, she found herself stuck midway through the chimney-like passage.

Her hands and feet were braced against the cylindrical walls that only had space enough for her to cram inside with her knees bent up to her chest. Her tail was used as a third leg of sorts to keep herself from slipping. She was facing straight down into the pool, sixty feet away, but from her vantage point, could see as far as Diava's altar.

All five of her limbs began quaking from the white-knuckle stresses of keeping her body suspended in such an uncomfortable position. And how much more so this uneasiness was exacerbated when she heard slipper-clad footsteps against the marble floor below, casually coming closer to where she was hanging. She and a nonplussed Diava locked eyes when the High Priestess stood by the southern edge of the Purifier.

Kasra's grip gave when she had been caught, just enough to allow herself to fall to the very edge of the oculus. She bit her lip and prepared herself for the fall when she felt her fingers loosening their tension. But with an unspoken fygidia from the abbess below, she opened her eyes to find herself crouched on the floor, stuck in the same position she was in before she was teleported.

Of all the things the High Priestess could have asked, the first one that came to her mind was, "What were you doing out at this hour, Kasra?" The emotion in her softly spoken words were like the rumblings of faraway thunder.

Diava's voice raised the rigid violette from her funny bow to bear her eyes on the abbess' stiff countenance. "I was on a date, your holiness," Kasra's speech trembled, knowing that any excuse wouldn't satisfy her.

"You were supposed to be in by now," came the High Priestess' next, coldly austere statement. "Where is Raia?" The air around the quietly fuming lady was rife with electricity; The ire in her face rose the fine hairs on Kasra's skin.

"She came with me," the violette said, pointing to the closed doors behind her. She stepped back, as if expecting a vulcan reaction from the High Priestess. "She's still outside."

This unsatisfying answer elicited a surly rumble from the back of Diava's throat. With another fygidia, Diava summoned Raia to her side. The brunette squeaked with surprise when she saw that it was not Kasra, but the High Priestess, who called her into the Purifier Hall. "Uh, y-your holiness--!" She couldn't think of anything to say fast enough before Diava's patience had expired.

"I am very disappointed in you," the abbess began. "I thought you and Kasra would be better influences on each other. But now I am not certain if I have made the right decision letting you room together. You are now forbidden from leaving temple grounds, under *any* circumstance."

An aghast Kasra's anger inwardly boiled. The violette sighed out her frustrations, knowing such would be her fate if she was caught. She despondently accepted her punishment with a bow of her head. "Yes, your holiness."

"The same goes for you, Raia," Mother Diava added. "Teacher Rozha will be in charge of Kasra's obedience. During that time, if I find out that either of you have partaken in any unsupervised activity outside temple grounds, you *both* will be expelled from the convent."

Kasra's eyes upturned with bewilderment to the abbess upon hearing this stark stipulation. Raia, too, gaped her mouth as if wanting to argue her point. She wanted so badly to say how Layna never faced so harsh a penalty for any of her wrongdoings, but she also knew that Layna was never caught breaking into the temple before. *'That must've scared Mother Diava, to think that such an entrance could be possible.'*

"Until then," Diava started, "you get to sleep, Kasra."

"Yes, your holiness," came another saddened purr from the violette, as Diava took her leave.

When the two vixies were left alone, Kasra raised her head with a groan. "I'm sorry, Raia... You gave me fair warning of what to expect and I did it anyway. I thought I could've gotten away with it easier than that."

What she was expecting to be a compassionate response was soured by the punishment Raia was dragged into along with her. "I don't know what you thought you could've done," the brunette brashly replied. "I mean, I think you gave yourself away when you screamed up there, but even if you *hadn't* made a sound, I don't think you could've fallen into the pool without alerting *someone* to your presence."

Kasra shot Raia an angry, quizzical look as if her very eyes were telling her to shut up. "Gee thanks," she shook her head with a sarcastic tone. "If you didn't think I had a chance at making it, why didn't you try to stop me?"

"I *would* have, if I thought there'd be any point in *trying*," Raia dismissively laughed. "You really are just like Layna when it comes to things like this. She wouldn't want me getting in her way, either. Whenever she was presented with a challenge, I'd just let her have at it. What's the point in wasting my breath trying to talk sense into you two?"

"Sheesh, sorry I asked," a hurt Kasra turned away from her, but Raia only continued her ranting barbs.

"I mean, I only made myself a reputation for being nice and wanting to help everyone, and what's it gotten me other than *trouble* from one day to the next?" The pace of her speech was so fast that it made it seem like she didn't really care about being understood. "They say here that nobody's hopeless -- that a good priestess can turn even the coldest hearts to see Sanguina's light, but the longer I've spent around you and Layna the more I've come to *doubt* these maxims."

She wasn't looking to anyplace in particular as she waved her arms with a gradual raising of her voice. "I don't get any rewards for doing the right thing; my payment is a slap on the wrist and a reminder to count my blessings, only every time I do, there are fewer and fewer. When will there be none? Probably when I finally go *stark raving mad* and get myself *kicked out* of this place!"

Watching the angry brunette pace about and lose her temper was truly a sight to behold, and Kasra wasn't sure whether to feel sorry for her or laugh at the fulmination of her suffering. She wasn't sure if anything she could say could top her friend's meltdown, and thought maybe a cooldown was what she needed. While Raia's back was turned, her hands clutching the hair draping over her shoulders, Kasra swept her tail at the brunette's ankles to trip her into the Purifier.

The unsuspecting Raia yelped as she was dunked head first into the holy water, and thrashed about in her soaked outfit. An alarming amount of darkness washed away from her into the scarlet waters as the Purifier relieved her of her sinful contemplations. What Raia said when she dragged herself to the side of the pool was something Kasra didn't expect to hear.

"Thanks for that," the brunette genuinely panted, accepting Kasra's hands to pull her back to her feet.

"Look, I didn't mean to get you tangled up in this mess with me," Kasra said, giving Raia a folded towel. "I know you're tired of being pushed around. You're tired of feeling used and never getting anywhere. I get that. It's my fault you're being held back, and unlike Layna, I'm going to set things right."

Chapter 27: Alien Visitor

When Kasra and Raia returned to their room, the violette placed the bouquet she received from Laritat on a nightstand by her bed. *'I wonder what Yalikai meant when she said these flowers grow better in darkness?'* Seeing that their petals remained open, despite the night sky out her window, she added, *'Maybe they're nocturnal blooms?'*

Raia had precious little to comment on as she changed into her pajamas and got ready for her rest. "It'll be another normal day, tomorrow," she sat on her firm mattress.

"Except," a smiling Kasra waggled her tail, "my sister will be having her first class in the morning!"

"Ah, this is true!" Raia nodded from the recollection. "We never did find out what she got into this evening. Mother Diava seems to think everyone is at the temple, safe and sound."

"I guess I'll have to ask her, tomorrow," Kasra shrugged. The violette laid down and proceeded to restlessly stare at the ceiling; all the exciting things she experienced earlier were still racing through her mind. Turning over to Raia, she propped up her head on her bent arm and asked, "Would you mind telling me the rest of the story about the adventure you and Layna had last winter -- the one you started this morning? It's been bugging me all day that you didn't end it yet!"

Raia rolled over to face her friend, flattered by her request to finish her narrative. "Now we're getting to the interesting part of the tale," Raia proudly smirked with the raise of a didactic finger. "It was at that point in our conversation with Voxus that we noticed we weren't alone. The owners of the outpost we had found had returned and took us all off guard."

~~

Two different kinds of alien speech, both from languages unknown to any part of Vitiosa, were conversing with each other in an almost argumentative tone as their speakers approached the egg-shaped craft they had left behind. Raia, Layna, and Voxus held their ground -- too shocked to move even if they wanted to, when the strange beings breached the clearing. One of them resembled a man of a species they had never seen before, clad in a curiously fragile-looking gray and black armor that probably would have been broken by any weapon that struck it. The wearer's head was concealed by a round helmet featuring a single window to show his face. The 'creature' had a much smaller nose than those of belhuayns and a much more defined chin line. He really looked nothing like belhuayns at all, but his body was similar enough that if he never showed his face, his lack of a tail would be the only thing that could give him away.

Beside him stood a tall, avian creature covered in white feathers and a similarly humanoid build, clad in a kind of fragile suit of his own. The bird man wore an assortment of scanty plating; half of a red breastplate was endowed with long, wing-like markings that curved over one shoulder. His three-toed talons were left uncovered by footwear of any kind, and were currently raised up on their toes as if preparing for a confrontation. Unlike his teammate, he wasn't reaching for a weapon on his belt; rather, he seemed quite confident in the devastation his four-fingered claws could commit upon his adversaries.

Then, in the most shocking exchange yet, the fully-armored man said in a fluent but oddly-accented belhuayn: "Friend or foe?!"

Raia and company were so taken aback, they almost forgot to say anything. Layna was the first of the trio to regain her composure enough to respond. "I could ask the same of you!"

At this, the first astronaut pulled out a short, blunt weapon from a holster on his belt. It looked reminiscent to guns Layna had seen in use on board sailing ships from the Ontevallian coast, but it was made in a stylistic fashion that was far more advanced than anything she had seen before. The nervous man's trigger finger twitched untrustingly, and had it not been for his more level-headed compatriot, Layna would have seen what the business end of the weapon was like. The bird man placed a clawed hand on his friend's wrist to push his gun aside. "Don't shoot," he calmly stated in a belhuayn of his own. "Can you not see they're only children?" His beak flexed into a smile as he turned his peaceful attention toward their interlopers.

"My name is Kaitora," the avian crossed a hand over his chest. "I am a cleitean from planet Saja. I am joined by Captain Yibesh, of planet Aedaria. We mean you no harm."

Raia seemed to believe them, but Layna wasn't about to let up her guard so easily. "Then for what reason are you here?"

"To meet members of your race, believe it or not," the diplomatic cleitean turned a disapproving scowl to the jumpy aedarian. "I am a scientist from my world. I was asked by Captain Yibesh to join him on an expedition to your 'Forbidden Planet.'"

"Forbidden?" Raia repeated.

"What's a 'planet?'" Layna blinked.

Kaitora looked like he was trying not to chuckle at their primitive knowledge. "A planet is just one of many surfaces in the Qualarian System that supports life, like yours. We are all a part of Qualaria's embrace -- that is the name we gave to our sun."

"Your world is known by many names in our cosmic community," Yibesh squeezed his way into the conversation. "But to the Xallian Space Federation, you are called 'Forbidden' because of your race's proclivity to violence."

The Safiric Voxus smirked, very tempted to demonstrate a little bit of that 'violent proclivity' to his otherworldly visitors, but restrained himself for the moment. "So if we're supposedly so 'dangerous' and 'forbidden,'" the novitiate priest began, "why are you risking your lives to 'meet' with us? What's in it for you to come all this way out here, in the middle of nowhere?"

"I beg your pardon," Kaitora said, "but this is hardly 'the middle of nowhere,' for the sake of our research," he gestured to the surrounding wilderness. "The city merely two miles from here is a mecca of development, unlike anywhere else we've studied on this world. While we have observed larger, even more populated regions on this planet, there are none with a population diversity greater than that we've found here. We have found these differences rather intriguing and we want to know why cultural segregation is present everywhere else in your world."

"This benefits us for a couple of reasons," Yibesh answered Voxus' second question. "One, it answers a very old question we of the Qualarian Community have had about your people: why are they so... underdeveloped, compared to the rest of us who seem to be on the same page, so to speak. Once we have found the source of the problem, we can work on correcting it. But as it stands... the people of this world do not seem ready for such a revolution to take place."

"You're right," a defensive Voxus threateningly scowled. "Nobody here needs the 'assistance' of untrustworthy outsiders to set things right when they have no place muddling in our affairs. The Dark Men and other visitors like them have been capturing and beleaguering we belhuayns for centuries." He raised his hands to chest level, equidistant apart, to begin conjuring the spiral of a spirit blast. "The day we become like you is the day the Father has turned His back on us. We of the Safiric Brotherhood are taught to hate and destroy anything that is unlike the members of our sacred community.

Now I'll send you to meet whatever aberrant gods *you* worship! Say your prayers, 'cause I'm your slayer!"

Before Raia could say 'astapsyxi,' Voxus thrust his arms forward to throw a white blob of mist into Yibesh's helmet. With a splash of this Safiric energy, the glass shield protecting his face shattered as the astronaut was sent onto his back. His unarmed sajan compatriot squawked something in his own language as, with a flap of the wings on his arms, he bounded to the top of his spaceship on the rightmost edge of the clearing. Its door lifted open to reveal a white interior bathed in light. Before Raia or Layna could get a good look at it, three armed men came rushing out in single file. They were each clad in a bulky, black and gray armor that fully concealed their bodies. Their helmets were made to cover a xallian head. Their visors and vents were stylized to look like glowering eyes and a downturned, open mouth. Maybe it was due to the metal suits that their voices were corrupted into sounding like they did, but their speech hardly had a natural tone; it was loud and had no rise nor fall in pitch. Their alien words were unrecognizably garbled to their belhuayn adversaries, but the three of them were able to get the gist of what was coming next.

The first guard was wielding a weapon that could've been mistaken for an advanced musket. The one behind him to his left carried a shoulder-mounted gun that looked like it could've been used on board a sailing ship. The one to the right of Cannon Shoulder had a wrist-mounted implement that seemed rather tame by comparison; every clenching of his fingers caused the gun on the back of his hand to fire a small bolt of red energy. Instead of using the large space ship behind them for cover, Musket knelt and took aim at Voxus so that his backup could fire over his head.

In the interest of self-preservation, instants before the hail of gunfire could ensue, Layna and Raia protected themselves with a tandem masalida -- the wide barrier was constructed by intertwining both of their Sanguinic magic. But it was not they who the guards saw as the aggressor; Wrist Gun's fire was trained on Voxus, who as soon as he was targeted, repeatedly vanished and reappeared in V-shaped puffs of smoke to avoid his shots.

He disappeared only to reappear an instant later crouching on the high branch of a nearby tree. Wrist Gun's automatic fire trailed up the trunk while Musket took a more pinpoint shot. The branch was severed from the tree by a streak of blue energy, forcing Voxus to teleport again.

Cannon Shoulder decided he'd had enough of these games and risked the collateral damage from firing his weapon. With a thunderous burst, out from the long barrel of his gun was fired a giant, laser cannon ball. The whole clearing was consumed in a white flash from the detonation this missile made upon contact with the ground; the nearest trees were knocked down after their roots had been disintegrated by the blast.

Raia's and Layna's shield barely saved them from being knocked off their feet by the dissipating wave of energy. There was only a bowl-shaped crater remaining where Voxus had been standing.

Raia and Layna were silent with shock when everything calmed, but still there was an undeniable tension that held everyone still and alert. During the fireworks of the skirmish, a wounded Yibesh had lifted himself back up to a more-or-less standing position. His face was marred by the glass shrapnel, dark blood trickling from his light lacerations. He had no less collected his bearings before he was entangled by roots, as if the trees had gained a mind of their own.

Voxus then reappeared directly behind him with an arm wrapped around the neck of his hostage, using him as a deterrent from being attacked. The struggling Yibesh barked incomprehensibly to his guards, causing them to shake with uncertainty.

"Take him alive!" Kaitora repeated this command in belhuayn, so that the kids would know his peaceful intent. The guards withdrew their fire to avoid hitting their commander, leaving them open for Voxus' retaliation. The novitiate stomped a foot on the ground, summoning a line of jagged icy stalagmites to rise in a path straight for his bunched trio of attackers.

Musket suddenly found himself encased in a shell of frost and unable to move, but his two allies were able to nimbly roll aside to avoid being entangled with him. While his adversaries were taking cover, Voxus advanced toward the vulnerable Musket and empowered a massive haymaker by focusing a white ball of Safiric energy around his fist.

With a primal cry, Voxus smashed the Musket ice sculpture into frozen chunks. His audience was stunned as they watched the pieces of the guard fly off into separate directions; a severed arm still encased in a crystalline shell plopped before the protected Raia and Layna. Any of the dismembered limbs, once settled on the ground, emitted a black smoke from the joint at which they would have attached.

Voxus pushed away Wrist Gun's arm before he could fire a point-blank salvo, which were then deflected off Raia's and Layna's masalida. The teenage priest stepped back to dodge an overhead chop of Cannon Shoulder's forearm, seemingly unable to be caught off guard by his flanking opponents.

A quick-thinking Raia decided to give their alien allies a helping hand by holding avast their common adversary with an astapsyxi. In doing so, the novitiate had lost her concentration on her shield, leaving both she and Layna defenseless as it disintegrated. A speechless Layna cast her friend a bewildered glare; while they didn't wish death upon their alien visitors, they had no reason to assume their safety would be guaranteed if they turned against Voxus to save them.

Even after what the Safiric novitiate said about Vitiosa's history with these alien beings, she was more apt to believe in Yibesh's good intentions. She doubted the worlds he and Kaitora were from would have only sent two, barely armed astronauts to seed an invasion of a whole planet. Seeing Kaitora so fearing for his life, Raia couldn't allow these visitors to be harmed if she had the power to help.

The bulkier Cannon Shoulder did the honors of capitalizing on their telekinetically frozen enemy, and sent an uppercut into his jaw so fierce that it broke Raia's astapsyxi and took Voxus off his feet. As if somehow expecting to be struck in such a manner, the young novitiate flourished with an acrobatic flip and disappeared in mid air to return directly in front of Cannon Shoulder.

This time, Raia was not fast enough to stop him. Voxus attacked with an empowered whip of his glowing tail, spinning around to clash his strongest limb into the torso of his taller enemy. A surprised Cannon Shoulder was knocked clear into the air and slammed against the side of his space ship with a loud clang.

Wrist Gun forewent shooting his adversary point blank and instead, with a flick of his left wrist, projected a shimmering blade of blue light. A minutia of respectful concern crossed Voxus' countenance, this technology reminding the nascent priest of Safiric elites.

Though flanked, he was nonetheless prepared with his reflexes to raise an arm and use an invisible buckler of energy. The small, hexagonal barrier flashed into existence when Wrist Gun's sword collided against it, inches away from slicing through the belhuayn's limb. Safiric power swirled and tightened around Voxus' fist as he hooked his arm back, threatening to drive it through the stout guard's gut.

Ribbons of light followed his hand as the sound of energy fizzed louder, like an engine spooling up. With the peal of a galvanic burst, Voxus was suddenly and inexplicably blown away by the reversal of his own power. He was taken immediately into the ground as if crushed by a wall of force. Dirt, ice and snow were blasted skyward like the detonation of a grenade as his body excavated for itself a mud casket in the frozen earth.

When the smoke from this localized devastation had cleared, Raia and Wrist Gun were surprised to see a disc-shaped barrier unlike any either had seen before whirling between the guard and their downed adversary.

A bewildered Layna froze in her arcane posture: her left hand was tied around her other wrist, the palm of her right hand faced forward. Her eyes were wide with disbelief at what she had done -- what she was expecting to be an ordinary masalida was transformed into a special mirror shield of which no one present knew any comparison.

Voxus' exhausted, agonized groan let everyone know he was still alive, but that he had more than had it for being ganged up on. "You turned on me," he breathed to the priestesses. "You fools, we were in this together! Are you not going to stand in their way to take this world over?"

Now that they had seen firsthand what these advanced races were capable of with their technological prowess, Raia and Layna were starting to doubt the astronauts had peaceful intentions. Seeing that the smoke had cleared, the scientist sajan fluttered down from his hiding place atop the spaceship to assess the damage. Yibesh eased up as well and signaled for his guards to do the same.

"We have no ambitions of domination," the captain said to the friendlier belhuayns.

"We are much more your allies than your enemies," Kaitora added. "Our worlds," he pointed between himself and Yibesh, "were vital in the survival of yours, nearly 100 years ago. We never had an interest in conquering your lands, but the Xallian Alliance was started to prevent the Inmarisians from taking away the sovereignty of Vitiosa."

"So what," Layna quirked an eyebrow, "are you saying we owe you something now?"

Kaitora's laugh came in the form of a funny, avian warble. "Not in the least. Our protection of your world was done with the utmost altruism. The Xallian Alliance believes that all intelligent races, no matter how advanced, should retain their neutrality if they desire it."

Layna wasn't entirely sure if she could believe what he was saying. "And yet you've come to our world to 'revolutionize' it, as you put it earlier," she commented.

The sajan paused for thought, not helping the case Layna made for his double standard. "But I also said, 'as it stands,' it is not a possibility; the royalty of this world are too closed-minded for such deals to be made. They wouldn't be ready to join our cosmic community."

"I don't get it," Layna shrugged. "What would be in it for us to join your 'Xallian Alliance?'"

Kaitora explained, "The further you allow yourselves to fall behind, the more increasingly hostile outsiders will become to you. You cannot afford to wallow in the primitive technology to which you have mired yourselves. You must assimilate into the Qualarian System, or be destroyed by those who see you as nothing more than insects to be exterminated." After preaching this rather candid bit of information, the sajan glanced over his shoulder to see Yibesh crouching beside the placated Voxus. The astronaut was holding to the novitiate's neck what could be best described by its belhuayn viewers as a glass mosquito. Its transparent innards were filled with the crimson ooze of Voxus' life force, but left no visible wounds on its host.

"I have collected the sample from the hostile," Yibesh told his partner. "Are you ready to depart?"

Eyeing sideways his teenage acquaintances, Kaitora replied, "Yes, but I know I will regret the shortness of my stay. I will not be satisfied until I have seen the results of my work." Then addressing Raia and Layna more properly, he continued, "I feel I have come to know a lot about you, people of the 'Forbidden World.' I have hope that my research will prove untrue the assertions my colleagues have made about this planet being condemned by its own people. Once we can lift the ban placed on Vitiosa, we can forge a real connection between our worlds. I think this will be to the betterment of us all." Once again leaving his audience with heavy considerations, Kaitora finally regrouped with Yibesh. "I am ready, now."

With that, the door to their spaceship reopened; they and their guards marched back inside. Layna, Raia, and a prostrate Voxus watched with awe as the grand structure folded in its landing struts and began lifting above the forest canopy. Its near soundless takeoff was like watching a cloud rising from the ocean into the sky. Once it had cleared the trees, its slow hover became an instantaneous acceleration; the whole craft vanished like a white streak through the air.

~~

"And from then on, was never seen again," Raia finished her story. "We heard people talking about it around town for months afterward; apparently, lots of people saw it and had no idea what it was. On the ground where it had been standing, it left behind a funny, spiral-shaped etching. When Layna and I went back to revisit the landing site in the spring, the spiral was still there -- nothing grew around it."

Even though it was all explained to her in a very believable way, Kasra still had a hard time imagining everything Raia was telling her. She would have been much more convinced if, "Can I see it for myself?"

"You want me to take you back there?" Raia tipped her ear. "You know we just got forbidden from ever leaving the temple, right?"

"Not right now, of course," the violette chuckled at her friend's bewildered expression. "Just sometime after this whole thing blows over."

Raia disdainfully shook her head, wanting to reprimand her friend's determination, but couldn't help admiring it slightly. "I swear, you and Layna…" she trailed off with a mutter, then said more clearly, "I'm sure it won't 'blow over' until after we both pass our initiation into the clergy." Holding her notched tiara in her lap, Raia gazed wistfully at her bronze-colored reflection. "I only have one notch left, but I feel like it could have been removed several times, months ago, had Layna not been holding me back."

After a minute of deliberation, Kasra asked, "When do you think they'll release her?"

Her friend defeatedly raised her shoulders and twisted her lips with puzzlement at her novitiate crown. "I don't know. But I'm going to make the most of my time without her, to do what I should have done when she was still here." She glanced up to see Kasra's encouraging, inquisitive eyes, prompting her to add, "I'm going to focus on the path Sanguina has set for me, rather than the adventures Layna wanted to take me on. I realized all too late that she was distracting me from achieving my goals. I can't have both frivolity and fruition; too much of one leaves no time for another. I've enjoyed these games long enough; now it's time to get serious about who I am and what I want to be."

Kasra's tail gave a slow, limber wag as she filled with pride for her friend. Seeing her on the cusp of making a difference in her own life was enthralling to the violette, who had a very similar awakening when she first came through Sachelvae's doors. *'Everyone has a moment like that, sometime in their lives; it just takes longer for some people than it does for others.'*

Having caught her friend enraptured in her thoughts, Raia's next question slightly startled Kasra. "I know everyone here thinks that you're going to make something special of yourself, Kasra, but I want to know what you want that special something to be."

Truthfully, it wasn't a question Kasra herself had thought too long about. Her eyes vacantly blinked as her gaze shifted to her knees; her tail wrapping subconsciously around her waist while she stammered, "Uh, I don't know… I honestly don't feel like anyone terribly important. But, there are questions about myself that I want to have answered. And I don't feel like I'm going to find them by staying here."

At this, Raia cast her a rather worried look. "What are you saying, Kasra?"

The violette realized what this statement would have entailed, and gave the brunette the most genuine smile she could manage. "I'm not going to leave you, Raia! But I feel like there's some searching I have to do elsewhere. I think the only reason Layna stuck around is because she wanted to know what she was, too."

Drawing in a deep breath to release a heavy sigh, Kasra spiritually prepared herself. "Before I came to Sachelvae, I didn't know anything about myself and was craving answers, but I didn't know where to look. There were a lot of things I could do that I couldn't explain. Learning about the magic of Sanguina and the Safiric Brotherhood has helped me understand where these powers come from. But I never felt connected to either deity…"

She trailed off to collect her thoughts. "I'm not like the other novitiates because I don't feel beholden to Sanguina like they do. They call me a Pure, but I don't feel like one. I never felt like the alternative, either; I just did what I wanted to and felt no guilt for either action."

The way Kasra ended that statement had Raia worrying what her friend did that she could have been guilty about. "Layna knew you were like her when we all first met," Raia admitted. "I've believed, from the beginning, that's why you two could never get along. I'd never bother telling her that, though --" They both knew thawing Layna's heart to reason was as fruitless as puffing warm breath to open a locked door in an ice storm. She laughed off the memories of certain arguments she had with her aforementioned friend in the past, then waited a few seconds before turning her attention back to Kasra. "What do you feel you must do to get closer to the answers you're looking for?"

The violette longingly gazed out the round window above the headboard of her bed, a little ripple of thought flowing through her tail. "I think I have to look for Layna's sister."

"Viasarria??" Raia gaped at the sudden change of subject. "What does she have to do with anything? She's not even at the temple anymore!"

"She attacked Rozha and I, after my first date with Malkinos," Kasra explained. "She said she was sent by our mother to find us. We scared her off, and we never knew what became of her since." Kasra pensively sighed as Raia tipped an ear for what the violette really wanted to say. "I want to know where she went."

Recognizing that stubborn, mission-oriented fire in her friend's eyes, an exasperated Raia threw up her arms. "Oh no, I *knew* you were going to say that! You're not seriously considering going out and looking for her, right after you've been sworn to never leave the temple again?"

"What other choice do I have?" Kasra turned to her with a bit of aggression. "Viasarria is the only person who can tell me of my past. If I don't take a step to learn more about myself, I'll just resign myself to staying here and wondering what could have been."

Raia didn't like where this conversation was going; her stomach was getting that familiar ache it would have when Layna was about to pull her into some dangerous situation. "If you get kicked out of here, you won't even see your sister ever again! You were hardly even alive when you came into Sachelvae, and now you want to potentially risk the chance you might regress into the same life you had before you found the temple? You don't care at all about coming back, do you?"

"That's not true!" Kasra's voice softened when she saw Raia's eyes glistening. Gripping the edge of her mattress, she continued, "Now that I know Rozha is alive and well, I have nothing to fear; I can start living for myself. I'm in the greatest health I've ever been in in my whole life. Besides, I wouldn't have even considered leaving if there was any chance it would cause permanent separation from my sister and the friends I made at Sachelvae. I'll always come visit you and keep in touch somehow."

"No, you don't understand!" Raia blurted. "I--" Realizing what she was about to say, the brunette caught herself. She listened to her heart pound in her ears until fervid heat welled up in her cheeks. "Fine…" she eventually squeaked. "If you're gonna leave, don't expect me to join you. I told you I'm done with all this stupid adventure stuff."

Seeing her ears wilt and a hand rising to cover her tearful eyes, jerked Kasra from her seat to hold the distraught brunette in her arms. She let Raia cry into her shoulder, her sobs and sniffles convincing her that she was worse than Layna ever was for hurting the poor thing's feelings. She was so shocked by Raia's catharsis that words completely failed her; she wanted so badly to say something -- anything that would turn everything back the way it was. After some time of rubbing circles into the vixy's back, Raia rested her head against Kasra and dried her tears on the violette's soaking sleeves. Her voice was weakened by the strain of her sorrow. "What is it like, those feelings you have for Malkinos?"

Kasra's misunderstanding of her friend's unexpected question elicited a quizzical curling of her tail around Raia's waist. "I-I don't know…" she awkwardly stammered, unsure of what exactly the brunette was looking for in her answer. "It makes me feel happy to be around him."

"Yeah…" Raia breathed, as if having expected Kasra to say that. Her fingers pensively tightened on the violette's narrow side as she spaced out into the floorboards. "That's how I feel to be around her."

"Who?" Kasra's expression hardened from the suspense.

Raia swallowed nervously, before she mustered the courage to embarrassedly squeak, "Layna."

Kasra's eyebrows raised. Her mouth gaped, but no words escaped. "You… *like* Layna?" Her inflection was not meant to denote surprise for Raia's wanting to be the troublemaker's friend -- rather, her wanting to be *more* than that.

The brunette uneasily nodded, brushing the side of her face against Kasra's arm. "Everyone wonders how I'm able to tolerate her," she started. "I never say it because I know they won't understand. Layna was being mean to others to protect me from them… I never told her my feelings for her, but I think she's always known."

Thinking about the way Raia was treated by many of Sachelvae's student body, Kasra gently asked, "Does anyone else know how you feel about her?"

Raia stayed silent for a moment, then raised her shoulders for a defensive shrug. "I think Lavelle does. She's the only vixy I ever kissed."

Kasra couldn't contain her eureka purr, as suddenly the chartreuse novitiate's attitude was starting to make sense. "You had a bad experience with her?"

Raia thoughtfully hummed, not really wanting to be reminded of it. "She said she didn't mind… at first. She let me do it, but I don't believe she liked it. I think she started spreading rumors about me, and that's why everyone else gives me a wide berth."

Kasra gently stroked her friend's ear and offered her a smile when Raia finally looked up into her eyes. "I don't care if you like other vixies. I'll still be your friend, no matter what!" Lying down, she borrowed from her sister's language and invitingly patted Raia's side of the pillow. "You look like you could use a snuggle buddy."

Raia's breath caught in her throat. She was so embarrassed yet relieved, she sputtered for some heartbeat-quelling levity, "O-Okay," Raia weakly nodded, as if unable to believe what had happened. "As long as you promise me you won't leave, tomorrow."

With an affectionate bump of their noses, Kasra said, "I'm not going anywhere without you."

Chapter 28: A Healer's Mettle

Kasra stood in a white-out of clouds. "Where am I?" But the odd thing about her own question was, she didn't feel like she was actually there. She felt no temperature, no wind, no atmosphere. It was as if she was viewing a place through someone else's eyes, but she didn't know whose. As the white clouds began to disperse, she could see sparkling strips of a rosy sky unfolding around her. There was no ground and no horizon. She was standing, but no weight was on her feet. While hardly a believer in an afterlife, it looked like the closest thing she imagined a heaven to be.

"So you're finally here," a feminine voice fluted from the beautiful nothingness. Kasra clung to the familiar tone, trying to remember where she'd heard that voice before.

"Who are you?" Kasra wanted to ask, but no words escaped her mouth. Her response was contained in her thoughts.

Her speaker did not appear, but Kasra could have sworn she was talking right to whomever it was. *"You are truly one of a kind, Layna. I've been watching you since the moment you were born. This world needs you. But I have no Path for you. You've known that you're not like everyone else for some time. The time has come for you to learn the reason you're here."*

"Layna?" Kasra's eyes widened. She tried to look for her aforementioned rival, but saw nothing apart from the sparkling, pink sky.

The mysterious voice was unperturbed. *"I gave you the powers to change the world. Anything you put your mind to can be done. I will show you how."*

The white clouds returned to obscure Kasra's vision. She began to feel faint, as if she were being pulled away by an unseen force and falling asleep. "Tell me! Tell me!" she begged. "Wait! Don't leave me!"

"Kasra, Kasra!" Raia yelped, shaking her friend awake. "You're kicking me!"

The sleep-thrashing violette gasped when her eyes opened back to reality. "Raia," she caught her breath. "I'm sorry -- it was a weird dream."

"Some nightmare you were having," the brunette squinted at her, rubbing her forehead. "I took an elbow right to the face."

Kasra's lips sputtered, her brow furrowing with an apologetic laugh as she nuzzled Raia's cheek. "I didn't mean to hit you!"

"I think this is the last time we share a bed," Raia bitterly chuffed, hoisting herself off the squeaky mattress. "What was that dream of yours about, anyway?"

"Um," Kasra stammered. After thinking about what happened just last night, she knew mentioning something like what she heard in her stranger say would only frighten Raia again. "Nothing -- I can't remember."

The dubious brunette gave her an over-shoulder look, then proceeded to changing into her novitiate mantle. "Well, today's supposed to be Rozha's first class as a Teacher. Maybe you were subconsciously excited about getting to hit things?"

Kasra chuckled. "You don't seem terribly excited about it. What's wrong?"

Raia sighed, looking at the floorboards for a few seconds of deliberation. "I know Mother Diava is trying new things, but it has me worried. It's like she's gearing us up for a Crusade, and I don't think anyone's ready for it."

Kasra tilted her head, interested by her friend's new insight. "You think she wants to launch a preemptive strike against Travestas?"

Considering the wall that was being built around the Safiric side of Tresantia, and the arming up that was being done among the Brotherhood, the logic sickened Raia. Seeing that she was clearly disinterested in talking about it anymore, Kasra held her friend's hand and said, "Let's get to the Purifier. It's best to just handle these things one step at a time, you know?" Cracking a little smile, she added in a language that she knew Raia could understand, "I doubt it's Sanguina's Will for you to live in fear of what the future will bring."

Raia's cheeks dimpled as she gave Kasra a distracted little half smile, to at least let her know she appreciated what the violette was saying. "You're right. I can't let this stuff bother me so much." Gazing at their interlocked fingers as they walked out of their room, she quietly said, "You're not still entertaining the thought of leaving us, are you?"

Kasra gawked at her. "Where'd *that* come from?"

Judging by the concerned frown Raia returned her, she was in need of a more comprehensive answer. "What'll you do if you stay here? You said yourself that Sachelvae is not where you want to be." With a funny, howbeit intentionally flirtatious batting of her eyes, Raia brushed her shoulder against the taller Kasra's arm. "I hope you're not staying here just to be with me~"

Taking advantage of the opening she was given, the violette grinned and gave the brunette a peck on the nose. "Maybe I am!"

After Mother Diava guided her followers through the daily Purification process, all the priestesses prepared to do their chores. All of the novitiates, however, instead of walking single-file behind Teacher Xanne, were sent to walk with their newest Teacher, Rozha. The benched Xanne gave Rozha a look that could only be described as hopeful, yet distrusting at best. Mother Diava had remained behind her old Teacher while Rozha was walking away with her students, leading them to her newly finished classroom.

"I never noticed it before," Xanne quietly said, "but watching those kids walking with her like that reminds me of someone."

"Someone?" Diava forthrightly repeated, knowing Xanne could be more specific.

The Teacher turned around to face the High Priestess once Rozha and her entourage were no longer in sight. "Doesn't Teacher Rozha remind you of Saint Sevasmia? Just a little bit?"

For the first time in the fifteen years she'd known Mother Diava, the High Priestess' lips twisted into a noticeable scowl. The taller velta stared over Xanne's head. "No," irate gravel ablated her throat, earning the raised brow of a very taken-aback Xanne. The Teacher had nothing more to say to test the High Priestess' patience thenceforth and settled for a proper curtsy to excuse herself from further comment.

Meanwhile, Rozha's class had organized themselves amid clay and straw dummies made in the waist-up likenesses of potential adversaries. They were each endowed with the familiar, indigo robes of Safiric priests, taken from the recently Purified followers of Bidarius. There were twenty opponents in all -- one for each of the novitiates. Of course, due to Layna's absence, the last one at the back of the room was left open and unoccupied. At the furthest wall from the doorway, was a rack full of wooden practice weapons with which the students could take a whack at their Safiric effigies.

Teacher Rozha stood before her students at the left wall of the room, where beside her was what appeared to be a tree stump with bald branches taken down to short nubs. "At this time every day, you're used to Xanne telling you all about your Sanguinic powers and then teaching you the ethics thereof. You've been shown how to use your goddess-given blessings, then you've been told not to get into a fight. When the crap hits the waves, and all that ethics stuff doesn't matter, there's only one thing you need to know:" Unrestricted by the long hems of her dress, Rozha delivered strikes with her fists, wrists, forearms and legs to every limb on her target. In a matter of seconds, the log was left spinning on its swivel, dizzied by Rozha's fury. "That's how to kick ass."

The Red Dancer's swift moves wowed her students. Raia nervously gulped; the last time she hit something that hard, she only hurt herself. She couldn't imagine moving that fast and still being so precise. But Kasra was enthralled with her sister's performance -- she couldn't wait to learn her blade dancer skill.

Rozha thumped a foot as she began pacing back and forth. "On your mannequins, you will see circles highlighting basic pressure points and vital regions. I want you to practice striking those areas with your dummy weapons until it becomes second nature to target them on a real adversary." The Red Dancer watched her sister with interest as she and her fellow classmates each went to retrieve a wooden dagger from the mock armory.

An apprehensive Raia stood out as the last one of the room to follow suit. Upon returning to her spot in the class, her weapon grasped firmly in a sweaty palm, she eyed her faceless target as if it were a breathing belhuayn.

Drawing a real dagger from her belt, Rozha used her mannequin to set an example for her students. "I want you to start high and work your way down," she brought the edge of her blade to the dummy's neck. "Your finished result should look something like this:" she proceeded to give the bust a gash-inflicting whack -- a direct hit connecting with each of its designated pressure points in barely a couple of seconds. "When you're really good," she added, "you'll be able to use multiple weapons for an even better effect -- one on every limb, so no matter the situation, you'll be able to fight your way out."

Lavelle attacked her dummy just to see Raia skittishly recoil. Kasra glanced over and could see her friend clutching the wooden dagger's hilt up to her chest. Kasra's eyes narrowed at a cackling Lavelle, while Raia focused her worsening tunnel vision on the task at hand.

"Begin!" Rozha declared.

While the whole class was converted into a cacophony of clacks and bangs, with varying degrees of gusto, Raia's energy was decidedly the lowest of them all. She didn't even have the nerve to hit her mannequin with the blunted edge of her weapon, and instead settled for nervously tapping its pressure points with the mock pommel. The lightness of her rigid shots came as if she were meaning to say "sorry" with every blow. Even though she was trying not to draw attention to herself, her pitiful performance earned an embarrassed slap of Rozha's forehead.

"Are you trying to *dance* with the bastard, or knock his ass out?!" the Red Dancer shouted at her.

"I'm sorry, Teacher Rozha!!" a blubbering Raia cried.

But the stern taskmaster was having none of her excuses. "You wanna be pushed around?! Hit him like you *hate* him!"

Before Raia could complain any further, she heard Lavelle laughing at her. The brunette gave the mean vixy a teary-eyed sneer and turned her dagger's business end toward her fake foe. Upon visually substituting its head with Lavelle's, it was suddenly much easier for Raia to throw full force at her target. Her first hit was hard enough to make whole the dummy wobble on its stand.

"*That's* more like it!" Rozha cheered.

Raia continued venting her pent-up frustrations into the straw soldier, striking slow but with impressive strength. Her display of bravado even caught the proud attention of Kasra, but it also elicited extra scorn from Lavelle. "Careful you don't break it when you put all your *weight* into it~!"

The brunette flaunted a before then unseen aggressive posture. "You know what?! Screw you!" She punctuated with a shove to her mannequin, before taking a step toward her real enemy. Lavelle shrank back when Raia surprisingly advanced and called her bluff.

Something about seeing this transformative process on her most pacifistic student was enjoyable to the new Teacher. But upon witnessing the tempestuous vixy about to take her anger out on her classmate, Rozha came back to her senses. "Alright, that's enough. You can save all that aggravation for our next bit."

"When you're in close quarters, and your masalida doesn't matter," Rozha began, "do everything you can to keep your enemy on the defensive. Put your weight on his feet and your forearm across his face to blind him and knock him off balance," she demonstrated her technique on the mannequin before her. "When you feel leverage, sweep your tail under his legs and put him on the ground. Make sure he doesn't get back up. If you're armed, you can finish him off quickly." Rising off her prone opponent, Rozha whisked her tail behind her and looked down her nose at her shaky students. "I want to see you practice this skill on each other. It's not my goal to turn you into killing machines, but it *is* my goal to make sure you don't *get* killed." After a short pause and a scan of her room, Rozha added, "Lavelle, since you seemed to like goading Raia into picking a fight with you, I think you two would make perfect rivals for this session."

"Rivals, huh?" Lavelle's eyes gleamed, while Raia suddenly turned blank with trepidation.

"Clear the floor," Rozha whisked a hand to her students, gesturing for them to move the mannequins to create an open square. "I want you to use your false weapons to practice on each other. You can't use your Sanguinic powers for this session. This is to train your reflexes so that you won't need them when you find yourself under pressure."

"But Xanne said as a priestess," Raia weakly protested, "that we must rely on our goddess-given --"

"I believe the *opposite*," Rozha interrupted, looking down her nose at the smaller vixy. "The more you come to rely on these powers, the greater a chance they'll fail you when you need them most. You need to be able to defend yourself in more than one way."

"But it will tarnish our spirits to use such implements of malice," Raia argued again, before being silenced once more.

"Mother Diava and I have already had this discussion," an impatient Rozha twitched her tail with a raise of her brow. "Our goddess will not punish us for not allowing ourselves to become cannon fodder for our enemies." With that, she earned the collective silence of her students. "Lavelle, you will defend yourself against Raia; try to prevent her from landing a blow on you. Raia, don't use full strength; those weapons are only wood, but if they hit someone hard enough, it could put them on their ass." The new Teacher cut the air with her hand to pit Lavelle and Raia against each other. "Commence!"

Raia gave one timid look at Lavelle, unable to properly steel herself when it was time for her to make a serious effort to attack her rival. It wasn't difficult, however, to feel the proper ire one should have for an opponent; just looking at the chartreuse vixy's sneer was enough to make her fingers wrap tighter around the hilt of her fake sword.

"Well?" Lavelle readied herself, holding out her own weapon at an angle in front of her. "Come at me then."

Rozha judgmentally crossed her arms and tapped a foot out in front of her as she watched Raia shuffle toward her enemy. The brunette's ears were plastered to her back; she had to fight her tail from curling around her legs as she stood face to face with Lavelle, thinking more about how everyone was quietly watching her more than how she was going to get through her opponent's guard. Maybe she'd wait until she fell asleep from boredom? As much frustration as Lavelle had caused for Raia, she couldn't turn her angry thoughts into actions.

"Would you just take a *swing* at her already?!" Rozha groaned.

"Fine, I will!" Raia then suddenly raised her practice sword above her head, taking Lavelle by surprise, but the other novitiate had plenty of time to respond before Raia's muscular tension weakened. The brunette's war cry was reduced to a whimpy squeak as her weapon ineffectually coshed off the edge of Lavelle's, who barely had to resist Raia's strength.

"Okay…" Rozha trailed off, trying not to sound too underwhelmed. "Maybe you'll make a better counter-puncher, then? Let's switch roles -- Lavelle, why don't you give it a shot?"

Lavelle gleamed at the opportunity to attack the flat footed brunette. With swiftness, she threw a perfunctory chop into the side of Raia's arm, causing her to squeal and take a step back. Rozha coached from the sidelines, "Parry! Keep your block up!" Raia ducked her head into her shoulders and tried not to look directly at her enemy as she held her sword out in front of her, as if expecting it to be a magnet for Lavelle's wrath. After getting jabbed in her soft stomach and taking another hit to the forearm, her classmates were starting to laugh at her inability to fight back. "You're getting murdered over there!" One of them jeered. "Take her down, Lavelle!"

"Open your eyes!" Rozha barked. "What're you doing?!" Almost as soon as she said that, Lavelle whipped her tail at Raia's ankles and had her falling straight on her bottom. Watching the poor brunette fall down earned a demure giggle from the student body, except for Kasra. Knowing the history between Lavelle and Raia made the violette dislike the hotheaded vixy all the more when a cocky Lavelle turned and brushed her feet at her dizzied foe.

"Alright, alright," Rozha ushered Lavelle back onto her side of the square. "Return to your corner, champ; there's no reason to showboat." Turning her attention to a red-faced Raia, she went to kneel by her side. "You alright, kid?" She comfortingly rubbed the brunette's back.

"Um," Raia sniffled, brushing a wide sleeve across her eyes, "n-no, Teacher Rozha. I… I feel sick."

Her eyes flicking over Raia's head to a concerned Kasra looming over her, Rozha said, "Take her to the Quarantine Bay." While her sister was carefully helping Raia steady herself, Rozha stood back up and addressed the rest of her class. "As for all of you, I will choose another pair of sparring partners, and we will continue this session until I have had a chance to coach everyone here."

Meanwhile, Kasra continued to lead Raia down the hall to the Quarantine Bay, keeping an arm slung around her shoulders to make sure her friend didn't faint. "How come you didn't fight back?" Kasra raised a brow at her. "I thought you and Lavelle hated each other?"

Raia held a hand on her stomach and kept her pace slow to prevent getting queasy. "I'm such a loser," she berated herself. "I couldn't even handle myself in a practice fight."

"What do you care about any of that for?" Kasra asked. "You were saying yourself that you didn't believe fighting had any place in Sanguina's faith."

"I know!" Raia heaved a sigh. "And I was made to look like a total fool in there."

"Rozha wasn't picking on you, Raia," Kasra detected the bitterness in her friend's tone. "She knew you were the one who needed the most work; that's why she chose you and Lavelle as sparring partners first. She was expecting you'd turn some of that aggression you were showing each other into something productive for her class."

"I can't force myself to be something I'm not," Raia shook her head. "It's not that easy for me to uproot from my principles. I'm comfortable with my faith the way it's always been taught to me; I don't want it to change just so it'll be more palatable to current events."

"So you'd rather everything just stay the same, so long as it makes you happy?" Kasra frowned. "I think following Sanguina's Path is supposed to do more than just make you feel good about yourself."

"Sanguina doesn't want us to *kill* each other!" Raia angrily argued.

"I didn't say that!" Kasra shot back. "I was saying that if you want to make something of yourself, you will have to face and overcome challenges. The road to success is not paved with sunshine; you sometimes have to do things you don't like to get what you want. If you keep looking for easy ways to get around something, you might never achieve your end goal." Her expression softened as she saw Raia calmly listening to her. "You won't be a novitiate forever if you want to be a priestess, one day. When that happens, you'll be expected to go on missions like the Pericula Initiative -- then sparring with your peers will be the *least* of your worries."

Pointing at the sanrisma pendant hanging from Raia's neck, Kasra finished, "Someone thinks you've got an amazing chance at turning your life into something special. If a complete stranger can believe in you, then it's only a matter of time before you find out what that special thing is."

Raia couldn't deny the profound points Kasra was making; their rendezvous with the mysterious Yalikai girl was indeed eye-opening. "She really did seem to know a lot about us..." Raia's mulling caused a quizzical cocking of Kasra's head. "Who do you think she was, Kasra?"

Before the violette could begin to speculate, Platina's stoic voice had them both turning around to see the sneaky nurse peering from the curtained room behind them. "Raia, Kasra? Are you both faring well?"

Kasra looked to Raia, who let herself step away from the violette to show she was not any longer worse for wear. "I was overcome with a bit of a dizzy spell during Teacher Rozha's class," the brunette gracefully explained with a curtsy. "Kasra was told to escort me to your office, Nurse Platina."

"Is this another stress-related fainting episode?" Platina guessed, placing a hand atop Raia's head. "Yes, you appear to have been shaken up, but are recovering quite nicely. I do not think this condition requires medical attention, but I would suggest some water to hydrate your system." The assistant healer led Raia and Kasra into the Quarantine Bay, and shared with them both a cup of water from the sink.

"If I can't do well in Teacher Rozha's class," Raia lamented, "I will never become a priestess."

"Do not besmirch the quirks of having a healer's heart," Platina consoled the novitiate. "You should focus your talents on restoring wounds rather than inflicting them."

"You think I have what it takes to be a healer?" Raia blinked.

"If you would like," Platina acknowledged, "I can contact Kyrana, and she can help you find your latent abilities."

An elated Raia clasped her hands together, her wagging tail nearly slapping Kasra's back as she raised up on her toes. "That would be wonderful! I want to see her as soon as I can!" Grabbing Kasra's hands, the short brunette bounced up and down on her heels. "Kasra, I'm going to be a nurse!"

Platina raised her communication ring to her chin and said, "Kyrana, if you are not terribly busy, I have a student who wishes to join our staff." Seconds later, with a fountain of white sparks, Kyrana was summoned to Platina's side via fygidia spell. The Arch Healer couldn't have had a more relieved nor impressed beam on her face when she saw the student of whom Platina spoke. "Raia dear," she began, almost sighing with admiration. "Somehow, I'm not surprised you're the one I needed to see."

The brunette hid her cheeks as she started blushing from Kyrana's flattering praise. The Arch Healer then turned her attention to the unexpected violette standing beside her. "Kasra, is there something you needed to see me about as well?"

"I wanted to be here for Raia's important revelation," Kasra smiled, rubbing a circle on her friend's back.

"Indeed you may," Kyrana nodded. "You two have established quite a connection since the day you met." Turning to her new pupil, she said, "Raia, I'm going to test to see if you truly have a healer's meddle. Bear in mind that only a small ratio of priestesses can even pass this test; it requires not only a strong connection to our sacred Mother, but also an extensive knowledge of Her power. If you can pass this test… its honor will end your time as a novitiate, and you will be officially inducted into the Sachelvian Sisterhood. Are you ready?"

Raia's eyes couldn't have been wider as she fearfully looked to Kasra with bated breath. "It's all happening so fast, I --" she swallowed her timorous stammering and reached deep to calm her mind and accept the task. "Tell me what I must do."

"Kasra," Kyrana gently ushered the violette to one of the firm beds of the Quarantine Bay. "I am going to put you into an induced stasis known as a *metoza*. No harm will come to you, but you will not be able to awaken unless I or another healer is able to revive you."

Gazing toward Raia's worried, howbeit determined stare, Kasra willingly offered herself as the bridge for her friend's long-awaited initiation. "I'm ready."

Kyrana began by cupping Kasra's cheeks with both hands, closing her eyes and meditatively bowing her head. Shortly thereafter, a faint, pink glow outlined Kasra's body from head to toe, until the violette began feeling overwhelmingly tired. In just three, long breaths, she dozed off and was carefully reclined against the stiff, white mattress she was sat upon. She was still enveloped in the rosy radiance Kyrana had placed on her even after she was no longer touching her patient. Kasra's whole figure, albeit peaceful, appeared rigid under this spell, as if frozen by an astapsyxi. Kyrana then turned to Raia and motioned for the nervous vixy to come forth. "Now," the Arch Healer instructed, "hold her wrist and concentrate on her pulse. Then synchronize your heart to beat with hers. If you have the will for her to live, it shall be done."

Raia followed Kyrana's directives and despite the distraction of her trepidation, was able to sharpen her focus under pressure. When she began listening to Kasra's slow heartbeat, all other sounds faded away until it was the only thing she could hear. It began getting louder as more of her senses were being numbed. She couldn't feel herself standing any longer, but didn't feel faint. The only thing she could feel was a sensation of nearly burning warmth, rushing from the core of her body from the tips of her fingers.

Kyrana tried not to gasp with glee as she exchanged looks with a solemn Platina, both healers watching Raia's body absorbing the pink light of Kasra's metoza. Instead of falling victim to its effects herself, the burgeoning nurse assimilated Kyrana's power into her own spirit. Then, Kasra suddenly took a deep breath as she was snapped back awake. She and Raia locked eyes, both just as surprised at what the brunette had accomplished.

"Congratulations, Raia," Kyrana hugged the short vixy around her side. "You are one of us, now!" Raia's mouth gaped as the Arch Healer removed the last notch from her novitiate tiara.

"I am?!" The brunette was unable to decide whose arms to throw herself into first. "I did it! I'm a healer!!"

Kasra got up to join Kyrana and her friend for a group hug. "Look at you! We've gotta celebrate this!"

"And we shall," Kyrana replied, petting both vixies between the ears. "Mother Diava will know about this as soon as she returns from Mediona. Then you, Raia, will be able to accept your full responsibilities as a member of the Sachelvian Sisterhood."

Diava, presently, was busy supervising her priestesses as they performed their daily chores around Tresantia's fabled market median. But most of her disapproving stare was concentrated on the perfidious progress being made on the night and day construction of Travestas' barrier. It was three quarters of the way done and featured many more turrets than it did before.

The wall even boasted a gated barbican, lit by blue torches on either side of the large doorway. Some priests, placed every few yards abreast from each other, were standing guard to ensure no outside interference could be made with their building schedule. They inconspicuously eyed Diava and the other priestesses milling about the shops and tents of Mediona. Everyone was respectful if not fearful enough to give them a wide berth as they passed on by.

"It won't be long now, until it is all done," Deniechus' voice startled Diava, as he approached from behind. His walking stick, which wasn't fooling anyone by now, tapped on the xanthic stones at his feet until he was within an audible, yet unsettling distance from the High Priestess.

"And to what end?" the elder abbess retained her composure.

"What business is it of yours?" The corners of Deniechus' lips crinkled.

"You're *making* it my business," Diava retorted. "For what reason would you come here to gloat if you did not expect me to ask about your intentions?"

"Have we not settled a dispute about this already?" the High Priest leaned on his black staff. "I'm aware of many things your temple does that you need not share with me… like the recruitment of a new Teacher, of self-defense no less." He craned his neck to one side and gave her a smugly knowing look. "What would a temple that preaches the peace and forgiveness of Sanguina need a fighter's discipline for?"

"Is it not obvious that we are living in different times?" Diava replied.

"Exactly," Deniechus grinned. "We are answering the vocations of our deities. We are fulfilling the roles we are meant to play." Slouching slightly, his pupils watched her from within the shade of his hood. "You cannot defy Their Will forever. The Vytameta is meant to come to our side and set the gears of change in motion. You cannot stop this revolution from taking place, no matter how much you want our world to stagnate and suffer."

"It is Mother's Will that our world not perish!" Diava argued with a sweep of her arm.

"Our world has been slowly dying since the end of the Great Civilization," Deniechus despondently looked away. "It is time for this madness of two faiths to end. I knew every leader of Sachelvae since its founding… and *you* have been the most difficult one of all to work with. If you will not cooperate, I will have to continue taking matters into my own hands."

"At no time in our history--!" Diava was about to end her tirade, but Deniechus was unhearing and turned to take his leave.

Chapter 29: Moving On Up

"Mother Diava won't return until next dinner hour," Kyrana told Kasra and Raia, as all three were leaving the Quarantine Bay. "At that point, I will be able to inform her of the feat you have accomplished today." She smiled at Raia's notchless tiara.

"I couldn't have done it without you, Kasra," the new healer thanked her friend.

"Oh, that reminds me," Kyrana said. "For having helped Raia with her initiation, I believe that calls for a removal of your first notch, Kasra." The Arch Healer then did the honors of clipping one of the round teeth of the violette's bronze crown. "Four more to go, now; keep up the service of others as you have been, and you might be our newest priestess by the end of the year."

"How exciting!" Kasra flashed a grin, retrieving her circlet back from Kyrana. "Since we pretty much skipped Rozha's class," she looked between the Arch Healer and Raia, "what shall we do, next?"

"All classes are scheduled to run no longer than one hour," Kyrana said. "I believe recess would have begun by now," she checked the position of the sun through the windows in Sachelvae's roof, as they continued their way to the Purifier Hall. "You should go to the orchard and get yourselves some lunch. It was a little tradition of mine to sit in the shade of the old Teakrent Tree when I was still a novitiate; it was where I met Wanystha."

The lack of an honorific title when referring to the Teacher had Kasra pausing for thought. "You and Teacher Wanystha are long-time friends?"

"That's right," Kyrana nodded. "She was born in Fort Pericula, and her family came to Tresantia when she was twelve years old. We met when we were your age, Raia."

Raia pleasantly hummed as she tried to imagine the members of the faculty as teenagers. "What will you be doing, meanwhile, Arch Healer?"

The pink velta in question replied, "I will be meeting with our newest Teacher so that I can assess the quality of her first class and suggest lesson plans for the next. I meant to be there to see it firsthand, but I was stuck a bit longer than expected, trying to convince Mother Diava to give me the permission to take medicines to the Laeyudi."

"Laeyudi?" It wasn't the first time Kasra had heard that odd name. She knew her sister had tried to explain something about it as it pertained to the Pericula Initiative, but she never did hear the end of that story.

"They're a tribe located in Virluti Forest," Kyrana explained, "a people forgotten by time and civilization. They've established their own sanctuary in the darkness of the swamp. It's quite an impressive culture I had the honor of visiting briefly when Teacher Rozha and I were on our way to Fort Pericula."

"Why would you have had a hard time getting Mother Diava's blessing to help them?" Raia asked.

"They're not a chiefly Sanguinic population," Kyrana started, "nor do they recognize the deities the same way Tresantians are familiar with them. To convert people from such a primitive society would mean amalgamating them into our own, first. Mother Diava didn't believe there would be any real benefit in going through all that trouble to proliferate the Goddess' Will."

"With all due respect to Mother Diava," Kasra frowned, "that sounds terribly short-sighted."

Kyrana breathed a chuckle at the vixy's agreeable brashness. "Truthfully, it's what I thought, too. But I've known Mother Diava for a very long time; such an attitude isn't unlike her. Before she was High Priestess, she was an Arch Healer like myself. She was always having brazen ideas and was unabashed to share her selfish opinions with our then Mother Vathita. I think Diava had convinced herself a long time ago that she was next in line, and was letting her ambitious drive get the better of her."

Stopping to see her reflection in the waters of the Purifier, the Arch Healer continued, "While Wanystha was still a priestess, I was the temple's Teacher of History and Lore, and resided with Diava in the dorm I currently share with Teacher Rozha now. Because we spent a lot of our time together, she became quite candid with me in the information she shared, regarding her personal goals. She told me once of a recurring dream she had, in which she was recalling a past life. In these visions, she said she was trying to collect an artifact of great power. The way she talked about it made it seem like she knew more about it than she wanted to avow. She believed that in these dreams, she was meant to hide the artifact from others who would wish to use its awful powers. But upon collecting this object, which she later described as a 'fragment,' she said she started drifting into madness. The power she wished to keep from others was slowly consuming herself."

She paused. To make a long story short, Kyrana concluded, "This dream she shared with me changed when Mother Vathita abdicated her crown. In her initiation speech as the new High Priestess, Mother Diava claimed to be Saint Sevasmia in the flesh. From the very beginning, she wanted to make something special of her legacy at Sachelvae. Even I don't know what her end goal is."

While the High Priestess would certainly remind her that it is not circumspect for a member of Sanguina's Order to be gossiping about authority, if the Arch Healer were feeling especially confrontational, she might riposte that it is equally scornful to lie about oneself to gain the respect and adulation of one's servants. Perhaps with this unseen ammunition at each other's disposal, they could be considered even? Still, the thought of this vindicated behavior made Kyrana's stomach turn; she knew that the immunities she was granted from her relationship with Mother Diava meant nothing to Sanguina. Even now, she could feel the Goddess' eyes bearing down on her.

It was a bit of an ironic thing, that the Arch Healer could suck all the oxygen out of a room like that. She may have stolen all the words from Raia's lungs, but Kasra was never short of questions. "Why did you say all of this to us, in such confidence?"

Kyrana soullessly smiled, finally addressing the students with her eyes. "As someone who has raised children all her life, I know when someone has grown up and is ready to hear the truth. Raia, as our newest member of the clergy, it's important that you know what's going on. And Kasra, as our star student who has a relative in the faculty, there's no hiding this truth from you. I'm sure Teacher Rozha could divulge many secrets to you." Looking to the corridor ahead of them, on the opposite side of the room, Kyrana added, "Speaking of... I have important matters to attend with her." Starting on her way, the Arch Healer nearly forgot to give the vixies her parting curtsy. "I will see you both again, later in the week."

The lack of a definitive deadline was a bit unsettling for Raia, who had a hard time waving her off. "Bye, Kyrana!" She exchanged heavy looks with Kasra, neither one having the energy to do or say much else after having received such decisive revelations.

"Not that I'm very hungry anymore," Kasra said, "but I guess we should go to the orchard now, huh?"

"Yeah," Raia rocked to and fro on her heels. "Since Kyrana mentioned her history with the Teakrent Tree, I've been wanting to visit it."

"When Kyrana told me about it was the first I'd heard of it," Kasra tried to imagine where she might've seen anything in the gardens that stuck out to her. "Where is the tree she was talking about?"

Raia explained, "I think it's the one that stands by itself near the well in the corner. Its large leaves are slippery -- they secrete a kind of oil that can be used as a reagent for tonics. Only someone like Platina would be able to make any use of it. On its bark often grows a moss and a shelf fungus, both having their special uses as well. Teacher Wanystha said it can be seen in artwork of Sachelvae, spanning a hundred years. You can see all these paintings in the hallway leading to the orchard, itself."

Truthfully, Kasra had always noticed these aforementioned artworks in all the times she had been to Sachelvae's backyard, but had come to appreciate their historical significance. The paintings featured a white tree with a thick trunk standing amid fruited plants. No matter from what the angle of perspective was, the Teakrent Tree could be seen at different stages of its life. The frames in which the canvases were placed on the walls were like time capsules, showing the dates that the paintings were created.

The Teakrent Tree looked even older in person. It wasn't the first time Kasra had seen it, but she was endowed with a new sense of appreciation for its existence with the wisdom she had acquired for its significance. Knowing the tree had been alive for so long and had served the people of Sachelvae for many lifetimes made it almost seem like a priestess, itself. It was a beautiful plant, standing over thirty feet tall with a large dome of leaves from branches that started high up out of arm's reach. Raia would have needed to stand on Kasra's shoulders to touch one of the lowest leaves, any of which were half the size of either vixy's forearm. Kasra could see, upon closer inspection, that the leaves did indeed appear slick -- shining in the sunlight as if wet with morning dew. Some of the lower branches didn't produce any leaves at all; a couple of them, closer to the wall, looked like they were hanging on by threads of bark.

"Layna once vandalized Old Teakrent when she tried to use it to climb out of the orchard," Raia bitterly reminisced, still shaking her head at the shameful memory. "It didn't support her weight when she crawled on one of the withered branches, though. I remember spending almost all evening helping her pick thorns out of her gown after she fell into that bush," the brunette pointed to a rather deflated-looking flowered shrub.

Kasra let out an airy chuckle, holding her elbows as she easily imagined the aforementioned troublemaker getting into the hijinks her friend described. Raia made a seat for herself in the U-shaped arms of the Teakrent's exposed roots, the base of its trunk almost acting as a chair while the dirt served as a cushion. She gazed up at Kasra pensively admiring the corner of the orchard, trying to picture her as the young Wanystha that Kyrana met all those years ago. Kasra gathered a handful of red blooms from Layna's shrub as a sort of keepsake before joining Raia on the ground.

"The way you talk about her makes it seem like there was never a time you didn't know her," Kasra observed. She followed Raia's eyes as the vixy elegiacally smiled and looked down at her knees. "It sounds to me like you're starting to miss her."

Raia dismissively shrugged. "It's true that I'd never been without her since the day I came to the temple. I have a lot of my life's experiences invested in the time we spent together." She looked at the bouquet in Kasra's hands, and her cheeks puckered. "Those flowers of yours reminds me of one of the chores Teacher Xanne had us doing last summer. Those bushes you see in the gardens, lining the walls, grow twice their size in the hotter seasons of the year. It was our task to trim them and keep their flowers in wheelbarrows. We'd take these carts to the cemetery and leave them on every headstone."

"Sachelvae has a cemetery?" This was news to Kasra. Of course, she knew it must've had a place to bury the dead, somehow, but she didn't really think about it until it was mentioned. Kasra wasn't fond of dwelling on death.

Raia looked to the wall and pointed out to the east, as if her friend could somehow see through it. "Below the hill behind the temple is a small acreage guarded by broad trees serving as windbreaks. You could probably walk by it and not know it was there, unless you came into it by hopping over this wall."

Kasra turned to Raia with a knowing smirk and a raised brow. "...Which is what I'll bet Layna was trying to do?"

The brunette laughed at her insightfulness. "When we were told of the cemetery's maze gardens, Layna wanted to prove that she wouldn't get lost if she tried to find the Matron Sanctuary -- the place where all former High Priestesses are buried. She of course was not interested in doing her chores with the rest of us, so she wanted me to help her escape. That wasn't the way she asked me, however; she just made it sound like she wanted to climb Old Teakrent, here."

Vintage Layna, for sure. "How long's it been since the last time you were there?"

"Well..." Raia trailed off, grimacing a bit. "This may not come as a total shock, but I'm not really a fan of the cemetery that much. I visited it maybe once a week for two months; I wasn't afraid of getting lost in there anymore. But it's not a place I'd visit at night -- you know what I mean?"

Perhaps Kasra was showing her true naivete when her response was anything but an immediate shudder. "I thought the temple was protected, both inside and out, from the Safiric Brotherhood? What would you be worried about getting you in there?"

Raia looked at the violette as if she had grown a second head. "Ghosts, of course! Not that I have any reason to believe there's any in there, besides stories that Brynita tells. But the prospect was yet another thing that just *totally* fascinated Layna... That was the one adventure she couldn't take me on, because I'm *terrified* of ghosts."

"Have you ever seen one?" Kasra asked.

"N-No..." Raia stammered, realizing that maybe her fears were seeming a bit unfounded. "But I don't want to, either. They say that ghosts linger where their bodies are laid to rest because they don't want to suffer Safiro's wrath, or they don't want to be reborn. I think either excuse is cowardly, to be honest... but ghosts are known for being defensive and mean. They don't want anyone traipsing into their territory. Brynita said that if they were powerful when they lived, they can still use their powers when they died."

Kasra was only becoming more intrigued from all this lore. She had no reason to fear these spectral entities that Raia spoke of. Rather, she was all the more excited to meet one. "And you say there might be the ghosts of priestesses wandering about the cemetery?" Her eyebrows raised.

"Oh no, not you too!" Raia groaned, hitting the back of her head against Teakrent's trunk.

"What's the big deal?" Kasra touched her friend's shoulder. "If they were children of Sanguina, they're not gonna do anything to hurt us! I'd love to talk with them and ask what it was like to live when they did."

Truthfully, that didn't sound like a terrible reason. In fact, "That sounds a lot better than why Layna wanted to go in there. At least you have some level of interest and respect." Checking the time by the sun's position in the sky, and by the shadows on the ground, Raia said, "Alright, if you want to go, I'll take you. We probably have about another half hour to look around."

While they were on their way to the cemetery, Kyrana was fixing herbal medicines she was to deliver to Laeyudi Town in Sachelvae's pantry. After concocting these special samples for the past two days, she had just now finished putting them all together, and had the various bottles arranged in a neatly-packed carrying case to ensure they would not be damaged during the trip. But she knew Mother Diava would never let her make the journey alone, even with the extra power of her Branch of Life. So she called upon the assistance of Rozha, to help her make the adventure again. The blade dancer currently had her shoulder leaned against the doorway, her tail patiently tapping on the tiled floor as she watched Kyrana at the other end of the cluttered room.

"All set?" The Arch Healer turned, closing the metal clasp on her utility box.

"Are you sure you're prepared to go back out there?" Rozha tilted her head toward the exit. "It's barely been a week since we went to Fort Pericula."

"What's that got to do with anything?" Kyrana curiously raised a brow. Then, seeing the slight unease on her friend's countenance, added with the slightest smirk, "Is The Red Dancer nervous? With my Branch of Life," she glanced toward the staff in her hand, "I'll be the one keeping us safe, this time."

"Great, so I'm just coming with to let Diava be at ease," Rozha bitterly spoke her mind.

"Don't think of it so negatively!" Kyrana chided her. "It's not just to follow protocol. I could've had anyone come with me. I just like your company."

"Aww," Rozha cooed with a kittenish wag of her tail. *"You* wanna be friends with a murderous heathen like me?"

Kyrana sighed and looked skyward, "After I *tried* to be nice…" "Yes, because you're a damaged soul that I believe needs fixing. There, are you satisfied with my excuse?"

"Well let me tell you, nurse," Rozha straightened herself to a normal standing position. "It's going to take a lot more than someone who wants to be my friend to save me from myself." Her tail elegantly swirled around her legs as she turned with arms raised, performing a ballet stretch.

"I figured as much, but you have to start somewhere," the Arch Healer followed her out the door.

"Start where?" Rozha curiously quirked a brow.

"Nevermind," Kyrana dismissively replied. "We shouldn't be wasting any time prattling on, anyhow. I'd like to arrive in Laeyudi Town before nightfall."

While Kyrana and Rozha were gathering their steeds from the stables and preparing to leave Tresantia, Kasra and Raia finally entered Wanystha's classroom, interrupting the Teacher's history lesson. The frizzy-haired azurette placed her hands on her hips and feigned having taken offense to their tardiness. "Oh, *there* you are! Late again, I see?"

Pretending that she didn't understand the Teacher's sarcasm to use it against her, Raia pleaded, "Please forgive us, Teacher Wanystha -- I was using our recess to show Kasra the beautiful Matron Sanctuary of the temple's cemetery. It was a bit larger than I remembered, so we got a bit lost trying to find our way out of the maze gardens."

"That's most thoughtful of you, Sister Raia," Wanystha dipped her head with respect for her novitiate's courtesy. She then waited for Raia and Kasra to take their empty seats on either side of Lavelle, who couldn't wait to poke fun at them. "Why are you always late to these classes? Were you two *kissing* each other out there?"

"Screw you, Lavelle!" Raia snapped.

"Whatever you've been doing must've gotten you somewhere," Lavelle eyed the notchless tiara atop Raia's head. "Looks like someone's about to be a priestess. Congratulations."

It was a bit hard for the brunette to accept the strangely stoic admiration she received from the jealous vixy. Lavelle had been waiting as long as Raia had to have her last notch removed. "Uh, thanks," she breathed, barely audible.

Their quiet exchange ended in just enough time for them to hear Wanystha say, "Now that that's out of the way, we can begin this week's art assignment! Every week, we've been trying a new medium; for this week, I want you to work with watercolors. I will pass around wood carvings that you can use for inspiration --" as she said this, she handed a stack of small tablets to the first student on her left. "Your drawings don't have to look exactly like the references themselves. I like this liberty of design because it allows the personality of the artist to come through their piece." She then walked to the desk in the corner of the room, where she had stationed all her paints, brushes, and inkwells full of water. Her paints were stored in small containers of seven colors, made to look like rainbows. She had one of these rainbows for every student, as well as two brushes of different sizes. She then passed around the canvas on which they would create their piece, which was a 6x6 card of thick vellum.

"Since I knew our time was short," Wanystha explained, "I wanted to try and keep the workload small to give you all a fair chance to create something without feeling rushed. If you wish, after class, you can show and describe your piece!"

Teacher's pet that she always was, regardless of setting, Raia raised her hand and chirped, "When will we get to see your own masterpieces, Teacher Wanystha?~"

The brunette's flattering charm tugged at the corner of Wanystha's lips as she tried to play it off with a rolling of her eyes. "Oh, Raia, you know I'm not one to bluster! But if anyone here would be interested, I'd gladly bring one of my original works to class every week to have a little show-and-tell of my own." Clasping her hands by her waist, the Teacher finished, "Call me modest, but I'm more interested in seeing what *you* can create! So get to it!" She added a little, energetic fist-pump.

Doing what she thought would get her the most attention and a good grade to boot, Raia ignored her prompt and decided to try her hand at drawing Wanystha, instead. Meanwhile, Kasra's quantitative mind was accustomed to the precision of pencil and had little appreciation for the pigment's fluid performance. The strokes refused distinction; instead, color floundered across her canvas, seeping into the fibres and blending for an unrealistic stain. From negligence, sly droplets escaped the bristles of her instrument and swam towards the floor, leaving a trail of imperfection in their colorful wake. As Kasra observed the abstract jumbles of impression gawking from her easel, she feared that the watercolors had a separate agenda, and that she was merely the medium of self-expression.

Alternatively, avoiding the possibility that her work could be tarnished by gravity, Raia kept her canvas on her desk. She risked the chance that the hardwood surface would be ruined forever by the pastels dripping off her brush, for what seemed like a much more gratifying chance of appreciation by her teacher. She might've cheated slightly when she used a pencil to sketch the outline for the drawing she wanted to make before applying the soft colors over them. But when it was all said and done, her attempt at trying to emulate Wanystha's dress through her unpracticed medium resembled a belhuayn face attached to a vaguely bell-shaped blob of red with some black mixed in to endow a third dimension. She couldn't shake the feeling that her work wasn't going to impress the Teacher as much as she fantasized it would, but she was fooling herself if she expected that she'd be an expert at her first try.

When it came time to review their work, Wanystha returned to her spot center stage. "Alright you guys," the Teacher energetically locked her hands, "let's see what you've got for me! I'll start with you, Lavelle," she daintily pointed her way.

"Well you see," the vixy replied coolly, having long awaited this opportunity to show up her rival, "when I gazed into the reflective depths of this proverbial eyeglass, I could nary but admire its reflective perception..." She contemplated her 'audience' wistfully, assuming the pose of a tortured artist, then spun her easel outward; it teetered to the left and finally settled to reveal an unrealistically beautifying self-portrait. She straightened her spine, arms held midway to hip, and palms facing the ceiling as if to catch the praise and collective awe of her silent classmates, she waited. Undaunted by their lack of reaction, she picked up her canvas, swivelled on her heel and sauntered out the door. "Catch ya later, chumps~" she dramatically sighed, confident that her work could not be outdone. She eyed a speechless Kasra as she took her leave; the door glided shut and the clatter of her feet faded to hush. When she was gone, no one was able to surmise whether her theatrics had intended ruminative or comedic essence.

Wanystha returned the raised eyebrows of her students as she tried to refrain from making a snide comment. "Well, I do have to say, while it may not be the most accurate depiction of the artist herself, she does have quite a talent." Having successfully retained her professional demeanor for the nonce, she turned to Raia, next. "Hopefully you followed the rules more closely, Raia dear?" She asked, her tone somewhat wishful.

The brunette then sheepishly raised her completed canvas to viewing height, admitting with her expression that she didn't adhere to Wanystha's spoken rules. "I didn't use the reference you had provided me," she began, "but I decided to use one more immediately available instead." Raia left it at that with a little grin, hoping that Wanystha would notice whose image she tried to capture.

Indeed, it didn't escape the Teacher's attention, but her response lacked the enthusiasm that Raia had grown accustomed to. "Is this supposed to be yours truly?~" the flattered Wanystha chirped, getting a closer look at the finished piece. "It looks good, Raia! I can only imagine how your abilities will improve by the end of the quarter."

"Th-Thanks," the brunette deflated, recognizing all-too-well the seldom heard but very feared 'Wanystha-burn.'

"So Kasra, what have you got for me this time?" Wanystha leaned close, curiously peering around her student's easel.

"Nothing!" She gasped, clutching the easel as if it were more precious than her beating heart. She noted the impatient gaze of her teacher along with the inquisitive stares of her friends and swallowed, surmising that there was no point in doing the assignment if she didn't turn it in. With the velocity of liquid mercury, her arms unhinged and she positioned the canvas for Wanystha's judgment.

What laid before the Teacher's eyes was an incomplete yet amazingly drawn sketch of Kasra kissing Malkinos from a bust-high viewpoint. Despite the attentive detail and anatomical accuracy only capable by practiced fingers, disappointment was evident in the illustrator. Guilt was oozing from her pores as she tried to read satisfaction on the Teacher's lips.

"This is remarkable," Wanystha purred at the romantic scene. "Why do I have a feeling this boy is not from your imagination, but that this actually happened?" Analyzing Kasra's nervousness, the Teacher added, "and recently, by the looks of it…" Trailing off again, she took another moment to admire her student's artwork. "What do you call this piece of yours?"

It embarrassed Kasra even more to think that the entire time she was creating the emotional scene, she actually had been thinking of a name for it. As if confessing a terrible sin, what had been smoldering at the back of her throat erupted from the tip of her tongue. "Lovers," she creaked, her soul nipping at the last vowel as it escaped her.

"That's a good word for it," Wanystha agreeingly nodded. "I want to see this piece finished -- it's not fair that it must be left broken like this by time constraints." She placed a finger on the smooth canvas, as if tracing the image she was envisioning. "Yes, I think a Sanguinic, moonlit background would fit perfectly… perhaps with a pair of unborn spirits swirling overhead, representing how the two were meant to meet." She clasped her hands to her chest as she heaved the dramatized sigh of a hopeless romantic. A motionless Kasra wished she could sink into the floorboards, her nerves set aflame by Raia's piercing flush from the corner of her eye.

"Will you continue working on this, tomorrow?" An agog Wanystha requested. "It would be my pleasure to feature it in this room, along with the other favored works of my students," she motioned to the walls of framed artwork.

Though it pained Kasra much to speak at all, she forced a quiet response: "Okay," and left it at that, having not the energy nor the inclination to express any gratitude for the honor of her superior.

"Feel free to leave it here overnight," the Teacher offered, "so you can continue working on it next class period." Checking the windows outside once more to see that half an hour had elapsed, Wanystha concluded the day's exercises and allowed the students to have the rest of the evening for relaxation -- what little of it Kasra could have, anyway. The minute she fought her stressed muscles to stand herself up out of her seat, all of her fellow students came flocking to her easel to see what earned it such accord from the Teacher. While Kasra pretended not to notice and was in the process of sneaking her way out with Raia in tow, she was suddenly stopped by a beseeching Wanystha.

"Raia," the curly-haired azurette smiled. "I received a message from Mother Diava. She has a special gift for you. We are all required to be at the Purifier Hall for her announcement."

Mother Diava awaited Raia's arrival atop her plinth. She stood to the right of her podium, overseeing the full body of her clergy kneeling around the Purifier below. Directly before her altar stood Teacher Xanne, holding a folded square of red cloth in her arms, on top of which was a silver tiara. Nurse Platina came behind the altar, bearing a torch of pink flame. Raia and Teacher Wanystha led the procession of novitiates to the Purifier Hall; Diava motioned for her followers to rise and bear witness to the ceremony about to take place. The High Priestess waited for everyone to take their places around the pool, and for all motion to cease, before she gesticulated her next directive.

"Raia, would you come to the stage?" She asked, softly smiling at her newest priestess.

The brunette in question gave Wanystha a fearful glance over her shoulder, to which the Teacher responded with an encouraging hand on the vixy's back. "Yes, your holiness," Raia started with a short curtsy before raising her dress and shuffling her way up the short staircase to meet Mother Diava. It was hard not to feel intimidated by the High Priestess towering over her, despite her matronly composure. "It has come to my attention that you have passed the test of a healer. That would make you the youngest novitiate to have ever received this honor. I, myself, was eighteen years of age when I was inducted into the staff of the clergy... Saint Sevasmia must be proud of you." Diava directed Raia to move so that to her audience she would be standing on the left side of the podium. "As a healer of Sachelvae, you shall bear the traditional vow of 'protector,' which has been traditionally upheld by all healers since the founding of the Sisterhood. From this day onward, you shall sustain this sacred promise to Sanguina by letting no harm come to those in your care. This includes all of your fellow Sisters in the clergy."

Diava silently waited for Raia to show her that she understood the tasks expected of her. Though the brunette was standing right in front of her and listening as intently as her ears would allow, the powerful gravity of the moment was sinking in so thickly that the information could only squeeze into her synapses at the speed of sap. "Yes, your holiness," her response was as thoughtless as the breath that left her lungs to make it heard.

"Your novitiate mantle shall be exchanged for your new priestess *mantamina*," Diava explained, cuing Xanne to come forth. At the same time,

Teacher Wanystha helped a nervously stiffened Raia disrobe. "This special cloth shall protect your soul from being seen by members of the Safiric Brotherhood." She then gestured for Wanystha to place Raia's novitiate gown on the altar. "Your old clothing shall be burned to signify your initiation into the Sisterhood, for from this point in Sanguina's Path, there is no turning back."

Platina used her torch of pink flame to immolate the red garb laid upon the altar, along with Raia's notchless tiara. It was almost painful to watch them be destroyed right before her eyes; she had lived with those pieces of attire for her two year existence in Sachelvae. She didn't have terribly long to think about her past as with more urgency she was shoved into the future; the next thing she knew, she was being clothed in her new mantamina and crown by Wanystha and Xanne.

"This is a truly momentous occasion," Diava admired Sister Raia. "Tell us all what inspired you to become the youngest healer in Sachelvae."

Because Diava addressed the audience, stage-frightened Raia wasn't sure whom she was speaking directly to when she was supposed to give her answer. She fought her hands from fidgeting with each other and her tail from curling around her legs as she slowly forced herself to turn toward the entire clergy -- sixty faces all staring back at her with varying levels of interest. She could spot Lavelle and Kasra standing at the farthest corner of the pool. Lavelle, whose arms were crossed as if wanting this whole thing to be over, and Kasra, whose eyes couldn't have been glistening with more admiration. Raia bit her cheeks as she tried to imagine Layna making distracting faces at her to ease her spirits.

"I knew from a very young age that I wanted to be a priestess." Her crestfallen tone softened, "My dad said it was my mother's dying wish to join Sachelvae. I've come all this way to live the dream she could not. Though I never knew her after I was born, I feel like she has been holding my hand down the path Sanguina has made for me."

"That's a beautiful promise, Raia," Mother Diava said. "It sounds to me you knew how to be a priestess long before you came to this temple. But now your trials as a student are over and your responsibilities of being inducted into the Sisterhood begins. The Teachers and I," her eyes flicked between Wanystha and Xanne, "have agreed that you're ready to leave the classrooms; you will now be participating in the daily chores around town and in Mediona. However, the Safiric side of Tresantia is still strictly off-limits." She raised her nose, waiting for Raia to acknowledge her order. "At the beginning of each day, after Purification, you will be given a sheet of tasks to complete with an assigned partner." Turning obliquely so that she was facing somewhere between Platina and Raia, the High Priestess continued, "Because Viasarria is no longer rooming with Platina, our nurse will be your partner for these tasks."

Raia wasn't sure if she visibly gulped or not when she locked eyes with Platina's chilling visage standing behind the burning altar. The glow of the flames against her skin and glinting off her glasses gave her an almost demonic appeal. She had a hard time unfixing her stare when she needed to bow to Diava. But just as she was about to bend her knees, she caught a glimpse of a red light over the High Priestess' shoulder; the red, crystal dome on her podium was glowing.

"Your holiness," Xanne was the first to bring it to Diava's attention. The elder abbess turned and saw the foreboding illumination beckoning her toward it. Diava stepped behind her stand and placed her hands on the seeing orb, closing her eyes and concentrating her psychic mind on what it wished to show her.

"There is Safiric activity in the Black Swamp," Diava's face blindly upturned, as if finding her bearings. "They have established a small base there. It's underground -- I cannot see what ritual they are performing, but I believe it is a sacrifice."

Xanne and Wanystha silently awaited the High Priestess' command as the abbess' fingers lifted from the now slowly dimming crystal. "A Pure's life is in danger," she opened her eyes with severeness unto her gathered clergy. She began pointing to the priestesses, "Brynita, go to the pantry and gather provisions for two. Raia and Platina, this will be your first time working together."

Though Raia knew better than to argue Mother Diava's wishes, she couldn't help feeling a little unprepared for such a daunting task. "Just the two of us? Did you not once say yourself that the Black Swamp is a terribly dangerous place?"

"I detected that their hideout is a small one," Diava sternly replied. "It would do no good to have several of us waiting outside while only one or two would be able to delicately traverse the compound. As this is a rescue operation, stealth is always key. But you have your communication rings; if there is to be more trouble than anticipated, everyone here will be waiting for your call. A Sachelvian priestess is never alone; one Sister has the strength of all sixty." That being said, she adjourned the gathering and let the rest of the clergy retreat to their quarters for the night.

When everyone's backs were turned, Kasra took her opportunity to escape the single file lines of her more obedient peers and hid behind one of the marble columns nearest to the doors of the temple. She watched Diava guide Platina and Raia to the grand entrance, where they waited for Brynita to return with their packs of supplies. The green-haired velta, after handing the provisions to her volunteered colleagues, said, "There should be enough in there for two days, if you ration it right. The Black Swamp is a treacherous place at night, and is the largest forest in all of Tresantia's outer lying wilderness. If you run out of supplies before you're able to complete your mission, you must fygidia back here. You cannot forage off the surrounding area; everything there is nasty and inedible at best."

With attention to Raia, Diava said, "Remember what I told you and steel yourself. Remember that Platina is there to help you; she is an experienced member of the Sisterhood who has participated on missions such as this for five years."

The High Priestess disengaged the invisible barrier spell with which the temple was sealed so that the doors could open for her brave servants. Before they started on their way, Platina turned to Raia and shared some encouraging words of her own. "Have no fear, young one; I took a vow of protection as well. If need be, I will be your sword as well as your shield."

Holding a magic ball of light in her hand, the nurse was the first to set foot out into the night, letting Raia follow a couple paces behind her. As soon as they were gone, Diava shut and sealed the doors again. Kasra had to quickly duck her head back behind her hiding place as the High Priestess swirled around and breezed by her down the hall. She was so close, Kasra could smell her perfume; she was surprised that Diava did not notice her presence before she departed. When the abbess was gone, Kasra approached the daunting doors and tried once again what she was told Layna could do before: just push them open. But no matter how hard she shoved, they wouldn't budge. Perhaps she made too much noise when the iron slabs creaked and clanged, reverberating throughout the Purifier Hall.

"What're you still doing out here?" Brynita's unexpected voice caused Kasra to turn her back to the doors and clutch a hand over her jumping heart. Instead of being faced by a tattletale scowl, she was greeted by an understanding, if not somewhat helpful smirk. "You should know better by now than to try sneaking out at this time of night. Besides, you couldn't get through that spell if you wanted to, anyhow."

"I'm not going to remain stuck in here while Raia's being sent out on a fool's errand," a determined Kasra crossed her arms and tossed her head.

"After everything you said about how dangerous the Black Swamp is, what makes Diava think that sending someone freshly inducted into the clergy is a good idea?"

"I can't believe you haven't figured out what she's up to by now," Brynita berated the now quizzical violette. "She's trying to remove everyone who gets close to you."

As shocking as this sounded, Kasra wasn't convinced. "Remove?" She squinted her eyes into a sideways leer and raised her shoulders into an incredulous half shrug. "Why?"

"She knows you're like Layna," Brynita cryptically smirked. "She could control Layna before you arrived. But ever since you stepped through those doors, everything began changing -- much too fast for Mother Diava's liking. She got anxious. You see, people around here don't like change. Tresantia has been the way it is for four hundred years because nothing ever threatened the cycle from breaking."

"What cycle are you talking about?" a frightened Kasra frowned.

Brynita's voice became more complacent as she had succeeded in earning the novitiate's full attention. "Life and death; the temples are protected from one overtaking the other. This kind of dual dominance -- this ruling of both faiths is maddening to the Safiric Brotherhood."

"But why does it?" the student of history couldn't understand, "If we were all on the same page in the Great Civilization, why wouldn't we want to come back together again instead of remain broken?"

"Isn't it obvious?" Brynita gave her a look as though it should have been. "Safiro's gone mad. All of his followers are just as nuts as he is. He thinks he can create a sustainable world where only the most powerful can exist. He's completely beyond reason, just like his worshipers. There's no getting through to them. But Sanguina doesn't want to destroy them. So the cycle continues in perpetuity..." she made a wheel-like gesture with her hand.

"What's this got to do with what I am?" Kasra finally turned the conversation full circle.

"Still haven't caught on yet?" Brynita apparently relished being one step ahead. "Mother Diava knows you're different. You are not Pure, you are not Safiric... but you can enter both temples proofed against the opposing faiths. I don't know what you are, or even if you're belhuayn at all... but the potential for great change is evident in your abilities. Mother Diava is scared of you."

Chapter 30: Fallout of Pericula

Mounted on their black striders, Rozha and Kyrana had started on their way to the westbound wetlands. Heschel and Vanix looked eager to stretch their legs for the first time in a few days. They even recognized the direction they were headed and, like their riders, were undaunted by the memories of their previous journey. In fact, they seemed a bit more determined and strengthened by the harrowing experiences they had undertaken before. They were confident the same dangers wouldn't get the best of them again.

Once they reached the cloak of darkness cast on Virluti Forest, it didn't seem so threatening anymore. That was until, breaking the melody of amphibians and insects, there was the sound of footsteps creeping through the water. Heschel and Vanix stopped to look in the direction of the noise they heard. They were able to smell the presence of a creature that their uncertain whinnies suggested they couldn't identify. Rozha and Kyrana too were on full alert. The sounds were getting closer, and their source was getting clearer. The footsteps they heard were as if someone were slowly dragging something through the muddy water. In preparation for what was to come, Kyrana used her scepter to cast a golden masalida around herself and Rozha, supplying light as well as a ward from Safiric monsters. But the creature steadily advancing was not a monster native to the Ontevallian swamps. Kyrana and Rozha could hear its voice echoing through the trees, muttering to itself. Its garbled speech was unintelligible, yet familiar; Rozha knew she had heard it before. "It's one of the Dark Men," she surmised with bated breath, whispering to her companion.

Rozha turned Heschel to face their oncoming foe. Its voice grew louder; its red, almond-shaped eyes could be seen flickering in the misty distance. The entirety of its body couldn't be seen, but once it knew it had been spotted, it stopped right where it was. Its languid stature suggested injury and possibly starvation. It probably hadn't eaten since it was left behind by its brethren. The fact that it had come this far -- this close to Tresantia -- was a concern for Kyrana. "It was probably following the lights of the city after Pericula was destroyed," the Arch Healer stated. "Even if it is wounded, it is still a danger to our civilization."

"I'm going to run it down," Rozha said, jolting Heschel's reigns. The black strider sallied forth, splashing up the water to give chase to the fatigued Dark Man, whose lame leg stunted any movement greater than a feeble hobble. The tall, thin creature frightfully staggered back -- it didn't even appear to be armed.

The Dark Man's small, insectoid head was just high enough off the ground that Rozha could catch it between the eyes with her forearm saber as Heschel charged between the trees. She heard its exoskeleton crunch as the massive force of her strike split its skull like a coconut. With a burst of green blood and a splash into the stagnant water, the Dark Man fell unceremoniously dead into the foliage-ridden murk.

The knee-deep water was just enough to hide its body, but that wasn't enough to satisfy its murderer. Rozha dismounted Heschel and pulled the creature out of the water by its arm, only to accidentally tear off its fragile limb. Oddly, no gore had come from the stump once it had been removed; it was as if its corpse had already mummified the instant it died. Its arm felt light in her hands, like a long-dead branch having fallen from a tree.

"Have you had enough fun, now?" Kyrana quit averting her eyes.

"This isn't a game to me," Rozha argued. "Come here and look at this," she began examining the Dark Man's armored limb.

"I'd rather not..." Kyrana trailed off. She held her dress so it would not touch the water when she teleported to Rozha's side. She risked her stomach a glimpse of the creature's quartered arm, and what was most striking about it was the bracer it wore. The metal from which it was made was so light as to be aesthetic, but on it was what appeared to be a green, rectangular window emitting its own, soft illumination. On this window was a series of white glyphs written out like one might find on a piece of paper. Beside these small lines of letters was a white outline of a body that looked very similar to a Dark Man's silhouette. Only the right arm, left leg, and head were colored in red; the rest of the outline was left transparent.

"Isn't that something," Rozha remarked. "That picture there has highlighted the spots I damaged. Was he keeping a record of the places where he was in pain? Why would he need to do that?"

"I don't think that's what it is," Kyrana observed. "He couldn't have colored those spaces in *after* you killed him."

"Are you suggesting this picture colored in *itself?*" The Red Dancer gave her companion a quizzical glare.

"What other explanation is there?" The Arch Healer said. "These people don't come from our world. Who knows what they are capable of?"

To think that a small swarm of them could completely annihilate Fort Pericula made Rozha nauseous with dread. She doubted if even one of the four Emperors could do something like that. "If they wanted to conquer us, what's stopping them?" The doomsayer wistfully wondered.

"You must remember that our world is watched by Safiro and Sanguina," Kyrana replied. "What happens below these skies are the works of Their Will. They control the destinies of the faithful. They who are without faith to either deity will have the protection of neither." With a shrug, she matter-of-factly concluded, "It's why bad things happen to neutral people. You can't live on this world with a lukewarm mind."

After giving her sermon, the Arch Healer returned to her mount and Rozha did the same so they could be on their way once more. That single interruption put them back in their time slightly, so by the time they saw the lanterns and walkways of Laeyudi Town, it was nearing Sachelvae's dinner hour. Instead of the nice meal the temple's chefs would have prepared, Rozha and Kyrana got to enjoy a ration of salted meats. Their steeds traded their dinner-time grain for the lilies floating around their ankles. But the excitement of getting to make her long-awaited delivery to the estranged Laeyudi tribe was greater than Kyrana's spoiled appetite. She and Rozha roped their steeds to the first posts siding the stairs of the walkway before they sauntered up the mossy, moldy bridges to find where the elder lived.

Enroute to their destination, as they navigated the wavy, elevated roads, they found a large, open space built around a tall tree serving as the centerpiece for the raised village. Nestled into an alcove carved into the tree's trunk, was a stage draped with vines like an apron. Around this stage was a box formation of Safiric priests carrying blue flag banners emblazoned with a maroon-colored eye. There were probably a dozen of them, standing in two groups.

They appeared to be waiting for someone to show up. Their presence caught passersby like insects to tree sap, until a crowd of curious Laeyudi had gathered around them. Rozha and Kyrana were relegated as distant observers, in the back of this small, tightly-clustered audience. The faces of the Laeyudi people seemed tired and wary, as if having recently dealt with some strife already and untrusting of what extra troubles these Safiric newcomers had to bring. When a few of them saw the holy robes of Rozha and Kyrana, it made them all the more tense; they would glance between the priests and the Sisters with puzzlement, trying to figure out if their arrival was correlated.

Rozha and Kyrana exchanged looks of their own, wondering where these monks came from. "I can't recognize the insignia of their temple," the Arch Healer said. "They aren't from Travestas. Pericula wasn't far from here, but in the chaos of the devastation, their temple couldn't have survived. Where are they from?"

An imperious, metallic clunking, like the stately footsteps of someone clad in heavy armor, commanded everyone's attention. All eyes were brought to bear on the stage between the Safiric priests, as a scelan of gray skin and long, indigo hair came traipsing up the stairs behind the raised platform.

The imposingly tall priest stood in a slightly hunched posture that made it hard to tell what his full height may have been, but there was at least eight feet between the toe of his boot to the top of his head. Intimidating bone armor wrapped around the sides and shoulders of his uncovered upper torso, flaunting the scars on his well-defined body. Hanging from his neck was a golden amulet featuring an eye-shaped jewel, similar in appearance to the sigil on his servants' flags.

A modified robe was cut just above his knees to allow both legs freedom of movement, which were encased in matching greaves and boots of the thick bone material he wore on his back. His face was partially hidden inside a helmet made to resemble a horned skull; the deep sockets barely showed one eye at a time, depending on which angle his head was turned. The lower mandible of this helmet framed his jaw and covered his mouth, so that when he spoke, his voice was somewhat muffled, causing his audience to come closer.

"I am here because of what you heathens suffered," he cast a critical gaze over the heads of his barbarian audience. "The attack on your putrid village was a merciful warning sent by Safiro, urging you to seek His guidance and repent for your lack of worship."

'Attack?' Kyrana thought. *'Did we miss something? What's happened here?'*

The High Priest continued, "The Father does not give His graces freely. The God of Death demands a sacrifice for His forgiveness to be shed upon you, for as of now, He finds you undeserving. Safiro has sent me to this place, to winnow the weak from your population. Once all pestilence of Purism and old age has been exterminated from this village, recourse for the rest of you can be made. Until then, you can expect more attacks in the future from the Forgotten Ones and beings like her."

Many raucous arguments among the Laeyudi tribesmen broke out at the end of this speech as they quickly decided among themselves what to do. But some of them weren't so willing to capitulate to the stranger's demands.

"We make sacrifice to demoness many time for over decade. You say is not enough? She want more?"

"Safiro does not commend the worship of false idols," the High Priest corrected him. "What you call 'the Mire Fiend' is merely one of the Father's creations. She has no clout in His order. Only Safiro Himself matters. *He* is the one to whom your sacrifices shall be made."

"Why we trust you?!" came another uneducated, howbeit righteous yawp. "Who you be, so special to come here and tell us what to do?!"

"My name is Kada'timor," the regal ordinator deigned to introduce himself. "I am one of the original Holy Warriors for Lord Zercius. I was there the day Sevasmia died. I was here before the days of Tresantia. I am one of the last Keepers of Truth for the Safiric faith. I know all there is to know about The Father's Will." The slouched scelan turned his head once more to sweep a glimmering, red iris across the faces of the unwashed plebeians before him. His tail impatiently swished behind him, the chains in which it was wrapped clinked together like fingers tapping against a table's surface. "I will answer no more questions from the likes of you. It is now you who shall be taking orders from me. I command you to find your weak... your tired... your children of Sanguina, and gather them before me... so that I may slay them all."

Though many of the tribe were frightened into doing nothing, the braver and more recalcitrant among them made sure their opinions were heard. "I refuse!" shouted one, who was joined by several more stepping forth from all directions. As they advanced on Kada'timor's position, the priests in his service bound them to the spot with ghastly entanglement spells. With swirling motions of their hands, the Safiric servants tied wisps of bluish energy around the bodies of their would-be attackers, holding them in place, for Kada'timor to finish them off with a power of his own.

By merely intertwining his clawed fingers, with no forcefulness nor even an effort at concentration, Kada'timor issued forth a barely-visible pulse of air that immediately stole the life force of his enemies and drew them into his body. As they watched their fellow fighters drop dead, the rest of the crowd backed off with a unanimous gasp, at last granting Kada'timor the reverence he desired.

"I gave you a chance to choose your own fate," he told them. "Don't make me choose it for you."

Bereft of the bravery to challenge him anymore, the survivors of this violent sermon scattered throughout the neighborhood to round up whoever they could to be offered as Kada'timor's Safiric penance. But he wasn't left alone for long; Kyrana and Rozha finally entered the town square once the crowd had dispersed, earning the intrigue of the High Priest and his small congregation. "You came by yourselves?" He asked them, as if biting back a chuckle. "Where are the rest of you?"

"We're the only ones here," Rozha narrowed her eyes at him. "And that's more than enough for you."

With that, Kada'timor could no longer restrain his guffaw. "Surely you jest, haughty priestess! You might as well be the sacrifice I ordered --" A sudden pitch of anger raised his voice, "Do you not know who I am?!"

"I don't *care* who you are," Rozha replied. "But I know what you're *about* to be --" Throwing off her robe with a single sweep of her arm, the blade dancer drew her sword and lunged forth with surprising speed. It was enough to even take Kyrana off guard; the Arch Healer's knees buckled as she watched her companion leap over the heads of Kada'timor's servants. The High Priest himself, however, was unperturbed. He nary flinched before he raised out a hand to stop Rozha in mid-flight. Just inches away from the tips of his fingers, he froze her in a telekinetic vice.

"Did you say something, velta?" He mocked his immovable adversary, but soon thereafter lost his composure when Kyrana uttered a "koptigma" to break Rozha free. The forcefulness of his spell's disruption caused Kada'timor to step back, allowing the blade dancer to land on his platform and give her the opening to knock him off of it with a powerful slap of her tail. Upon the humiliating disthronizing of their leader, the Safiric priests separated into equal groups -- one targeting Rozha, the other aiming blasts at Kyrana. The Arch Healer was quick to use her masalida to reflect their ghostly mist projectiles back at them, at the same time her Branch of Life resisted the effects of their entanglement spells.

Meanwhile, Rozha found herself restrained from both sides by a pair of Safiric priests. Before she could fight out of their grasp, she was suddenly met by the frightening glare of Kada'timor, who had appeared before her in the blink of an eye. He would have slashed her in half with a rising of his clawed hand had the blade dancer not flipped backward, twisting her arms out of the interlocked elbows of her foes, at the same time catching Kada'timor's chin with her heel.

At the end of this single, fluid motion, she landed on her feet before the High Priest's stage. Instead of pursuing her, his servants held her still with another telekinetic trap, this time for Kada'timor to summon a spell from the sky. The first warning Rozha had was a beam of blue light aimed directly upon her. She hardly had the chance to wriggle free before the unseen hammer was dropped directly between her feet, smashing a hole in the wooden road. With a splash, Rozha fell into the waters beneath Laeyudi Town, and before she could recover or collect her bearings, she was attacked in the darkness by the same two priests who helped put her down there.

While she was fending them off, Kada'timor set his sights on Kyrana. With a full-body spin, the chain he wore on his tail lashed out thirty feet to pass like a poltergeist through Kyrana's masalida and strike through the unprotected priestess within. She was so shocked by the unexpected pain that she dropped her staff when she was knocked over.

The Arch Healer's shield disengaged, allowing her to be ensnared by the Safiric priests standing on either side of their leader. Now holding his chain whip in both hands, with a massive swing, Kada'timor prepared to smash the length of cold steel down upon his held adversary. Kyrana blew her holders away with a sudden "koptigma," allowing herself the instant she needed to step aside and avoid being fully struck by the High Priest's weapon.

The chain was unimpeded by the floorboards, splitting the town square in half with a thunderous sunder. While Kyrana and the Safiric priests were buried underneath the wooden road crumbling into the swamp's shallow waters, Kada'timor slightly more gracefully fell on his feet to join his foes in the Laeyudi sewers.

There, in the dark, the menacing glow of his eyes and the blue fringe of his weapon could more plainly be seen, spoiled only by the weak rays of cloud-choked sun filtering in from the damaged platform above. The debris from the street still splashed into the waters, like droplets after a rainstorm. He had no time to capitalize on the dazed healer, before Rozha's arm locked around his neck.

The Red Dancer had leapt upon his back, sinking her spiked heels into the vertebrae of his armor, to cross a dagger against his throat. But Kada'timor could not be so easily blindsided; the moment he was accosted, he tossed his opponent over his shoulders with a forward lunge. Rozha was taken into the water and held to drown while Kada'timor prepared to finish her off with a thrust of his right hand -- not before he was stopped by Kyrana's astapsyxi freezing his arm.

His angered gaze up at his troublesome opponent provided Rozha the opening she needed to throw a punch right under the High Priest's chin. Kada'timor staggered back, allowing the Red Dancer to rise to her feet and keep him on the defensive, delivering multiple slashes with a ferocious vengeance across his torso, adding fresh wounds to the scars decorating his chest. The back of Kada'timor's hand ended the rapid succession of attacks, smiting Rozha with such force that she lost the agility to keep herself from hitting the ground.

He retaliated with a multitude of strikes of his own, sending Safiric ghost bullets from the ends of his claws like a gatling gun to pelt his foe. A whip of water followed his foot as he prepared to stomp Rozha with his heavy boot, but once again found himself frozen by Kyrana's astapsyxi. He nearly lost his balance from being so uncomfortably suspended in mid-motion, but was able to recover in enough time to punish the Arch Healer's annoyance with a larger ghostly blast he had saved just for her.

Kyrana deflected Kada'timor's attack with the sudden projection of another masalida, breaking the astapsyxi's hold on him and causing him to bend like a tree in a hurricane as he tried to keep himself from falling over. But the Arch Healer finally cut him down when she threw her dome-shaped barrier with the power of a cannonball. With a mighty burst of air, Kada'timor was taken off his feet and splashed down like an iceberg splitting from a glacier.

Rozha regrouped with her ally with a fygidia spell, so that the priestess could restore her vitality while they waited for Kada'timor's next move. The furious High Priest fought his way to his feet, breathing heavily through his helmet as he stared his enemies down. A mystic, smoky light drifted from his body, before his skin was set ablaze in a blue fire.

Taking his chain, he spun like a corkscrew, whipping everything around him as he flew back to the surface of Laeyudi Town. His destructive re-emergence caused all buildings nearby to explode into clouds of splinters as his whip lashed through them.

He continued his tornadic tantrum near the heights of the forest before crashing back down like a plane-dropped bomb, issuing from himself a dome-shaped blast of blue, forcing Rozha and Kyrana to retreat lest they be caught up in the explosion of his enraged assault. Town square had now become a hole in the ground, and everything close to it had been leveled. Houses and other buildings had been cut in half; what was left of their walls resembled the stakes of a henge enclosing anything on the floor that wasn't immediately destroyed by Kada'timor's whip.

Kada'timor himself stood exhausted amid the wreckage he caused, his fire now reduced to wisps of smoke drifting off his hunched form. His eyes flicked between his terrified enemies standing at the fringes of the sewer's darkness, neither Rozha or Kyrana daring to advance on him. For that while, Kada'timor appeared to recognize them as equals, or at least, worthy of less underestimation. The High Priest laughed, humored by their respectful apprehension. "Now I see why my brother had so much trouble with you. The Sachelvian Sisterhood is more than just a name -- it actually lives up to its old reputation. Yes, the true disciples of Sevasmia you certainly are. The Saint herself would be impressed by your heroism."

Rozha barely had the desire to consort with this deranged scelan; if she had any more energy left in her, she would have been taking her blade to him right now. It was left up to the more civil of the duo to take the High Priest's invitation to a truce. "What do you know about Saint Sevasmia?" Kyrana asked him, albeit with some guarded suspicion.

"Did you not hear me earlier?" Kada'timor began. "I was one of her original slayers, along with Deniechus and my brother, Atherator. I was there when Lord Zercius took her life. It was there we learned the Shield of Sanguina was all a lie." He chuckled in a mocking tone, "That 'sacred artifact' she held did not make her invulnerable! Once we lured her to our turf, she showed her true colors. She died in the Black Swamp, along with her followers."

"Yeah, and if your 'Master' is so great," Rozha spat, "where is he, now?"

"Contrary to what I'm sure you've been told," Kada'timor smirked, "Lord Zercius still lives. Immortality is closer within his reach than it has ever been. It is up to us, his most trusted, to make it all possible."

"What do you care if he gets what he wants?" Rozha continued her snide interrogation. "What's in it for any of you?"

"While it is true that many of the Safiric Brotherhood are out for themselves," Kada'timor calmly explained, "Lord Zercius knows an organization cannot function if everyone seeks to undermine each other. Indeed, the High Priests, such as myself, are meant to give order to the Brotherhood by keeping the bloodlust of our members satisfied. So long as they are told what to do and are allowed to destroy to their hearts' content, they are not aware of the strings being pulled above them. They continue to fight amongst themselves and die for a cause they are too foolish to achieve, while we the wiser remain untouched. Meanwhile, the world trembles before our power and dares not to oppose us. We control the militaries, we control the minds. Soon, Lord Zercius will control everything."

To Kyrana, there was only one thing missing from this grand picture that Kada'timor had envisioned. "If what you say is true, that the Safiric Brotherhood already owns this vast loyalty, what's standing in the way of Zercius securing his victory?"

Thinking that he had perhaps told too much already, Kada'timor chose his next words carefully. "The Emperors have been historically unwilling to give what they owe Lord Zercius. Even as powerful as our mighty master is, he cannot defeat they who... sit on so much power. He requires... outside intervention -- something that comes not from the Brotherhood to assist him in this mission. It is the job of we, his trusted to... procure this champion for him. Maybe this champion does not even reside on our own world?... At least," With his head turned skyward, he said, "Atherator seems to think so."

Kyrana and Rozha were collectively floored by this revelation. But their storyteller would have to leave them in suspense, for now. "It appears, as of right now, we are at a stalemate," Kada'timor observed, turning the conversation full circle. "However, upon our next meeting, we will be enemies again. And I promise you, the next encounter will not end in a tie." Arms spread out and one knee raised, the High Priest levitated a few feet off the ground before he vanished in a loud burst of sparks.

Chapter 31: A True Laeyudi Warrior

Sometime after Kyrana and Rozha had clambered back onto the dry bridges of Laeyudi Town, they were greeted by the survivors of the explosive conflict, all asking them in a panicked, foreign language how they were able to drive back the Safiric Brotherhood. The villagers and warriors were impressed by how the two priestesses held their own against 'the demonic invaders,' and implored them to stay so that they could protect the tribe.

"Bone man say that more attack will come," one of the villagers said. "If next attacks like first, how we defeat them?"

"You let us worry about that," Rozha confidently stated.

"I will seek Mother Diava's guidance on the matter," Kyrana added her own assurance. "It is not my place to order occupation of one land or another, but if your elder would desire the Sisterhood's presence, I am sure the High Priestess would gladly order the construction of a temple for your town."

"Speaking of the elder," Rozha tapped the Arch Healer's shoulder, "we should be seeing him now, right? The whole reason we came here in the first place was to deliver your medicines to him."

"Yes, this is true," Kyrana trailed off, her mind obviously in another place.

"Are you still thinking about what Kada'timor said?" Rozha studied Kyrana's vacant countenance.

The priestess nodded. "It worries me that Mother Diava would not have warned us beforehand of any Safiric activity in this area. How could she not have known of a congregation developing here?"

"She did tell us about the gathering in Pericula," Rozha pointed out. "Perhaps it simply wasn't of a size that she could detect?"

"That's what scares me," Kyrana said. "If she couldn't have known about a High Priest attempting to take over a small town such as this, how many other areas around Tresantia might the Brotherhood have claimed?"

"I guess we'll find out when they try to start something in one of their outposts," Rozha shrugged. "We can't stop them all from taking hold of everything; we can only be in so many places at once. But," she smiled and patted Kyrana's arm, "I think we did wonderfully at stopping this one, all by ourselves!"

Albeit with her usual half-heartedness, the Arch Healer agreed, "Yes, we handled ourselves quite well, didn't we? Except... Kada'timor is still out there," she looked to no direction in particular. "Who knows what he's doing, now."

"He hasn't lived as long as he claimed because he could get his ass handed to him by people like us," Rozha held her hips. "He may not know how to pick his fights, but if there's one thing he's good at doing, it's knowing when to quit. He was right; next time we meet, one of us is dying. And it ain't gonna be us!"

Kyrana could have rolled her eyes. *'So long as she's still alive, she's going to think nothing can kill her.'*

Every Laeyudi in the village couldn't have been nicer to them as they wandered about town, looking for Ghanius' house. It was as if everyone knew about their heroic deeds, whether they were part of the crowd or not. It would've surprised them if anyone didn't know of all the damage Kada'timor had caused, but it was quite apparent that Ghanius hadn't heard of what happened merely fifteen minutes ago.

It was also apparent that the elder wasn't expecting any guests at this hour, for when Kyrana poked her head in through the leather door to make her surprise greeting, the old scelan nearly choked on the tail of a fish he was eating. His wife stood up from the table, which amounted to a wooden board on top of a barrel, to pat his back and help him swallow the bite stuck in his throat.

"Healer priestess!" He cried with a fit of coughs, outstretching his arms. "You come back!"

"I have a gift for you, Ghanius," Kyrana dipped her head as she offered the metal case to him. "These are medicines for you and your people. You can use them to cure and prevent the spread of disease that may be prevalent in the village."

"Ah, Sister," the elder raised a hand to respectfully decline, "You no need! We Laeyudi adapt. We born to live here. My illness age. When die, son take over. Rokior best fighter in village. Only one to survive against Mire Fiend. He tell all tales of awful creature."

"You won't have to worry about that ugly thing anymore," Rozha proudly poised. "I dealt with it, just as I said I would."

"You no do good job," Ghanius shook his head. "Demoness still live."

"What?!" Both Rozha and Kyrana gasped. "But that's impossible!" The blade dancer argued. "I killed it with that tinvath dagger -- I watched it die!"

"Mire Fiend no die," Ghanius said with a fearful growl at the back of his throat. "She angry. She attack Laeyudi village night after you leave. Warriors wound her and chase away with fire. She make big wall around Mordax. No one see her since."

"I can't believe it," Rozha glared at the floor, just slowly shaking her head.

"If she contained herself in her home turf," Kyrana began, "you won't be able to stop her from making another attack like that if she ever chose to. Since our *Safiric* methods have unsurprisingly *failed*," she cast a critical glance at her blade dancer friend, "I will now attempt to stop her the way I know will work: I will cast a Sanguinic warding spell on the walls the Mire Fiend has made. That way, so long as those walls remain standing, she will not be able to leave them."

Ghanius grinned, "When you do this for us?"

"Even with my new powers," Kyrana minded her Branch of Life, "such a powerful spell can only be done on a night of Sanguina's full moon. Sanguina is currently in the last quarter of her powering phase. Tomorrow night, I will be able to perform this power."

"*Tomorrow* night?" Rozha groaned. She mumbled something to herself about how this trip was all a waste of time. *'First the old fart didn't take the medicine, and now we gotta wait a whole day just to take care of something I could do right now!'* At least the evening was waning; Rozha was tired from the fight and her stomach rumbled with hunger. Perhaps it was for the best that they rest first.

"I'm sure there's something we can do around here in that span of time," Kyrana optimistically suggested.

Finally noticing Rozha's existence, the Laeyudi elder pointed at her and asked, "You Healer's fighter, yes?"

"Yeah, I guess so," the redhead tried not to huff her response.

"You see Rokior -- I take to him," Ghanius ushered her along. "It do you good to meet. He share skill with you."

"What're you trying to say?" Rozha stubbornly frowned. "You don't think I'm any good because I couldn't kill your Mire Fiend for you?"

Ghanius wheezed through a long-winded laugh. "*No one* kill Mire Fiend. You *survive* against her, like Rokior. You at least strong as him. You both learn from each other. Come, I show you where he live."

Though the Laeyudi elder looked every bit as rickety as the bridges he walked on, the speed of his movement was unaffected by his age. Rozha didn't have to break her stride for her to keep up with him as he led her to the higher levels of Laeyudi Town. Intertwined through the great canopy of Virluti Forest were more residences built into the sides of the trees, far above the water. An untrained eye would probably not have spotted the camouflaged housing were it not for the lanterns hanging by roofs to give them away.

The pathways winding underneath the houses were built like figure eights; the bridges between them were constructed with rope and supported by nothing beneath them. Only two or three people could walk through at one time to avoid collapsing the hanging bridges. Many of these higher houses were built out of reeds or other hard stalks of Virluti's vegetation. Their roofs weren't the best designed for keeping out leaks in a rainstorm, but the interwoven leaf shingles added a natural appeal to the buildings, making them resemble unusually-shaped lumps on the sides of the trees.

One of these modest, higher tree houses was the residence of Rokior, fabled fighter of the Laeyudi tribe. His home, much like Ghanius', was scantily furnished but surprisingly much cleaner and boasted less of a draft for having an actual door made of hard materials. Rokior himself was sitting on his knees in the middle of the strawmat floor, fletching an arrow with the sharpened fang of an unknown creature. Only when his concentration was disturbed by the footsteps of his approaching visitors did he blink his brown eyes to see them come in. Rokior was a leanly-muscled scelan whose half-naked body earned Rozha's captivation almost immediately. His black hair flowed to his shoulders. His darkly-tanned skin was decorated with tattoos from the base of his neck to the upper half of his arms. The strange symbols, though not written in any belhuayn tongue, all seemed to mean something. He said nothing when he saw Ghanius and Rozha come inside his home, but offered them a quizzical, stoic stare demanding explanation.

"This fighter seek your knowledge," Ghanius said, motioning for Rozha to step forth. "She do battle with Mire Fiend, like you."

"Did she?..." Rokior's accent sounded much more proper than his father's, as if he knew more of the common belhuayn language than he did. "Join me," he invited Rozha to sit with him. "You may leave," he whisked his father away, and without question, Ghanius stepped back outside. "You are... not Laeyudi," he paused between phrases, as if trying to remember the words to say. "Where do you come from?"

"I'm a priestess of Tresantia," the redhead replied. "They call me Teacher Rozha."

"What do your student learn from you?" Rokior asked.

Rozha said, "I teach self-defense to my clergy, to help them do battle against Safiric evils."

"Are all evils of Safiro?" Came Rokior's next question. A quick glimpse into his narrow eyes revealed his Wild nature.

"That's only the way it seems," Rozha stiffly responded, unintimidated by his insinuations of offense.

Rokior could tell by her body language that she had a long memory for slights, and had only bad experiences with those of Wild blood. "Is that what all priestess believe?"

"I'd tend to agree with them," The Red Dancer doubled down again.

At first, Rokior seemed displeased by Rozha's comments; his lowered brow suggesting that he was merely a finger point away from telling her to leave his house. Instead, his composure relaxed with a small smile. "You have strong faith," he finally said. "It good to have conviction. Conviction create anger against foe. In fight, anger is valuable as courage. If no hatred toward enemy fuel your fist, you no kill him. I did not hate Mire Fiend when I first fought, I was scared; I lose. I hate her and brave when we fight again; she flee. Now *she* hate and brave. She come here and kill warriors. I chase her off with fire. Not without wounds," he pointed to the half-healed acid burns on his torso. "Mire Fiend fear fire. It is only way to defeat her."

'That's all it takes?' Was what Rozha said on the inside. "How do you guys make torches in a damp environment like this?"

"I take moss from tree outside," Rokior explained, "then take here and wait 'til dry." He demonstrated the desired effect by retrieving a clump of desiccated, leafy foliage from his table. He methodically tied the dead moss to the end of his arrow with practiced fingers. "I have single bow for hunting," he pointed to the recurve on the wall. "I gave it new string after Mire Fiend came. I made arrows to set aflame, for when she come again."

"Why wait for her to make the first move?" Rozha confidently squared her shoulders. "I'll go out there and kill her, myself!"

"No!" Rokior suddenly stood to shout her down, "It is my fight!" Then with a pained grunt, he doubled over and reached for his ankle. Rozha saw a terrible burn where his shin connected to his foot; it looked like the Mire Fiend grabbed him with one of her slime whips during their battle.

"You're not going anywhere like that," the Red Dancer observed, easing Rokior back down. "Don't be stubborn about this. Now that I know how to win, there's no reason for me not to go."

Wincing from his subsiding pain, Rokior loosened the tension of his gritted teeth and breathed, "I go with you…"

"You'll need my friend's help," Rozha said. "Kyrana can heal you." Using her communication ring, the blade dancer sent a telepathic message to the aforementioned healer. "I've got one for you to do your magic on." After shortly explaining the situation to her, Rozha finished, "Fygidia to me."

After a quick reply of acknowledgment from the nurse, Kyrana's sparking emergence into the room had Rokior jumping with surprise. "Relax," she calmed him with her voice. "I am here to help you, Rokior."

The Laeyudi warrior quelled his beating heart as his widened eyes were affixed on the matronly velta, perhaps only so quickly placated because of her fair appearance. Kyrana knelt to his level so that she could place her hands on his wounds. At first, Rokior obeyed his instinct to shrink away, but after he felt the soothing energies of her Sanguinic magic flowing into him, he was certain he could trust her.

"Are you not angel?" The bewildered warrior asked with wonderment.

Kyrana gave him a playful smirk as her eyes flicked up to meet his shocked, if not admiring gaze. When she removed her hands from his ankle, she and her patient beheld that it now looked as if it had never been scathed. "Sanguina is with me," she stated, upon the completion of her task.

Rokior couldn't believe the miracle that had been performed -- injuries that would have taken a month to heal with all the right medicines were vanished in instants. "What is your name?" He asked pleadingly.

"Kyrana," the nurse replied. "Arch Healer of Sachelvae." Judging by the look on her company's face, he'd probably never heard of the place. "It's been my pleasure to do this service for you."

"You here with her?" Rokior pointed between Kyrana and Rozha, as if disbelieving their connection. "You hunt Mire Fiend, too?"

Kyrana gave Rozha a frustrated, sideways glare, knowing what she had gotten herself into. "I am not," she failed to hide the rising anger in her tone. "My mission is to *banish* the creature from ever attacking your lands again."

"But Kyrana!" Rozha petulantly argued, "I know how to win, this time! Rokior taught me!"

Before Kyrana could retort, Rokior added in Rozha's defense, "This fight is special to me. I avenge my people."

The Arch Healer knew war as a response to anger was only typical among Safiric children, but she chose not to educate him on the matter. "We were at an agreement that this was to be settled *properly*. We gave your way a try; now it's *my* turn to end this."

"And what if your banishment doesn't work?" Rozha stiffly crossed her arms. "What then? We might as well play it safe and do the deed!"

"Listen to how desperate you are to *murder* this monster--!" Kyrana's burgeoning tirade was then interrupted by a diametrically calm Rokior.

"Why not both?" The warrior suggested. "We go in case banishment no work."

"I like that idea," Rozha gave an irritating smile to Kyrana, as if expecting her to reluctantly agree. "What do you think, Ky?"

Not only was she being snarky about it, but she had to throw in a pet name on top of that. *'The unmitigated cheek of this child,'* the Arch Healer's grip tightened on her staff. "Alright, I realize how important this is to you, Rokior. Normally I would let cooler heads prevail in a situation like this, but I feel as though I have no choice but to let you accompany me." *'Oh dear,'* her expression turned vacant as she gave herself a moment of realization. *'Now I know how poor Kasra feels...'*

"Since we will be here a while," Kyrana said, "I will go out to make arrangements for a place for us to stay. We will need to rest overnight after our journey into Mordax." Before she turned to head back outside, the Arch Healer gave Rokior a bow. "It was good meeting you."

Having lacked the formal politeness of Tresantians, Rokior settled for saying nothing while he watched Kyrana disappear out his doorway. When she was gone, the Laeyudi returned his attention to his remaining guest, Rozha. "If we do this challenge, I need know your ability as warrior. When I see your strength, we make better teammates."

"Agreed," Rozha acknowledged. "How do you want to test me?"

"We fight," Rokior stood, a bit awkwardly balancing on one foot. Once he overcame the mental hurdle of his ankle no longer being in excruciating pain, he planted both soles of his feet on the floor, assuming a natural combat stance. "You say you fighter; I want see your spirit."

The double entendre this statement presented had Rozha a bit taken aback. She clambered to a standing position to ready herself, but hadn't much time to ponder how deathly he expected this battle to be, before Rokior was already coming at her. The next thing the spry blade dancer knew, she was acrobatically dodging a massive uppercut, starting low and aiming high. During her backward somersault, she discarded her priestess robes and revealed her stealth suit. Upon seeing the weapons she kept concealed, Rokior stopped his advance and showed a hand, gesturing for the battle to halt.

"You no fight with swords," he demanded. "I unarmored and unarmed; so should you be."

Seeing the fairness in this request, Rozha unclasped the belts tying her saber to her forearm and unbuckled her spiked knee pads. Once her unfair advantages had been removed, she was down to fighting bare-handed and bare-footed. Still, this lack of weaponry did little to deter Rozha's confidence; she was taught to fight without blades before she was taught to fight with them. She wanted to show Rokior just how capable she was with a blinding kick to his temple, taking the tall Laeyudi down to a knee before she whipped her tail into his stomach to knock him onto the floor. She immediately pressed the attack, going to cover her downed foe, but Rokior kept her back with his legs curled protectively toward his chest.

While she was leaning over his knees to grasp at his head, he used his tail to sweep her off her feet, thus allowing him to turn the tide and grapple her on the ground. With his superior strength and technique, Rozha quickly found herself in a painful and virtually inescapable vice that had her head pushed down so close to her chest that she could feel her teeth about to snap against each other.

The way he had wrapped himself around her from behind, bending her legs around his, disabled her from kicking at him to break free. Her tail didn't have the room nor the leverage it needed to take a swipe at him, either. She was forced to develop a new technique. Her arms were locked above her head -- she could just barely grasp at his face, although she couldn't see where her hands were moving.

She thrust a palm under his chin to painfully crane his head upward, causing his grip to loosen as his leverage was decreasing. It was just enough to allow Rozha's arms the flexibility they needed to push harder against him, until the Laeyudi finally relinquished his hold. Once Rozha had disentangled herself from him, both fighters returned to their feet and spun around simultaneously to meet each other's eyes. With a renewed respect for each other's skills, they continued testing their techniques.

Rozha sampled Rokior's block with a high kick that he deflected with his wrist. Rokior then saw an example of Rozha's reversal, when he threw a kick straight out that she caught under her arm. Using his forward momentum to her advantage, Rozha tumbled to the floor, thus taking Rokior down with her. But neither stayed down for long; as Rokior crawled forth to wrap her up into another of his punishing grapples, Rozha rolled out of arm's reach back to her feet so she could thrust a knee into his forehead.

The dazzling shot knocked the Laeyudi off all fours, which Rozha capitalized on with a swing of her tail. She spun full circle to wind up and build her momentum, but Rokior was able to catch her strongest limb's haymaker in a single hand. As he rolled to his feet, he took Rozha back to the ground. But before he could drop on her, she sprang back up -- with her tail still firmly in his grasp. She pulled him toward her with the limb he refused to release, and punished him for it with an elbow to the neck. With an awful choking sound, Rokior doubled over and presented his head to once again get jump-kicked by Rozha's knee, sending the tall warrior flailing and staggering back.

Rozha lunged forth, taking a diving kick at Rokior's chest to take him down, but the Laeyudi protected himself with a strong sweep of his tail, swatting the blade dancer from the air. Rozha's body buckled; the massive hit taking all the wind out of her. She hit the floor rolling with a painful thud, unable to react fast enough to break her fall. Perhaps ruthless for a sparring session, Rokior lifted her by the ears just high enough to give her an uppercut with his bicep, sending the stunned velta flying through the open window of his house. With a shriek, he heard her falling outside.

Immediately losing his combat seriousness, he leapt through the window after her, to find Rozha precariously dangling by a single hand off the side of his house's surprisingly sturdy foundation. After the exhausting fight, Rozha lacked the strength to hoist herself up the damp, wooden boards. Rokior lent a hand to the frightened blade dancer, saving his worthy opponent from plummeting sixty feet to the watery floor. Both fighters took a minute to breathe and relax their beating hearts, chuckling through the ebbing adrenaline that came with with a riveting encounter.

"You show your spirit," the impressed Rokior sat with his friend and rival. "You indeed strong warrior. You not hold back; your strikes hurt," he laughed, rubbing the bruises on his arms.

"You could've killed me twice!" Rozha grinned, unperturbed rather than angered. "You're no slouch, yourself; I can see why you're the best warrior in this village."

Rokior smiled at her flattery. "It my pleasure to battle you. You more than pretty face."

"You know it!" The redhead dismissively, albeit playfully shoved him. She admired the muscular man, finding him rather endearing, if she were to be honest with herself. Not many men were able to defeat her in combat, and this Laeyudi had done so with magnificent skill. If nothing else, he could satisfy an urge Rozha couldn't deny she'd been seeking to fulfill for some time. "You're not bad looking yourself, Rokior."

Chapter 32: Differing Opinions

The blade dancer's first night in Laeyudi Town ended with the most satisfying meal she had all day, as well as the most satisfying sleep she had in the past few months. Rokior had been sleeping peacefully with his arm behind his head until he felt her moving against him. She found herself wanting to simply lie there and enjoy his warmth, but Kyrana's voice interposed.

"Did you have a good rest?" The Arch Healer's tone had an irked, knowing gruffness to it. "If you're about done, I'd like to have a word with you."

"We've still got all day til we hit Mordax," Rozha groggily protested. "Can it wait?"

"You are a member of the faculty, now, Teacher Rozha," Kyrana tersely reminded her. "You represent the clergy of Sachelvae. It's time to act like that means something to you."

'It doesn't mean anything to the Laeyudi people...' Rozha kept her argumentative response to herself. "I'll be right with you," she settled for a frustrated sigh. Then glancing up at Rokior's wanting gaze, she offered an apologetic nuzzle. "Sorry, I've gotta go." As nice as continuing to rest with the handsome warrior would have been, another bout ephemeral pleasure wasn't worth losing her home at Sachelvae. Rozha looked over her shoulder as she gathered up her clothes, noticing an embarrassed look on Rokior's face. She offered him a smile when he seemed worried that he had done something wrong.

As soon as Rozha was dressed and made her hair somewhat presentable, she fygidia'd to see a very disappointed Kyrana sitting at the table of Ghanius' house. The elder's wife was in the process of washing dishes at the kitchen sink on the rightmost wall. The elder himself was seated at the table just across from the Arch Healer. Upon seeing Rozha's figure softly shadowed by the dim light pouring in from the leather door to the slovenly abode, Kyrana pushed herself from the table. "Mother forgive my anger," the gravel of her words boiled in her throat. "Do not tell me what you have done."

Rozha confrontationally poised as the Arch Prude stamped her way toward her, placing a hand on her hip as she leaned back on one foot. She lifted her chin to stare Kyrana down with narrowed eyes as the staunch priestess homed in on her like a swooping bird of prey. "After everything

Diava has taught us, you run off with the first man you meet in town?! Do you have *any idea* what your irresponsibility has done to sully your spirit?"

Kyrana knew better than Rozha that it was nearly impossible for a Pure to carry Wild-blooded offspring. Having premarital intercourse with a Wild scelan wasn't as frowned upon as if it had been a fellow Pure. But these mollifying facts didn't help the Arch Prude's narrative to give her friend the hell she thought she deserved. "Even if you don't care what *my* opinion is of you, so long as you wear that *mantamina* and continue to reside in Sanguina's temple, you must abide by your Mother's rules. It is to Her that you ultimately must hold yourself accountable at the end of the day. Mother is patient and willing to forgive, but she does not give her graces freely to those who refuse to find it."

As much as Kyrana hoped her heated sermon would drive Rozha to see the light, the only thing the redhead heard was her heart pounding in her ears. *'If she's unwilling to hear me out and let me explain myself, then I don't need to take this from her.'* With a jerking motion, Rozha turned away with a dismissive "Fine," her boots clopping on the floorboards. Kyrana meanwhile shook her head while she watched the tempestuous blade dancer take her leave. *'The more I see her like this, the harder of a time I have understanding -- accepting Mother Diava's decision to make her one of the faculty. She hasn't matured enough in herself to represent the clergy.'*

"You no expect change warrior's heart," came an unexpected teaching from Ghanius. "She not be what you are."

"No," Kyrana agreed, "instead, we have been changing what *we* are so that she can fit in. It doesn't make sense for Mother Diava to bend over as much as she has for the sake of this child. I have a better idea," she concluded, following Rozha through the strider skin door.

" Rozha," the Arch Healer appeared, standing in the midst of a populated bridge. She sauntered toward her as Laeyudi locals politely brushed by her, peacefulness seeming to have been restored to the pace of her amble. "I thought I might help you find Mother's Grace by giving you an assignment that we can do together."

"Oh really?" Rozha tried to sound interested. "What is this 'assignment,' exactly?"

"We will sell these mock guidance charms," Kyrana held out a couple of the ruby pendants in question, "to educate the people of Laeyudi Town about Sachelvae, the same way Sanguina is said to educate the people She visits during her monthly sojournings. At the same time, we will collect these profits as a donation to the temple."

"That doesn't sound like it'll annoy anyone here," came Rozha's caustic sarcasm, "especially after what just happened when the Safiric Brotherhood came to town."

"Now that they've seen the powers of both the Brotherhood and the Sisterhood juxtaposed," Kyrana didactically raised a finger, "they will be able to make a better choice between the two of us. They will want to accept us as their protectors, after what we did for them."

"I suppose we can give it a shot," Rozha shrugged. The idea of being a Sanguinic salesperson wasn't quite what she had in mind when she thought of the fun activities a Teacher of Sachelvae would have the privilege of doing.

"I was planning on doing this when I got here, anyway," Kyrana admitted. "Sanguina must've been smiling on us, to have given us such a golden opportunity."

Since the only town square in Laeyudi village had been demolished by the Safiric Brotherhood, Rozha and Kyrana weren't left with many locations they could use to set up a merchant's booth. Laeyudi Town was bereft of a Mediona-like avenue, since all shops were done out of someone's residences. "I say we look for a high traffic area and start there," Rozha offered her first, helpful suggestion to the cause.

They set up shop in the middle of the single, longest bridge in Laeyudi Town -- a straight shot through the center of the village, with many residences and businesses on either side. They made sure to have everything ready by lunch hour, when Rozha and Kyrana expected there would be the highest concentration of people wandering around. While the amount of their potential customers wasn't quite as numerous as the bustling metropolis of Tresantia, Laeyudi's busiest commercial time of day still provided a good amount of people to flag down and strike up conversation with. It was at that point that they ran into their first vital problems: the speech impediments of many Laeyudi made it difficult to communicate with them. Even if they were interested, they were too poor to afford any kind of significant payment; most could only part with one or two divitias -- if they had any at all to give.

Laeyudi worked on a trade system; rather than barter with coin, they'd give something they saw as equal in value to what was being offered them. But since a mystical pendant of questionable power was hard to put a price on, many of their customers turned them down because they couldn't think of anything worthy to give.

"This isn't working," a bored Rozha groaned. She lazily reclined in her seat and stretched her legs out under the table. "You have all the personality of a moldy boot. It's no wonder they're not interested in buying anything from us."

Rozha's ears perked up as her new friend came by their makeshift 'shop' and frowned at the wares. "No one buy this," Rokior said lifting the charms with a sour look. "You bring promises, no can keep. No respect Laeyudi traditions, Laeyudi no respect you."

Kyrana snorted, "And what traditions would those be?" she narrowed her eyes at Rokior and Rozha together.

"You see, there is pride in being Laeyudi," Rokior explained. "Anyone here respect you when you show spirit."

"You mean I have to fight *everyone* in town, like you?" Rozha asked, with some disbelief.

"There is another way," Rokior replied, pointing toward his tattoos. "Artist Graxifen no can see. But can see spirit of others. He make it visible on skin, so that everyone else can see. When you wear spirit, everyone can see your strength."

"Blasphemic!" Kyrana turned a face at the coiling barbs of ink strewn across his skin. She tried to make out a word--any word along the curls and juts of symbols, but it almost seemed like a different language completely. However mysterious they were, Rozha certainly found them quite enthralling.

"Those tattoos *are* pretty cool," Rozha blithely remarked. "Where does this Graxifen guy live?"

Kyrana gawked at her as if she'd just offered to slay Mother Diava herself. "What in the name of Sanguina are you thinking?" she snapped. Rozha ignored her pink friend.

"I take you to see him," Rokior offered.

"I'd love to meet him," Rozha said with a twist of her tail, taking his arm and striding away to leave Kyrana with her fake charms.

The warrior led Rozha across the bridges whence she and Kyrana came, down to the ground level of Laeyudi Town. Judging by Graxifen's purported blindness, it was probably for the best that he didn't reside over 20 feet off the ground. "He no leave home much," Rokior explained, "mostly to eat, otherwise, no other reason. Most come to see him. He used to visitor. Gets many every day."

Near the center of town, where the elder lived, was the quaint shack that Graxifen called home. Even though its occupant couldn't see to clean it, the exterior was surprisingly well-kept. Its most notable feature was the four vine overhangings that had attached themselves to the top of its banana peel-shaped roof. "Because he is respected Laeyudi," Rokior said, "Others come look after him." He continued to explain that Graxifen was born blind, but was ironically known as the village seer. Through his dreams, he could detect the comings of strangers and even predict disastrous events. "Though he no have eye to see, he have other sense to replace it. All Laeyudi adapt. We no have weakness we not overcome."

This statement made Rozha curious of something and decided she'd stop Kyrana from whatever she was doing to ask her via communication ring. "Can you cure blindness?"

"Oh, are you talking to me now?" Kyrana huffed vengefully before sighing an answer, "I have before, but I cannot heal what was never broken; if he was born unable to see, I can't do anything for him."

As bad as Rozha felt for the old scelan's troubles, she was nonetheless excited to meet him when Rokior brought her into his dark abode. It made sense that the house was devoid of windows, given who lived there. The only light it had was what came from the open door -- and even that wasn't much. The chilly fog of Virluti forest dimmed any sunlight that managed to seep through the canopy. Indeed, the brightest hour of midday more closely resembled a coming dusk.

From what could be seen within the soft cone of illumination in which Rozha and Rokior stood was a ragged, green rug decorated with white rings. In the center of which sat a middle-aged scelan, perhaps in his early fifties, wearing one of maybe two dark green and brown robes he ever owned.

It looked like it had been worn and washed many times through many years. His long hair of earthy colors had a liveliness untouched by age, and was meticulously braided -- one down his back, and one over either shoulder. His chest-length beard had the same style of healthy keeping, and grew seemingly in a straight line from his chin. His bangs reached to his eyes, but there was barely just enough space between the curtain of tresses for his visitors to see the pair of pale gray irises vacantly staring behind them. Though they never moved, they didn't seem to have a focus on just one single space; it was more like they were surveying the entire world around him.

Graxifen seemed to be in some sort of meditative stance, sitting cross-legged in front of another scelan who was fully disrobed and seated calmly before the master. Graxifen's breathing was perfectly controlled to long, in-and-out inspirations. His concentration was unperturbed by the unexpected entrance of his guests; not even his ears twitched at the sounds of their footsteps.

"Graxifen," Rokior said, as if needing to get the artist's attention, "I have guest for you."

"I know," the seer replied, making no effort to move from the spot. "What her name?"

Rozha's heartbeat fell out of synch momentarily; how did he know what her gender was if he never met her before? She was suddenly reminded of the psychic she and Kasra met -- the creepy perfume lady -- and immediately bristled at the thought. "My name is Rozha," the Red Dancer tried to sound polite.

"You been here before," Graxifen hummed. "I feel your spirit many sleeps ago. You have big, old spirit."

"Huh?..." Rozha couldn't help uttering a quizzical yawp. "What does that mean?"

"You must be Pure, yes?" The seer dodged the question.

"Yeah, so?" As Rozha's patience dwindled, her defensiveness came through in her tone.

"That why," Graxifen answered. "You have many life cycles."

"This is true for every Pure," Rozha said. "Mother Diava taught me that."

"You not just *any* Pure," the seer slowly pointed at her. "I seen lots over long time. Their spirit no big as yours."

"What difference does that make?" Rozha quirked an eyebrow.

"You have big capacity for much powers," Graxifen raised his arms, as if trying to show the size of his guest's soul. "You have them before in other life. You have them again, later."

During a pause in their conversation, while Rozha was trying to understand just what in the world this blind scelan was going on about, Rokior stepped up to get their minds back on track. "She came for you to show her how big her spirit is," he motioned to the tools adorning the walls of the hut.

"I hoping you say that," Graxifen smiled. "But I no have time today. You come back tomorrow for spirit draw. I have many scelan come today." His fingers curled over the flesh of his next appointment, drawing an unseen pattern over the scelan's skin as if he were tracing an image that were already present.

Rozha frowned, her eyes sliding towards the nude man sitting on the floor awaiting his turn for the fantastical inking.

"Alright," she nodded, "Tomorrow. I can stay an extra hour or two-"

"You stay more day after. Spirit draw take many day recover; hurt lots. You no ready, don't come," Graxifen warned.

"I am not afraid of a little pain," Rozha said with a hand on her hip.

"Then you come tomorrow."

Rokior saw Rozha off and let the blade dancer return to her friend, though reluctantly so. Upon her arrival, Kyrana immediately shot up from her chair at the shop, planting both hands over the table angrily.

"What happened to you?!" Kyrana shouted over the bustle of the street.

"Calm down, Ky!" Rozha put her own hands up as she approached the healer. "Rokior took me to see someone who could reveal the image of my soul through body art."

"And what? Did you do it?"

"Tomorrow. I made an appointment," Rozha said blatantly.

"Are you doing this to *impress* him?" Kyrana shot a glare towards Rokior's house, her tail coiling vainly under her dress.

"I'm not some damn teenager, seeking acceptance from a man!" Rozha shot back, getting up in the other velta's face. "He wants to make me a part of his tribe. I'm doing it to show my dedication to our mission."

Kyrana disapprovingly shook her head. "Your hypocrisy is unbelievable -- you who were just lamenting having to stay in this village for a couple of days, now you want to stay longer to do something so goddess-forsaken and self-serving."

"What?!" Rozha restrained her temper just enough to slam her fists over the table, making the faux charms rustle and clatter. A hint of fear flashed over Kyrana's features. "Are you substituting your own opinions for what Sanguina Herself believes?"

Kyrana scowled as she felt heat flowing through her ears, causing her fingers to clench and her tail to curl. "A test of pain, such as body art," she forced herself to calmly explain, "is a Safiric custom that should *not* be observed by a member of the Sanguinic Sisterhood. The symbols you will bear on your skin, no matter what they represent, shall forever leave their traces of Safiric evil. You will only be able to remove them once Purified by a priestess, such as myself…" The way she said this made it seem like she wouldn't have been at all opposed to demonstrating what exactly Purification entailed. "If you die without being Purified, Sanguina will not recognize you as her child and you will be tortured in between realms for all eternity."

Throughout this diatribe, Rozha had ignored Kyrana's words with her own convictions. "How ridiculous," she bitterly spat. "I've never heard of such a silly thing like that. You're making a big deal out of nothing, all because you can't trust a man of Wild descent. These people aren't of the Brotherhood and were willingly refusing their demands when Kada'timor came to their town. What they're doing is not made with the intention of destroying Purity."

"It doesn't have to be made with the conscious intent to make it sinful," Kyrana argued. "The Safiric Brotherhood has been poisoning and conditioning the minds of Safiro's children from the beginning of their community's history. You don't need to be a member of the Brotherhood to have been tainted by their influence. Though Rokior and his kind may not realize it, they are living by the Father's Will."

The Laeyudi traversing the streets were beginning to pause awkwardly and stare at the fiery Arch Healer, after hearing her powerfully condemning statements. Rozha finally had enough of listening to Kyrana using Rokior as an exemplification of this apparently abhorrent evil that only the Arch Healer perceived. The blade dancer was a good enough reader of emotions and body language that she could tell that this purported sin Kyrana was reprimanding her for wasn't the only source of her friend's outrage. But she was too angry to care about what it was she had done, this time, to earn the priestess' ire.

"You know what," Rozha aggressively puffed through her nose. "I'm gonna go get a drink. You can curse my stupidity for the rest of your days if you like." She spun on her heel and strode away to the nearest tavern without a backwards glance.

Chapter 33: A Poisoned Mind

Rozha approached the entrance to a tavern named Solientus, where an imposing bodyguard outside stared them down with his blood red Wild eyes from six and a half feet high.

"What're *you* doin' here?..." the mistrusting scelan kept his head craned to one shoulder and crossed his burly arms. "You've come to *'evangelize,'* have you?"

"Nah, I've had enough of that for one day," Rozha waved a hand at him. "I'm just here to relax."

"What about her?" he nodded behind Rozha to the Arch Prude who had been following the blade dancer with folded arms and a haughty upturned snoot.

Rozha glowered at the healer, "If you're coming with me, you better be ready to have a drink and chill out."

Kyrana huffed, "I have no intention of causing problems."

The bodyguard calculatingly closed an eye and grumbled broodingly. "See to it that it stays that way," he warned them, stepping aside, "or there will be consequences."

The inside of the bar was every bit as shady as the people loitering around outside. It was sparsely illuminated by small candles attached to wooden support beams, their wicks so close to the thatch roof it was a wonder the place hadn't burnt to the ground, yet. The carefree clientele were scantily clad and heavily tattooed, wearing more scars and bruises than clothing. They could be seen sitting at the short, round tables or on the stools by the bar, cackling or chattering about something undoubtedly risque.

While Kyrana timidly held her hands behind her back, her knees shivering under her gown, Rozha couldn't have been more laid back, looking around as if it had been years since she had seen the beloved establishment. Kyrana naively cast her virgin eyes all over the dark interior, trying to dodge the eyes of anyone nearby. She leaned toward Rozha to whisper over all the ambient noise, "What is this? I don't feel safe here..."

"Are you kidding?" the redhead gave her a sideways glance. "This is my kind of place! It brings back fond memories."

Almost immediately losing herself in the intoxicating atmosphere, Rozha shouted out,

"Anyone up for a game of cards? Come right over to this table, if you're feeling lucky."

Kyrana took a seat with her friend near the door as curious bar flies started buzzing in, beginning to feel cornered. "Rozha," the out-of-place priestess squeaked, "what're you doing?"

"Relax, I'm just making us some easy money," she said, drawing up her pack of cards and shuffling them in her hands. "It's been a long time since I've laid bets with the peshed."

"This is terribly taboo," Kyrana's ears nervously wilted. "I want no part in this!" Her mind wanted her to leave, but her body was too weak with fear to carry her anywhere.

"You'll thank me for it, later," Rozha assured her. "In about an hour, you'll be thinking this is the best idea you've ever had."

Kyrana couldn't stop fidgeting while the seats around the table were taken by a few roughnecks with half-filled mugs in hand, setting down their money to pay their way into Rozha's first hand. The redhead even dealt Kyrana in so she'd have something to hold onto and take her mind off the situation. She was absolutely mortified to be in the kind of place Diava would absolutely forbid any priestess from ever entering. Now she knew exactly the kind of person Rozha really was -- the kind of thing she always feared to think about and liked to pretend didn't exist in the darker areas of society. She subconsciously clung to Rozha for most of the time she was there, just to feel some semblance of protection from the tipsy and sometimes collapsing customers sitting near her.

After winning a few rounds of poker, Rozha used the small sum she had collected from the chain-smoking lot to pay for her first drink of venio -- a translucent and somewhat tasteless alcohol with a burn so unpleasant it was best described as an all-out attack on the drinker's tonsils. The glass Rozha had ordered for her friend had been flavored with fruit juices to mellow the venio's scathing bitterness until it masked enough of the alcohol to be virtually undetectable.

"What is this?" The Arch Healer eyed the drink suspiciously.

"It's just frupom juice," Rozha lied.

Kyrana trustingly took the glass into her hand and drank down its contents rather quickly. She had been quite thirsty since most of the water to drink in Laeyudi Town was so nasty, she could barely stomach most of what Ghanius offered. She hardly even noticed the tingly feeling in her belly after she had finished her first drink. She even asked Rozha to get her another. About thirty minutes later, Kyrana was holding her head, leaning back in her chair as the whole room seemed to be spinning around her. A still very dry

Rozha caught the lightweight by the arm when it looked like she was going to fall out of her seat.

"Woah, you alright there, Ky?" she slowly helped her stand up. "It's time to go; we've had enough for one day."

"I feel very odd..." the nurse weakly protested, most of her weight leaning against her friend. "And funny," she gormlessly snickered into Rozha's shoulder. "What's wrong with me?"

"I'm going to get you some water before you get sick," the redhead hurried her out of the tavern.

"Wait, what was it you had me drinking in there?!" Kyrana chortled at the sound of her own overreaction. "You said it was frupoms!"

"I thought you could handle more than that!" Rozha replied. "You asked me to keep giving you more."

"I'm telling Diava you tricked me!" The nurse angrily yelled. "You're no better than the Brotherhood! *Astapsyxi* to you!" Her inebriated intonation stopped Rozha in her tracks and caused her to accidentally drop Kyrana to the ground. The spell broke as soon as the priestess' forehead bounced off the wooden floorboards of the Laeyudi walkway. She laid a healing hand on her crown as Rozha helped her back to her feet and picked up her tiara for her.

"Just calm down, and sit right here," her friend chided, leading her back to their table. "I'll go buy some water for you -- I'll be back in a moment."

"And it better be water this time!" Kyrana shooed her off with a sloppy admonition. But 'a moment' didn't come quick enough for the drunk nurse, who grew tired of watching all the people walking by, not sparing her a minute of their time to browse her store. So she decided she'd bring them to her with a bit of advertising.

The priestess stood up and shouted as loud as she could, "Get over here and buy our stuff, or you'll go to hell! Safiro doesn't love you! He wants you all to die and suffer forever! But if you buy these things from me, Sanguina will like you! She's a good mother like that -- She knows you're a piece of crap, yet She's willing to give you life again and again!"

A small crowd began to gather around the velta's strident sermon, more entertained by her blithering than they were interested in picking up her artifacts.

"Don't be stingy, give it a chance!" she beckoned them. "It won't cost you a single divitia!"

Some were convinced it would be worth their while, as a souvenir and conversation piece if nothing else, and left whatever they could afford to pay on the table, as if Kyrana were some kind of street performer. By the time Rozha had returned with the drink she promised to retrieve for her friend, their inventory had been cleared out and was exchanged with a pile of money that Kyrana was having a hard time counting.

"Wow, you made a killing!" The impressed blade dancer exclaimed, reclaiming her seat beside her. "I told you all you needed to do was loosen up."

"You're going to be in big trouble when Mother Diava knows what you've done," Kyrana held her head, taking the pitcher Rozha brought. The redhead had to hold the sloshing container so that the nurse wouldn't spill its contents all down the front of herself. "I can't believe you talked me into this," the priestess slurred, wincing at the sunlight.

"You're acting like I've turned you into monster," Rozha laughed. "How're you supposed to tell your followers not to do something if you don't even know what it looks like or how it feels? Just consider this an exercise in advanced Safiric studies -- I am a Teacher, after all."

"That's what frightens me..." Kyrana groaned. She rested her head on her arms crossed on the table to hide her face from passersby. Although the position wasn't terribly comfortable, she found herself nodding off soon after. Rozha hadn't realized when Kyrana had fallen asleep until she asked if she was feeling better, when it was starting to get closer to dinner time. Having not received a response from the sleeping priestess, Rozha nudged the now sober Kyrana awake.

"Hey, you feeling hungry?" The blade dancer casually asked.

Kyrana confusedly blinked as she tried to recall where she was, as she gathered her bearings. "Yeah, a bit," she started. "Was I asleep?"

"I can't blame you for taking a nap," Rozha indirectly affirmed. "We'll have to get as much rest as possible now so we won't need it later, when we go back to Mordax."

"I can barely remember what I did earlier," the Arch Healer yawned.

"Don't worry yourself too much about it," Rozha stood up from the table, encouraging Kyrana to join her. "Let's go back to Ghanius' place to have some more of our rations, if he's not making anything particularly edible."

"Good idea," Kyrana chuckled, then starting on their way. "You know, I was worried about you, when you ran away from me earlier. I'm not used to seeing you as anything less than cheerful. When we argued, I felt uneasy -- I saw a side of you I'd only ever seen directed toward our enemies. Indeed, I was hoping I would not become one of them to you."

Rozha smiled and offered an apologetic flickering of her eyes. "I didn't mean to lash out at you like that," she tapped her tail as they walked in step. "I guess I don't understand what it's like to be mothered."

Kyrana's expression softened. The Teacher had never told her about her childhood, but the more she made mentions like that, the more the pieces of the puzzle were coming together. She could tell, even as inviting as Rozha's voice made it seem, that the Red Dancer wasn't ready to avow this particular history with confidence. "Us priestesses are responsible for each other," the Arch Healer replied. "Mother Diava always stressed developing trust within the clergy, so that we can always depend on one another. Our admonitions are never meant as an attack on our fellow members. The harshness of our reprimands are balanced by the evil that results from not heeding our warnings."

Rozha could count on all her digits how many times she'd heard that from her peers in the last two years. "Just because I don't have the typical priestess broomstick shoved up my ass, doesn't mean I'm not every bit as 'devout' as you are." She almost chuckled as she caught a flash of shock crossing Kyrana's visage, as if she was somehow defiling the Arch Healer with her 'foul language.' "After having seen a few veltas enter and leave the clergy in my time at the temple, I know the difference between someone who was *told* to join, versus someone who *wanted* to be there."

In all the time Kyrana had known of Rozha, the one thing she was never made privy to was where the Red Dancer came from. Mother Diava was always good about retaining a new member's anonymity. Even with as close as her relationship was to the High Priestess, she never avowed anything a student or cleric told her in confidence. It was a rule of Sachelvae to let any novitiate's past be left behind them; it was why the burning ritual of old clothing was so integral to the temple's traditions. "If you do not mind me asking, Teacher Rozha," the Arch Healer was suddenly kindhearted once more, "what ever happened that brought you to Sachelvae?"

In spite of Kyrana's vexation that her question would be met with a snide or indirect answer at best, Rozha couldn't have been happier that someone would finally ask. "I've never told *anyone* the secrets of my past," the Red Dancer rolled her eyes and cracked a smirk as she placed a hand on her chest, realizing that she was being a bit melodramatic. "But since you consider me a friend and I trust you, I'll tell you something I've not even told my own sister." At this fact, Kyrana's ears finally perked up. Having received the full attention of her fogy, Rozha sat up straight in her chair, assuming the pose of a fabulous storyteller with a leg crossed and an elbow rested on the table.

"At the age of seventeen, I used the skills I learned as a blade dancer to escape my clan, after it was discovered that my commanding officer showed favoritism toward me. As you might imagine, it was frowned upon in the military for a scelan of Wild descent to be fraternizing with a Pure."

Rozha grinned, no doubt pridefully recalling her taboo relationship. "He provided me with ample time to flee my pursuers at his own risk, allowing me to begin my journey to the only land where Pures like me would find freedom: Tresantia. I had left Onteval's royal capital city and spent much of my time slogging it out in the damp, ever thickening forests on my way to the center of the continent. I roughed it every night in the wilderness as she traveled, always spending outside my means to live luxuriously as I went, often resorting to gambling to make ends meet. I couldn't afford to stay in one place too long, and had to remain incognito at all times."

She paused, looking to Kyrana as she knew this next part would irk her. "I frequently impersonated priestesses in order to avoid tolls and other traveling expenses. I'll leave it up to your imagination how I was able to procure a disguise for myself."

~~~

It had been a month since her adventure began. The only obstacle on the last leg of her journey was the lakeside city of Vavio. At the edge of the temperate forest, just a quarter mile away from the lights of civilization, she gazed into sully skies to see Safiro's morbid light shining upon her. The ex-blade dancer shook with consternation at the omen of malice, suddenly feeling as though she were being watched by an evil presence. She uncomfortably held her shoulders and fearfully glanced back to the darkness, certain that she was being followed.

The wind was gentle, yet loud enough to hide whispers and all but the closest footsteps. She listened intently as she moved slowly through a shallow valley of tall grass moist with dew, taking extra time to ensure the crunching sounds she heard were her own and not echoed by a sneaking assassin. The paranoid velta only felt safe when she had reached the dirt road above the vale, where she was bathed in the orange light of two torches on either side of the wall's opening. She turned to the grasses from whence she came and watched for signs of motion, but not a blade quivered out of place. The only sounds to be heard were of the fires flickering in their cressets from the tepid zephyr.

Her tension was somewhat eased by the scent of the ocean, leading her into town. Hungry and strapped for cash, she leisurely strolled down the vast roads, looking for the nearest inn where she could quell her nerves. She gamed with anything she could place a wager on, be it dice, cards, or even the spontaneous bar room brawl, and out-drank most of her competition before those who had not already passed out on the floor could call it a night. After she had her fun and collected enough money to support herself for another day, she rented a room and crashed there til dawn.

When she reawakened, slumped more-or-less in her bed, she checked in a bronze mirror on the wall that she didn't look as hung over as she felt, before fixing herself up enough to be presentable while wearing the robes of a priestess from her rucksack. She figured that disguise would suffice to escape notice of the officials and give her a free ride on the ferry she'd take to Onteval. She knew that this was the week Sanguina would be at rest, and perhaps her sacrilege would escape her notice, but her guilty conscience disallowed her from breaking her tradition of asking for blessing and exoneration every day she could.

She was greeted kindly by the genuine, Sanguinic priestesses on her way through the open doors of a chapel, and bowed before an altar underneath a small, stained glass painting of the goddess to whom she silently prayed. When she looked up, she caught the solemn smile of the elder abbess standing behind the altar. As if she were able to see the trepidation hidden in Rozha's countenance, she said, "Mother always forgives."

Taken aback as her mind was trying to cogitate all the reasons for such a suspicious phrase, Rozha hadn't the presence of mind to force a smile in return, and merely uttered a quiet, "Thank you," before continuing on her way out. The paranoid imposter kept her head down, her eyes on the white sands as she walked in the direction of her destination.

Her ears perked up at the sound of a feminine voice calling her from behind. "Sister!" cried the unknown woman. Rozha turned and saw a Pure possibly no more than 24 years old, with albicant skin and long, white hair, dressed in drapes of translucent red, rushing toward her with a troubled look on her face. The cerise rosage on her nose was almost entirely pink with irritation; her crimson eyes appeared thoroughly rubbed and watery. She tried to catch her breath as she stopped before the false priestess.

"I am very ill," she sniffled, her squeaky voice tainted with congestion. "Last eve, I was accosted by many symptoms with which I am unfamiliar and know not the cause thereof. I am unable to smell, taste -- even breathe at times! I fear it is the work of Safiro, and if I am not cleansed of His curse, I will surely perish! Although Sanguina is at rest, She must have guided me to you so that my soul can be saved."

Rozha's brow furrowed, knowing she had really gotten herself into it this time. Whatever was ailing this albino woman must have been very serious -- enough to get her to run out in the hot sun without fear of burning. She couldn't possibly reveal her true identity to her, but she could never forgive herself if she let this poor person die by giving her some placebo blessing and sending her away. Thankfully, the illness which had worried this stranger so much could be easily diagnosed with a simple touch to the scared velta's unusually warm forehead. The albicant woman trepidatiously raised her fists to her chest, as if expecting an exorcism.

"Do not fret," the redhead confidently smirked.

Easing up slightly, her patient cautiously eyed up at her and asked, "Am I cured?"

"You merely caught cold," Rozha chuckled, a bit relieved it was nothing more serious. "I understand your worries, granted what unspeakable time it is. However, I believe you will be back in good health by the end of the week."

"A cold?" the stranger curiously repeated, as if having never heard of one. After a short pause to collect her thoughts, she laughed, "Ah, what luck! I doth feeleth a fool, having mistaken it for something it w-wasn't..." she trailed off, her eyes distractedly flickering. Without much warning, aside from a long breath, she rose the back of her hand to her chin and clenched her torso with a sharp sneeze.

Rozha blinked, trying not to titter at the sick velta's surprised expression. "May you have Sanguina's grace!"

"After these seven days, hopefully I shall!" she retorted, wiggling her nose. "I thank thee, Sister. Accept my sorrows, for I hath kept thee from thine quest."

"Don't be," the redhead courteously replied. Although she was in a hurry to leave, she couldn't bring herself to just abandoning a fellow Pure until she knew she was alright. "May I walk back with you to your house?"

"I hath no dwelling in this land," she answered. "I was merely crossing to visit my kin."

"You have relatives in Tresantia?" Rozha raised an eyebrow with intrigue. "As it turns out, I was just heading there, myself. Would you like to share a cabin with me?"

"T'would be my pleasure!" she jovially chirped. "I would feel much safer on waters so treacherous around a practiced priestess. Thou art a connoisseur of excitement to evangelize in perilous lands," the stranger proudly tipped up her head, impressed with her bravery. "Alas, a few of mine own babes were led astray -- they are want of your wisdom to see them true. Would I know your name, so that I may refer thee?"

Rozha stammered, honestly having not expected a question like that. "I'm hardly experienced enough to proselytize those who are misguided!" she acted flattered to give herself time to create a false identity. "My work is to help those who are already in the faith."

"Hath not such modesty," the pale velta grinned. "Thou should feel proud to be who thou art -- tis all Sanguina ever wanted of thee."

The ex-blade dancer couldn't wait to be rid of this stranger so she'd no longer have to worry about keeping up this sinful facade for her, but at the same, she found her so fascinatingly different that she wanted to know as much about her as possible before they parted ways.

"My name is Sacyrella," she finally answered. "And may I know with whom I'm sharing a room during this excursion?"

The short albino smiled. "Yalikai," she stuttered, giving Rozha a subtle tell that she wasn't being honest, either.

Normally, the redhead would have become worried that this woman may have been a spy trying to blow her cover, had the name she used not been so unusually archaic. *'No one's named their daughter something like that in a thousand years,'* Rozha curiously contemplated.

Yalikai watched Rozha study her visage, and tilted her head. "Shall we sally forth?"

"Indeed," she confidently lifted her chin.

She took the first step to lead the way across the gray sands, inside the Vavio Port admissions building. Because of the town's rather quaint population, probably no more than 500, there wasn't much of a line to wait through at the end of the roped fence at the open door. It didn't take the two veltas long at all to meet the captain standing behind the moldy, wooden desk up front, which had on its surface a record of all the passengers who were boarding his ferry. His ship could plainly be seen sitting in the boathouse behind him, anchored to a pier on which a single-file line of people were waiting their turn to ascend a short flight of stairs to the deck.

The captain, himself, was an aged scelan with a slouched stature, who was probably much taller in his years of youth. But now he stood a mere six feet, even, barely looking over the heads of most passengers on his ship through squinted eyes. His white fu manchu, like a catfish's barbels, reached past his neck in length.

The floorboards beneath his cane creaked when he shifted more of his weight onto it, to keep his balance as he reverently placed a hand over his heart for the faux priestess. "It does me great honor to have ye sailin' with us, fair lady. And who be this friend of yours? If she be ill, I cannot risk having her spread disease to me shipmates."

A bracelet of prayer beads around Rozha's wrist slid up her forearm as she solemnly raised her hand to the captain. "Fear not, sage seaman; as long as I place blessings on her sickness, her condition will not be contagious. It is for this reason I have her in my care, to ensure that Safiro will not take her life."

Yalikai's lips slightly parted, as if she had something to say, until she snapped forward with a sudden sneeze, then turned and pleadingly stared at Rozha over the handkerchief covering her face.

"Salvii," Rozha gave the sick velta a customary blessing, who somberly closed her eyes and placed a hand atop Yalikai's crown.

The captain fought the urge to raise an eyebrow, unsure of what was going on but was unwilling to question a holy servant's conduct. "Mayhap you would shield our ship from Safiro's rays during its voyage 'cross the Ontevallian channel?"

"Of course," Rozha courtly curtsied, "I will pray for Mother's protection over all crew and passengers."

"For that," the captain cracked a smile, "I welcome thee aboard the Nexuna, free of charge, with our safety in your hands."

"May it be Sanguina's will," were Rozha's parting words, walking off to the pier.

"I cannot thank thee proper!" Yalikai happily squeaked. "Thou art much too kind, dear guardian."

"It must have been by divine kismet that our paths intertwined," her defender explained -- trying to believe it, herself. "Sanguina sent you to me. I will look after you as long as She needs me to." Her ragtag homily seemed sufficient to convince the faux priestess' follower of her genuineness, who smiled in the comfort of her placebic providence. Seeing how blindly she trusted her had Rozha awash with compunction, stronger than ever before.

Once the two veltas had reached the ship deck, they were approached by a sixteen-year-old sceli wearing a sailor's striped uniform. "May I show thee ladies to your cabin?" His light voice developed a slightly gruffer accent, no doubt influenced by his fellow crew. "The anchors will be aweigh shortly."

"Certainly, my brother," Rozha followed him below deck into the passenger level.

She and Yalikai were the last to be guided to their room by the steward, who braced himself against the rocking of the ship between the narrow walls. The vessel's hull echoed with the sounds of small waves crashing starboard. Their cabin was located at the aft end, where a window provided them a view of the wake parting around the stern.

"Here you are, m'ladies," he opened the door for them. "We should arrive at Port Zelguun tomorrow. You will receive three meals 'til then, which will be provided by our kitchen staff at the times posted on the wall of your room. Is there anything I can get for you?"

Minding Yalikai's condition, Rozha asked, "May I have a bowl of soup, for my charge?"

"Of course," the young sailor assentingly nodded, before turning back down the hall.

Walking into their cabin, Rozha gestured to one of the beds connected to the wall. "Make yourself comfortable. You probably didn't sleep too well last night, huh?"

"Tis not a luxury I know fair," the albino admitted with a somber sniffle. "I hath developed accustomization to a full day's awakeness."

"You and me, both," Rozha laughed, momentarily breaking her refined priestess act. "Getting some rest will help you kick this cold, quicker. It's about the only decent thing about being on a ship, is that you can get plenty of sleep."

Yalikai softly smiled for a moment. "I hath not the comfort of being one's charge before," she embarrassedly raised her shoulders. "I always am looking after my own children."

"It's time someone returned the favor, huh?" her caretaker smiled.

Yalikai grinned back with a batting of her eyes, before both of their attentions were diverted to the knocking on their door. Rozha stood up to see their steward standing on the other side, with a bowl of broth in his hand.

"Here you are, m'lady," he said.

"Thank you, dear," the redhead bowed, taking the soup she ordered.

"Do you need anything else, priestess?"

"No, you have done well," was the end of their brief exchange.

Rozha took a spoonful for herself, first, to test the flavor before returning to her charge. Kneeling by her bedside, she held the next spoonful of bouillon to her lips for her. "It tastes pretty good! How do you like it?"

Yalikai leaned forward to slurp the warm liquid. "I appreciate this much! I thank thee again, Sacyrella." She took in a larger mouthful and added with a liberated sniff, "I doth feel good health!"

"I'm glad I could be of assistance," the redhead tenderly kissed the tip of her friend's nose.

"My sister," she albino velta breathed, "is not a buss of affection taboo for a priestess?... There is difficulty in pretending to be something thou art not, yes?" she gave her a knowingly sidelong glance.

"Wh-What do you mean?" Rozha's heart skipped a beat, a cold chill shot up her spine like a dagger.

The albino dropped her chipper lilt, her voice sliding into a deep, almost mollifying tone. "What kind of priestess cannot recognize her own mother?" she cast a judgmental glare. "Sanguina knoweth all Her children -- even those led astray."

The redhead fell on her bottom as she backed off in complete shock. "What are you talking about?..." She shook her head in bewilderment, refusing to believe what she was saying. "What do you know about me?"

"Thou art flying from authorities," the goddess revealed herself. "Thou hath forsaken Me. Thou hath believed I left you, so thee doubted Me. Thou blaspheme as a priestess to mock Me... It doth not feel well to be deceived, yes?"

A frozen Rozha swallowed her fear, feeling as if she were weighed down by Sanguina's presence. "You have come to condemn me?" the shivering redhead managed.

"Mother always forgives," Sanguina tersely reminded her. A bright light wrapped around her body as she delivered her last message. "Thine penance shall be My Path for thee: Upon thy arrival in the city of Tresantia, thou shalt meet with the High Priestess of Sachelvae. She shall teach thee the way of a *real* priestess, and follow thy Path thenceforth."

~~~

"That's why I came to Sachelvae," Rozha finished. "To atone for my sins."

Kyrana's eyes were filled with a soft lister, pensively paying attention to the Red Dancer's story as everything she ever thought about Rozha's attitude was tying together with her upbringing. "You think you met Sanguina, Herself?" Unlike the High Priestess, Kyrana didn't believe Rozha had any reason to embellish the details of her past. "I'd doubt if even Mother Diava has seen the Goddess with her own eyes."

"They say that the most devout never do," Rozha ironically stated. "She uses those who seem ill-fitted to carry out a meaningful existence, so that those weakest in the faith can come to her. Sanguina favors the humble, while Safiro favors the proud. Children are used to asking for permission and guidance, but adults are accustomed to looking after themselves -- they need to be reminded that we are all Sanguina's children. Mother knows what's best for all of us."

Kyrana's countenance could not have shown a more delighted beam. For once, she agreed with the redheaded heathen. "Mother Diava may be the High Priestess, but you're much wiser than she is."

The blade dancer's cheeks dimpled. "Wow, you must still be drunk," Rozha joked with a chuckle. "Diava only knows what she has read, but I learned of the faith through my own experience. I would sooner put my trust in an unchaste vixen than rely on a sanctimonious celibate like her."

Kyrana pursed her lips in thought; perhaps the frupom juice still lighted her heart, but she couldn't help the small smile creeping up her face as she blinked up at her friend. "Rozha...if Sanguina has led you to the Laeyudi tradition in hopes of forming a bond with their people, who am I to doubt your decisions while you are here."

"Are...are you telling me to get a tattoo?" Rozha raised her brow aghast.

"I will deny that in front of anyone, especially Mother Diava." Kyrana said with a subtle smirk.

Chapter 34: Return to Mordax

After they enjoyed a small dinner at Ghanius' house, Rozha and Kyrana relaxed and spoke with the elder and his wife about how they knew Laeyudi Town in their childhood. The old couple gave a hard-to-understand history lesson about all the different people who helped shape Laeyudi Town into what it had become, then they checked out for the evening. Night had barely fallen by then, but Rozha and Kyrana decided to be on their way. Kyrana grabbed her Branch of Life and touched her forehead against it to utter a prayer, wishing for good fortune on their journey.

When the two travelers had made their last preparations, they left Ghanius' house and beheld the ominous lights of the Laeyudi lanterns, creaking in the gentle breeze. The midnight air was fraught with a wintry chill, causing Rozha to shudder under her robes. Even the light of Sanguina's full moon didn't provide much warmth to the sublunar landscape. Their enjoyment of the nighttime symphony of swamp-dwelling creatures was disturbed by the sound of someone walking toward them.

The darkness of the outdoors and the fog rolling in made it nearly impossible to see the owner of the footsteps the veltas heard advancing toward them. Were it not for the torch he carried, the onlookers wouldn't have been able to recognize him at all. The wooden planks rattled with every step, getting louder as their visitor came closer, until Rokior's visage emerged through the shadows of obscurity. He carried with him, reclined against his shoulder, the long recurve Rozha had seen at his house the day before. On his back, a quiver of arrows were tied to a sash -- he had apparently completed a whole set of new ones during the day, evidenced by the tired, howbeit determined expression he wore. Dressed for war, he was clad in a boiled leather cuirass -- the only armor he allowed for himself besides a fresh slathering in the remnants of the Mire Fiend's last victims.

"Prepare self, friends," the warrior said, handing them what was left of the gel, within the waterskin he stored it in. "This only protection against demoness' power."

Once again, Rozha declined to inquire about the substance's origins, and Kyrana again refused to put any on herself, saying, "With the tactic I wished to use, I should not require this greasy bane."

Gathering their steeds awaiting at the edge of town, Kyrana was prepared to prove the effectiveness of her strategy. Even though she couldn't see the moon's fullness in the sky, she could still see the redness of its glow upon the trees and the waters below. The priestess could feel the warmth of the goddess smiling upon her, causing the Branch of Life to glow with Her holy energies. She too, felt a springtide of confidence that she would not fail; she had prayed for her success throughout the day, requesting Sanguina's wisdom for the task at hand.

While Kyrana and Rozha rode their striders through Virluti's waters, Rokior settled for traveling on foot beside them, his legs accustomed to the muddy traps beneath the stagnant murk. It was a night brighter than the one before, when Rozha and Kyrana first visited Mordax. Even the Safiric creatures of the night had sense enough to remain hidden; indeed, the melodies of the deeper wilderness were thus quieter as the priestesses pressed onward.

They knew they were getting close to the realm of the Mire Fiend when these sounds began to fade entirely behind them; the once friendly fog began turning hatefully green with the demoness' putridity. It was Rozha's cue to raise her facemask, as it was Kyrana's and Rokior's to down their tinvath potion to prevent asphyxiation. Even with the protection of their gear and special tonics, their eyes still burned from the acidic clouds wafting around them. Heschel and Vanix became recalcitrant to go any farther, and it was there that Rozha and Kyrana had to abandon them to continue. They'd know where their steeds were, this time, for both were given a guidance charm that would allow their owners to find them.

Unlike the last time they set foot in the Mire Fiend's lair, the further they went in, the warmer and thicker the waters became, until the ponds were almost sludge-like and bubbled like hot tar. As safe patches of land were becoming more scarce, avoiding these boiling pits of a drowning death became more difficult, forcing Rozha and Rokior to climb the trees while Kyrana stayed behind, so that she could fygidia to one or the other once they had already forged a safe path ahead.

But their creative progress was soon stopped by the legendary barrier of slime that Ghanius had spoken of. It resembled a thick spider web of greenish yellow gunge, hanging between every tree around the clearing before them. Although their surroundings had changed much in the short time they had been away, Rozha and Kyrana could recognize, through the nearly opaque curtain, the place they had first encountered the Mire Fiend.

"This must be where she has hidden herself," Kyrana surmised. "When I cast this banishment spell, it is where she will remain for all time, never to harm anyone again." Staring at the impressive, intimidating wall, Kyrana momentarily had an inward minutia of doubt. *'I just hope I can do it...'* With a mighty strike of her magic staff into the sodden earth, she raised her hands above its twisted branches until the small rubies dangling from each one shone brightly in Sanguina's moonlight. The Arch Healer concentrated, then recited a phrase in the ancient belhuayn tongue.

A shining symbol appeared at her feet, resembling a hexagon and a triangle merged together, with her standing in the center of the vertices. From this sigil's striations, cracks of light formed a translucent wall around her, causing her body to glow a pale white. The Branch of Life began to rise from the ground of its own accord, levitating over Kyrana's head, when from the fractured Sanrisma fruits on its limbs it fired threadlike rays into the Mire Fiend's barrier, filling the large wall with a red hue.

Rozha and Rokior were shocked by the power they were witnessing. It was unlike anything the blade dancer had ever seen being used by any member of the clergy in all the time she had resided at Sachelvae. Certainly the faculty glossed over much of the details when they told stories of their faithful exploits. The anemic recountings of Mother Diava's adventures did events like this no justice. Rokior was truly in awe; he gazed at his bow as if considering breaking it upon his knee right then and there. But before the ritual could be finished, his trained ears turned in the direction of a sudden splash breaking the stillness behind them. His whole body froze with fear when he saw the Mire Fiend's eyes rising from the waters. He took a step back and wasn't even able to bring his weapon to bear as he shakily warned his friends of the demoness' approach.

The radiant Kyrana could not stop the preparation of her powerful spell in enough time; the acidic darts that the Mire Fiend slung from her slimy arm burned holes into her backside, taking the unprotected Healer to the ground.

An off-guard Rozha faced the towering monster and was blinded by a ball of slime hurled into her eyes. The terrible burning of the flesh-melting gunge had the blade dancer shrieking and falling onto her back, trying to crawl toward the refuge of the Arch Healer. Rokior struggled to pull an arrow back along the string of his bow as he fearfully stepped back.

He ducked under a tendril of slime that the Mire Fiend extended from her hand like a whip, lashing against the tree beside him; the acidic splash split its trunk in half and crashed down before him in a cacophony of creaking bark and shattering leaves. He used the fallen trunk as cover when he shot an arrow through its branches for the Mire Fiend's chest, but it never made its mark.

The demoness, with agility unparalleled to anything in nature, swatted the arrow out of the air, breaking it like a twig against her forearm, as she came charging forth in a single, solid motion. She loosed a gurgling cry as she cleared the distance between them with a single bound, leaping over the tree and landing on Rokior feet first, taking the Laeyudi to the ground.

She gnawed through his bow as he raised it to keep her teeth from crunching his skull, her acidic saliva dripping on the warrior's face before he threw a punch into her cheekbone. Even as strong as he was, the force of the blow was barely enough to make the Mire Fiend flinch; her eyes flashed with anger as they returned their glare upon him, and affixed her hand around his neck, expecting him to be decapitated by her slime.

But the grease he wore on his skin allowed him to survive what would have spelled instant death for those without his protection. Out of frustration for her surviving adversary, the Mire Fiend raked her claws across his face with a spiteful slash and a hateful screech, right before a recovered Rozha came to her partner's defense with a bladed uppercut for the monster's jaw.

Now the Red Dancer had earned herself the Mire Fiend's wrath. Before she could exact vengeance on her foe, Rokior gave Rozha another opening to strike by sending a punch into the demoness' unprotected gut. The Mire Fiend doubled over for Rozha to lash her tail into the side of her head, knocking the monster off her downed prey -- but not for long.

As Rozha pursued with a stomp of her spiked heel, the Mire Fiend rolled out of the way toward the trees to her right. But as she was attempting to climb them, she found herself stopped by an expertly placed "Masalida" by Kyrana, deflecting the monster back to Rozha's feet. The enraged blade dancer kicked the demoness to the ground and now was on top of her to send her sharp blows of her fist and bladed forearm. These two strikes were all that the Mire Fiend allowed before she retaliated with a breath of acidic steam right into Rozha's face, blinding the dancer once again before she wrapped her in a cocoon of flesh-eating gunge. Rozha was only able to escape by Kyrana's assistance, when she was fygidia'd from her trap and brought to the Healer's resuscitating embrace.

This left Rokior with the opportunity he needed to grab another arrow out of his quiver. Even though he was bereft of an apparatus with which to fire it, he still had the means of using it as a weapon. Wielding the arrow like a small spear, he charged and came face to face with the devilish creature, threatening to plunge its demon-slaying tip through her sternum.

But the Mire Fiend wasn't going to let him get that close. She spun around to trip him up with her tail, and in the same spiraling move, caught him by the arm to sling him to the ground. Before she could tear the lower mandible from his skull, Kyrana halted her with an astapsyxi, enabling Rokior to fight back against his frozen foe.

The demoness broke free of her Sanguinic vice just after Rokior had delivered a few sucker punches to push her off of him. But he wasn't back on his feet for long; as soon as the Mire Fiend was able to move again, she cornered the warrior up against a tree and tied his hands to the trunk with a slimy coil that would have eaten through unguarded wrists. When she felt him vainly struggling, she gave him a toothy grin and made an almost cackle-like sound as her long tongue unrolled from her mouth.

Paying no mind to her adversaries still standing by, the Mire Fiend was unexpectedly brought to a knee when Rozha swept a leg at her shin, then with the same leg, sent a spiked knee into the demoness' chin. The spike didn't even puncture the monster's flesh, but the force of the strike had her falling on her bottom, cuing Rozha to slap her face with her tail to cut her the rest of the way down.

Like a contortionist, the Mire Fiend performed a sickeningly limber, backward somersault, allowing her to return to her feet before Rozha could stomp her abdomen. With an interesting semblance of practiced technique, the demoness bent Rozha's body over her knee as she thrust it into her midsection, then sunk her claws into the blade dancer's neck -- one second away from ripping out her esophagus, had it not been for another of Kyrana's astapsyxies.

Rozha took this opportunity to remove her neck from the Mire Fiend's hand at her own discretion, and capitalized on the opening she was given to entangle her tail around the monster's legs as she gave her opponent a headbutt, sending the stiffened demoness to the ground.

The Mire Fiend used the slickness of her skin to push herself against the muddy grass, leaving a slimy trail behind her, as she slid toward the safety of the trees. She tossed a sticky coil up to one of the branches above her and used its springy tension to hoist herself back up. But in the time it took for her to do so, Rozha had already cornered her again, pinning the Mire Fiend against the tree trunk. The demoness grinned, as if her opponent should have known better for coming so close. But before Rozha could be taught a lesson, she surprised the demoness with a tinvath-steeped dagger aimed straight for her throat. The shocked monster gagged, spitting up acid as she choked on the blade dancer's rigid steel, buried up to its handle in her neck.

"Rokior!" Rozha turned to her entangled comrade. "Where's the fire?!"

The warrior didn't want to tell his friend that he dropped his torch when the Mire Fiend attacked him. His eyes desperately scanned the ground, looking for any signs of fire near the tree he was nearly buried under before he saw the smoke from his torch. He broke the slimy cuffs keeping his wrists bound and made haste to secure what was left of the dying flame from the soggy soil, before relaying it to Rozha.

By the time the wooden stump was in her hand, what was left of its flame was barely more than burning embers. The Red Dancer refocused her attention on the Mire Fiend to see that the knife she had stuck in her throat had fully disappeared. Instead of laying her eyes on an unconscious demoness, the evil creature was very much still alive, albeit struggling on her breath.

She coughed and gagged, her esophagus flexing as if something were crawling within, until through the acid frothing at her mouth, she expelled the dagger from her body. Shortly thereafter, the slimy film on her skin seeping into the puncture wound across her neck began to close the laceration right before Rozha's eyes.

Rozha and Rokior were shocked at the Mire Fiend's seeming immortality, but that had no comparison to when they heard the demoness making words with her damaged vocal chords. "Staaahhp…" came a long, growling vowel, extended by exhaustion as she rested against the tree. A guarded Rozha almost felt like backing away from her, but not without a good excuse. "Why should we let you live?!"

"I buiiiild wall, keep hunterrrr out," The Mire Fiend slowly breathed, her head tipped back. "Daughter… went missing. I attack Laeeeyudi… no find her. Nnneed her back… cannot leave without."

"You did all this for your child?" Rozha exchanged looks with Rokior and Kyrana, who had tried to stay out of the action as much as possible until now. It was only then that the Arch Healer decided to properly join her friends around the dangerous demoness. "Why should we trust you?" The nurse sternly asked.

"You are seen as evil to the Laeyudi," Rozha added.

"Laaaeeeyudi… untrusting," The Mire Fiend snarled. "Very… stupid, too." Her eyes moved to the warrior, staring at him from their corners as she loosed a painful laugh, having not forgotten the taste of Laeyudi bones. "They not knowwww… what I am. They like aaaall lander: murderous… of what sssscare them."

"Landers?" Rozha repeated the unfamiliar term, then familiarizing herself with the aquatic features of her adversary -- the Mire Fiend's gills and fin-like appendages. "Where are *you* from, then?"

"I haaiiil... from darkest depths," The Mire Fiend's head returned to an upright position. "We come... from abyss. My name... Viunnatha."

"Abyssal belhuayns?" Kyrana unknowingly coined the name. "Why are you here?"

"To rrrraise my young," Viunnatha replied. "Ourrr home... too dannngerous to rear child. I brrrring her here, where safer... to nurture." As the abyssal's emotions were being soothed by conversing, her company noticed that the globs of slime falling off her form did not scorch the dirt where they landed. It seemed she could control the acidity of her secretions to some extent.

"You created these ponds to protect her?" Kyrana guessed.

"Yeeess," Viunnatha gravelly hissed. "Sheeee eat what fall in water. She eat *anything*, not know what is," she darkly cackled.

Though Kyrana was clearly disgusted, she couldn't side with Rokior who only wished the Mire Fiend and all things related to her to die. "I kill you both now!!" The warrior aggressively exclaimed. But before he could take Rozha's torch to finish the job, Kyrana stopped him with an astapsyxi.

"No, Rokior!" The Arch Healer quickly reprimanded him. "We will settle this without bloodshed."

Viunnatha gave all three of them a suspicious, sideways scowl. "Whyyyy I trust *you*?" She interjected. "Thisss is second time... you hunt me."

"You can trust me a lot more than you can the likes of Rokior and his tribe," Rozha sneered. "If I were truly hateful of you and your kind, I would not have been listening to your excuses to let you live."

The Mire Fiend laughed, seeing the logic in her reasoning. "Yeeesss... mercy is weakness of Pure. You *can* kill me, but you nnnno want to."

"We came here to settle this matter my way," Kyrana narrowed her eyes at her more violent counterparts, "the way Sanguina would have intended."

"Sanguinnnna...?" The Mire Fiend incredulously repeated, as if the name were oddly familiar to her. She then curiously gazed at the moon, now in full view through the large clearing. "Weee of the Old Faith call her 'Blood Mother.' That is whyyyy you here... to purge me -- to make me... one of you."

"Purification?" Kyrana clarified with her own proficiency.

"Centuries ago," Viunnatha explained, "Priestess start Purify child of Bone Father. Theeey remove... what make them strong. We call weakness... Purity. This why Pures... pestilence to our race."

"I've never heard of this," Kyrana defensively retorted at the aged abyssal. Although, her history lesson inspired wonderment in the priestess. "What is this special quality you say we lack?"

"Wild Spirit... is what it called," Viunnatha said. "Iiiit make us strong... and give us want to kill. They who not have Wild Spirit... are Pures. My daughterrr... one of them. This why she not survive... alone."

Admittedly, Rozha was unused to hearing about a Wild parent being so caring about their Pure children. As awful as the Mire Fiend was, with the horrible reputation she had made for herself, she was still a much better parent than either of hers. "How long were you keeping her here?" Was her roundabout way of asking her daughter's age.

"Fifffteen yeeear," the abyssal replied. "Child with Wild Spirit survive alone... at fourteen year old. Child without... take longer. That why... even nowww... she still too weak. I havvve raised... thirrtyyy children, each one to different mate. Onlyyy motherrr raise young; male only breed with female. Male not care what happen to offspring after."

Rozha scoffed with a quiet snort as she crossed her arms. She was beginning to wonder i her own parents had adopted the abyssal family praxis. "You don't raise families?"

"Rarrrrely," Viunnatha began, "wwweee form community underwater or in oceannn cave. We solitary, innndependent hunter; not need neighborhood like lander do. Biggest community of abyssal is Origin Depths."

The way she said it sounded almost like an accented corruption of 'ocean,' but Kyrana knew that's not what she heard. "What is this place you speak of?" the Arch Healer inquired.

"Mmyyy birthplace," Viunnatha proudly lifted her head. "Iiiit what left of... Holy Land, wherrrre Bone Father and Blood Mother ruled together." As if she suspected that her audience may have had a different name for the territory she described -- if they were aware of the ancient lore at all. "Aaaafter Hellfire Fall, onllly water breathers livvve. Aaall life on land gone... for long time. Nnnno sun for many year. Wwwwe adapt to dark. We thrrrrive at bottom of world..." She took a dramatic pause before continuing. "Wwwwe come to surface... after first generation. Wwwwe see the night... and find the moons. Bone Father and Blood Mother lllleave the world. Bone Father no come back, unless all Pures destroyed. Blood Mother no come back, unless all Wilds destroyed."

Chapter 35: The Slimy Sylph

"Mother Diava said where they're going is an underground base in the Black Swamp," Kasra palavered to Brynita, during their short journey to the pantry. "Even if we tried to follow them, with as far of a head start as they've gotten on us, we'd have no way of knowing where they were going."

"I've tailed them to their hideouts, before, outside of town," Brynita proudly stated. "There's a cave located deep in a swamp a few miles from the walls. I've only ever seen its entrance, but I've watched monks walking in and out of there when the day is late."

"Sneaking out to spy on the Brotherhood?" Kasra smirked. "You're a lot more mischievous than you look, priestess!"

A flattered Brynita purred. "Well, how else do you think I know all the stories I tell? I don't just make them up -- I've seen them all, myself! Once you're no longer a novitiate, you're not as deep under Mother Diava's radar. There's a lot you can get away with when you learn how things operate around here -- you just have to know when the faculty's back is turned."

Kasra's eyes inspirationally glistened, as she facetiously summoned her inner Raia. "Wow, you're *terrible*!" Her comment elicited the laughter of them both.

Getting back on task, Brynita said, "After we pinch some leftovers from the pantry, I'll get you a communication ring so we can keep in contact, in case we get separated. Once we're all packed, we'll head out posthaste!"

"Won't we have to be *quiet* about it?" Kasra whispered, reminding Brynita not to raise her voice. "If anyone hears us sneaking out, we'll be in big trouble!"

"They'll punish us?" Brynita sputtered her lips. "For what? Trying to be heroes while they all stayed inside? Who are *they* to take pity on us when *we're* the ones taking the initiative to do what's right?"

Kasra swallowed, as suddenly her heart's ambitions seemed to be getting ahead of her body's capabilities. "Are we really prepared for this?" she started second guessing their mission. "We don't even know what's waiting for us inside that cave. If it turns out to be bigger than we thought, we could be in serious trouble."

"This priestess stuff is risky business," Brynita waggled a finger, "in case no one ever told you. Sometimes, you can't wait on Mother Diava to tell you what to do. It often behooves you to follow your instincts and take the initiative to do what's right. Even if the High Priestess doesn't reward your valor, Sanguina will. *She's* the only one you really need to answer to."

The provisions for their outing collected, Brynita took Kasra to the daunting, iron doors sealed by Diava's powerful magic.

As much sense as what Brynita told her had made, the estranged Kasra only hung her head, lacking the personal experience to give her any motivation. "What if I've never felt the Goddess calling me to action?"

Brynita laughed at the violette's naivete. "Oh, you poor thing -- if *only* it were that clear! Just because we take a vow, say our prayers, and bathe in the Purifier, doesn't mean we're in direct contact with Sanguina Herself."

Her voice softened. "It shouldn't come as any surprise that, being what you are, you haven't received any guidance from the Higher Powers."

She looked over her shoulder to see the perplexed, howbeit inquisitive gawk from the teenage vixy. "Do you still not know what you are by now, kid? Have they really been keeping you in the dark that long? It's not a big secret: there was an old legend passed down by the most pious among us for generations. They saw the coming of a time when our warring religions would anger the gods. They would seek to end our conflict with the birth of a hero -- a champion -- who would have the powers of both gods, but the protections of neither. Someone who, by merely *choosing* the side they were on, could change the world for better or worse, however they saw fit. The gods called their champion... *the Vytameta*."

The speechlessly stunned Kasra felt her whole body break out in chills. "And you're it," Brynita continued, as if she needed to convince her further. "If you have not proven it enough to yourself, I will show you how you can."

"This spell cannot be undone but by the caster, herself," Brynita dramatically expounded. "Or so you've been told. But I've seen Layna do so much as simply push open these doors before. Once you're really strong in Sanguina's ways, and have a firm grasp of the goddess' might, you don't even need to say the word to use the power it's named after. If you've never heard it be said, you'd have no idea how to use it. The sacred word is *Arcignum.*"

"If you know the word," Kasra asked, "why can't you disable the spell?"

"It can only be undone by its caster, or someone equal to the caster's power," Brynita explained. "Mother Diava already knows Layna could do it. Now I want to see you try."

Kasra faced down the iron portal standing before her, watching the water-like shimmer coating its surface. She placed a hand on either door, causing a rippling effect to appear around her wrists. She closed her eyes and tensed herself to shove, at the same time uttering, *"Arcignum."*

As if the spell was never established, the large doors slowly creaked open without the seal ever being broken. Every noise their old hinges made echoed through the silent gathering hall. Kasra hesitated, fretfully scanning behind her for any signs of awakened life.

The shimmering lens of the Arcignum spell still coated the tall, metal slabs, but did not prevent neither her nor Brynita from leaving the temple. Kasra finally locked eyes with her mentor's proud visage staring back at her. Kasra's heart sped, the blood pounding in her ears. *'I am the Vytameta? No, impossible! She had been a homeless girl on the street; she had been thrashed about by life itself and spat into a world she didn't belong in.'*

'Maybe that was it...maybe that's what the Vytameta was -- a soul spat into the world without goals, only one purpose. According to Brynita, the Vytameta could save the world. Change it. Fix it. She'd never have to hear of another child going hungry on the streets again. She could end the war. She was the catalyst for a better life for all belhuayns.'

'But...how? She didn't know how to do anything! Not really...'

Kasra's eyes drank in the spell she had just surpassed with a small smile. *'Maybe I don't need to know anything...just do it...'*

She turned glistening eyes to Brynita who beamed back at her, all the hopes in the world in her one starry gaze. "You ready for your first assignment, hero?"

With their meager supplies ready and organized, the intrepid duo started on their way out of Sachelvae. The cool air of the foreboding night saturated their gowns, causing them to shiver.

Up in the center of the sky, the waning gibbous sphere of Safiro's moon could be seen shedding its light of misfortune upon the city rooftops. The strong winds were the only source of sound in the otherwise quiet desolation. Torchlights flickered and lanterns were blown askew from the signs and overhangs under which they were hung.

Certainly a spooky evening such as this was not the proper time to be out and about. Kasra already was looking back in the direction of safety, but she had already come this far.

To make matters even more difficult, they had to make the journey without the assistance of a light source. A torch or lantern would only make them easy prey for the Safiric Brotherhood. Without a steed to ease their travels, they had to make the whole jaunt on foot, which didn't seem too terrible of an idea until they found themselves starting to get tired, after having barely just left Tresantia's city gates. The outer lying wilderness was still nearly three miles away, down the grassy hill upon which the city stood. Getting back home would prove to be a more arduous pursuit than getting to their destination in the first place.

At the city gates, Brynita could see a very faint glimmer of light coming from her guidance charm. The pinkish glow could hardly penetrate the thin layer of fog surrounding both her and Kasra. "Raia and Platina aren't very far," the priestess said, looking to the distant entrance to the Black Swamp. "We can still catch up with them if we hurry."

By the time they reached the bottom of Tresantia's hill, Brynita seemed to have an uncanny sense of direction in the fog's near-total blindness. Kasra found herself following her guide very closely through the sloshing waters of ever increasing depth. She suddenly hated herself for wearing her robe, which was now half soaked and dragging behind her in the unseen murk.

Brynita was beginning to regret not having searched for taller boots she could wear as she plodded through the mossy, knee-deep water below Tresantia's hill. The slippers she wore underneath her mantamina were made more for keeping cool in the summer time and were far from waterproof. She couldn't wait until they reached a patch of dry land on which she could take off her footwear and ring out her socks. The grimace on her face said it all for her with every mud-sloshing stomp through the dark waters.

The winds seemed to grow colder the further away they traveled from Tresantia. By the time they reached the first trees of the Black Swamp, Kasra was unable to keep her hands off her elbows as she rubbed them up and down her arms. *'If we're not being attacked by any Brotherhood spooks, then we're not in any real danger,'* she coolly thought. Looking up at the tops of the trees, ever rising in height with shrinking proximity, she confidently smirked and said aloud to her friend, "I don't see what's so frightening about this Black Swamp place. I'll bet those rumors were spread only to keep the faint of heart from finding some valuable treasure down there."

"Wishful thinking, for sure," Brynita scoffed. "That's a pretty bold statement for someone who hasn't even been inside the forest, yet."

It had already been a couple hours since they left Tresantia. Midnight was upon them; Safiro shed His lunar light to cast a warning glow upon the Goddess-forsaken territory. But as the travelers progressed through the first and youngest trees of the Black Swamp, the flickering stars began disappearing one by one, until even the blue radiance of Safiro's moon was choked out by the shaded leaves of the canopy. Once inside the fabled lands of secret, Safiric activity, the weary travelers were greeted by the first sights of land they had since they entered the wetlands. It was the first opportunity Kasra and Brynita had to sit and rest their tired feet. It had become so dark by then, that the only indication the adventurers had that there was ground under their feet was the crunching noise the dead foliage made under their shoes.

What they hoped would be a tranquil sit down was constantly interrupted by spine-crawling skitters across their legs or buzzing wings flying over their heads, causing them to frenetically swat away whatever nasty insect was threatening to hide in their hair or nibble on their ears. Sometimes they could hear these invisible pests coming when the leaves would shift, or when the bark of the trees around them would be scratched by tiny claws. The only illumination to be seen in the blackness between the tree trunks were the coming-and-going wisps of light created by bioluminescent bugs, flying up and fading like embers off the forest floor.

The travelers shared their rations, but they weren't the only ones having a bite to eat at that time of night. When Brynita decided she'd had enough of being made a meal out of by pesky parasites creating itchy welts on her skin, she sealed up the bag she brought with her and urged her comrade to continue on their way. She only wished it was tiredness, or maybe simply standing up too fast, that caused her to see what looked like a bluish blur vanish in the distance. From the corner of her eye, it appeared like the top half of a person's shadow, walking from behind one tree, and disappearing behind the next. While the nocturnal music of the Black Swamp's creatures was indeed loud to belhuayn ears, she was certain she nor her friend noticed any footsteps beyond where they were standing. She would have loved to have confided in the thought that it was just her imagination, but being the respectable leader that she was, she had to play it safe and ask, anyway. "Did you see anything, just then?"

Kasra gave their surroundings a curious once-over as she stood up alongside her, but caught no sight of Brynita's potential stalker. "What do you mean?" the violette tilted her head. "Do you think you spotted a Brotherhood goon?"

"I don't know," Brynita felt a cold bead of sweat trickle down her brow. "I guess not."

With a coy smirk, Kasra jabbed a finger into the green-haired velta's shoulder. "You're not gonna tell me you're getting scared, are you?"

"Heh, *no!*" Brynita bristled at the mere mention of weakness. While it was true that she had been to the Black Swamp before, she had forgotten to mention that her previous visits were done in broad daylight. Now that she was getting a glimpse of what the Black Swamp was like under the cover of darkness, she was starting to believe more and more the legends of its hauntings. *'I hate ghosts,'* she shivered. *'The Brotherhood spooks only live once, but even if they die, they don't go away.'*

Nothing in the immediate vicinity sparked their interest for further investigation; they continued trudging onward to find what they were looking for. Safiro's blue glow on all the verdant vegetation filled them with an ominous sensation, like dark clouds about to deliver a storm. Everything in its sublunar radiance was awash with danger --

Kasra's head turned toward the sound of a splash. In the dark, stagnant waters full of logs and foliage flotsam, she saw the evidence of motion stirring ripples throughout the round pool. It was much darker the further on they went, even though the spaces between the trees grew wider. The land was also less scarce; it was getting more difficult to avoid the waist-deep water.

She and Brynita both were frightened by the presence of unknown creatures swimming near the dissipating shores. They could feel other such slithering beasts trying to rise up underneath their feet. As they stayed true to their course, wondering where Raia and Platina could have gotten to by now, the adventuring duo could have sworn that they saw a ball of ghostly light rising up like an ember from a flame, just in the darkness between a pair of trees.

Brynita heard a creaking of timber above her. She looked up, and saw a rustling of leaves -- as if something had jumped from the branch she was about to see. Now she knew they were being watched. But by what? Brynita suddenly stopped and gestured for Kasra to halt behind her, the back of her hand accidentally bumping against the vixy's nose. "Wait, I just heard something."

Kasra took a moment to listen, but was too busy panicking from her own illusional fears that she couldn't possibly focus on what both of them thought they were hearing. "What is it?"

"It sounded like a twig snapping," was the best way Brynita could describe it. "You didn't hear that?" A confused Kasra shook her head, prompting her friend to look upward again. "Come on out, you Brotherhood *bastard*!" Brynita cried. "If you're looking for a fight, you've *got* one!"

Brynita's challenge was answered by a girlish giggle, resounding everywhere and nowhere in the darkness above her. A sudden, chilly zephyr shivered the leaves on every tree, causing them to curl and brown. She and

Kasra heard behind them what sounded like tree bark creaking, as if it were being peeled off the trunk. They quickly spun and took a step back. Descending like a marionette hanging by its strings was a teenage vixy of light blue skin and leaf-like hair, attached to a web of thin, yellowish slime. She was scantily clad in clothes hewn from moss, vines, and ferns. Her oily skin secreted a thin mucus, dripping off the flukes of her long tail, her large, fin-like ears, and white, webbed fingers.

"You talk funny…" The girl mischievously grinned, her amber-colored eyes glimmering in the dark. Her ties of slime severed with an unheard snap, almost like spider silk, when her toes touched the muddy ground. The amphibious life form crept a bit closer to her visitors, but kept her distance when she saw Brynita's aggressive poise. "Who you be?" She inquisitively craned her head; her melodic voice was carried through the wind and inspired skin to crawl.

Kasra tipped an ear and offered her a softened smile. She didn't see the stranger as frightening at all -- in fact, she thought she was rather endearing. "My name is Kasra Jantica. I came from Tresantia -- the great city on a hill," she pointed southward.

"And I am Brynita Plendor," her not-so-nice acquaintance introduced herself next. Though she was more tempted to say 'what' first, she settled for a more polite, "*Who* are you?"

The slimy creature dripped mucus off her fingertips as she crept just a bit closer, her long tail writhing behind her. A golden light emanated from the angler tentacle sprouting from her forehead, revealing her face in a dim glow. "My name Morvenia," she breathed. "You want be friends?"

Brynita exchanged looks with Kasra, undoubtedly dubious as to this uneducated stranger's intentions. But Kasra was not in the least concerned with malice of any sort coming from this outwardly innocent vixy. The violette even took the initiative to close the gap between them, which instead of inciting Morvenia to attack her, actually had the much smaller sylph recoiling somewhat. "Yeah, I'd be happy to be your friend!" Kasra bravely extended a hand toward her.

Morvenia covered her mouth to contain an excited gasp; suddenly, a weak, cold wind blew behind her visitors, as if echoing her voice. "We friends now!" She purred, hesitantly accepting Kasra's hand with a cold, slimy palm. "I not make many friends here," she batted her large eyes. "They think I like my mom, but I no eat anyone."

"Your mother... *eats* people?" Kasra slowly withdrew her fingers from Morvenia's slippery grasp. She tried not to be rude and resisted the urge to fling the gunk now coating her hand.

"Hunters think my mom bad, but she only protect me," the young abyssal's ears wilted to her back. "She no let me leave home, but I bored of staying in pool. She no like that I Pure; she think I weak. I run away to prove her wrong."

Kasra's brow worriedly furrowed. "You don't think she's out there looking for you?"

"I no want her find me," Morvenia shook her head. "Momma *scary* when angry! I no want go back home to her. But... it lonely here. I want leave forest, but I scared of people. I no meet anyone nice as you. You my first friend."

Kasra sympathetically pursed her lips at the vague mirror of her former self and softly cooed, "If you don't like it here, why not let me take you to Tresantia? You'd have a wonderful time at Sachelvae, where Pures like you are protected."

Brynita couldn't believe what she was hearing and pulled Kasra aside to rethink the deal she was making. "You cannot possibly be considering letting a monster like this into the sacred city!" she hissed under breath. "Imagine what Mother Diava would say! Pure or not, she would not be accepted by the local population."

"But she claims to be just as belhuayn as any of us are," Kasra tersely argued, rolling her shoulder away from Brynita's grasp. "Certainly you can understand that, if Morvenia is truly a Pure, then you'd need to rescue her as a favor for your fellow child of Sanguina."

Morvenia stopped shifting her focus between the two priestesses deciding her fate at this point in the conversation. "You no need rescue me! I *strong* vixy --" she flexed an arm. "I live out here all by self!" With an inquisitive drip of a tilted ear, the slimy sylph added, "Say... why *you* two here?"

Exchanging another look with Brynita, this time Kasra deferred to her friend to do the talking. "We are on a sacred mission to stop a plot of the Safiric Brotherhood. We know they have established a stronghold here and are about to cause... trouble for us."

"Safiry... Bother... hood?" Morvenia's eyes nearly crossed as she tried her hardest to sound out the multi-syllabic name.

Even if she'd never heard of them, Brynita was willing to bet that someone who traipsed around the Black Swamp every night would have had to have spotted them, before. "Yeah, they're really creepy guys who go around wearing indigo robes," the priestess pulled at her own gown.

"Hmm…" Morvenia crossed a finger to her chin, thinking hard enough to perspire another couple of drips from her skin. "I *have* seen Botherhood!" she snapped her fingers with a squidgy sound. "Last night, I see them take black-dressed velta through woods and down into scary cave." Before Kasra and Brynita could begin to speculate on the identity of the victim in question, the sylph reached another excited epiphany. "Oh! Before I met you, I see a red-dressed velta with younger vixy come through here. They wear clothes like you!"

Brynita gaped, losing the capacity to speak for a second before finally stuttering, "Y-You wouldn't have happened to see where they went, did you?"

"Ummm," came another prolonged, mental blank from their private eye. "No, I sorry… I no follow them far. You look for them?"

"Yeah, they shouldn't have been out here by themselves," Brynita sternly replied. "They should've been heading in the same direction we are. Morvenia," she started, the utterance of her acquaintance's name causing the sylph's ears to lift. "You said that you've been to this cave, before?"

"Mmhm," Morvenia confidently nodded. "I know exactly where is. But I no go in. I hear bad noises from cave."

Kasra took her turn to convince their new friend to assist them. "If you help us look for it, we'll protect you. We can never have too many brave, strong vixies on our side!"

Morvenia's yellow-tinted cheeks puckered under her glistening eyes. "You say my words~" she purred in a sing-song voice. "I excite for adventure! I follow you wherever you go!" The slimy sylph faithfully held Kasra's hand.

Brynita continued to stay alert, her walking speed a little more careful than it had been before. She tried everything she could to keep herself on dry land and avoid walking in the water as much as possible. Something about the stillness of the Black Swamp made her feel like she was being watched from every corner; if she made too much noise, something would try to sneak up on them. "Tread soft and careful," Morvenia admonished her travel mates, "and stay close. The cave is just a hole in ground. If you no watch your step, you fall in."

The tension of their fears grew stronger as the size of the unknown became larger. Visibility was cut down to barely three feet in any direction. Not even the lights of Tresantia could be seen in the distance. There was nothing to be seen. The groaning tree branches above made it seem as if someone or something were stalking them. In the winds squeezing through the swamp, the adventurers thought they heard voices, like whispers being carried in the breeze.

Brynita cast a pool of soft illumination around her allies so she could see where they were going as Morvenia took point, looking for any creatures or traps that could have been hidden in the leaves blanketing the forest floor. The bright contrast of Brynita's light was enough to ward most creatures from entering their safe zone, but was abhorrent to Morvenia as well, who decided to climb the trees where she'd have a more familiar vantage point of the cave they were trying to locate.

"I usually see entrance from afar," the sylph explained. "Is easy to see from high up."

Some time into their travels, Kasra had almost forgotten that her friend was no longer walking by her side. The abyssal's pace was normally so sneaky, it was hard to tell where she was most of the time.

Morvenia had no fear of the darkness; instead, being unseen endowed her with an empowering sensation. It was a kind of bravery she did not have in any other situation. Her abyssal instincts encouraged her to scout ahead and begin foraging off the weaker denizens of the dark. It made her proud to feel like a real 'Mire Fiend' when she could sneak up on something and give it the scare of its life.

Her spine-crawling giggle could be heard in a cold zephyr, causing leaves to fall from the ends of their branches. Even though Kasra had heard it before, it still made her hesitate and pause for thought. Brynita stopped to take twenty; her nerves were tested by the orb of light she held in her hand like a torch, casting long shadows against the trees around them. The first warning she had was a cool drizzle matting down her hair. Her face twisted with disgust as she felt a clear thread of sallow ooze trickle down her forehead, alongside the bridge of her nose. She gazed upward. A glowing pair of ambers and rows of silver teeth fell directly on top of her, putting her to the ground with a surprised shriek.

Kasra immediately turned to her accosted ally, preparing to attack the creature with everything she had. The light could hardly reach their eyes fast enough to give Morvenia her saving grace. The effervescent swamp vixy had pinned Brynita under her knees, her long tail flicking slime to and fro as it wagged behind her. "I got you~!" the slimy sylph laughed. "You so scared!"

A koptigma fizzled out from Kasra's palm as she relievedly eased up with a slump and a sigh.

"You idiot!" Brynita exclaimed. "We could have killed you! And for what? A childish prank…" she used a glowing hand to brush off Morvenia's offensive secretions.

"Why did you do that?" Kasra incredulously eyed the guilty sylph, rising up to let Brynita to her feet. "Have you forgotten the seriousness of our undertaking?"

Morvenia mocked Brynita's behavior by charading her poise and brushing dirt off her imaginary dress. "She start it…" whispered the petulant vixy.

"I don't care who started *what*," Kasra's ears twitched with a hint of impatience. "We're all in this *together,* and it's time we started acting like *teammates.* Agreed?" She waited for Morvenia to submissively nod, but Brynita, even if she agreed, wouldn't show it.

Almost immediately thereafter, the 'fearless' leader felt a tight grasp on her ankle; a pallid, half-rotten hand reached up from the water's edge, threatening to pull her in with it. Losing her balance, she staggered back and screamed with terror as she suddenly disappeared from sight. Her voice seemed to echo, as if through a long tunnel directly underground.

"Brynita!" Kasra called to her friend, but couldn't find where she had gone. She and Morvenia glanced all around the forest in a chaotic whirling, until their quickly moving eyes glanced into the empty sockets of a ghostly face suddenly looming over them. With the shove of an icy hand, they found themselves falling down the slippery esophagus of a cave. They slid for what could have been over twenty feet down a steep angle before coming to rest against a dazzled Brynita, sitting in the dark.

With a terrified screech, the curled-up velta blindly lashed out with punches and kicks toward her unseen friends lying on top of her, striking Kasra multiple times before the violette could slap sense into her. "Cut that out, it's us!" she held Brynita down until the panicked priestess stopped squirming against her.

"Don't go bumping into me like that!" the green-haired velta cried. What looked like tears could barely be seen in the darkness, glistening in her eyes. "I thought I was going to die!"

"Fine time to grow a conscience!" Kasra shot back. "*Now* you're worried about dying?"

"Something dead-looking grabbed me!" Brynita argued.

"Yeah, and now we're stuck here because you freaked out," Kasra huffed a warm breath into the cold air, rubbing her hands up and down her arms. "And we don't even know if this cave is the one we were looking for."

Morvenia forged on ahead of them, her feet leaving small puddles of goo with every step she took on the ribbed, rocky floor. The echoing drips of her slime leaving her skin accompanied the rhythm of water falling from the stalactites hanging from the ceiling. The sylph discovered a curious light source around a bend further down the narrow passage. The angler light on her forehead glowed with intrigue. "Hey, I find something! Come and see!"

Surprised that she would have been capable of identifying anything in near-absolute darkness was interesting enough to cease their squabbling. Brynita and Kasra both joined up with Morvenia where the cave's trail dog-legged to the left and indeed saw a cyan light, albeit faint, flickering like a torch at the end of the hall. The cave's path widened to a circular opening full of tall, luminescent mushrooms on the floor and the walls.

"This must be how the Safiric monks were able to stay here for extended periods of time," Brynita surmised.

"Where are they now, I wonder..." Kasra worriedly scanned the area, taking a few steps ahead. "You don't think they'd come here tonight, do you?"

Brynita was trying not to think about their likelihood of getting jumped, especially in a confined space where running away was not a possibility. "It shouldn't take us long to get what we need. We'll be out before anyone even knows we were here."

Almost immediately after she said that, both she and Kasra jumped slightly to the sudden sound of Morvenia's loud sneeze. The cavern vibrated from the high-pitched noise as Kasra and Brynita spun to see liquid dripping from Morvenia's steepled hands covering her face. "I allergic to *gloegus,*" she squeaked.

Brynita narrowed her eyes and sighed at a sheepish Kasra, as if to say 'you just *had* to bring her along.' "We'd better get a move on, then," she said instead, "before we run into any more issues."

A few paces further on, they saw a shimmering tapestry hanging over a half-open doorway -- an alcove in the wall as the path narrowed again. They stopped to listen for activity, nervous now that they realized how much noise they had been making. What they first mistook for the wind outside was quite apparently coming from a mysterious source of its own within the cave's halls. The whispering they heard in the forest was much more pronounced, but all the same unintelligible. The voices seemed to have been guiding them to the room ahead.

"I'll bet they booby-trapped this chamber," Brynita suggested with a whisper. They couldn't be scared into turning back, even with the fear they'd be running into a nest of the Safiric Brotherhood.

With suspenseful steps forward, they approached the oddly flowing tapestry and prepared themselves before Brynita brazenly pulled it from the doorway. Kasra's heart jumped in her throat, but Morvenia's reaction was a much more audible gasp. The slimy sylph shifted back as if ready to bolt rather than stand and fight, but thankfully for her and the teammates she was so intent on leaving behind, the small hideout was empty besides the vases and urns along the rocky walls.

An armoire was left open to show its dusty interior full of old spear-like weapons and what appeared to be fire pokers. Another tapestry was placed on the floor like a throw rug, but the dirt and dust clouding its blue-hued imagery was a fair indication that this room had been vacant for some time. The smell of smoke from a fire place still lingered in the chamber, likely from the ashes permeating the ceiling.

"Someone live here, for while," was Morvenia's expert observation.

"What were they doing in a place like this?" Kasra asked the more intellectually bracing question.

"I don't know enough about this stuff to say for sure," Brynita started, taking a step inside the room, "but whatever they left behind is ours for the taking." Her eyes glittered at all the possible loot.

"Brynita, should we really be thinking about that?" Kasra reached out a cautious hand. "Stealing someone's belongings was not what we came here to do."

"Can I not make it worth my while?" Brynita snapped at her over her shoulder. "I'm the leader of this party; I can do what I want. You wouldn't even know this cave existed had I not brought you here."

Kasra and Morvenia were still hesitant about looting any belongings of the Safiric Brotherhood. Kasra knew if anyone were to come back to this dwelling that their items would have been tampered with. Unfortunately for Brynita, nothing of value were in any of the pots she checked. "Damn, not a single divitia," she disappointedly sighed, returning to her anxious friends impatiently standing in the doorway.

"Well, gee," came an unusual amount of derision from Kasra. "Who would have thought that no one would just stash their cash in a place they'd never come back to?"

Before Brynita could give the smart-mouthed vixy a piece of her mind, she was distracted by a sudden move Morvenia made, when the sylph turned her head in the direction of a noise she heard. "Someone coming..." she whispered.

"What?" Brynita disbelievingly came forward, trying to hear whatever Morvenia was listening to. In the distant depths of the darkening cavern, the triad of explorers could hear something stomping, echoing to the chambers above.

"It doesn't sound like a person," Kasra started, "or even a living thing. It sounds more like... running water?"

The three adventurers continued on down the path, further away from the glowing mushrooms until they reached a funnel-like opening in the narrow passage, like a doorway into a much larger space. They could hear faint voices, emanating from the vast room up ahead. The closer they came to the open corridor, the colder the air became. The curious whispers began to resemble much more like mischievous cackles of the deceased.

"Kasra," Brynita's beckoning voice caught the distracted violette off guard. "Do you see that, up ahead?"

After removing her gaze from the soundless space of her thoughts, Kasra was surprised she hadn't noticed it sooner. Standing just forty feet ahead of them was a great, granite arch built into the cave wall. The thirteen foot archway was lit by a row of blue torches -- a calling card as obvious as any for the Safiric Brotherhood. Their architect had even went through the trouble of engraving a picture of a downturned, ceremonial dagger into its keystone.

It was a bit of an odd touch, Brynita had to admit, as from her personal experience, "the Brotherhood usually denotes their presence with tapestries of Wild eyes or blue moons." Indeed, labeling their purpose in such a way was telling for their mission. "They must've been planning this for a while." Curiously brushing away some overgrowth that had begun splitting one of the tightly-hewn stones forming the base of the arch, she wondered, "Why would they only start now?"

Chapter 36: Calming the Waters

At this point in their discussion with the Mire Fiend, Kyrana's and Rokior's tinvath potions and anti-corrosion gels were beginning to wear off. Upon the subsiding effects of their protective ointments, the noxious air of Mordax Swamp began to elicit burning sensations on every uncovered portion of skin. Even Rozha's specialized stealth suit was losing its buffer from the acidic mists.

"We should probably get going soon," the Red Dancer said to her company. "I doubt we'll be able to last much longer here. We need to return to our steeds, as well; I don't trust that nothing would have tried to attack them in our absence."

"We will not leave until I have done what I have set out to do," Kyrana replied, bringing her Branch of Life closer to her chest. "I promised Ghanius that I would ensure there would be no future attacks on their village."

Viunnatha couldn't help smirking at Rokior as the warrior flashed her an untrusting scowl. "Hooowwww you do that…?" the old abyssal smugly cocked her head, threads of gunge hanging from the corners of her ears. "Yooouuuu expect treatyyy?"

"I had another idea in mind," Kyrana narrowed her eyes, "before you waylaid my plan of action. I was about to cast *Iterniam*," she looked to Sanguina's full moon, hanging above the clearing. "It's a spell that can only be used by a wielder of a Branch of Life, in the light of the Goddess. It ensures that any Safiric evil trapped in its consecrated area can never leave it."

"Yooouuu would be… *fool* to try," Viunnatha frowned, holding her elbows with webbed hands. "Yooourrr spell break… upon first face of Bone Father. You no have Ssssaanrisma," she pointed to the magic staff Kyrana held. "Cannot use… fuuuulll magic, without it."

Kyrana was taken aback with silence at the Mire Fiend's surprising breadth of knowledge regarding Sanguinic powers. She was only moderately embarrassed that she didn't know better the facts that Viunnatha was educating her with; she only had recently acquired her Branch of Life after all.

Now that the abyssal had put her Sanguinic rival in her place with her superior wisdom, she made an ultimatum of her own. "Yooouuu want me promise… peace with Laeyudi?" Seeing how she curled her lip and snarled just at the sound of her own words didn't bode well for her enemies' chances. "Theeennn, you come with me. I llliiive in cave, short distance... from here." Without giving them a chance to discuss it, the Mire Fiend went to her round pool of acidic water and disappeared beneath its rippling surface.

After she was gone, Rozha and her friends could hear Viunnatha's voice whispering to them from the wind: *"Norrrttthhh... through treessss..."* Her succinct directions were not easy to decipher, but left her guests with no choice but to follow them to the best of their ability. Through the trees of the clearing they were standing in, the group arrived into another, seemingly identical spot of land. The pool they found in the center momentarily frothed with bubbles and shimmered, as if someone had exhaled into its depths. With that, the adventuring party heard their next directive: *"Turrrrnnn west..."*

The simple heeding of this request brought the eyes of Rozha's team to bear on a very distinct, almost wedge-shaped opening in the foliage separating this clearing from the next, allowing them to see, through a curtain of vines and hanging moss, a space of untrimmed grasses unlike anywhere else in Mordax. These prickly, bluish blades seemed to have adapted to the acidic environment and secreted their own version of abyssal slime, like a natural shielding from the corrosive elements.

Rozha experimentally brushed her fingers along the knee-high stalks to sample their clear extract. "These are tinvath grasses..." she mused with intrigue. "This is the first time I've ever seen them in the wild. I was told by my mother, when she was training me to be a blade dancer, that they only grow in the deadliest places in Onteval.

"You mean your trainer was aware of areas like this?" Kyrana gestured to the forest all around them.

"If what Viunnatha said about coming here to rear her child was true," Rozha started, "then others of her kind have probably constructed hideouts like this all over the world." Another thing the astute blade dancer noticed was that the burning mists were not as intense in this small pocket of natural growth. She surmised it must've had something to do with the fact it was missing an acid pool, unlike the rest of the swamp.

"Innnn heeerrre..." Viunnatha's whispered voice guided the eyes of her followers to the entrance of a small cave, as the curtain of moss drew back by phantom hands to unveil its dark interior.

"I have to admit," Rozha thought out loud, as she and her team made their uncertain approach, "the small, flowering vines going through the rocks here are a nice touch." She gestured to the green lattice of multicolored blossoms framing the mouth of the den.

Both Kyrana and Rokior looked at their friend, neither one able to believe what the Red Dancer just said in such a shaky situation. Rozha paid them no mind, leaving them to continue exchanging incredulous glances at each other, as she continued on inside. The darkness of the room lifted as soon as the shade was upon her eyes.

There was probably thirty feet of space between the doorway and the back of the vaguely peanut-shaped chamber. At the end where Rozha stood, the floors were comprised of smooth, gray slabs of natural stone. Large stalagmites looked like they had been eroded into earthen tuffets and stools. On table-like rocks, glowing mushrooms took the form of lamps, providing Viunnatha's den with its only sources of light.

"I never would have taken Viunnatha for a decorator," an impressed Kyrana wound her tail around her waist, admiring the Mire Fiend's personal lair. She was pleasantly surprised and equally relieved that she could breathe normally in this cave, without fear of her throat being corroded by acid gas.

The soles of Rozha's boots clopped with a nearly dizzying reverberation; sounds bounced off the craggy stone walls with no effort. *'I'm worried my thoughts might have an echo in here,'* the Red Dancer risked her theory by inwardly commenting.

At the back of the room, Rozha could see blue lights of bioluminescent lichen casting a soft glow to fill a crystalline pool. Along the edges of the pool were halves of barrels, that looked like they had been forcibly broken into to get after whatever food they once stored. Now they took the role of ornamentation as they were left to gather mold from the humidity. But they certainly were not empty. Instead, they were filled to the brim with gold, silver, and copper specie of divitia.

A certain, avaricious blade dancer could have very well salivated at the glistening hoards of coins framing the back edge of Viunnatha's pool. She never imagined that riches of these kinds would have been hiding in the depths of the deadly Mordax Swamp. Now that she knew, she was willing to bet that many Laeyudi expeditions were not meant to hunt the Mire Fiend as much as they were after her cash. No doubt these treasures were taken from traveling merchants and other victims that the Mire Fiend had killed in her 15 years of residence there.

Rokior seemed the most silent and the least comfortable of any of his friends, staring at every corner of the chamber with disdain. Doubtlessly, all he could think of was the horrible deaths his friends and fellow Laeyudi suffered at the hands of the Mire Fiend. Now he was deeper in the Demoness' territory than any of them ever had been. His pounding heart was like the rallying call of a drumbeat in his ears. The spiritual energy of his tattoos burned on his skin; his greatest chance to avenge their deaths was upon him. He must have been daydreaming of taking Viunnatha's treasure for himself as proof of having slain the monster that had plagued his people since some of his earliest memories.

As if able to sense his Wild desires leaking through his unspoken emotions, Kyrana turned to the seething Rokior, squinting at his thin pupils as they glared with intensity to the pool -- expecting Viunnatha to rise from its calm waters. "Rokior," the Arch Healer snapped his attention to her. "Please don't do anything rash when our hostess comes." Kyrana threateningly twirled the sparkling energies of an astapsxyi around her fingers.

It was odd that Viunnatha wasn't already waiting for them inside her house. Rozha and her team would have assumed that she would have been way ahead of them by now. Just before they could think about making themselves at home and sampling the Mire Fiend's furniture pieces, their spines were stiffened by the Demoness' voice rasping at them from the doorway.

"Yooouuu... eennnjoy my hospitalityyy?" Viunnatha showed her guests an unsettling grin as her long fingernails curled around the arch-shaped jamb. Her slimy tail slithered along the wall beside her as she leisurely made her way to the depths of her den, where she sat on a stone recliner of sorts. Resting her elbow on an armrest, she crossed a leg over her knee and splashed her webbed toes in the water. She motioned a hand for her guests to find their own seats nearby.

While Rozha and Kyrana had no measure of difficulty answering the Mire Fiend's simple request, Rokior's knees bent like rusty iron, as if it was against every fiber of his being to relax rather than take immediate vengeance. He glared at the treasures that Viunnatha had accumulated in the back of her chamber, his stomach souring as he imagined all the lives that had to have been taken to have accrued such an amount of loot. He could recognize some tribal necklaces and bracelets that would have been worn by some proud Laeyudi warriors. He subconsciously clutched his own necklace of fangs, taken from the creatures of the rivers.

The small gems of Kyrana's magic staff glistened in response to the Safiric activity emanating from Rokior's anger. She turned her attention to the seething Laeyudi, whose eyes took an extra moment than normal to catch her forewarning glare. His transparent emotions had him looking like a caged animal. His tail slapped into and curled around his seat as his fingers dug restlessly into his knees.

His unspoken aggression didn't escape Viunnatha unnoticed, who revelled in his apparent anguish. She mockingly fanned herself with a webbed hand, as if she could feel his temperature rising. "Sommmething the matter, warrrrior maaaann?"

Following the Mire Fiend's narrowed eyes to where they rested on Rokior, Rozha too could feel the tension now permeating the room. She quirked a brow at Viunnatha, knowing something needed to be said to distract from the anxiety being fueled by everyone's unbearable coexistence.

"You said before that you were a worshiper of the Old Faith," was the mollifying question that Rozha finally asked.

Viunnatha turned a wry grin to the voice of reason; droplets of her skin's slimy film splashed with a quiet echo on the smooth floor. "Yeeesss… I was once Hiiiigh Priestess… of Bone Father. Fiiive huuunndred years ago…" She took a breath for a dramatic pause, expecting her audience to be surprised by this fact. While Viunnatha might've seemed elderly from a glance, Rozha nor Kyrana would have pegged her for a day above 60, much less centuries more than that.

The Mire Fiend continued, "My grrrandparents told me… the fall of Great Civilization. It was therrrre… that Old Faith firrrst practiiiiced…" Every time she exhaled, a wisp of acidic steam floated from her mouth. "Children of Blood Motherrr… born to raise many offsprinnng. Love and fertilityyy… paramount to Blood Mother's faith. Children of Bone Fatherrr… born to facilitate peeeaaaceful death. Reeecccycling of spirits… paramount to Bone Father's faith. Nooowww… New Faith depart from… oooollld principles. Newww worshipers of Bone Father… proud of kill. They becommme… soldier, just to murrrder with Bone Father's power."

She frowned, turning her head to the side with a tilting ear. "New Blood Mother faith… *choooosssyy* about each gennneration. Child must be 'Puuurre;' that is, grannnted 'blessing' by High Priestess. This not how it worrrk before; aaaall child born 'Pure --' no child need 'blessing.'"

This was certainly news to Kyrana, who before now had never questioned the tenets of her faith, as taught to her by Mother Diava. But apparently, "this New Faith did not start with the current owner of Sachelvae. It must have started much earlier than that."

"Yeeess…" Viunnatha confidently smiled. "Foouur hundred years ago."

Rozha's eyes widened, but Kyrana didn't want to believe it. "With the beginning of Tresantia?" the Red Dancer guessed.

Viunnatha confirmed with a slow nod. She leisurely readjusted her sitting position on her stone recliner. "Tresantia make... Mysssstic Rrrresonance. Resonance change... many things. Newww Faith no want returrrrn... to way things werrre. Theeeyy want Bone Father... or Blood Mother; onnne or otherrrr, not both." She exhaled again, with a tone of mild frustration. "Ouuurrr world... need cycle. Caaannnnot function... with onnne idealll."

This was starting to sound familiar to both Rozha and Kyrana. "So you know the legend of the Vytameta, as well?" the Arch Healer asked.

Once again, Viunnatha gave her affirmation. "Forrr thouuusand years... it prophesied. I was heeere... whennn Vytameta was borrrn. I was carrryying daughter," she pointed indicatively to her stomach, "whennn I sawww... both moons. I knewww... I would meet Vytammmeta sooonnn..."

Rozha and Kyrana glanced at each other, before returning their eyes to their hostess. "We have been preparing for the Vytameta's advent for some time," Kyrana began to say, before she was interrupted by Viunnatha's interposing hand.

"Runnnn and hiiiide..." was the spine-chilling warning the aged abyssal gave, "forrr 'advent' spell dooommm of New Faith." Her lips curled into a smirk that relished the starstruck expressions on her guest's faces. "Ifff... Bone Fatherrr's Champion... has her way."

The fact that she knew enough about the Vytameta to assign it a gender was reason enough to earn even more of Kyrana's full intrigue. "Her? What do you know about the Vytameta?"

"Theyyy are twinnnss..." Viunnatha explained. "Sisters: onnnne heal... onnnne destroy. Onnne value peace... onnne value vengeance. Theeeyyy are judge... annnd our worrrlld... is courtroom. Weeee... are jury. It ouuurrr onus... to help judge maaake... theirrr decision. It is Vytammmeta... who shall brinnngg... condemnation."

Though the oxygen was very much depleted from the room by this startling augury, Rozha found enough air left to ask another question on the tip of her tongue: "Do you know what the Vytametas look like?"

Viunnatha hummed, a smile forming on her lips as she rested on her elbow. "Theeeyyy are young... like my daughterrr. Theeeyyy not know... their power, yyyeet. But... theyyy come know it, soon. They cannot find power… by themssselves. They need… be 'unlocked' by Blood Motherrr or Bone Fatherrr. But onnnly after… they choose… which deity to serrrve."

"When will that be?" Kyrana implored her, scooting to the edge of her seat. "How long do we have?"

"Sooonnn…" was the concise response Viunnatha gave to both of these concerns. "You nnnooo want be… wherrrre they meet."

Of course, Rozha's next question was naturally, "Where will that be?"

"Wherrre you expect it," came Viunnatha's abnormally cryptic answer. "Youuu knowww them both, after all…"

At this, the Red Dancer swallowed thickly; her brow was suddenly laced with a cold sweat. "I… what?!" A shock was sent through her tail from along her spine. Kyrana, too, was very much enraptured with the same gawk. "How do you know who they are? Or that we know them?!"

Viunnatha gave a nonchalant shrug as if she weren't wearing a giddy grin at the prospect of schooling two priestesses of Sachelvae. "I sssee Vytametas when theyyy leave homesss…I like followww themmm…sssee for ssself what comessss. They both vvvveryy differenttt but alsssso ssssame…" she nodded approvingly, "True ffforcessss of the godssss…"

Kyrana's impatience was reflected by a thump of her staff on the stone floor. "Who are they?" she asked, feeling as though the question shouldn't have needed to be asked.

But Viunnatha this time was uninterested in carrying on any farther. She reclined with a stretch and an unheard yawn, brushing a slimy secretion on her chair. "I grooowww tired; dawwwnnn approaching." She pointed a sharp fingernail to the brightening sky through her cave doorway. "I nnnooo eat much tonight… is hungry. Youuu leave nowww… orrr I make meal of *you*." As quickly as her kindness came, it was just as swift to leave. Viunnatha gave her guests a surly, sideways glance as she rose from her seat, before slipping into the comfortable shallows of her pool.

When the Mire Fiend had disappeared, Rozha, Kyrana, and Rokior decided it would be best if they took the opportunity to do the same. They couldn't leave the same way they came, now that their protective ointments had expired. Thankfully, Viunnatha's den was far away enough from the dangers of her lair to where when they were back outside, they weren't exposed to the corrosive mists. Rokior seemed to know a way to navigate back to Laeyudi Town from where they were, but as soon as they had left Mordax Swamp and were trudging through the familiar dark pools of Virluti Forest, the Laeyudi warrior couldn't stop regretfully looking over his shoulder.

Upon observing this behavior a couple of times, Rozha couldn't help wondering aloud, "You think she's coming for us?"

"No," Rokior replied, "I thinking about turning back."

"Why?" Kyrana asked. "We did what we needed to do there. What rock did we leave unturned?" Her eyes narrowed at the Laeyudi warily, as if she might've already known the next thing he was going to say.

"Treasure," Rokior said, with a gleam in his eye. "You are thief, yes?" He pointed to Rozha. "You help us take gold. Laeyudi Town is poor. If we have such riches, our people prosper greatly."

Somehow, Rozha saw no harm in this very tantalizing prospect. Now that they knew Viunnatha slept during the daytime, and the location of her den, they could come back any time to snatch her stash. "I will agree to this only if I can keep a share of the loot: as much as my pack can carry!"

Kyrana couldn't believe what was being discussed behind her back. She stopped and turned around to face her two comrades with offended aggression. "*Teacher* Rozha," she sternly interrupted their dealings, "you do not think this is most unwise? As a priestess, and much more a member of the faculty, you should be more circumspect when discussing an agreement with a *Wild*-blood." The Arch Prude certainly had not forgotten Rozha's and Rokior's night together.

"What's the big deal?" Rozha spread her arms and swished her tail behind her. "The Mire Fiend just *took* that stuff for herself; she doesn't *use* any of it."

"Listen to how your greed speaks for you!" Kyrana came stepping forth, grasping Rozha by the jaw. Her fingers sunk deeper when the Red Dancer instinctively tried to jerk away; Kyrana held her face from a different angle so she could see more clearly the narrowness of her pupils. "I think a trip to the Purifier might be exactly what you need to refresh your spirit, when we return to Tresantia."

"What are you talking about?" Rozha quirked a testy brow, her tail twitching with aggravation.

"Your ease of temptation is uncharacteristic, even for you," Kyrana squinted an eye as she gave her friend a curious, sidelong leer. "It must have been our battle with Viunnatha that has reduced your Purity," she hummed with concern.

"Yeah, and what about *you?!*" Rozha slapped Kyrana's arm away from her. "How come it is that only *I* am a victim of these transgressions? You fought Viunnatha, too, and before that, we fought Kada'timor! And your 'Purity' has somehow remained unaffected?"

"That is because I battle in the way the Mother intends it be done for her children," Kyrana self-righteously explained. "You use weapons of war and death," she pointed to the scabbard of Rozha's new kris, "like a Wild blood. You murder rather than placate. *That* is why your Purity has been reduced." The two veltas stared at each other with equal anger for a few seconds, neither one budging for the other. Since Rozha had nothing to say in her own defense, Kyrana gave an ultimatum: "If you like it better that way, then you can surrender your guidance charm, your communication ring, your tiara, and your mantamina, because you won't be needing them anymore."

Rozha's breaths became deeper as she fought back a rage that was starting to make her shoulders shiver. Despite her increasing aggression, her fists remained at her sides. "You wanna kick me out that bad, huh?"

"I didn't become an Arch Healer to 'kick people' from Sachelvae," Kyrana bitterly explained. "But if to be a Wild blood is what you want, I'm not going to stop you."

Rozha swallowed, her brow furrowing as her adrenaline was beginning to leave; her skin started feeling colder as she took a moment for honest stock. The last time they had an argument like that, Kyrana was willing to fight for her. Now it looked like she couldn't have cared less whether Rozha stayed or not. "You've given up on me? Just like that?"

"I'm not giving up on anyone," Kyrana's voice was soothed by seeing her friend calming back down. She took another step closer to gently hold Rozha's hand. "I've been at the temple long enough to know when it's in someone's heart to stay or leave. I believe you told me something similar, Teacher Rozha," she smiled, for once using the Red Dancer's formal title in a non-pejorative sense. "It seemed to me that you were proud of being what you are. And if I recall your story correctly, you believe you were sent to Sachelvae for a special purpose. Are you willing to give all that up over acquiring some treasure?"

Rozha's lips guiltily twisted when she followed Kyrana's gesturing arm to a silent Rokior, watching this conversation with an amount of compunction of his own. Her eyes were brought back on her friend when the Arch Healer went on to say, "I may not always know the nicest ways to say what I need to convey, but I only warn you because I care. If I did not, I would have let you to your own devices every time you wanted to go off and do something against Sachelvian conduct. But now that I know how important the temple is to your salvation, I am doing everything I can to ensure you can remain a part of it."

Chapter 37: Threads of Fire

Continuing on inside, they saw that this deeper part of the cave had been refined into a beautiful example of belhuayn masonry. The smooth tiles of whitish gray stone echoed their footsteps as they cautiously walked through the narrow access passageway. The hall was just wide enough for two people to stand abreast between the walls, both of which were covered in colorful hieroglyphics, depicting two very similar scenes. The wall to their left showed a full, blue moon in a sky that was split between day and night.

Directly under the ominous face of Safiro was a belhuayn figure, its arms poised upturned with its fingers raised like claws. Red balls of fire spewed from its hands like fountains, raining like meteorites upon a burning town where terrified villagers ran for their lives. All the villagers, upon closer inspection, had the eyes of Pures. A Safiric cathedral could be seen in the distance in this landscape, perfectly unhindered by this destruction.

The other wall, to their right, mirrored this image with a belhuayn figure floating below a red moon, its hands outstretched and turned down to magnanimously spill forth a fountain of unborn spirits. The town in this savior's midst was prosperous; its buildings were tall, but its people were unhappy. Upon closer inspection, most of the downtrodden people of this town had Safiric eyes. In the shadows of their tall buildings, they could be seen burying their dead. In the distance of this landscape, could be seen the ruins of a Safiric temple. On a higher hill across from it, a Sanguinic cathedral stood proudly, waving a red flag from its steeple.

Neither of these scenes were particularly pleasing, from Kasra's perspective. Instead of choosing which looked better, she found herself wondering which looked worse. While she didn't think a new age of prosperity would've been contemptible, she didn't think all Safiric belhuayns were inherently evil, either.

The young veltas had to watch their step on the wet stone floor as they emerged into the next, huge chamber, lest they slip on its wet surface into the churning river before them. The water was not deep, but it was quickly being pushed through sharp stones jutting from its choppy surface. A large waterfall to their immediate left, probably fifteen feet wide, emanating from an artificial dam comprised of clean tile, was the source of these subterranean rapids.

The flowing water rushed off the side of another cliff to their right, separating the homey stonework from the natural cave. They appeared to be standing on the second of two terraced stairs in this cave: the bottom being where the river was spilling into. Looking over the edge to their right, they could see the surface of the crystalline lake below them. Under the glassy surface, only slightly misted by the fog of the falls, they could see the jagged spears of stalagmites, threatening to impale anyone who might get the idea of jumping in.

Their astute observations could only be made in thanks to the bowls of bonfires lighting the floors, and the shining spider webs hanging from the ceiling like threads of fire. Within this mass of blazing webs, they could see the skeletons of long-dead prisoners.

"I've never seen spiders spin glowing webs," a disturbed Brynita raised an eyebrow.

"How do we cross the river?" a concerned Kasra peered over the running water. "Nobody could swim through that…"

A curious Morvenia stepped up to the challenge, fearlessly leaning her head over the edge of the splashing current as she absently tapped her squidgy fluke on the ground behind her. "Lander no like fast water?" A vaguely condescending purr escaped the abyssal's pursed lips. "I make it safe to cross for you."

Rubbing her palms together in a circular motion, she began conjuring a rope of slime between her hands. She continued extending her sallow tether by continuing to spin it like a jumprope as she kept outstretching her arms. Once her creation had reached a satisfactory length, she lashed her completed rope like a whip at the nearest, flat rock poking out of the river's surface.

With a wet splat, the slime whip connected to the natural stepping stone and formed a makeshift tightrope bridge between it and where Morvenia was standing. The abyssal seemed quite pleased with herself as she posed her arms behind her back and waited to receive the adulation of her impressed audience.

"I have to say," Brynita began, "that was a pretty cool trick. But it's not quite safe enough for one of us to be standing on. In fact, it looks quite dangerous…"

"No judge so fast!" a pouting Morvenia reprimanded her critic. "It not done yet!"

With an energetic leap, the aquatic vixy threw herself into the rapids, leaving Brynita and Kasra on their toes with suspense as they watched her swimming form power through the buffeting current. Morvenia stopped at the flat rock where her bridge had been connected and began stringing another slime rope right next to it, pulling it taut as she swam back to the starting shoreline.

Instead of being exhausted, Morvenia seemed to be rather enjoying herself upon the completion of her task. She grasped the edge near where Brynita was standing and gave her a look as if to say 'so there!' "You test now -- I catch if you fall~" the slimy sylph flicked a spot of gunge onto the uptight priestess' dress. The prankster then ducked into the white water to hide from her victim's wrath.

"Ugh, the *nerve* of that thing!" Brynita disgustedly swatted at the mess on her clothing, leaving a very entertained Kasra to laugh at her expense.

"Well since you don't seem to trust our new friend," Kasra straightened herself out, "I'll lead the way." The violette started with a somewhat timorous touch of her toes on the sticky web to see if it would hold her weight. Once she had a single foot down, she moved her second foot to join in. Having steadied her balance, she turned back to her Brynita and nonchalantly spread her arms wide. "Seems sturdy enough!" she shouted over the roaring surf.

Her excessive confidence getting the better of her far too soon, she quickened her pace when traversing the second step, which was about the same distance as the first, and tried to keep this pace on the third step, which was much further away than either. Brynita was right behind her the second she saw her slip when she tried jumping from one stone to the other. She was just barely able to reach for the end of Kasra's tail to keep her from being swept away by the current. Kasra was just one foot away from falling into the river; her other leg was precariously left dangling over the splashing waves. Once she realized she had been rescued, she calmed down and eased herself onto the flat rock of the segmented bridge.

"Wow, that was some pretty quick thinking!" Kasra exclaimed. "I owe you one!"

"If I let you die here, who's gonna save the world?" Brynita shrugged with a smile.

"So you still believe in me, huh?" Kasra teased, having not forgotten her friend's sour attitude toward her bringing Morvenia along.

Brynita laughed, "There's a lot about what's going on that I don't fully understand. Who am I to berate you for thinking outside the box?"

During their chatter, Morvenia had completed the other half of her bridge, starting from their midway point and ending at the other side of the river. "Not much farther, priestess friends!" the helpful abyssal pointed to their destination. She made sure to stay close to her creation as she shadowed Kasra and Brynita during their crossing, just in case one of them took a spill into the river. Once all three of them had reached the other side without further complications, they found the room's only exit dead ahead: an arch-shaped doorway closed by a curtain of glowing spiderwebs.

Giving their obstacle a closer look, Brynita said, "If there's supposed to be a sacrifice going on down here, I'll bet anything the Pure we're looking for is being kept beyond this door."

Just the very look of the creepy door made Morvenia shudder. "I no like it. It bright and look like fire." Indeed, the webs radiated a faint warmth; they looked unadvisable to touch. Lacking weapons with which they could cut through the tangled mass, the three adventurers were running short of options.

"Any chance you could push through this, Kasra?" Brynita quickly suggested.

The violette just gave her a look. "I've got a better idea." With a twisting gesticulation of her hands, she prepared a full-strength *koptigma* blast aimed for the barrier of webs blocking their path. The star student's exceptional telekinetic shove was repelled by the unwavering door and was reciprocated back on its user, causing a shocked violette to stagger and almost lose her balance. "Woah, what *is* this stuff?!" She recovered her footing, gaping with disbelief.

"Ahh, it bounce magic, like mother's slime…" hummed an intrigued Morvenia, stroking a webbed hand against her chin. "You no get through easy. Maker of wall was worshiper of Bone Father. That why Blood Mother spell no work."

The abyssal's educated warning came as a bit of a surprise to Kasra, who hadn't expected her to know much about Safiric and Sanguinic magic. "How did you know that, Morvenia?"

The slimy vixy proudly hummed, interlacing her webbed fingers behind her back as she raised her shoulders and thoughtfully tipped her head from side to side. "Momma is old High Priestess of Bone Father. She teach me much thing about both parent god magic. She tell me I child of Blood Mother, so she tell me how use Blood Mother spell by speaking certain word." However, upon telling this interesting fact, Morvenia's eyes lost their luster and began trailing to where the cave floor met the wall. "But… I no good at magic," she bashfully purred. "It no work when I try."

"I'm sure you know something that will break down this spider web," Kasra pointed to the shining barrier before them.

Morvenia's wet feet plapped against the smooth stone as she walked back to stand at Kasra's side. Cradling her chin between her finger and thumb, she sized up the door of burning telae and puffed out her chest, crackling her webbed fingers together as she dramatically prepared her mind. A pleasant aroma wafted from her as she eased her mind. "No can use unless calm," the abyssal loosed a meditative breath. "Okay, here go:" she gesticulated her hands together and pursed her lips as she recalled the magic word, before vociferating it to the best of her ability. *"Koteema!"*

She thrust her hands out as her shout filled and reverberated through the narrow hallway, causing Kasra to jump slightly. But that was it; no great burst of power, no nothing. The spider wall seemed utterly amused at Morvenia's attempt to break it down. Perhaps if she could make it laugh, it would fall apart on its own.

"I, um…" Kasra nervously bit her lip at her friend's aghast expression. "I don't think you're saying the word properly."

"What you mean?!" an offended Morvenia squeaked. "I say 'koteema' good!"

Kasra tipped her head, trying not to show her nervousness through her grimace. "I think the word you're looking for is *'koptigma!'*" The violette showcased the proper pronunciation and the power itself with a stretching of a single arm, causing the rocks around the doorway crack as they were struck by her invisible shock wave.

The Vytameta looked rather impressed with herself as her hair relaxed in the stilling breeze. "Now you try."

Brynita crossed her arms with a puff of air through her nose. "A spell is only as strong as its maker," she gave a judgmental wink to Morvenia, causing the sylph's cheeks to angrily puff. "If we all three try our best *koptigmas* together, we'll *have* to break through!"

Holding her hips with a nod, Kasra saw the sensibility in this plan. "Alright then, I like the sound of this. I'll count to three so we can be ready at the same time."

So on the count of three, the trio of adventurers stood shoulder to shoulder and prepared their full-power *koptigma* spells one more time. On the shout of the sacred word, a great shockwave fulminated from the palms of their hands, causing a wave of distortion to ripple through the air before them. With a thunderous crash, this cone of invisible force struck the barrier with the power of both young priestesses.

Before they could even see the results of their teamwork, they were blown back off their feet by the recoil. The echoes of their activity rumbled throughout the cavern for several seconds, and even caused vibrations strong enough to loosen small stalactites from the ceiling. Amid the rain of falling stones, they lifted their heads and rose to their knees, only to see the undaunted spider barrier before them.

Their collective shock was answered by a slow applause, given by an unseen viewer, that drew their attention to an old altar standing before the waterfall on their immediate left. This large slab of white marble looked to have been there a very long time; it was broken out in mold from the moisture of the air and rivers running around it, and was coated in the same webs as the ones that hung from the ceiling. All around the altar were piles of bones. Not long after they laid their eyes on the structure, an apparition began to form in front of it.

First to appear were the person's aged hands, wearing two rings on both middle fingers. They were attached to sinewy arms of pale blue skin, reminiscent of a long-dead corpse. Tied around the biceps of these arms were heavy chains, attaching the wearer to the altar. Next to appear was the figure's masculine upper body, of which only its shoulders were clothed in long, cloth pauldrons.

Hanging off these fashionable shoulder pads was a long and tattered cape. A hood was tied to the pauldrons using a blue, gem-like clasp. Inside this hood, no face could be discerned until the stranger raised his head into view. His pale face had a stiffly disinterested countenance; his eyes, though no more than white almonds below his brow, showed a distinct jadedness for the world around him. His hands came together one last time when he was in full view; his lips crinkled as if about to speak, but with some unease, as if he might've forgotten how to.

"Visitors," was the first word he said, his voice light and raspy. "It's been a long time since I have had so many guests."

Morvenia was too scared to offer any semblance of a reply; she glanced to her friends on either side of her, who seemed more willing to try a confab with this denizen of the darkness. "Yeah, I guess so!" Brynita crossed her arms, leaning weight on one foot. "Who'd wanna come into a place like this?"

Kasra tried to save the sour first impression that Brynita gave her group with a more friendly question of her own. "Who are you?"

"My name?..." The wraith paused for thought. He tilted his head and turned his blackened eyes toward the ceiling, his mouth left half open as if surprised at himself how difficult it was to answer. "I can faintly recall... yes, my name was Nohvaias. This place has been my tomb so long, no one even knows it is mine, anymore. I have seen three generations of the Brotherhood use this burial ground as a place to deliver sacrificial offerings. I have watched bodies rot to their bones. I have watched stalactites grow. I have watched drips from the ceiling become a waterfall. I have watched rock be eroded by rivers. I have been here a very, *very*... long... time."

"You can't leave this place?" Kasra astutely asked.

The wraith chuckled, lifting his arms to show the clinking shackles to which he was bound. "Such is the punishment of those who displease the Master. I was to be one of the five original slayers of Saint Sevasmia. I was told to spy on her -- to lure her to our ambush site. I was heralded for my ability to control the minds of Pures; the Master had full confidence that I would not fail my mission. And perhaps I wouldn't have... had I not fallen for Sevasmia."

Even after all this time, recalling the one he lost brought sorrow to the dead man's eyes. "She was every bit as legendary as they said... beautiful, too. She knew I was coming to get her, but she showed no fear when she pulled me from my hiding place. She had that... 'forgiveness' that Sanguina had sullied her heart with."

He longingly chuckled at his jocular derision. "She told me about her faith. She converted me to her way of thinking without even berating mine. It felt so nice... how could I not have fallen for her? But the longer I tarried in my mission, the more my cohorts came to remind me of my obligations. They threatened me if I did not bring her to them as I was entrusted. It was never against the Old Faith to love a Pure. But Zercius had been getting interesting ideas about how to revolutionize the faith into something he believed would be more efficient to Safiro's Will. He was starting to go mad with his delusion about recovering the Annihlus; to be the new Chaos God was all that mattered to him."

"He's looking for the Annihlus?" Kasra sounded disbelieving. The only time she'd ever heard of that object was from Raia's Creation Story. "The four fragments were taken by Sanguina's Trusted after the death of the Chaos God, weren't they?"

Nohvaias chuckled at the teenage vixy's naivete. "You obviously do not know the whole story. The information the Sisterhood either lacks or refuses to acknowledge is only made privy to those who have my privilege: being the Keeper of Ancient Knowledge that I am." The priest finished his blustering to continue, "Sanguina's Trusted *did* take the Annihlus and move them to the four corners of the world. They then became the first Emperors of Vitiosa, burying these artifacts deep within their respective tombs in the hopes that concurrent generations would never find them. The tenets of keeping a royal bloodline was made so that the Annihlus' protection would only fall to those who know of its existence and fear its power. However, no Pure is immune to the Father's Will…"

"The Annihlus calls to anyone around it. No amount of ground nor distance can muffle its voice. It *wants* to be wielded; it desires to be recombined. It is the Father's Will in physical form. It was made to imbue its holder with all His Power. And even when fragmented, as it has been, it still has the same strength of temptation. The current Emperors of Vitiosa no doubt have taken its power for themselves. But they are not the rightful owners of the Annihlus; they have no want for its full glory to be remade. It's Lord Zercius who is the rightful heir to the Chaos God's might."

'Rightful heir?' Kasra repeated to herself. *'What does he mean by that?'*

"It is why Lord Zercius places curses on those who fail his mission," Nohvaias' fable finally reached the purpose for its beginning. "He would rather the cycle of Life and Death be broken, if it would mean that he could come one step closer to inheriting his dream of becoming almighty." His face fell as he bowed his head, but not in prayer. "Members of the faith can avoid this punishment if they are strong enough; their spirits will forever be anchored to the place they were killed. The Master killed us all after placing his geas on us, so that we would be forever beholden to his mission."

Nohvaias paused once more, watching the faces of his audience silently begging him to elaborate further. "The Master became obsessed with acquiring the Annihlus -- he told me once that he believed the ruler of the Brotherhood should wield Safiro's weapon. I thought his ramblings that of a naive novice and paid him little heed. I was…distracted. Love had made me a brave fool. I could not refuse to leave her side. I brought her to the most beautiful place I could find… a forest full of life and light, just outside of a secluded cave -- no more than a hole in the ground." The familiar description earned the widened eyes of Kasra and Brynita. "That's when he attacked me…" He scowled, bottled anger built over centuries crawling back up his throat and manifesting as a guttural growl. "Deniechus…"

Seeing his anger for the familiar name sparked a greater hatred of the same man in Kasra's own mind. "They desecrated this land when you and Sevasmia were killed?"

Nohvaias slowly nodded, "into the very place you now call the Black Swamp," he finished for her. He took advantage of his stunned audience's silence to recover from his burgeoning rage. "I am not the only one here.

My brethren litter the surface, forever trapped in the Black Swamp to find something that is not there."

"What is this artifact they cannot find?" came Kasra's next question.

Again, Nohvaias uneasily stared to another corner of the chamber. "For as much suffering as it has caused me, you'd think I could remember, but I cannot. I gave up looking for it centuries ago. I have just remained here, in the purgatory of the mortal world, because I fear what awaits me in the afterlife."

"Hell?" Kasra guessed, but her host only gave a slow shake of his head.

"Worse. They who have sworn to Lord Zercius' oath will have their spirit be used to empower him, if they die before his mission is achieved."

Upon hearing this Safiric servant's plight, Brynita found herself in an emotional quandary. She shouldn't have felt pity on this evil worshiper, but she could see the pain in his recollections. She could see that he was willing to turn, if given the chance to. "Is there no way to rid yourself of this curse?" the green-haired priestess asked him.

Nohvaias despondently slumped and doubtfully shook his head, with a pessimistic sigh, "Alas, there's nothing I can do from my current position... I would need the body of a Safiric blood to transfer my spirit into their physical form. If such a person presented themselves, I could easily rid myself of this place. However, only members of the Safiric Brotherhood have ever come down here. If I took one of their cadavers as my vessel, the Master would find me again. If I could possess a Pure like one of you, I would have my perfect opportunity with the veltas on the other side of that door." He pointed to the stalwart spider webs that the three vixies tried opening, earlier.

At that, both Brynita and Kasra perked up to attention. "You mean," the violette started, "that Platina and Raia are down here, too?"

"Yes," Nohvaias folded his fingers together. "I knew you were looking for them, from the moment you set foot in this cave. That door is sealed with a powerful magic -- it can only be opened with Safiric power." Then, with a gleam in his lifeless countenance, he came to a hopeful realization. "While in the ethereal state you see before you, I cannot interact with the physical world, I can assume the form of the weapon given to me by the Master, when I first became one of his Trusted."

Sheathing himself in a ball of radiance, Nohvaias transformed into a large sword with a beautifully decorated hilt, and a double-edged blade. As it levitated above the altar, a white, fiery glow drifted off its bluish steel. "Now anyone of Safiric blood can share my power."

"What good is that going to do *me*?" Kasra defeatedly threw up her arms with an impatient swish of her tail. "All of us here are Pures."

"Except you," Nohvaias confidently asserted. "Together, Vytameta, *we* can rescue your friends."

The use of the cryptic title that up til now only Brynita had called her had Kasra pausing for thought. "You... know who I am?"

"As astute as I am regarding occult knowledge," Nohvaias began, "would you expect me *not* to? As the Vytameta, you have the freedom to use both Safiric and Sanguinic power at will. All this time, you've only seen one side, correct?" he asked, obviously minding her priestess attire. "You've no doubt been told how taboo the Brotherhood is, but you've never met one of the Old Faith like me. I have sworn off my allegiance to Lord Zercius; it would do me no greater pleasure than to assist in the destruction of what he has created!"

The sword glowed brighter with its decidedly twisted laughter, then suddenly ceased when it caught the funny look on Kasra's face being reflected against its shining surface. "Y-You *will* take me along, won't you? What other option do you have?"

While Kasra was thinking it over, Brynita injected a voice of reason into her decision. "Even if he does seem willing to help us, trusting a member of the Safiric Brotherhood seems a bit unwise. How do we know he didn't put that spell on the door in the first place?"

With another dramatic moment of deliberation, Kasra's determined stare hardened. She could feel her round pupils narrowing closer to Safiric slits. "I trust him. We have no other choice but to." And with that, her mind was made. She grasped the hilt of Nohvaias's sword, completely expecting that the heavy blade would take her to the ground, but was pleasantly surprised to feel how light and balanced it felt in her hand.

"Swing me at the door, and I'll show you what I can do!" Nohvaias excitedly exclaimed.

"I..." the violette nervously gripped the sword's handle, "I've never used a blade like this before."

"Oh, come now, it isn't difficult!" Nohvaias impatiently sighed. "Look, I'll make it easy for you -- I will guide your arms with an expert's finesse! It hasn't been so long that I forgot how to fight."

Kasra nodded before finally answering his request, thrashing the air before her with an unpracticed wave of her arm. Through the Safiric steel, an icy wave of blue energy ripped the stone floor and even parted the river as it shattered to pieces the cobweb curtain blocking their path. Kasra and her friends were amazed and stunned at this destructive and impressive unleashing of power. They were all the more relieved that this priest, at least for now, was on their side.

"It feels incredible, doesn't it?" Nohvaias chuckled. "You priestesses are so naive, you don't know what you're missing out on. *This* is how belhuayns are meant to live."

Chapter 38: The Face of One's Spirit

With Rokior's navigational assistance, Rozha and Kyrana were able to skirt the edges of Mordax Swamp whilst following their guidance charms back to their steeds. Heschel and Vanix looked eager to be reunited with their riders after having spent a nearly sleepless night standing watch from the trees they had been roped to. Admittedly, Rozha nor Kyrana assumed it would have taken that long for them to return, but their 'in and out' missions never were that simple. However, they were still proud of what they accomplished through *almost* non-violent means.

"We have the Mire Fiend's word that she won't attack Laeyudi Town anymore," Kyrana recapped, "now all we need to do is ensure the Laeyudi warriors will uphold their end of the bargain."

"Alright, but we're not leaving until I've gotten my spiritual markings from the Laeyudi seer," Rozha said, climbing into the stirrup of Heschel's saddle. "He told me to wait a day for my appointment. It'll be morning by the time we get back in town, so I want my tats."

As much as Kyrana would have rather rested instead, seeing as how she was awake all day and night to fight and speak with Viunnatha, she wasn't about to leave her friend in an uncertain situation. "Then I'll accompany you."

Even though she and Rozha were both confident that the Red Dancer could have held her own in case a couple of people wanted to take advantage of her, knowing that Kyrana was going to be there made Rozha a lot more comfortable with what she was getting into. "Thanks, Ky." Her smile then turned into a smirk as she prodded the Arch Prude with the tip of her tail. "So long as you promise to behave yourself in front of the 'heathens.'"

Kyrana stifled a chuckle, rocking from side to side as Vanix started moving onward. "We have already had this discussion; you know I am not upset with the decision you made. But you are still getting Purified when we get back to Sachelvae, alright?"

"Fiiine," Rozha facetiously rolled her eyes, making it sound like this deal was more trouble for her than it really was.

She, Rokior, and Kyrana returned to Laeyudi Town near lunch hour -- the brightest time of day in Virluti Forest, when the night time fog had fully cleared and the sun was shining directly above the gaping tree tops. Rozha thought it would be wise to have something to eat before she went to see Graxifen, not knowing how long it might've taken to get her ink done.

Rokior had admonished her that it could take many hours, "at worse," depending on "how big spirit is." It didn't give Rozha a warm and fuzzy. Not to flatter herself, but she decided to err on the side of caution and give herself as much time for preparation as she could. Hopefully she'd still be on the waitlist by the time she and her friends found Graxifen's parlor again.

"You come back," the seer smiled. "Someone else with you. No meet her before."

"Her name is Kyrana," Rozha introduced her friend.

"Arch Healer of Sachelvae," the pink priestess added for herself.

"She here to see her spirit as well?" Graxifen asked.

"She isn't here to partake," Rozha explained, "only to watch."

"Hmm," Graxifen's pale eyes upturned as his face tipped toward the ceiling. "Rokior can be assistant, then."

Rokior nodded, "I do what I can," and found a seat for himself in the corner of the room, near the doorway.

"I feel greater presence from you," Graxifen's attention returned to Rozha. "Yes, you stronger now than before. You grow very fast; it because you have very big spirit. I never draw spirit so big -- it will be honor to make you proud Laeyudi warrior." He reached his hands out to gently feel the contours of the Red Dancer's face. His fingertips tingled at every pressure point; his face gained a look of wonderment as a picture was starting to form in his mind. "I see you..." he breathed, "Many layers. You have many names. You born with favor. You no can see it because it on your back... I want show you."

"Alright," Rozha uncomfortably glanced between him and Kyrana, "but the underwear is staying on, got it?" As vulnerable as it made her feel to disrobe in their presence, even with Kyrana's scrutiny, the redhead unzipped the top portion of her stealth suit and peeled the padded leather to her waist. As Rozha turned her back to Graxifen, she respectfully covered her chest to at least be decent in front of her chaste priestess companion. Meanwhile the Arch Healer sat in a corner to observe Graxifen's work from a distance.

Rozha looked over her shoulder to see the older scelan feeling around his dark surroundings, as he searched for something on a table by the back wall of his house. He collected what appeared to be a menagerie of colored dyes pooled on a thick palette, and a sharp, pen-like instrument.

"Rokior," Graxifen called to his newly appointed assistant, "bring me torch." At that, Rozha's eyes fearfully widened. What would a blind man need a torch for? Rokior, meanwhile, left the house to grab one of the glass lanterns hanging underneath Graxifen's roof and set it down beside him. She opened the lantern's door so that Graxifen would be able to reach the small flame inside. "I never make mistake," he said, "but can never be too sure. I not make spirit scar so big."

"Scar?" Rozha thought aloud.

"It take warrior to not shrink from pain," Graxifen replied. "This make you true Laeyudi."

Rozha worriedly turned her head toward Kyrana, who was now sitting protectively by her side, and began to think that acquiring his body art must've been a rather unpleasant experience.

"You no can move," Graxifen warned. "Not even little bit." Like any self-respecting blade dancer, she wasn't going to say no to a test of strength and steeled her nerves when Graxifen's left hand braced itself against her shoulder blade. It was just to its side that she felt the sharpened bronze pierce her skin -- it felt like a small claw slowly working its way through her flesh. With every tap, Graxifen injected black ink into the stylized wound he was etching into her body. He kept his canvas clean with a moist towel -- no doubt dampened by the less-than-clean swamp water outside.

After what felt like an hour, and a thousand needle pricks later, Graxifen had finished carving the ancient, belhuayn message across Rozha's back. Of course, being illiterate, he couldn't read what it said. Rozha, not understanding ancient text, couldn't translate it either. Rozha's jaws felt sore from having ground her teeth all this time, whilst trying not to make a sound of pain. She only hoped it was still dark enough to where Rokior couldn't see the teardrops that had rolled down her face. "Is it done?" She finally let her breath go.

"First one, yes," Graxifen began washing his implements. "Now I do other side. I saw face under neck," he traced the invisible pattern he saw with his fingers, spanning from shoulder to shoulder just under Rozha's collarbone.

"Really?..." The exhausted blade dancer bit her lip. "Can I let my first one heal before we continue?"

"I no will have inspiration, by then," Graxifen shook his head. "You stay, or you not Laeyudi."

As badly as she wanted to curse at herself, Rozha sucked up her pain once again and turned back around to face him. "Alright," she acceptingly sighed.

Seeing that the Red Dancer was having trouble, Kyrana was impelled to hold her hand. At any other time, for any other undertaking, the violent tomboy would have rebuked such caring behavior. Seeing it come from the

Arch Prude herself, who at first shunned the idea of this 'sinful' body art, made it all the more endearing.

Just like before, Graxifen's technique, howbeit careful and precise, spared his customer no agony from start to finish. Her only hope was that she wouldn't have to see what he needed the lantern for. But weathering the pain was much easier when she could dig her fingers into Rokior's calloused palms; he nary took his eyes off her throughout the process.

When her second design was finished, it resembled a segmented necklace of odd patterns and symbols, bearing some similarity to wisps of smoke drifting off a dead flame, or pieces of clouds detaching from a storm. Her relief was short-lived, for when Graxifen sterilized his instruments in the dirty bowl of swamp water, he said, "Now another," and focused on her face, next. Just imagining what she'd have to suffer made her swallow with fear. Even Rokior seemed worried for her, seeing as how his face was devoid of any stylized scarring.

"Not often I do this," Graxifen muttered, "Maybe first time."

'Oh great,' Rozha squinted her eyes shut, *'This better not be when he needs to cauterize anything...'*

She hadn't made a sound so much as a squeak the entire time for either tattoo she had received, so far. But the ultimate test finally broke her resilience. His pen started just under her left eyebrow, and within a few jabs toward her forehead, she couldn't restrain a short scream. Though she let her sound of pain escape her lungs, she remained steadfast and refused to move; she wanted to see it through. Not to impress either scelan, but to prove she wouldn't back down. The whole side of her face felt like it was on fire after Graxifen was done with his latest, and certainly longest tattoo yet. This shape resembled a star with long, curled spokes, extending as high as her scalp and as low as her chin.

But she'd be lucky if the whole experience were to have ended there. This time, for the artist's next design, he aimed his attention for her sides -- both of them -- and copied the pattern he made on one perfectly on the other. The entangled, root-like markings started just under her arms and worked their way down to her waist, and curved inward toward her navel. Between these roots, extending across her midriff, were markings resembling two bridges of hanging chains. Rozha could have easily forgotten the passage of time through this whole ordeal if it weren't for her growing hunger reminding her how long it had been since her last meal.

'We've been at this for hours,' she inwardly commented. *'And he's still not done. Will I be here all day?...'*

It seemed like every time he was finished with one design, his attention would be drawn to another part of Rozha's body that was not yet in excruciating pain. He gave her upper arms a design that extended to her elbows and resembled a barbed wire double helix. He gave the outside of her thighs a red crescent shape, with its convex side pointing downward. Beneath it, he drew stars, as if to depict Sanguina's moon in the night sky. It was the only tattoo to have a color other than black, and it was the last one he made before speaking again. "I am done. You now see your spirit."

"Thank you, Graxifen," Rozha breathed through gritted teeth, uncertain if she should have been thanking him at this point. She was all the more ready to leave this place after being subjected to this voluntary, spiritual torture. But not before Graxifen did her the favor of generously applying a slimy, clear ointment to her skin that soothed somewhat the burning pain of her tattoos.

"You are now honorary Laeyudi," he continued. "Now all can see your strength."

After the artist was done clothing her in the medicinal goop, Rozha needed Kyrana's help to stand up, so that she could see herself in the polished bronze surface of a mirror hanging beside the doorway to Graxifen's place. Her body art glistened behind the shiny film applied to each ink-laden wound. Though it pained her much just to move a muscle, Rozha's cheeks puckered under her eyes at the beautiful imagery coating her upper body.

She really did feel like she could have blended in with any of the Laeyudi warriors patrolling the streets. She opted not to bring her black stealth suit back up to clothe herself since merely touching the markings carved into her skin would have been very uncomfortable. She was starting to see why walking around half-naked in loincloths would have been preferable to the Laeyudi.

"You have done some amazing work," Rozha looked back to a smiling Graxifen. "Hopefully we will meet again." Albeit not feeling in the least like walking anywhere, she started on her way out.

Before she could leave, Graxifen imparted her with a precautionary statement: "It hurt many days," a mixture of compassion and admiration in his eyes. "No wash for week," he held up a single finger, instructing her on how to care for her new artwork.

"We are needed back at the temple soon," Kyrana reminded her. "I will do what I can to reduce the pain of your body art so that it will not cause an impediment to our travel through Virluti Forest."

Virluti Forest had turned much darker with the waning daylight. With each step, Rozha could feel the tug of pain arcing across her marred skin, as if the needles hadn't quite left their inked wounds. She was getting tired of gritting her teeth, but she pressed onward nonetheless.

"Before we leave," Kyrana said, "we need to report to Ghanius the successes of our mission. We must also warn him to call off any future expeditions to Mordax."

"First, fighter promise she kill demoness," Ghanius scowled, "then healer promise to banish demoness -- neither work! I no trust you anymore! When Mire Fiend return, *we* kill her!"

At this, Kyrana had reached the end of her own rope. She suddenly stood from her chair and slammed both hands on the table between them, causing the elder to frightfully jump back. "You are not listening to me, you old *fool!!*" the Healer shouted him down. "I have given Viunnatha my protection from your savagery, and this is a promise I *will* keep! When I find her missing child, I will make sure you are *Purified* before you *ever* see her!" Kyrana then stormed away from Ghanius, brushing by an equally aghast Rozha now exchanging looks with the silenced elder.

Rozha joined the enraged Healer back outside, where she found her taking a moment to cool down in the humid fog. Kyrana's hands rubbed up and down the long sleeves of her arms as she stood there, shivering -- not from anger, but from the chilly air. Her tail was wrapped around her waist underneath of her dress for extra warmth, but even still her stocking-clad legs shivered as their knees touched together.

It was the most piteous Rozha had ever seen her Healer friend be; it caused the Red Dancer to sympathetically purse her lips as she came toward her, offering the comfort of a single-armed embrace. She managed a little smile when Kyrana's hatefully upturned eyes settled somewhat blankly on hers.

"You gonna be okay?" Rozha rubbed a circle on the pink priestess' back.

"I... I suppose..." Kyrana blinked, unused to seeing such a compassionate look on her companion's face. "I'm sorry," she exhaled, the corner of her lips dipping into an apologetic frown. "I got into an argument with Ghanius, in my best efforts to defend our decision to save Viunnatha from the Laeyudi. The elder is not willing to swear off any more huntings of her. But I fear more for the huntsmen than I do for Viunnatha."

"I don't doubt that Viunnatha can take care of herself," Rozha acknowledged, "but I'm more worried about you. You've been acting strangely ever since you came here."

Once again, the Red Dancer's concerns took Kyrana off guard. "It's just the stress of what's been going on lately," the Healer's ears wilted as she slowly shook her head. "Long gone are the days of 'business as usual.' There's a new crisis every week. Of all the time I've served at Sachelvae, I've never seen anything like it. Things are changing very fast. But to what end?" Her downcast expression hinted that she may already have had a grave answer to her own question.

Chapter 39: Cleansing Evil

The new chamber before them was dimly lit by spiderwebs along the walls, laced with silken sacks. A particularly large web covering a hole in the middle of the floor looked oddly fresh, as if it had been made earlier in the day. At the furthest corner of this web was a small tear, as if something had been caught and tried to break free, before being contained in a fiery cocoon. At the far end of the room, stuck to the walls coated in burning curtains of silken threads, were other such sacks with the heads of their victims exposed. Even from the distance they were standing, Kasra was able to recognize the both of them right away. "It's Raia and Platina!" she cried, readying Nohvaias above her head.

"Don't just go running in there!" the sword shook in Kasra's hands. "This place belongs to a great demon they call 'The Arachniath.' "

Unhearing to his warnings, Kasra swiftly circumnavigated the huge trapdoor web in the center of the large chamber, followed distantly by Morvenia and Brynita. The justified violette was about to tear open the cocoons holding her unconscious friends by compelling Nohvaias' Safiric sundering spell, until she happened to glance up at just the right moment to see three, spindly legs dangling just inches from her face.

They were adorned in orangish red, scar-like stripes that seemed to glow like embers in a fireplace. They were attached to the body of a rather large spider -- its thorax was about the size of Kasra's head. It was suspended in the air by a red hot, silken thread spun on the shadowed ceiling.

Kasra grimaced, Morvenia screamed, and Brynita hardly had the nerve to move before Kasra sent Nohvaias' edge straight through the nasty creature.

With a splash of red blood, the spider's head was split from its thorax and plopped onto the ground. The rest of the large insect swayed on its thread while the last half of its legs trembled and curled inward, causing Kasra's skin to crawl. She blew the creature's corpse away with a koptigma blast, splattering its husk against the stone wall.

"Yuck!" a shivering Morvenia wiped her slimy hands on her thighs. "I no like spider!"

Brynita couldn't help laughing at the abyssal's terror; Kasra breathed a sigh of relief as she relaxed her sword against her shoulder. "Oh please, it wasn't all that bad!"

"I hate to be the bearer of bad news," Nohvaias hesitantly said, "but that wasn't The Arachniath." A spark of light shot up from the base of the sword's blade to the tip, as if pointing for Kasra to look upward.

Kasra's eyes followed the glint of Nohvaias's sword to the ceiling; she and her teammates gasped at what they saw. There in the darkness, they saw a cluster of eight red eyes, like balls of fire. As the monster to which they belonged silently descended upon its prey, its face came into view; its large fangs rubbed hungrily together, resembling a pair of clawed fingers steeped in venom. The pointed tips of its legs reached for the walls across from where Kasra and her team were standing. They watched this giant black spider of crimson, crack-like stripes and bristle-like hair stretch itself out over sixty feet wide.

Morvenia nearly fainted when she and Brynita were immediately thereafter accosted by The Arachniath's spiderlings from above. Each one of the blazing spider's children were large enough to wrap around a person's skull. The first fell right on Morvenia's head from the ceiling; she could feel her hair getting singed as its legs latched around her face. The panicked abyssal ran aimlessly away from her friends, and fell face-first into the web in the center of the room.

A quick-thinking Brynita thrust a hand forth and uttered, *"Koptigma!"* summoning a current of air like a fist-sized bullet to knock away the spider from the back of her friend's head. The Arachniath, upon seeing its child attacked, lurched across its web and grabbed Kasra with two of its front legs to pin the small velta underneath of its body.

Kasra was about to strike the giant spider with a swipe of her blade, but in mid-swing she was interrupted by a warning from Nohvaias: "Careful when attacking this demon," he said. "Its blood is like fire!"

Shortly after making this remark, Kasra's leg was tightly hugged by the hairy arms of one of the Arachniath's lackeys crawling up her shin. She plunged the point of her sword into the spiderling's face, causing its boiling hot blood to burn holes in the wide sleeve of her wardrobe as it nearly split in two.

Seeing what the monster's innards had done to her clothing, Kasra was wise to shield her eyes before taking a swing at the Arachniath's nearest leg. The side of her steel brushed through its exoskeleton and freed its lava-like life force, but it had no greater effect than making her the Arachniath's next target.

Brynita was released from the spider's clutches when it turned on Kasra, who announced *"Astapsyxi!"* freezing the Arachniath's outstretched fangs for just the moment she needed to lop one of them off with her sword. Kasra flinched with a small shriek when its blood sprayed her torso and scorched her unprotected face. She staggered back into the grasp of another spiderling, jumping onto her back with its slender legs wrapped around her sides. It sunk its teeth into either side of her spine, causing her to go rigid with pain as its venom coursed through her veins. With a whip of her tail, she whacked the large vermin into the wall beside her and stabbed it through with her gladius. But she soon thereafter faced more rappelling from the roof, like embers falling from a flame.

Brynita rolled out from underneath the recoiling Arachniath, to find Morvenia vainly struggling against her sticky trap as a horde of spiderlings were bearing down on her. *"Fygidia!"* her voice rang out, instantly calling Morvenia to her side and out of harm's way. The abyssal's oily skin was scarred with a grid of burns from having been caught in the Arachniath's web, but apart from some burns on her arms and face, Morvenia appeared to be little more than shaken over what had just happened.

The two adventurers had no time to recover, for as soon as they had a moment to stand back up, the Arachniath had already turned back around on them. Brynita tossed a koptigma from her hands, piercing The Arachniath's eyes, causing it to pause and stagger. The angered, half-blinded demon thrashed forth its front legs, knocking the priestess down. Before it could sink its one remaining fang into her torso, Morvenia stopped its deathly advances by spitting a gout of acidic slime into its mouth, allowing Kasra to blast it with a crescent wave of power from Nohvaias' blade.

The power of the attack was strong enough to get the giant spider back off her, but hardly long enough for Brynita to return to her feet before it stabbed its teeth at her again. The quickness of its lunge sent Brynita's back to the wall; she found herself pinned once again as its fang sunk into her shoulder, pumping so much poison that the left side of her body turned numb.

The other half felt like it was turning on fire -- all of it was wrapped in excruciating pain that took the priestess to her knees. She was rescued by Morvenia, who lassoed her with a whip of gunge to the safety of her side to stop The Arachniath from envenomating her further. Kasra then lashed a cleaving saber of energy from her Safiric sword to take off a pair of the demon's back legs.

"*That's* what we needed!" Nohvaias cheered her on. "Hack off *all* the ugly beast's legs!"

The Arachniath had a hard time standing upright as it turned to meet its adversary. Its vengeance was taken by one of its spiderlings, which leapt on Kasra's back while she was distracted facing down the giant demon; it wrapped its legs around her sides and sunk its fangs on either side of her spine. Her vision was enclosed by darkness as she watched The Arachniath begin to bear down on her. She could barely maintain her grip on Nohvaias as she crumbled with pain, strength sapped from her muscles by the spider's venom coursing through her veins.

"Get ahold of yourself, kid!" the sword coached her, glowing with excitement. "If you don't fight back, this'll be the end of you!"

Nohvaias endowed her with enough healing vitality to allow his wielder to whack away the smaller spider on her back with her tail. But she nearly fell over as the giant Arachniath bore down on her; Nohvaias commanded her arms to straighten against the demon's advances, using his edge to parry the spider's fang and push it away from her.

"You're doing good, hero!" Nohvaias sounded genuinely proud of the budding Vytameta. "You're not as bad at fighting as I thought you would be, for someone whipped by the Sisterhood. Now I will show you how to use the power of Safiro!"

Through the sword shining brightly in her hands, a strange feeling of pressure was exerted on every inch of Kasra's body, as if she was submerged in ten of feet of water. She could feel her round pupils tighten to slits as she was suddenly awash with a sensation of liberation. An aura of darkness began growing around her like a cloud of black smoke.

Kasra shoved away her giant attacker with a supersonic explosion, stunning The Arachniath as it knocked onto its back. Kasra watched balls of shadow rise from her palms; she waited for the monster to roll back to its remaining feet before she unleashed a storm of diamond-shaped darts from her fingertips right into its eyes. Fire spouted from the orange stripes twisting around its legs and thorax in an effort to defend itself while it stomped about in search of refuge. It blindly found its way back to the web where its prey was held and stood over its victim, as if using its hostage as a shield.

"Yes, *beautiful*!" Nohvaias quivered with excitement. "The Father would be pleased to see what you've become... Set me loose and *I'll* slay the beast!"

Heeding the sword's request, Kasra tossed Nohvaias like a bullet with the assistance of a koptigma burst, driving the point of its blade up to its handle between the eyes of the blind Arachniath. A tower of flame shot up from its back to the ceiling as the monster loosed an agonized cry, its legs curling toward its underside as it fell on its back through the web on which it stood.

The hole it made tore the telae from the edges of the pit, so now the mystery cocoon dangled precariously over the black abyss. The Arachniath itself entered its grave with an echoing crash. A few seconds later, Nohvaias returned to Kasra's hand from the pit, laughing with glee to have performed such a stunt.

"Did you see that?!" the Safiric steel reverberated with his voice. "I've never felt more alive since the day I died! You and I make an excellent team, don't you think? Yes, you should take me along with you for lots of adventures!"

"I'd love that," Kasra said, "but first, I have to free my friends." *"Fygidia!"* she intoned, teleporting the two cocoons keeping the bodies of Platina and Raia before her. Immediately thereafter, the weakened violette collapsed to all fours.

A worried Morvenia held Kasra's shoulder to keep her upright, gripping where the spider had bitten her. "You hurt!" Instead of causing the violette to grit her teeth and groan with pain, the cool slime of the abyssal's hand seeped into her wound to sooth her pain.

"You're quite versatile," Kasra smiled up at her ally. "Thank you again, Morvenia." She hadn't recuperated enough of her strength to open the silk caskets herself, so Morvenia took the initiative to try to free Kasra's friends.

The resourceful abyssal cautiously drizzled acid from her fingertips to gently perforate the coffins in which Platina and Raia were being held, until the thickly-wrapped threads were breaking apart at the seams. The cocoons were slowly undone like the zipper of a jacket, revealing the unconscious, yet relatively unharmed bodies inside. The only wounds they suffered were scathing bite marks; twin holes on their necks and arms from where the Arachniath's minions had no doubt latched onto them.

"Nrrghh," Raia and Platina both sleepily blinked awake, as if having recuperated from a long rest. They were unsurprisingly confused with their surroundings, disbelieving their eyes as the first things they saw was Kasra wielding a Safiric sword and the familiar face of Brynita staring down at them. "Kasra!!" Raia elatedly cried. She winced with pain as she raised her arms out for the violette's embrace; her back twinged like it was being stabbed with a thousand pins and needles.

A smiling Kasra chuckled as she helped Raia into her arms, already feeling her shoulder dampening from the brunette's misty eyes rubbing against the crook of her neck. "I'm so glad you're okay!" the violette's breath was squeezed out of her by her exhausted friend.

"I can't believe I'm alive, either!" Raia exclaimed, finally pulling away from Kasra's comforting hug. "What are you--?" she started babbling. "Where are we?"

Nohvaias' voice echoed within his sword, "We are in the Cave of the Arachniath, friends."

"Who said that?!" Raia's eyes shot all over the room.

"Calm down," Platina placed a soothing hand on her fellow healer's shoulder. "There will be plenty of time to explain all that later."

But Raia was not content with the idea of 'calming down' for anything. Especially not after seeing the crouched Morvenia curiously tilting her head at her, rubbery fluid dripping from her ears. "Wh-Who are you?" Before her question could be answered, the brunette's hair flipped over her shoulder as she glanced back at Kasra. "How long have I been down here?"

"Most of the day," Kasra's lips tightened, her brow furrowing with an awkward frown. She wrapped her tail around the small of Raia's back when it looked like she was going to pass out.

Platina then tried again to ease Raia's worries. "Try not to trouble your mind so much. The most important thing about our situation is that we survived our ordeal."

"You is all injured," Morvenia finally contributed her own words to the conversation. Raia's widened eyes were fixed on the abyssal as she came crawling before her; the brunette instinctively struggled against Kasra and Platina, feeling like she was being held hostage between them. But her concerns were suddenly mollified when Morvenia laid a healing hand on Raia's arm, letting her slick wetness coat the shivering priestess' wounds.

Raia watched with a flabbergasted fish mouth as her bite marks were being sealed within seconds. "You have a healer's touch..." she gasped.

A flattered Morvenia softly purred, giving the now settled Raia a winning smile. "I is very versatile," she winked at Kasra, earning a Rozha-esque tweak of her squidgy ear from the violette.

Quick to ruin the lighthearted mood being generated by the young Pures, Nohvaias spitefully rang, "In case you've all forgotten, we're still stuck here... So getting *out* would be a good first course of action."

Once again, Raia found herself perplexed by the unknown source of the speaker's voice. Kasra finally waggled her blade as if to make Nohvaias wave at her. "This is a new friend of mine," the violette only slightly sounded insane when talking of the inanimate object. "He was a former member of the Brotherhood who helped us rescue you."

"And he's a sword...?" Raia clearly didn't understand.

"Watch your tongue, little Pure!" Nohvaias rattled. "I am an Elite of Lord Zercius -- one of the original members of the Old Faith!"

"What've you been doing down *here* this whole time, then?" Raia raised a brow to test the sword's patience.

"That's none of your business!" Nohvaias shot back. "I will not be interrogated by someone so disrespectful."

While Raia's negotiations were getting the group nowhere fast, Platina was swift to make her own suggestion. "We will achieve nothing by staying here. There's a chance that members of the Brotherhood will be sent here. The best course of action now is to return to Sachelvae."

"Good luck trying that," Nohvaias muttered. "Your fygidia spell might work to leave this cave, but you'll have no chance of using it in the Black Swamp." Suddenly all eyes were on the gleaming sword to hear its sage advice. "The Black Swamp has been enchanted with a labyrinthian spell; any attempt at using a fygidia there will bring you anywhere but where you want to be. You'll have to hoof it back to wherever it is you're from."

The very thought of having to traverse the entire Black Swamp, in addition to the wetlands outside, had all the tired veltas in attendance collapsing to their rears with a collective sigh. They assumed at first that the faint, muffled cries they heard from the Arachniath's pit was merely an echo of their complaints, until their ears perked up to hear the same struggling again.

The young priestesses all clambered across the floor to the edge of the Arachniath's dark grave to see the webs it broke through barely sticking to the slippery wall -- the only thing keeping it and a thrashing cocoon from a perilous drop of death.

They weren't even sure which of them said 'fygidia' first, to bring the mystery prisoner to the safety of the surface. But it didn't take Kasra long thereafter to open the silk encasing with a whisk of Nohvaias' edge. She couldn't have been more shocked to see the exhausted body of Viasarria lying at her feet.

"Hmmnn..." Viasarria groaned. "Great timing... I'm glad there's still some mercy in the world."

With a clenched jaw, Kasra checked her old enemy for wounds, astoundingly enough finding the blade dancer to be completely unharmed even after being trapped for so long in the burning coffin. "What are you doing here?" the violette asked her with a narrowed gaze.

Viasarria looked around at her surrounding company, biting her lip with a soft frown. "I could ask you the same…" Kasra expected there to be malice in her tone, but the green-haired velta's words were punctuated with a sorrowful gratitude that had Kasra pulling back her ears with pity. Viasarria looked the violette up and down. "You...you're Rozha's little sister, right?"

"My name is Kasra," the violette replied, staring daggers into the assassin's eyes.

Viasarria couldn't blame the kid for harboring such ill will and aggression for her, but she knew if Kasra still hated her, she wouldn't have risked her life to save hers. "I know you still see us as enemies after what I did to you and your sister, but rest assured I have nothing against you, Kasra." The green-haired velta took a formal stance and put a fist to her chest. "It would besmirch my honor as a blade dancer if I did not owe my life to you. Please accept my servitude as penance for my actions."

Kasra admittedly was quite taken aback by Viasarria's humble statements. She couldn't imagine anyone who had willingly consorted with her mother would have had an ounce of goodness in them. "I don't want a mercenary," the violette respectfully declined. "But I wouldn't mind letting you be my friend."

"Ughh…" the steel of Nohvaias' blade rang with a metal sigh. "Look, we can all go outside and find a rainbow to skip under later. Right now, we're still neck deep in a spider cave."

Following a perplexed Viasarria's eyes, glaring at her sword and the abyssal standing behind her, Kasra apologetically waved at her rescuee. "Never mind them, it's a long story. Speaking of, how did you get stuck down here, anyway?"

"I was caught by the Safiric Brotherhood," the veteran rogue explained. "They brought me here and left me to die. Four monks ambushed me; I couldn't hold them off. I don't think they realized I had stolen anything because they didn't frisk me when they had tied me up. They were more interested in collecting the bounty they had put on my head."

"How did they find you?" Brynita asked. "You've been able to evade them for years!"

"It was a selfish mistake," the blade dancer replied with a solemn shrug. "I was trespassing in an encampment of theirs on my way through these woods. It was oddly abandoned when I had arrived. I found a message sitting on a table in one of their candle-lit tents." She trailed off, rummaging in a belt pouch for the object in question. "Apparently it was important to them, but I never had a chance to read what it said." She held out a roll of paper and handed it to Kasra for her to unravel.

Kasra was a bit surprised that it would be her honor to read the rogue's prize, but did so anyway with gusto. "These are the days The Master has awaited. These are the times The Father foretold. The Vytameta lives among us; it is ours to decide who it benefits. We live in the era of legends; it is ours to decide how it ends."

"...Sounds like a bunch of mealy-mouthed mumbo jumbo to me," was Viasarria's quick critique of the manuscript. "But all that cryptic guff means something to them, at least."

"It means," came a familiar voice, echoing from the shadows above, "That the Vytameta is crucial to undoing Sanguina's faith."

The dark and raspy sibilance belonged to Deniechus, who floated from the ceiling's darkness like a poltergeist wrapped in fog. He carried his scythe against his shoulder as a free hand held an orb on an iron chain, similar to the ones carried by the Safiric monks the priestesses had seen near Travestas. The four veltas backed away as he came descending toward them. He grinned at their fearful and untrusting deference, not in the least perturbed that he was outnumbered.

"Deniechus..." Kasra lowered her head with a confrontational growl. "You set this as a trap, didn't you?" Her friends were taken aback that she seemed to have history with this creepy stranger.

"I knew she would bring you here," the High Priest confidently exclaimed, looking down at his cowering audience, with special attention to Kasra. "For you, the line is not meant to be walked, but crossed. You can't stand being boxed in. You can't stand authority. While the rest of us are content with our religion, you refuse to be classified... You think that makes it difficult to analyze what you are, yet your identity couldn't be clearer."

It was apparent that no one had any comprehension of what he was conveying. But being understood was obviously not his intention. The monk grinned, "It pains me to see how your talents are being wasted. You are stuck in a pestilent place that seeks to do naught but hide and repress what you truly are... But I am here to save you from the shadows -- to lift the wool pulled over your eyes so that you can see what you were meant to be." Taking it upon himself right then and there to decide who was worthy for whatever cause he was speaking of, he charged toward Kasra with his scythe turned upside down, his feet not even touching the ground.

Raia and Platina cringed, lacking the energy to use their Sanguinic magic. It was up to Kasra's more battle-able comrades to stop Deniechus in his tracks: *"Astapsyxi!"* but their combined powers had absolutely no effect on him this time. He was unimpeded from nearly running Kasra through, had it not been for the use of a silently-summoned shield that was able to stop his momentum before breaking. The sudden cancellation of his attack resulted in a forceful blast of pressure that sent his foes flying back against the walls, and had Kasra falling onto the floor.

"Your powers are useless, so long as I hold this dilitrivanni," Deniechus taunted them. "Sanguina cannot save you now." The Reaper of Travestas raised his scythe with a single hand and swung it down at his grounded target, who was able to roll herself back up to her feet in time to get away from the blade's electric fulmination against the cave's bedrock.

Kasra retaliated with a supersonic whip from Nohvaias' edge, but Deniechus tore through the current of air with a swing of his blade. He could see the Safiric steel angrily undulating with a powerful, smoky glow. "Nohvaias, you miserable fool," the High Priest disappointedly berated his traitor. "Not only would you dare to oppose the Father's Will by refusing the afterlife, but you would pick a fight with your own superior? You have no idea what Lord Zercius has planned! Stay out of the Brotherhood's affairs if you do not wish doom upon yourself!"

"I've been waiting four hundred years to exact my vengeance!" Nohvaias righteously exclaimed. *"I couldn't care less what happens to Safiro's world, so long as the Vytameta kills you all!"*

Deniechus answered the sword's taunt, silently flying forth with his large scythe carried upside down to deliver an upward swing. The massive force of the fast attack had Kasra reeling as she was just barely able to deflect her opponent's blow with the edge of her blade.

In the time it took for him to recover from the flinch she suffered, the High Priest had disappeared. Alerted by Nohvaias quivering in her grasp, she was saved at the last possible instant by her unholy weapon when Deniechus' deathly sickle came falling from above. The weapon spiraled back to its airborne wielder's hand like an angry boomerang, before, with an upward thrust, he threw a giant wave of slashing force. Kasra's sword was knocked from her grip after its blade had absorbed the brunt of the blow; simultaneously, the powerful hero was taken clear off her feet and slid across the cave floor, as if she'd been kicked in the chest by a strider.

"Which ideal do you value more?" Deniechus asked his struggling foe. "Forgiveness or vengeance?" The aged skin around his lips wrinkled as he smirked, watching Kasra grit her teeth as she was sapped of all strength to even rise on all fours.

After her hero had been defeated, Brynita desperately crawled away on her backside to escape Deniechus' wrath. The High Priest shoved Kasra to the floor with an invisible burst of energy before he prepared to slice Brynita into ribbons. The fearful velta panicked and shielded her eyes as she reached out toward him, crying *"Astapsyxi!"*

Suddenly, there was quiet. Brynita risked her safety when she hesitantly lowered her arm from across her face to see that Deniechus' weapon-bearing arm was lassoed back by what appeared to be a yellowish green rope. The confused and startled priest snarled at his unknown attacker over his shoulder, but before he could get a good look, a burning slime was spat upon his face. An angry Morvenia flew with a tremendous leap, latching onto Deniechus with all her limbs as she sank her teeth into his neck.

The blinded priest yowled with agony as he slammed Morvenia's abdomen with an open palm, leaving puncture wounds in her torso as he knocked the growling sylph to the ground. His fingers singed as he scratched at the sticky gunge burning his eyes, but wasn't able to remove it before Morvenia came back for seconds. With a whip of her tail, she took Deniechus off his feet and pinned him down as she bit ravenously at his face.

Deniechus' body burst into a hot blaze of blue fire, setting Morvenia aflame and causing the shrieking abyssal to back off him. The High Priest's marred face was slathered with his own blood, but enough of Morvenia's mucus had been removed to where he could glare with a single eye at his adversary. With a burst of smoke, the prone Deniechus appeared to his feet, his scythe back in hand.

He reeled back for a mighty cleave, and as Morvenia dove away, the priest swung his weapon wide, casting forth a massive crescent of destructive energy. With the sound of dynamite, the scythe's deathly rend smited the walls of the cavern. A shower of boulders shot from the great gash it left behind, one of which toppled on Morvenia and pinned her to the ground.

The undaunted Deniechus shifted his manic eyes upon the unconscious abyssal. His ghostly blaze began to shrink as he waited, listening for the clatter of steel raking the cave's roof above him. His head upturned at just the moment Viasarria leapt from the darkness with her sword raised above her head for a sneak attack. The High Priest was perfectly still one second, then the next, had turned to catch Viasarria's blade now vibrating between his clawed fingers before her feet even hit the ground. With a flip of his wrist, he sent Viasarria flying back, hitting the dirt in a daze from the intensity of her landing.

Viasarria acrobatically lifted herself back up, using the momentum of her rising to charge her opponent. "I won't let you destroy Kasra!"

He blocked a swipe of her sword with the edge of his scythe suddenly appearing into his hands. "Our Master destroys nothing," he calmly replied. "Lord Zercius will use the Vytameta to usher in a new age. A world without Purity."

"What a load of shit!" The angry velta's weapon parried the priest's with a few more clangs of steel, before she was pushed back on her heels.

Her opponent charged forth, using the reach of a single arm to repeatedly swing the curved blade of his long pole arm, forcing Viasarria to step back to dodge or have her sword be knocked from her hands. She came back to return an upward swing of her katana, but was blocked by the handle of his scythe, before he raised it above his head to have it come down on hers.

Viasarria hopped aside to let its sharp edge bite into the dirt and become stuck, allowing her to capitalize with a powerful kick to the man's sternum, separating him from his weapon and knocking him back into a cobweb against the wall. Just as she was about to capitalize on her adversary, readying her sword to run him through, Deniechus summoned his scythe to come flying at Viasarria's ankles like a boomerang.

With clairsentient reflexes, Viasarria backflipped over the whirling weapon and stuck a landing on the wall with the spiked heels of her boots. Deniechus then gave her chase with a volley of mist-like energy blasts from his hand, crashing into the wall as the blade dancer sprang off the stone surface.

She knocked the starstruck priest flat on his back by lunging her knee into his chin, then covered him with a roundhouse elbow into his temple. The High Priest pushed Viasarria skyward with a thrust of his palm into her stomach, sending her crashing against the wall while he punched a crater into the smooth stone to stand himself back up.

"You dare to mar the beauty of Deniechus?!" he self-righteously bellowed, a cut above his eye oozing blood down his cheek. He grabbed the slowly-rising blade dancer's face in his iron claws and squeezed hard enough to make her think her skull was being crushed. His metal fingers to digging into her skin kept the fighter pinned to her knees.

Though she was in terrible pain and could not see past his palm, Viasarria thrust her hand into Deniechus' locked elbow, breaking it inward with a sickening snap that had him releasing his hold. Viasarria face was adorned with five puncture wounds from her opponent's claws; four streaks of red spanned her brow. Her vision, albeit slightly obscured by the sanguinary veil dripping over her eyes, she still had perception enough to sweep her tail at his shins to have him falling down while she came back to her feet.

As she charged forth, she was tripped by Deniechus' scythe spinning into her calves on its way back into his hand. He raised his weapon for the finishing blow, but Viasarria got to her knees first, throwing a jab under the armored loincloth hiding his crotch. His breathless wheeze was subsequently followed by a jaw-crushing elbow strike, sending the elite fighter reeling back.

"Yes, that's right!" Nohvaias cheered her on from the proverbial sidelines. "Kill him! *Kill him!!*"

An enraged Deniechus lurched once again, extending his scythe to take another swipe at Viasarria, but with the grace of her profession, the blade dancer flourishingly evaded his deathly strike and countered with one of her own. In the same motion, she cartwheeled to grab Nohvaias from the ground and as she arose, she used the Safiric blade to cut through Deniechus' outstretched arm. The precision and speed of her swing had the High Priest feeling an unusual loss of weight from his now phantom limb, lying in a gory mass behind him.

Nohvaias was overjoyed at the injury he had caused to his former colleague, his blade excitedly shining in Viasarria's hand. "I've never been happier in all my years! To think I'd live to see this day…"

A panicked Deniechus sputtered with disbelief as he clutched the stump of his shoulder, eyes flashing with harmless rage as he glowered at his blood dripping off the traitorous sword. "What kind of priestess are you?!" he backed away as the vindictive Viasarria came closer. "It will corrupt your soul to do us harm! Don't you care?"

"Mother will forgive me," Viasarria closed in to give him the guillotine with her blade. Before her attack could connect, he vanished into a choking burst of smoke. When the cloud cleared, she saw Deniechus hovering above the great pit that the Arachniath had fallen into, holding a compromised Kasra under his single arm. Above his head, a black disc full of cosmic ribbons all coalescing into a starry galaxy in the center spiraled into existence. The flat portal was wreathed with an angry blaze that brightly glowed in five colors.

"We are all here because we are all a part of Their grand design..." The loftiness of Deniechus' declaration was stunted by his pain and lack of vitality. "We all have a finite role to play in Their Will... the Father's Power, the Mother's Love. The only fate that rests uncertain is which will win in the end. That is for us to choose, and for the Vytameta to accomplish." At the end of his sermon, the High Priest ascended into the portal he created. Viasarria watched him disappear into its deceptively endless recesses, as if falling down a bottomless pit, until he and Kasra were completely vanished from sight.

The blade dancer indecisively glanced to the prostrate bodies of her rescuers, with whom she'd fought alongside before this situation unfolded. She had no idea if they were still alive and didn't believe she had much time to check before Deniechus' doorway would close. She watched it begin to shrink as it hovered far beyond arm's reach. She knew that her one chance to not only save Kasra but perhaps the whole world rested within wherever that gateway would take her.

Was she ready to make the blind leap all by herself?

"Viasarria," Platina called her name, "you cannot be considering such a foolish venture!"

"What other choice do I have?!" the ex-blade dancer shot back over her shoulder.

"None of us are fully rested!" Raia added her own voice of reason. "Most of us aren't even conscious!" she addressed the slightly shifting bodies of Morvenia and Brynita. "If you jump in there now, who knows what kind of ambush is waiting for you on the other side!"

"There is no time to leave this up to someone else!" Viasarria had enough of their hesitations. "You should either come with me, or die wishing you had!"

The cords of fate were coming loose, like the failing sinews of a rope, threatening to drop her if she missed this opportunity. It was hers to seize. The portal was calling her. With acrobatic finesse, Viasarria leapt and bounded off a web-slathered wall, ricocheting headfirst into the infernal entryway -- the access point to a dimension she never could have imagined. She was weightlessly conveyed through a wormhole of clouds, watching the light of the world she knew fading behind her as she was brought into a new realm of darkness.

Chapter 40: Gathering Reinforcements

Having reached the end of her rope, a stressed-out Raia collapsed defeatedly onto her bottom, knees to her chest and her hands clutching the insides of her ears as she was tormented with the thoughts of where her life had went wrong. There she was, sitting on the cave floor of the Arachniath's terrifying domain of blazing spiderwebs, in what had very much became a deathtrap for not only her, but her own rescuers, who had went out of their way to save her from this peril.

The much more experienced priestesses, Platina and Brynita, seemed to have recovered markedly better and had retained their outward sanity for the most part. Their postures were undaunted by the fatigue that would have done a lesser member of the clergy in. Indeed, they had seen their share of tragedies and had overcome difficulties of a similar caliber before. It was all a part of being one of the Sanguinic Sisterhood. But poor Raia, who had been catapulted from the classrooms and into the field, was simply not ready for this harrowing experience.

Raia was suddenly stirred from her mental, emotional turmoil by a wet slap of Morvenia's fluke on her shoulder. "Raia girl," the abyssal's voice had the small brunette perking to attention, tears misting her eyes. "You want help Kasra friend, yes?"

"Yeah…" Raia meekly squeaked with a sniff, her tail curling powerlessly around her bent legs.

"Then I help you," Morvenia's angler light emitted a happy glow. "Nice Kasra girl was my first friend~" she sang and swished her tail, painting the floor behind her with yellowish globs. "If she like you, I like you too." The abyssal offered Raia a slimy hand.

Even though it was initially against every instinctive fiber of the brunette's being to touch what she assumed would be an unpleasantly cold, wet object, the fingers in which she intertwined hers as refuge were warm enough to where the dampness dripping off them was hardly noticeable.

She found herself being pulled to her feet by the abyssal, who was maybe an inch or two shorter than the brunette herself was. Raia blinked down at the smiling Morvenia's large, amber eyes, as if the height difference was suddenly the most interesting thing about this very alien belhuayn. Truthfully, she wasn't used to looking down at many people other than children half her age. But Morvenia didn't look that young; in fact, Raia would peg her for about the same age she was.

"You know where she is, Morvenia?" Raia tried not to sound too impressed. If anything, she was willing to take any savior she could get at this point.

Even though Morvenia tried to say this fact at a hushed enough tone to where Brynita and Platina would not overhear, being just a couple paces away, it was hard not to be made privy to these juicy details. Both priestesses turned attentively in Morvenia's direction to hear what she was about to tell her newest pal.

"My momma High Priestess of Bone Father; she make portal like Botherhood man, all the time with special key," the abyssal explained. "But she no let me go to Malumai because I Pure girl; Pure no allowed there."

As curious as Raia was about Morvenia's mother, her next question of concern was: "What is this 'special key' of hers that we need to make this doorway?"

From a sackcloth attached to a vine around her waist, serving as a belt of sorts, Morvenia pulled open the small bag by its thread of twine, allowing her to dig a finger and a thumb inside to retrieve her prize: what appeared to be a wand, crafted of a simple tindertwig, topped with the skull of a shrunken head.

"I take from momma when leave home," she blithely stated, juggling the ancient and fragile-looking artifact in her hand. "She still no know where is~"

"Why *did* you leave home, Morvenia?" Raia asked, starting to feel sympathy for the slimy vixy.

"Was no fun there!" the abyssal replied, arms outstretched before wetly clapping back to her squidgy sides. "I no get do *anything*! All because I Pure girl. I want be temple priestess~" She batted her eyes with a dreamy gaze, folding her webbed fingers together. "I be healer girl and serve Blood Mother!" Her expression fell once more to a petulant pout. "But momma no let me! She no want me go to Tresantia! She no let me leave Mordax! I angry!"

She punctuated her statement by raising her arm high to throw her mother's important scepter key into the rocky floor. Raia's heart jumped in her throat as time seemed to stand still; she had expected the wand to break in half the second it clacked off the ground.

Luckily, the tiny skull on its end stayed intact. Raia would have had a mind to slap the tempestuous abyssal if she didn't think she'd splash herself with her yucky secretions in the process.

"Get ahold of yourself!" a much less patient Brynita grabbed Morvenia by the shoulders, rattling the young vixy's head. "We need that thing to rescue the Vytameta! She's a lot more important than *you* are! So you'd better --"

The next thing Brynita was about to say was silenced by a thick lump of sticky gunk Morvenia spat over the mean velta's face. Brynita's screams of horror and disgust were muffled by this mask of mucus as she blindly flailed into Platina's austere embrace. While the nurse was assisting the mortified lorekeeper, Raia approached her seething friend, silently watching the whole kerfuffle as if to say 'that'll show her!'

"Morvie," Raia called the abyssal's attention, "I know that you and *Meanie*ta haven't gotten off to the best of starts…" her use of a funny nickname earned a soft giggle from Morvenia, "but I promise that the rest of the Sachelvian clergy isn't like her. If you wanted to join our temple, I'd put in a good word for you!"

"You do for me?" Morvenia's angler light flickered as she pointed a sharp nail to her chest. "Now I know why you is Kasra friend; you is nice girl too."

Raia's cheeks dimpled at the abyssal's kind words, always pleased to make another acquaintance. She was finding that she had a lot more in common with the poor estranged thing the more she talked to her. "You can help us save her. Do you know how to use that portal key?" She pointed to the thankfully unbroken wand by Morvenia's foot.

Morvenia uttered a thoughtful purr and crossed a finger against her lips. She grasped the stick between her toes and lifted it high enough to where she could transfer the wand into her hand. "Momma teach me how use Bone Father magic, but I no like it much. It hurt people, and I no want that. But I can try make portal for you."

She pointed the scepter at the pit of the Arachniath's grave and began to roll her wrist in a stirring motion. The darkness began reacting to this telekinetic swirl; blue and purple lights churned as if stirred by a giant spoon. Within the center of its shimmering vortex, a disc-shaped gateway began to appear, highlighted by a white fringe. Raia watched this hypnotic creation become progressively larger, until it was more than large enough to swallow whole the short brunette.

Upon successfully completing her task, Morvenia seemed to lose her nerve when she was faced with the decision of whether or not she wanted to take the plunge into the ominous unknown. "I no know where portal lead…"

she admitted, a grave tone quieting her voice. "Is to Malumai, but where you be in city is big guess."

"Malumai is a city?" Raia asked.

Morvenia affirmingly nodded, "Momma went to different place there every time. She know how to make portal go where she want to."

Intrigued by this fact, a recuperated Brynita suggested, "Maybe it'll take us to the last place your 'momma' went?"

Judging by the mean sneer Morvenia gave the velta, she was blatantly hoping that whatever place Brynita went to would be terribly perilous. "You want find out, Meanieta?" she flicked slimy globules on the priestess' mantamina with a switch of her tail.

Before the fuming Brynita could wrap her claw-like hands around Morvenia's neck, Raia interposed herself in what the experienced mediator could see was an ensuing conflict. "Hold it you two!"

Composing herself with a short prayer, the side of her hand resting on her forehead, Raia added, "Mother forgive me, but we're plunging *butt-first* into *Sanguina-knows-where*, to rescue a legendary hero from certain death or *worse*, and we couldn't be *less* knowledgeable about the dangers we're facing."

Her ears wilting and eyebrows furrowing, she glanced between her two scowling compatriots, both staring daggers at each other over her head. "We need to call upon someone more skilled and more capable than we are if Kasra is going to have a chance of being found and brought to safety. I'm… sorry to say that it isn't going to be me…" With a more apologetic tone, Raia touched Morvenia's shoulder and gazed solemnly into her eyes. "Morvie, I thank you for opening that portal, but I have to leave this to someone who I know is more qualified than we are for what lies ahead."

Raia raised the communication ring she was wearing on her left hand under her chin, so that she could send a message to the Arch Healer Kyrana.

Kyrana and her friend Rozha had been spending the morning resting in Laeyudi Town, preparing for the return trip to Sachelvae. Suffice it to say, after their heated argument with Ghanius in regards to their mercy of the Mire Fiend, they weren't welcome guests in his house anymore. Thankfully, Rokior was willing to provide them the shelter his father wouldn't in his lofty tree house.

However, the space he had available wasn't quite as nice as a more spoiled Kyrana would've liked; his domicile lacked a real bed to speak of. Instead, he made do with a mattress of straw and large leaves sewn together into a kind of blanket of sorts, which was remarkably more comfortable than it looked. That being said, the bedding was rather itchy and tended to poke holes in clothing that was made of any substance less rugged than leather.

Gentleman that the Laeyudi warrior was, Rokior happily lent his mattress to the two priestesses for the time being. Rozha tried not to tease Kyrana too much about being her bedmate, especially since she wouldn't have been able to get any rest at all were it not for the Arch Healer's medicinal touch, soothing the otherwise unbearable pain of her full body tattoo. Truthfully, Kyrana couldn't have felt any less comfortable about nestling down in the same bed that Rozha and Rokior had committed some rather unchaste acts just two nights before.

She wondered if those aforementioned 'acts' had anything to do with why she could smell a strong amount of maleness from the leafy sheets she had pulled up to chest level. She was feeling borderline defiled albeit fully clothed, her sweatiness keeping her from doing any more than dozing off periodically. It didn't help that it was so ridiculously humid this time of day in Virluti Forest. At some point during her restless nap, Kyrana had pushed off the blankets from herself and Rozha so that she would lose one layer of overheating garb.

A half-naked Rozha awoke to shivers shortly thereafter. The sunlight attacking her squinted eyes through the mossy curtains triggered her full alertness to the extent she wouldn't have been able to return to sleep even if she wanted to. She shook her head disdainfully at the Arch Prude and stretched her aching muscles, having become stiff and sore from laying on the hard bedding. At least she was feeling rested enough. But just moving beside the other velta caused Kyrana to wake up again with a rather disgruntled stir; Rozha answered the priestess' vindictive leer with an apologetic grimace.

"Arch Healer!" a squeaky voice bumping through Kyrana's throbbing head pressing a palm into her ear. It took her a minute to realize it was coming from her communication ring.

"Raia?" the pink priestess asked into her jewelry's glistening gemstone.

The troubled brunette in question couldn't have been happier to have gotten through. "Oh thank goodness! I was so worried a signal from my ring wouldn't leave this place!"

"Where are you, Raia dear?" Kyrana asked, trying to calm the girl's excitement.

"I… I don't know what this awful place is called," the young healer stammered. Kyrana could hear the tears in her eyes straining her speaker's voice. "Platina is here with me. We were rescued by Kasra and Brynita and --"

"What?" yawped an incredulous Kyrana, earning the raised brow of Rozha, listening in to her friend's half of the conversation. "Kasra was there? Why did she come for you? She shouldn't have even known --"

"I don't know why she showed up," Raia blubbered, "but now she's gone -- that scary High Priest Deniechus took her away somewhere!"

"Deniechus…" innumerable thoughts raced through Kyrana's head, wondering why Kasra of all people was kidnapped. "Fygidia to me! It's too dangerous for you to stay there any longer!"

"I can't!" the sniveling Raia complained. "There's a spell on the forest that scrambles fygidias."

Kyrana looked to Rozha, who shared her horrified expression when she quickly explained the situation to her. Bringing her ring far away enough to where Raia couldn't hear her next comment, she hissed, "What was Mother Diava thinking, sending such a young priestess to a place like that?! She's barely entered her initiation into the clergy, for the Mother's sake!"

Kyrana heaved a deep, almost reluctant sigh. "We must fygidia back to Sachelvae and report this to Mother Diava." After everything they'd already been through the last couple of days, she wasn't looking forward to heaping on another day's worth of troubles on top of that. "Sanguina's moon will be entering its resting phase in a matter of nights; the Safiric Brotherhood will be getting more active and brave, soon."

Truthfully, Rozha could wait to give that report. The earlier mentioning of her sister had her more worried for Kasra than anything. "I want to know why Kasra was sent to rescue them. She's still a novitiate…" Then the realization struck her. "She was acting on her own… *damn* her!"

Despite her empty stomach, the Red Dancer could wait no longer. She left Kyrana in her dust as she stormed off toward the edge of town, where their steeds were tied and waiting by the edges of the elevated piers.

"Leave the steeds here where it is safe," Kyrana ran after her, lifting her dress so she would not trip over it. "The Black Swamp is no place for them."

"How do you expect to get there to rescue Raia posthaste without them?" Rozha snapped at the Arch Healer, her hands still clinging to Heschel's lead rope.

"Only my Branch of Life has the power to carry us to where Raia and the rest are," Kyrana proudly swiveled the magic staff she spoke of, causing its ruby gems to dangle off its crown-shaped limbs. "She may not be able to bypass the Safiric holding spell, but these traps are only as strong as the caster who made them. An Arch Healer such as myself, when armed with this scepter to magnify Sanguinic power, should be able to get through easily." Rozha must have missed that class in Teacher Xanne's room, because her response to this little known nuance came with a perplexed head tilt.

Kyrana continued to clear the muddy waters by reminding her, "Because Raia's communication ring is synchronized with my own, I will be able to fygidia us both to wherever she is."

And no sooner did she say that than did Raia and her company immediately find themselves showered with the white fountain of sparkles denoting Kyrana's emergence. When the lights dimmed, they could also see Rozha standing by her side; it took the two teleporters an extra moment to overcome their post-fygidia fugue, as they were taken aback by the new environment they found themselves in.

They weren't sure what they were expecting to find when Raia told them that she had been holed up in a Safiric encampment, but it certainly wasn't like anything the seasoned veterans had seen in their time serving Sachelvae. These were signs of the changing times indeed.

What was almost as startling as all that was the face of a certain young abyssal, looking up at them from two feet below their heads. "Hey…" Rozha was the first to make a remark of any kind, speaking what was on Kyrana's mind for her. "You wouldn't happen to be Viunnatha's kid, would you?"

The familiar name of her mother had Morvenia perking an attentive ear; a ripple of intrigue was sent from the base of her tail all the way to its fluke. "You know momma?"

"Yes," Kyrana replied, "she asked us to look for you."

"She worry about me?" Morvenia pursed her lips, as if this was unbelievable to her.

"You've been missing for a long while," Rozha placed a hand on her hip, her upper body leaning in the direction of her raising eyebrow. "What're you doing down here? How'd you get mixed up in all this?"

Her expression hardened, her nerves galvanized by having her motives questioned. "I want be hero!" Her webbed fists clenched with a squishy sound. "All this talk of Vytameta, and no place for Morvenia! I important, too!"

Rozha could recognize that determined spark in the abyssal's glare -- the kind of look that was tired of taking no for an answer. But the fact that she hadn't run off into the portal with a head full of steam showed the Red

Dancer that this brave vixy had better sense than to throw her life away for a cause she didn't even know she was fighting for. As Sachelvae's Teacher of Self Defense, Rozha could see bountiful potential in the small being, and wasn't about to let any of that go to waste.

For probably the first time in her life, Morvenia heard a pair of words come from an unlikely source: "You're right," Rozha gently held the abyssal's fists, causing the slimy vixy to stiffen her neck. "You can do a lot more than you think. If you're anything like your mother, you could become something very special -- especially if you use the powers Sanguina has gifted you," she pointed to Morvenia's eyes indicatively. "You might find now that everything seems to be way over your head, but when it really comes down to it, nothing is as complicated as it seems. Once you've unlocked your potential, everything you now find daunting and scary will become doable." Rozha's encouraging smile fell slightly. "But you have to start somewhere. You can't 'be hero' right away."

Morvenia let all these profound teachings sink in, registering in her mind with a dreamy blankness on her countenance everything that the inspiring blade dancer was telling her. She was such a sponge for her new role model that she was willing to believe anything Rozha told her now. "What I must do?" she breathed, threads of warm gunge trickling from her balled hands.

Rozha let her go to pet the abyssal's ear, as if not even perturbed in the slightest by her secretions. It was as if she was looking at a younger Kasra staring back at her. Indeed, she had certainly said things of a similar nature to someone before. "If you want to prove you're capable of saving people," the Red Dancer began, pointing at the three priestesses she had come to rescue, "I want you to guide them out of here and to Tresantia."

"Y-Yes ma'am…" Morvenia weakly replied, only forgetting to salute at her. "I do that for you." She didn't want to look too upset, however, when she realized she'd have to be escorting Brynita back along with the two she liked more. But at least Raia would be good company; she could rely on her friend to protect her from Meanieta.

Satisfied with her new trainee, Rozha returned to an upright stance and turned back to Kyrana with a smirk. "I think we're all set."

The Arch Healer only lingered so that she could give the apology she felt she owed to Raia, Platina, and Brynita. "I would have brought you back myself, but without one of us here, I would have no way to follow a signal back to the portal…" she looked to the swirling colors draining down the pit. "I am sorry I cannot help you expedite your travels, but you all have Platina to ensure your safety."

Vytameta

The taciturn nurse acknowledged the order of her superior with a curtsy. She watched Kyrana and Rozha both step forth into Morvenia's portal, entering feet-first into what was shaping up to be the most dangerous challenge they had faced in their Sachelvian careers.

Chapter 41: Eaves of Malumai

Viasarria felt like she was being weightlessly suspended and stretched like a strand of spaghetti as her body was conveyed through a colorful tunnel vortex, in an almost dreamlike state. She was nearing slowly a twisting star of light at the end, feeling more and more nauseas from dread at what she might face at the other side. Once the light was fully upon her, she had to shut her eyes to avoid being blinded by its all-consuming radiance.

"You'd better wake up soon," she could hear Nohvaias' voice. "Or they'll find us lying around out here."

When clarity was restored to her vision by the ambient light source, Viasarria found herself standing in a quadrant of a ring-shaped city, all of which was built concentric to a tornado of stones floating in an endless, alabaster sky. This asteroid belt of debris orbited a floating, lone mountain, stretching too high for Viasarria to see its peak, which pointed directly toward a black spiral, slowly swirling in the broken firmament above.

The whole place seemed distorted. The whole dimension defied her common sense. She could hardly believe she was even standing there. She forgot that she was there at all, until she saw some cloaked figures ambling about the streets of light yellow dirt, to and from their sandstone houses.

It was surprising to see any amount of civilization could thrive in a barren zone like this. The whole city was built into the side of a large, bowl-shaped cliff -- the likes of which was probably the only of its kind in this whole dimension. For as boundless as the sky appeared, it didn't seem to have much in it aside from the city Viasarria was standing in.

"Oh, good, you're awake," a gleaming Nohvaias got her attention. "You're lucky you didn't give me a dent when you dropped me! Now pick me up; I don't like the taste of dirt!"

Viasarria did as the mewling High Priest requested, lifting the talking sword from the ground and replacing it with the one currently in her scabbard. A superpowered weapon like him was certainly an upgrade from the measly scimitar she had been wielding before.

"You're lucky you're not the Purest of folk," Nohvaias' voice was slightly muffled by the sheath's leather walls, "or you would already have been spotted by anyone traipsing about the streets, here."

It was true that Viasarria's violent lifestyle had earned her the slit-shaped pupils of a Wild blood, but she was still Pure enough to have been taken prisoner once before. She'd rather not get captured in the worst place for any Pure to be, which had her wondering, "Where are we, exactly?"

"You, young missy, have entered the Brotherhood's paradise: Malumai," Nohvaias explained. "It was a place created by Safiro Himself, as a refuge and haven for His most devout children. Only a High Priest can open a gateway to this realm, and only a High Priest can open a door to leave it. When you're here, you can converse with any member of the Brotherhood, and go to any Safiric temple in all the world."

A gear clicked in Viasarria's mind, as what he mentioned suddenly had her coming to a eureka moment. "That's why I saw so many of the spooks leaving the small chapel in Fort Pericula," she gasped. "I knew there was no way they could all have been living in one space."

"Very observant of you," Nohvaias flatly replied. "Indeed, you will see priests of all kinds here, hailing from the four nations of Vitiosa."

During Nohvaias' exposition, a crowd-watching Viasarria picked out some seemingly out-of-place female members of the Brotherhood as well, heading toward the entrance to what the blade dancer could recognize all too well as a tavern. "The only thing I'm not seeing here are the people I came in here after," she impatiently replied. "It's time to collect some information from the locals."

She made sure the hood of her indigo cloak was covering enough of her face before making her way across the dusty street. She thought it fortuitous that the Brotherhood goons who found her sneaking into their camp hadn't removed the Safiric robes she had stolen, after they captured her.

The tavern she entered was quaint but clean on the inside, showing a craftsmanship she wouldn't have been expecting from its exterior. The wooden floorboards were dusted from the grains of dirt and sand tracked in from its patrons. The walls were obviously carved out of the rock of the cliff encircling the ring-shaped city. Someone was playing a piano near the back of the square-shaped room, no larger than forty feet wide. To her right was the bar, where six patrons were seated at stools, their tails curled around the wooden legs of their tall chairs.

To her left was a colorful trio of chattering priests sitting at a round table, seeming to be celebrating in a less-than-hushed tone some sort of special occasion. "The Master's going to be making an appearance on the mountaintop, soon," a dark-skinned Ontevallian took a swig. His arm was decorated with a swirling, black tattoo, but it wasn't a Laeyudi spirit marking. He sported a long, thick hairstyle that started as what appeared to be a mohawk between his ears, but widened as it spilled down his lower back.

"Do ye think'eel invite us?" asked his Lasuisian friend. He seemed to look like a younger version of Reaventyr, come to think of it. He featured a much shorter, dark beard that was braided tightly along the sides. He wore a bandanna on his head, probably to cover up a bald spot forming prematurely at his age. But judging by the bulging muscles in his arms, he probably wasn't teased for it much by his peers.

"Paugh, not a chance," the Ontevallian shook his head. "VIP stuff, for sure. I hear The Elites are gonna be there -- Master Deniechus and his lot. We'll all get a nosebleed seat for the beginning of the new world!"

"That Vytameta they've got," the Lasuisian brought the conversation back to Viasarria's subject of interest, "they say she's just sixteen years old."

"And she's s'posed ta bring about all dis change for us?" a skeptical Cataenian scowled. He had the shortest hair of the bunch, but that wasn't really saying a whole lot; his spiky, aqua blue locks were styled in a way that if he was viewed from the side, it would almost look like beach wave was rushing down his forehead. He was certainly the youngest of the trio, probably no older than Viasarria, herself.

"What could some *kid* know about the troubles dis world's bin facin'?" the Cataenian continued. "How can Lord Zercius trust some little thing like dat?"

"Shush," the Lasuisian waved a hand at him. "Don't be questionin' the Lord's will! He ken it better than you; he's got this 'ole thing sorted."

The group seemed to be detracting from their original commentary, and Viasarria needed to know more before it was too late. She slipped into their small circle and piped up softly. "So, when is this supposed to take place?" she asked under her hood.

The Cataenian tried to sneak a peek at Viasarria's visage, but couldn't get a good look at her face in the shade of her attire. "By midnight, I'm thinkin'," he replied. "It'll be a few hours, but what's a short wait like dat compared to da whole sixteen years dis Vytameta has been keeping us in suspense? Lord Zercius is makin' sure he's got everythin' ready for his big show."

"For sure," Viasarria nodded, remembering to clasp the bronze button of her hood. The last thing she wanted to do was let them have a good look at her eyes.

This stranger's unusual dialect had all four scelans at the table leaning closer to her, forcing the poorly-disguised velta to uncomfortably shrink into her shoulders.

"Where'd ye say yer from?" the Lasuisian drawled.

"I hail from Tresantia," Viasarria cooly replied this time. It wasn't a total lie; it was true that her different dialect was a result of her birthplace on the Ontevallian coast, but she had lived in the central continent for so long now, it almost felt like a new home to her.

"Yeah, who *ain't* from there?" the priest didn't seem perfectly content with her answer, but was willing to let it slide.

However, his Ontevallian friend wasn't so willing to let the stranger go so easily. "What's your name, priestess? We don't see many ladies strolling around Malumai."

"I'm…" Viasarria balked at using her real name, thinking that there was a chance she was on a wanted list for having once masqueraded as a Safiric Priestess. "Kumara," she said.

"Y'know something, Relnigan," the Cataenian jabbed a finger at his equally suspicious Ontevallian, "her accent don't sound right for someone from Tresantia. They have that… lower swamp tongue. She sounds more *refined…*"

"Uh...thanks?" Viasarria wondered whether this was truly a compliment at this point.

"Didja take a vow of secrecy, priestess lady?" the Lasuisian asked, still trying to peek under her hood.

Viasarria lowered her head defensively, blocking his view. "I uhm...yes…" she said warily, having not realized members of the Safiric clergy took their own vows. "I can't tell you a lot of stuff, but yeah I did do that." She could catch out of the corner of her eye, a gray-skinned, musclebound scelan wearing half of his robes tied around his waist. He seemed to be giving her a funny look with his forehead reclined into his palm, and his elbow against the table in front of him. He was practically screaming 'are you kidding' without verbalizing it.

Viasarria's hecklers continued their curious assault. "Who's your High Priest?" the Lasuisan shot his question at her. Before she could give an answer, she was hit with another from the Cataenian. "What weapon did the Father give you upon your initiation? By the look of your robes, you've obviously passed novitiate training…"

'Dammit,' Viasarria grumbled to herself. She should have paid closer attention to the disguise she took before walking in there. "I...I can't say," she begged. "Vow of secrecy~" she held up her fingers in a small wave.

This caused all four scelans to now exchange looks. The Ontevallian suddenly stood from his seat and began reaching for her hood. "I don't trust you. I'll bet you're a spy sent from Sachelvae!"

"Hey!" Viasarria leapt to her feet, pulling at her hood. "No way! Diava's a *bitch*! Like I'd spend a damn *second* in her stupid temple!"

"Yeah, a likely story," Relnigan frowned, backing Viasarria into the wall behind her. He grabbed her ankles with his tail to ensure she couldn't make a sidestep to the saloon-style doors so closely within reach. "So you know the name of Diava, but not the High Priest of Travestas? Alright, your jig is up, priestess." As soon as he reached for her hood, Viasarria slapped his arm away and threw a jaw-cracking shot right into his chin. The table's leader found himself staggering back, but the pain-resilient priest was hardly dazed.

With a loud scuffing of chair legs across the wooden floor, the rest of Relnigan's company stood up to aid their leader's defense. In the Cataenian's hands appeared a magical bow and arrow, comprised of blue light. Just as he was about to shoot the already notched arrow at point blank, Viasarria engaged her invisibility power and ducked out of the way. The thin projectile of Safiric energy zipped into the wall behind her and shattered like glass upon making its markless contact.

When Viasarria reappeared into the sighted world, she had her own weapon drawn, in both hands and at the ready to deflect the Lasuisian's overhead bash with his light mace. The Lasuisian's weapon was outfitted with an unusual ice pick on its heavy head, that he used to hook onto Nohvaias' blade with a scraping of sparks.

"Ugh, what an awful sound!" the High Priest's complaint could barely be heard over the metal screech.

Viasarria dislodged the Lasuisian from her weapon with a kick of her spiked heel into his knee, causing the priest to drop his mace and gasp with pain. With a single motion, Viasarria then tripped up her weakened foe with a lash of her tail at his compromised leg, whilst also ducking underneath the Cataenian's next arrow. She was, however, caught completely off guard by Relnigan's reckless advance: with a graceful leap off the table, he jump-kicked Viasarria in the side of the head, knocking the blade dancer into the wall behind her.

Relnigan then pinned his cornered foe, slamming into her temple with his forearm while a knee kept between her legs kept her from kicking back at him. With his free hand, he was winding up a punch to hit the gut of his helpless adversary. Just when the hit was about to connect, his arm was stopped by Viasarria's tail blindly hooking into his bent elbow. The confused priest then found himself being shoved back and spun on his heels by the impressive strength of the blade dancer's flexible limb.

The angered Relnigan exuded a black smoke from his arms, his eyes turning whiter after he recovered his balance. He brushed a claw-like hand between his ears to comb back the tangled, brown tresses falling over his face, puffing through gritted teeth as he summoned a blade of his own into his grasp. As Viasarria was readying herself for a collision, her defensive posture slackened slightly at the sight of the lone scelan she had spotted earlier, staring both of her enemies down with bored contemn in his burgundy eyes.

The large stranger at least had chivalry enough to tap the Ontevallian on the shoulder before he decked him across the face. With that high class 'how ya do,' the swordsman's weapon fizzled out with a burst of sparks as he spiraled off his feet. He crashed through the wall beside Viasarria with a burst of splinters and raining lumber, then tumbled onto the boardwalk outside. It was at this point that the pianist's music stopped, and all eyes in the establishment were on the huge bruiser sticking up for the Pure interloper.

The Cataenian archer wasn't so swift to be cowed by his taller adversary. But he couldn't ready another shot of his magic arrow befoe the quick-thinking brawler was able to stop him with a mere shove to his face. The archer stumbled off his feet, knocking over the table he was once sitting in, and almost thereafter trampled by his Lasuisian friend when he came hobbling forth. The upward swing of his pick-mace missed as his tall opponent barely had to step back to keep the curved blade away from his chin.

The massive fighter retaliated with a lung-deflating whip of his tail into his fellow Lasuisian's midsection, causing the priest to double over his limb, where his opponent's chin would be in range to be scooped up by his hand. The priest was risen over seven feet in the air, the top of his head brushing the dusty ceiling before he was sent like a lawn dart into the table the Cataenian was leaning against.

The wooden furniture piece was smashed into a hundred pieces with the force of the impact. The Cataenian would have been flattened underneath of his ally had he not been endowed with the swiftness to tumble out of the way. The shaky archer rose to his feet in just enough time to see the bar-fighting scelan reeling his next punch with a current of cold wind around his wrist. The Cataenian was met with a face-full of knuckles that had the priest's hood flinging off his head as he went flying across the bar room. He sailed over the sitting patrons and invariably knocked over a waiter on his destructive way to the rocky back of the building.

And now there was finally quiet. But it was a far cry from the peaceful kind; rather, the tension was so thick now, Viasarria began to wonder if it was deafening her. Somehow, the piano player, who had the unconscious archer merely paces away from his seat, mustered the nonchalant bravery to begin hammering away at the keys again in an attempt to restore the dignified calm the bar once had. The barkeep, and the rest of the patrons however, were not so immediately content to act as if nothing happened. They all were giving Viasarria and her hero the dirty looks that suggested they might prefer it if the rowdy customers were to leave soon.

Paying their sour attitudes no heed, Viasarria came to clap her tail on her towering savior's back to get his attention. "You're really something else, big stranger!"

He gazed down at her with a kind of calmness that simply was not normally found in those who had Wild eyes like his. "Yeah, I know," he was so bashful, dusting himself off like trashing three priests was no big deal. "So who are ya, anyway? I heard ya feedin' those guys a line of shit like nothin' I've *ever* heard."

"It's all a part of my trade," the blade dancer held out her hand with a grin. "I'm Viasarria Sladervorn."

"Name's Terrin Desmagni," he accepted her gesture with far greater gentleness than he handled the ruffians earlier. Now came his own interrogation. "What brings a Pure like you to a place like this?"

"Heh," Viasarria chuckled, batting her eyes that perhaps were not Wild enough to fool everyone. As grateful as she was to this man, she didn't want to be too blatant with her desire to 'save the Vytameta,' especially not when the whole bar seemed to know about Kasra's coming to Malumai. "I lost a friend here," she said quasi-truthfully. "I'm looking for her."

"A 'friend,' ya say?" Terrin squinted an oblique eye at her. Apparently he was very familiar with the recent goings-on around town, as well. Before he could blow her cover again in public, Nohvaias came to Viasarria's defense.

"Yes, and I brought her here!" the sword rattled in the blade dancer's scabbard.

Unsurprisingly, Terrin looked a bit shocked to hear a voice coming from no one he could immediately perceive. His eyes settled on Viasarria's fingers, clutching the hilt of Nohvaias as if it were someone's hand. "This is a friend of mine," she said with a comforted smirk, relieved that the sword was on her side. "I found him in the Cave of the Arachniath. He told me he was through with serving the Brotherhood after he was killed by his own acolytes and buried there."

She obviously wasn't telling him the whole story, but Terrin didn't need to know it to believe her. "Looks like I'm not the only traitor 'round here." He suddenly looked crestfallen, as he stared to the daylight outside the swinging doors. "Must feel nice t'have the freedom t'enter and leave this place as ya please. I was put here 'cuz I refused to take the lives of the weak."

He paused as if expecting Viasarria to comment something out of intrigue, but she didn't appear as surprised as he assumed she might be. Perhaps defending her from the Brotherhood was proof enough of the reason for his punishment. Terrin continued with a small shrug and a nostalgic smile. "Before I was sent here, I was the Prince of the North -- the only heir to Praeira's throne."

Now Viasarria really had a reason to interrupt his storytelling. "A Prince?" her mouth remained open, as if the proverbial wheel slipping off was the only thing keeping her jaw shut. "You certainly don't look like royalty to me…" She didn't mean for it to sound as crass as it did, but Terrin's sporty attire and makeshift kilt wasn't what she would have called fit for a prince. "What in the world would a member of an Emperor's family be doing down here?!"

Following Viasarria's judgmental gaze up and down his body, Terrin's lips embarrassedly sputtered at his own motley look. "I realize I don't look like much now," he rubbed the back of his neck, "but that's what happens when you defy an Emperor's will. I had no real will to join the Brotherhood… but my father insisted that I have the power to rule, both authoritatively and physically. He gave me…" his voice quieted, "a fragment of his Annihlus, to see if I could handle its power."

Viasarria was surprised she hadn't noticed it before, that Terrin was wearing a silver ring on his right hand. But when she was allowed closer inspection of the gemstone embedded into its lustrous surface, she was nearly pulled in by its enthralling sight. The cyan diamond contained what looked like a black hole in its center, that created a sensation of depth that made

Viasarria feel like she could stick her pinky right through it. In fact, the longer she stared at it, the more she wanted to take it for herself.

Her Wild eyes gleamed all on their own at the thought of harnessing the power that Terrin wielded so amazingly. *'And to think... each Emperor has a slice of the Annihlus much larger than Terrin's ring.'* If just a fragment no larger than a fingernail gave him the abilities he had, she couldn't fathom what the entire Annihlus could do if it was all put together.

Before she could start salivating at the tempting enterprise, Viasarria felt like she was yanking herself back by the ponytail to wrench her gaze from the hypnotic gemstone. "So, you can't leave here? Are you still in trouble with your family for being such a damn softie?" she grinned toothily at him, earning a chuckle and a snort from the scelan.

"I was told to remain here 'til a certain Lord Zercius deemed me fit t' perform my duties to the Brotherhood," Terrin explained. "This place is meant to 'recondition' unworthy servants and 'remind' them of Safiro's Will." Looking to the other patrons of the bar, he added, "Now, that don't mean *everyone* here's a prisoner, but I've been here long enough to tell the inmates from the passersby."

Terrin pointed to a long, serpentining tattoo of black ink, swerving from his shoulder to his elbow. Each bend of this curving mark was accented with a spine, as if it were a strand of barbed wire. "This is a mark they give to all the prisoners here. This 'inner circle' we're in," he traced a ring above his head with an upturned finger, "is Malumai's jailhouse. Everyone ya see traipsin' round these roads ain't allowed to leave. Now the outer circle... that's for the rich folk. Some higher-ups in the Brotherhood use Malumai as a vacation home, where they can hobnob with each other and trade valuables from other lands around the world."

Everything she'd learned about this odd, off-putting dimension since she got here had Viasarria wondering just how long this place had been around. It certainly was quite developed and seemed to serve more of a purpose than just a giant prison. It was a self-contained community, offering a sort of free trade with its own bartering system.

"How do people live here?" came a bewildered wonderment from Viasarria. "How did a whole city get built in a place where there are no resources?"

"Oh *please*, you can't even guess?" Nohvaias' voice rang the steel of his blade. "It was all *brought* here, from the outside world. When a High Priest opens up a portal to Malumai, it can be large enough for not only his entire clergy to come inside, but for everything they're carrying as well. A whole bunch of building materials could *easily* be transported into this little world."

Terrin nodded with agreement to what the older High Priest was saying. "It don't look it on the inner circle," he started, "but the *outer* circle boasts some ambitious development. They're always buildin' *somethin'* up there," he looked to the ceiling, as if he could see the buildings of the outer circle from within the bar.

While Viasarria was never normally curious to learn about the upper echelons of a society, the total strangeness of Malumai was worthy of asking as many questions as possible. She figured why not continue to make conversation; maybe she could pick up a hint as to where Kasra was being kept. "Who runs everything down here? Or... *up* here?"

"All the progress the city makes is under direct guidance of Lord Zercius. He lives atop Mt. Malumai itself, where he oversees everythin' that goes on 'round here. Funny thing is... no one's claimed to see 'im. Not even in all the time I've been 'ere, have I ever seen the head honcho make a public appearance."

Even though Viasarria had a satisfactory answer, she wasn't in the least happy with it; she didn't like the prospect that she might've had to scale that daunting mountain in the center of town, but she'd be fooling herself if she thought the Vytameta herself would've been kept in any place other than the most dangerous and secure.

"So Zercius serves as the warden of this jail?" Viasarria twisted her lips and tilted an ear. "If you can be a prisoner for something so meager as not taking someone's life," she smirked at Terrin's raising brow, "how did those aggressive jerks like the ones you beat up get down here? Their jerkass attitudes seem to be right up with the Brotherhood's standards."

"Relnigan and his crowd," Terrin motioned to the barely stirring bodies scattered throughout the bar, "they've been here a while. Probably for pride-killing -- giving the Brotherhood a bad name."

As far as Viasarria was concerned, "The Brotherhood already *has* a bad name. How much worse do they think their reputation can get?"

Terrin smirked with a shrug of a single shoulder. "I'm sure ye'd think that if yer a priestess. But the first thing the Safiric Brotherhood teaches is humility with their craft; yer not supposed to use yer powers to cause indiscriminate death. We pious Safirics all have an innate sense when death is imminent; we can feel the suffering of others. It's our job, as children of Safiro, to usher in a gentle repose when we hear the silent calls of the dying."

"And there was more to it than that, in the beginning," Nohvaias added. "But ever since Zercius took over as leader of the Brotherhood, the balance between Pures and Wilds has been undone. Now it's harder to keep tabs on the members who have gone astray from their principles. These forbidden 'pride killings' that Terrin mentioned go unchecked more often than not."

Terrin nodded with agreement to what the elder sword was saying. "Brotherhood goons who are kicked out of their temple for likin' to kill too much go off to use their powers in the military, where they're even more dangerous."

Viasarria laughed, "You say 'Brotherhood goons' just like Sanguinic priestesses do." She pointed at him with a smirk, "You sure you're a priest here~?"

Terrin once again spared a chortle of his own. "Well I guess it's pretty obvious I've got a few ill feelin's fer my colleagues. I've been lookin' forward to leavin' this place, but somethin' tells me Zercius likes havin' me right where he wants me." He nervously rubbed his fingers against the ring he was wearing.

"How would you know when it's your time to leave, anyhow?" Viasarria curiously cocked an ear, jabbing a thumb to the sunless sky out the window. "How long have you been here?"

Terrin finger-combed the flowing tresses on the back of his neck as he paused for thought. "I've been here a long time, but I've never seen a day go by. I measure time by resting periods; I still get tired like I would at the end of a regular day, anyhow." Suddenly, he wished he'd been keeping a calendar. "It's not like I mark off the days… but it's been a while, I guess."

Viasarria tapped her lips thoughtfully. "If you're getting tired of living here under Zercius' foot, I…might have a proposition for you…" she pushed the words out of her mouth, hoping she wasn't about to get herself thrown out of the bar.

Now Terrin was really interested. A chair groaned as he perched a foot atop its seat, and rested an elbow against his raised knee. "Alright, I'm game for a deal," he said.

Viasarria swallowed and let out a breath to gather her courage. She didn't want to risk the chance that anyone else could hear what she had to say, so she stepped forward to whisper, "I'm here to save the Vytameta." She watched his face for a reaction, from which at first, there was blankness -- she could almost hear the wheel slipping off.

There was a long pause of pure disbelief; his head shook so slightly, that only his shifting hair over his shoulders could provide any indication of movement at all. "What? You and... *who* exactly? The Vytameta has been the only talk this town has had fer... as long as I've been here. And you..." This Pure's very existence in Malumai should have been reason enough to believe what she was saying. He'd never seen an undercover priestess before, much less would he expect to see one deep in Brotherhood territory. She must've been something tremendous if she could have even found a way to come to Malumai, and end a doomsday scenario on top of that.

She already broke the seal, she might as well continue. "That's the problem," she finally said despondently. "I don't know if anyone else followed me through that gate when I came here. I had five other friends with me, but they were all badly beaten when someone came to stop us. Even if they're here, I don't know where they'd be. But with Nohvaias, and your Annihlus," she gestured to her weapon and pointed to Terrin's ring, "We don't have a better chance to save the Vytameta from Zercius. And if anyone tries to stop us, we are going to take them down."

Chapter 42: Through the Floating Mountain

Standing outside the bar, Terrin and Viasarria now gazed at the daunting heights of Mt. Malumai, casting its enormous shadow on the entire city below. The longer she had been there, the more she was willing to bet that Kasra was holed up somewhere on that mountain in the middle of town. The only problem was getting there; the swirling debris surrounding the mountain didn't seem to be safely traversable, even for a blade dancer's acrobatic finesse. She could imagine herself getting whacked by one of the flying boulders on her way to and from another, and falling to her death down the abyss below the city.

Though she'd need binoculars to see if she could actually climb it, she spotted what appeared to be an upside-down spire attached to the bottom of the mountain. It was encircled by what she assumed to be a spiral-shaped staircase, that featured no sort of handrails on which to steady herself, nor was it even really attached to the spire itself. She couldn't be certain whether the curious protrusion was merely decorative, or if it served the intended means to access Mt. Malumai.

As if not even worried about the asteroids forming a rather painful barrier between the commoners and the mountain, Terrin poised his hands to his hips and said, "Won't be easy to get up there, for someone who can't fly, but I can get us there."

"Y-you can *fly*?!" Viasarria blinked up at him.

Terrin nodded, nonchalantly levitating a couple inches off the dusty street, as if standing on his toes to get a better view of the challenge he faced. "But just flyin' there ain't the hard part. That spinnin' wall of boulders is protected by an invisible barrier; ye'd need a large chunk o' Safiritem to break a hole just big enough fer us to squeeze in."

"Safiritem?" a quizzical cheek puckered under Viasarria's squinted eye. "What's that? Where are we going to find it in a tiny desert like this?"

"Ye'll actually find a lot of it here," Terrin swept an arm across the town, pointing to the marketplace. Vendor carts on the other side of the the cliff-facing street were outfitted with striped umbrellas to draw as much attention as possible to their wares. A few of them advertised their purpose with fetching flags fluttering in the mysterious, Malumai wind.

"Every priest has got somethin' magical on 'em," Terrin explained as they made their approach. "All of it is empowered by a gemstone called Safiritem. They say it glows blue and can hold Safiric energy because it comes straight from Safiro's moon. I'm sure you could get a good unrefined chunk of it from the markets around here. But they'd want a very good price for it; any Safiritem is very valuable before it is turned into a weapon or any other kind of material. It's worth all of its untapped potential."

Terrin led Viasarria to one of the carts whose flag was emblazoned with a roughly-painted blue stone, insinuating that it may have been a place to search for the wares he spoke of. But it didn't take him long to see that it certainly wasn't the premier shop to go perusing. The Brotherhood acolyte standing behind the service counter wore the robes of a Teacher.

"Hello hello!" the thin, mustached scelan prompted Terrin and Viasarria over, his voice endowed with an accent that made Viasarria think of Onteval's northern beaches.

Viasarria slapped her palm on the table and beamed up at the scelan's lilt. "Hey there, love!" her sudden burr seemed oddly natural. "Whatcha got here?"

The shopkeeper seemed equally elated by the newcomer's familiar tone. For sure this would earn her a discount at his store. "All kinds of *hotly-acquired* Safiritem jewels, m'lady! Won't you sneak a peek?" he stepped aside to let his customer do just that, take a look at the rack of gems, hanging inside tiny fishnets with belhuayn price tags attached to them. They all seemed rather high, most of them four figures. The larger specimens at the top of the display had prices worth 10,000 gold divitias each.

"Your values seem a little steep, fella," Terrin cast him a wary look. "Are ya sure yer even a Teacher with them robes, 'r did ya pinch *them*, too?"

The shopkeeper squared his elegant pauldrons and puffed out his chest, poising his hands to his hips as if to size up the much taller adversary. If he were any more offended, his mustache would have flown off his face by now. "How dare you insult me like that!" He was overcome with an aghast series of coughs. "These fabulous gems came from all corners of the world. I'd bet my hat on it that these are the best quality you've ever seen."

Viasarria raised her brow at him and scowled, "You say all that, but your product doesn't come with a warranty?" She feigned a soft gasp. "What kind of establishment is this?! I could report you to the Emperor for tax evasion! Iminsun's cronies will have your paycheck for *years* unless you clean this mess up right now and sell these things for the *proper* price!" she pointed an accusatory finger at him, tilting her hips as she spoke fervently.

"Waugh?!" the shopkeeper nearly lost his monocle as he bounced in place. Were his tail not curled to the floor to catch him, he would have fallen over by now. "What a preposterous thing to say!" his mustache fluttered as he coughed through his words. "And what would a 'fair price' to *you* be, *m'lady...?*"

"I'll give you *four* gold divitias for that one," she pointed at the biggest, oval-shaped chunk, "and you'll be *damn* lucky for that much! Without proper paperwork, you'll never get a better price for it than *that*!" Viasarria threw her nose in the air haughtily as her fists found her hips with a pop.

He acted like he had been shot in the chest as he clutched both hands over his heart. "I will have no more of these insults! You will pay *my price* and that is that! If I sold these artifacts for any less, I would be *giving* them away!"

Viasarria pursed her lips at him. "How long have you been trying to sell these...?"

"Hmpphhh..." he breathed uncomfortably. "I, uh... w-what does that matter? Are you interested or not?" His bejeweled monocle twinkled. "Well, you most certainly have to be! Yes, you haven't walked away yet..."

"I *will* walk away, like all of your other customers if you don't sell me something I can *afford*," Viasarria stared him down, despite her much smaller size.

He stared longingly at the ridiculous prices he expected of his customers, then glanced defeatedly back to her with a quivering of his mustache. "Fine, you win... dirty haggler. *F-Four* gold divitias, was it...?" he held his stomach, as if it made him physically ill to say such a thing.

Viasarria slid four gold coins over the table with a proud smirk and a puff of her chest. "Thank you for a *reasonable* transaction, sir," she said with a nod as he reluctantly handed her the Safiritem chunk.

"Ya certainly know how to handle the swindlin' type," Terrin raised a brow at her. "Where'd ya learn how to barter like that?"

"Travel is a big part of a blade dancer's life style," she said, tossing the unpolished blue gem into the air and catching it with a victorious grin. "When you're always a stranger in a strange place and a small fish in a big pond, you've gotta know how to talk to people so they won't take advantage of you. Sometimes you don't need violence to solve problems, just good wit and a bit of--"

"Scuze me, pardon me, comin' through!"

A quick, robed scelan ducked right by Viasarria and Terrin, excusing himself with a shove to the proud blade dancer as he breezed on past.

"Hey, what the shit!" Viasarria growled as she was knocked teetering to the ground, losing her grip on her prize as her hands flew to catch herself before she went down. She barely caught a glimpse of the thief whisking up the Safiritem with his tail before he took off again. "HEY! That's *mine!*" she shouted after him.

"Lemme handle this," Terrin took off after the speedy thief with a burst through the air. His feet looked like they never touched the ground until he had grabbed the small scelan by the hood, tripping him up and stopping him in his tracks.

The surprised thief groaned with pain as he was choked by his own clothing, his voice sounding like it belonged to a younger teenager. Terrin turned him around with a sharp grasp of his upper arms.

"Ya can't be serious, child," the tough scelan tipped an ear at the squirming thief. "What're you tryin' to get away with here?"

The young priest wriggled his way out of Terrin's hands and backed himself into a rock, as Viasarria approached them with her arms folded across her chest. Glancing between his captors, he never once relinquished his white-knuckle grip on the stone he stole. "What's it to you?! That snooty jerk at the stand would *never* let me buy these things for cheap like *you* guys got away with! I've been wanting these things *forever*! I want to be a real priest -- I can't do that if I don't have a magic item!"

"Why don't you just make it through the ranks like the rest of us?" Terrin simply suggested, crouching to his level. He held out a hand, waiting for the teenager to surrender his Safiritem, but he still didn't seem willing to let it go. "C'mon, ya too good for your own temple, are ya?"

"They're not fair to me!" the priest shook his head, unable to scoot any closer to the rock he was leaning against. "They don't think I have what it takes because I'm just some kid to them."

"Then show them you aren't," Viasarria said blatantly. "Do something yourself; don't cheapen your abilities by mooching off of someone else's success. Find your own and they'll accept you."

"She's right," Terrin agreed with a tip of his head in her direction. "You respected the temple enough to join. You go through all the daily motions of wearing the robe and worshiping, doing your chores --"

"That's the *boring* stuff!" the thief complained. "It's all the same, every day. Meanwhile, the 'real' priests are out there doing what a member of the Brotherhood is *meant* to do."

496

"Yeah well!" Viasarria stomped a foot, almost thinking she was reprimanding Layna. "If you don't learn how to do the 'boring stuff' right, how are you going to prove that you can handle more?"

"Are you gonna tell me that you learned how to haggle meanies like Stufflewurt by doing boring chores?" the young priest didn't seem willing to believe her story. He crossed his arms as if waiting for a better one.

"No, but I had to make enough money to pay for what I wanted until I *learned* how to haggle for better prices," she spat. "If you really want one of those things, go talk to the guy like an *adult* and try it for yourself. If you can't handle that yet, guess it's back to scooping strider crap for a while, right? Either way, you can't just run around grabbing people's stones."

Terrin coughed boisterously at the double-entendre.

"Fine..." the thief brought his knees to his chest. "I see what you mean. Here..." he looked away as he handed the unrefined Safiritem to Viasarria, its rightful owner. He sighed when he felt its promise of power lifted from his palm.

"You have an impressive way with words," Terrin said, rising to a standing position by Viasarria's side.

"Fighting isn't everything," the blade dancer explained. "Being a special operative like me requires many skills. Gathering information so you know where to go, and having the charisma to weasel your way out of getting captured are more important than how well you can kick ass."

"When I first saw ya, I'll have to admit, I didn't have the strongest of faith that ye'd handle yerself here," Terrin bit back a grimace, remembering the bar room scene. "But'yev done pretty good." He now looked to the swirling stones, forming a hectic blockade below and around the entirety of Mt. Malumai. "Now comes the difficult part..."

Terrin led Viasarria around the ring-shaped town until the buildings forming a wall around the abyss between them and Mt. Malumai's asteroid field opened up on either side of an arch-shaped trellis, forming the gateway to a tiled bridge. This bridge looked to be suspended using the same kind of magic or whatever freak force of nature was keeping the mountain staying aloft, because no kind of guard or beam was fastening it to anything but the sky around it.

Though it didn't look the safest, Terrin seemed to be confident that the thin straightaway path would hold his weight when he pressed a foot upon its flat surface. Viasarria was only keen to follow behind when she saw him trying first, but was honestly only more surprised that no one had come to stop them, or even ask what in the world they were trying to do.

'It's not like they had a sign out there saying 'employees only,' or whatever,' the blade dancer kept her dismissive snark to herself. "Hey Softie," she called to Terrin before he could get too far ahead. "Why don't you just fly over this, eh?"

"I didn't want to put your life in that kind of risk," Terrin admitted, looking at her sheepishly. "It's much safer to walk the distance." He stopped suddenly, placing an outstretched hand on a flat, invisible wall of air. "But first," he said, clenching the safiritem stone in his fist. He let his next action complete his sentence for him: reeling back his arm, a rush of wind flipped back his long hair and almost had Viasarria staggering behind him.

With an expert turn of his fist, he crushed the safiritem in his curled fingers, absorbing its total power within himself to be then immediately expelled in a single, tremendous punch. A horrendous sound, like glass shattering inside a tornado, accompanied the breaking through of the barrier that once barred their further movement along the bridge. Only after this happened did the magic barricade turn visible: Viasarria could see the jagged edges of the open wall of air, still crumbling down in sharp shards like a broken window pane.

What appeared to be a honeycomb pattern could plainly be seen, fading away from the opening. This pattern enabled the curvature of the wall to be seen, giving Viasarria the impression that the barrier was shaped like a giant bubble, surrounding the whole of Mt. Malumai.

"We've gotta hurry, now," Terrin turned back to warn his partner. "They'll know we're here." His eyes then jumped when he caught the shape of a blue robe standing at the entrance to the hovering walkway.

His heart stopped momentarily, his fingers pricking to be turned into his palms. His bristling nerves were quelled when he came to the well-timed realization that the person he spotted was not a 'goon' coming to impede their progress; rather it was the thief kid from whom they had recollected their Safiritem key.

Viasarria, who had been rendered speechless until now, followed the direction of Terrin's soft stare to the face of the priest boy behind them. They stood silent, waiting for the rebellious teen to come up and say something to them, but the kid was fine with relegating himself as a starstruck observer for now. He'd obviously not been anticipating that breaking through Mt. Malumai's shield would've been the purpose for their special artifact.

Viasarria's and Terrin's eyes met each other, exchanging looks with a small shrug before continuing on their way. The blade dancer couldn't resist the urge to make a comment in an attempt to alleviate her growing stress. "I can't imagine that everyone's supposed to get in here the way you just did."

"They don't," Terrin admitted. "It's keeps out e'ryone but Zercius' Elites; only they can move through that wall. But I figured a good amount of Safiric oomph could break us in just fine."

Viasarria incredulously gaped, "You mean you *never* tried before?"

Terrin shrugged. "Prisoners have in the past, because they believed that they could leave Malumai if they went to the top of the mountain," he pointed to its distant summit. "But they didn't get very far. I knew I could break out if I wanted to… but I never had a reason to pick a fight with Lord Zercius."

Someone certainly was interested in picking a fight with him, however. A swirling cloud of dark fog was issued from the bridge at Terrin's feet and began rising around him. This thickening snake of a black nebula pulsated with purple lightning like a thunderstorm as it grew around the aeromancer's body. Terrin's knees bent in a guarded stance as he threw a rather vain punch at the pernicious fog, his fist doing naught but sliding right through. His hooked arm in fact turned numb where it touched the thundering snake, and fell limp as if paralyzed.

The now frightened Terrin's next reaction was to step back, but he had nowhere to move but skyward. Instead of risking his safety by leaping into the river of asteroids above, he summoned the powers of his Annihlus ring to shoot a burst of air pressure from his body. With a loud *thump,* like the pop of a bomb, the nebula snake was pushed away and disseminated into the atmosphere -- for a second. The numbing fog then returned with significantly more aggression and speed than it exhibited before.

The next thing Terrin knew, he was immediately restrained by the constricting cloud, sapped of all strength and unable to move. Unable to stand by any longer, Viasarria reached for Nohvaias' handle, but the High Priest's sword advised her against interfering. "Don't let *yourself* get caught up in it too!" he cried. "Find its caster!"

With a confused quirk of a brow, Viasarria pulled the Safiric steel from her scabbard as if demanding further elaboration. Instead of wasting time with an explanation, Nohvaias simply gestured for her to look upward by wiggling himself in Viasarria's hand. The blade dancer followed his prompt to see a cloaked priest, floating within the torrent of asteroids. He was gesticulating his hands in a kind of rolling motion, as if telekinetically stirring the cloud that was wrapping itself around Terrin's paralyzed form.

She couldn't reach her flying adversary from where he was. His cloak was blowing in the nonexistent breeze behind him. He was somehow able to dodge the various stones by simply remaining there, as if he was deflecting them with an invisible barrier. Viasarria tested the range of Nohvaias' power by unleashing a curved saber of sundering force with a swing of the Safiric steel. The blackish purple wave of energy distorted the air as it sliced on through, but was blocked by one of the asteroids passing between them. It cut a deep, wedge-shaped scar into the thick boulder, but did nothing more than get another priest's attention on her.

Viasarria found herself blindsided by another of the flying bastards, shooting her clear off the bridge with a blast of blue light. Her ears rang as if she had been struck by a grenade, leaving her momentarily disoriented as she tumbled into the air. She couldn't tell if she was falling or rising until clarity was restored to her senses.

She watched the choppy surf of rough stones passing her by, the sensation of gravity weighing on her cranium and in the pit of her stomach, telling her that a painful impact was imminent. She tried to twist her body to orient herself upright, but was unable to stick the landing as a flying boulder passed under her feet. She tumbled once more and landed neck-first on the next small rock to come zipping through.

The resilient blade dancer was somehow able to blink the stars from her eyes just quickly enough to reach with a single hand to dig her soft fingers into the craggy surface of another, larger stone. She could see the bridge she had fallen from was now very much above her, but without the presence of an atmosphere, it was almost impossible to cursorily gauge the distance.

As she fought to pull herself onto the carriage-sized rock, utilizing her tail and her free arm to hoist herself up, she watched the other speedy boulders nearby turn black. Pools of darkness grew all around her, and from them emerged the wraith-like servants of Safiro.

"You cannot take her back!" they hissed. "The Vytameta is ours!" "The Father's Will shall be done!"

As they began conjuring their ghostly bullets between their fingers, Viasarria lashed a whip of cutting force from her Safiric blade, splitting in twain the first of her foes. She was able to dodge the oncoming projectiles being launched by his friends by acrobatically leaping and diving to the other rocks flying around her. Every shot they made with their exploding spheres of white fog blasted craters into any asteroid she was standing on, forcing her to keep moving.

Just when Viasarria thought she had found a place to rest, when it seemed that her enemies were no longer in pursuit, she saw her newest boulder haven darkening from below. It was crumbling apart beneath her feet. Her eyes darted for a means of escape, but either the closest asteroids were too small for her to hold onto, or they were moving too fast for her to grab onto safely. She had no more time to react; cued by the sound of the rock splitting apart, she dove backward, as if in the hopes something would catch her fall. But her confident leap of faith was unanswered. Her stomach sank as the wind rushed through her hair, unimpeded by gravity's embrace. Her once rigidly outstretched limbs were now fearfully flailing for anything to grab onto. Her breath caught in her throat, her eyes only remaining open because she forgot how to close them.

She hardly even felt it when it happened -- a stinging pain in her backside caused her whole body to buckle backward. She barely remembered the back of her head snapping into an unforgiving surface. Her prone form was rested like a pancake upon a lumpy rock no more than six feet across. Her arm dangled off the side of her flying stone bed; if her platform were to make even the slightest of intimate contact with any of its brethren breezing by, she would be pushed off into the abyss.

Her victorious foes circled her like vultures over a carrion feast, watching the dust settle while they waited for signs of life, but her unconscious body did not do so much as stir. As they closed in to pick her apart, a gradually strengthening wind began to blow through, before the horde of blue wraiths were whisked away by a cinder-laden whirlwind. They crashed into the hovering cliffs and barely had time to collect themselves before one of them was annihilated by a tremendous impact from a black blur.

The massive boulder on the other side of the crash was smashed into pieces, scattering like a volcanic eruption. The source of this spectacular destruction momentarily revealed itself before taking off again in another burst of speed: Terrin wore a confident grin, showing his obsession and increasingly apparent success at winning fights.

His breakneck flight was only interrupted to deliver rapid attacks on his enemies one after the other, slicing them apart with his blades of ice attached to his forearms, tackling them into walls of rock, or whipping them away with his tail. He had all the grace of a wrecking ball, shattering whatever he hit in whichever direction he was moving. It was clear he had no thought of strategy nor of tactics; he only thought of how he could end his foes as quickly as possible, with no consideration for the world around him.

Having scared off his enemies for the nonce, Terrin's eyes softly fell to the unconscious form of Viasarria, before he lazily drifted down to rescue her. Positioning himself lower than her resting place, he turned the boulder she was lying on so that her body would tumble into his outstretched arms. He cradled her against his chest and floated away from her uncomfortable location to find a place significantly less precarious. He fixed his gaze on the bottom of the spire, poking out of Mt. Malumai's underside. Now that he was closer to it than ever before, he had a better appreciation for how much larger the spiral stairway really was.

But this wasn't the time to be admiring the sights; the Brotherhood was already on to what he was doing. He had to act fast and get out of the open before anyone else could zero in on his position. Moving quickly and dodging flying rocks was difficult with dead weight in his arms; he had to tuck his head close to Viasarria's body to shield her in case he was struck by any wayward asteroid.

As the spire's upside down point and the base of the stairs were getting closer, he was starting to feel the sensation of pressure against his back -- a sixth sense telling him that someone's approach was imminent. But it wasn't as reliable of a sense as the one had as a Safiric acolyte, that was informing him of Viasarria's nearing death. He could check over his shoulder a hundred times to see no one coming at him from the roaring sea of stones, but he could look to the unconscious Pure in his arms and know that she couldn't survive long as she was.

The spire's stairway was large enough for two people to walk abreast, but not without fear of falling; there was no safety rail on which to ensure someone walking on the outside would not take a tumble off the side. But there was space enough on the landing, where Terrin's feet had finally touched, to sit himself into a comfortable kneeling position. He had no healer's touch, and no real chance to save her. Maybe Viasarria was more right than she realized, about Terrin being a 'Softie,' when tears started pricking at his eyes. He risked his own life to save hers, and had nothing to show for it. For as useful as the Annihlus was, with all its power, he felt utterly helpless in this moment of total weakness.

"You really have grown far from the Brotherhood, haven't you?" Nohvaias' voice almost sounded jeering, as his sword rattled inside Viasarria's scabbard. "Crying over a dying Pure... I'm proud of you. You remind me of when I was young."

Terrin was so choked up he could hardly speak. He sniveled and dried his tears until he was certain he could manage a response without his voice pitifully breaking. "Who are you?"

"Who I am…" Nohvaias despondently began, "is of no consequence. Not when compared to what I yearn to be right now: alive. I want your permission for me to take her body for my own, Terrin. Her soul will be leaving it soon. Were it not for her, I would not have my newest chance at life. I want us both to live on, together. Through each other and with you, we will save this world. What do you say?"

Terrin couldn't have said anything at all in this moment. All he could do was give his affirmation by a shaky nodding of his head, before bowing over Viasarria's lifeless form, overcome with shuddering sobs. He was not able to see, through his veil of tears, the light from Nohvaias' sword leaking into Viasarria's body, one particle at a time, like a swarm of fireflies. He was not even made aware of what was happening until he felt warmth emanating from the blade dancer, resting across his lap. His sniff of awareness was accompanied by the reassuring grip of Viasarria's hand against his wrist, straightening the crying scelan from his sorrowful genuflection.

He couldn't have looked like more of a mess when his tear-flushed face was brought to bear on the diametric, if not mischievous grin, of the scelan of light blue skin he now saw lying beneath him. His features were so fair; his leeringly narrow, Wild-blooded eyes seemed to have stolen the same, green luster that Viasarria's once had. His long, silvery hair was endowed above his brow a single, black stripe of the deceased blade dancer. His cheeks were pale white, yet endowed with a healthy flush. Truthfully, the handsomeness of the other male was enough to make musclebound Terrin jealous.

"Suck it up, won't you?" Nohvaias smirked, patting his wet cheek. "You look ridiculous. C'mon, tough guy, we're almost there." the former High Priest pointed to their skyward destination, encouraging Terrin to finally brush his forearm across his face so he could see it for himself.

The underside of Mt. Malumai had been entirely excavated out; the mountain had been hollowed into a giant, floating cave, through which the spire formed an axis leading all the way to the summit. There were lights inside the cave that resembled stained glass windows, shining on the spire so that someone traversing its heights would be able to see the inside of the cave. There appeared to be structures, like chapels, built within the cave's walls. Small bridges suspended by thin air were the only things connecting the stairway to the buildings.

"The Brotherhood certainly likes its unsafe architecture, huh?" Nohvaias spoke Terrin's mind for him.

However, the pugilist Prince's pensive mood was unperturbed. Nohvaias rolled his eyes at Terrin's lack of a response and snapped his fingers at him. "Stop standing around! The Vytameta needs us, you know!"

Chapter 43: The Champion of Safiro

Going to the top of Mt. Malumai would prove to be an even greater hassle than just getting there in the first place. Even without any asteroids to dodge, the spiral stairway winding through the entire mountain's hollow interior wasn't exactly a straight shot. With all the churches and buildings bulging out of the concave cliffs like burs in a tree, Nohvaias worried that, "They'll see us climbing up these stairs for sure, and when they come for us, we'll be too winded to fight them."

"Not if we get up there really fast," Terrin suggested, taking a knee to bring himself to her level. Nohvaias quirked a brow as he offered his arm like the seat of a swing. "Make yourself comfy. I ain't hoofin' it up the stairs."

Nohvaias's crossed his arms at the thought of perching his rump upon the other scelan's forearm. But seeing as how he had no other choice, he secured himself to his new sitting position by wrapping his tail under his arm and around his back, making sure he wouldn't fall when he rose to a standing position.

"You won't use me as a meat shield if we get waylaid, will you?" Nohvaias jokingly barbed.

"I'll think about it," Terrin smirked at him. "Just don't be mouthy and we won't get caught."

When Terrin and Nohvaias had risen into the golden fog of noxious air, they reached the summit of Mt. Malumai, which was entirely flattened like a plateau. A huge summoning circle was etched into the ground, made to represent the likeness of a half-closed Wild eye. This etching was filled with blood; a black altar in the center of this symbol formed its slit-shaped pupil. The convex table was built so that when its sacrificial offerings were exsanguinated, their blood would drain into the artistic trenching. The bodies of the last sacrifices had been reduced to their skeletal remains, and were suspended by chains on six columns encircling the summoning circle. There were just enough strips of red cloth hanging on the skeleton prisoners to indicate their prior attachment to the Sanguinic Sisterhood.

This truly horrendous sight was accompanied by another, which offered bittersweet relief to the rescuers who had come this far. Standing just outside of the Safiric summoning circle, was a wheel-shaped torture rack made of wood and fashioned into the likeness of a strange clock face. Runic symbols resembled the digits 12, 3, 6, and 9.

Hanging by its shackles, her limbs extended into the shape of an X, was the comatose figure of Kasra. Her face was covered by a black leather mask to protect her from the thickening miasma at these heights. This mask was fashioned with U-shaped horns to resemble some kind of demonic being; a pair of white, stylized eyes wrapped around either side of its face.

"Viasarria," a voice entered Nohvaias' mind. "We're here. We're coming to help."

A loud noise, like the crack of a whip or perhaps a sudden lash of lightning, turned the two's attention to Rozha and Kyrana standing just outside the summoning circle.

Nohvaias now shared the same mixture of disbelief and bewilderment that Terrin was. "Who the hell are they?!" He then caught the glint of red light off the communication ring on his hand -- he must have taken it for himself without realizing it, after using Viasarria's body as a gateway to the physical word.

"Yeah, I'd like to know the same thing from you, creep!" Rozha confrontationally started, tromping toward the two Brotherhood-dressed scelans. "What did you do to Viasarria?! You've got her ring! You must have some nerve trying to lead us into a trap!"

"Trap?" Nohvaias yawped, bringing a hand over Terrin's chest to stop him from charging the two priestesses. "You are mistaken -- I..." Realizing quickly it would take a long amount of time that they didn't have to explain what had happened, his hair flipped across his face as he resigned to shaking the thought from his head for now. "Look, it's not important right now! You have to rescue The Vytameta!"

"The *who?*" Rozha's raised brow was then pointed in the direction of Kasra's body, hung up on the torture wheel behind her. At first, nothing would have stopped Rozha from leaping to free her sister, until she heard Kyrana bleating at her from behind.

"Don't go *running* in there!" The Arch Healer fearfully warned her friend. "Just because it doesn't *look* like there's anyone here, doesn't mean they're not waiting to ambush us." Shifting her eyes to the foreboding surroundings, she added, "I'll bet anything they already know we're here."

Before Nohvaias could lend any assistance, he was stopped by a black, curved staff hovering above the poisonous fog. It was adorned with jagged, blade-like protrusions near the top and crowned by a round, sapphire gem that seemed to glow of its own accord. The second they laid eyes on it, the walking stick began to move, as if it were being carried by someone. It made a single revolution in a clockwise manner, revealing behind it as it went the now visible figure carrying the weapon. Deniechus returned their gaze with his lifeless eyes, exhuming malice with his smile.

"Ah, Nohvaias… how good of you to join the land of the living once more. You have come just in time to watch the beginning of the end."

Immediately thereafter, another one of the High Priests made his own appearance: emerging from a doorway of smoky darkness came the glowing eyes of Kada'timor. "You should feel privileged to witness the conception of the Master's grand creation."

Their statement was concluded by the both of them simultaneously. "A WORLD WITHOUT WEAKNESS; A WORLD WITHOUT PURITY."

The Master's Elites turned to the summoning circle and bowed their heads in silent prayer. After a minute of calming their minds with this dark concentration, they extended their hands toward the center of the circle and began slowly chanting a long verse. As soon as it began, Terrin, Nohvaias, and their newly-arrived allies found themselves unable to move.

With every repetition of their chorus, their voices grew louder. With the second verse, the flames of eight torches turned alight of their own accord. With the third verse, a tall gateway of flames manifested in the middle of the summoning circle, just a few paces away from the unconscious Kasra. With the fourth verse, a swirling portal of blackness and aubergine stars grew within the gateway. With the fifth and final cry, vociferous and more intense than any before it, the doorway to another dimension began to hum, louder and louder with every second until its pulsating vibrations rattled the pebbles on the floor.

Larger stones began to lift as if gravity had inversed when the sound of thunder struck from an omnipresent source. Amethyst lights like fireflies floated from the gateway and comprised a humanoid form standing over eight feet tall. The solid shape they assumed was sheathed in a bright blue light like an eggshell until this husk of light instantly dissipated with a flash to unveil a terrifying figure clothed in armor of purple and silver, laced with spines like a thistle. A golden smog swirled around his form; every crevasse of his carapace issued a deathly cancer.

"THE MASTER IS HERE," his faithful disciples whispered and genuflected. *"LORD ZERCIUS HAS COME."*

The focus of Zercius' amber eyes was fixed on Kasra and she alone. The steps he took with his metal boots crunched the small stones underfoot. The only indication the High Priest gave that he was aware of his audience's presence was when he started speaking. His every word was meticulously calculated. With every breath, flaxen fumes fell from the vents in his helm.

"Beautiful, is she not?" he began, placing a hand on the wheel to which she was bound. "I never imagined The Father would have chosen such an... *unassuming* Vytameta to cultivate this world into what it should have been... from the very beginning. When the Vytameta awakens, she will destroy all Pures and claim this world for the glory of Safiro."

Zercius caressed his knuckles longingly under Kasra's chin. "I've pined for the power you will give me, Vytameta. For such a long time, I have been awaiting the day you would free me from this hell."

Rozha aggressively growled under her restraints, "What you're talking about sounds like nothing more than the culmination of a delusional faith of *lies*! Kasra is not anyone's tool!"

Zercius heartlessly chuckled, holding his arms behind his back as he finally turned to face her. "Quite the contrary... *my Sister*. Throughout her life, she has been groomed to serve that very purpose. She was never meant to decide for herself; only to be sent in the right direction. Perhaps I cannot impute your ignorance alone for her destiny's incomprehensibility. You are just another piece of a grander image; your confusion in regards to her divine providence is reasonable, insofar. I am just as much of a sympathizer as you are. I do not wish for her to be harmed. I, too, wish to end her suffering."

He began to approach Rozha, wanting to have a closer look at the curiously familiar interloper. "We have always had a difference in opinion from the day we first met. Four hundred years have passed, and you're still the same... Sister Sevasmia."

Rozha's eyes widened, her muscles tensed with fearful disbelief. "What... did you say?"

"Ah... I see you're suffering memory loss," Zercius continued. "How pious of a priestess could you be, if you could not even remember your past life? You were the one to whom Sevasmia gave her Shield of Sanguina, to ensure it would not be lost when she was murdered by my hand. Was sealing me here in Malumai really worth the sacrifice she made?" He laughed, humored by the memory of which Rozha was not privy to. "How far do you think you can go to claim your precious paradise in such a weak, *faithless* body? When I kill you, Sevasmia, I will corrupt your soul so that you will *never* be reborn again."

With a slow raising of his hand, he summoned a blue thunderbolt to enter his palm from the clouds of poison in the twisted sky. And with this flash of light, a magnificent naginata appeared in his hand -- a golden blade of cancer on one end, and a mallet of unmaking on the other. "I was promised... by the new entity I serve, that the Vytameta would be the key to unlocking the shackles that bind me to Malumai. I will give her mortal form to The Postrekadas, so that It Who Judges the Gods shall be freed from his own imprisonment. Yes... the Vytameta will be more than the Champion of the Gods. She will have a power much greater than either. She will have... the Power Apocalypse! She will bring balance to this *universe...* and END the aberrant deities!!"

Outstretching his limbs and clenching his fists, Zercius meditated along with the rising wind, lifting him on a pillar of alabaster smog. This pillar grew tendrils of smoke, whirling around his levitating body like roots of a tree. From these roots sprouted fog-like fruits of miasma; bulbs of golden light edible only insofar that they would cause death to their consumer. These proverbial bulbs then blossomed and unleashed spores of sunlight to come dancing around their creator: Zercius, the Incarnation of Death.

The cyclonic wind hummed along with the meditating priest, growing in its intensity as he prepared to empower his vassal. Wreathed in his unholy radiance, Zercius used his naginata to tear a spatial rift in the very sky itself. From this black wound in the cancerous firmament, a crimson red fog fell like a jagged bolt, piercing into Kasra's form, filling her with so much energy and power that the torture rack behind her developed stress fractures from the amount of pressure she unwittingly exerted.

Kyrana and all her allies struggled harder against the mystic force to which they had been bound, to watch this satanic spectacle unfold. The sanrisma gems on the Arch Healer's branch of life shone brightly through the miasma cloud, threatening to engulf her. This pinkish red radiance flowed from her staff of Sanguinic magic to flow throughout her body, endowing her muscles with heat and strength, unlike anything she had felt before. She felt as if she had the might of Sanguina herself, pushing her arms through her invisible vice like a heavy net. Even her tail lifted as her whole body straightened. Both hands grasped firmly the branch of life as it issued an even greater light than it ever had before.

With a cacophonous clash, the foot of her staff crashed into the floor before her, sending forth a koptigma like nothing she had ever seen. This vast ripple of energy flowed through to not only free her, but all her friends from the entangling spell.

Zercius was knocked from his arborous fog from the force of the barrier's blast; his body careened backwards and knocking him dizzy against a crumbling pillar. He shook off the dregs of pain and watched in anger as the group of Sanguina's followers recovered from the paralyzing grip. Panicking slightly, the High Priest reached animatedly towards Kasra whose body was now filling with the blood red smoke, her eyes leaking soft clouds of wispy fog.

"Your ascension is almost finished, Champion of Safiro. Soon you will have all the powers you need to conquer this world."

Kasra's bindings then lifted, but instead of falling to the ground, her floating form disobeyed gravity. She remained suspended, her hair sparkling like the stars at night as its voluminous tresses weightlessly flowed behind her.

A tremendous peal, like that of a cathedral's bell as her struggle sent a pulse from the ritual site strong enough to ripple the ground under everyone's feet. Silence stole the breath from her witnesses' lungs, as they now watched globules of light lifting off the thin, white aura around her form.

A heavy clunk of Zercius' boot snapped everyone's eyes to focus on him. His open hand facing toward his Champion, the Master commanded, "Almighty Vytameta... Show me your power! Face your enemies... and DESTROY THEM!!"

At the palms of Kasra's outstretched arms, she focused a pair of black orbs, pulsating with white energy as shining particles, like cosmic dust, flowed into them. These black holes were then pushed together and combined with a mere closing motion of the Vytameta's hands. A great gale immediately rushed from her form, scattering small rocks and debris as if pushed by a tornado. Then, with a thrusting motion of her arms, from this gateway of darkness, a black pillar of fire slashed through the ground, creating a trench as it carved a destructive path straight to Lord Zercius himself.

The starstruck cultist was taken off his feet from the enormous clash of energy, ripping through his armor of purple and silver plates. He bounced once before tumbling to a halt, his crumbling armor continuing to tear apart like strips of flesh with each collision. Lord Zercius slowly lifted himself to his knees, thick miasma spilling through his clenched teeth. With the fury of a supernova, he lifted his gnarled, partially exposed visage, his eyes catching ablaze with golden smoke as they fixed their molten pupils on Kasra.

The traitor discarded her mask in a further act of outright defiance, disrespectfully tossing the leather wrap into the dirt while Zercius watched with hellacious contemn.

"You are merely a vessel for The Father's Will!" He struck the stone floor with a mighty peal as he returned to his feet. "You... are just a weapon... to free me so that we may undo the evils of this ROTTEN WORLD!"

A vortex of multicolored energy spiraled under Kasra's feet as the Vytameta began conjuring another attack. "Then I will start by destroying *you*."

"You naive creature..." Zercius snarled, his growl like an avalanche. "This Fang of Death is fashioned from a fragment of the Annihlus itself. It cannot be broken. And so long as I hold it, I cannot be defeated." He summoned the strength of Safiro himself as he raised his legendary Fang of Death and bit its all-powerful steel into the ground at his feet. From this single point, the entire asteroid on which they stood was fractured into thirds, causing Kasra's allies to be separated from either side of her.

Rozha and Kyrana found themselves staggering to maintain their balance on their own floating island, which happened to be shared with the large and imposing Kada'timor. "Priestesses..." he smirked under his skull-like helmet, "we have... unfinished business." The ghostly chain on his tail unbound itself into his hands, allowing him to lash it through his two old foes.

Kyrana could barely deflect the entirety of his chain whip with the projection of her masalida. Her shield shattered when the whip transferred its awesome force, but Kyrana's power was just able to slow it down enough to where she would only be knocked over without suffering injury. Rozha, meanwhile, was forced to duck under the oncoming weapon's overhead sweep. The long time it took for Kada'timor to regain control of his heavy chain's momentum was just enough for Rozha to draw her kris and come in to plunge it through the High Priest's abdomen. But even as satisfying as it felt to take advantage of such a beautiful opening, the massive scelan did not even bleed while the sword was buried up to its hilt in his body.

In fact, Kada'timor hardly flinched. The ghastly, blue light in his helm's empty socket twinkled with suspicious intelligence before he shoved Rozha away, at the same time prying the Red Dancer's weapon from his torso. She barely managed to tumble backward to break her fall, but her attempt to soften her landing only made it that much more precarious; forgetting the space she had to work with, Rozha somersaulted clear off a ledge of the floating island.

"Rozha!" Kyrana cried, as she watched her friend disappear.

"Help me up!" the Red Dancer shouted back, dangling precariously upside down by her tail, whose end was wrapped just barely around a small outcropping.

As fast as Kyrana could yell "*Fygidia*," Kada'timor was already upon his foes again. With another round swing of his huge chain, he broke the already small floating island in half. He was barely able to balance himself onto one of the floating land masses before his legs would have him doing the splits into oblivion. Now Kada'timor found himself on a platform no larger than five feet wide, staring down a very much cornered Rozha. Kyrana, meanwhile, was separated on her own personal island, and called Rozha back to her with another "Fygidia" spell, before Kada'timor could stomp her friend underfoot.

Suddenly, the High Priest realized he was alone and now drifting into the nothing sky, while his two opponents were huddled a safe distance on their little chunk of land, waving goodbye at him.

Nohvaias and Terrin only wished they could be so lucky. They were currently stuck on their own sky flotsam, cornered by a more uncomfortable member of Zercius' Elites. But Deniechus didn't seem terribly interested in starting a fight with them just yet; there seemed something rather thoughtless in his usually quite intellectual eyes. Right now, he was perfectly content to keep them busy just conversing with them, leaning lazily against his staff as if they had nowhere else more important to be. "In just a few short moments," he began, "you will see the beginning of Safiro's new world. There's nothing a pair of traitors like you can do to stop it."

As much as Terrin would have liked to show Deniechus exactly how capable he was to end their evil scheme, Nohvaias, sensing his aggression, once again moved his hand to block his advances. "Why aren't you on our side, Deniechus? Are you really still so blinded by Zercius' will that you have no mind of your own? Can you not see what he's up to? He does not serve Safiro! It is not his mission to let the Vytameta create Safiro's world!"

"Stop your nonsense," Deniechus hadn't the patience to even question Nohvaias' warnings. "Your mind was poisoned long ago by that vile Saint Sevasmia. You are still cursed by her Sanguinic delusions; like her, you seek to undo the progress the Brotherhood has made. Once the Champion of Safiro has removed Purity from this world, the Father's followers will be given everlasting life. We undying few will become the most powerful beings under the stars. We will be feared by all outworlders and conquer the Dark Men. Safiro will be the only god there is, and our power will be absolute."

"That is *not* Safiro's Will!" Nohvaias raucously shouted him down, holding his ears to stop the blasphemy. "The God of Death does not seek to undo the balance he has made! The Vytametas were meant to restore the cycle of Life and Death --"

"Silence, Sanguinic sympathizer!!" With a dexterous twirl of his walking staff, unmitigated by the loss of his arm, Deniechus' black magic branch transformed into his electric scythe. "I will slay you for the Glory of Safiro!"

The Reaper of Travestas chose his foe with a headlong charge; a bolt of lightning followed the curved blade of his large weapon as it crashed into the arena's rocky soil, but Terrin sailed away from their small platform. Seeing his opponent now suspended in the air, Deniechus threw his spiraling scythe to give him the chase its owner could not.

Terrin grabbed the wrist of his ring-bearing hand, his chip of the Annihlus reacting to his unspoken command with a black, flickering glow. The aeromancer's body was instantly enveloped by a thin layer of ice, like armor, to protect himself from Deniechus' spinning saber. Terrin flinched, his arms held out as if to block a fighter's punches as the dancing sickle took a mind of its own to hack away his frozen carapace.

The scythe was able to act independently of its caster, as now Deniechus was faced by Nohvaias, coming to Terrin's defense. He twirled his ancient sword as he began his acrobatic assault. The weaponless Deniechus raised the gauntlet of his forearm to block Nohvaias's energized, overhead chop, the force of which shuddered the Elite as a disc of blue light flashed from his opponent's steel.

Nohvaias swiftly sidestepped mere inches away from Deniechus' countering, outstretched palm, threatening to grasp him with its sparking claws. The swordsman answered with a swipe of his tail across his midsection, knocking him back the space he needed to capitalize further. With an upward sweep of Nohvaias' sword, he tore a black scar into the air itself, and telekinetically sent it forth to deliver its wrath.

As if having been pushed by a cyclone at his feet, Deniechus suddenly flew into the sky to dodge Nohvaias's attack. At the end of his flourish, he caught his scythe when it from nowhere reappeared back into his hands.

Terrin, now without much of his armor left from parrying Deniechus' possessed pole arm, re-entered the fray with astonishing speed and an uppercut of a forearm blade, comprised of his Annihlus' icy energies. Albeit flanked, Deniechus' reaction speed was unwavered by the surprise attack; a translucent globe sparked into life around him, emanating from his scythe when Terrin's white saber shattered against the Elite's defenses.

Deniechus punished his adversary's attempt with a jolt of his staff against Terrin's chest, breaking what was left of the plating covering it. His scythe looked like an electric wing spinning over his hand as he prepared to plunge it through his staggered foe, but Terrin recovered just quickly enough to summon a powerful gale at Deniechus' back with a sweeping motion of his arms.

The Elite found himself uncontrollably careening back to the floating arena, where Nohvaias was waiting to deliver his pent-up vengeance. Deniechus crash-landed on his knee, giving the swordsman the perfect range to slice right through his skull. But the High Priest was able to back off with a standing step, just in time for the very tip of his blade to leave a horizontal scar across his foe's face.

Deniechus let out a harrowed cry as the stinging pain took an extra second to fully sink in; he covered his face with a wide sleeve and turned his back to his adversaries. He barely had a moment to check his arm for the crimson ooze staining his indigo cloth before Terrin was upon him again. The flying brawler kicked the High Priest down with both feet thrust atop his head, crushing Deniechus underneath him with a burst of alabaster dust.

Something about this small victory was satisfying enough to warrant a high-five between Terrin and Nohvaias, but they perhaps had begun their celebration a little too early. Terrin felt what he initially assumed to be Deniechus' corpse shrinking under his boots, prompting him to look down and see that the Elite's robed figure had turned completely into liquid shadow. Shortly after Deniechus' startling disappearance, the looks Terrin and Nohvaias exchanged were averted to the inharmonious bomb detonated on the summit of Mt. Malumai.

They looked with horror to see a great cloud of purple smoke creating a blinding haze, disallowing anyone from the outside to see the altercation between Kasra and Zercius within. The clouds seemed to have been caught under the contours of a dome, as if contained within a giant snow globe spanning the area of Zercius' battlefield.

The henge of sacrificed priestesses were brought down, the altar destroyed, and the summoning circle around it ruined by the scars of combat. Zercius stumbled back as he was struck by a volley of silver stars shooting from Kasra's right hand, denting his armor as it rang out like gunshots.

Upon having been taken by this attack, Zercius slumped slightly, his shoulders sinking. Clouds of yellow gas fumed through his sharp teeth as he tiredly puffed. He looked as though he was waiting to be finished off, albeit his naginata was still firmly in hand. But his enemy had not the energy to give her coup de grace.

Zercius stood his staff on its end and clenched his free hand in meditation. Suddenly, as if by a vacuum, all of the alabaster fog covering the summit of the mountain was sucked into the cracks of his armor. Then reeling his arm back, he opened his hand, his clawed fingers upturned to wrap around a golden orb of poisonous mist. This ball of fog-like energy was being fed to grow larger by the wisps of thick, yellow clouds seeping through the plates of his armor.

Kasra tried to lock him still with an astapsyxi, but instead of his attack fizzling out at his fingertips as she had expected, she found herself having to dodge a destructive beam of pulsating power -- the likes of which she'd never seen used by any member of the Brotherhood. She could feel the heat of its intense radiation as it rushed by her side. Fearfully she turned, just to watch with bewilderment as this unspeakable power crashed into the ground behind her. The gust of wind from its violent detonation had her long hair whipping across her face.

Holding his naginata in both hands, Zercius swooped down on his stunned foe, but the sound of his approach swiftly brought the Vytameta back to reality. She prepared a purple masalida on her right forearm like a buckler shield, raising it up above her head to deflect Zercius' Fang of Death. With her free hand, she pushed him away with an intense koptigma, the force of its telekinetic burst rippling the air like a shock wave as it caused the huge High Priest to tumble through the air.

Zercius showed an athleticism unexpected of such an old and large scelan, especially one clad in armor, as he in midair orientated his feet to point groundward, so that he would slide back on his heels. He then bit the point of his Fang of Death into the ground between his feet to slow down his backward momentum. But he was only able to stop himself in time to see Kasra's next attack coming: Three Star Bolts bursting like white fireworks tore open his damaged armor from his waist to his head like a tin can. Zercius' muscular body underneath bled yellowish blood from the hole-shaped wounds in his dark, veiny skin. His face was fixed in a gnarled grin from lacking lips, exposing his sickly gums and sharp teeth. His eyes looked like molten steel with small white pupils.

Zercius gaped with astonishment as the protective dome he'd created to surround their arena shattered like a floe of ice breaking up in a swift river. All of the poison gas inside was released into the endless atmosphere. The High Priest slouched, a single arm wrapped around his torso as the other hung limply by his side to drop his Fang of Death to the ground. His tail laid limp behind him, his knees buckling under his own weight.

Every move, every motion, every single muscle working in his body seemed to cause him excruciating pain as he forced himself, as though possessed, to walk toward the Vytameta. It seemed as though every living fiber were slowly withering away, as though every string of muscle were separating from each other. He shivered uncontrollably with every labored breath, his limbs tensing up and spasming intermittently.

"Th-This... *Khh*, none of this sh-should be possible," He coughed up blood down the front of himself as he struggled to speak. "I was meant to... bring in the new age. Life has -- *hhhkk* -- no other purpose." His teeth gnashed together from a quivering jaw forcing him to stutter. "What is your p-purpose, Vytameta? I must know... wh-why you -- *khhhxx* -- could end what was once fated."

Kasra took a cautious step back away from him, pressing her weight guardedly on one foot as she looked down her nose at her hyperventilating adversary. "How does my being a 'Vytameta' grant me the right to control destiny? Believing that having some special power somehow entitles you to the world is the disease of tyrants and demagogues. A power's purpose is defined by its user, not by divine providence. I am not some delusional demigod guided by predestination. I rightfully earn what I have because I make my own path in life; nothing is 'fated' to be mine."

Though it pained him much to speak at all, Zercius couldn't help but to bellow a restrained laugh. "The world th-through your agnostic eyes... is nothing but black a-and white. You're always kh-concerning yourself with matters of... good and e-evil... but, fate and destiny free the universe of malice. Within the i-invisible forces that govern... e-everything and everyone, we live in a world of order."

Zercius' posture gradually slouched as his willpower was fading. Kasra watched him unblinkingly as his eyes lazily drifted open and shut, struggling to maintain consciousness. He slowly raised out an open hand and said, "T-Take my power and you shall... be e-endowed with my knowledge. Then... then you'll see... what you were meant to be."

From where she and Kyrana were Rozha was able to silently watch Kasra take some time for careful consideration. Even though she had known the Vytameta all her life, she had a hard time recognizing the sage being as her sister. She was endowed with a certain, inexplicable splendor, the likes of which could not have belonged to a mortal person. The powers she used to vanquish her foe were unlike anything she'd ever seen. And the words she spoke were unlike any she'd heard from either the Safiric Brotherhood or the Sanguinic Sisterhood.

Having reached her conclusion, Kasra's thoughtful gaze trailed away from the soundless space of dispersing clouds and was now fixed on Zercius' broken, languid body. "I knew from the moment I was born that I have no place in this world. I've always known I can't trust anyone -- and certainly not anyone who'd use me as an expedient to their own ends. I want to know what I am and what my purpose *really* is. Supremacy cannot be evaluated by serving an intangible, yet supposedly omnipresent entity. I was not designed with a 'sacred path' at all. That is why I cannot commit to either Safiro or Sanguina, not because I'm a 'Vytameta,' but because I fight for some*thing*, not some*one*. Whoever has their own philosophical and moral compasses to follow become leaders and emperors. Anyone who is not guided by a direction of their own become the zealots and the crusaders who die for them. I refuse to be indoctrinated; I refuse to ingrain myself without knowing both sides of every story. I only believe what I know, and what can be proven."

"A wasted lifetime is spent in ignorance," Zercius replied. "It's easy to be agnostic when you're young, but you can't go through life refuting all faith. This world has no room for people who are on the fence."

"Why would I want to spend the rest of my existence serving gods who've forsaken me?" Kasra immediately returned with an angry start. "The servants of Safiro believe that our race must sharpen itself against each other and destroy anyone opposed to violence. The servants of Sanguina believe that our race must live in harmony and forgive those who commit wrongdoing."

Her voice softened again before she added, "But the servants of either god have one thing in common: a vision that this world cannot sustain itself unless the principals of one deity defeats the other. Perhaps, in order to change the world, our people will need the assistance of both? Like plants need both dirt and sunshine to grow, a mind needs both bad and good ideals to expand its horizons. Once I have practiced the ideals of Safiro and Sanguina, I will determine which is dirt and which is sunshine."

The Vytameta held both hands forward, before them focusing a great ball of sparkling energy that looked like a hole punched out of the night sky. From this shining orb of many colors, a bright, purple pulse shot forth like a quasar. On contact with Zercius' exposed body, it immolated the High Priest where he stood. He loosed a terrible, agonized screech as he was completely disintegrated into embers, so that not even his sordid soul remained. Every fragment of flame and tattered cloth left over was then drawn into a black rift his body left behind. This hole of inexplicable darkness provided the only exit from this backward world.

The white aura surrounding Kasra's body faded; as if it were the only thing keeping the Vytameta in her upright stance, she dizzily wobbled on weakened legs the moment she was no longer bathed in its ethereal radiance. She clumsily fell to a sitting position, barely remaining conscious as she placed her hands flat on the ground behind her. Her ears had just enough sensitivity to stir her head in the direction of a rushing wind -- the sound of Terrin's flight coming toward her as he carried Nohvaias in his arm.

"You alright, young hero?" The big aeromancer knelt to her level, at the same time letting Nohvaias step onto solid ground.

The bedazzled Kasra couldn't manage a response. Her now purple eyes seemed glazed over as she listlessly stared at him, her lips parted slightly. It was obvious she wanted to say something, but words were failing her.

With the intonation of a fygidia, Kyrana and Rozha suddenly appeared before Kasra. Both priestesses were equally relieved that she was safe and for the most part uninjured. But they knew they couldn't stay at the horrible heights of Malumai for long. As if echoing Zercius' roar of death, the Anticosm erupted in an uproar caused by the Safiric Brotherhood, swarming in like a dark cloud to avenge their fallen leader.

"Go, now!" Terrin shouted to his team, thrusting a finger in the direction of Zercius' portal. "I'll cover your escape!"

"What?!" Nohvaias resisted. "Don't be stupid! Come with us!"

"I won't make it! It's more important that the Vytameta lives!" the scelan argued as the horde closed in. "I ain't dyin' here," he promised, pushing his friends toward the doorway. "If Zercius was right about each of us having a destiny, then perhaps it was mine to stay behind so you could go on."

Without letting Nohvaias nor his other allies have any time for further argument, he shoved them into the portal with a whip of his tail as he turned to face his innumerable adversaries bearing down on him.

As if waking from a dream into the night, none of the travelers knew how much time had passed since they had been away from the real world. They found themselves lying face down in a bed of soft grasses, on the incline of Tresantia's hill outside the city's western gate. From there they could see the city lights of both the Sanguinic and Safiric sides of town, on either side of Mediona's upbeat melodies in the distance.

Sanguina's moonlight was upon them, turned to a crescent sliver as if the Goddess were giving them a little smile, proud of Her resolute followers for having escaped Malumai alive. Rozha coughed weakly as she tried to stand, slinging Kasra's arm around her shoulders to help her up alongside her, but simply hadn't the strength to carry their weight. She spat up blackened blood from the toxic air having poisoned her lungs; she began to feel faint as she tried to press on. She was the only one fighting to stand; Nohvaias and Kyrana were gasping on the cool, crisp air, watching their friend with bewilderment.

"Stay put," Kyrana warned the Red Dancer. "You are much too weak to be going anywhere. You mustn't move when your blood has been steeped in such toxins."

"I'm not..." she eked out her words as she dragged her feet, and a fading Kasra, toward the open gate of the city. "I won't let his sacrifice... be in vain. We have to pull through, together..."

After taking two steps, she was reduced to crawling, sinking lower and lower until Kasra slipped from her grasp. Her focus slowly fading, the last thing she saw was her hand reaching toward the night sky before she expired her last and fell face down, her withering muscles unable to be pushed any farther. Moments later, an angelic light washed over their motionless bodies lying in the tall grasses on the hill, as if from a lantern being carried by an unknown but wholly benevolent visitor. Though none of them were any longer awake -- possibly not even alive -- the stranger spoke to them as if they could hear her voice.

"The path I made for you does not end here. There is still more yet to be done."

Chapter 44: Revelations, part 1

The morning after Kasra and Brynita had left for the Cave of the Arachniath, Mother Diava called all her priestesses to the Purifier Hall for the daily ablutions and headcount. What with Rozha and Kyrana also absent, it was a bit easy to overlook someone missing at first. But when she noticed the two extra, vacant spots around the natatorium, her usual frown soured substantially. "Where are Kasra and Sister Brynita?"

Upon receiving no response from Teachers Wanystha and Xanne, who were every bit as puzzled as everyone else exchanging looks with them, Diava returned everyone's attention to her with a thunderous slamming of her hands on her podium. Everyone's eyes were wide with fear from the silent, yet impatient rage darkening the High Priestess' countenance. She didn't need anyone to tell her what happened. She knew what Kasra was capable of. She knew she couldn't have kept the Vytameta in these doors forever. The only thing she didn't know was why she took Brynita with her. But what did that matter?

*'The most powerful being in the world is set loose -- **beyond my control** -- and now could the only chance we have to stop the Brotherhood's evil is gone!'*

In a single motion, exhibiting untold strength, Diava lifted her marble podium and cast it off the side of her plinth, causing its sanrisma dome to shatter against the floor. All of the veritably shocked priestesses sitting around the pool rose to their feet and stepped back. Even the Teachers posed no resistance to the abbess' angered outburst. For the first time in any Sister's memory, both Wanystha and Xanne showed a collective look of absolute fear.

Despite their efforts to stay out of the way, the High Priestess targeted them with an imperious directive. "Drain the Purifier!" Diava's shrill voice pierced the heavens of the hall. She didn't much care who did her task, but Xanne wasted no time racing to the far end of the pool to escape Diava's wrath.

Wanystha meanwhile tried to maintain the peace as best as she could, rallying the scared novitiates and shaky priestesses through the open corridors before sealing them off with a powerful masalida.

Xanne turned the spoked wheel on the faucet faster when she saw Diava advancing toward her, the speed of the drain's opening not quick enough for either of their likings. The High Priestess' silver hair billowed behind her as if taken by a rush of air from beneath her fluttering gown. Her bright blue eyes shone intensely as her whole body was surrounded by a smoky white aura. A pulse of power around her outstretched hand caused the air around it to shimmer like an event horizon.

With a fulmination of enraged energy, she cast a mighty koptigma at the small maelstrom forming in the sinking Purifier. The explosion of wind instantly drained all the water in the natatorium by splashing it like a tidal wave clear back to the walls. The whole floor of Sachelvae was swamped by the violent deluge; an unsuspecting Xanne was taken off her feet and was rushed into the closed doors by the torrent.

Mother Diava stormed down the stairs of the empty Purifier and began her descent through its drain into Sachelvae's secret subchamber. Her normally elegant walk was overtaken by her shivers of anger; each step she took was not so much a controlled motion, but rather a convulsive twitch urging her forward.

The secret chamber itself seemed to react to her uncontrolled mood; the pink globes of magic light being held by Sevasmia's statuary flickered like candlelights dying in a cold breeze. The square-shaped indentation in the center of the room -- the summoning circle for the Elnastha Gate -- emitted a red light around its frame, as if warning oncomers to stay clear. But Diava was unhearing to these unspoken warnings.

As soon as she set foot in the indentation, the globes of light being held by the statues of the Saint started turning red. These thoughtless sentinels then encapsulated Mother Diava's body in an astapsyxi -- the strength of which was as impressive as the action was shocking. But the High Priestess' minutia of fear did not outlast her confident rage.

Her whole figure shivered within the muscle-tensing vice, as if beginning to overcome its effects by her mere will. Her aura came back with greater intensity just seconds before she released another koptigma to not only break the astapsyxi holding her still, but to also snap the statues in half with the loud burst.

She glared at the dying lights in Saint Sevasmia's eyes of stone, and waited for the red glow around the summoning square to disappear before she shared any words with the likeness of Sachelvae's holy matron. *"I'm* in charge now."

Mustering the most concentration her troubled mind would allow, with a spiraling gesticulation of her hands, she began muttering a prayer she hardly believed anymore, enunciating its sacred words almost blasphemously, as if twisting the arm of Sanguina Herself to open the Elnastha Gate. Even now, she could feel the Goddess' ire bearing down on her from Her ethereal realm.

She ignored the mystic pressure being exerted on every inch of her being. Despite her guilt trying to crush her from the inside, the High Priestess lacked the full compunction to ask for her Goddess' forgiveness.

"This is *my* world to save."

The Elnastha Gate twisted into life with a cyclonic force that almost had Diava losing her balance and staggering toward it. The High Priestess steeled herself against the magic wind's growing intensity. She could hear the rush of air escaping through the hole at the top of the stairs, creating an almost tornadic whistle as it grew and grew until...

With a sound like a crack of lightning, the portal had reached its full size -- the pink disk swirled with white waves and sparkles of light dancing toward the center. As it just floated between the ruined statues, it continuously emitted a melodious ring, like windchimes settling after a gale. Then, this transient peacefulness was abated by a new sensation -- rumbling, like a distant stampede, shook pebbles and grains of dust littering the floor.

These tremors grew until even the fist-sized rocks and debris from Sevasmia's statues joined this frenetic jumping. Streams of dirt fell from the ceiling as cracks began to form along the walls. Diava took a step back toward the stairs, and turned around as she heard the iron comprising the stairwell creaking. Her chance at escape was crumbling right before her. Her faith once again tested by her returning senses, she timorously raised her communication ring, about to beg for the assistance of her terrorized friends.

But what she feared had already emerged.

A blinding flash and an ear-splitting screech had Diava collapsing to her knees. When the light had faded and sight was slowly returning to her eyes, she blinked away the dark spots floating through her vision and held the insides of her ears, wondering if the quiet in which she was suddenly immersed was due to deafness or the end of the storm. She would receive her answer one way or another -- and far too soon.

"Mother... Diava..."

That voice was clear as day. Diava's back stiffened, almost too scared to face whom she knew was standing behind her. Now the abbess was not shaking from rage, but from heart-skipping fear. Her spine tingled with rigidity so strong, it felt like it would snap if she twisted it to turn around. Her breath caught in her throat when she saw a strikingly angelic figure floating where the Elnastha Gate once stood.

Diava's eyes narrowed against the white radiance shining off the stranger's body with such splendor. The angel silhouette's arms were folded, its head bowed in prayer. The disc of light behind the shadowed angel faded into an iridescent halo.

Diava was graced and at the same time stunned by the features revealed to her by the retreating darkness, fading away from the angel's form.

"Layna."

A solemn smile of inner peace graced the vixy's countenance in such a way that it almost seemed beautiful.

"Come hither, neophyte, and say a prayer to your new... goddess." The awakened Vytameta's lips curled at one corner as her eyes slowly began to open. The vixy's once green eyes had changed to red and blue, and almost gleamed in the low light. Undeniably, her once Pure pupils had narrowed into Wild slits. The red robes she once wore were replaced by a more form-fitting outfit of black and green. Despite their difference in height, Diava felt like Layna was the one staring her down.

"You..." The High Priestess began with a chilled breath. "You are the Champion of Sanguina -- *not* the Goddess' replacement."

Layna's smile immediately fell. The dark Vytameta relaxed from her posture, letting her arms hang to her sides as she kept a single knee bent, her long tail waving like ripples in a pond toward the ground. "I will not debate my purpose with the desperate masses, especially not the likes of she who hath summoned me to right the world's wrongs." Her nose wrinkled as her scowl deepened. Diava was silenced by her judgement. The Vytameta continued, "I was *made* unto this world for one purpose: to decide the fate of its people."

"Why do you speak as if you are not one of us?" Diava protested. "Are you not belhuayn first? Do you not represent us?"

"I am as belhuayn as I am Wild or Pure," Layna lifted her head. "I am attached to no place, I belong to no people, and I worship no deity. I have no need to find a 'Path' of enlightenment when I can forge my own and end the Paths of others at will… because I am a goddess, myself." Her smile returned, daring the abbess with contempt, "Behold my brilliance and know what I say is truth. Lies are made by those who wish to gain power over the deceived, but I need not stoop to such cowardice for I already *have* all the power in the world."

Diava frowned with denial, the vixy's words only serving to regalvanize her faith. "I do not believe the Goddess would have told you such things. To rule us was not the reason you were made! If you betray your sacred Mother, She will--!"

"Sanguina can do ***nothing!!***" Layna suddenly snapped with a commanding boom. Black, heatless fire exhumed from her body as she held a clenched fist out to her side and pointed down at the High Priestess. "I was made to be *beyond* Their Will! What I decide is *ultimate*! My powers *cut* the strings of destiny!" Layna watched Diava's nerve shrink under her manic grin. The righteous Vytameta's sudden calm was as foreboding as it was sardonic. "And as I promised before… *you* will be the first to experience them all."

With a raising of her hand, a tornadic wind even more powerful than that of the Elnastha Gate began flowing into her palm. Ribbons of black and white energy swirled from every corner of the room and converged above her head like a shrinking pinwheel, transforming into an ever growing, pulsating spiral of black and purple light.

Diava cast aside her white gown with practiced speed and replaced it with a holy armor made of Sanguina's light -- in an instant, a whole suit of masalida steel appeared over her body. In her left hand, a Branch of Life had been summoned with a fountain of sparks. Entangled in its wooden tresses was a brightly shining sanrisma -- a Purifier Beacon. "You are not above Sanguina's Will. The sacred Mother prepared a contingency for Her rogue Vytameta. I am Her last line of defense."

"The more you talk," an enraged Layna twitched her head to the side, *"the more I want to **KILL YOU!!**"* Bringing both hands together and aiming them forth, she fired her power spiral like a bullet that, as soon as it was detached from her grasp, multiplied into five more projectiles.

All six flying saws each took a different path on their way to slice up Mother Diava from all directions, but the High Priestess deflected them all with a well-timed golden masalida. With a twirl of her Purifier Beacon and an outstretched hand, Diava slammed Layna back into the wall with a powerful koptigma blast. However, the Vytameta was equally prepared with an invisible shield of her own, glowing with a purple light that refused recognition by either Safiro or Sanguina.

No matter how powerful her unholy barrier was, it could not protect her from Diava's astapsyxi, freezing the struggling Champion in place. This special astapsyxi, blessed by the Purifier Beacon, began siphoning Layna's energy into its sanrisma. Layna grit her teeth as she felt herself slowly weakening under the bone-locking suggestion of this magic vice; she could even see her draining shield constricting toward her, as if threatening to crush her within it.

With a koptigma of her own, Layna blew away not only Diava's astapsyxi but cratered the wall behind her as if it had been shot by a giant cannon. Huge chunks and boulders of debris blasted toward Mother Diava and struck her masalida, causing it to flux and shimmer as her secondary line of defense was being brought to its knees.

Layna finished it off with a supersonic rush, discarding her own shield to deliver the slash of a black blade of fire through Diava's masalida. The forceful disengagement of the High Priestess' shield rang through the chamber and caused its owner to stagger. The next swing of Layna's hellacious sword put a crack in Diava's Purifier Beacon when she used it to parry her attacker.

Recognizing that her holy staff would not be able to weather another sort of this punishment, when she saw Layna coming back for another thrust, Diava froze her with an astapsyxi. She then sent her enemy flying, bouncing off the floor with a point-blank koptigma blast. Seeing that the Vytameta had the air taken out of her lungs, watching her have a bit trouble standing back up, Diava took this opportunity to call in reinforcements through her communication ring. "Fygidia me out of here! Prepare for confrontation!"

Just as Layna returned to a languidly hunched stance, she fixed a vindictive glare on the retreating High Priestess in time to watch her disappear with a flash of light. Blood trickled between her teeth as her lips parted into something between a grimace of pain and a grin of excitement as she stared at the light coming through the hole in the ceiling, leading back to the surface of Sachelvae.

Jagged wings of red light flashed from behind her back as a transparent sphere of darkness faded into existence around her body, enabling her flying form to crash through the ceiling like a cannon ball. A thunderous explosion of stone debris denoted the Vytameta's arrival to the Purifier Hall, where the dark angel was surrounded by Diava and her company of priestesses.

"That's right, call in reinforcements! *Send more meat to the grinder!*" Layna mocked her foe. "No hell can hide you from my *divine judgment!!*"

524

Spreading her arms outward, the Vytameta closed her eyes and tipped her head back as twin pinwheels of black energy began twisting into her open hands.

The vacuum being drawn into her shield stole the air from her opponents' lungs and snuffed the fires of the swinging chandeliers now crumbling to the floor. Marble stones began levitating into the air as if gravity were being inversed. What was left of the Purifier itself crumbled into the abyss of the secret chamber beneath it, forming a gaping hole in the floor of the desecrated temple.

"Now!!" Diava commanded, thrusting the shining sanrisma of her Purifier Beacon toward their foe. "Seize her!"

Simultaneously, all priestesses and faculty locked an astapsyxi onto Layna -- the might of all forty of them combined created a suffocating pressure so intense, the Vytameta could feel its weight being exerted on every inch of her bones. But her overflowing energies could not be contained. The effects of her powers were undaunted; Diava's followers found themselves increasingly short of breath as they watched the bright, pink fringe of their astapsyxies beginning to fail.

Layna's limbs quaked inside the mystic vice, resisting its crushing power with rapidly released koptigma bursts. Each one felt like the stomp of a mountain, causing powerful tremors that extended stress fractures from the temple's floor to its walls, until -- with a deafening detonation of wind, every one of the priestesses were sent flying back into the walls as the entire ceiling exploded into the sky. It was as if a tornado had suddenly formed above Sachelvae's roof, with just as much ruination left in its wake.

The Purifier Hall was rendered an unrecognizable pit of dust and debris. Anyone who was not immediately crushed underneath boulders from the roof or impaled by the smaller, bullet-like stones that had been scattered in every direction, were slumped against the corners of the temple and buried underneath what was left of their sacred sanctuary.

Were it not for Diava's quickly timed masalida, she and her Teachers standing on either side of her would not have survived the devastation. Behind them, stood the broken entrance to the temple; the massive iron doors had been bowed out as if kicked by a giant and were barely hanging on the busted hinges of the ruined jambs. A terrified Xanne and Wanystha watched a whirlwind of smoke and dirt swirling around the floating Layna -- the Vytameta's eyes were transfixed on her remaining victims, glowing like green lights from the twisting clouds.

"Hear the will of your new goddess!" came Layna's conceited decree. "No longer shall your Sisterhood be allowed to stymie the growth of a greater specie. As you have been a blight to this world, you shall be *cleansed* of it!"

"This cannot be Their Will!" Wanystha disbelievingly cried, cowering against the doorway as she watched Layna's cyclone darken with fury. "Why would Sanguina condemn us?!"

"Have we never had the Goddess' favor?" Xanne fearfully twisted her tail around herself, keeping her quarterstaff outstretched. "Where did we go wrong? What warning did we not heed? Why does Sanguina wish this be our fate?!"

"ENOUGH!" Diava raucously interjected. "If you want to live, retreat while you still can!"

Any action the bewildered priestesses were about to take was shuddered from their spirits by Layna's demonic cackle. "Has the great Diava lost her nerve? You can run, but you will still DIE!" The Vytameta then unleashed all the power she had stored as an all-engulfing whirlwind of invisible blades -- a blinding Sunder Torrent. Everything that stood in the Purifier Hall was torn to pieces. The walls of Sachelvae crumbled and now bore testament to Layna's new power with the glyphs of their deep scars. The evil Vytameta seemed rather impressed with herself; she gazed with a smirk to the exhaust drifting off her palms. She had never felt more alive.

Diava's once radiant armor of transparent shields was broken apart to sharp shards of glass, dissolving into the air like a swarm of fireflies. She weakly coughed and barely stirred as Layna slowly made her approach. Lacking all ability to move a muscle, the bleeding, broken abbess resigned herself to lying in the ruins of her temple, soon to become her grave. As her eyes went blank, she started to see something beyond the present, physical world. She could see her own past, as far back as the life she had as an unborn spirit in her maker's realm. The anger of her expression softened as she summoned the last thread of her strength to reach for the skies, as if longing to be reunited with the heavenly fane she left behind.

"I was supposed to be… the voice of Sanguina," she meekly rasped. "I was meant to keep Her world from being destroyed. Why has She… forsaken me?"

When Diava's last breath left her lungs, her arm fell to the ground. Her face was as still as the wind, her corpse as quiet as the crowd surrounding the fallen sanctuary. Layna gazed up at the fearful strangers having gathered to watch this historic apocalypse; an event so unspeakable, none of them imagined they would have lived long enough to see it.

The cowed Pures of Tresantia's Sanguinic side seemed to be awaiting the orders of their new, self-appointed ruler. Layna was not going to keep them in suspense. Like the goddess she believed herself to be, the dark Vytameta raised herself upon an invisible column of air, to stand up high before the crowd, shining like the north star. "I will bring all belhuayns to their salvation. Sanguina and Safiro have left you to die in the darkness of disorder. But I shall save you with my enlightenment; I am the one you shall worship."

Chapter 45: Revelations, part 2

Morvenia had led Platina, Brynita, and Raia all night through the fearsome woods of the Black Swamp. Their first sign of daybreak hadn't come until they had cleared the last trees of the infernally haunted zone. Their shivering travels through the wetlands were gradually warmed by the rising sun, sending down its welcoming bands of heat to the lonely travelers below.

"You say food serve at Sachelvae?" Morvenia asked her winded group, straggling along behind her. "I is hungry after so long walk!"

"We wouldn't have had to walk the whole distance if anyone was answering their damned communication rings," Brynita scornfully shook the jewelry in her hand, as if trying to wake it up.

"The fact they haven't answered in hours worries me," Raia pursed her lips into a small frown. "What's been going on that they would've been unavailable to heed our call?"

From where they were standing, halfway up Tresantia's hill, they were able to see a cloud of smoke, flowing into the sky like an ashen pillar. It was hard to tell, from its size alone, where this ominous cloud was emanating from.

"Did volcano erupt?" Morvenia asked, pointing to the large object of interest.

The urge of a teacher overtook Platina, as the young teenager's genuine curiosity elicited what she felt to be a didactic response. "A volcano of active status has not been seen in this locale for thousands of years," she was about to go further, until she was interrupted by a more grounded Brynita.

"Damnit, nurse, Sachelvae is burning!"

"Mother Diava!" a fretful Raia called into her non-responsive ring. She left her friends in the dust as she summoned a new wave of energy to go racing in the direction of the temple.

Morvenia and the two other priestesses made haste to follow after, insofar that their tired legs could carry them. They could have just waited to teleport themselves to the scene once Raia had gotten there, but they were not about to miss a moment of the horror doubtlessly unfolding further inside the city.

They found Raia pushing her way through a crowd of starstruck spectators, their numbers flowing down the terraced heights of town. It looked like every Pure resident in all of Tresantia had gathered to see the destruction of their most sacred building. Every one of them was facing up at what appeared to be a second sun hanging over where the eaves of Sachelvae should have been. The cathedral had been entirely transformed into a funeral pyre.

Raia nor her friends knew how this devastation occurred, but this was not the time to be asking questions. They tried to ignore the whispers surrounding them of "It's the priestesses," "Where were *they* when this happened?"

Once they had moved beyond the bystanders and had entered the fore of the crowd, Raia and her group finally beheld what had been captivating all their attention. It was not the scorched husk of Sachelvae, nor was it the unrecognizable interior. It was instead the culprit for all this destruction: Layna, floating like an angel of madness, splotched with blood from head to toe.

Her eyes opened to unveil their shrunken irises and Wild pupils. "We should not regress into a laissez-faire society that breeds weakness into every generation, by letting everyone live by their own baseless ideals. I was born with the divine destiny to unify our people under a single, absolute principle."

"Layna Sladervorn!" Raia called up to her to get her attention.

"Oh, Raia dear," the bloodsoaked angel looked down at her girlfriend with dangerous eyes and softly smiled, bathing the brunette in her divine radiance. "I was wondering where you were! You were late for the spectacle. I was hoping you'd be there to see it all unfold."

Tears filled Raia's eyes and spilled down her cheeks as she weakly crumbled to her knees. She didn't want to believe Layna could have been responsible for all the devastation surrounding her. "What have you done?!"

"Don't be so histrionic, sweetie," Layna dismissively flicked her tail at the terrified Raia. "Shouldn't you be happy for me? I've never felt more relieved… After so long of being left in the dark, I feel like I've finally been brought to light. Everything I didn't know before has been unveiled to me." She closed her eyes and raised her head into the rays of the dawn sun, to feel its warmth upon her face.

Raia knew that Layna had been pining for the answers to unravel the mystery of her existence, but she never expected that this dark exhibition was what this great revelation was leading up to. "They did nothing to deserve this!" the brunette cried.

Layna's face fell with a judgmental glower. "Of course they did. I was through with trying to impress some sanctimonious High Priestess. It was fine with her if I never passed my initiation -- only Diava's favorite ass-kissers ever got the spot that *I deserved!*" the dark Vytameta self-righteously bellowed.

"Their sacrilege went beyond the mere sins they committed against me," she added. "I was given these powers to punish them for much more than that. They did more than misguide me; they lied to all their servants as well.

They blasphemed Sanguina's Will. They attempted to subvert the prophecy of the Vytametas. They tried to deny the inevitability of legend. They tried to avert the cataclysm that would spell the end of their sinful ways... but I am now here!"

Taking advantage of her audience's collective silence, Layna used this moment to stare upon the gathering that Raia had brought to her. Standing behind the brunette were the familiar faces of Brynita and Platina, but she had never seen an abyssal belhuayn before, much less knew the name of Morvenia.

"What you speak of sound like Old Faith," the slimy vixy began. Her knowledge surprised Layna almost as much as her ability to speak at all. "You say that Blood Mother not happy with New Faith. Vytameta story been told for long time; my momma tell me story that grandparent tell her. For long time, Blood Mother and Bone Father not like New Faith."

Layna graced the abyssal with her smile. "Then we are at an agreement; you believe that the world cannot be sustained as it is. You believe that a return to the Old Faith is what it needs. Well, this cannot be done as things currently are. The religions need to be wiped out if they are to be reset. As someone who understands the Old Faith intimately, you would be crucial to my cause! You could join me! What is your name...?"

Morvenia squinted and obliquely turned her head away from Layna's untrustworthy gaze. She defiantly folded her arms across her chest and swatted the air with a slimy fluke. "I no need tell name to mean stranger. Just because you think same thing, no mean you is nice person. I no trust you. You *murderer!* You Bone Father *evil!* Blood Mother *ashame* of you!"

"Ashamed?" Layna incredulously tilted her head, her confusion soon thereafter replaced with mocking laughter. "Sanguina has the *gall* to be ashamed of *me?* Her finest creation? The most *powerful* being in this god-forsaken *world?!*" Layna's humor shifted to unmitigated contempt.

With a closing of an outstretched fist, she lifted Morvenia from her feet and telekinetically choked her out. The strangled abyssal's slime thickened instinctually in her thrashing to escape, but no amount of her slippery gel could disentangle herself from Layna's unforgiving grasp.

"How dare you judge me, you disgusting creep!" Layna bitterly seethed through gritted fangs, watching Morvenia flail and flop about. "Maybe you need to see why I am *not* to be questioned?!"

Above her free hand, Layna materialized what appeared to be a black dart in a clear, red bubble. As its point was turned to face her foe, and her arm reeled back to throw, Morvenia's allies came to her rescue.

Raia called Morvenia to her side with a fygidia as Brynita's koptigma broke through Layna's chokehold to set her free. Platina prepared a wide shield around all three of them, expecting Layna's retaliation, but perhaps underestimated its ferocity.

Layna released the attack she had created to end Morvenia's life -- her Vytameta Dagger splitting into six clones when loosed into the air. All seven missiles destroyed Platina's masalida from their destructive collision, popping the thin barrier like a pin to a membrane engorged with air. All the priestess huddled behind it were knocked off their feet and scurried to sitting positions.

"You couldn't be more eager to die, could you?" Layna sneered, conjuring a disc of visible wind with a stirring of her tail. "You had the unmitigated arrogance to *push* me with your insults, when you knew the source of my ire! When you see Safiro in hell, tell him that the Vytameta sent you!"

Before Layna could remove Tresantia of its 'undesirables,' she was entangled by an astapsyxi of an unknown kind. A wheel of stars orbited her frozen form, each stabbing her with a paralytic ray. To ground-bound observers, she looked like the center of a spoked wheel.

The crowd dispersed to reveal Kasra's tiny form standing among them. Upon seeing her old rival in the distance, Layna's lips struggled against her bindings to turn into a gradually-forming grin -- the first, real smile Kasra had ever seen from her. "There you are..." the dark angel longingly breathed. "The faker... the deceived; the *False Vytameta*."

There was something unsettling about seeing her opponent so comfortable in her bindings; it made Kasra wonder if they were having any effect on her at all. Yet she felt comfortable enough with the advantage she had over her rival just to see if she would make an act of aggression. "Even now that you've been awakened, you still resort to name calling and throwing made-up titles around to feel better about yourself."

Layna's jaw clenched, her expression maddening as she responded to Kasra's taunt in the exact way the violette assumed she would; with a whisking motion of her arms and a sweep of her tail, she disabled Kasra's astapsyxi. With the sound of a snapping rope, the stars that once spun around her scattered through the air and dissipated out of sight. "You look at me now and you still delude yourself into thinking that nothing has changed between us? We are more different now than we've ever been, Kasra. You went to your realm to receive your powers, and I went to my realm to receive mine. Because... in the end, it was meant to be this way."

"When I was imprisoned in Elnastha, I was told by the Goddess Herself that I was born to study this world -- to see the sides of Safiro and Sanguina

and to them be judge and jury. I have received my powers and I have reached my verdict..."

Kasra lowered her head and grit her teeth. "You killed them all."

Layna grinned at the accusation, the satisfying memories still fresh in her mind. "While speaking with Sanguina, I was confronted with many questions: What am I, and if I'm so important, why is there room for two...? I didn't want to believe it; I didn't want to believe I had an equal..."

Just the very thought of competing with Kasra made her vengefully snarl. "You had done *nothing* but *humiliate* me since the moment you strode into town. Everyone just fell in *love* with you and *forgot* all about me. You had them believing that *you* were the legendary Vytameta -- she who was prophesied to remake the world in her image. I... am the *TRUE Vytameta!!*"

Black fire burst around Layna's feet, forming a tower-like aura all around her. "Everyone on this world, Wild and Pure alike, believe that only *one* deity can bring them to salvation. But neither religion can exist without the other. The True Vytameta was made to rid this world of their *feckless* gods! If it is truth and guidance you seek by an omniscient and omnipotent being, your search ends with me!"

With a powerful shriek, Layna commanded an intense wind to flow around her open palm. White ribbons manifested from thin air, twisting into a ghastly sphere in her hand, which was then thrust into the ground before her, causing the earth to split toward her enemy. Silver flames spouted forth from the fissure, burning Kasra as she barely escaped being swallowed by the earth. The hellish rift tore a jagged path behind her on its way toward Raia and her group -- her teammates were able to dive away, but she was left right in the middle of the arrow of destruction.

Kasra used a well-timed fygidia to pull the girl to safety on her side of the infernal fissure. "Raia, get away from here!" Kasra declared to her shaken friend. She held out a starry shield to cover Raia's escape, but the brunette was too terrified to move.

Neither Kasra nor Raia wanted to believe this is what had become of Layna, but the violette immediately started blaming herself. She wondered what would have happened if she had just let herself perish in that swamp the night before she came to Tresantia. She wondered if all the people who were dead now would still be alive if she were not around. She wondered if the world really was a better place now that Zercius was gone.

"Have you lost your nerve, *hero*?" Layna jeered. Seeing Kasra at a disadvantage brought the confident smirk back to the evil mistress' face. "That which is empty caves under that which is full," she lectured her weak foe. "As hollow threats have no authority, so too does a body bereft of spirit lack strength."

Layna raised a hand above her head and over it, a pinwheel of light began to form. In the center of this spiral, a sparking ball of energy slowly grew. Her dark hair whipped around by an invisible breeze as the

preparation for her powerful spell had been completed, but just when she was about to launch it at her bitter rival, she was distracted by Raia's voice.

"I won't let you do it!" the young healer bravely charged forth, interposing herself between the two fighters.

"Raia!" Kasra cried. She reached out to manifest a shield before her reckless friend while Layna cast her grand spell. The Black Missile manifested as a tremendous arrow, piercing through Kasra's shield to strike its target. The only thing Kasra could see was Raia's disintegrating silhouette; the only thing she could hear was her anguished screams. When the fulmination of light had faded, Raia was nowhere to be seen.

All Layna's unholy arrow left was a speechless Kasra in its wake. Even Layna, herself, seemed for a moment taken aback by what she had just witnessed. The vacant look in her starstruck visage softened, as if having justified in her own mind the murder of her friend. But when her expression soured, it looked more like she had found a way to blame Kasra, instead. "She only cared about saving you. She didn't do it to stop me -- not because she cared about me. She only cared about YOU!"

With a diagonal outstretching of a single arm, she coalesced energy from thin air to form like a long blade of white fire in her awaiting hand. With a primordial cry and a full body spin, the very atmosphere itself had been given a black scar; air was sucked into the distorting event horizon of this spatial rift, to seal the absence of matter. When it was closed, certainly nothing was left where it had been.

Except, the Vytameta she had targeted was still very much alive; Kasra was floating just beyond the range of Layna's severing wave. The dark Vytameta's narrow pupils shrunk even tighter as her eyes flashed and her teeth bared. Rings of the same cutting energy appeared around her wrists like deathly bracelets as Layna prepared to give chase.

The ground beneath her rippled when she bent her knees; with a slap of her tail, she kicked off the surface of the arena and launched herself like a bullet for her skyborne adversary. She led her hand-to-hand assault with the pair of circle blades, forcing Kasra to dodge with a zigzagging motion as Layna swiftly closed in.

The dark Vytameta conjured a punching dagger of energy before thrusting a fist into Kasra's abdomen, but her rival once again avoided with a midair sidestep. Kasra immediately countered with an empowered strike of her knee into Layna's midsection, curling the other velta around her leg, before crashing her fist into the back of her opponent's head.

Layna tumbled down through the sky, but stopped herself in time to turn around and suddenly answer Kasra's one-two punch with a dazzling blast of wavy energy. Kasra so barely avoided contact with Layna's attack that she

could feel its sizzling radiation leave a red scar across her skin. Seeing Kasra on the defensive returned a grin to Layna's face, but it was about to be erased by a power blast of the Vytameta's own.

With a reeling motion of Kasra's arm, she collected a sphere of energy on her fist that manifested itself as a shower of stars when thrust forth. These star-shaped blasts struck with unwavering accuracy; no matter how fast Layna tried to move, they followed her every motion with precision and greater speed. Upon being struck by the first two, she projected a black shield around herself to absorb the last three.

Once the shield had taken this damage, Layna threw the spent barrier at Kasra -- an attack that the violette was not anticipating. She was bowled over by the improvised energy bomb, leaving her helplessly hurdling further skyward. Layna gave chase to her foe, striking her in the back in mid-revolution, but not without getting her wrist entangled by the end of Kasra's tail. Layna then suddenly found herself being pulled into a straight-arm punch for the face that had her seeing more than the stars of Kasra's power blasts.

Layna retaliated by reaching her own tail around Kasra's midsection and bringing the Vytameta into a deathly, spiraling embrace, allowing neither combatant any defense as she thrust her forehead into her opponent's. Despite the mark of blood now spilling down her face, Kasra was unperturbed to lay into Layna with shots to her jaw and chin. Layna countered with another vicious headbutt, before projecting another barrier to forcibly tear Kasra apart from her entanglement.

An enraged Kasra knocked on the wall of Layna's protective bubble with a volley of star bolts, but this time they didn't seem to do more than make it fizzle. Without the trickery she used before, Layna dismissed her shield perhaps with a bit of overconfidence, but when Kasra saw that her opponent had fully healed her wounds, she understood the reason behind Layna's smug expression.

"You realize you're going to die here, right?" Layna cackled. "Who can you protect with empty powers like yours? Look at you, so *weak* from renouncing the truth! Why do you bother defending this population of ugly, misguided mouth breathers? What have they done to be worthy of saving? Why would you go through all the trouble of defending these thankless, *gormless* masses, when you owe them nothing?"

Looking to the spectators of whom Layna spoke, Kasra was met with the largest task she ever had to overcome since realizing she was this Vytameta figure: her self-legitimization. At no other point in her life would she have

been able to answer this question with any measure of confidence, but upon this precipice of clearness, her reasoning was as blatant as the all-embracing terror throughout Tresantia.

"I was not put here on this world to condemn strangers for crimes they did not commit. Anyone, when faced down by a tyrant like you, has a natural impulse to destroy such an unconscionable oppressor. No one is too mighty to be defeated; no one's will is absolute enough to be untested. Just because those who disagree with you cannot appeal to your bloodlust with an answer of equal violence against you does not mean your ways are the truth. They need someone to represent their sanity -- to stand up for them in times of terror and uncertainty. That is why they will call me a hero."

Although her question was met with a heartfelt response, Layna felt there was something missing, if not entirely bland about Kasra's answer. "Is that blind, pointless faith of yours the only justification you have? A baseless, moral duty to defend your 'fellow man?'" the dark Vytameta derisively stuck out her tongue at the intentionally saccharine sound of her words. "Nothing is more revolting than watching a people mindlessly following antiquated traditions which have lost their origins and purpose to the annals of history. Even now, our species insists on adhering to rules laid out for them by ancient superstitions unproven and unprovable. Others seek refuge in authority figures and confide in them for their direction and purpose in life. Obviously, a perfect medium must be reached if all belhuayns are to be satisfied with serving one ruler. She must be a tangible deity who is perfect and superior in all ways, to be fit for worship…"

Her smirk indicated that she had a fair idea of who this 'perfect person' was. She held out an open palm, as if imagining the planet shrunken inside of it. "I am the goddess who shall call an end to the perpetuation of this world's mistakes… by destroying the temples responsible for its turmoil and removing the rulers who have washed all nations in waves of war and fear."

The very fact that Kasra had come to avenge the fallen Sachelvae was proof enough that she opposed Layna's ideals. "If you seek to defend this toxic society, then you are no better than Diava herself. If you do not wish to change the powers that be, you wish to see this world continue to rot and die."

The dark Vytameta poised the knuckles of her fists together, rolling her head back with a rising motion of her arms. "This world does not need more than one Champion." Above her grew a portal of swirling energy, being fed black ribbons of light from all directions.

"I am the only recourse Vitiosa needs."

Once this portal had grown to the caster's size, it unleashed a dark purple column, pulsating with white light.

Kasra's starry shield was barely able to block and resist the magical energies colliding against her small barrier. She countered by throwing star-shaped bolts of magic with a sweep of her arm, but their precision was undone by a shield of Layna's own; an invisible barrier that only showed at the points it was struck as it deflected Kasra's rapid attack.

With a forward sweeping of her crossed forearms, Layna shot an X-shaped scissor of slicing energy that would have torn Kasra in four pieces had the Vytameta not dodged. With acrobatic finesse, Kasra turned her downward spin into continuing momentum that had her corkscrewing a flying, energy-powered punch for Layna's chin. She added a falling, whirling slam of her tail to her aerial onslaught, grabbing hold of the dark Vytameta as she sent them both hurdling to the ground.

She was intent on using Layna's body to soften her landing, but her rival was swift enough to spring Kasra away and save herself with a single projection of her shield. Her bubble-like barrier allowed Layna to harmlessly bounce off the stone floor right before it shattered from the intense duress it withstood.

Having her shield being dismissed without her control sapped Layna of her energy and left the dark Vytameta in a momentary daze. She crumbled to a dizzied knee, left vulnerable for Kasra's clincher: the violette's hands were spaced equidistantly on either side of a transparent orb, that within its confines, contained a glowing galaxy of multicolored lights. Sparks of purple and pink electricity jolted from around this orb, like shocks of plasma, as Kasra's hair blew behind her like a starry cloud.

"I do not believe in a destiny that cannot be changed," Kasra said, flying steadily higher and back away from her swaying foe, "but I do believe that the course evil has set cannot be reversed if we do nothing. Justice disregards location and time; it doesn't matter where, it doesn't matter when, and it doesn't matter who. But rest assured that justice will be done. Right here. Right now. By *my* hand."

With an outward thrust of her arms, Kasra commenced her ultimate power to be unleashed upon her enemy. The Quasar Blast was, however, detonated halfway by an unseen force; its explosion cast an intense, white light on everything in the region. What was left behind, when this radiance faded, was a colorful nebula -- that in its midst, stood a tall, silhouetted figure.

Layna and Kasra watched the remnant of the Quasar Blast be blown away with a single burst of wind, like a shock wave, revealing the identity of the figure it concealed. He was close to eight feet tall and proudly clothed in scant armor of blue hues, the likes of which did not appear to have been made on this or any other world. His body was perfectly toned, to a level not achievable by mortals. On his shoulder, he had rested the head of a great warhammer that spoke its name without words: all who saw it knew it was called The Unmaker.

His likeness had been seen in many forms in tapestries, in murals, and in all windows of Safiric temples. His praises had been sung throughout millennia by Wilds the world over. Every language had a word for his name. He didn't even have to say it for all in attendance to know that he was Safiro, the God of Death.

"Cease this meaningless conflict," Safiro's coldly irate eyes shifted slowly between the bewildered Vytametas. His voice carried like a rumble of thunder, emanating from everywhere at once. "Come and speak to Me, as a Champion to its Creator." The God of Death held the head of his warhammer like a walking stick as he imperiously motioned a hand to invite the floating Kasra to solid ground.

Time was standing still; the only bystanders allowed to move were the Vytametas themselves. "It displeases the Mother as it does I, to see Our Vytametas engaging in combat."

Still surging with adrenaline, Layna bristled at being called a relative to her hated rival in any fashion, even if such a title was given by the God of Death Himself. "You waited all this time to make yourself a part of our lives? What kind of 'Father' are you, to leave me suffering in confusion and squalor, waiting on the answers? What kind of 'Father' are you, to then *punish* me for exercising the prerogative I was *born* with, to cast my judgment as I see fit?!"

While Kasra's saucer-shaped eyes insinuated that she might have been expecting Layna to have become a pile of ashes at any moment, Safiro instead exhibited a kind of patience one would not have thought a God of his kind possessed. Safiro disdainfully shook his head. "Woe to you, Vytameta, for you have never known what true suffering is. It was for this very reason, this bias, that a second judge was made." An open hand gestured to Kasra, as if the violette should have been taking a bow.

Layna squared her shoulders and took a vindictive breath like a sizzling pan, her fingers curling one at a time into her palms. "Please tell me there was a point to you coming here 'Father,' *other* than to enrage me?"

If Safiro had visible pupils, he probably would have been rolling his eyes. "I have come to educate you, as I see there still is much you both have yet to learn about the mission you have been created to undertake."

Now that having professed the gravity of the situation had earned the disrespectful teenager's obedience, Safiro continued, "Up to this point in time in the short whiles you both have lived, you have enjoyed the safety from the outside world that this sanctuary city has to offer. That is why the Mother and I chose it for you both to live; you would be given the greatest chance to survive the turmoil while at the same time learning about the problems that face this world. So that, in time, you would know enough to reach your verdicts when you attained your powers -- through service either to the Mother or Myself."

While Kasra was fascinated to hear Safiro's enlightening words, Layna showed a diametric impatience. "So you said there was something we had *yet* to learn...?" the dark Vytameta wheeled her hand forward.

"There are wars being waged between the four nations," Safiro started, "as there have been for centuries. They ebb and flow like the aftershocks of an earthquake -- an earthquake that started with the creation of the Annihlus."

"You mean that horrible thing that *you* created?" Layna treated the God of Death to some more of her incorrigible lip. "Are you admitting that all the problems *we* were made to fix were *your* fault?"

Safiro's patience was slowly unraveling, like a rusty nail being pried from a board. A testy twitch of his tail was the only indication that Layna had successfully struck a nerve. "The Annihlus was a desperate solution to a cataclysm that could have caused the full *extinction* of the belhuayn race," he said, his words frustratedly strained albeit sounding rehearsed. "Perhaps you do not think you owe me gratitude because this secret has not been explained to you in satisfactory detail?"

"Alright, spill it then," Layna brazenly commanded the deity. "If you came here to school us, please don't let *me* stop you."

Safiro's fingers tightened their grip on the head of his Unmaker. Were it not part of his reason for being here, he wouldn't have deigned to the whims of this child. "That is why it is to the Vytametas that I have come and it is to them I must defer. Yes, it is you both who have the final judgment with what happens to our world."

Kasra and Layna exchanged uneasy looks between each other, knowing full well as Safiro Himself that they hadn't the best track record of working together. Especially now, after what had just occurred this horrible day,

Kasra could say with total assurance that she couldn't trust her counterpart at all. "You want me to work with she who *killed* my best friend? Right in front of me?!"

"I *loved* her!!" an incensed Layna spun on her, with terrible vengeance contorting her countenance. Black orbs of fire wreathed her fists as her hair started flowing behind her. "And you took her away from me! Once you came into her life, all she ever talked about was *you!*"

"ENOUGH," Safiro's powerful voice knelled as his warhammer delivered a shock wave through the ground to separate the quarreling judges. "The Vytametas were meant to make decisions beyond the affairs of mortals," he said with a calmer tone. "You mustn't let your feelings for others distract you from your mission. The Mother and I created the both of you... to work together."

From the look Layna gave him, it was evident to see she thought some sort of mix-up had taken place. But the motormouth was never short of disrespectful remarks. "Why did you bother giving us free will when you designed us with this destiny of yours?"

Safiro cracked the kind of smile that looked like he could have almost chuckled. He rolled his shoulders with a complacent shrug as he tilted his head to one side. "The Mother and I believed that... if I were to create My Champion to live a sordid existence, she would come to know her Father through her desire for vengeance. And the Mother believed that if She were to create Her Champion to live a perfect life, she would have no desire to murder others. However," his eyes shifted between the two Vytametas, who looked significantly less humored than Safiro did about what he was telling them. "As you can see, the opposite came true."

In truth, it was at this moment that Kasra and Layna had finally come to agreement on the very same thing they were thinking. But it was Layna who made her opinion vocally heard. "So this is just one big fucking game to you?!" she finally snapped. "We're just pawns in some little social experiment?! I was right -- you 'deities' are totally corrupt! Without you, the world would actually prosper!"

With as much power and anger as the dark Vytameta had behind her, none of her apocalyptic abilities could match Safiro's mortal form. Her attempt to attack her rival's maker was undone by an unceremonious swing of Safiro's warhammer, taking Layna off her feet and sending her skidding back to Kasra's side.

Instead of continuing to punish the Vytameta's vengeance, Safiro seemed more proud to reward her for it. "It pleases me... to see how far you have come. You may have been made by the Mother, but your mind is more like Mine the more I test you. Yes, had I been in your position, I would have exhibited the same aggression."

The way Safiro looked at Layna seemed more like the smile of a scientist beholding his masterpiece rather than a father beholding his child. "What you must understand… is that it is not just the creations of the Mother and I who function in this predetermined way. Indeed, the products of *all* creation were made to serve specific purposes, at specific points in time. The Mother and I could have made Our children on *any* world, around any star," he motioned a hand skyward, waving to the celestial bodies themselves. "But it was Qualaria who called Us first, to propagate Our children on *this* world. As you can see, even gods must obey their superiors."

Safiro looked to the clouds, as if he could see the Mystic Plane from there. "What you must do now," he addressed both Vytametas, "is recombine the Annihlus."

Kasra was reminded of the Creation Story that Raia once told her, that mentioned how the Annihlus was being kept hidden at the four corners of the world. "The Emperors are the ones hiding the pieces of the Annihlus," she said, looking for Safiro's confirmation.

The God of Death replied, "It is true, that the present generation of Sanguina's Trusted has been keeping the Annihlus fractured. It is for their greed and their ambition to compete to become the new Chaos God that their wars shall remain in perpetuity. It is from them you must collect their legendary weapons, but they will not give these artifacts freely."

Safiro needn't to say it for it to become obvious that this would prove to be the hardest challenge for the Vytametas yet. Kasra had already fought one such wielder of an Annihlus fragment; the blade of Zercius' weapon, the Fang of Death, was made from a piece of this terrifying power gem. If the Emperors possessed the four main quadrants of the Annihlus itself, there was no telling what any one of them would have been capable of.

"What will happen when all the pieces are recombined?" Kasra finally asked. "Will Layna and I not be driven mad like the Raging Chaos God?"

"It is the special privilege of the Vytameta to suffer no ill when harnessing the might of either I or the Mother," Safiro explained. "Your purpose for collecting the Annihlus is to ensure it never again is used by mortals who cannot handle its might. What you do with it once it is recombined will be a decision left up between the two of you. I trust you will not use it for malicious intent... but you mustn't tarry. There is no telling how much time we have left."

Without giving his audience any more time to discuss their new obligation, he raised a hand above his head and commenced a wreath of slowly blinding light to surround himself. In those short moments, he had blinked from existence as if he'd never been.

Chapter 46: After a Cataclysm

The frozen, frightened faces of the bystanders watching and fleeing the Battle of Champions resumed their previous actions. Only now there was a sudden, inexplicable calm between the Vytametas, where just an instant before, there was not. The smoke had cleared and they were both still standing right where they were before Safiro had departed.

When Kasra gazed upon the fearfully bunched masses, she started to feel as if she had become a monster. She began to understand what Zercius meant when he said that "this world has no room for those who are on the fence." It was not because she was born a 'Vytameta' that gave her the right to change the world, but it was because of everyone's consternation of her powers that she'd have no choice. It wasn't her 'promise' that everyone was after; it was their desire to ensure she was on their side.

Seeing that the fight between the Vytametas had ended, the crowd started backing away. They were vexed that the two, terrifying entities had reached a truce and it would be the innocent bystanders that they would target next.

However, even the more violent Layna had no interest in pursuing them. She said nothing further as the crowd and Kasra glowered at her to leave this place at once. She did as they silently asked; she turned to take her leave and seemingly vanished from thin air -- not in the fashion of a *fygidia,* but of a different power altogether.

When her detestable rival had departed, Kasra began to gather stones from the ruins and stacked them into pyres for the priestesses Layna had selfishly murdered. After the crowd watched her for a while, some of them came to help her dig through the rubble of Sachelvae and give a proper burial to Layna's victims.

During the exhaustive building process, some food caterers thought they'd make the most of their captive audience by wheeling their meal carts around the build site, hoping to attract the attention of any hungry workers looking for a break.

The building's remains were turned into a short, brick wall around the cemetery it had become, and were used as gravestones inscribed with the names of the deceased. Kasra knelt into the fresh mound of soil marking Raia's resting place, calmly accepting the terrible sight that would no doubt haunt her dreams for the rest of her life. Reclining her forehead on the marker that bore her friend's name, she wept; she could smell the stench of smoke still rife within the ashen dirt. Kasra's friends sat with her to join in her hour of grief, awash with the painful phobia of having to recount her memories of the awful tragedy.

Once she had time to grieve the losses of her friends and acquaintances, she lifted her head from the graves. The pensive Kasra's vacant expression was startled by Kyrana's hand touching her shoulder. "Are you alright, my child?"

Though the Arch Healer was trying to be strong for the young hero, the redness to her cheeks and the darkness of her eyes suggested that she had been quite emotional about the disaster as well. Kasra couldn't manage any response; her silence alone was sufficient, to let Kyrana know how empty she was feeling. With Sachelvae gone, it felt like there was nothing left for either of them in this city.

"What happens now?" Kasra asked her mentor.

Looking to the headstones of the dearly departed, Kyrana wistfully replied, "That's up to you, is it not? I can do no more for the Vytameta than hope she goes in the right direction."

An overwhelmed Kasra shook her head, having not the first clue where to start. "There's so much I don't know about this world."

"Then I will help you," the Arch Healer smiled down at her. "Just tell me your mission and I will guide you there."

"Kyrana..." Tears entered Kasra's eyes; she was feeling so vulnerable and lost, anything could have sent her to the brink of crying once more. She tried to retain her 'heroic' composure, brushing an arm across her face. "You are willing to leave this place? To follow me?"

"I have no better choice," Kyrana said, looking to the cemetery once more. "As much as I'd like to, there is no way to rebuild the temple that Sachelvae once was. Its replacement would forever be haunted by the memories of what happened here today. No, to pick up the pieces would be an affront to Their Will; Safiro and Sanguina sent the Vytametas here to do what they wish with the world."

Kasra frowned almost piteously, her ears falling and her tail drooping to the ground. "I don't want to destroy anything. I'd rather save as many people as possible. There has to be a way to reverse the damage and make things better without adding more war and causing more death. Violence will only beget more violence and cause more hate..."

A soft purr of admiration escaped Kyrana's lips. "You speak the words of a true Vytameta, my child. But... the Gods are well aware of a truth many like to ignore, and that is that a revolution cannot be done without appealing to pre-existing bloodletting. They created a second Vytameta in the hopes that one of them would exercise this usage of power."

Determination galvanizing Kasra's gaze, she said, "I can stop her. Just because she *can* ruin everything, doesn't mean she *should*. I don't care what Safiro was thinking when He gave us the powers He did. I have the right to use them in any way I see fit."

Kyrana couldn't have been beaming brighter for her young hero. "Well then, my child, I feel all the better about following in your footsteps. I am confident that no matter where you go, I will be on the right side of history. The more people who you can rally behind you, the greater your chance of success shall be."

Reaching into the wide, V-shaped collar of her gown, Kyrana retrieved a brass locket attached to a string. "There is no telling what we will face when things get under way," the Arch Healer's tone turned more grim. "That is why we should exercise caution by always remaining in touch." By pressing her thumb against the crease of the clam-shaped container, its thin lid lifted to unveil the ruby ring it was carrying inside.

"This is a communication ring," Kyrana explained. "So long as we are both wearing one," she pulled back her sleeve to show her own, "you will be able to telepathically message me, no matter how much distance comes between us. That way, we cannot be separated."

The magic ring, though it didn't look properly fitted for Kasra's small, slender fingers, shrunk to their approximate size the moment she plucked it from the locket. "This is incredible," the violette breathed.

"They are standard issue for all priestesses," Kyrana replied. "Everyone carries two, just in case we are to be captured and happen to lose one."

"I can join too?" came the hopeful chirp of Morvenia, eavesdropping on the conversation. The sneaky sylph stood up from where she was crouching behind a nearby headstone, trying to look as unassuming as possible. Her slimy tail anxiously hugged the grave marker, her hands poised behind her back as she attracted the stares of Kyrana and Kasra.

"I also have speaky ring~" Morvenia smiled, as if this were initiation into some sort of club. "Look, I show you!" She lifted a finger, asking her friends to wait, before reaching into a small, brown sack cloth attached to a rope tied around her waist.

From its ragged insides, she retrieved what was certainly a very old communication ring of a rather crude make; its band, if it was ever gold at all, had been tarnished long beyond recognition. It looked more like it was hewn together out of two twigs. The sanrisma it held was unpolished and uncut, yet still maintained its magic luster when held nearby the newer rings on Kasra's and Kyrana's fingers.

"That's… really neat, Venia," Kasra tilted her head, her face a mixture of humor and praise for her friend. "Where'd you find that?"

"Momma find it long ago," Morvenia answered, slipping her ring on and admiring it, as if she had just been engaged. "She give to me because I Pure girl. I always want to be priestess, though…" her eyes glittered, her attention returning to Kasra and Kyrana. "If you is priestess, and I join you, I become priestess too?"

Kasra couldn't refuse the drippy abyssal's sweetness; her knees were touching and her fists were held so nervously to her leaf-clad chest, it looked like her heart would have been utterly crushed if she gave her any other answer than the one she was looking for. "Of course I'll let you come with us!"

She hardly got the words out before Morvenia had burst with excitement; Kasra found herself tackled by the smaller vixy, who now lovingly nuzzled her wet face against the violette's cheek. While Kasra was being slowly crushed by the strong abyssal's arms and tail, wrapped tightly around her back, Brynita and Platina arrived to her aid.

"You'll need to keep that thing on a leash," Brynita stared down at the struggling Kasra, her comment earning her a vicious look from Morvenia.

"You not come with!" The abyssal pushed herself away from Kasra, accidentally slapping her in the face with her fluke as she spun on her rival. "Is *our* group, now!" she spread out her arms, as if to block Kasra and Kyrana from the two other priestesses.

"Good, because I wasn't about to send myself on your deathtrap anyway," Brynita scoffed.

"Oh?" Kyrana tipped an ear, earnestly curious. "What are you going to do?"

Even though the question was not directed at her, Platina answered for the both of them. "We believe it would be best for us to stay in Tresantia. The city needs us more than ever to do our duties for the Pure population here."

Kyrana couldn't argue with their sense of responsibility. Now that Sachelvae was gone, Platina was the only healer the town had left. "I believe you both will serve this place well," the Arch Healer respectfully bowed her head to them. "I hope, in time, these children of Sanguina will join your ranks and learn to help themselves, what with the dangerous times we now live in." She cast a suspicious look to Travestas, in the far distance. "There is no telling what the Safiric Brotherhood will do, now that Sachelvae is no longer here. They may become more bold than ever to stake a claim to these unprotected lands."

Upon hearing this, it only made sense for Kasra to ask, "Then should we not rally our children of Sanguina together to leave this place at once? They have no safe bastion in Sachelvae anymore; there will be nothing defending them from the Brotherhood's retaliation."

Although Kyrana's smile showed she might've had a bias in opinion, the Arch Healer once again showed loyal deference to the Vytameta's will. "If that is your choice, I shall abide it and assist you in any way I can."

"And I shall, as well," came Nohvaias' unexpected voice. The former High Priest was the last of Kasra's group to make himself apparent, now standing with the circle of his new cohorts. His sudden emergence grabbed the attention of Kyrana in particular.

"You were the one I saw with the other large scelan, when we first met at Mt. Malumai," Kyrana recollected. "We never properly introduced ourselves before. My name is Kyrana Rejinam," she gave him a priestess' curtsy. "I am indebted to you for having helped us all save Kasra."

"Ah, think nothing of it, my Sister," Nohvaias respectfully smiled and closed his eyes. "It was my pleasure to give the damned fool Deniechus his come-uppance... I've waited four long centuries to return his little *favor*." For as long as he had spent being a ghost, the former High Priest still maintained his strong, Wild-blooded vengeance. "However, I can explain all that later. Right now, planning our next step is more important."

"Next step?" Kasra tipped her ear, clearly overwhelmed enough already by everything that just happened. The last thing she wanted to think about was starting up another big adventure while the evening was still young. "What do you think is going to happen here?"

"You left Malumai in *shambles*, remember?" Nohvaias started. "Killing the founder of the Safiric Brotherhood is going to have its consequences. Every Safiric spook in the world knows what you've done and knows the name of the Vytameta..." It didn't do him any pride to have clued her in on all this. If anything, Nohvaias was every bit as worried for her as Kasra herself was. "You'll need all the help you can get to fight off *that* kind of attention."

Everyone stayed silent, their eyes either shifting to each other or looking to different places of the street around them. They knew Nohvaias was right, but they couldn't just live in fear of what was to come.

It felt strange for Kasra not to know what their next course of action should have been, but the Vytameta was still very much a greenhorn when it came to her new responsibilities. She couldn't have been expected to suddenly become a tactical genius. She barely escaped her fight with Layna alive.

Luckily, Nohvaias already had an idea for what their game plan should have been. "I say we gather up as many troops as we can. Anyone who wants to stay alive will fight with us and help to build up our side of Tresantia's defenses. The Safirics already have their wall built and their forces ready, by the looks of it. They probably saw this day coming for a while."

Seeing Kasra's terrified nervousness widening her listless eyes, Kyrana placed a comforting hug around the violette's side. "There is no need to get yourself worked up about it now, my child. There is still plenty of time for us to make decisions and prepare ourselves. We should take this time to have a well-deserved rest this evening."

Kasra had been so caught up in the excitement of the emotional exigency that she hadn't even stopped to look for Rozha, who was oddly missing from the group of friends she had left behind at the town walls.

"What happened to Rozha?" Kasra asked.

Nohvaias uneasily grimaced at her. "The idiot got away from me and ran off to try to help you fight the evil Vytameta. I don't know what happened to her after that."

Kasra's sinking stomach made her feel faint; all she could think about was what happened to Raia, and she began to worry that Rozha might have been caught in the crossfire at any point thereafter.

Detecting the Vytameta's inward panic, Kyrana gave her shoulders a reassuring squeeze. "Your guidance charm will help you find her, as it always has," the Arch Healer raised the ruby pendant Kasra was wearing, for her to see it before her eyes. The sanrisma dangling from its looped string did not do so much as flicker when she thought of Rozha.

Kyrana stroked a hand down Kasra's wilting ear. "We should keep an eye on the guidance charm for any signs of your sister's whereabouts. We can check it once at night and again in the morning." The forlorn look on Kasra's face had Kyrana creasing her brow. "You must rest, young hero. Take some time to reflect on what you've learned."

The Arch Healer brought Kasra and her group to the Jolly Kelvor Inn, located near the eastern edge of Mediona. It was such an ironic name, when compared to the feeling Kasra was filled with. She couldn't have felt less happy, unlike the bucking likeness of the four-legged creature painted onto the establishment's wooden sign, hanging above the door.

The Jolly Kelvor was in the midst of its dinner time rush, and they were serving their evening special: buuntash cake. Nothing could have been more appealing to Kasra's empty stomach than the strong odor of raw-cooked meat stacked up in piles of brisket at every round table. Among the sitting patrons, Kasra saw some familiar faces of the people who helped her turn the rubble of Sachelvae into a graveyard.

The management had apparently changed hands since last time Kasra had seen its sunny interior. Instead of there being an old, balding ardinsulaian standing behind the counter, there was a young and loud cataenian scelan of long, turquoise hair. "Heyo!" he waved over his new lot of customers with a dark hand. He fixed his straightened bangs and blew them away from his green eyes. "Name's Pochino -- what can I do for ya?"

His Wild eyes gave an unafraid once-over to the dower face of the Vytameta in Kyrana's company, and the rather imposing Viasarria standing by her side. "Well say, ya brought in some fresh faces! Good tah see a referral of business! I'm feelin' like a nice guy today -- what say I just charge ya a flat fee for a whole dinner for the bunch of ya?"

Kyrana exchanged a pleasantly surprised look with her friends and didn't take much longer to accept his terms. "Well you *are* quite nice, Pochino! How much would a dinner and a few rooms be?"

"I ain't got a VIP suite upstairs to be fittin' *your* types," he gave them a twinkling smile, "but I got three rooms I can spare -- two beds each, if that's good enough for ya?"

"Sure, that'll work fine," Kyrana nodded, opening a bag of coins.

"Ten silver divitias is the total price," Pochino said without batting an eye as the Arch Healer gave him a double take.

She normally didn't like spending a hefty sum, and only showed a moderate reluctance in sliding the payment across the counter. But she was in the right mood to let some of her currency go for the sake of trying to help Kasra relax from all the chaos she had gone through.

Their party was given the largest table the Jolly Kelvor had to offer, which was tucked back somewhere near the corner of the main dining area, near one of the fireplaces that kept the building warm and lit.

Kasra took her seat with a heavy sigh, unable to stop thinking about the last time she, Rozha, and Raia had come to this place to try the very same meal they were about to have once more. "It was my first date with Malkinos," she recollected. "That was the day everything turned upside down. It was when Viasarria attacked Rozha and I, and it was when Layna was put away in Sachelvae's dungeon."

It didn't make her feel much better about everything that was going on to reminisce about all the bad times that led up to what she was being faced with now. Especially when all she could really think about was what happened to her sister. In spite of all the energy she burned fighting Layna and building Sachelvae's graveyard, she simply didn't have the appetite to enjoy any of the nice food laid out for her.

Morvenia, sensing Kasra's discomfort, placed a wet hand on the Vytameta's shoulder and offered a sympathetic purr. "You want be alone, yes?"

Kasra was stunned at how well the abyssal could read her body language, but she wasn't about to deny what she was feeling. "I wouldn't mind a little bit of company," the violette smiled at her.

Morvenia scooted her chair back with a commanding screech across the wood planked floor, and helped Kasra out of her seat to start them both off for the second floor. Kasra was brought to the room Kyrana had rented for her upstairs, where she pensively sat on her bed and thought about all the chaotic events that had transpired earlier.

"You is okay, hero girl?" Morvenia asked, earning a belated reaction from Kasra, who took an extra moment to pull away from her thoughts.

Kasra shook her head, but circled her tail on the mattress beside her, inviting Morvenia a place to sit down. She, unlike many might've been, was unperturbed by the abyssal's slimy touch leaning against her. It actually smelled pleasant, for some reason. "I stay by you, no matter what. We look for sister girl together."

Just knowing someone cared was all Kasra needed to bring a little smile back to her face. She wet her nose with a nuzzle against her friend's cheek, and brought an arm around the sylph's side. "Thanks, Venia," she started. "Wanna stay with me for tonight?"

Morvenia batted her eyes with pleasant surprise. "Yes, I be here for you~" She chirped, clinging to Kasra. "I wake all night; I keep watch out for you." She lied atop the blankets behind her, turning onto her side. In doing so, she accidentally covered her friend's face with her ears.

Kasra swiped at the mucky belhuayn appendage, moving it off of her cheek with a mock scowl. She couldn't stop looking at the dark guidance charm sitting on the nightstand, finding it increasingly hard to sleep when her mind was still racing. As she stared at the ceiling, her eyes growing heavier as she pondered the whereabouts of her friends, her guidance charm started emitting a glow. It was faint, but she knew she had to follow it.

Epilogue

As the shadow of Vitiosa encroached the rubescent lands of Sanguina's ethereal fane, the Goddess of Life sat in a low-hanging swing hewn on the boughs of her holy Life Giver tree. Around the flowered vines of her perch were twisted the incorporeal tails of unborn spirits, the joyous cherubs frolicking along with their sacred Mother.

Other spirits made snacks of the large, pinkish fruits plentifully provided on every leafy limb of the Life Giver. Their stellar heights provided a picturesque vista of the moon's curved horizon, full of scarlet lakes sparkling on the lush valleys and verdant hills. The black skies were full of stars and swimming spirits, excited for their turn to be conceived into the Physical Plane.

One of Sanguina's many, winged children passed her by with a playful nuzzle, as it gracefully arced its way into the Life Giver's shady marquee. Another was soon thereafter inspired to vie for her attention in a similar manner, slithering down the vine of her swing to curl itself in her lap. Normally, the Mother Goddess would have shown no exhaustion in answering to the fickle spirits' harmless whims, but knowing her week of sublunar vigilance was nigh, her concerns were on matters significantly more pressing than she would have liked.

Sanguina moved her eyes from the oncoming wall of darkness to set her sights on the waxing light of her husband's moon. As hers was now entering its waning crescent, his was already half full.

After he left his realm with the promise to speak with the warring Vytametas, she had become curious to hear of what news he'd have to bring her, now that their battle had successfully been stopped. At least, for the time being.

"What have you learned, upon speaking with Our Champions?" Sanguina sent her voice across the spacial void between their heavens.

Reclaiming his throne, Safiro disinterestedly leaned his elbow against its armrest, as ripples of contemplation flowed through his long tail. "They lack discipline," a fist pressed up against his cheek. "They are too young to wield the authority they were bestowed. We should have extended their trials so that they would have received their powers later in life, when they understood more of the task at hand."

In spite of the seriousness of their conversation, Sanguina continued entertaining her children as if nothing would have distracted her from their whims. "Drastic times and traumatic life experiences are boons to one's wisdom and maturity. I knew Our Vytametas would have the information they needed at the time they could no longer be kept from the truth about what they were. But your concern is that they are incapable of cooperation. What was it you hoped to do that would guide them together, without risk of turning yourself Aberrant?"

Even if Sanguina could have seen Safiro's smile, she wouldn't have been able to tell whether it was prideful or mischievous. "As of now, I have seen only emotional bias in their decision-making, and this is troubling to me. So I gave them a chore to do, that would better serve to test their teamwork and judgment -- a mission that is more neutral and that will require a greater understanding of the world. I asked them to gather the Annihlus."

Safiro waited, anticipating his wife's incensed reaction. However, Sanguina landed an unexpectedly softer blow. "You really have changed your ways?" The slight incredulity of her tone indicated that she was humored by the improbability of this statement. Nevertheless, she went on to say, "You do not see this end goal backfiring, do you?"

"It is true that I sacrificed much to create the Annihlus," Safiro mused, "and that its power could be used as harmful leverage against me... But it has been for the Annihlus that the world has been split into four warring nations, and my children now see an armageddon on the horizon."

It was from that admittance of her husband's wrongdoings that had Sanguina pausing all action for quiet rumination. Her pendulous perch slowly dangled to and fro to a gradual halt. Her blank stare earned the curious coos of her unborn spirits, now stopping their bubbly spirals to accord her countenance with an inquisitive scrutiny.

Having now gained his wife's undivided attention, Safiro concluded, "Once its evil is contained... a vision for recourse can be devised for Our faiths. Until then, the Vytametas have no hope of uniting Our world... to the way it was before the fall of the Great Civilization."

To be continued in Volume II

Glossary

Abyssal: This slimy species of nocturnal belhuayn are native to the darkest depths of the ocean, and can be found all over the world. They are immensely strong and tough; their bodies are built to withstand the crushing pressures of their undersea habitat. They are capable of seeing perfectly in total darkness, but abhor the sun and hide during the day. At night, they come to the land to breed, birth their young, and forage for food.

Annihlus, the: The giant gem that Safiro created to endow whoever held it with all his power. It was an important part of the belhuayn Creation Story, and was said to have been broken when its holder was killed by the four heroes Sanguina sent to destroy it. The four, largest fragments of the Annihlus were said to have been taken by Sanguina's heroes to the furthest corners of the world, thus begetting the Cardinal Emperors of Vitiosa.

Arachniath: A giant, demonic spider who casts glowing webs of flame in the bottom of a cave, near the heart of the Black Swamp.

Arcignum: A powerful Sanguinic spell, usable only by a High Priestess. It places an invisible seal on an enclosed structure, preventing anyone from getting in or out. If this spell is to be disabled by anyone other than its caster, a psychic alarm rings in the mind of the person who established it.

Ardinsulai: The southern, volcanic archipelago of Ardinsulai is owned by Emperor Signus and is home to a subterranean race of belhuayns whose bodies are accustomed to the intense heat of their lava-laden lands. These most resourceful and ingenious belhuayns have mastered an early form of geothermal power to run their cities. These hot-blooded belhuayns are characterized for having hair colors ranging from a bright orange to a deep red, and skin tones ranging from bronze to light pink.

Astapsyxi: A Sanguinic entrapment spell. Usually requires invocation to be used. The user entirely and immediately ceases the momentum of her target.

Belhuayn: A member of the belhuayn race, and a native of the planet Vitiosa. Belhuayns are notoriously hardy lifeforms, strengthened by their homeworld's lack of atmospheric bastions against the harsh radiation of their great blue star. They are endowed with exceptionally heightened senses of smell, and a very highly attuned sense of hearing. Just by scent, they can recognize friend from stranger, and can even identify someone by the sounds of their footsteps. Their tail is the strongest limb on their body; one whip by the average scelan could crack a brick wall.

Bizkah: A belhuayn card game that features the Emperors, soldiers, priests, and priestesses of all four corners of Vitiosa. The hierarchy of each card tends to change depending on which country the game is being played, as well as the religious demographic of that particular city.

Black Cloud, the: What the belhuayns call an Inmarisian spaceship. Black Clouds are large vessels that can turn transparent during space flight and can travel soundlessly in an atmosphere. Their empty hulls are made for storing belhuayn captives. There are at least thirty inmarisian poachers on board, who leave the vessel to round up belhuayn targets with paralytic tractor beams.

Black Strider: A beast of burden native to the swampy heart of Onteval. These horse/deer-like steeds are slender and elegant. Their tall legs are made for walking above water and won't sink in muddy terrain. They have very highly attuned senses of touch and sight. They can see perfectly in the dark and can feel slight vibrations in the ground, alerting them to advancing predators.

Black Swamp, the: A very dangerous territory to the north of Tresantia, said to contain a stronghold of the Safiric Brotherhood, as well as a slew of the worst monsters in Onteval.

Blade Dancer: A female assassin of Iminsun's military. They are highly skilled spies and saboteurs capable of using most any bladed weapon on any limb of their body with exceptional efficiency. They are called 'dancers' because of the way they twirl their whole body as they fight, to use all the weapons on their arms, legs, and tail.

Branch of Life: A magical Sanguinic staff. Endows the user with the ability to use a golden masalida. Can be equipped with a sanrisma to become a Purifier Beacon.

Brown Strider: A beast of burden native to Onteval. These big, woolly mammals are immensely strong and are capable of pulling whole wagons through muddy terrain. They don't move very quickly, though, and tend to rest frequently. They are sometimes used in the Ontevallian cavalry.

Cardinal Emperors: The four sovereigns of Vitiosa, so-named because each one controls a separate hemisphere of the planet -- one for each direction on a compass.

Cataenas: The Royal Isles of Cataenas are a tropical archipelago in the western hemisphere of Vitiosa, owned by Emperor Tentitum. It has been said that Cataenas boasts the most tame wildlife and the most beautiful wilderness of any place on Vitiosa. Its people are said to be carefree and generally happy individuals, if not a bit prone to laziness. Cataenians are very outspoken people who like music, dancing, and art.

Chaos God: The Raging Chaos God was the original wielder of the Annihlus, and was an integral character in the belhuayn Creation Story. It was said he traveled the world, leaving destruction in his wake until he was slain by Sanguina's four heroes.

Communication Ring: Made from a fragment of a sanrisma crystal, these small gems allow their wearers to telepathically communicate with each other.

Dark Men, the: Insect-like humanoids from the planet Inmaris, aka Inmarisians. They are hated and feared by the belhuayn race for shanghaiing whole villages under the cover of night.

Divitia: A belhuayn unit of currency. They are coins no larger than the last joint of someone's thumb. They usually depict an embossed image of the Emperor of the lands in which they were minted. The currency of one nation shares the same value as the currency of another, therefore all four types are commonly shared worldwide.

Ectobolt: A Safiric power blast that is manifested by the strength of the user's spirit. They can be fired in volleys when used by particularly powerful casters, and track fleeing enemies without fail.

Elite: One of a rare number of Safiric Priests who have a special, godly connection to a certain, favored implement of death. Wild-bloods naturally have a fascination with violence and are often drawn to devices that can murder others. An Elite can permanently attach his spirit to his favorite weapon; this allows him to draw his weapon from nowhere and endows the device with his own intelligence. An Elite's spirit weapon can use any of his powers and function independently from its owner.

Forest Strider: The native specie of strider for the Royal Isles of Cataenas. These tropical steeds are clothed in leafy camouflage and are equipped with long, antenna-like whiskers that it uses for quickly feeling its surroundings as it speeds through the trees faster than any other land creature can move.

Fort Pericula: The small military town built around its landmark, the Thunderstone, founded 200 years ago by High Priest Atherator.

Fygidia: A Sanguinic teleportation spell. By invoking the name of the magic power, a priestess can instantly pull a friend within their line of sight to their side. A fygidia spell's range can be increased through a communication ring. Certain, powerful casters of this spell can use it to move vast numbers of willing people from one place to another.

Great Civilization, the: In the belhuayn Creation Story, this was the idyllic city in which Wild and Pure belhuayns were said to have lived in peace and harmony until a terrible catastrophe from the stars caused such terrible ruination as to nearly wipe out all life on Vitiosa.

Golden Masalida: A Sanguinic shield spell. Can only be used by higher members of the clergy, especially when wielding a Branch of Life. Works like a standard masalida, but with the added effect of warding Safiric monsters with its radiance. Can englobe multiple users at once.

Guidance Charm: Made from a fragment of a Sanrisma crystal, these small gems glow when within at least a mile of one another. They are like compasses that keep Sanguinic priestesses from being separated when on holy missions.

Healer: (aka nurse) A healer is a rare breed of Sanguinic Priestess who has the special ability to mend any wound or even cure disease by simply touching her patient. The severity of the injuries that a healer can repair is dependent on the skill of the healer, herself. As powerful as they can be, healers do have their limits: they are incapable of restoring death to life, replacing severed limbs, and curing ailments from birth. Only a Healer can become and Arch Healer, and only an Arch Healer can become a High Priestess.

High Priest: A high-ranking member of the Safiric Brotherhood. They are typically in charge of entire temples and lead a congregation of Priests and Monks. Only an Elite can become a High Priest, once that Elite has satisfied a certain trial of strength and dedication. High Priests gain the ability to live forever through their spirit weapon; if they die, their soul is transferred to their sacred implement, but they lose their physical body forever.

High Priestess: The highest ranking member of a Sanguinic church, who typically leads a congregation of priestesses and novitiates under her. They are often older but are intensely powerful, as they have dedicated much of their lives to serving Sanguina and learning the Goddess' magic. They know every power the Mother wills them to have and they are capable of using spells exclusive to High Priestesses.

Iterniam: A powerful spell that can only be cast by a high-ranking priestess on a full moon of Sanguina. The very use of it must be ordained by the Goddess Herself, but once a priestess receives this blessing of permission, she can cast this power to permanently prevent anyone from entering or leaving a specific area. The size of this banishment circle is dependent on the size of the physical wall it is cast upon. Once this power is set, it cannot be reversed or undone.

Laeyudi: One of a tribe of primitive belhuayns who lives in Virluti forest, to the west of Tresantia. These people have developed an immunity to the molds and fungi that permeate their domain, and are even comfortable with hunting the dangerous creatures that inhabit the evil bayous around them.

Lakusha: A yellow, pear-like fruit that grows on a blue, corn-like stalk. It can be eaten like an apple or juiced like a lemon, and tastes of citrus. They're expensive cash crops in Onteval and earned rancher Drathnifere his fortune.

Lasuis: The largest continent in all of Vitiosa is located in the planet's northern hemisphere: a frozen, unforgiving tundra of all the largest and most dangerous wildlife the planet has to offer. It is home to the rugged lasuisian belhuayns, and is owned by Emperor Praeira. Lasuisians are characterized for being the tallest and longest-lived belhuayns. Their bodies are conditioned to withstand the harshly cold temperatures of their environment. Their skin color ranges anywhere from dark gray to pale white, depending on how close or far from the coasts they live.

Lava Strider: The native specie of strider for Ardinsulai have charcoal black fur like steel wool and hard, heavy hooves made for walking on top of liquid magma. Along their backs is a fiery mane -- candle-like fires are said to glow at the tips of their antlers.

Life Giver, the: The sacred tree of 10,000 limbs, said to reside on the north pole of Sanguina's moon. It's believed the very first Branch of Life was made from the Life Giver by Sanguina, to be given to Saint Sevasmia for her sacred quest.

Lord Zercius: The founder of the Safiric Brotherhood. Heralded for having killed Saint Sevasmia on her journey to the promised land.

Maestiga: These 'swamp demons' are the most feared predators of Onteval. They are Safiric monsters native only to the heart of the Black Swamp, and are hunted by Priests looking to prove themselves as Elites. They are tremendously strong and powerful.

Malumai: A backwards dimension of Safiro's creation, deadly to all Pures who enter. It is where Elite members of the Safiric Brotherhood can meet each other and access any Safiric temple in the world. It is also the home to many prisoners who live within the realm's inner ring, surrounding the mountain of Malumai, where Lord Zercius is said to reside.

Mantamina: A protection cloak worn by Sanguinic priestesses. It prevents the wearer's "Purity" from being seen by members of the Safiric Brotherhood.

Masalida: A Sanguinic shield spell. Usually requires invocation to be used. The user is englobed by a transparent ball of energy that blocks all attacks from entering it. They can be shared with someone else and, if used skillfully, even reflect an attack back to where it came. Multiple users can increase the size and power of a single masalida to englobe and protect a larger area.

Mire Fiend, the: The name the Laeyudi people gave to the frightening 'demoness of Mordax Swamp.' It was said to have preyed upon anyone and anything that ever set foot in its horrific lair.

Monk: A young member of the Safiric Brotherhood, or one who is still achieving their rites of passage into the clergy.

Mordax Swamp: The fabled domain of the legendary Mire Fiend. Mordax's water is tremendously acidic and within seconds, can completely devour anything that touches it. The very fumes the water emits can burn belhuayn travelers from their insides out.

Novitiate: A young member of the Sanguinic Sisterhood, or one who is still achieving their rites of passage into the clergy.

Onteval: The continent on which much of this book's story takes place. It is owned by Emperor Iminsun -- the richest of all the world's sovereigns. It is geographically noted for its swamps and wetlands in the central region of the continent. Closer to the coasts, the climate becomes more temperate and mountainous. Toward the south and near the west, the beaches boast brown sands, whereas in the north and in the east, the coasts are cold and rocky.

Origin Depths: The birthplace of the Mire Fiend, and legend has it, the birthplace of the modern belhuayn race.

Overlord Deimos: The Xallian Overlord who waged war against planet Inmaris and started the Vitiosa Dissention. He was slain in a hand-to-hand battle with King Pulsar before he could abdicate his ruling to the next in line. Because of Deimos' demise, no Overlord is allowed to serve in his seat of power longer than 50 years.

Priest: A member of the Safiric Brotherhood who has completed their rites of passage to enter the clergy. They are characterized as wearing blue or indigo cloaks with hoods that tend to cover their facial features. They move in processions outside their temples, led by an Elite, whilst carrying special equipment made to cast unholy blessings where they walk. They practice offensive spells and few have the ability to receive a 'spirit weapon.'

Priestess: A member of the Sanguinic Sisterhood who has completed their rites of passage to enter the clergy. They are characterized as wearing red and black cloaks with very rank-conscious insignia. They typically wear a tail band inscribed with a sacred vow upon their induction into the Sisterhood, and a silver tiara. They practice defensive spells and few have the ability to heal the wounds of others.

Pulsar, King: The royal head of planet Inmaris, Pulsar was responsible for the beginnings of the black market belhuayn slave trade, which earned the ire of Xall and sparked the Vitiosa Dissention. Pulsar was notoriously hateful of belhuayns, but saw them as perfect for serfdom and for powering his mercenary war machine. Inmarisians like Pulsar have an inherent advantage against belhuayns, allowing them to easily bend the strong and proud race to their whims.

Pure: A belhuayn with rounded pupils. This denotes a natural closeness to Sanguina, and the ability to use Sanguinic magic. Pures are likely to have an aversion to violence and value forgiveness over vengeance.

Purifier Beacon: A sacred staff made by a High Priestess of Sanguina. These powerful, magic items enhance greatly the Sanguinic energies of their wielders and can permanently overturn the effects of Safiric evil upon any land to which they are established.

Qualaria: The name of the great blue star star around which all six planets of the Qualarian System orbit.

Rakshasti: A Sanguinic spell that can only be used on an opponent within arm's reach. A short, invisible sonic pulse is emanated from the user's hand and fills the target's body from head to toe, causing numbness at first and eventually sleep-like unconsciousness. The duration of the spell's effects are typically determined by the expertise of the caster.

Sachelvae: The Sanguinic cathedral of Tresantia, around which the whole city was constructed 400 years ago. It is home to over fifty priestesses, not including novitiates and faculty. The convent is led by Mother Diava, who has been High Priestess of Sachelvae for over

Safiro: The belhuayn God of Death, and the name of the blue-colored moon on which he resides. He wields a weapon known as The Unmaker -- a great warhammer capable of leveling mountains and raising continents from the ocean. It was said He and His Wife, Sanguina, built all of Vitiosa and designed the belhuayn race in their image.

Safiric Brotherhood, the: Worshipers of the God of Death believe that the belhuayn race should be limited to the strongest people. Their tenets are built on power and self-sufficiency. Members of the Brotherhood strive to be as mighty as possible by destroying the enemies of Safiro and winnowing weakness from the population.

Sanguina: The belhuayn Goddess of Life, and the name of the red-colored moon on which she resides. She wields a magic staff called The Sinews of Creation, created from the roots of The Life Giver. She tends to the unborn spirits of belhuayns and delegates them to their bodies at the time of their conception.

Sanguinic Sisterhood, the: Worshipers of the Goddess of Life believe that the belhuayn race should be unlimited in its prosperity. Their tenets are built on wisdom and altruism. Members of the Sisterhood strive to leave the world better than they found it before the end of their lives, so that they can be reborn at a different time to carry out a new purpose.

Saint Sevasmia: The founder of the Sanguinic Sisterhood, heralded for having fought and died against Lord Zercius during her holy quest to find the promised land.

Sanrisma: A large Sanguinic jewel, meant to be attached to a Branch of Life for the purposes of becoming a Purifier Beacon. By itself, the Sanrisma can be carved into guidance charms and gems for communication rings. Sanrismae are precious stones that are difficult to mine and can be consecrated by high priestesses.

Sevasmus: A merry holiday celebrated near the end of the Vitiosan year by members of the Sanguinic Sisterhood to honor the death of their Saint Sevasmia.

Scelan: A male belhuayn, when at least 18 years old.

Sceli: A male belhuayn below the age of 18.

Shield of Sanguina, the: A legendary artifact that Saint Sevasmia was said to have worn, that gave her protection and immunity from all Safiric powers. It was believed to have been given to her by Sanguina Herself, so that she could lead her disciples to the promised land.

Spirit Weapon: A Brotherhood Elite's weapon is not only attached to their owner at all times, but it is capable of storing the soul of its wielder upon death. In this state, the spirit weapon cannot move unless someone else wields it, and the dead Elite's soul can only restore its physical form through the last person to have used their weapon.

Teacher: A member of a Safiric/Sanguinic faculty, responsible for imparting knowledge of Safiric/Sanguinic spellcraft.

Tinvath: A Sanguinic potion made to resist Safiric elements.

Thunderstone: The large meteorite around which Fort Pericula was founded. The residents of Pericula believe it is imbued with cosmic energy, and was delivered to them by Safiro.

Travestas: The Safiric cathedral of Tresantia. It is led by its founder, High Priest Deniechus. The Safiric side of Tresantia was built around Travestas to mirror everything built on the Sachelvian side of the city.

Tresantia: Said to be the most sacred city in all the world, Tresantia was founded 400 years ago, in the very location where Saint Sevasmia had died. It is most famous for having the two largest cathedrals in Vitiosa -- one for Safiro and one for Sanguina -- coexisting in the same area. Its population is exactly half Safiric and half Sanguinic, and attracts members of either faith from all over the world who seek the city's protection and prosperity.

Tribummatia: The promised land that Sanguina sent Saint Sevasmia to find, and relocate her travelling Pures. It was said they would have the protection of Sanguina herself forevermore upon their arrival. However, it was founded by the only survivor of the mission, Aurina, who later became known as the first empress of Tribummatia.

Velta: A female belhuayn, when at least 18 years of age.

Venio: A rather harsh, belhuayn alcohol.

Vitiosa: The 'forbidden' homeworld of the belhuayn race. It is a planet three times the size of Earth, with at least three times its gravity and an atmosphere nearly 100 times denser. Even still, its atmosphere is considered lacking by the standards of most Qualarian planets, and does not shield its natives as much as the other worlds of the stellar community. Indeed, it is said that the much higher radiation is what gives belhuayns their seemingly limitless adaptability, allowing them to dominate all corners, heights, and depths of their world.

Vitiosa Dissention: The great conflict that occurred between planets Xall, Saja, and Voir vs Inmaris and Marden to contest the neutrality of Vitiosa's sovereign lands. The war ended 100 years ago when Xall used their ultimate weapon: the Harbinger of Dominion, to force Inmaris' surrender. Inmaris' king, Pulsar, was captured at the end of the battle after he had killed Overlord Deimos of Xall.

Vixy: A female belhuayn, under the age of 18 years old.

Vytameta: One of two heroic figures that, in legend, was said to come at the time of a great calamity to decide the fate of Vitiosa.

Wild-blood: A belhuayn with slit-shaped pupils. This denotes a closeness to Safiro and the ability to use Safiric magic. Wilds are likely to take vengeance when dealing with enemies and prefer violent solutions to their stressful dilemmas.

Xall: Planet Xall is home to the most technologically advanced race in the Qualarian System. The Xalls are famous space explorers and have established colonies on many worlds outside their parent star. They have a close and long-established alliance with the worlds of Saja and Voir.

Vytameta

Vytameta